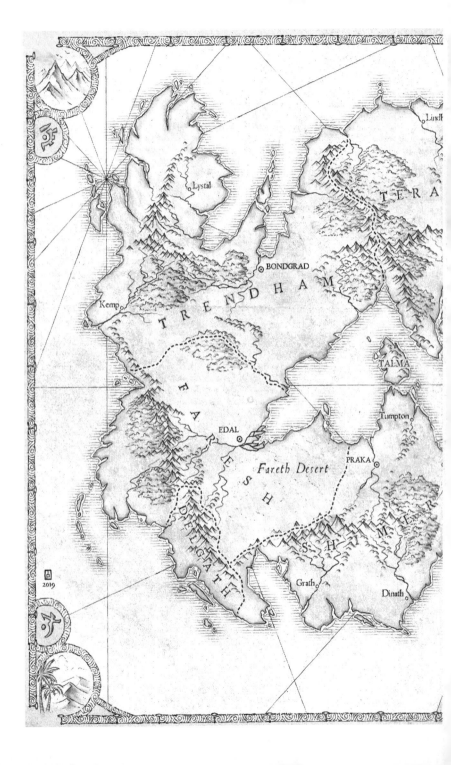

CHAPTER 1

Will, along with most of the other children, followed the carriage as it rolled through the village. Newcomers of any sort were always a major event, but a gilded carriage was big news. He had never seen anything like it before. Unlike a wagon, the carriage was entirely enclosed, and it was constructed with such delicate craftsmanship that it was hard to believe the conveyance was made of ordinary wood and metal.

Whoever rode inside had to be extraordinarily important—and wealthy. The driver was dressed in expensive clothing, and a footman rode at the rear. Both men looked wealthy to Will's eyes, and if they hadn't so obviously been acting as servants, he might have thought them lords.

The village children followed in the carriage's wake like a swarm of friendly—and very dirty—bees, waving and calling to the unseen occupants. The driver ignored them, but a small window in the back opened, the wood panel sliding to one side, and Will caught sight of a pair of bright blue eyes staring curiously out at them.

The moment passed quickly, as a hand appeared with slender yet masculine fingers, and slid the window shut once more, cutting off Will's view of the girl who had been staring out.

Unlike the children, the adults of the village of Barrowden studiously avoided the carriage, and parents who spotted their own offspring quickly caught them and herded them into their homes. While ordinary travelers or merchants might have drawn a crowd, the ostentatious carriage was a warning sign to them. No one old enough to understand the ways of the world wanted to catch the attention of whatever lord or lady might be within. Nothing good ever came of interacting with the rich and powerful.

By the time the carriage had passed through and reached the opposite end of the village, only a few children remained to follow it. One of the few who remained was his friend and cousin, Eric, who stopped Will by tugging on his arm.

"We should stop here," suggested Eric. "They're just passing through, and that man on the back looks mean. He might do something if we keep following."

Will gave his friend a look of amazement. Usually Eric was the wilder of the two of them. It was rare for him to caution restraint. "Really?"

Eric shrugged. "I have to go home anyway. Dad's waiting for me to help him."

That soured Will's mood. Ever since they had turned twelve, Eric's time had been more and more restricted as his parents began asking their son to take on more responsibilities. Eric's dad, Johnathan Cartwright, was relatively prosperous by their village's standards, making a good living as a wainwright and wheelwright.

Will shared the same last name, since his mother, Erisa, was Johnathan Cartwright's sister, and had never married, but the similarities between him and his friend Eric ended there. Unlike Eric, Will didn't have a father, or a trade to inherit. His mother's work didn't require much help, and as a consequence he was still relatively carefree—carefree, and with little hope for the future.

"Go home then," said Will flatly.

"What are you going to do?" said Eric, squinting suspiciously at his cousin.

Will grinned. "Worried I'll have an adventure without you?"

"As if you could!" said Eric in disbelief.

Will deflated. "You're right. I'll just go home. It's in this direction anyway."

"Don't follow them down the road. They might get angry."

"I won't," said Will. "It's quicker to cut through the woods." With that, he waved goodbye to his friend and took to his feet, running through underbrush that bordered the village and into the deeper shadows of the forest of Glenwood.

Weaving and ducking through the heavy brush, Will followed a route that was not so much a path as a game trail. Like all the children of the village, he was well acquainted with the territory and he knew the easiest way to reach his destination, particularly since this was his usual way home. He reached the house in less than ten minutes.

His home sat not far from the road he had left, but since the road followed a curving route, he was confident that the carriage wouldn't pass by for several more minutes. He stopped and hid in the bushes to get one more good look at it when it came by.

Sure enough, he soon heard the sound of horses, and the carriage appeared shortly thereafter, but to his surprise it didn't pass by his home. Instead, the carriage turned and pulled into the wide path that lead to the house and stopped a short distance away. The footman jumped down from his seat and moved to open the carriage door for the occupants.

"Why are they stopping here?" muttered Will quietly to himself.

Will's mother, Erisa Cartwright, made her living growing herbs, tending the sick, and acting as a midwife whenever one of the village women gave birth. Hers was a humble life, especially since she was a single mother with no husband. Will couldn't imagine what a strange nobleman would want with her.

The man who stepped out of the carriage was a prime example of wealth and privilege. Slender and of medium build, the man had light brown hair and a sharp nose. He exuded pride and arrogance with every breath he took. His clothes were a rich burnt orange, heavily embroidered with gold thread; even in the dappled sunlight of Glenwood he seemed too bright to look upon.

A girl in a yellow dress tried to follow him out, but the man turned and stopped her. "No, Laina, stay in the coach. This place is filthy. You'll ruin your dress."

Laina had warm brown eyes and matching hair. She pouted unhappily. "But, Father, I'm bored. I can't stand another minute in the coach!"

The man pressed her firmly back. "That's why Selene came with us. Be a good girl and play a game with her inside." He shut the door before she could protest further, then he turned and strode toward Will's home.

Is he going to buy Mom's herbs? wondered Will. That made no sense. A nobleman from the city could buy anything he wanted in the markets there. There was nothing special about his mother's wares. Certainly nothing that would warrant a nobleman coming to buy them in person. He was torn by the desire to go in and discover what was really going on, but the stern looks on the faces of the driver and footman made him hesitate.

The driver left his seat and stood by the door to the carriage, while the footman followed his lord to Will's house. The footman knocked, and then opened the door without waiting for an answer. He ducked inside for a moment and then stepped back out. "Only the woman is home, milord. It should be safe."

"As if I need your protection," said the nobleman dismissively. Going inside, he shut the door behind him. The footman took up a guard position by the door.

Fear touched Will's heart and he worried for his mother. Erisa Cartwright was a strong woman, but strength mattered little when it came to men such as these. *That lord could kill her and walk away, and no one could touch him,* he thought.

What to do? At twelve years of age, Will didn't have the size needed to protect his mother. Any one of the three men was more than a match for him, and the footman and driver looked exceptionally vigilant. Briefly, he considered circling around and trying to enter his house from the other side, but then movement from the window at the back of the carriage drew his attention.

The wood panel slid to one side, and a pair of slender legs appeared as the girl in the yellow dress eased herself through the opening. She hung from the edge for a brief second before dropping lightly to the ground and waving her hand at a second girl looking out.

Once again Will spotted the blue eyes he had seen before, framed this time by raven-black hair as a second girl poked her head out the window. This girl seemed older, somewhere closer to Will's age, and she seemed unhappy with Laina's escape plan, but she kept her silence.

Laina motioned to her friend again, and the second girl turned around and eased out the same way, feet first.

The two girls were hidden from the view of their guardians by the carriage itself, and they carefully snuck towards the bushes across from where Will watched. He couldn't help but admire their craftiness, for both the driver and the footman seemed oblivious.

Backing away from his home, Will began stealthily circling through the woods, working his way around so he could watch the girls and see what they were up to. For a moment he thought he might have lost them, since he had to take a longer route to avoid being seen, but then he heard a rustling ahead.

He grinned. They were good, but it was nearly impossible to move without making some noise with so many leaves on the ground. Reaching down, he pulled his thin leather shoes off. Barefoot, he could probably get much closer without alerting them. Trying to sneak up on others in the forest was a game that he and his cousin Eric often played with each other, and he was fairly certain of his skills.

If I can't follow a couple of spoiled brats from the city, I'll eat my shoes, he thought confidently. He wedged his footwear into the crook of a familiar tree so he could find them later, then set off after his quarry.

Will wasn't perfectly stealthy—that sort of silent movement just wasn't possible with the early fall leaves carpeting the forest floor—but he didn't have to be. He only had to be quieter than the two girls, who were no longer even attempting to move silently.

He couldn't keep them in sight, either. From his games with the other children of the village, he knew all too well that the human eye was designed to detect movement, so he had to follow them by staying at a distance and keeping them within earshot. Over the course of the next ten minutes, he thought he had lost them several times, when they got too far ahead, but he had the distinct advantage of knowing the area. He was able to guess which way they would go, because he already knew the easiest way through this part of the Glenwood. The two strangers would follow the path of least resistance.

They'll probably stop at the mossy rock, he told himself.

Chapter 1

The mossy rock was a large, flat monolith that sat in a clearing not far ahead, and it was a popular spot for the children of Barrowden. In the spring it was a beautiful place to picnic, when all the wildflowers were blooming, but even now, in early autumn, it was a magical place to play or relax.

"Look, Selene! It's a castle!" That was Laina's voice, so Will assumed the other girl must be Selene.

"It's just a big rock," responded Selene dryly.

"A *magic* rock," insisted Laina. "In fact, it's probably a fairy fortress, disguised by illusion to prevent our eyes from seeing the fair folk."

Selene snorted. "Bollocks. I don't sense the slightest bit of magic coming from it. You should know better, Laina. You've already begun your training."

Laina sighed. "Can't you play pretend anymore? Why do you have to be so boring?"

"If you want magic, call Tyranil," responded Selene. "You don't have to pretend."

"He'd just burn everything," said Laina, her voice sounding glum. "That's not very fun."

"I'll show you how to make a grass wreath," suggested Selene.

Will was at the edge of the glen now, and he could see the two girls sitting on the sunny side of the big, mossy rock. A thought came to him and he smiled. He'd give them a scare.

The ground of the clearing was soft and damp, and there weren't many leaves. Working his way slowly to the left, he crept out into the open from the opposite side, where the bulk of the stone would keep him out of their view. Moving ever so slowly, he made his way forward, taking care to avoid rustling the grass. Once he reached the rock, he could come around from one side and surprise them.

His plan worked, and soon he was just a few feet from the two unsuspecting girls, peering at them from around the rock. Will paused then, studying them. The older girl, Selene, struck him as particularly beautiful.

Will had never cared much for girls—most of those in the village were either much older, much younger, or extremely annoying—but Selene seemed cast from a different mold. She had a certain grace to her movements, a calmness and surety about her that he wasn't used to seeing. That combined with her glossy black hair and the somber, midnight-blue dress she wore made her seem almost otherworldly, like one of the fair folk that Laina had been rambling on about before.

Selene's hands were deftly weaving long blades of grass into a wreath while her friend watched. *Too bad it isn't spring, or she could have put flowers in it,* thought Will, having forgotten his plan to scare them. He was thoroughly entranced.

"I want to try," said Laina, inspired by Selene's efforts. The younger girl turned in Will's direction, and but for the fact that she was staring at the ground, she would surely have spotted him. Moving forward while bent over, she searched for a good patch of thick grass to pluck.

Utterly still, Will watched her approach, until he spotted a sinuous, green length on the ground just before her. Oblivious, Laina's hand reached for the grass that was hiding the viper.

"Look out!" shouted Will, leaping forward and shoving the smaller girl to push her back.

Laina stumbled and fell hard, several feet away, and after recovering from her first shock, began to scream.

Selene jumped up, dropping her wreath. "Don't touch her!" she yelled, rushing forward to defend her companion. She produced a small dagger, which she held in front of her, though Will hadn't noticed her wearing one previously.

Will's eyes grew wide at the sight of the sharp steel pointed at him. "It was a snake!" he announced, trying to reassure them. Looking down, he spotted the viper near his feet, beginning to make an escape through the grass. Without pausing to think, he bent quickly, his hand snapping out to catch the reptile just behind its head. Straightening back up, he held it out to one side. "See? It would have bitten her."

Laina, who had just begun to recover from her first fright, screamed again at the sight of the reptile. Selene's response was more measured, though. The older girl's eyes widened, but she stepped back and lowered her knife.

Grinning, Will twisted at the waist and threw the snake toward the far side of the clearing, where it couldn't threaten them. "In another month they'll be asleep, but it's still warm enough right now that you have to be careful," he told them, confident in his knowledge.

Then Will heard a crashing noise coming from behind him. The bushes shook and branches broke as the carriage driver charged into the clearing. Spotting Will, he ran forward. "Get away from them!" shouted the driver, his face red with anger.

"I was just—"

The world exploded with pain as the driver's fist caught Will in the side of the head, sending him tumbling to the ground. Stunned, Will stared upward in confusion, trying to clear his head. In his ears he could hear the girls yelling, but he couldn't make sense of their words.

"How dare you?" continued the driver. Then he raised his right arm, unfurling the coachwhip he carried and bringing it down in a long, sweeping stroke that caught Will across the face. He cried out in pain and rolled over, trying to shield his wounded cheek, then felt a second line of fire as the driver whipped his back.

Everyone was yelling, but the driver lashed him once more before the girls finally calmed the enraged man down. "There was a snake, you idiot!" yelled Selene, hanging onto the driver's arm. "He saved Laina from being bitten."

Selene continued to berate the driver while the younger girl cried, a reaction to both the shock of seeing the snake and the sudden violence she had witnessed. Will gradually pulled himself together and got to his feet, tears of pain running from his eyes and mixing with the blood of his cut cheek.

"We need to return," said the driver coldly, taking Laina by the hand and leading the girl away.

Selene stayed still for a moment, then started to follow. "We can't just leave him here!" she insisted. "He's hurt."

"He's a peasant," snapped the driver. "If you cared so much, you shouldn't have left the carriage. Lord Nerrow will have my hide for letting you two slip away."

Will watched them go, his vision blurry. "It's all right," he said. Taking a step forward to follow, the world spun around him, and his right leg collapsed under his weight. Crashing to the ground, he wondered what was wrong with his leg. It was throbbing with pain, but he couldn't remember the whip striking him there. His heart was racing and beating so hard it felt as though it might burst from his chest. *Why can't I catch my breath?*

"Something's wrong!" said Selene loudly, running back to him.

Will tried to focus his eyes, but nothing seemed to work properly anymore. All he could see were the girl's blue eyes staring down at him. She looked worried.

He felt cold fingers on his leg. "He's been bitten." His vision narrowed to a tunnel and then vanished entirely as his consciousness surrendered to darkness.

CHAPTER 2

"What happened to his face?" demanded a deep voice that Will didn't recognize.

"My apologies, milord, I thought he had attacked your daughter," said the driver apologetically.

Opening his eyes, Will recognized his surroundings; he was home, in bed. The unfamiliar voice had been that of the lord who had come to see his mother. The lord looked distinctly unhappy.

"Do you realize what you've done? Do you know who he is?" demanded the lord.

The driver stared at his feet. "Just a peasant boy from the village, milord."

"He's Erisa's son!" shouted the lord. "Her *only* son. You know why I'm here. Think about that for a moment."

The driver's face paled. "Forgive me, milord. I didn't realize…"

"Get out!" shouted the lord. "I'll deal with you later."

In the silence that followed, Will slowly became aware of someone crying in the background. Turning his head, he saw his mother sitting on a small stool at the foot of the bed. The lord was standing over her, his features remorseful.

"Erisa, I'm sorry," said the lord.

Glancing up, his mother begged, "Can't you do something? Please, Lord Nerrow, he's all I have."

"This is beyond my power, Erisa," answered Lord Nerrow sadly. "There is no magic that can heal this. If your herbs cannot help…"

"It was an emerald viper," cried Will's mother. "Don't be a fool! If magic cannot help, what good do you think herbs will be?"

"Then his fate is in the gods' hands," said Lord Nerrow. "Perhaps it is better this way. Even if he dies, I'll see to it that you're taken care of." He pressed a small leather pouch into Erisa's hand.

Will's mother shot to her feet and she flung the pouch against the wall. The seams burst, spilling gold and silver coins across the floor. "I don't want your *money*! I never wanted it! I just want my son, healthy and whole."

"And what kind of life could he have had?" said Lord Nerrow. "Stuck in this filth-ridden village. It's better this way, for both of us. You're still young, Erisa. You could find a husband—"

Furious, Erisa turned on the man. "I don't want a husband! I want my son!" She looked as though she might attack the nobleman then and there, but after a second, she clenched her hands into fists and grew still. "That's right, though, you have your daughters. You wouldn't care."

Lord Nerrow started toward her, but Erisa held up her hand. "Leave. Please leave."

"Erisa, I never wanted this…"

"Go," said Will's mother firmly. "Save me your guilt and pity. You can keep them. I regret the day I ever laid eyes on you."

"Very well," said the lord, and then he left the room.

Will's mother followed him out, and he could hear her parting words from the other room. "Don't come back here," she said. "I don't want to ever see you again."

He thought he was alone, but a small noise made him refocus his eyes, and he saw the dark-haired girl was beside the bed. Will's eyes met hers for a moment, and then she leaned over, pressing her lips to his forehead. "Thank you for saving Laina," she said, and then she was gone.

Darkness swallowed him, and Will slept, grateful for an end to the pain.

***

He awoke in darkness sometime later, vaguely aware that people were talking close by, just outside his room.

"Please, Master Arrogan, if you can help him…"

"You have a lot of nerve calling me here, Erisa," answered a gruff voice.

Will's mother didn't relent. "There was no one else I could turn to. If anyone can save him, it's you."

"You know how I feel about this, Erisa. Why should I do anything to help that man? Do you have any idea what his kind have cost me? Why should I help his cursed spawn?" answered the man.

Erisa's voice was strident. "Please! He's my son. He's done you no wrong. Don't condemn him for the sins of his father."

"There are no herbs for this, nor alchemy either. The venom will have spread throughout his body by now," argued the man's voice.

"I know that," agreed Will's mother. "You taught me everything I know of herbs and medicine, but I also know that you can do more. Please, you have to try, Master Arrogan."

"Silence," commanded the old man's voice. "Don't say that name, and don't mention other things either. Don't you realize what will happen if they discover my presence here? You worry for your son, but what of the rest of the village? They'd burn this place to the ground and raze the village if they heard I was here."

"I don't care!" declared Erisa. "If you won't help him, I'll run into the streets shouting your name. I'll run all the way to Cerria if I have to, until everyone in the world knows you're here!"

"Fine," growled the old man. "That's enough. There's no reasoning with you."

"Then you'll…"

"I'll do what I can," answered the old man. Will heard the door open, and then the man cautioned his mother one last time. "Stay outside. Make sure no one comes near the house."

"Thank you," said Will's mother, tears in her voice.

"Don't thank me yet," said the old man. "I can't make any promises."

The sound of the door closing came to his ears, and Will felt the presence of the stranger beside his bed, though there was no light to see by. A rough hand touched his forehead, cold against his fevered flesh.

"You're awake?" said the old man, sounding surprised. "Been listening, eh, boy? That's a good sign, but I'm afraid it won't do. We can't have you watching this."

Watching? I can't see a thing. It's pitch black in here, thought Will. Then he felt the newcomer press a finger against his chest, and something cool rushed into him, passing through his body like ripples across a still pond. Will's eyes closed, and then a white light flashed before him.

He felt as though he was floating, and his dark room was now well lit by the afternoon sun splashing in through the window to paint his room in bright colors. Everything was crisp and clear, and something about the light bothered him, though he couldn't put his finger on what it was.

An old man leaned over him, and Will recognized the man's face. It was the hermit of Glenwood, an old man who lived in the forest. The children of the village had lots of stories about the hermit, most of them bad, claiming the old man was a warlock who stole the souls of those who ventured too close to his abode.

Will had never believed the rumors, though. He had met the old man on several occasions in the past, usually when the hermit had come to trade with his mother, but he had never spoken to him.

He tried to say something, but his voice didn't work, and it was only then that he realized how strange his position was. He was floating *above* his body, looking down on the room, a disembodied observer. Will got the sense he should feel panic at his unexpected situation, but he didn't. In fact, he didn't feel much of anything. He was surrounded by a sense of serene calm.

With mild curiosity, he watched as the old man traced a quick pattern in the air, his fingers trailing lines of blue light before he brought them down to rest on the body in front of him. The old man's eyes were closed, and he seemed to be concentrating with strange intensity. Motes of light sparked around, and *within* Will's body.

What is he doing? wondered Will. *Is that magic?*

The old man worked over his body for an unknown period of time, and Will could see the swelling in his leg going down visibly. Even the color improved, going from a purple so dark as to almost be black, to an angry red. Eventually, the man stopped, sitting down on the stool and breathing heavily, as though he was trying to catch his breath. He seemed to have finished.

Then the old man's eyes drifted upward, and he seemed to stare at the place where Will hung in the air. The door to the room opened and Erisa looked in.

"Is he…?" she started to ask.

The old man turned at her voice. "I said to stay out. I'll call you when I'm finished." He waited until she had closed the door before looking up at the ceiling again. "I wondered why you weren't waking up. Now I see why. You've been spying on me, haven't you?"

Will tried to protest his innocence, but again, his voice failed him.

The hermit smiled wickedly. "I should have expected as much. I'll be keeping my eyes closely on you in the future, boy. Now, it's time for you to go back where you belong." Standing, the old man brought his hands together in a clap that sent a heavy bell-like tone shivering through the air. The world spun, and Will felt nauseous as something hemmed him in, pressing him down into a warm darkness.

When he opened his eyes again, he discovered he was back in his body, looking up from the bed. The old man leaned over him, staring at him with hard eyes. "This isn't over, boy. I'll be seeing you again, one way or another." Then he left, and Will was finally alone.

CHAPTER 3

Will recovered quickly after the old hermit's visit, and his mother warned him not to mention either the snakebite or the man who had saved him to anyone in the village. Will chalked it up to the fact that people didn't survive emerald viper bites—they were invariably fatal. His mother was probably afraid of starting rumors, since the villagers were prone to superstition.

What did strike him as odd was her emphatic insistence that he not mention the old man's visit. She almost seemed more worried about that than having people find out he had survived the snake's venom.

He brought the subject up several times, hoping she would explain what had happened, but Erisa always evaded, refusing to give him answers. More than a month after his recovery, he tried again. "Why did that lord come to visit you?"

Erisa looked up from her needlework. "He wasn't visiting *me*. He just wanted some herbs."

"But you knew his name," countered Will. "You called him 'Lord Nerrow.'"

She sighed, and then, putting down the shirt she was mending, stared intently at him. "Baron Nerrow was a customer. I make it a point of learning customers' names."

Will frowned. "Our lord is Lord Fulstrom. Why would another lord come to our little village?"

Erisa picked up the shirt again, resuming her work calmly. "How should I know? Noblemen do as they please."

"Do you think he knows Arrogan?" asked Will, trying a different line of questioning.

His mother looked at him in horror before standing up, heedless of her work falling to the floor at her feet. With two long strides, she crossed the room and put her hands on his shoulders. "Don't ever say that name again! Do you hear me?"

The fear and anger in her features shook him to the core, though he couldn't understand what had provoked her reaction. "Why? It's just a name…"

She shook him. "Listen to me, William Cartwright! You are never to say that name again. Do you understand? This isn't a game."

Will tried to twist out of her grasp, for her fingers were digging painfully into his shoulders, but she wouldn't release him. "Fine," he answered. "I won't repeat it."

"Ever!" insisted his mother, shaking him again. "If that name reaches the wrong ears, we're dead. They'll kill us, William, and not just us. Everyone in the village would be at risk."

"All right!" said Will forcefully. "I won't say his stupid name. Who do you mean by *they*?"

She ignored his question. "Promise me, William. Swear it. Swear you'll never repeat that name again."

Frightened by her strange behavior, he agreed, but he crossed his fingers behind his back as he said the words. "I swear, Mom. Can you please let me go?"

Erisa seemed to remember herself then, and she took her hands away. Returning to her chair, she quietly gathered up the shirt she had been mending. When she looked up at him again, her face was calm, but Will would never forget the quiet fear he saw hiding deep in her eyes.

He didn't ask again after that.

Of course, he didn't forget his questions, and his curiosity was even worse after his mother's desperate insistence, but as with anything, time and a lack of new information eventually forced him to stop thinking about the subject constantly. After a few months, it was just one more of life's mysteries, tucked away in the back corner of his mind.

He had other interesting things to keep his thoughts occupied anyway. Since the day of his near-fatal snake incident, he had gradually become aware of something unusual. The world had changed, or perhaps he had. Will couldn't really be sure which was the case, but he was definitely beginning to notice things that he hadn't been aware of previously.

His mother grew a large assortment of herbs in their back garden, and as fall progressed, many of them had to be harvested and either dried or processed into tinctures. Only a few of the plants were perennials that would survive through the winter. As her son, and only assistant, much of the work fell on his shoulders.

He had been helping her for years, but this fall he began to find differences in the plants, things he hadn't noticed before. In the past, it had always been his mother who made the final determination regarding which plants were fit to be dried or kept. Years of experience had given her a fine discernment when it came to spotting plant diseases and sorting out the best of their harvest, but this year Will had the advantage.

Not only was his initial sorting and grading of the plants nearly perfect in his mother's opinion, but he also spotted problems with some of the herbs that escaped her attention entirely.

"What's wrong with this mint?" asked Erisa, picking up a small bundle he had set aside for the discard pile.

Will looked at it again. "Root fungus," he answered after a moment. "The leaves look all right, but they won't taste good."

His mother gave him an odd look. "Did you check it?"

He shook his head. "No, but I'm sure."

She plucked a few leaves and chewed them before making a sour face. "You're right," she admitted. "How did you know?"

Will wasn't sure how to answer that. To his eyes, the plant in her hands looked almost identical to the healthy ones, but when he concentrated, he could see something else, a faint, sickly glow. It was like a different color, but it wasn't really a color, and he was at a loss to describe it. All the plants displayed new colors to him now, but they weren't colors he could see with his eyes. It was as though he had discovered a new form of light, one that came from within them, providing information about their health and properties that he was unable to explain. Trying to tell his mother how he knew was like trying to describe a painting to a blind man.

"I'm not sure," he answered finally. "I could just tell."

Erisa looked at him curiously. "Is there anything you aren't telling me?" When he didn't say anything, she continued, "I know this is a confusing time for you. You're about to turn thirteen and your body is going through a lot of changes. You can talk to me—about whatever, whether it's physical changes, or strange new feelings—"

"Mom!" Will interrupted. "Please, stop. It's nothing like that." *And I wouldn't tell you if it was,* he thought silently.

His mother pursed her lips. Then she changed topics, "If you're done with the mint, you can check over the yarrow and pennyroyal. I want to finish this today.

Tomorrow I'll go into the village and see if the spirits I ordered have arrived. If so, we can start making tinctures."

"Why do they call them 'spirits' anyway?" asked Will. "Isn't it just alcohol?"

Erisa smiled. "The alcohol people drink is more than half water. For tinctures, I need something closer to pure alcohol, and that isn't easy to get. It requires a special process to make."

"Why don't we make our own then?" he queried. "It would save a lot of money."

She sighed. "If I could afford distillation equipment, I would just make spirits and sell those. Better still I'd make essential oils—those fetch an even higher price—but the copper and glassware costs more than our home."

"But you know how it's done?"

Erisa shrugged, and her eyes stared into the distance. "I've seen it done. My teacher had the equipment."

"Who was your teacher?"

That question brought her back from her reverie, and her eyes narrowed as she turned her gaze on him, as though she suspected him of having an ulterior motive for asking. Will kept his face smooth and tried to look innocent. After a few seconds she answered, "My great-grandfather."

Something felt off about her answer, though whether it was a half-truth or an outright lie, Will couldn't be sure. He accepted her words, though, for he had the distinct feeling she would react badly if he pushed her for a better answer. *More secrets,* he thought. *What is she hiding from me?*

Swallowing his questions, he went about checking the yarrow and pennyroyal, but it still bothered him. The more he thought about it, the angrier he became. If he couldn't expect the truth from his own mother, who could he expect it from?

He hurried through the rest of the herbs and then excused himself. He needed a walk to clear his head. The brisk autumn breeze cooled his cheeks and did in fact make him feel better, but no sooner than he had stepped outside he felt a prickly sensation down the back of his neck.

It wasn't a new feeling, and if he hadn't known better, he would have thought someone was watching him. Will glanced around at the bushes and trees surrounding his home, but he couldn't find any obvious cause for his suspicion.

"Between that strange old man and my mother, I'm starting to imagine things," he told himself, but he couldn't quite bring himself to believe it.

Will decided to visit his cousin, Eric. The feeling of being watched didn't go away, though. *If someone is bored enough to waste their time spying on me, there's no reason to make it easy for them,* he thought. Increasing his pace, he broke into a run and didn't slow down until he had reached Eric's house.

The feeling stayed with him until he was almost there, before vanishing as mysteriously as it had appeared.

 CHAPTER 4

Winter came and went, boring and uneventful, with little to do and even less to talk about. During the cold months, Will's mother's work was limited to tending the sick and the occasional childbirth. Unless a patient showed up on their doorstep, there was no relief from the tedium for him, for she rarely took him with her when she went to someone's home.

Spring was a welcome relief when it arrived. Will didn't even mind the rain and mud, so long as he was free of the confines of four walls, hemmed in by the unforgiving cold. Spring meant freedom. Once the garden was planted, there wasn't much to do other than watch the plants grow, and there were few colds and illnesses, so Will was free to visit Eric or roam the woods as he pleased.

Except today. Becca Taylor had gone into labor, and Will's mother had been called to her home to oversee the delivery. That meant Will was tied to the house, in case anyone else showed up wanting to buy a remedy.

It wouldn't have been so bad if one of his friends had been able to visit him, but they were all busy helping their own parents. At thirteen, most of them had begun working nearly every day. Will was the only one that still had a modest degree of freedom and leisure.

He was sitting in front of the house, staring up at the sky through the slender branches waving in the wind, when his day became a lot more interesting. Several people came down the path from the road, moving in haste. It only took him a second to recognize them. It was Tracy and Joseph Tanner, who lived in the village.

The young couple was a relatively new addition to Barrowden, having moved there only four years ago. Erisa had delivered their first child, a boy named Joey, only two years past. Joseph was carrying their young son in his arms as they hurried toward Will's house.

"Where's your mother?" called Tracy as soon as she saw Will, a tone of desperate urgency in her voice.

Will jumped to his feet. "She's at the Taylors', delivering a baby. What's wrong?"

"It's Joey," answered the young mother. "He's got a boil on his leg."

"We wasted our time," said Joseph, giving his wife an angry glance. "It's a half day's walk to the Taylor house."

Will had relaxed slightly when he heard the word 'boil.' At first, their faces had made him fear it was something more serious.

"Do you have anything that might help?" asked Tracy, ignoring her husband's complaint.

"You'll need a fresh poultice to draw it out," Will informed her. "But I know how to make one. Bring him in the house and I'll do what I can."

The father glared at him. "He's just a boy. We should go home. He'll only make it worse."

"It can't get much worse, Joseph," declared Tracy. "Everyone trusts Erisa. Her son must at least know a little about these things."

Will didn't like the sound of that, but he opened the door and ushered them in, directing them to place their son on the small bed he called his own. When Tracy drew back the blanket to show him the small boy's leg, he almost hissed in alarm.

That's no boil, he realized. *It's a septic wound.* There was a large, puss-filled abscess on the child's thigh, surrounded by red and inflamed tissue. Tentatively he pressed on it, noting the thick, yellow fluid that oozed out at the slight pressure. Red streaks ran up and down the boy's leg.

"When did it start?" he asked, trying to hide the tremor in his voice.

"Two days ago," answered the boy's mother. "He came in after playing and had a small scratch. I didn't think much of it at the time, but it's gotten steadily worse."

Will was hardly an expert, but he knew enough to know the boy's chances were poor. Putting one hand against Joey's forehead, he noted the heat there. *He already has a fever. This is bad.* Short of removing the boy's leg, Will didn't know of anything that would help once a wound had turned septic. Poultices were nearly useless once the sickness had moved into the blood.

He was also afraid of how Joseph Tanner would react if he told them the truth.

Joseph grew impatient waiting on him. "Can you do anything or not?"

Squaring his shoulders, Will decided to be honest up front. If the boy's father lost his temper, it wasn't really his fault, and if he gave the man false hope, it would be much worse later. "I won't lie. I think it's bad. I can make a poultice for the wound and try to bring down his fever with some tea, but the wound has sickened. My mother has more knowledge than I do, but I think it might be too late, even for her." He kept his eyes firmly on Joseph's as he spoke, then bowed his head respectfully when he had finished.

Before Joseph could reply, his wife put her hand on his arm. "Don't be angry with the boy. It isn't his fault. Maybe we can take Joey to the Taylors'..."

Her husband let out a long, pent-up breath. "No. That would take too long, and most of her medicines are here." Then he put his hand on Will's shoulder. "Thank you for being truthful. Do what you can and I won't blame you. The fault lies on me. I should have brought him yesterday." Looking back at Tracy, he added, "I'll go to the Taylors; and see if Erisa can come back sooner. You stay here with Will and see if he can help Joey in the meantime."

The man left soon after that, leaving Will alone with Tracy and her sick son, but he felt as if he were alone, and the weight of the world was resting on his shoulders.

Going to the back of the house, Will soon returned with a small packet of willow bark, which he handed to Tracy. "Can you make a tea while I work on the poultice? This should help with the fever. I'll do something about his leg."

But what? he thought to himself, fighting to suppress a feeling of panic. He went back to the storeroom and looked at the dried herbs hanging in bundles there. Compared to what they had been like when freshly cut, they felt dead and nearly useless to him. In his strange way, he could sense that they retained some of their properties, but not the ones needed to cleanse a wound such as the one he had just seen.

He returned to the boy and studied the wound, trying to capture the feeling he got sometimes when harvesting and inspecting fresh herbs. The exercise left him frustrated, like trying to draw a picture of something without being allowed to look directly at it, but he felt as though he had learned something, even if he couldn't describe it. Then he went outside. He needed something fresh.

A quick perusal of the garden told him what he already knew. None of the plants were ready. He was about to give up and go back inside when his eyes fell on the lilac bush growing by the corner of the house. His mother kept it mainly for ornamental purposes, but he knew the leaves could be used for rashes. Moving closer, he examined it closely. What he found seemed promising. He ripped off several large handfuls of leaves, and as he did, he saw a large, green garden spider hanging in its web just under the eaves of the house.

The web seemed to sparkle, pulling at him, and an idea occurred to him then.

When he returned to the house, Tracy already had the kettle close to boiling, so he borrowed some of the water to scald and clean the lilac leaves before putting them in a mortar to crush. Then he used a little more to clean a sharp knife his mother used to harvest particularly delicate plants. Tracy watched him worriedly while brewing the willow tea.

"What's the knife for?" she asked.

Will had been trying not to think about that, but he answered anyway, "We have to clean the wound out first. Otherwise it won't matter what else we do."

Her jaw firmed. "You're not cutting my son."

Will's own fear and uncertainty turned to anger as he replied, "Fine. We'll wait for Mom. If she leaves as soon as your husband gets there, they'll be back by midnight. She'll tell you the same thing, but it will be too late by then."

Tracy Tanner chewed her lip nervously. "Are you sure?"

No, thought Will. *I'm not sure of anything.* He nodded confidently instead. "I don't know if we can save him, but I know if we don't clean it out he will die for sure." *I can't believe I just said that!*

Something about his attitude convinced her, and ten minutes later they were sitting by the bedside where Joey lay. They had already coaxed him into drinking some of the bitter willow tea, though not as much as Will thought he needed.

Will took up the knife. "Try to keep him still. I'll make a small cut. After that, you pour some of the water over it."

The next few minutes were a nightmare. The abscess was sensitive and painful; the boy jerked and began to thrash as soon as he felt the knife touch his skin. "Hold him still," ordered Will, grinding his teeth together and praying he wouldn't faint himself.

The second attempt was more successful, although his cut was slightly ragged due to Joey's movements. The pus emerged in a sudden rush, followed by a thin, sanguineous fluid. The smell made Will's stomach turn, but he forced himself to keep his eyes on the wound as Tracy poured clean water over it.

Will could see a deep hole where the pus had been, one that rapidly filled with blood whenever the boy's mother stopped pouring water. He suspected his mother might have tried cutting deeper, to make sure the wound was clean, but he didn't have the nerve. *This will have to be enough.* "All right, stop," he said.

He reached for the mortar filled with bruised lilac, but he kept his eyes on Tracy. As soon as she took her eyes away, he picked up the small bundle of spider silk and pushed it into the wound. Then he covered it with a handful of ground lilac leaves and put a clean cloth on top of that.

"Will it be enough?" asked Tracy.

"I don't know," said Will, but he had a strong feeling it wouldn't. In some strange way, he could still feel the sickness in the boy's body. Cleaning the wound had been a good start, but it wasn't likely to be enough. The lilac and spider silk felt right to him—they would stop the wound from festering—but they couldn't reach the poison already circulating in the child's bloodstream.

He's going to die, thought Will. It would take a day or two, but it was a near certainty, and when it happened they would probably blame him. For the first time, he began to understand the burden his mother carried every time she went to care for the sick or deliver someone's baby, and he felt a new respect for her.

"I can do that," suggested Tracy, indicating the hand he was using to keep the poultice pressed against Joey's leg. "You've done all you can."

"Let me hold it a while longer," he answered. "Then we can wrap it in place with a bandage."

She nodded and sat back, but Will couldn't relax. Staring down at the little boy, he wished he could do more. He could feel something stirring within him, a desire to reach out, but he didn't understand it.

Closing his eyes, Will kept his mind on the wound, and in his imagination it seemed as though he could almost see the essence contained in the spider silk and lilac flowing outward, ever so slowly, but it wasn't enough, and it wouldn't travel far.

There needs to be more, he thought, and then he began pressing harder on the wound, but not with his hand. From deep within, he felt something move, flowing through his hands and cloth and into the poultice. It was as though his own life was pouring into the boy.

It wasn't quite right, though; it needed to match the feeling he got from the lilac, from the spiderweb. He imagined it shifting, becoming more like the essence within the poultice, complementing and expanding it.

I'm delusional, he thought, but in his mind's eye he could see it working. The essence was expanding, moving through the small boy's body, and wherever it encountered the sickness, it eliminated it.

A quarter of an hour passed, and Will grew steadily weaker, as though the strength was leaving his body. He felt as though he had run several miles without stopping. *That's all I can do.* Letting go of the poultice, he looked up at Joey's mother. The woman was watching him with a strange look in her eye.

"I think he's going to be all right," he told her. "Can you wrap it? I'm really tired." Standing up, he started to leave the room—he needed some air—but after only a few steps the world began to spin, and the floor rushed up at him. He was unconscious before he landed.

***

Erisa and Joseph Tanner showed up sometime after midnight. They were surprised when it was Tracy who answered the door to let them in.

"Thank goodness you're here," said Tracy with obvious relief.

"How is our son?" asked Joseph.

"He's much better," said Tracy Tanner, but her face retained its worried expression. "But something happened to Will."

"Will?" said Erisa, looking past the other woman's shoulders. "Where is he?" Tracy stood aside, and they entered. Erisa found her son moments later, stretched out on the floor beside his bed. A pillow had been placed under his head and a blanket covered his body. Joey slept peacefully in the bed itself. "Is he sleeping?"

Tracy shook her head. "I don't think so. He passed out after putting the poultice on Joey. He had the strangest look on his face. I haven't been able to wake him since, so I did my best to make him comfortable."

Erisa checked Will's breathing and listened for his heartbeat, reassuring herself that her son was still alive. Then she shook him and called his name several times but failed to rouse him. Opening his eyes, she watched to see if they dilated in response to light. They did, which was a relief, but he still showed no signs of waking. Looking up at Joseph, she asked, "Can you help me get him into my bed?"

Joseph Tanner was a slender-built man, but he didn't lack for strength. He bent and lifted Will before carrying him to Erisa's room and laying him gently on the bed. Once he was settled, Erisa turned to Tracy. "Can you tell me what happened?"

Tracy described Will's efforts, from lancing the abscess to preparing and placing the poultice. Erisa was somewhat surprised that her son had had the courage to take a knife to the wound, since he had never done anything like that before, though he had watched her a time or two in the past. She felt a quiet sense of pride in her son, while simultaneously hoping he hadn't made the wound worse through his inexperience.

Tracy wasn't finished, though. "After that, he held the poultice in place for a while. It seemed a little strange, almost as though he was praying over him. It was maybe a quarter of an hour, then he told me to wrap it up, but he passed out as soon as he stood up."

Erisa's heart sped up as she heard the story, but she tried to keep her face calm. "Would you mind making some tea for us, Mrs. Tanner? You'll find everything in the cupboards there. I'll check on Joey in the meantime." She left the two of them and went into Will's room, where Joey lay, shutting the door behind her.

Her first impression was that the little boy's condition wasn't nearly as serious as his father had described. Joey was sleeping peacefully, and when she laid her hand on his brow, she felt no sign of fever.

That wasn't too unusual. If he had been on the mend already, his fever might have broken naturally, but it didn't match up with what they had told her. Chewing her lip, Erisa began to unwind the bandage around the child's leg, her eyes widening when they saw the wound.

It looked as though it had been healing for several days, with no signs of redness or swelling. The edges of the knife cut Will had made were already puckered and starting to draw together. "No, no, no," moaned Erisa. "This can't be happening."

Examining the poultice, she recognized the lilac leaves. "Why did he use this?" she muttered to herself. "The yarrow would have been better." She shook her head to clear it. There was no time for wondering at what he had done. Her first priority was covering her son's tracks.

She returned to the main room and gathered up a fresh cloth bandage from a drawer and went back to the small boy. Judging by the progress of the wound, it needed only a light dressing. Air would be more important than herbs at this stage, so it could dry out and close properly. She wrapped it carefully and went back to the Tanners.

"Joey should be fine in a few days," she told them. "It wasn't as serious as you described."

Tracy frowned. "Your son said he might die."

Erisa put a hint of condescension into her smile. "My son is a quick learner, but he lacks experience. Boys his age enjoy excitement too much. It might have been serious if you had waited longer, but fortunately you didn't. I'll keep Joey for a day or two and he can go home after that."

"I'll stay with my son," declared Tracy.

It took Erisa almost a quarter of an hour to convince both of the Tanners that there was no need for them to spend the night. Their home, after all, was less than twenty minutes away, and Erisa's house didn't have any extra beds or other accommodations for two extra people.

"I'll be back in the morning," conceded Tracy at last. She had been the more difficult of the two to convince.

Erisa nodded. "That's fine, but there's no rush to get up early. You haven't slept. Whenever you wake up will be all right, or even the next day. I'll take good care of Joey."

As soon as they had left, Erisa climbed into bed next to her son. She made sure to leave her curtain drawn, though. She was tired, but she wanted to get up early. There was someone she needed to see before the Tanners returned.

CHAPTER 5

Will woke slowly. The sunlight was streaming through the window of what he soon recognized was his mother's room. From the angle of the shadows, he could tell it was quite late, close to noon, though he had no idea why he would have slept so long. When he tried to sit up, the room began to spin, and he quickly lay back down.

Why am I so tired? he wondered. He had quite a few other questions as well, such as how had he gotten in the bed, whether his mother was home, and how Joey was doing?

It was about then that he became aware of the voices talking outside the room, which answered one of his questions. His mother was definitely home. Holding perfectly still, Will strained to make out their words.

"You're lucky he isn't dead, Erisa," said an older male voice, one he recognized as belonging to the hermit.

"How was I to know he'd do that?" returned his mother. "You said this wasn't supposed to happen."

The old man sighed. "I said it wasn't likely. Left on their own, they usually go on to live normal lives. Stressful events have a way of bringing these things out. If he was grown, this wouldn't have occurred. Puberty is a sensitive time."

"Next time I'll take him with me," said Erisa, "and to hell with my business."

"There won't be a next time."

Erisa's voice went up in alarm. "What do you mean?"

"He'll have to come with me," answered the old man. "He can't stay here any longer."

"He's my son!"

The hermit's voice grew harsh. "Do you think you can protect him? The first time is always uncertain, but now that it's happened once, it will happen again. The next time he probably will kill himself, or worse, be noticed. If word gets out, they'll either lock him up for unlicensed magic or execute him as a warlock."

His mother sounded angry when she replied, "My son is no warlock!"

"Do you think they'll care or bother to check?" pointed out the old man. "Besides, no one starts out a warlock. If he fully awakens, who knows what might happen? They'll be on him like flies on shit, all sweet words and irresistible temptation."

"You don't know that," Erisa argued, but she didn't sound confident.

"The hell I don't!" swore the hermit. "They're everywhere, even in this house. Just because you can't see or hear them doesn't mean they don't exist. If he learns to notice them, they'll notice him right back. Do you think a thirteen-year-old boy has the maturity to make sound decisions?"

"So, what? You'll make him like you?"

"Hah!" said the old man, raising his voice. "You think I'd train that pox-ridden bastard's son? That I'd teach him the keys to power? Not likely. I'll teach him enough to hide. With a little luck, he could still have a normal life."

"Oh? You've finally given up on your private war?" asked Erisa.

The old man snorted. "I gave up on the world a long time ago, just like it gave up on me. As far as I'm concerned, it and everyone in it can all go to hell. It's none of my concern."

"You still sound bitter," Erisa pointed out. "You've never given up your grudge. That kind of hatred will shorten your life."

The hermit laughed sourly. "My life is almost done. And it isn't a grudge—I simply don't give a fuck anymore. I'm not bitter, I just don't care. I did my best and all they want is easy power to further their stupid games, like mud-covered swine fighting for slop."

"If you really don't care, why are you helping us?" asked Erisa.

"That's your misconception," said the old man. "I'm not helping you. If I leave this alone, he might do something and draw them down on the village. Then I'd have to move again. I'm getting too old for that crap. I just want to live out the last of my days with what little dignity I have left. I'm doing this because it's less trouble than the alternative. I don't give two shits about your little bastard in there."

"Don't forget what I said before," warned Erisa. "If you hurt him, I'll shout your name from one end of—"

"That threat is getting old, girl," interrupted the old man. "If I were as cold hearted as that I'd just get rid of both of you, especially with you continually trying to extort me for help. It would be a damn sight easier than putting up with an apprentice. Give me a couple of years. By the time he's fifteen, he'll know enough to hide it. After that, you can have him back and I can get on with forgetting the world and all the stupid people in it."

Will heard the door open and immediately closed his eyes, pretending to still be asleep. Heavy footsteps sounded as the old man crossed the room to his bedside.

"You'll have to do better than that boy," said the old man. "Get up. You're coming with me."

Erisa put her hand on the hermit's shoulder. "He's still sleeping. Let him rest."

"I may be ancient, but I'm not addled. He's been awake for several minutes. There isn't even a trace of dreaming about him." The bed shook suddenly as the old man kicked the mattress. "Get up, boy. I don't have any more time to waste on you. We're leaving."

Will opened his eyes warily. He was pretty sure his acting had been perfect. "How did you know?"

The old man smiled down at him maliciously. "That's one of several things you'll have to learn, or else…"

"Or else what?"

"Or else you'll wind up dead," said the old man.

Erisa started to protest, "Don't threaten him…"

"Stay out of it, Erisa. The boy's mine now." Glancing around the room, he searched for something with his eyes but didn't find it. "Oh, this is your room, isn't it? Go get a bag and put his clothes in it. I don't think he's fit for packing right now."

Will's mother left. While she was gone, at the old man's urging he made another attempt at sitting up. This time he succeeded, but he still felt weak as a kitten. The old man didn't let up, though. He kept prodding and poking until Will got to his feet, where he stood swaying for a moment.

"You'd better pull it together, boy," said the old man harshly. "If you pass out on the way back, I'll leave you in the woods. I'm damn sure not carrying you. It's your spirit that's tired, not your body. Learn the difference. You'll feel worse than this before I'm done with you."

Will felt the first stirrings of anger at the rough words. "I'm not faking it," he protested. "I'm doing the best I can."

The old man reached out with one hand and lifted Will's chin so he could stare into his eyes. "You think I should feel sorry for you? Maybe I should be nicer? After all, you're like this because you saved that little boy. Is that what you're thinking?"

Will pursed his lips for a moment, then answered, "I didn't say that."

"But you were thinking it, weren't you, you selfish little prick?" accused the hermit. "What you didn't stop to think about was how dangerous what you did was. How would your mother have felt if she had come home to find you cold and dead on the floor? That never crossed your tiny little mind, did it?"

"I didn't know it was dangerous," protested Will.

"Then you shouldn't have done it!" said the old man. "Lesson number one, if you don't know what the fuck you're doing, then don't do it."

Will didn't understand why the old man was so angry. Especially since it was clear he hated Will. If saving Joey was dangerous, then Will's action was all the more heroic. "I'd do it again," he said rebelliously. "At worst, it's a life for a life."

Erisa returned with a sack stuffed full of his meager belongings. The old man took it and slung it over one shoulder, then ushered Will out the door. He stumbled trying to keep up. For some reason, he was extraordinarily clumsy today.

His mother followed them a short distance, uttering an endless stream of advice and warnings. "Be good for him, Will. Learn whatever you can. He may seem rough, but he's not as bad as all that. I love you."

"I will, Momma," he told her, wishing he could reassure her. The old man said nothing at all, ignoring both of them equally as he walked.

Eventually, Erisa stopped following them and they were left alone, following a small trail through the Glenwood. Will knew it well. He had followed it often in the past, during his many adventures with Eric. The hermit's home had been a favored destination since it seemed strange and dangerous.

Now he was going to live there. It boggled his mind. *I wonder if he'll let me visit Eric,* thought Will idly. Almost as soon as his thoughts drifted, he stumbled and fell.

"Get up, fool," snapped the old man.

Will stared sourly up at his antagonist, then shakily got to his feet again. "You could help me," he said bitterly.

The old man stretched, running his hand through the bristly white hair that stood out from his head. "I am helping you."

"You could have fooled me, then."

"This is a lesson," said the man. "A lesson in consequences. Don't forget it. Learn it well and you won't do this to yourself again, or at the very least, if you do, you'll do it knowing the price you'll pay." He watched Will struggle to coordinate his legs as they began walking again. There wasn't an ounce of sympathy in his hard, grey eyes.

They walked for fifteen minutes without a word when Will's new guardian broke the silence without warning. "The worst isn't a life for a life."

Startled, Will replied, "Sir?"

"Earlier," said the old man. "You said at worst it was a life for a life. That isn't true. There are worse things than dying in this world."

"Such as?"

"You'll learn about those things later, if you live long enough," said the hermit. "For now, you just need to do as I say. Pay heed to my words, and I guarantee the worst that will happen to you is dying."

"You're a real charmer," said Will sarcastically.

"You want me to be nicer? Fine. Here's another lesson for you," said the hermit. "There's nothing wrong with your body. It's your spirit that's worn thin. It's a big surprise to most, learning how hard it is to function when

39

your heart and soul are grey and empty. You'll recover in time, but for now you'll have to put all your attention on your movements. Focus on putting one foot in front of the other. Don't let anything distract you. You don't have the energy for stray thoughts."

Will did as he was told, and it did seem to help. So long as he kept his attention firmly on his body, it worked properly. His muscles weren't tired, though it still felt as though he was walking uphill. It was some sort of internal resistance he had to fight against.

He couldn't keep his thoughts from straying completely, though. After a short while, he asked, "Is this what happened to you?"

"Pardon?"

"Did you use up your spirit? Is that why you're so crabby and mean?" explained Will.

The old man began to laugh, long and loud, a hearty laugh unlike anything Will had heard from him before. When he finally stopped and caught his breath, he continued walking without answering.

 **CHAPTER 6**

When they finally arrived at the hermit's house, it was just as bad as Will remembered. It didn't even merit the name 'house.' A better term would have been shack, for the place had certainly seen better days.

It was about twenty feet across when viewed from the front, and perhaps as long as that from front to back, although it was hard to tell. The back of the dilapidated structure was completely overgrown with small trees, brush, and a stupendous quantity of thorny brambles. If there had ever been a back door, it was certainly no longer accessible.

"Wait here," said the old man before stepping up to the front door.

"Can't I come in?" asked Will. It wasn't that he was particularly keen on seeing the inside, but even a dirty shack would be better than sleeping outdoors.

"I don't want you fouling up my home," said the hermit bluntly. Then he went in and shut the door.

Will stared at the door, angry and confused. *Fouling up his home? Is he serious?* He was near certain he was cleaner and better smelling than the old man had been at any point in the last ten years.

The door opened again, and the hermit stepped back out, a small glass vial in his hand. He held it out to Will. "Drink this."

"What is it?" asked Will suspiciously.

"Something to make you feel better, unless you'd rather be a wet rag for the next few days. You're of no use to me like this."

As soon as he took the vial in hand he felt something, and when he unstopped it he could see a strange though faint light stirring in the dark fluid. It reminded him of one of his mother's herb infusions, except that the energy within didn't remind him of any plant. It reminded him instead of the old man who had just handed it to him.

"Is this blood?" he asked in alarm.

The hermit began to laugh again. "Why would you think that?"

"Because it feels like you," said Will, unsure how to communicate his feeling.

The old man's eyes widened slightly. "You're a little more perceptive than is good for you." Then he chuckled. "Blood—that's a good idea. No one's done that in a long time. It might be easier to make that way, though I doubt it would keep as long. Drink it."

Will clenched his teeth. "No."

"Suit yourself," said the hermit. "You can sleep out here tonight. We'll call that your second lesson." He turned away and started to go back inside.

"Wait," exclaimed Will. "I don't want to sleep out here."

The old man looked back at him. "Then drink it. Those are your choices. Drink it and come inside, or don't and sleep on the ground."

"What is it?" asked Will sullenly.

"Elixir of turynal," answered the old man.

"I don't know what that is."

The hermit sighed. "Turyn is what the old wizards called the energy that fueled their magic. Think of it as mana, spirit energy, or just as magic, if that helps you understand. Drinking it will help restore what you've lost."

Will's eyes lit up. "This is magic?"

The old man nodded, his face serious.

42

Tilting his head back, Will drank the contents in a single gulp, ignoring the bitter taste. It burned as it went down his throat, and he felt a warm glow begin to radiate from his belly. A moment later, a wave of nausea passed through him.

The old man stepped close and grabbed his head then, gripping his skull with one hand and holding his mouth shut with the other. Will struggled in his grasp, but the man's hands seemed impossibly strong.

His stomach rebelled, sending their contents upward, but the old man wouldn't release him. "Hold it, boy. Just a few seconds, that's all it takes," said the hermit. Then he began to count backwards from five. When he reached 'one,' he released Will and leapt back with surprising speed.

Choking and coughing, Will began to vomit, emptying his stomach onto the weeds at his feet. Even after his belly was empty, he continued to heave for several minutes, retching and spitting. His abdomen was sore and tender even once the heaving had stopped, and the nausea was far from gone. "You poisoned me," he gasped at last.

"That's a valid observation," said the hermit, grinning down at him. "From your limited perspective, at least. I prefer to think of it as teaching through experience. The sickness you feel is called 'spirit poisoning,' but my intent wasn't as malicious as you might think. Once your body recovers from the shock, you'll find that you feel much better."

Will's stomach contracted once again. It relaxed a moment later, and he drew a deep breath. "I think I'm dying."

The old man arched one brow, then replied, "I highly doubt that, but given your lack of ability, I suspect you'll feel ill for half an hour or longer."

"Why?" asked Will, spitting to clear his mouth of the taste. "Why would you do that to me? What did I ever do to you?"

"Besides being born?" stated the old man, answering his question with a question. "Nothing. I don't hate you, boy, though I'll admit to disliking you. But that isn't the reason I gave you the elixir." He sat down on the porch and stared at Will thoughtfully. "My real reason was to get you back on your feet quicker, and to illustrate a valuable lesson. The turyn in that vial was mine, as you correctly observed. If it had been yours, you would have suffered very few side effects, or even none at all. Why do you think that is?"

Glaring at him, Will answered, "Because you're evil."

The hermit laughed. "Guilty as charged, but that isn't the reason. Try again."

"You aren't human," Will suggested. "Or maybe you're a half-fiend, the wicked product of the union of a demon and a human woman."

"Better," said the hermit. "You certainly don't lack for imagination. Still wrong, though. At least your answer has a testable element to it."

"Testable?"

The old man nodded. "If you could convince a half-fiend to produce the elixir of turynal for you, you could take it and see how it affected you."

Will was dumbfounded. "But, demons aren't real. Right?"

"Oh, they're quite real," said the hermit matter-of-factly. "And while I've never had one make the elixir for me, I did devour the essence of a demon once, which amounts to almost the same thing. It wasn't too different from that of another human."

"You what?" Will gaped at him.

Waving his hand, the old man went on, "That isn't the point, boy. The important thing for you to know is that even if the elixir I gave you had come from your mother, or a saint, the effect on you would have been much the same. Try to reason out why that is."

"I don't believe you," said Will abruptly.

"As if I give a shit, boy," said the hermit dryly. "Stick to the question at hand."

Will stared at the dirt in front of him, then scooted back to put some more distance between himself and the mess he had expelled from his stomach. He didn't know what to make of the old man's claim regarding demons. *It couldn't be true. He's just trying to scare me,* he decided. Glancing up, he saw that his new guardian was still waiting for an answer.

He thought about his mother's herbs then. Each one was different from the others; they all had their own subtle properties. Even plants of the same species were different, as he had come to learn from his newfound insights. If people were the same, or rather the magic within them, would that account for the sickness he felt?

"Because they're different?" said Will hesitantly, unsure how to explain his thoughts.

The old man's eyes perked up, sending his bushy brows to new heights. "What's different?"

"Their turyn, or whatever you call it. If everyone's is different, maybe that's what makes you feel sick when you get someone else's…"

"Now you're starting to think," said the hermit. "Here's something else to consider. Long ago, some mages would make the elixir of turynal and sell it to more skilled wizards. Even today, warlocks use it to barter with their patron spirits. If it makes the user sick when they imbibe someone else's turyn, why do you suppose it has value to others?"

It sure isn't the taste, thought Will sourly. Then he remembered something the old man had said a few moments before. "You said I lacked ability. Maybe someone with skill can use it without getting sick?"

The hermit smiled. "You're not as stupid as you look. A proper wizard would never drink a vial like that in a single draught, unless it was his own. He would sip it slowly, taking time to absorb and convert its essence. Very few, and only those with great skill and experience, could manage to take an entire dose all at once like that."

"Then why did you tell me to gulp it down?" exclaimed Will angrily.

The old man smirked. "I didn't. I never said anything about how you should take it."

"Well you could at least have warned me!"

"It's better this way anyway," said the hermit. "If you had tried to drink it slowly, you'd have wasted most of it. I doubt you could have taken a second sip."

Standing up, Will kicked loose dirt over the products of his insulted stomach. "I don't see how it's better. I threw it all up."

"How do you feel?" asked the old man innocently.

Will paused in mid-thought. He hadn't noticed before, but his bone-weary fatigue had vanished. Even the nausea had faded into the background and seemed to be rapidly disappearing. In a word, he was better. Much better. He looked at the old man in surprise. "How? It came up almost immediately."

"The elixir is just a vector or intermediary," explained the hermit. "It contains and sustains the turyn until it reaches its destination, which in this case was you."

His head was spinning with unfamiliar words. "Vector?" asked Will.

The old man frowned for a moment. "Vector has several meanings, but in this case, I'm talking about a substance used to convey something from one place to another. Once you swallowed the elixir, it only took a few seconds for the turyn to diffuse from a small area of high concentration into the relatively empty space of your half-dead body. I'm using alchemical terms to describe it, but the principles are the same, although true drugs take quite a bit longer to diffuse, but I won't get into osmotic pressure right now." He paused, scratching his beard for a moment. "Actually, I suppose I should say 'etheric pressure,' since we're talking about turyn."

Will stared at him as though he were speaking a foreign tongue. "Huh?" was all he could manage.

The brief speech seemed to have improved the hermit's mood somewhat, because he gave Will an apologetic look. "Pardon me. It's been a long time since I had occasion to talk about any of this. I forget you're not versed in it. Not to worry, I'll loan you a primer this evening. Reading through it will help improve your vocabulary immensely."

"Primer?" asked Will.

The old man nodded. "A book meant for learning."

"Oh," said Will, understanding at last. "You'll have to just tell me. I can't read."

His new guardian stared at him as though he had grown a second head. "You can't—what? Didn't Erisa teach you?"

Will shook his head. "She says talking is faster anyway, so there's no point in it," he replied confidently.

The old man growled. "I don't have years to sit around *telling* you everything. Besides which, since I've been alone so many years, speaking only to myself, I've forgotten how to communicate with ignoramuses. So, if you intend to learn anything from me, the first thing you'll do is learn to read. We'll start in the morning. I'm too tired to even think about it right now. I'll show you the stove and you can start dinner."

Will shrugged. "You expect me to cook? I don't know how to cook."

This was too much for the hermit. Throwing up his hands he shouted at the boy, "Then what good are you?" The sudden movement, combined with the noise, spooked a doe that had been grazing nearby, and the hermit's eyes tracked her as she sprang away. In the space of an instant, he forgot about Will entirely. "Deer?" he muttered, as though he had forgotten the very existence of such an animal.

Seconds later his face reddened, and his eyes seemed to catch fire. Furious, he sprang to his feet and began running around one side of the house. "Fucking deer! Get away!"

Will watched him go with wide eyes. "He's mad, utterly mad."

From the far side of the house, he could hear the old man screaming, "Nooo! Stop! You bastards, what have you done to my squash?" The voice receded slightly as the hermit got farther away, but the volume of his voice was such that the words were quite clear to Will's young ears. "I'll kill every last one of you misbegotten wretches!"

CHAPTER 7

The next morning arrived bright and early, and Will greeted it with muscles stiff from spending a night on a cold, hard floor. The old man's home had turned out to have two rooms. The front room, which Will had at first assumed was the entirety of the small house, was dirty, cluttered, and without a bed. Its main feature had been an old stone hearth that he had been forced to cook dinner over.

His efforts had been rewarded with singular praise from his new guardian. "That was by far one of the worst meals I have ever been forced to endure."

"You didn't have to eat it," Will responded sullenly.

"Trust me, I won't again," the old man said. "But I did so out of respect for your talents. You have a lot of promise, boy."

"Huh?"

The hermit nodded. "Definitely. When I eventually kick you out for laziness, stupidity, or some other yet undiscovered fault, you have a great career ahead of you. You could do well as the chief cook for King Lognion's dungeon. One taste of your food would have his prisoners begging to confess their guilt. They'd probably entreat him to send them to the gallows just to escape your culinary torment."

Will pressed his lips together firmly. He was quickly learning that the old man loved to goad him to anger. He wouldn't reward the bastard this time.

"Let me ask you, though," continued the old bastard. "Where did you get the inspiration to combine raw turnips with oat gruel?"

Will ground his teeth, refusing to respond.

"And not peeling the turnips, that was pure genius." The old hermit sighed. "I can still taste the dirt and grit in my teeth. Do you think you could make it again?"

"You said you wouldn't eat it," Will replied.

"Oh, I won't! I was just thinking that if we spread it around the garden, it might keep the deer away from my plants."

The old man laughed long and hard after that, before eventually retiring to what must be his bedroom—the door to which Will had somehow failed to observe until the hermit rose and opened it. When he started to follow, the crotchety bastard had turned back to face him. "You sleep out here." Then he shut the door and locked it.

With no blanket and no bed, Will slept on the floor beside the slowly dying hearth fire. Stretching to relieve the soreness in his shoulders, he glared unhappily at the old man when the door to the back room opened the next morning.

The cruel bastard's first words of the day were, "Do you know how to cook eggs?" When Will shook his head 'no,' the old man showed him, supervising this time to prevent a repeat of the previous night's disastrous dinner.

After that, he brought out a large flat piece of dark grey slate and a piece of chalk. He began scratching symbols onto it. "This morning you'll learn the sounds of the alphabet."

Will frowned. "Shouldn't you be teaching me something more important?"

Large, bushy brows went up questioningly. "Such as?"

"Magic," said Will immediately.

"Why the hell would I do that?" said the old man in genuine astonishment.

"But…"

The hermit went on, "You can't cook or read. Your vocabulary is so poor as to be nonexistent. At this point, I wouldn't be surprised to find you'd never learned to wipe your ass. You have far more important things to learn than magic."

Will was beginning to get used to the insults, so he refused to take offense. Instead, he asked, "After I learn to read, you'll teach me magic, though, right?"

"I'll teach you herbology, and if you're lucky, a little alchemy."

Will's shoulders slumped. "If I wanted to learn that, Mom could teach me," he complained.

The hermit's eyes twinkled with hidden mirth. "Who do you think taught her?"

Surprised, Will answered, "She told me it was her great-grandfather." Then he remembered his previous doubt. "She lied, didn't she?"

The old man grew still, his face taking on a serious expression and his eyes misting slightly. After a long pause, he said, "No. No, that's the truth."

Will couldn't believe it. "You're not old enough!"

"Hah!" said the old man. "I don't look my age. How old do you think I am?"

Trying to think of the oldest person he had ever met in the village, Will guessed, "Sixty?"

The hermit began to laugh. "I'm a bit older than that, but if anyone asks, sixty will do."

Something else occurred to Will then. "What should I call you? Mom says I can't use your name."

Hard eyes bored into him. "She told you my name?"

Will shook his head. "I overheard the two of you. Your name is Arrogan, right?"

"No," declared the old man. "Arrogan died a long time ago. He's a historical figure. Best to forget him.

Someone mistook me for him once, and it's caused me all sorts of trouble ever since."

"Who was he?" asked Will, his curiosity piqued.

"The betrayer of Darrow," said the hermit, referring to a country that neighbored Terabinia. "After you learn to read, you can look him up in one of my books. I'm not interested in talking about him."

He could sense that the topic was considered closed, so Will went back to his previous question. "Well, what should I call you? You do have a name, don't you?"

"You're barely weaned from your momma's teat. Calling me by my name would be disrespectful," said the old man, deflecting the true question.

Will thought for a few seconds. "If I'm your apprentice I should call you 'Master,' shouldn't I?"

"Probably," admitted the hermit, "but I'd die of embarrassment if anyone heard you and attributed your idiocy to my teaching."

"How about 'Grampa'?" suggested Will, watching the old man carefully.

The hermit froze a second, then blinked, his face taking on a strange expression. "Why would you do that?"

"Well, if you're Mom's great-grandfather, then you're my great-great-grandfather, so we're family," said Will hopefully. He wasn't sure why he had made the suggestion. The only family he'd ever had were his cousins, his uncle, and his mother. For some reason the thought of calling someone 'father,' or in this case, 'grandfather,' appealed to some inner need he didn't fully understand.

The old man coughed, then cleared his throat. When he answered, his voice seemed thicker than before. "Fine. You can call me Grandfather if you want, but if we're ever around other people use 'Master.'"

"You said that would be embarrassing," Will reminded him.

His grandfather glared at him. "Not as embarrassing as having people know I'm related to a lackwit." He pointed at the slate. "You need to learn these ten letters. Once you've managed that, I'll show you the rest. If you can name them all and tell me their associated sounds, I'll teach you something interesting after dinner this evening, assuming you don't poison us."

"Magic?" asked Will hopefully.

The old man paused. "Why are you so damned interested in magic?"

Will looked evenly at his grandfather. "You and Mother both seem to think I've got some talent. That's why you brought me here, isn't it?"

"I brought you here to teach you to be an herbalist," said his grandfather. "Along the way I hope to teach you only enough magic to keep you from killing yourself or getting yourself put in prison."

Defiantly, Will spoke up, "I don't want to be an herbalist! I want to be a sorcerer, like you."

The old man's face hardened. "What did you call me?"

"You're a sorcerer, aren't you?"

His grandfather stood, towering over him, his face angrier than Will had yet seen. "I'll take your ignorance into account this once, boy, but if you ever call me that again I'll cut your ears off and sew them on backwards. Do you hear me?"

Confused, Will nodded. "Aren't the most powerful mages sorcerers, though? Like the king?"

The old man's eyes lit with fury. "Sorcerers are the weakest, most morally corrupt, vilest, and most despicable examples of humankind ever to crawl mewling out of their mothers' wombs. They aren't even fit to be called 'mages.' I'd sooner be accused of trafficking with demons and named a warlock as to be called a sorcerer."

The vehemence in his grandfather's voice set Will back on his heels. It made little sense to him. All the most powerful nobles, and even the king himself, were sorcerers, commanding powers so vast they could wipe out entire armies, or even level mountains, if the stories were to be believed. It had been King Lognion's distant ancestor, the first sorcerer, who had defeated Darrow and established Terabinia's independence. By comparison, warlocks were known to be degenerate magic wielders who traded with demons and evil spirits for their powers. Being named one was a capital offense.

So what does that make him? wondered Will. He remembered the old man saying he had once devoured a demon's essence. Was he really a warlock?

The old man noted the fearful expression on his face. "I'm not saying I *am* a warlock, dunce! That was a rhetorical device."

Will wasn't sure what 'rhetorical' meant, but he got the gist of the old man's statement. "Then what are you?"

"Someone who isn't going to teach you magic," spat his grandfather. "You'll learn to be an herbalist, and I'll teach you just enough magic to keep you alive and to understand why you don't want to be a sorcerer." Will didn't reply, and after a moment the old man took his silence for acquiescence. Pointing at the slate, he said, "I'll go over the letters again. Pay attention. I expect you to use the rotten gourd you call a head."

Will did his best, reciting the sounds as his grandfather repeated them to him. Fortunately, he had a pretty good memory, not that the old man would ever praise him for it. Once he could repeat back all the names of the letters and their related sounds, the old man stood up to leave.

"I'm going to check the garden," said his grandfather.

A few minutes later, he could hear the old man bellowing from behind the house. "Gah! Get away! I'll hunt every one of you demon-spawned quadrupeds down and exterminate you if you come back again!"

There was a short silence, and Will laughed quietly to himself, imagining the old man running around behind the house in a panic. Then his grandfather started yelling again, "Fuck off! I'll curse you and your offspring unto the tenth generation!"

CHAPTER 8

That evening, after a dinner of peas, roasted carrots, and yet more turnips, Will's grandfather sat with him in front of the hearth. "Ready to learn something interesting?"

"How was the food?" asked Will warily. Their latest meal had been bland, but the old man had walked him through the preparation step by step. He suspected his grandfather might be planning to punish him if the food wasn't up to his standards.

His grandfather replied, "Barely edible, but if you keep this up we might not starve to death."

"As if you could do any better," Will huffed.

The old man sat up straight, affronted. "I'll have you know I'm the best cook from here to eastern Darrow. Watching you mutilate vegetables is downright painful for me."

Will's eyes narrowed. "First you said you were an herbalist, now you claim to be a chef. I don't know what to believe anymore."

"The best chefs are herbalists," declared his grandfather self-righteously. "Now, do you want to learn this or not?"

Cautiously, Will nodded.

His grandfather rose and went to a side cupboard before returning with what appeared to be a tallow candle. Sitting back down, he placed it on the floor in front of Will. He glanced to one side suddenly. "Look over there!"

Will did, jerking his head around, but the moment his eyes left the old man he felt a sharp pain in his chest.

Whipping his head back around, he saw that the candle was now lit. He glared at his grandfather. "Did you pinch me?"

The old man smiled evilly. "No."

"Then what did you do?"

His grandfather picked up the candle, holding it in front of Will's face. "I've linked your life to this candle. The flame represents the turyn within you. Whatever happens to it represents what is happening within you."

Will wasn't impressed. Then his grandfather reached over and pinched his arm. The flame shot several inches into the air, flaring in correspondence with Will's temper. "Damn it! Stop!" exclaimed Will. "That hurts." The flame died down slightly, but continued to flicker angrily.

"Did you see what happened?" asked his grandfather excitedly. "Do you understand?"

Will rolled his eyes. "You'd make a great entertainer, if it wasn't for your foul attitude."

"They're linked, idiot!" said the old man. "Your life and the candle flame are one and the same." When that statement failed to impress his grandson, he reached out with two fingers, as if to snuff the candle out.

Will slapped his hand away, suddenly afraid.

His grandfather laughed, then leaned forward and blew hard on the flame. It jumped, burning higher in response to a jolt of adrenaline as panic ran through Will, but nothing else happened. The fire didn't even respond to the sudden puff of air. "It reflects *you*," said the old man, "not the other way around."

Awed by the strange behavior of the candle flame, Will blew on it himself. It didn't move at all. "So it isn't real?"

"Oh, it's real," said his grandfather. "Or rather, it represents the reality within *you*. Nothing out here can affect it." He waved his hand through the flame, which remained perfectly still. "The only thing that can change it is *you*." Bringing his hand up suddenly, he smacked his palm against Will's forehead, and the flame guttered and swirled.

"Enough!" exclaimed Will, annoyed. "You made your point. I thought you were going to teach me something interesting. This is a party trick."

"You said you wanted to learn magic," said the old man.

"You said you wouldn't teach me magic," Will shot back.

His grandfather rolled his eyes. "And I won't, but if it makes any difference to you, this lesson is the first lesson any wizard learns. It's the most important thing I could ever teach you, whether you ever become a wizard or not; the first and greatest knowledge you will ever gain."

Will glanced sideways, impatient and annoyed. "Why are you talking about wizards? I don't want to be a wizard. They're just librarians and assistants. They can't do much of anything."

The old man closed his eyes. Will could see the muscles in his jaw working as he cussed under his breath. "Give me patience to deal with fucking morons," muttered the old man. Will waited, expecting his grandfather to explode once again, but after a moment the old man let out a long breath and opened his eyes, his face calm.

"Listen up, boy," said his grandfather. "I'm only going to give this speech once, so pay attention. I've been making allowances, since you're entirely ignorant. I'm going to explain a few things. Interrupt me and I'll rip your tongue out and use it to make breakfast tomorrow. Do you understand?"

Will nodded, afraid to speak.

The old man smiled at his caution. "First, do you know the difference between mages, warlocks, sorcerers, and wizards?"

Still unsure whether he should open his mouth, Will shook his head no.

"Mage is a general term," continued his grandfather. "Anyone capable of magic is a mage. Mages aren't born, they are trained. Almost anyone has the necessary potential, but very few ever become aware of it, and fewer still gain the skill to do anything.

"Wizards are mages who have learned to control their turyn, and with it they can affect the world around them. Through training and practice, they can accomplish a wide variety of things, including the use of spells and the creation of potions and other magic items.

"Warlocks are mages who bargain with external powers to gain advantages." His grandfather pointed at the candle flame. "This flame represents your turyn. As you might have guessed, it isn't a large amount of power and can easily be exhausted. Warlocks seek to augment this power via agreements with supernatural agents. They may deal with spirits, the lords of faerie, demons, or any number of other beings. In general, I think this is a bad idea, as you almost always give up far more than you gain.

"Long ago, most of the early mages were shamans, which was basically a type of warlock dealing with primal nature spirits, but over time, some became more skilled. Magic was studied and better understood. It was codified, and spells were created. This was the beginning of true wizardry.

"The candle flame spell I just showed you is the beginning of that new understanding. It was the foundation that all wizardry rests upon. That may not make sense to you now, but someday, you'll understand why.

"Sorcerers are mages who hold the heart-stone enchantments of one or more elemental spirits. You can think of a heart-stone enchantment as a leash or binding. It gives them absolute control over an elemental. Elementals range in power from very weak to extremely powerful, but controlling any of them grants a vast amount of power to the mage, crude though it may be.

"A few centuries ago, there were no sorcerers. The first was a wizard of great skill, who designed the heart-stone enchantment and trapped the first elemental. Most of the sorcerers of today are no better than leeches, resting on the achievements of their ancestors. The heart-stone enchantments are passed down through the generations, and those that receive them gain vast power through no effort of their own. Many of them can barely manage a spell, if they have any training at all." The old man stopped for a second, then asked, "Any questions?"

"What are you?" asked Will directly.

His grandfather sighed. "I'm an herbalist, and an old man who knows a little too much for his own good."

It was clear he wasn't going to say more about himself, so Will changed tactics. "Why do you hate sorcerers?"

"None of your damned business," snapped the old man. "All you need to know is they're lazy, useless individuals. Also, what they do is morally repugnant."

"Why?"

"It's slavery," said his grandfather. "Rather than develop their skills and use their own innate gifts, they trap and enslave the most basic spirits of nature. The most benign of warlocks makes a victim of himself, at the very least, but a sorcerer violates the purest and simplest spirits in the world. Compounding their wickedness, the power they gain is generally used to exert control over others."

Will thought about it for a minute, then tried to summarize his thoughts. "So, you're saying that all mages are evil, except for wizards, and they're the weakest of the bunch."

"If wits were food, you'd starve to death," answered his grandfather, "but at least you're trying to think." He sighed, staring up at the ceiling. "No. It's entirely possible for a warlock to be good, though he or she would still be a fool. A good warlock trades only what they already possess—elixir of turynal, blood, or even their own soul—but most of them wind up stealing to gain more than they deserve. They'll take children, or other helpless sorts, and use them for their own ends. A good sorcerer, by contrast, would no longer be a sorcerer, because he'd free the elementals that serve him.

"As for wizards, I guess that's true, these days at least. Most of them spend their time bowing and scraping for the sorcerers, hoping to be given scraps. Not one of the current lot has the courage to rely on their own strength or learn the secrets of true mastery."

Will stared at his feet, feeling sad and deflated. He had never expected magic to be so depressing.

"So now you understand why I won't teach any more than you absolutely need to know," said the hermit. "You can't be a sorcerer because unless you're born into one of the noble families, they'd never give you an elemental, and I certainly wouldn't train you to become a wizard capable of enslaving one on your own. Far better for you to be an herbalist. At least then you can help people."

Something about that statement caught Will's attention, for it implied the old man had far more knowledge than he should. "You know how to create the heart-stone enchantment?" he asked suddenly.

"Hah!" barked his grandfather. "Only the most skilled of today's sorcerers can manage that. If I did have that knowledge, I'd certainly never allow it to be used again. No sense in repeating the mistakes of the past."

"Oh," said Will, dejected. But he noticed that the old man didn't actually answer the question. *He could have denied it, but he didn't.*

"We've spent enough time on bullshit," said his grandfather abruptly. "Time for you to learn. Stare at the candle flame."

Will did so, but nothing happened. "Now what?" he asked.

"That's it," said his mentor. "Just keep a close eye on it from now on. Pay close attention to any changes."

Frowning, Will asked, "For how long?"

His grandfather scratched his bearded chin thoughtfully. "That depends on you, but most likely for a couple of years or so. Actually, I take that back. As dumb as you are, it will probably be even longer."

Jumping to his feet, Will exclaimed, "What? That's crazy!" The flame flared up briefly, then swirled violently in response to his anger.

"See that!" said the old man, pointing at the candle. "That's the sort of thing you need to observe."

"But why?" said Will, exasperated.

"So you can control it," said his guardian smugly. "For you to keep from doing magic, you first have to learn the difference between your insides and your outsides, and how one affects the other. Now, go get the broom and sweep the room out before you go to bed."

"I don't have a *bed*," Will announced, bitterly.

"And you never will, with that attitude."

Chapter 8

A low growl rose from Will's throat, but he did as he was told. Snatching up the broom from one corner, he began vigorously sweeping.

"Watch the flame, idiot!" shouted his grandfather. "Were you paying attention to anything I told you?"

"How can I do that and sweep at the same time?" said Will in frustration.

"Hold it in one hand. It won't burn anything. It isn't a real flame. If that's too awkward, just put it somewhere in your line of sight. You really are daft. Why do I have to explain every little thing?"

Swallowing an angry retort, Will moved the candle and resumed his work, beating angrily at the floor with the broom. The flame danced in time with his movements, flaring now and then as he silently cursed his tormentor.

"That's better, moron," encouraged his grandfather. "Make sure you finish before you go to sleep. I'm off to bed. I want eggs and toast for breakfast. If you're smart, they'll be ready when I get up."

Will's temper finally snapped. "We don't have any bread! How do you expect me to make toast?"

The old man ignored his insolence. "Oh, right. One second." Leaving the room, he stepped through the door into his bedroom. When he returned a moment later, he held a large, relatively fresh loaf in one hand. "Use this."

Dumbfounded, Will asked, "Where did that come from?" The bread was obviously less than two days old and he knew for a fact the hermit hadn't gone to town in that time.

"None of your damn business," said his grandfather. Then the old man gave him a smile and added sweetly, "Good night." Disappearing into his bedroom, he shut the door and Will was left alone.

CHAPTER 9

Will woke the next morning, cold, sore, and irritated. The candle sat a few feet away on the floor, still burning and with no sign of having gotten any shorter. Remembering the old man's words, he got up and started breakfast.

There weren't any eggs in the house, so he went outside and walked to the back. A small trail led through the brambles and into a wide-open space where his grandfather grew a variety of beans, squash, turnips, and other vegetables. The chicken coop was at the far end, farthest from the house, though still within the defensive, thorny barrier. Idly, he wondered how deer managed to get in, since there was a small gate to prevent them from entering through what he assumed was the only opening.

He managed to collect a handful of eggs with only minor injuries from the offended hens, then went back to make breakfast. His grandfather was waiting on him. "You left the candle behind."

"I just went to get eggs," explained Will.

"Leave it behind again and I'll cook dinner without letting you have any," warned the old man.

"Fine with me," said Will sullenly. "You never cook anyway."

"It wouldn't be a punishment if I cooked it," said the hermit dryly. "Speaking of which, why isn't breakfast ready?"

"I just woke up a few minutes ago."

The old man scowled. "If you have that much trouble rising, you can start sleeping on the porch. The sun will wake you up that way."

Will stared at him, trying to decide if his grandfather was joking or not. *Knowing how mean the old bastard is, he probably does mean it,* he reasoned. The candle flame burned violently.

"Stop cussing me and get busy," said the old man.

Will glared at the flame, realizing it had betrayed his emotions. "Stupid candle." He got busy, heating an iron skillet and cutting the bread into rough slices.

"Have you never handled a knife before?" The old man's tone was belligerent, as usual.

Will gave him a blank stare. The old geezer had watched him cutting turnips up just the day before.

His grandfather stepped closer and took the knife from his hand. "Gently. Don't cut bread like you're trying to chop through a carrot. Use a light touch and pull." Under his skillful touch, a perfect slice emerged from the loaf of bread.

The old man never ceased to surprise him. Will was about to say something when he felt a sudden movement against his leg. Looking down, he saw a large, grey cat. "What's this?" he asked.

His grandfather glanced down. "Oh, him. That's the goddamned cat."

"You never mentioned having a pet."

"Pet? Hell no," protested the hermit. Cracking one of the eggs into a small wooden bowl, the old man placed it on the ground, whereupon the cat began to eat.

"If he isn't your cat, why are you feeding him?" asked Will, puzzled. "If you feed strays, they won't leave."

"Who says I'm feeding him?" quipped the hermit. "I'm just paying rent. And don't call him a stray; you'll piss him off."

He really is crazy, thought Will. Reaching down, he tried to pet the grey feline, but it hissed and bared its teeth at him.

"See?" said his grandfather smugly. Cracking the rest of the eggs one by one, he began frying them in the pan.

"You just called him the 'goddamned cat,'" argued Will. "How is that any better than 'stray'?"

"He's got his pride," said the hermit.

"Is he your familiar?" The cat looked up at Will's words and hissed at him. If he didn't know better, he might have believed the creature understood him.

His grandfather slid the eggs from the pan to a waiting plate with a smooth, practiced motion and then used his other hand to swat the back of Will's head. "Don't be a jackass!" Then he addressed the cat, "Don't mind him. He's a charity case I picked up. He'll learn better manners."

The stray blinked once, slowly, then returned to eating the raw egg.

The old man split the eggs between two plates and then arranged the toast beside them and began spreading butter on the slices on his own plate. He pointed the knife at Will. "No butter for you."

Will was very sure his grandfather didn't have a cow. "Where did you get butter?"

Predictably, the old man replied, "None of your damn business." Then he lifted a knob of butter on the end of the knife and offered it to the cat, who had just finished his raw egg. "Want any?"

The cat turned its head away and began cleaning one paw.

"Suit yourself," said Will's grandfather. Turning back to his grandson, he added, "Let's get one thing straight. The goddamn cat owns this place. We're his tenants, so mind yourself when he's around."

Will wasn't sure whether to laugh or cry. It seemed every day that his guardian showed a new facet of his personal insanity. "What's his name?"

"How the hell should I know?" responded his grandfather. "He's a cat. If you feel the need to be formal, call him 'the goddamn cat.' He likes that."

Will shook his head. "I can never figure out if you're being serious or not."

The old man looked up, spearing him with pale blue eyes. "I'm dead serious. The goddamn cat comes when he pleases, leaves when he pleases, and if he wants anything, you damn well give it to him." Stuffing more egg into his mouth, Will's grandfather mumbled the rest.

Will wasn't sure, but it sounded as though he had said, "I don't want to have to move again."

The cat soon wandered off, with nary a goodbye, and Will put thoughts of the strange conversation out of his head. The eggs and toast made that fairly easy to do, since they were perfectly cooked. It would have been better if he'd had some of the butter for his toast, but the eggs were so tasty he almost didn't care. *He really is a good cook, despite being nutty.*

After breakfast, and the inevitable washing of dishes, they moved on to Will's literary education. In spite of the fact that Will had only just learned the alphabet, his grandfather insisted he begin trying to puzzle out words from a small book. As if that weren't enough, the old man occasionally interrupted him with reminders to keep an eye on the candle flame, as though something might happen while he was trying to puzzle out the meaning of the writing.

In fact, the flame did shift and change while he was concentrating. Most of the changes were subtle, but at times, usually when his frustration began to build, it would grow noticeably brighter.

He got so engrossed in his task that he lost track of time, so it was a surprise when his grandfather's voice broke him out of his reverie. "I'm stepping out. The garden needs some tending."

The old man was wearing a leather cap with long thongs tied under his chin to keep it in place. Sticking out from the top were two rather large deer antlers. The effect was simultaneously frightening, and ridiculous. "Wha— what?" Will stuttered. "What is that?"

"A hat, obviously," spat his grandfather. Then he was gone.

It was a strange testimony to the fact that Will had gotten used to such weirdness that he spent no more than a few seconds thinking about it before returning to his study. Or perhaps it was that he genuinely enjoyed trying to figure out the words in front of him. He had never been confronted with a purely mental task before, and he found considerable satisfaction as he sorted out some of the simpler words by sounding out the letters.

Some time later, he was startled when he heard a voice calling his name. "Will!" It was Eric.

Picking up the candle, he stepped outside. The flame became smooth and stopped flickering when his eyes fell on his best friend's face. "Eric?"

"There you are!" said Eric. "I got worried when your mom said you were living here. Why did she kick you out?"

"I wasn't kicked out," insisted Will indignantly. "It's sort of an apprenticeship."

Eric's eyes grew round. "Is it because you healed the Tanner kid?"

"I didn't heal him. I made a poultice for a bad abscess."

His friend nodded, knowingly. "That's not what Mrs. Tanner is saying. She thinks it was magic." Then he noticed the candle in Will's hand. "What's that for?"

Will shrugged. "I'm not really sure. Grandfather is a little strange."

"Grandfather?"

"He's Mom's great-grandfather, so he's my great-great-grandfather," he explained.

Eric paused, staring into the distance for a moment. "If that's true, then he's my great-great-grandfather too. Are you sure that's right? He doesn't look old enough, and my dad never said anything about it. He always called him a crazy old hermit."

Will hadn't thought about that, but Eric was right. Eric's father was Erisa's older brother, so his cousins would also be the old man's great-great-grandchildren. "I dunno," he admitted. "Mom said her great-grandfather taught her about herbs, and the old man says he was her teacher, so—"

"I'll ask my dad when I get home," said Eric. Then he held up the bundle in his hands, pushing it toward his friend. "Your mom asked me to bring you this."

"What is it?"

"A blanket."

Unrolling the bundle, Will found a heavy wool blanket along with a thick quilt, the same one that had once adorned his bed at home. He sighed gratefully. "Thanks, Eric. I really needed this."

His friend laughed. "I told her she was worrying too much, but she was afraid you might be getting cold at night."

"I don't even have a bed," admitted Will.

"What?" Eric seemed shocked. "Where do you sleep?"

"On the floor," answered Will.

"That's just cruel," said Eric indignantly. "Does he think you're a dog?"

Remembering the goddamn cat, Will replied, "If I were a dog he'd probably treat me better."

Eric clapped him on the shoulder. "Tell you what. When I get home, I'll talk to Dad about building a cot for you. No one should have to sleep on the floor."

Will felt a surge of gratitude and the candle flame shrank slightly, becoming round and changing to a warmer orange color. He had never felt closer to his cousin than he did at that moment. "Thanks, Eric."

His friend smiled. "Think nothing of it." Then his eyes lit up. "You said this was an apprenticeship—what are you learning? Are you going to be a sorcerer?"

Will felt a moment of panic and glanced around, making sure his grandfather hadn't returned. "Don't say that word! The old geezer gets really mad if you say anything about sorcerers. He hates them for some reason."

Eric frowned. "Then what are you learning?" His voice dropped lower. "Is it black magic? Is the old man a warlock? He is, isn't he?"

"Shush!" warned Will. "You're going to get me in trouble. I don't know what he is, but he doesn't seem to like magic very much, even though he definitely knows some. He says he's going to train me to be an herbalist."

"Boring," sighed Eric in a long breath. "Is that what you're learning now? Your mom could teach you that stuff." He pointed at the candle in Will's hand. "What's that anyway?"

Will grinned. "It's magic, some sort of spell he's teaching me."

His friend's eyes lit up with excitement. "Really? What does it do?" Eric leaned forward to examine the candle more closely.

"Nothing, as far as I can tell," admitted Will. "It's not even hot. You can touch it." He demonstrated for his friend by putting his fingertip in the flame.

70

Eric didn't bother hiding his disappointment. "That almost makes growing lavender sound more exciting."

Feeling defensive, Will replied, "At least I'm never in the dark. I have to keep it with me at all times."

"For how long?"

Grimacing, Will answered, "A couple of years."

"Wow," exclaimed Eric with mock enthusiasm. "Only two years to learn such an amazing piece of magic? That's amazing, and in only twenty more, all of this could be yours!" He swung his arms wide to encompass the dilapidated shack and weed-filled dirt yard.

"I'm sure making carts and wagon wheels is a *lot* more exciting," replied Will in a surly tone.

"Dad says cartwrights and wainwrights make good money in Cerria," said Eric, unfazed. "When I make journeyman, I can move to the city and make a fortune. Then I'll come back and settle down, marry Annabelle Withy, and have a houseful of kids."

Annabelle Withy was a sore point between them, since Will also fancied her, but he decided not to get into that argument again. He shifted directions instead. "Do you really want a houseful of kids?"

Eric winked. "Kids aren't so bad, but it's the making of them I'm looking forward to."

"Too bad," said Will. "While you're off working in the city, I'll marry Annabelle first."

"And do what?" said Eric. "Whisk her away to your own hermit's cottage in the Glenwood? The only thing you'll do is learn how to be a crazy old man who talks to his cat."

That brought Will up short. "How did you know about that?"

Eric began to laugh. "What? He really talks to his cat? You'd better start running, Will, or you'll wind up just like him. I'm sure Dad would take you in. We always need more help."

"I'll think about it," said Will, just before a distant scream of rage floated to their ears.

It was his grandfather's voice. "Fucking deer!"

"What was that?" asked Eric.

Will pushed him toward the edge of the porch. "You better go. He gets really pissy when he finds deer after his garden."

CHAPTER 10

Summer passed quickly as Will settled into a routine living with his grandfather. Each morning he made breakfast, after which he continued his literary studies. His afternoons were taken up by math and measures, and if he had time after that he was expected to clean the house before he made dinner. Through it all, he was expected to keep the candle close at hand. Any time he was caught without it, he would be scolded and punished.

The punishments were rather odd, though. Most commonly, his grandfather would cook dinner while he watched, then refuse to let him have any. Whenever this happened, the old man would show off his culinary skills by turning the most ordinary of ingredients into what appeared to be a masterpiece of the gustatory arts. Will couldn't be sure if it actually tasted good, since he wasn't allowed to sample the food on these occasions, but it certainly smelled amazing.

Those incidents put a fire in his belly, and not just the ache of his empty stomach. After the first few times, he began to pay close attention when his grandfather cooked, hoping to learn some of the old man's tricks. At the very least, if he couldn't eat during his punishment, he would learn to replicate some of it so he could make it for himself the next day.

As summer turned into autumn, he became grateful for the blankets his mother had sent. If the nights were cold in the summer, they were far worse in the fall. He didn't want to think about what winter would be like.

73

Without a bed to keep the floor from leaching the warmth from him, he didn't think the blankets would be enough.

Winter was fast approaching, and with it his fourteenth birthday, though he had little hope it would be marked by a celebration of any kind.

He was sitting on the porch one afternoon, pretending to add and subtract fractions, while his grandfather was off chasing deer—or whatever it was he did when he went out—when Eric appeared.

Will jumped up in excitement. He hadn't seen another human being aside from his grandfather in months. "Eric!" he shouted.

Eric was hauling what appeared to be a wooden frame of some sort, and another of Will's cousins, Sammy Cartwright, was holding up the other end. Sammy, short for Samantha, was Eric's younger sister by two years. She smiled at Will, hazel eyes twinkling above a nose dusted with a light sprinkling of freckles.

The two of them brought their burden to the porch and deposited it. "Sorry this took so long," apologized Eric.

"Hi, Will," said Sammy brightly, using one of her now free hands to push back her strawberry blond hair.

"Hey," said Will, giving her a brief nod. He wasn't particularly fond of Sammy. Through most of his childhood, she had been an annoyance, always wanting to tag along when he and Eric were looking for adventure. Worse, when they were forced to accept her, usually by Eric's mother, they weren't allowed to go very far. Instead, they became glorified baby-sitters.

He turned to Eric. "What is this?"

"A cot," said Eric proudly. He had a bundle tied over one shoulder, which he now pulled off and rolled out. It turned out to be a large sheet of canvas designed to fit over the wood frame. "I would have finished it sooner, but we had a busy summer."

"Let's take it inside and set it up," suggested Sammy.

In spite of himself, Will was somewhat glad to see Sammy as well. Despite their history, she had obviously matured quite a bit over the past year. She wasn't as gangly and awkward as he remembered her being.

As they unfolded the wood frame and stretched the canvas across it, he noticed that his cousin had changed as well. Eric's formerly skinny arms now displayed an impressive bit of muscle, the product of his labor no doubt. Will couldn't help but look down at his own arms and feel slightly envious. As far as he could see, he hadn't changed at all. If anything, his occasional missed meals had made him skinnier than before.

Sammy had a bag as well, and she opened it to reveal a linen pillow. "Here, I thought you might need this too."

Will turned it over in his hands, touched by the gesture. The pillow was off-white in color and stuffed with old, but clean, rags. One side had been embroidered with green and yellow thread, creating a simple design of grass and flowers. "Did you make this, Sammy?"

She nodded, then looked away. "Momma let me have the scraps for the stuffing. She's been teaching me embroidery, but I'm not very good at it yet."

"I think it's amazing," said Will, genuinely impressed. "It's probably the best present I've ever gotten."

Sammy blushed, but Eric gave him an abrupt shove. "Have you forgotten the cot already? I put a lot of time into that."

Will grinned. "All right, the *two* best presents I've ever gotten. Honestly, you've probably saved my life. I'm sure I'd freeze to death if I had to keep sleeping on the floor this winter."

"That's better," said Eric. "If you're done giving Sammy a big head, I have something to talk to you about." He glanced around for a moment. "Is the old man around?"

Will shook his head. "He's off somewhere. Probably chasing deer again. What is it?"

Lowering his voice, Eric leaned close. "He isn't our grandfather."

Will frowned. By now he was firmly convinced the old hermit was insane, but he hadn't shown any signs of dishonesty. Sure, the old geezer had a mean streak a mile wide, but as far as Will could tell, he was honest, often brutally so. "How do you know that?" he asked his cousin.

"I asked my dad. He said the first Cartwright to live in Barrowden was his grandfather, Nathan. Before that they lived in Branscombe. He said all his great-grandparents are buried there," answered Eric somberly.

"That can't be right," said Will. "Mom said he was her great-grandfather. Did you tell your dad that?"

"No," responded Eric. "He seemed so sure, I was afraid it might start an argument between them. He said he's seen all their graves, though they died before he was born."

Sammy pulled on her brother's sleeve. "Tell him what else Dad said!"

Eric hesitated, looking uncomfortable.

"What is it?" asked Will.

"I probably shouldn't say," said Eric. "It's not my place to talk about your mom."

"Just tell me," said Will impatiently. "I won't get mad."

"Your mom ran away from home when she was sixteen," blurted out Sammy, unable to contain herself. "She didn't come back for almost four years, and they don't know where she was. When she did come back, she was pregnant with you."

Will grimaced. He hadn't known much about it, but he had expected something along those lines. "Did he say who my father is? Maybe the old man is my great-great-grandfather on his side."

Eric seemed embarrassed. "He doesn't know. He said he thinks your mom worked as a barmaid in Cerria. She probably got pregnant from one of the customers."

Will's cheeks flushed, and the candle flame flared. His hands balled into fists. "You're saying she was a whore?"

His cousin held up his hands. "Look, I'm sorry. That's just what he said. I don't think he really knows what she was doing while she was gone."

"He also said he doesn't know anything about her being taught by the old man," put in Sammy.

Will let out a long breath, calming himself. "I don't know why she would lie about that. Plus, the old man said the same thing. Why else would he visit our house over the years?"

"You do know he doesn't visit anyone else, right?" said Eric. "He's never come into the village. Not once that I can remember."

That seemed odd. *Where does he get the butter then?* wondered Will. His grandfather never seemed to lack for necessities like soap, salt, dried beans, flour—the list went on. The old man had to be buying things from somewhere.

Sammy broke in, "Dad says there's been a hermit living here since he was a boy, and according to him, there was one here when his dad first moved to Barrowden, but he doesn't think it's always been the same old man."

"What does that mean?" asked Will.

"The hermit in the woods was an old man when Dad was a boy. He'd have died of old age by now, so the one you're living with has to be different," explained Sammy.

"Anyway, Dad said the old man who lived here when he was little had dogs."

"Just because he had dogs back then doesn't mean he would still have dogs," argued Will. *Though it is a good idea.* Putting that aside, he had to admit it seemed unlikely it was the same person living here back then. People just didn't live that long. "I'll ask him about it later."

"Be careful," warned Eric. Sammy nodded in agreement beside him. Both their faces displayed worry.

"Careful of what?" said Will dismissively.

"Remember what we talked about before?" reminded Eric. "He might be a warlock."

Will laughed. "He's a grumpy old bastard, but I don't think so."

Sammy grabbed his hand. "He might be fattening you up for later."

"I doubt it," said Will confidently. "Aside from eggs, I've never seen him eat anything that didn't grow out of the ground."

"As a sacrifice," added Sammy, wrinkling her nose.

"Well he's got a strange way of doing it, then," said Will. "His favorite punishment is not letting me eat. I've missed dinner twice this month because of that."

"Maybe his demon likes skinny virgins," suggested Eric.

"Then you should probably get out of here," returned Will with a sly grin. "He'll want to capture both of you."

Eric sniffed, lifting his chin haughtily. "I don't have to worry for long. Annabelle let me dance with her at the harvest festival."

Sammy's features grew angry. "I'm telling her you said that!"

"I did dance with her!" insisted Eric.

"No, I'm telling her what you *meant*. She'll never talk to you again if she hears what you said!" declared Sammy.

Will listened to them bicker without interrupting. It made him feel good to hear their voices, and sad at the same time. Especially the part about the harvest festival. He had completely forgotten it, and it sounded as though Annabelle had forgotten him as well.

His cousins stayed another quarter of an hour, chatting and filling him in on the doings of Barrowden. When they finally left, he felt more alone than ever, and it was hard to get back to his fractions. Math seemed pointless to him. What use did anyone have for numbers, aside from being able to count?

When his grandfather showed up that evening, he seemed to be in a good mood, until he saw the cot. "What the hell is that?"

"A cot," answered Will simply.

"I can see that, dumbass! Where did it come from?" demanded the old man.

His grandfather's angry reaction sent a quick surge of adrenaline through Will, and the flame on his candle began to flicker wildly. "E—Eric brought it for me."

"Eric? Who's that?"

"My cousin," explained Will. *He doesn't know anything about my family, does he?* Will realized.

"Why did he bring it?" asked his grandfather, his tone more even now.

"Because I told him I've been sleeping on the floor. I'll freeze this winter if I have to keep doing that."

That brought the old man up short. "You don't have a bed?"

Will just stared at him as if he'd gone mad. Then he spread his arms wide, gesturing at the small room as if to say, 'do you see a bed?'

"Oh," said his grandfather. "No, of course you don't. I had completely forgotten. Next time remind me. You shouldn't take things from strangers. Did you pay him anything?"

"Eric isn't a stranger. He's my cousin."

"Strangers, family, friends, it's all the same," insisted the hermit. "From now on, you are to take nothing from anyone without paying. Do you understand?"

Will did not understand. Family was how one survived, at least as he understood it, but he simply answered, "I don't have any money."

His grandfather nodded. "Then you take nothing." He paused then, staring at the cot. "Still, you're right. You can't keep sleeping on the floor. How much do you think a cot is worth?"

"Eric doesn't want money for it," insisted Will.

The old man fixed him with a hard stare. "Listen up. I'm not going to repeat this a third time. From this day forward, you accept nothing without paying or trading something of equal value. As long as you're my apprentice, you will owe nothing, you will accept no debts. Consider it part of your training."

Will was staring into the corner, muttering angrily to himself. "He's crazy, absolutely nutters…"

His grandfather disappeared into his room for a moment and returned with his hand outstretched, a gold coin in his palm. "This should cover it."

Will's eyes bulged. A single gold crown was worth dozens of cots—hell, it might be worth more than the hermit's entire ramshackle dwelling. He reached for the coin, but the old man snatched it back.

"What did I *just* tell you?"

He stared at the old man in confusion.

"Accept no debts!" said his grandfather emphatically. "Tomorrow you'll take the axe and saw and go cut wood. You'll do so every day until you've cut enough to last us the entire winter. *Then* I'll give you the coin, which you will take to pay your cousin for his generous gift."

The payment was far more than the work was worth. "A cot isn't worth an entire gold crown," said Will at last.

"It is to a man about to freeze to death," said his grandfather.

CHAPTER 11

It took Will nearly two weeks to cut enough wood to satisfy his lunatic grandfather. During that time, he was still expected to keep up his reading practice in mornings, arithmetic in the evening, and as always, he was not allowed to leave the candle behind at any time.

The old man did give him one break, though. He didn't make Will cook during that period, and he got his first real chance to try his grandfather's cooking, which was a revelation in and of itself. The first meal the old man made was a simple affair; roasted carrots, peas, sliced radishes, and an assortment of greens.

It didn't look like much, though it was arranged artistically on the plate, but the first bite to reach his tongue told a different story. "Wow!" exclaimed Will. "Oh, wow! What did you do to it to make it taste like this?"

"Not much," said his grandfather nonchalantly. "A little oil and vinegar for the greens. The peas I blanched and sautéed with butter. Most importantly, I didn't cook the carrots into flavorless mush as you seem so fond of doing."

For the first time, the hermit's complaints about Will's cooking made sense. If this was what his grandfather expected, then what Will had been giving him wasn't much better than pig slop. He cleaned his plate and was delighted when he was given more. His compliments seemed to sit well with the old man.

After he finished he sat back, feeling replete with food and warm in the heat coming from the hearth. He almost didn't mind the fact that his entire body was sore from chopping and hauling wood. Relaxed, he asked a question, "Why don't you get a dog?"

The hermit looked quizzically at him. "A dog?"

"You're always fussing about the deer getting into the garden. A dog would solve that," offered Will.

His grandfather stared into the embers, his expression somewhat sentimental. "I used to have a couple of dogs, but they died a long time ago. I haven't had the heart to get any since then. Plus, I don't think the landlord would appreciate it."

"Landlord?"

"The goddamned cat," clarified the old man, picking his teeth with a splinter of wood. "He really doesn't appreciate dogs. He'd probably increase the rent."

How much could one cat eat? wondered Will, but he didn't bother voicing his thought. Instead he asked, "How long ago was that? When you had the dogs?"

"Oh, it's been a while," said his grandfather. "Before you were born." He chuckled, then added, "Before your mother was born."

"You must have been a lot younger then," suggested Will.

"Not so much," said the hermit. "It's all relative I suppose, but I was already pretty old by then."

Unable to restrain his curiosity, Will was direct with his next question. "How old are you?"

His grandfather looked up sharply. "None of your damn business." Then he stood and dusted himself off. "Time for bed. Make sure to clean the dishes before you sleep."

***

83

The next morning Will rose early, and after stuffing himself full of eggs and buttered toast, he began his reading. After a couple of hours of that, his grandfather informed him that he was free to go and finish the woodcutting. With any luck, he thought he might get enough to finally finish the task.

As he started out the door, axe in hand, the old man reminded him, "Only dead wood. I know you've scoured the woods clean close to the house, but don't be tempted to cut a live tree. You couldn't afford the payment. Take your time and go farther out if you have to, even if it means you need to spend another day at it."

His grandfather had been giving him similar warnings every morning, though Will really didn't understand the prohibition against cutting live trees. He knew better than to go against the old man's orders, however, and he couldn't think of much worse than spending a day at hard labor only to get no supper. "I won't forget," he assured his guardian.

He set off toward the west, the direction opposite that of the village, since it hadn't been scavenged for wood quite as much. He remembered seeing a fallen tree in that area previously, which should provide more than enough wood. The only downside was that it was farther away than he would have liked, which meant a lot of extra hauling to get the wood home.

The ground had a gentle upward slope, since the hills that separated Barrowden from the village of Branscombe lay in that direction, but Will figured that was a good thing. It meant the trip back, while carrying a load, would be much easier.

Despite the cold wind of late autumn, the sun was shining brightly and there were no clouds that day, making his hike an almost cheerful affair. Will found himself whistling as he went, and he began to study the plants along his path. At this time of year most of the trees had lost their leaves, but some of the hardier perennials that lived beneath them were still green. Mentally, he named them as he went.

As he walked, a thought occurred to him. *He's supposed to be teaching me herbology, but I haven't had a single lesson on the topic. It's all been reading, math, and cooking.* He glanced at the candle in his hand. *And whatever this is supposed to teach me.*

His eyes fell on a tall plant he didn't recognize. "What's this?" he muttered. It was unusual for him to encounter something his mother hadn't taught him to identify already. *Ovate and dentate leaves, square stem...* Mentally, he made note of its features for future reference. It stood almost three feet tall and was still green despite the late season.

Concentrating, he focused on the plant, attempting to use his strange extra perception to learn something about its properties. He was disappointed, as he got the sense that it wasn't useful for much. It wasn't astringent, antiseptic, or good for any other purpose he could discern. It was edible, though, and it resembled sage, so he wondered about its taste. If it had a good flavor, he might be able to surprise his grandfather at dinnertime.

His mother had always warned him about trying new plants, but that had been before he discovered his special ability. Reaching out, he started to pluck one of the leaves, and as soon as his fingers touched it, he felt something new. A strange essence stirred within the plant, something he didn't recognize, mysterious and tempting.

Will plucked a large leaf and held it to his nose, noting a scent reminiscent of sage. *Maybe it's a variety of sage I'm not familiar with,* he thought, before biting a small portion from the leaf. The taste didn't match. It was more like lettuce, with a faint, thyme-like flavor. He pressed the rest into his mouth and chewed.

The flavor remained mild, but a slightly bitter aftertaste began to build. Despite his former caution, he picked a second leaf and began chewing it as well. The bitterness grew stronger, along with a smoky flavor that hadn't been noticeable before. "This would go well with some of the milder greens," observed Will.

The candle flame was shifting now, changing color. It had done that before, but in the past it had always been shades of yellow or orange. Now it had turned pink and was shading toward lavender. "That's odd," he muttered.

Then the ground fell away from his feet, and he found himself spinning. He opened his mouth to speak, but words failed him. He couldn't think at all. The world had become a swirling mix of colors, and he could only watch, mesmerized as his body melted into the earth that reached up to swallow him.

A timeless period followed, filled only by shapes, textures, and strange colors. His body was gone; *he* was gone. His self had faded away to join the infinite beauty that surrounded him. Emotions remained to him, but he felt no panic or fear, only peaceful curiosity, awakened by his newfound connection to the universe.

Eventually the experience faded, and he discovered himself again, lying quietly on the forest floor. The treetops swayed in the wind above him, somehow reflecting the gentle motion of his own soul. From the sun and the angle of the shadows, he could tell that less than an hour had passed, but although his mind seemed to have recovered, the world was not the same.

Squinting, Will tried to focus his eyes, but no matter how he tried, his vision remained a mixture of perfectly normal shapes and bizarre streamers of color. It was similar to the glimpses he had seen in plants before, but now it was everywhere. He could see energy pulsing within the trees, moving to a slow, steady beat. Wide, diffuse bands of light that were almost too faint to see floated through the air, moving around him as though he had fallen into some giant, ghostly river. More energy moved through the earth beneath his feet.

Everything was connected.

Then Will noticed the candle, which had fallen to the ground beside him. It hadn't changed, but he could see a slender thread of light connecting it to his chest. *Is this magic?* he wondered. *Am I seeing magic?*

The sound of laughter floated to him through the trees in high tones. *A girl?* Will stood and looked around but saw no one close by. Bending over, he reclaimed his candle and axe, then he took a step in the direction he thought he had heard the laughter coming from.

The sound vanished, and somehow he felt he had moved the wrong way. Stepping back, he heard the girl's laughter again. Turning his head from side to side, he could see the faint streamers of light diverged there, slipping into two similar but different forests. *Not that way, this way.* Acting on instinct, he turned a different direction—it was hard to describe, but he stepped sideways, entering the other forest. The laughter grew louder.

"Follow me!" said the girl, teasing him. Her voice sent a shiver down his spine, tickling instincts he hardly recognized.

Will looked around. "Where are you?"

"Over here!" she shouted, but when he looked, he only caught a flash of bright orange vanishing into the underbrush.

Leaping to follow, he crashed along at a reckless pace, trying to catch up to her, but she remained ahead, and always just out of sight. He continued the chase, his heart thundering in his chest, until he heard the sound of rushing water ahead. When he broke free of the trees, he saw a rocky river-bank, and the girl had stopped at the water's edge.

No, not a girl, he thought. She was a woman, young no doubt, but in full possession of maturity. When she turned to look back at him, his breath caught in his throat.

Hair the color of flames cascaded down her back and over her shoulders, but it did nothing to hide the sight of her nakedness. She smiled at him with pearl-like teeth that seemed to sparkle in the autumn sun, distracting him for a moment from her small but pert breasts. "You're alone," she announced in a delighted tone, clapping her hands together.

Will had no response for that. He continued staring, drinking in the view. When she gestured for him to come closer, he took a step forward. Moments later he found himself just inches away from her, so close he could feel her breath. It smelled of mint and lavender.

Her eyes were an unnaturally bright viridian, but it was the pupils that were most startling, for they were slits, like those of a cat. "You're not human," he mumbled.

"But you are," she responded, her lips curling into a smile. "Would you like to kiss me?"

Yes, yes I would, screamed his hormones, nearly drowning out his reason. Instead, he answered, "W— what?"

The strange woman pouted, then ran her hand down his chest, trailing her fingers across his stomach. "Are you afraid? My price is a small thing, though I can sense it growing as we speak."

For a moment he could hear his grandfather's angry voice, echoing in his memory. *"Accept no debts! Think of this as part of your training."* He took a step back, away from the woman. "I have nothing to pay you."

"Oh, but you do!" she returned, while her eyes silently devoured him. "What I want is something you would dearly love to give."

Despite himself, Will asked, "What is it?"

"A fair exchange," she said, her voice sly. Then she stepped closer and put one hand behind his neck and ran her fingers through his hair. "I will give you pleasure beyond measure, and all you need give me in exchange is your seed." Lifting her chin, she leaned forward to bring her lips to his.

Will jerked, turning his head to one side before she could kiss him. "No."

"But why?" she asked. "You have plenty. You can make hundreds of children when you return. I only need one." Her hand stroked his thigh, moving upward until it reached...

Startled, Will stumbled backward and fell, landing heavily on the rocks. He felt something under his hand and discovered it was the axe. He had dropped it without realizing it. Will lifted it as the strange woman started to settle down on top of him.

She hissed, making a sound like an angry cat as her eyes fell on the hard metal of the axe-head. Leaping sideways, she was suddenly more than ten feet away. "You dare bring iron to this place, mageling?"

The candle flame swirled, reacting to the chaos of emotions within him—relief, fear, and no small amount of disappointment. "I came here by accident," he managed to say.

The woman's eyes shifted as quickly as her mood, going from anger to twinkling with amusement. "No one enters the fae realm by accident, manling."

He could feel the truth in her words, and thinking back on it, he could remember the distinct moment he had chosen to step sideways, seeking to follow her voice. "I didn't realize what I was doing," he explained. "Now, I just want to leave."

"I could show you the way," she teased, "for a price."

"No thanks," said Will immediately, though deep down he couldn't help but wonder if he really meant it.

The woman was walking back toward him, this time more slowly, making sure to stay on the side of him as far from the axe as possible. "What is your name, manling?"

"W—" he started to answer, then caught himself. "You expect my name for free?"

Her laughter tinkled in his ears. "Fair exchange then, my name for your own."

That sounded fair, but he still hesitated. What if learning his name gave her some power over him? "What would you do with my name?" he asked.

"So cautious, so careful," said the fae woman. "You would be worth knowing, if ever you escape the sun-drenched lands. Names exchanged are no sinister thing. A name can be used for finding and calling, just as with friends in your own world."

Will's eyes narrowed. "Are you saying you could summon me?"

Her answering smile didn't quite reach her eyes. "So dark are your thoughts. Are you a warlock, mageling?"

He shook his head. "No." *Not yet, anyway.*

She moved closer and bent her head to his neck, inhaling. "You have no smell of wickedness. Very well. To answer your question, if I were to call your name you would hear it, wherever you might be. What you choose to do afterward is your own business, though you would be able to find the closest door to reach me if you chose to come."

"And if I called your name?" he responded.

"The same."

"Is there a price for calling?"

She whispered into his ear, sending shivers down his spine. "Only if one is set during the exchange. Would that please you?"

"That's not necessary," he stammered, finding it difficult to think with her so close.

"Then a simple exchange it is, are we agreed?" she asked.

Will nodded. The hand holding the axe handle was white-knuckled and beginning to ache.

"I am called Tailtiu," she responded. "And you are?" She breathed her words into his ear before taking the lobe between her teeth.

"William Cartwright," he blurted out, unable to help himself. Then her sharp teeth bit down on his tender ear, sending a tiny jolt of pain, and an even larger spasm of pleasure, through him.

Tailtiu pulled away, sighing. A single drop of blood on her lips. She reached up with one hand and wiped it away, then put her finger in her mouth to clean it. A purring sound rose from her throat and she licked her lips once more. "You taste good, mortal. So much potential..."

"That's my blood," said Will. "That wasn't part of our exchange."

Tailtiu pouted. "Then I am in your debt. What would you like in return? A kiss?" She looked hopeful.

Judging by his reaction to what she had just done, he doubted his reason would survive a kiss. For a moment, his mind pondered scenarios. Perhaps if she was tied and bound it would be safe. He shook his head to clear it. "Show me the way back." He regretted the words as soon as he uttered them. He really wanted the kiss.

"So stubborn," she replied. "Very well. Follow me." Turning away, she started walking at a leisurely pace, her slim hips swaying hypnotically.

To hell and back, thought Will, falling into step. Every part of her movement was entrancing, from her graceful stride to the way her hair shifted from side to side, giving him glimpses of her shoulders that made him want to take hold of her.

The candle flame was burning fiercely, twice as large as normal. It rose and fell to a slow, deep rhythm that matched his heartbeat. Seeing its odd behavior distracted him for a moment and he felt his lustful urge fade slightly. He focused on her feet after that, afraid he might lose his mind if he let his eyes drift upward again.

Damn, even her heels are beautiful.

Logically, he knew that the way back should be the same as the way he had come, but nothing seemed familiar. They walked for nearly half an hour, and when asked, Tailtiu assured him that they were taking the shortest path back to his world. *She wouldn't lie, would she?* he wondered. *She shouldn't have any reason to.*

The wind picked up suddenly, changing from a pleasant breeze to harsh gale, picking up the leaves and whipping them violently through the air. The trees bent under its strength, and Will was forced to lift his arm in order to shield his eyes. Tailtiu looked back at him, alarm written on her face.

"He comes!" she cried.

"Who?" asked Will, confused and suddenly anxious.

"Elthas, lord of this place," she explained.

"We should run," suggested Will.

Tailtiu shook her head. "It is too late. Forgive me. This is the fault of my greed, hoping to keep you for myself." Without warning, she leapt toward him.

Will struggled to avoid her, but the fae woman was fast, and once her hands were on him he discovered she was far stronger as well. Grabbing his head, she pulled it forward and planted her lips atop his.

Fire burned through him, sending waves of pleasure from his head to his toes. Her tongue danced between his lips, and the intensity of the sensation was so great that it became painful. It was ecstasy, a pleasure unlike anything he had ever experienced in his not-quite fourteen years.

And it was killing him.

From the corner of his eye, he saw the candle where it had fallen. Its flame dimmed and grew gradually smaller. He wondered how long it would take before it vanished entirely. Somewhere deep down, he wanted it to stop, wanted to push her away, but his arms had lost their strength.

Then she released him. Will fell to his knees, washed out and feeble. The air felt colder now and he shivered. Staring up at Tailtiu, he accused her, "I didn't give you permission."

"I owe you a debt then, manling," she replied, a strange light in her eyes.

"Who is this?" said a deep and frighteningly masculine voice behind him.

Weary to his bones, Will turned his head to see the man who had appeared behind him. The figure who stood there was tall, taller than Eric's dad, and he was also mostly nude. The newcomer had some clothing, if it could be called that—a leafy mantle that covered his shoulders and ran down his back. But it failed to obscure the more pertinent details of his manhood.

Will held up one hand briefly. "Hello."

The stranger stared down a long, arrogant nose at Will, and one corner of his mouth quirked up into a devious smirk. It was then that Will noticed his hair was green, and the multitude of leaves around his shoulders were *growing* from him, rather than being a separate article of clothing.

Glancing back, he could see that Tailtiu was kneeling, her eyes on the ground. "My lord, I found a manling within your demesne."

"Yet you didn't see fit to bring him before me, did you, child?" responded the fae lord.

"I owe him a debt," responded Tailtiu. "I was forced to lead him home."

"Nothing is owed to the dead," said the man looming over them. "Trespassers belong to me."

"I've done you no wrong, Lord Elthas," said Will abruptly. "I didn't know where I was."

"Silence," barked Elthas. "Do not taint my name with your tongue." Moving around him, the fae lord examined him, taking note of his candle and the axe in his hand. "A mageling, I see. It has been a while since one has been foolish enough to tempt my wrath, and you come bearing iron as well. Did you think that would protect you from me?"

"I meant no disrespect, sir," said Will. "I came here by accident." Following Tailtiu's example, he kept his face to the ground, but in his peripheral vision he could see more feet around him. Elthas had brought a host of servants with him.

Elthas laughed. "The hunter has no need of excuses. You are *prey* to me, manling. All I require of you is your life." The fae lord looked at the candle. "What's left of it, at least. Tailtiu has stolen some of my reward already."

A new voice called out from the trees. "The only reward you'll be getting is my foot up your ass, Elthas." Will recognized it at once. It was his grandfather.

CHAPTER 12

"You dare show your face here, Arrogan?" said the fae lord, his voice deepening with anger. He hadn't bothered turning around yet, keeping his gaze firmly fixed on Will.

The fae circling them opened up, and Will saw his grandfather walking forward, his face smooth and confident. He had to admit that the old man seemed sure of himself. He almost looked heroic, except for the ridiculous deer horns strapped to his head. "I'll make an ass of myself wherever I please," announced his grandfather. "My face is just tagging along for the show."

Elthas turned then, and his face darkened when he saw the horns. "You've gone too far this time, old man."

Will's grandfather winked and lifted his hand to touch one of the antlers. "You mean these? I'm the sentimental sort. I keep them around to scratch my backside. They really help to get to those hard to reach places. I'm sure you understand."

Will could see the turyn gathering around Elthas, streamers of power so intense they almost blinded him. The fae lord's power wove in and out, and then shot toward the earth at his grandfather's feet. Vines sprouted from the soil, but they didn't touch his grandfather; instead they snaked away from him, racing across the ground to bind the ankles and legs of the observers.

"Want to try again?" asked the old man. "Maybe this time I'll take the only horn you have left." His eyes traveled downward to stop on Elthas' disturbingly tumescent manhood.

"You're bluffing," said Elthas, but he didn't attack again. "You're long past your prime. Your flame is dying, just like the boy's."

"Think so?" asked his grandfather calmly. "You're welcome to test me. But I promise you, I only need a spark to whip your ass. I'll kick your teeth so far down your throat you'll be shitting them out for a week." He looked past Elthas. "Get up, Will. We're going home."

Will struggled to his feet, gathering up the candle and axe. He shuffled forward. "Yes, Grandfather."

The fae lord's hand shot out, circling his neck. Will could feel the man's sharp nails against his throat. "Grandfather?" said the fae lord, a wicked smile crawling across his face. "This child is of your line, Arrogan?"

His grandfather's eyes shot daggers of hate at him. "Didn't I fucking tell you to call me 'Master' when others were around?"

"Does the child displease you, Arrogan?" asked Elthas, his grip tightening. "Perhaps I should punish him for you."

The old man's gaze locked with that of the fae lord. "You spill one drop of his blood, and I'll spread pieces of you far and wide across the Glenwood. They'll need a hundred years to piece your carcass together."

"Always rude, always crass," said Elthas. "Has time given you no taste for diplomacy? Let us make a bargain, Arrogan, like the old days."

"Bargain?" said Will's grandfather derisively. Then he spat on the ground, and Will was surprised to see smoke rising from where the spittle struck. "I'm not making any bargains with you. If you're going to kill him, do it, but don't say I didn't warn you."

Will felt the nails dig into his neck painfully for a moment, but then Tailtiu ran forward. "Stop!" she cried.

Arrogan's face changed when he saw the fae girl, and Will saw his stance shift. The old man stared at the girl with an intensity he hadn't even shown to his opponent. "Tailtiu," said the hermit, the name almost catching in his throat.

And just like that we've lost, thought Will. *All because he turns out to be just another horny old goat.* He knew he was doomed. His despair only lasted a second, however, replaced almost immediately by shock when Tailtiu replied, "Father."

"She's your *daughter?*" exclaimed Will, disgusted. "What the hell is going on? She kissed me!" His eyes rolled sideways to glare at the fae woman. "That's incest!" Even as he said it, though, he couldn't help but note her erotic charm.

Both Elthas and his grandfather responded at the same time, "Shut up."

Will closed his eyes, wanting to block everything out, most especially the sight of his cousin's naked form. *Or is she my aunt?* He couldn't be sure. *Either way, I'm going to hell.*

His grandfather was the first to speak. "Did you say you kissed her, boy? Did you make a bargain?"

Will tried to shake his head, but Elthas' grip was too tight. "No. She did it without asking." Then he felt a need to add some clarification. "I didn't like it, either," he lied.

Arrogan looked back at Elthas, a wicked grin on his face. "That changes things, doesn't it?"

The fae lord scowled. "Not in the least. His life is still in my hands."

"It's obvious you just want to kill him so you can negate Tailtiu's debt," said his grandfather.

"This is my forest," insisted Elthas. "I do as I please. Your daughter's obligations are not mine."

Arrogan glanced around, letting his eyes linger on the other fae trapped around them. Then he faced Elthas again. "Do you think they'll believe that? Or do you think they'll realize that the oh-so-honorable Lord Elthas is nothing more than bog scum? Why don't we test it out? You kill the boy, I'll tear you into tiny pieces, and they can go tell the other fae what happened while you put yourself back together. I'm sure your reputation will still be just fine when you are eventually whole enough to tell your side of the story."

The fae lord simmered with rage. "All this rests on one faulty assumption, *old man*. I can kill both of you. Your threats are meaningless. This is my demesne. I hold power here."

"Is that right?" challenged his grandfather. Then the old man stepped closer, until he and Elthas were standing almost nose to nose. "Show me. I've been itching for this fight for a long time."

The moment stretched out, until Will began to grow impatient. Opening one eye, he saw Tailtiu and felt an immediate response. *This is so wrong,* he thought desperately. *I'm about to be choked to death and all I can do is fantasize about my faery aunt. Where did I go wrong?*

Without warning, the pressure around his throat vanished, and Elthas stepped away. "Go!" ordered the fae lord. "If I see either of you again, your lives are forfeit."

Will's grandfather grabbed his hand, pulling him away. "Empty words from an empty pus bag, Elthas." Arrogan cast one regretful look at his daughter, and then he turned Will around and marched him out of the clearing.

They hadn't gone more than twenty feet before Will asked, "Grandfather, was she really your—"

"Shut the hell up!" barked the old man. "Not one more word from you until we get home."

Will managed to keep his questions to himself the rest of the way back, even though they seemed to be multiplying by the minute. When they reached the place of entry, his grandfather grabbed his hand again and twisted them both sideways in that same strange way that Will had before, and they were back in the normal world again.

But the normal world was still slightly strange. Will's vision hadn't returned to normal. He still saw lots of things that hadn't been present before. His grandfather had an aura around him, the trees still thrummed with hidden power, and faint streamers of light flowed about them in the air.

His candle flame wasn't the same either. It was small and feeble, less than half the size it had once been. Considering his fatigue, that seemed to match up, but it had never done that before, not even when he had worked himself into complete exhaustion.

When they had finally gotten inside the house, Will couldn't keep it in any longer. "Am I dying?"

His grandfather was busy untying the thongs that held his bizarre antler cap on. He glanced Will's direction. "Huh? Why the hell would you think that?"

He held up the candle.

"Just when I thought you couldn't get any more fucking stupid. You never fail to impress. Don't you remember the day I brought you here?"

Will nodded.

"Well, if I had done the candle spell for you then, your flame would have been even smaller. Much smaller, in fact. You aren't dying. You just had some of your turyn sucked out." Then he cuffed the top of his grandson's head, *hard*. "Idiot."

"Was that really your daughter?" asked Will, rubbing the sore spot on his skull.

The old man passed one hand over his face. "I really don't want to talk about it."

"Does that mean she's my aunt?" prodded Will. "Or am I not really your grandson?"

"I'll answer one stupid question," growled the hermit, "then you're going to explain to me what happened. So choose wisely."

He thought about it for a moment. He was pretty sure the fae wouldn't have lied about Tailtiu being the old man's daughter, and besides, he was more worried about his own status. "Are you my grandfather?"

"I'm your great-great-great-great-grandfather, plus or minus ten or twelve greats. I don't know exactly anymore. I stopped keeping count of the generations a couple hundred years ago," admitted the old man.

Will was stunned, then he had a flashback of Tailtiu kissing him. "Was she your great-great-however-many-times-over granddaughter?"

His grandfather laughed sourly. "No, she was my youngest child. The fae are all but immortal. She'll still look like that long after you're dust in your grave."

"So who was her mother?" blurted out Will.

Arrogan's face blanched at that, an expression reminiscent of an old pain come back to haunt him. "Enough. I told you one question, yet I've answered two. How in the hell did you wind up over there?"

Will tried to describe what he had done. "I just sort of moved *sideways*. Just like you did when we came back."

"I'm well aware of how it's done, turnip-brain," shot back his grandfather. "But to do that, you have to be able to see things you shouldn't be able to see."

"I found this plant I didn't recognize," began Will.

The old man didn't wait for him to finish. "Do you always stick strange plants in your mouth?"

"Well, no, not usually. But I can tell if a plant is edible, and I thought it was some variety of sage I hadn't seen before…"

His grandfather's eyes narrowed. "How can you tell if a plant is edible? I haven't taught you that."

"You haven't taught me anything!" said Will in exasperation. "You said you'd train me to be an herbalist, but you haven't said one word about plants since I came here!"

Instead of reacting to Will's outburst with anger, his grandfather leaned back, his expression thoughtful. "I've taught you to read, along with basic mathematics…"

"What does that have to do with plants?" broke in Will.

Getting to his feet, Arrogan left the room. He returned a few moments later with two books in his arms. He placed them on the table and opened them up for Will to peruse. "What does this look like to you?"

The first was filled with colorful drawings that showed leaves, flowers and stems. Each was accompanied by a description. Will could read some of them, but many of the words were too long and unfamiliar for him to figure out. The second had lists of ingredients, along with instructions and numbers. Again, he couldn't understand all of it, but he got the sense that they were recipes of some sort. He looked at the hermit questioningly.

"There is more information in these two books than you could ever memorize," said his grandfather flatly. "This one, *Winton's Herbal*, describes hundreds of useful plants, showing their leaves, flowers, and recording their life cycles and growing needs. The other, *Gidding's Apothecary*, gives instructions for tinctures, potions, extracts, as well as specialized preparations that can be made with various plants and herbs. Does any of that strike you as useful?"

Bewildered, Will flipped through the pages. "Why didn't you tell me about this?"

"Why should I?" barked Arrogan. "Can you read them?"

"A little," said Will hesitantly.

"What's this word here?" asked his grandfather, stabbing his finger at one of the pages.

"Minim," answered Will immediately. It was one of many seemingly useless names for measurements he had been forced to learn.

"And here?"

"Dram."

"Here?"

"Two scruples," said Will, beginning to feel foolish.

"I've been teaching you the names, so eventually you will be able to follow the instructions in these books to prepare whatever you need. To do that, you will have to be able to read these books, along with others. Your mother has already taught you how to identify many plants. Why should I waste my time repeating her lessons when you clearly need to learn the basics to progress any further?"

Will didn't have an answer to that, so he just stared back blankly.

"Would you like to know what plant you so foolishly ingested today?" asked his grandfather.

"Sure," said Will meekly.

Arrogan flipped the *Herbal* closed and reopened it at the beginning. "This table at the front subdivides plants into groups. Was the plant deciduous?"

Will nodded and answered several more questions before his grandfather pointed at the book again. "It will be here, in either chapter fourteen or fifteen. I should make you look through them, but I won't bother. Go to page seventy-two."

Flipping through the pages Will softly recited the numbers to himself.

"I'll give you a hint," growled Arrogan. "It's between seventy-one and seventy-three."

Will looked up sharply. "I know that!" His angry response earned him a malicious grin from his mentor. *I should know better than to let him get to me,* thought Will. Finding the page at last, he laid the book down and studied the picture and its description. It definitely looked like the plant he had found. It even mentioned the square shape of the stem. "Diver's sage," he said, reading the name aloud.

"Diviner's Sage, moron," corrected his grandfather. "It's a powerful psychedelic. The early shamans used it to see visions, although personally I think they just liked feeling weird. The important thing for you to know is that it opens the mind, allowing you to see things normally invisible to the eye. For those who are already sensitive, or those who have had extensive training, that effect is permanent."

"Oh," said Will, unsure what to say.

"This is just one of several plants and mushrooms that teachers use to initiate their students into the arcane arts," explained Arrogan. "I already knew you were sensitive, which is why I took you in, hoping to prevent this. But *you,* in your infinite idiocy, took it upon your shoulders to turn yourself into a mage. There's no going back for you now."

Alarmed, Will asked, "I can't go home?"

Arrogan covered his face with one hand. "Of course, you can go home. I dream of sending you there every day. You can't go back to being *normal.*"

That didn't sound too bad. "Does this mean I can do magic now?"

His grandfather sighed. "You have several choices. One, you can go home, which would almost be a relief, because so far, you've been more trouble than you're worth. If you do, I'll start packing, since I don't want to be around when they find you and execute you as a warlock, which is almost certainly what they'll decide. Proof or no proof. Two, and slightly less stupid, you can go to Cerria and present yourself before the Royal Magister, Grant Haywood. He's the idiot running the Wurthaven College of Wizardry these days. After a few tests, he'd put you in classes and eventually you'd get to be a lapdog for one of the noble sorcerers running things nowadays."

Arrogan leaned back, lacing his fingers behind his head. "Personally, I like that option the best, since it means I'll be quit of you and I won't have to worry about moving."

Will could sense the old man wasn't finished, so he prompted him, "But…?"

His grandfather sighed. "The third option is the best for you, but a pain in the ass for me. Stay here and I'll train you properly. The only drawback is you'll still be an unlicensed mage, so if they catch you later, you'll wind up in prison at best."

"How is that better for me?" exclaimed Will querulously.

The old man grinned evilly. "Because by the time I'm done with you, there won't be a mage alive, sorcerer or otherwise, capable of putting you in prison. I can teach you to be a wizard the likes of which even King Lognion would be afraid to face—or would, if any of the fools knew what real wizards could do back in my day."

That reminded Will of one of his longstanding questions. "Exactly *when* was your day?"

CHAPTER 13

Arrogan leaned forward. "Before I answer that, I have to know whether you plan to go to Cerria or train under me."

Will spoke before he thought. "It's because they're hunting you, isn't it?"

"And that, my boy, has sealed your fate. You have sharp ears, don't you?"

"I heard you and Mom talking," admitted Will.

His grandfather grimaced. "Well, options one and two are off the list now."

He was beginning to feel slightly rebellious. "And what if I would rather study in the city?"

"Do you really want to test my patience, boy?" asked the old man, an angry gleam in his eye. "You saw what happened today. How many wizards do you think would dare to tweak the nose of one of the fae lords? Do you think any of the glorified sanitation workers that come out of Wurthaven would dare? They'd be pissing their pants at the thought! If you think anything that happened today was commonplace, let me be the first to disabuse you of that notion."

Will let out a long exhale, deflating. He really didn't know what to think about what had happened, nor did he have any idea how dangerous a fae lord might or might not be. As far as he knew, they might be pushovers. But he strongly suspected they weren't.

And Elthas had taken all of Arrogan's insults and abuse and then just let them walk away. That couldn't be normal. He studied his grandfather with new eyes. Just how dangerous was the old man?

"Are you really going to teach me?" asked Will at last. "You still haven't taught me anything about herbs. Will you really teach me magic?"

Arrogan thumped his hand on *Gidding's Apothecary*. "This book contains recipes for medicines and potions. There are other books that contain spells. You have to be able to read them. Not only that, but you'll need to learn a new alphabet, the runes of power, in order to work those spells."

Will groaned.

"Yes, I'll teach you," finished his grandfather, ignoring Will's moaning. "But you'll learn things in the proper order."

He nodded. "All right. Doesn't seem like I have much choice." Then he remembered his earlier question. "So when was your day again?"

The old man yawned. "I'm getting tired." He stood up, as though to retire to his bedroom.

"You said you'd tell me!" protested Will.

Arrogan sat back down, grinning at Will's frustration. "Somewhere around four hundred and fifty years ago."

"You're four hundred and fifty years old!" yelled Will, jumping up and knocking his chair over.

His grandfather shook his head. "No. That's when my *day* was, if by that you mean the period when I was at my peak, before the so-called Terabinian War of Independence."

"Then how old are you?" demanded Will.

"Still none of your damn business," replied Arrogan. "If you ever learn to cook something that doesn't make my stomach churn, I'll think about telling you."

***

The next day, after breakfast and his obligatory two hours of reading practice, Arrogan called him over. "Let's see your candle."

Will held it up. The flame was brighter today, but it still hadn't recovered completely from Tailtiu's kiss.

"You've spent plenty of time observing it as you go about your tasks," said Arrogan. "Since you're a mage now, it's time for you to learn to control it. Here's a question for you. Why is the flame still so small?"

That was easy. "Because I still haven't regained my normal amount of turyn."

His grandfather shook his head. "No, the real reason is because you're ignorant, but I'll try to correct some of that today." Then he added, "Try not to scream; this is for your own good."

"Why would I scr—" Will's voice cut off as a vivid green line of power shot from Arrogan's fingers and straight into his chest. He felt it bore into him, and while the sensation wasn't painful, it was distinctly unpleasant. Then he stopped breathing.

Panic rapidly overtook him as he tried and failed to make his lungs work. Seconds ticked by, and his grandfather watched him with the same sort of faint disinterest an evil child might display while squashing ants. Finally, the old man spoke. "I'm not controlling your muscles. Look at the candle."

The flame had turned green.

"Trying to make your muscles obey you won't work," said Arrogan. "First you have to make the candle return to its normal color."

Will's heart was pounding in his ears, and his face first grew red, then purple. He was beginning to see spots when suddenly his grandfather waved his hand and his lungs began working again. The candle was still burning green.

"I suppose you won't learn anything if I let you suffocate," said his grandfather. The green line of light still connected his fingers to Will's chest. "Right now, I have absolute control over your turyn. I can do anything I want with you. Your lungs take in air at my command. Your heart beats because I allow it. I could kill you with a thought." The old man reached back and began earnestly scratching his backside, seeming to have forgotten his grandson entirely.

When he looked back, there was a vicious intensity in his eyes. "It's disconcerting, isn't it? You feel helpless, violated. Those are perfectly normal feelings, but if you want them to stop, you'll have to learn. Watch the flame."

The candle flared, and Will felt a surge of energy. He couldn't remember ever feeling quite so alive. It was as though his body was bursting with vitality. The flame was now twice its normal size.

"That turyn didn't come from me," said Arrogan. "Just in case that's what you were thinking. It came from you. I'm just controlling it. Everything I am about to show you are things you are capable of doing for yourself, once you learn how.

"The turyn in our bodies comes from a limited source. Think of it as the candle. Make it burn faster, and the candle shortens more quickly, while the flame grows brighter. Ordinarily a wizard wouldn't do this, since I'm essentially causing you to age faster, but in a pinch it's a handy way to recover your turyn in a hurry."

Will's eyes lit with interest.

"It's also stupid," added his grandfather. "This is the main reason why wizards these days live such short, stunted lives."

Will felt a strange sensation, as though he had relaxed a muscle, though it had nothing to do with his physical body. The candle flame returned to its normal size and at the same time his strange vitality vanished.

Arrogan held up his left hand. "Would you like to see what my flame looks like? Here." A new flame appeared above his palm, though it was hardly deserving of the term. It was more of an ember, barely more than a speck of orange. After a few seconds, he let the illusion vanish. "Tiny, isn't it? Some would say it's hardly enough to sustain life, but controlling your flame is the secret to longevity—and power.

"Even in my day, many wizards would teach their apprentices simple magics first. Would you like to know why?"

Will could feel sweat beading on his brow, and his eyes kept darting back to the green flame. His brush with suffocation had instilled a deep terror in him, and the color of the candle was a constant reminder that his life was in Arrogan's hands. "Yes, please," he answered, trying to keep his voice even.

His grandfather smiled. "Because they were selfish. An apprentice who can't do magic is practically useless, much like you. So they taught them simple cantrips and spells, things to make their lives easier. Fortunately for you, I am not a selfish man. I'm not going to teach you any of that, even though it means you'll be a greater burden on my munificence." The old man leaned back, a self-satisfied look on his face. "You'll thank me later."

Despite his fear, Will complained, "But you said you'd teach me!"

Arrogan's expression shifted to annoyance. "I am teaching you, ungrateful wretch though you are. Learning any magic at this point will slow your progress. In the old days an apprentice might spend *decades* learning to master their turyn, and the main reason it took so long was because their teachers didn't have the patience to teach them in the proper order.

"You will learn control and discipline first, and with any luck you'll manage it in a couple of years, rather than ten or twenty." The old man sat up, and his fingers began to move. He was muttering under his breath, and Will could see tiny, yet intricate lines of power forming in the air.

Arrogan's right hand clenched into a fist, and Will saw the candle flame shrink slightly, so that it was slightly smaller than it usually was. The shift sent a wave of weariness through Will. Then the hermit's left hand went forward, pushing the small weave of magic toward him. It drifted through the air and sank into his chest.

The old man studied him for a moment, then snapped the fingers of his right hand. The line of power connecting him to Will vanished, and the candle flame returned to its normal yellow color. Will breathed a sigh of relief.

His grandfather gave him a smile that was pure malice. "Don't look so happy yet, boy. I've released your turyn, but the spell I put within you will cause you no end of trouble if you don't learn quickly."

Will's heart sank. "Spell?"

Arrogan gestured at the candle once more. "As you can see, I reduced the size of your turyn. Currently it's slightly smaller than normal, but it will try to return to its usual size. To prevent that, I've put a spell within you that will stop that from occurring, but if your turyn expands and puts pressure on the spell, you will feel pain—slight at first, but gradually growing in intensity.

"Your job is to keep that from happening. The pain will serve as your guide. The sooner you learn, the less discomfort you'll have to suffer," finished the old man.

He gaped at his grandfather. "Why would you do that?"

His mentor ignored the question. Instead he reached into his robes and pulled out a gold coin. "This is your payment for the wood. You can have the rest of today off. Go pay your friend for the cot and be back in time for dinner."

CHAPTER 14

Will didn't need any encouragement to leave. He had been aching to visit his friends for months, and the fear his grandfather had put in his heart that morning with his strange magic demonstration only made him want to get away even more.

The pain started just minutes after he left.

It began as an odd, itching sensation that covered his body but was strongest in his face and scalp, and it got immediately worse when he realized what was happening, going from itching to burning in just seconds.

He stared at the candle fearfully. He had no idea what to do, but he knew from long observation that strong emotions usually caused the flame to flare. *Calm down,* he told himself.

The flame stabilized, and the burning receded, becoming merely an annoying itch once more. He needed to figure out a way to keep the flame from growing. *Maybe if I burn off some energy.* In the past he had noticed that heavy exercise tended to deplete his turyn a little. Without waiting to think about it, he began to run.

He ran all the way to Barrowden. It would have taken almost an hour if he had walked, but he covered the distance in half that, dashing through the trees with reckless abandon. By the time he arrived, his face was red and he was covered in sweat, but the itching had faded. The cold autumn wind was a relief for his overheated body, but he worried what would happen once his sweat-drenched clothes began to leach away his warmth.

Walking down the one street that went through Barrowden, he was surprised when a familiar voice called to him. "Will!" Turning around, he saw Annabelle Withy step into the lane, two large wooden buckets in her hands.

"Anna," he responded, surprised. His friend had changed in the year and a half since he had last seen her. She was slightly taller than him now, and her figure had changed in interesting ways. He had always liked her, since she seemed friendlier and more practical than most of the other girls in the village. "How have you been?"

"I'm well," she answered. "Where have you been? Nobody's seen you in forever."

Good question, he thought. After a second, he replied, "I took an apprenticeship. I'm living with my teacher."

"Teacher?" said Annabelle, her face growing curious.

Master, Will chided himself. *I should have said 'master.'* Apprentices didn't refer to their masters as 'teachers.' "It was Mom's idea," he added.

"Where does your master live? Is he in Branscombe? What trade are you learning?"

All perfectly reasonable questions. None of which he wanted to answer. How could he tell her he was living in the forest with a crazy old hermit? Once the word got out, his friends would laugh themselves sick. It was a miracle they hadn't heard about it already. *I suppose I should thank Eric and Sammy for not telling everyone.*

Thinking of his grandfather, Will almost replied with 'none of your damn business,' but he caught himself before the words came out of his mouth. *I'm learning bad habits from the ornery old bastard.* He didn't want to lie, so he kept his answer vague. "Yeah, he lives near Branscombe. I'm learning medicine."

Arrogan *did* live in the direction of Branscombe, though his home was much closer to Barrowden, and

Will was supposed to be learning herbalism, so his answer wasn't really a lie. It just wasn't exactly the truth, either.

Annabelle's brown eyes widened, and he found himself marveling at how pretty she was. "You're going to be a doctor?" she asked.

Her assumption wasn't a bad one for Will. Being a doctor would command some respect, although many people treated them with suspicion. "Mom said it would be silly for me to become a midwife," he joked, letting her keep the assumption without actually confirming it. Then he glanced at the buckets in her hands. "Are you hauling water?"

She nodded.

"Let me help you then," he suggested. His scalp was beginning to itch again, so it wouldn't hurt to burn off some energy. Plus, he'd get to spend more time with Annabelle.

The well was located in the center of the village, so he walked there with her and then, after she had filled them, he took both the buckets. They were heavy, but holding one in each hand improved his balance and made it easier to walk.

"You don't have to carry both," said Annabelle. "We can share the load."

"Don't worry about it," he replied. "I need the exercise."

Tracy Tanner spotted him and called out to him as they walked back to Annabelle's house. "Come by after you finish!" she said loudly. "We have a gift for you."

Will nodded, and then noticed Annabelle looking at him from the side of her eyes. "What?" he asked.

"She's been talking about you for months," said the girl. "She tells everyone how you saved Joey."

"That's crazy," said Will, feeling uncomfortable. "I just made a poultice for him."

"She thinks you used magic to heal him," said Annabelle. "You'll probably make a great doctor."

"Doctors don't use magic," argued Will.

"You don't have to hide it from me, Will," she replied. "Everyone knows that sorcerer stopped at your house last year."

"He just wanted some herbs."

"I think he was there looking for a new apprentice," she opined.

Will laughed. "Sorcerers don't take apprentices. They pass their elementals to their heirs."

Annabelle gave him an odd look. "You seem to know a lot about how they work."

He put the buckets down in front of her door as he searched for an answer. "My master is pretty knowledgeable. He's taught me about a lot of things."

She gave him a sly look. "Mm hmm."

Will glanced around. "I'd better get going."

Annabelle put a hand on his arm. "Will you be coming back for the Festival of Elthas?"

He stopped dead in his tracks and his heart went cold. He hadn't thought about the name of the fae lord in connection with the holiday. Were they one and the same? It was held near the end of May, and from what he knew it was a holiday particular to Barrowden. Like most such events, there would be a lot of drinking and dancing and some of the village men would wear antlers on their heads in honor of the pagan god.

"What's wrong?" asked Annabelle. "You look like you've seen a ghost."

"Nothing," he answered, forcing himself to focus on the girl once more. "I was just remembering something I forgot to do. I'll be in trouble later."

Annabelle returned to her original topic, ignoring his remark. "I only mentioned it because Eric's been asking me if I would accompany him to the dance, but I haven't decided how to answer him."

He wasn't paying attention and he replied hastily, "That's wonderful, Anna. I really need to go."

The girl flinched, and he knew instantly that he'd said something wrong. Replaying her words in his mind, he felt like a fool. Apologizing, he backed away. "I have to hurry. Sorry!"

He crossed the lane and headed down it toward the Tanners', and when he looked back Annabelle had already gone inside. *She must think I'm an idiot,* he decided. *And I'm inclined to agree with her.*

Joseph Tanner opened the door to their home as soon as Will came into view; apparently, he had been watching for him. He offered his hand and Will shook it, feeling strange at the older man's show of respect.

"I wanted to thank you for what you did for us, and to apologize for how I spoke to you that day," said Joseph.

Will dipped his head. "You were just worried. You shouldn't apologize."

"I feel better doing it," said Mr. Tanner. "Come inside." He stepped back, holding the door wide.

Feeling embarrassed, Will did, trying not to wrinkle his nose at the smell. While he loved the smell of leather, going to the source of such goods was a pungent education. Since they operated a tannery behind their home, it was inevitable that some of the acrid smell from the tanning pits found its way inside.

He fervently hoped he wouldn't be offered food, for his appetite had all but vanished.

Tracy Tanner smiled as he came in and motioned toward her son, who was now over three. "He hardly even has a scar. I can't thank you enough."

"I really didn't do much," said Will humbly.

"Don't be so modest," countered Joseph Tanner. "Your mother tries to play it down, but we know you worked a miracle to save our boy."

Tracy held up a leather satchel in her hands, pushing it toward him. "I made this for you."

Remembering his weeks of cutting wood, Will felt a momentary panic. *The old man will work me to death if I accept this.* "I don't deserve something like that," he protested.

Joseph took the bag from her and pressed it into his hands. "It's made from one of my best hides. Tracy spent half the summer stitching it for you."

The leather felt soft, almost buttery in his hands, similar to doehide, though it was made of more durable cowhide. It was a wide satchel, with a sturdy flap closing it and a long strap for his shoulder. Feeling guilty, he looked inside and was amazed to find that it was divided down the center, with one side forming a large space while the other was subdivided into multiple compartments. Both sides of the interior had been carefully lined with linen. Will closed it again and then noticed that the outside flap was tooled and decorated with a pattern of oak leaves.

"I can't afford this," he stammered, still thinking of his grandfather.

Tracy clucked. "It isn't a matter of affording. We owe you a debt and this is the only way we have to repay you."

When he still looked hesitant, her husband chimed in, "It would be rude to refuse a gift like this."

Will bowed his head in defeat. "Thank you. I'll treasure it."

"I thought all the compartments might be useful for herbs or whatnot," said Tracy. "When you're out gathering."

That wasn't really true. If he was gathering wild herbs, he generally tied them into bundles and hung them over his shoulder; putting them into a bag would bruise them, but the satchel would still be useful for any number of other things. "It's very thoughtful of you," said Will.

By the time he left a few minutes later, Will was beginning to experience a burning pain all over his body. He ran all the way to Eric's house, hoping to use up more energy, but he was still itching when he got there. To his disappointment, neither Eric nor his father were home.

"It's been forever since I've had a chance to look at you, Will!" said his Aunt Doreen as she invited him in. She held him out at arm's length and studied him from head to toe, while Sammy smirked at him from behind her mother. "Are you eating enough? Why are you so skinny?"

"Well…"

"I can't believe your mother is letting you live with that old man," declared his aunt before he could respond. "It's shameful. She could do a lot better for you if she'd get over that willful pride of hers."

He had no idea what she meant by that, and the expression on her face when she saw his questioning look told him that she had said more than she meant to. She quickly tried to cover up her slip. "I just meant she could find you a proper apprenticeship in Cerria, if she just put a little effort into it."

Will's eyes met Sammy's and she shrugged, indicating she had no idea what her mother was referring to either.

"I'd appreciate it if you didn't tell anyone where I'm at," said Will. "I told Annabelle Withy that I'm studying medicine."

Sammy spoke up. "Don't worry. We've been pleading ignorance whenever the neighbors ask."

His aunt looked displeased. "You shouldn't lie, Will."

"Well, it's sort of true," he said helplessly. Trying to change the topic, he asked, "Where's Eric?"

"Johnathan took the boys to the city with him to deliver a new wagon to a buyer," responded Doreen. "They probably won't be back until tomorrow." She looked at him again, then added, "You should eat with us."

The smell of lamb was already beginning to drive him mad, but the pain of Arrogan's spell was steadily increasing. It felt as though ants were crawling over him. He didn't want to be there when it got too bad for him to hide. "I have to get back soon," he answered quickly. "I just wanted to give Eric and Sammy something for the cot and pillow they brought me." He held out his hand with the gold crown shining in his palm.

Doreen's eyes bulged slightly. "Where did you get that?"

"Gr—my master asked me to give it to you," said Will, silently kicking himself for almost saying 'Grandfather.' He knew Eric had already discussed it with his dad, but he was afraid of bringing up another uncomfortable topic.

"It's far too much," declared his aunt.

"Please take it," said Will. "He'll be upset with me if you don't."

"I can't even make change for this," complained Doreen. "Besides, it was a gift. You shouldn't pay us anything—hey!"

Will was backing out the front door. He dropped the coin on a shelf as he went. "Just take it. I don't think the old man cares about money, anyway. I really need to get going." He darted outside and started jogging away.

His aunt followed him out, calling to him, "Wait! You didn't even take any food. We can't take this!" Then she pushed her daughter in his direction. "Go after him! Tell him to come get some food to carry home."

He kept going, while Sammy chased his steps. With her shorter legs, she couldn't have caught him, but he pulled up once he was outside the village. She glared at him as she reached him, but she was panting too hard to speak immediately.

"Sorry about that," he told her. "I was afraid your mom wouldn't take the money if I didn't leave it and run."

"You've gotten really weird since you left home," said Sammy as she caught her breath. Then she pointed at his bag. "Where'd you get that?"

"The Tanners," he said simply.

She nodded, understanding immediately. "Oh." After another breath she added, "You really should take some food. There's too much with Dad and the boys out of the house."

"I really can't wait," said Will. The pain was getting worse, so he began jogging in place, earning him another strange look from his cousin.

"There's something else I wanted to tell you," Sammy informed him. "A messenger came from Cerria yesterday. He went to your mom's house. After that, he stopped in the village and asked several people about you."

A feeling of alarm passed through Will, and his pain increased for a moment. "What did he want to know?"

"Can you hold still for a second?" asked Sammy. "It's too weird trying to talk to you like this."

"Sorry, I have to burn off some energy," said Will honestly.

She sighed. "He was asking general questions. How you've been, where you're living, that sort of thing, but he spent several minutes with the Tanners. Who knows what they told him?"

Will had no answer for that. He couldn't even speculate, but he doubted it would be anything good for him in the long run.

"Would you just stop?" said Sammy, frustrated. "All that bobbing is making me dizzy."

He did, and she put her arms around him, giving him a hug. "I don't know what you're into these days, but be safe."

Will hugged her back, then broke away. "Thanks for the pillow, Sammy. I really love it." Then he began running, leaving her behind.

As he went, he heard her parting comment. "Weirdo."

CHAPTER 15

Will ran as hard as he could back to Arrogan's house, but despite his best efforts the pain continued to build. His body simply couldn't do enough to burn off his extra energy, and when he was forced to stop and catch his breath, things only got worse.

The old man began cackling as soon as he returned. "Oh, this is too good."

"It's not funny," insisted Will. "It really hurts!" He was jogging in place inside the house.

"It's hilarious from where I'm sitting," said Arrogan, grinning. "Maybe you should try dancing. It'd be more entertaining."

"Stop making fun of me!" said Will, desperate. "My body feels like it's on fire! Help me!"

His grandfather sighed. "Don't be so dramatic. Let me explain…"

"I don't need explanations. I need you to take the spell off of me!" Will was jumping up and down now.

The old man held up a hand, and once again a green line of power shot forth, spearing into Will's chest. A second later, his body stopped moving, and other than breathing, he was completely paralyzed. His mouth didn't work either, so he couldn't even protest. Arrogan stepped closer and pushed, causing him to fall backward.

He would probably have cracked his head on the floor, but something caught him in midfall and he found himself floating toward his cot, where he was gently deposited. His guardian walked over to stare down at him. "Now perhaps we can talk without all that ridiculous jumping and whining."

Will glared hatefully at his tormentor. The pain was growing worse, but he was entirely unable to move or otherwise express his distress.

"Apparently your best idea was to use your muscles to burn off some of your turyn," said Arrogan, "and while this shows that you do indeed have a capacity for thought, I'm afraid it's a hopeless solution for your problem.

"As you have discovered, physical activity does use some of your turyn, but it's a small amount. If you were a little smarter, you might have tried keeping your emotions in check, since those can affect it as well, but that's ultimately a dead-end also.

"The only effective way to use up your turyn quickly is by doing magic of one form or another," the old man smiled maliciously. "Which is why learning this lesson is much easier if you don't know how to do that. What you're supposed to learn here is how to *reduce* the amount of turyn you produce.

"Unfortunately, that's really hard to do. It's akin to learning how to not breathe. The longer you hold your breath, the more it feels as though your lungs are about to explode. Your body will fight you all the way." His grandfather straightened up and walked away. "I'll start dinner while you work on it."

It felt like he was dying, and he silently cursed the old man, until the pain grew too intense for him to even do that. Arrogan's voice carried to him over the smell of bacon frying. "Not to worry. I'll keep a close eye on you to make sure you don't die, but I doubt it will come to that."

Time passed with agonizing slowness, while Will sweated and suffered. The pain was even worse than what he had felt after being bitten by the emerald viper. *I'm going to kill him if I ever get free,* thought Will.

Once dinner was finished, his grandfather sat down nearby and began eating. "Would you like some?" offered the old man. Then he laughed. "No, I suppose not." He finished eating and then went about the chore of washing the dishes, all the while seeming as though he had not a care in the world.

Eventually, Will lost touch with the outside world. He was trapped in a prison of pain, without any hope of reprieve. In his mind's eye, he could almost see the flame of his turyn, burning and straining against a cage of green light. A voice intruded on his awareness, "Imagine you're squeezing a muscle, or maybe your fist. You have to tense it tightly, as though you're trying to squeeze the life out of something."

He couldn't tense anything, since his body was paralyzed, which forced him to do what the old man asked purely in his imagination. Will visualized it in various ways, as a fist, or as though he was hugging something tightly, but nothing seemed to work. In the end, he imagined his grandfather's neck and thought about choking the old man to death. That didn't work either, which seemed like a real shame.

As the evening wore on, Will found his mind disassociating itself from his body, making the pain feel distant, almost unimportant. He began to think more clearly, and then, almost by accident, he happened upon the solution.

It was impossible to describe, but once he found it, he knew it was right. A secret place inside himself that pulsed and burned, producing the turyn that was causing him so much agony. Mentally, he caught hold of it and squeezed. Nothing happened at first, but gradually his pain began to fade, and a refreshing sensation of coolness washed over his body.

His breathing became easier, and he knew he had done it. Opening his eyes, the one part of his body still under his control, he glanced around to see if his grandfather had noticed. From the corner of his left eye, he spotted the old man still sitting in the chair across from him. Arrogan was sound asleep.

He wanted to shout with frustration, but the paralysis made it impossible. *I did it, you ornery old geezer! Let me go!* In his anger, his grip on the source slipped for a moment, but he hastily got it back under control.

The rest of the night was less painful, but it was a misery nonetheless. Will was tired and weary from the long hours of agony, and he quickly slipped into slumber, but after a half an hour or so the pain returned. He woke as the burning began, and he was forced to reassert his control over the source of his turyn. The cycle repeated itself throughout the night, until the sun began to peek through the windows.

When he woke the final time, the room was bright and he could smell eggs cooking. He had become so accustomed to paralysis that it was several moments before he discovered he could move.

Arrogan greeted him with a smile when he sat up. "Are you hungry?"

"For blood, you sadistic bastard!" Will growled. "How could you do that to me? I nearly died!"

"Not even close," said his grandfather. "You should be proud. You learned in a day what some take months or years to manage. Of course, it was all due to my enlightened teaching methods, but still, you are due some of the credit."

Will cast about, looking for the axe. *Where did I leave it?* The porch, it was on the porch. Feeling a new determination, he got to his feet to go retrieve it. His mentor didn't even watch as he left the room, so intent was the old man on his cooking.

He returned a moment later, quietly, placing each foot slowly so as not to make any noise and alert his oppressor. With the axe held diagonally, close to his chest, he approached until he was only a few feet from the evil bastard who claimed to be his guardian, then he raised his weapon.

Arrogan was busy moving the eggs from the pan to a waiting plate, and Will knew his timing was perfect. Feeling only the slightest guilt, Will turned the axe so it would be the flat that struck. He really wanted to kill the wretched man, but he knew his conscience would bother him later if he did. *I'll just knock him out and run for it.*

He was just beginning his swing when his body froze in place. Unbalanced, he fell backward, crashing into the floor and nearly dashing his head against the floorboards. He stared upward at his grandfather with pure malice in his eyes.

The old man turned around and gave him an impish grin. "Next time, make some noise. The silence was far too suspicious." Snapping his fingers, he released Will and held out a plate. "Still hungry for blood?"

Leaving the axe on the floor, Will got to his knees. "I'm on to you now, old man. I've taken the measure of your evil. Someday I'll make you pay for your crimes."

Arrogan chuckled. "Whatever motivates you. Holding a grudge might help you learn faster. Once you're good enough to keep me from seizing control of your turyn, you'll be a lot closer to getting your revenge." He placed the plates on the table and nudged one of them.

"You should eat them before they get cold. They'll taste a lot better."

They ate in silence, but after Will finished his food he felt he needed to give his grandfather a reminder. "I've learned your lesson, so you can take your weird spell off of me now."

Arrogan 'tsked' at that. "Oh, it's far from over. That spell will be on you for months yet."

"But I can't sleep!" cried Will, despair seeping into his voice.

"Don't be so dramatic," rebuked his grandfather. "You're past the worst part. Once this becomes second nature, you'll sleep just fine. Until that happens, you'll just have to make do with a lot of short naps."

"You're insane," said Will. "I can't keep this up forever."

"Just until you die," said Arrogan dryly, "which, if you master this properly will be a very long time from now." Leaning across the table, he took Will's plate before fixing him with an intense stare. "Make no mistake, you vapid twat, I'm not training you to be one of those half-baked embarrassments that they produce in Wurthaven these days. I'm forging you into a true wizard, the likes of which brought humanity out of the dark ages of shamanism and obedience to alien gods. You'll either learn or I'll bury you in the garden out back to feed my plants. There is no middle way."

Will could see madness in the old man's eyes, and he shivered involuntarily before looking down at his plate to escape his grandfather's gaze.

"Now, it's time for you to start your reading practice," added Arrogan.

"How can I read? It takes all my concentration just to keep my turyn clamped down," he replied quietly.

"You'll manage. You'll learn to do everything like that. Reading is important. It's the best way to cure you of your ignorance. It's a pity it can't cure your stupidity as well. You're going to be a great wizard someday, skillful and well-educated." Arrogan paused for a second. "But you'll probably still be dumb as a stump."

Despite his poor mood, Will laughed a little at the remark. There was a certain pattern to his grandfather's insults and abuses that had grown on him over time. He still hated the crotchety bastard, but he couldn't help but like the man a little.

Arrogan's face remained still and serious. "That wasn't a joke," he stated, but after a second his eyes crinkled at the corners.

***

The next two weeks were a misery. The only thing good Will could find about them was that at least he wasn't in a lot of pain. He couldn't sleep more than thirty or forty minutes at a time at night before waking up with a burning sensation that told him his turyn was growing again. Consequently, he was constantly sleepy during the day and found himself nodding off at every opportunity, while reading, while cooking, and most especially while trying to learn math.

It came as a complete surprise to him the first night he slept eight hours without waking. He had thought it would happen gradually, but when his unconscious mind finally learned to maintain its grip on his turyn while he slept, it happened all at once. One day he was napping, the next he was sleeping without trouble.

Things got much easier after that, and his reading and math sessions seemed pleasant. His grandfather began to take him on walks as well, pointing out plants and trees that Will already knew, but giving him extra information about them. Many had uses his mother had never mentioned, primarily since she didn't practice magic. For a midwife, it wasn't particularly useful to know that ash and oak were helpful in creating protective wards.

What didn't happen, however, was any actual training in magic or spells. As winter came to a close, Will asked his grandfather about it. "When are you going to teach me how to do something?"

The old man was in a good mood that day, so he answered plainly, "Remember when I first put the spell on you to keep your turyn from expanding?"

He nodded.

"What would you have done if you could cast spells?"

Will already knew the answer. "I would have used magic to keep my turyn lower, but I've already mastered the trick. There's no reason to keep me ignorant."

"You aren't even close to being done," said Arrogan, his tone ending the discussion.

Will sighed, knowing it was useless to keep asking. That evening, the old man illustrated the point by removing the spell on him after they had eaten.

"Oh, that feels good!" exclaimed Will, but seconds later he saw the green line connecting to his chest again. "What are you doing?" He twisted in place, trying to escape the old man's control, but his best efforts were useless. The flame of his candle turned green, and he knew Arrogan had taken hold of him once more.

The flame shrank even more, as Arrogan manipulated his source. It was now a quarter of its former size. "This is your new goal," said his guardian.

Will felt tired and lethargic, his turyn too small to sustain him properly. "You're crazy," he protested. "I can't live like this."

His grandfather smiled, then recreated the spell-cage that would contain Will's turyn. It was sized to fit his much smaller inner flame now. "You'll be fine. As you will discover in time, you've been relying on your turyn to help you do everything: walk, talk, eat, shit, even think. That's what ordinary people do with theirs, but you aren't going to be ordinary. You're going to learn to live without it."

"What's the point? Why would anyone want to be so miserable all the time?" asked Will.

"Ask me again in a few years," said Arrogan.

CHAPTER 16

It was over a month before Will could sleep properly again. Keeping his source damped down properly was much more difficult given the new limit that Arrogan had imposed. His only solace was that he hadn't had to go through the same intensely agonizing period at the beginning this time. He already knew what to do; it was simply a matter of focus and discipline.

What he had more trouble with, though, was his lack of energy. It felt as though he was living underwater—every movement was difficult. Even walking took all of his attention, or he would trip and fall.

Naturally, it was at this point in his development when his grandfather decided that physical training would be beneficial. It began with brisk walks and culminated in Will being forced to run circuits around the house. By the end of the first two weeks, he was covered in bruises and scratches from tripping over vines and brambles that seemed to be everywhere.

When he could finally manage to run completely around the house without falling flat on the ground, Arrogan brought out two long staves of ash. He tossed one to Will, who skillfully caught it with his face.

"Ow!"

"Pick it up," said his torturer.

Will groaned but did as he was told. Then his grandfather began walking him through a series of staff forms. "Try to follow my movements."

The staff felt clumsy in his hands and though the movements his grandfather asked him to copy were fairly simple, he found himself having trouble. As usual, his body was incredibly awkward and he knew that if it weren't for the fact that his natural turyn was so thoroughly suppressed, he could have done it easily.

He got better, though. By the time summer arrived, he was able to follow the forms easily and his grandfather switched to active sparring, or as Will liked to think of it, 'supervised beatings.' It was a great relief to him when his cousin Eric appeared one day at the beginning of a training session.

"Will!" called his cousin.

Arrogan turned on Eric angrily. "What do you want? We're busy."

"Hi, Eric," said Will, grateful for the interruption.

"Baron Nerrow is at your mom's house," said his cousin excitedly. "He's looking for you."

"Tell that two-bit goat wrangler to fuck off," said Arrogan harshly.

Eric gaped at the old man's invective, then looked straight at Will. "Your mom told him that you were at our house. He won't leave without seeing you. Dad sent me to fetch you before Lord Nerrow loses his temper."

Will's grandfather was swearing quietly to himself. "Pompous ass! Who does the think he is?"

"I should go, Grandfather," said Will. "I don't want anything to happen to Mom."

"This is her fault to begin with," spat his guardian. "Erisa can take care of her own problems."

Eric spoke up. "If Will doesn't come, she might be forced to tell Lord Nerrow to come here."

Will was already moving. Leaning his staff against the house, he took a moment to brush the dust and dirt off his clothing. "Let's go," he told his cousin.

"Hold on," commanded Arrogan, his voice projecting authority. Will and Eric stopped and looked at him. The old man pointed at Eric. "Go stand over there. I need to talk to Will for a moment, privately."

Once Eric had moved off a short distance, his grandfather took him aside. "You need to be very careful when you meet Lord Nerrow. He can't know anything about your training."

Will understood. He hadn't forgotten that his grandfather was some sort of wanted criminal. "I won't say anything about you."

"This isn't just for my sake," said the old man. "It's for yours as well." He made a gesture with one hand and Will felt the spell encasing his turyn vanish. "We don't want him to see that spell, but don't think you're off the hook," warned Arrogan. "Keep your turyn tightly suppressed. The spell goes back on when you get back."

"He's a sorcerer," reminded Will. "Won't he see that my turyn is too small to be normal?"

His grandfather cuffed the side of his head. "Fool. Haven't you been paying attention? Can you see mine?"

Will shook his head. He had a vague sense that his grandfather's turyn was somewhat smaller than usual, but he couldn't visualize it directly. He certainly couldn't tell it was the tiny ember that the old man had once shown him.

"That's the point of the candle spell," lectured Arrogan. "In time, you'll be able to gauge almost exactly what your turyn is doing, based on experience and instinct, but judging someone else's is even more difficult. You can see the flows of magic around yourself and others, but seeing what lies within someone else is nearly impossible." He paused for a moment, then went on, "That's right, I almost forgot the candle. Give it to me."

He did, and the flame winked out, causing Will a moment of panic. He had grown so used to constantly observing it that seeing the flame vanish made him think he had died for a split second. Arrogan tucked the now-extinguished candle into a pocket. "I'll restore this spell as well, after you get back."

Thinking they were done, Will started to leave, but his grandfather caught his shoulder. "Not yet. You need to be ready for what *you* will see, not just what he might see."

"Huh?"

"The last time you saw Lord Nerrow, you didn't have the sight, and as far as he knows, you still don't," explained Arrogan.

Will frowned. "He's not going to know what I can see just by looking at me."

"He will if you act surprised," said his guardian. "Sorcerers usually have one or more elementals with them. They aren't visible to normal people unless they call on them, or when they want to impress people, but you are almost bound to see one around him, and it can be jarring. If you respond with shock or fear he's going to know."

"How bad could it be?"

"Mark Nerrow comes from a very prestigious line of sorcerers, even though his rank among the nobility is fairly modest. He will very likely have a major fire elemental with him. Seeing something like that can be very unsettling. Try not to shit yourself," advised his grandfather. "At its biggest, it could be as big as a large house, though it will almost certainly be compressed into a tiny form, like a ball of fire floating over his shoulder."

Despite the warning, Will found himself more curious than ever. His training with Arrogan had been singularly boring, except for the painful parts. Seeing an elemental sounded exciting. "I'll be all right," he assured the old man.

Chapter 16

Arrogan stared after him for several minutes after he left, then he went inside and got his travel boots and staff. As he stepped off the porch and started in the direction of Will's house, he spotted the goddamned cat. "I should have known you'd show up today," he told the feline.

The grey feline stretched and then sat up straight, fixing Arrogan with a serious stare.

"Don't worry, I'm not planning on starting anything," said the old man. "I've left that crap in the past, where it belongs."

The cat yawned, then stared up at him, closing its eyes slowly before reopening them.

"Trust me," said Arrogan. "I just want to observe."

The goddamned cat sneezed before walking away, seeming to have lost interest in the old man's conversation. Arrogan shook his head and started walking. As he went he muttered to himself, "But if that pompous prick tries to take the boy, I won't hesitate to start a war."

***

Will and Eric made good time through the woods on their way to Will's house, keeping their pace somewhere between a trot and a jog. When they got close, Will stopped and put a hand on his cousin's shoulder. "You should stay here."

"I want to see what happens," protested Eric.

"The man's a sorcerer," reminded Will. "If he's mad about something, or if something goes wrong, I'd rather you weren't there. It's bad enough that he's in the house with Mom."

"I'd like to see him try!" declared Eric, lifting one fist and shaking it defiantly. "I'd show him what the Cartwrights are made of."

Will couldn't help but be impressed by his cousin's loyalty, as well as a little envious as he saw the corded muscles of Eric's forearm. Even with his new staff practice, he doubted he'd ever develop that much muscle. Still, Will vividly remembered all the times his grandfather had rendered him completely helpless without so much as a word. If Arrogan could do that, how much could a powerful sorcerer do? "Please stay here, Eric," he said. "Neither of us can fight magic, and he'll have guards as well. I'd rather not risk anyone I don't have to."

Eric chewed his lip unhappily, but eventually he agreed. "All right. But if anything happens, I'll run and get Dad."

"If it comes to that, just run," said Will. He hugged his cousin briefly, then started through the underbrush. It was only twenty more yards to his house.

As before, the gilded carriage was parked in front and a well-dressed driver stood beside it. The footman stood guard at the door to his house. Squaring his shoulders, Will walked forward.

"Who might you be?" asked the driver.

Will wasn't sure if it was the same man that had whipped him two years before, but he turned his head to bring the scar on his cheek into view. "Will Cartwright," he answered. "I was told that Lord Nerrow wanted to see me."

The footman opened the door to the house and peeked inside. "The boy is here, milord." A man's voice responded, and then the servant looked back at Will. "You can go in."

It's my home, you asshole, thought Will, but he kept his words to himself. He was surprised by the number of people inside when he stepped in. The main room of his home served as both a kitchen and Erisa Cartwright's main place of business, so aside from the hearth there was a table with four chairs. The shelves around the sides of the room were crammed with dried herbs, and a variety of bottles and jars of ointment.

Erisa's favorite chair was occupied by an arrogant-looking man clad in orange and gold—the same one who had visited two years ago. Lord Nerrow had dirty blond hair, brown eyes, and a long, sharp nose that hung over a thin mustache. Seeing him in his mother's chair didn't do anything to improve Will's opinion of him.

Two of the other chairs were occupied by two young women, or more accurately, girls. The first looked to be close to Sammy's age, with brown hair and eyes. Will thought she must be the same one he had once seen escaping from the carriage, the one he had saved from the snake. He had no doubt about the identity of the other, older girl, whose raven black hair and startling blue eyes had caught his attention immediately. *Her name was Selene.* At a guess, he figured she was near to his own age.

More fascinating than the three strangers were the creatures hovering above their shoulders. Lord Nerrow and the younger girl both had ghostly flames beside them and when Will let his eyes settle on them briefly, he got the distinct impression that the flames were looking back at him, though they had no eyes that he could discern.

Even more interesting the older girl, Selene, had two spirits hovering beside her, one that seemed fluid and nebulous, and another with sharp, crystalline edges. Will could sense extreme concentrations of turyn within all four of the elementals, particularly the flame that hung beside Lord Nerrow.

While the three visitors were seated, Will's mother was standing. She shot Will a warning glance as he came in, though he had no idea what she might want to tell him.

No one spoke at first, so Will did the honors. "You called for me, sir?"

The younger girl corrected him, "Daddy should be addressed as 'Your Lordship' or 'my lord.'"

Lord Nerrow frowned and snapped his fingers. "Laina, don't interrupt if you want me to bring you on any more trips." He turned his attention back to Will. "Take a seat, young man."

Will glanced at his mother, who was still standing submissively at one side. "I'd rather not, Your Lordship, since my mother is still on her feet."

Erisa was alarmed as their attention shifted briefly to her. "I'll step outside," she offered.

Selene stood before she could move. "Take my seat, Mrs. Cartwright. My legs are tight from riding in the carriage. Standing would be a relief."

Laina gave her friend a look of displeasure, muttering to herself, "Both of them should stand in the presence of their betters."

Will moved closer and held the newly vacated chair for his mother, who radiated embarrassment as she sat, then he took the empty chair. Erisa looked at the girl who had given up her chair and said, "Thank you, Lady Selene. I don't deserve such treatment."

"She's not a—" began Laina, but her father held up his hand and looked a warning at the girl. She closed her mouth, and Will thought he saw a look of mild relief on Selene's face.

"Let's get down to business, William," announced Lord Nerrow. "After my last visit a couple of years ago, I wasn't sure you would live, but since you did I feel I owe you a debt for saving my daughter's life." He gestured toward Laina, whose face soured slightly at the comment.

Will decided he didn't care much for Laina. She gave every indication of being spoiled beyond redemption, as he would expect from someone born to her station. The older girl, Selene, he wasn't sure about. She seemed gracious and was more mature. Since she wasn't one of Lord Nerrow's children, he wondered what her status was, but he couldn't very well ask. He guessed she was a well-born playmate kept close by to keep Laina occupied.

If that's the case, I feel sorry for her, thought Will. "You don't need to thank me, my lord," he said at last.

"That's for me to decide, William," countered the nobleman. "I will thank you, and I would also like to offer you an opportunity to better yourself." Lord Nerrow leaned forward, putting his elbows on the table and lacing his fingers together before resting his chin on them. "Erisa tells me that you have studied herbalism with her, but that recently you've been taken under your uncle's guidance to learn the making of carts."

From the corner of his eye, he saw his mother glance nervously at him, probably worried he would spoil her lie. Will kept his attention on Lord Nerrow, though he was finding it difficult not to stare at the elemental hovering close to the man's shoulder. "Yes, my lord."

The Baron reached into a leather case and withdrew a folded sheet of parchment, which he then offered Will. "This is for you."

Will unfolded it and scanned the page. It was covered in elegant, flowing letters that were so artfully written that it made it difficult for him to decipher, but he did the best he could. His reading skills weren't good enough for some of the words, but he managed to get the gist of it quick enough.

As he struggled with the words, Lord Nerrow spoke again. "My apologies, I forgot you can't read. It's a letter of—"

Will nodded. "Wurthaven? You want me to study to be a wizard?"

"—introduction," finished the nobleman, who then stopped and arched one brow before glancing at Erisa.

"Pardon, my lord," said Will. "My uncle has been teaching me letters. I can't read all of it, but I caught the meaning."

Lord Nerrow smiled. "You impress me, young man, but then again, I suppose it's to be expected." He looked at Erisa once more, but she was keeping her eyes firmly on the table.

Will was thinking furiously, while trying to keep his face calm. While the offer would have been irresistible two years before, he was sure he didn't want to go there now. His grandfather was cruel and capricious, and he had yet to teach Will even a single spell, but he had come to trust the old man. It went without saying that he didn't want to leave his mother behind either. Though he saw her only rarely now, living in Cerria would mean he might not see her again until his training was over.

"I don't think I can be a wizard," said Will, looking for a decent excuse to refuse.

"Nonsense," said Lord Nerrow. "Most people have the potential, it's simply a matter of training and intelligence. You seem bright enough to me."

Hah! thought Will. *If only the old man could hear that.* "My uncle says I could make a good living as a wainwright in Cerria," offered Will weakly.

Laina snickered at that remark and Selene lifted her hand to cover a smile. Lord Nerrow glanced at the two girls then turned back to Will. "I'm sure they make a decent wage, but do you have any idea how much a wizard is paid?"

"No, sir," Will admitted.

"A journeyman wizard gets sixty gold crowns a year, William," Lord Nerrow informed him. "And that's the lower end of what they make. If they're talented or have good recommendations, they can make double that. It takes six years at Wurthaven to become a journeyman wizard. They only take twenty students a year, and I'm willing to cover your expenses during that time."

Will gaped slightly in spite of himself. Sixty crowns was a fortune. He could hardly imagine such wealth. *And grandfather calls them 'sanitation workers?'*

The nobleman smiled at his reaction. "Once you've been a journeyman for ten years, you can demand a trial to be raised to the rank of master wizard. You're what, fifteen years old now? With hard work and some luck, you could be a master wizard by the time you're thirty-one. A master commands ten times the money a journeyman can earn."

"I don't want to move to Cerria," Will replied, his tone plaintive.

"I won't take no for an answer, William," said Lord Nerrow. "Your future is too important to me."

Selene spoke up then. "We should make sure he has the basic potential before you push him into it."

"There's no doubt of that," said the nobleman dismissively. "He's m—" he stopped himself suddenly, then amended his statement. "Go ahead, Selene, examine him. It will be good practice for you."

Will didn't like the sound of that, but before he could protest, Selene raised her hands and said a word softly under her breath. A thin line of power flowed from the watery elemental beside her, meeting her hands and then forming a strange pattern in the air before her. The dark-haired girl peered through it as though it was a windowpane, her eyes fixed on him.

Maybe if she sees how small my turyn is, they'll give up, thought Will hopefully.

Selene frowned, narrowing her eyes. "That's odd."

"What is it?" asked Lord Nerrow.

"Give me a moment," said the older girl. Waving her hand, she dispelled the pattern and created another, studying Will even more intensely the second time. "I can't see it," she admitted after a moment.

"What do you mean, you can't see it?" demanded Lord Nerrow. "It's there, otherwise he'd be dead."

"The source," clarified Selene. "His turyn seems to be roughly what I'd expect, perfectly average, but I can't see the source at all. Everything within him is cloudy."

"Ridiculous," said the nobleman. "Let me do it." He performed a similar procedure and began studying Will as well, but after only a few seconds he stopped. "That is curious. It's almost as though someone has warded him, but I don't sense the presence of a spell."

"I didn't eat much this morning," said Will, at a loss to find a good explanation.

Laina giggled at that. "Your diet has nothing to do with it."

Will bristled at her remark. He knew from his early months observing the candle flame that being hungry could affect his turyn level, although only slightly, but he didn't argue. *The spoiled brat has probably never gone hungry in her entire life,* he thought to himself.

"Pardon me, William," said Lord Nerrow. "This is intrusive and may even cause you some discomfort." Then, without waiting for a response, he lifted one hand and a line of green shot toward Will's chest.

Will knew exactly what that was. Arrogan had done it to him many times already, and he despaired at the knowledge, but even as he flinched, the green line went through his chest and then slid away to one side.

The Baron grunted and tried again, but still failed to make the connection to Will's turyn. After two more attempts, he glared at Will. "Are you doing that on purpose?"

"Doing what, my lord?" asked Will innocently. It was hard pretending he couldn't see what the nobleman was doing. "Did something happen?" He had no idea why the man's spell was failing where Arrogan's had always worked, but he wasn't about to ask questions.

Lord Nerrow sat back, momentarily nonplussed. He ran his hand through his hair and let out a long breath. "Never mind. I can see you have a healthy level of turyn in you, so I doubt there will be a problem. The masters at Wurthaven can sort out whatever peculiarities you possess."

"I don't really want to be a wizard," said Will, "though I appreciate your kindness." Laina frowned at him, and after a second, he realized his mistake, adding, "My lord."

"You should leave him be, Father," said Laina, her tone condescending. "Birds fly and pigs root around in the mud. He'll be happier here."

"Laina!" said Selene. "That's enough!"

Lord Nerrow stood and stretched. "Fine, William. I'll give you some time. Keep the letter of introduction. You can think about it and give me an answer next year. If you change your mind sooner, come find me in Cerria."

Erisa stood and bowed deeply. "Thank you for understanding, Lord Nerrow."

Belatedly, Will realized he should be doing the same and he hastily jumped up. Laina laughed at his rush and he found himself scowling at the girl. The touch of fingers on his cheek startled him, and he turned to see Selene had stepped up beside him as the other two made for the door.

"It left a scar," murmured the young woman.

He understood her meaning then, for he often forgot about the mark on his cheek. "I don't even think about it most days," he told her.

Selene pulled her hand away, as though remembering her manners. "Thank you for helping her." And then she left with the others.

CHAPTER 17

His grandfather was coming out of his ramshackle dwelling when Will got back, a large, glass jar in his hands. "Oh, you're back."

Will was faintly disappointed by his mentor's bland greeting. "What's in the jar?"

"Troll piss," said the old man without even a twitch.

"What is it really?" said Will, repeating his question.

Arrogan lifted the small, wooden lid and held it out toward him. "Have a sniff if you don't believe me."

At five feet, Will already knew he wanted nothing to do with the foul odor emanating from the jar. "Oh, that's awful! What's it for?"

"I thought I'd use your absence as an opportunity to take care of some housekeeping chores. A little of this sprinkled around the edges of the garden should keep the deer away from my plants for at least a month," explained his grandfather. "But since you're back, I suppose I'll just have you do it for me."

Ugh, thought Will. "Aren't you going to ask me what Lord Nerrow wanted?"

Arrogan lifted his chin. "I have absolutely no interest in that man's doings, so long as he stays out of our business." Placing the jar on the ground, he stepped up to Will. "Time to put the spell back on you."

Will had been thinking about what had happened with Lord Nerrow at his mother's house and had planned a deliberate bit of rebellion. "No."

His grandfather's brows shot up in surprise. "Oh, really?"

Will began backing away, and as he had expected, his teacher reacted by sending a green line of power out to seize his turyn. A second later he found himself paralyzed. Arrogan wasted no time reapplying the spell-cage around the source of Will's turyn. Then he brought out the candle and redid its spell as well.

The old man studied him for a moment and then released him. "What was that about? You should know better by now."

"I was testing you," Will answered with a grin.

Arrogan's mouth went wide. "You? Testing me?"

He nodded, then handed his letter of introduction to his grandfather. "Lord Nerrow offered to sponsor me."

The old man scanned the page quickly then tossed the letter to the ground. "I should have expected something like this."

"He also examined me to make sure I had the necessary potential." After the words left his mouth, though, a second thought came to him. *Why would he have expected that?*

Arrogan snorted. "I bet that frustrated him. You're far enough along now that I doubt he got much of a read on you."

"He tried to seize my source, like you just did, but he couldn't do it," said Will, watching his grandfather's reaction carefully.

The old man frowned. "That would have been bad, but he failed, eh? Hah! I knew the fool didn't have it in him. The sorcerers these days are sloppy, even worse than those milksop mages they train at Wurthaven." He eyed Will. "You look like you have some questions. Go ahead."

"Why can you do it when he couldn't?" asked Will immediately.

Arrogan nodded. "The training you're undergoing has greatly increased your control over your turyn. Not only is it smaller, it's vastly harder for another mage to seize control of it now. In general, that trick is something only done to apprentices or non-mages, because if the target has good control of his own turyn, it's a waste of time. For it to work the one attempting it has to have much better discipline than the target."

"So I'm done with it?" said Will hopefully.

"Not at all," replied the old man. "I won't be satisfied until you can do far better than that. At the rate we're going, it will be another year or longer before I judge you ready for the next phase of training."

Will groaned. "That last time you squeezed it down, I could barely move, any further and I'll collapse!"

"And yet you're walking and talking just fine now, aren't you?" pointed out his mentor.

"That's the part I don't understand," said Will. "Not only that, but they were able to see my overall turyn and they said it seemed relatively normal." He pointed at the newly respelled candle with its tiny flame. "But that would indicate it's anything but normal. How is that?"

His grandfather sighed. "I wasn't going to explain this until later, but I suppose it won't hurt to tell you now. I told you before that normal people use their turyn to walk, talk, move, you get the idea, but you're at a point where you are no longer allowing yourself enough to do much of anything. If your turyn was like this when you started, you'd be flat on your back. You might even be unconscious."

"Then how am I moving?" asked Will.

Arrogan grinned. "That's the trick. You aren't using your own turyn anymore. By gradually starving your body of what it needs, it has begun to take turyn from your environment and use that energy in its place."

"Huh?"

"Here, look at this. It's easier to show than to explain." His grandfather lifted his right hand and a few seconds later a small flame similar to the candle flame appeared. "Let's pretend this is your native turyn, the energy you produce on your own. Watch." The flame turned blue and shrank until it was much smaller, while faint streams of energy flowed in toward it, forming a second flame, orange in color, that enveloped the original one.

"You're drawing in external turyn," said Arrogan. "The blue is you; the orange is what you're absorbing from your environment. The colors are just to show that they're different. Ordinarily, you can't use turyn that isn't your own, but your body is adjusting—it's learning to convert that external turyn." As he spoke, the outer flame shifted, becoming blue like the tiny inner flame. "This is what you're doing, the reason why you are able to function. It's also why those idiots couldn't see your source. It's too small, and the outer flame conceals it."

Will felt as though he was on a verge of a new understanding, but he still had questions. "So the reason he couldn't take control of my turyn was because it was small?"

"Yes and no," said his grandfather. "The actual size of isn't as important as the fact that you've developed much stronger discipline and control over it. Even though that sorcerer doesn't compress his own source doesn't necessarily mean he wouldn't be just as hard to control. Although, in my opinion, learning this technique is one of the best ways to develop true strength of will."

"Then what's the point of all this?" asked Will. "If my body replaces my turyn with external turyn and I wind up with roughly the same amount anyway, why go through the trouble?"

Arrogan showed his teeth in an almost feral grin. "Even in my day there were many who didn't want to bother, which is why this type of training is unheard of now, but a lot of advantages accrue for masters of this technique."

"Such as?"

"Well, I already told you that this is the secret to the longer lives that wizards used to enjoy," said his mentor.

Will wasn't impressed. At fifteen, he still had what seemed to be a lot of years ahead, and he couldn't imagine anything worse than the torture of his grandfather's training. "Is that it? I get to live twice as long? It doesn't seem to have done you much good."

"What does that mean?" said his grandfather suspiciously.

"You're bitter, mean, and you look like something the dog dragged in on a bad night."

Arrogan's face remained smooth for a second, then he smiled. Over the past year, Will had learned that the old man liked insults almost as much as compliments. "Well, that's true, I suppose," he replied. "But consider this. You're not just going to outlive regular people, but you'll outlive today's lazy wizards by an even bigger margin. The way they work shortens their lives, rather than extending it. Think about what you did for that boy, Jack."

"Joey," corrected Will.

"Joey, jackass, whatever he was called," said Arrogan, waving one hand. "Think about how you felt afterward; imagine what your turyn looked like. You exhausted yourself. What would happen if you did that now?"

Will thought about it for a minute. "The same thing. If I used up most of my turyn, even if it wasn't from my source, I'd still be exhausted until it recovered."

"With what you know now, that's true," admitted his grandfather. "But you would recover much faster, and you could cope with the temporary deprivation far better. What do you think one of those fools from Wurthaven would do?"

He could still remember their previous conversation on the topic, when the old man had showed him the candle flaring brighter. "He'd increase his turyn production for a while."

"And shorten his life in the process," spat Arrogan.

"Better than being so tired you can't move," argued Will.

"Since you like tests so much, why don't we try it?" said his grandfather suddenly. "You never believe what I tell you, so we might as well make a lesson of it."

Seeing the light of evil mischief appear in the old man's eyes, Will started to run, but the green line caught him before he could take more than half a step, and he was paralyzed again. Arrogan caught him as he started to fall and eased him to the ground. He set Will's candle on his chest. "Keep an eye on this. I think you'll find it interesting."

Arrogan stepped back and then held his left hand out toward his grandson before clenching it into a fist and pulling it backward. Will felt—and *saw*—the mass of turyn that emerged from his body. It followed the green line and stopped to hover around the old man's fist. Arrogan looked at it for a moment and then waved his hand as though trying to get rid of a bad smell, dispersing Will's turyn.

Will felt an intense exhaustion sweep over him, as he'd expected, but it began fading almost immediately. After just a few minutes, he was merely tired, and through it all the tiny flame on his candle remained steady, neither growing nor shrinking.

"Let's do it again," said his grandfather.

No! thought Will. *Not again, not so soon. Are you trying to kill me?* Unfortunately, he was unable to voice his objections.

Again the old man sucked the very life out of him, and Will was overcome with a bone-deep fatigue. A few minutes later, he did it again. "You would have been incapacitated for days after this when you first came to me," lectured the old man. "Now you can recover most of your turyn from the environment in just minutes, and you can do it over and over again. I'll show you something even more interesting this time."

He drew out Will's turyn once more, but this time rather than dispersing the energy, he brought it close to Will's body and released it. Rather than fading away, the cloud of turyn was drawn back into his body, as though a wind was blowing it toward him. Seconds later, Will's exhaustion faded.

"In the presence of higher concentrations of turyn, you can recover *much* faster," declared his grandfather. He snapped his fingers and released Will then.

Sitting up, Will brushed the dirt from the back of his tunic and gave the old man a sour look. "Every time we have a discussion, I wind up frozen while you perform experiments at my expense."

"All in the name of education," said Arrogan. "Besides, training an apprentice is a real pain in the ass. The only bright spot is that I get to have a little fun now and then."

Back on his feet, Will still felt tired, but it wasn't anything he couldn't deal with.

His grandfather pointed at the jar that supposedly contained troll urine. Will still hadn't decided whether he believe him on the identity of the contents, though. "You've had enough training for one day. After you spread the troll piss around the garden, you can rest for the afternoon."

"Yuck," commented Will. "I think I'd rather train."

The old man shook his head. "So far we've only talked about turyn and its source, but there's another important factor, something I call 'will.' Your will is a lot like a muscle. Training it to control your source makes it stronger—performing magic makes it stronger—but it has a limit. Push yourself too hard for too long and your self-discipline will crumble."

"How do you know when it's running out?" asked Will.

"You get irritable," said his grandfather. "Easy things seem difficult. Your mind feels fuzzy. That's if you're lucky enough to notice in time. Sometimes it falls apart so quickly that by the time you realize you've overdone it, it's too late."

"What happens then?"

"Depends on what you're doing at the time. If it's something big, the result can be bad, or even fatal," said Arrogan.

CHAPTER 18

Summer passed into winter, and Will turned sixteen without much fanfare. He wasn't even sure if his grandfather knew when his birthday was. The old man had never asked, and Will never brought it up.

Will went through two more cycles of having his turyn forcibly reduced, and while it was unpleasant each time, it was never as bad as the first had been. The flame on his candle was no longer even a flame—it more resembled an ember, much like his grandfather's. He hoped that meant he wouldn't have to go through any more compressions.

"We're done squeezing the life out of me, right?" asked Will, as the next summer drew to a close.

"Yeah," said his grandfather. "No one's ever gone farther than that, though I'm tempted to try since I have you as a test subject."

"Why haven't they gone farther?"

"They all died," said Arrogan in a bland tone. Then his eyes lit up. "I'm game to try, though, if you want."

Will gave him a sour look. "No thanks. Does this mean you'll be taking the spell-cage off soon?"

"Hah!" barked his grandfather. "You'd like that, wouldn't you? You lazy little prick."

Will sighed. "I knew it was too much to hope for. What's next then?"

"Well, since you've got enough nerve to ask, you must be ready. Next, you'll learn how to increase your available turyn," said his guardian.

"You have to take the spell off then," said Will. "I have to keep my source tightly clamped off as long as it's in place."

"That's where you're mistaken. The turyn you use now doesn't come from your source. Your body has learned to maintain itself without your source. What you'll do next is increase what you draw from your environment."

"This is going to hurt, isn't it?" said Will bleakly.

"It shouldn't," said Arrogan, "but I wouldn't put it past you to screw it up somehow."

"Can I ask what the point of this is?"

"You can ask, but it won't help you succeed, and you wouldn't understand either, so don't bother. It will make sense later. What you need to do is push your turyn outward, sort of like you did when you healed that boy."

It sounded simple. "That's it?" said Will.

Arrogan just smirked. "Try. We'll see how far you get."

An hour later and Will wanted to pull his hair out. No matter what he tried, nothing happened. It wasn't that he was struggling with a difficult task—he couldn't even begin, and his grandfather's advice was worse than useless.

"Imagine it flowing out through your hands. That helps some people," said the old man. When that didn't help, he offered different instructions. "Think of it like an empty wineskin. You're trying to push your breath out and inflate it."

After the second hour, Will was ready to give up. "Why don't you just take control like you did before? You do it and I'll learn from that."

The old man shook his head. "What I did before was compress your turyn, so it would fit within the spell-cage. You had to learn how to keep it that way on your own. This is almost the opposite of that."

That gave Will an idea. Forcing himself to release his inner grip on the source of his turyn might give him more power to work with. He was rewarded moments later when a sensation of intense pain built within him. He clamped down on his source immediately.

"Fool," remarked his grandfather. "You have to use the turyn you're absorbing, not the turyn from your source. That's why the spell-cage stays on, so you don't develop sloppy technique."

"I hate you sometimes," said Will honestly.

The old man grinned. "Time for some staff sparring, then. You can try this again tomorrow."

He didn't have any better luck the next day, the next week, or even that month, and to make matters worse, his grandfather delighted in taunting him about his failure. "The first-year students at Wurthaven learn to do this during their first week. It's the most basic step to creating magic. They don't even let them start learning the runes until they manage this," teased the old man.

Will was sitting down in the yard in front of the house, doing his best to concentrate. He was sweating in the heat, and a swarm of gnats seemed to have decided he would make great company. "Can you leave me alone?" he complained. "I can't focus."

Arrogan walked a slow circle around him. "Focus? A child could do this. If you weren't such a moron, you'd have done it by now. Stop thinking so hard and just do it!" He stopped in front of Will and a strange expression crossed his face.

As Will inhaled, he was assaulted by the stench of something akin to rotten eggs. When he glanced up, he saw the old man watching him, and on seeing his reaction, Arrogan burst into laughter.

His frustration boiled over, and for a moment the world turned red. Within him, his anger churned and twisted, spinning until he could feel it as an almost physical object. Snarling, he pushed his hand out and his feeling became real; an intense ball of crimson light shot forth toward Arrogan.

The old man's eyes widened in surprise, and he raised a hand just before the vicious ball of power struck him with a deafening thunderclap. Will was almost blinded by a flash of light, and when his vision cleared he saw his grandfather still standing, his hand outstretched, palm touching the ball of light. Arrogan's face was a picture of intense concentration and his brow was beginning to bead with sweat.

"You've made your point, boy. Let it go. Now!" ordered the old man.

Will was still angry, and it was a second before he realized he was still connected to the energy, that he was in fact pressing it forward against his grandfather's hasty defense. Meeting his teacher's eyes, he wondered what would happen if he didn't relent. *I'll teach the old bastard a lesson.* He pushed harder.

Arrogan grunted, and his arm bent under the pressure. "This is why I hate training apprentices," he growled under his breath. Sticking his left hand out to one side, he sent a red line of power out. It flowed with fluid grace and began to circle Will's ball of focused hatred.

Will felt his control beginning to slip as whatever Arrogan was doing began to eat into his spell. His anger turned to panic as he felt his determination falter.

"Let it go, boy!" commanded his grandfather. "You're just making it worse. If this goes much further, I won't be able to contain it, and I guarantee that I won't be the one who winds up a smoldering pile of ash. My kindness only goes so far."

Unsure what he was doing, Will let go of his anger and tried to relax. As he did, he felt something snap within him, and pain shot through his body. Gasping, Will fell sideways and lay on the ground. Looking up, he saw his grandfather still struggling with the ball of turyn he had somehow conjured. It was growing smaller by the second, with streamers of light trailing behind it like smoke as the old man guided it into a circle around his body. He seemed to be pulling energy from it as it traveled.

Arrogan's hair was standing out from his head, and to Will's eyes the old man seemed to glow with light that was shining through his skin. He grew brighter as the ball shrank, and wisps of steam began to rise from his body. When he could hold no more, he sent the now-diminished sphere away from the house, directing it into the forest. After traveling thirty feet, it struck a large oak and exploded, sending splinters of wood in all directions.

Will's ears were ringing so loudly he had trouble hearing anything else, but after a moment he asked, "Are you all right?" His grandfather was still standing in the same place, panting heavily and glowing like a piece of iron fresh from the forge. Then the old man took a deep breath and exhaled slowly. Flames sprang from his body, forming a shell of fire around him that slowly expanded before vanishing.

Arrogan sat down in the dirt, staring at Will. Streaks of red painted his face and arms where splinters had struck him, and he had begun to bleed. "Do I look all right to you?" spat the old man.

Will was having troubles of his own as a familiar pain began to build in him. He had lost control of his source, and no matter how he tried, he couldn't clamp it shut again. "I think something's wrong with me," he stated, trying to hide his panic.

"Your will is broken," commented his mentor. "Jackass." Raising one hand, he made a quick gesture and Will felt the spell-cage within him disappear. The pain vanished with it.

Letting his neck relax, Will's head sagged back to the ground. "Thank you."

"Nothing's ever easy with you," observed his grandfather. "You could have set something on fire or created a light show. No, you had to try and blow us both to hell and back."

"To be honest, I was only trying to blow you to hell and back," said Will, coughing into the dirt.

"Next time distract me first," said Arrogan. "If I see it coming, I'm just going to feed it right back to you and find a new apprentice."

"Is that what you were trying to do?" asked Will.

The old man snorted, reaching up to wipe away the ash that was all that remained of his eyebrows. "No. If I had, you'd be dead already. I was trying to defuse the anomaly you created, but you were fighting me all the way."

He wasn't familiar with that word. "Anomaly?"

"Accidental spell anomaly," said Arrogan. "Which basically just means you created something nobody's got a name for. If you want to give it a name, I suggest 'the idiot's ugly fucking death ball.'"

"You think I can do that again?"

His grandfather shook his head. "Shit like that isn't reproducible. It's too random."

"When you were learning, what did you do?" asked Will, suddenly curious.

"I levitated my master."

"That doesn't sound so bad," said Will.

"She would have disagreed with you. I sent her into a stone ceiling so hard it nearly broke her neck," said Arrogan, chuckling at the memory. "Served her right."

"Does something like that happen with every student?"

"God, no!" said Arrogan. "Most of the time it's not a huge problem—things like changing color, innocuous stuff. But I have seen worse."

"Like what?" asked Will.

"My last student, a guy named Valmon, he unleashed a really weird anomaly. It looked like a black spark, but it kept growing on its own, as though it was alive. I don't know what would have happened if I hadn't taken it apart, but it might have continued getting bigger and killed a lot of people. This was in a city, mind you," said the old man.

"If he was younger than you, is he still alive?"

"No," said Arrogan, his tone flat.

Will's head was pounding, and he knew he wasn't in any shape to stand up, so he kept asking questions. "What happened to him?"

His grandfather blanched, his expression one of profound unhappiness. Eventually, he answered, "He did well, for a hundred years or so, then we had a philosophical disagreement. I killed him."

Shocked, Will could only mumble, "Oh."

"Don't take it to heart, boy. When you get as old as I am, you collect bad memories like a dog collects fleas," said his grandfather.

"Anything I should know so I can avoid that sort of ending?" asked Will.

The old man laughed. "Don't piss me off, and don't mess with my daughter."

Will immediately thought of Tailtiu and blushed.

"I know what you're thinking," said his grandfather. "It wasn't Tally; she hadn't been born yet. It was my oldest, Ethnia. She was human. But while we're on the subject, don't get any funny ideas about Tally. I know she's amoral, nearly immortal, and wears less than a whore in Cerria, but as my student I expect you to keep your distance."

"She's my aunt, too," reminded Will. "Is Tally a nickname?"

Arrogan snorted. "She's so many generations removed you're probably more closely related to the people in the village than you are to her. Not that it matters; she isn't human. And the reason I don't use her name is that she might choose to show up if I do."

"How did that happen, exactly? If you don't mind me asking," said Will. "She has to be at least half-human, doesn't she?"

The old man wiped his face, which did little to clean it, but did serve to smear the blood all over his cheeks, giving him a barbaric appearance. "There are no half-fae. I guess I've neglected your education in certain matters. The fae can't have children. Their realm is rife with magic, and it's thought that besides making them nearly immortal it also renders them unable to reproduce with one another. That's why they like humans so much."

"So you were seduced by one of them?"

"Oh, hell no!" protested his grandfather. "Her mother was human too, but she gave birth over there. If you're born there, you grow up fae. Even if you just live there long enough, it will change you, though not as much as if you grow up there. The reverse is true as well, though it never really happens. If one of them gave birth here, the child would be human."

Will managed to sit up and regretted it. Everything hurt. "That makes no sense."

"I agree with you on that. When I was young, there was a scholar—I think his name was Angus—who spent a lot of time studying them. It was his opinion that the fae realm didn't originally have any fae in it, that they were the product of people who had gotten lost and trapped there."

"So how did she wind up being born there?" asked Will.

Arrogan scratched his head and when his hand came away, he had another long splinter of wood in his fingers. He tossed it away before answering, "That's another one of those things that goes firmly under the category of 'none of your damned business.'"

Persistent, Will kept probing. "Does it have anything to do with that hat with the antlers?"

His grandfather stood up, pointedly ignoring him. "Today's a special day. You've made a start at becoming a wizard, and it's also your first serious attempt at murdering me. That deserves a special meal. What do you think I should cook?"

CHAPTER 19

The next two weeks were unusual. Although Will felt much better the next day, Arrogan insisted he couldn't resume training for at least a fortnight. "Your will has to recover. While it isn't something you feel, like a torn muscle or an injured joint, it's just as serious," his grandfather had told him. As a result, he had been placed on the wizardly equivalent of light duty, which was a misnomer. Light duty for a wizard was apparently heavy physical labor.

Arrogan set him to clearing brush that had grown up in the front yard of the house, with strict instructions not to touch the brambles that protected his garden to the rear. When that was done, he was put to work collecting and chopping more firewood for the upcoming winter, even though it was far too early to be worrying about that in Will's opinion.

He also had more time to practice his scholarly pursuits, namely reading and math. He didn't mind the reading, but the math made him long to be doing something else.

After the first week of 'light duty,' Arrogan called him to his bedroom.

That in itself was unusual; Will had never been permitted to even see what lay beyond the door to his grandfather's private room. What he discovered shocked him, for the room was easily twice the size of the only other room, the one he had spent the last several years living in.

It was also clean. Not clean in the way that Will was used to, though. It was spotless, without a speck of dust to be found anywhere. Will couldn't imagine where his grandfather would have found the time to keep the room in that condition. The man spent almost all of his waking hours outside or in the front room with Will. *Another mystery to add to the list,* he thought.

The furnishings were impressive. A massive, four-poster bed dominated one end of the room while an ornate, hand-carved wood desk occupied the other. In between, the walls were dominated by floor-to-ceiling bookcases that were filled with leather-bound tomes of all shapes and sizes.

"What the hell?" Will blurted out when he first entered.

"What did you expect?" asked his grandfather.

He didn't answer for a second; he was too busy taking in the view. Will's mouth formed an 'o' as his eyes roved back and forth. Then he replied, "Something like the other room, only smaller and smellier." Pointing at the bed, he complained, "That thing is big enough for three people! Why did I have to sleep on the floor all those months?"

"Because it's my damned bed," retorted the old man. "Get your own."

"I can't believe you," said Will, disgusted. "You've kept me living like a dog while you slept in your little palace."

"Wrong tense," said his grandfather. "You're still living like a dog. The only reason you're in here now is because the entrance to my workshop is over there." He pointed to an expensive-looking rug in the center of the room.

Ignoring the old man, Will walked closer to examine the bed. The coverlet on top of it was fancier than any other article of bedding he had ever seen. Two large pillows were at the head of the bed, and the material that covered them was of a sort he didn't recognize. Unable to help himself, he reached over to touch one with his fingers. It was smooth to the touch and softer than anything he had ever felt. "What sort of fabric is this?" he asked.

"Silk," stated Arrogan. "Keep your hands off it."

Will noticed that the two pillows were different. Both were silk, but while one was fairly simple and undecorated, the other had frills around the edges. "Why do you have two pillows?" He leaned over to pick up the fancier of the two.

"Stop!" commanded Arrogan, making no attempt to conceal his anger. Will found himself paralyzed once again. "Touch that pillow, and I'll take your hands off and use them to make bookends."

A second later the paralysis ended, and Will stepped away, noting a pained expression on his grandfather's face. *Trying to kill him doesn't bother him in the least, but threaten his precious pillows and he's furious,* noted Will silently. *I'll never understand the man.* He started to say as much, but a second glance at the old man's face made him uncertain. Reading Arrogan's expressions was never easy. *Is he angry, or something else?*

Arrogan turned away, then bent over and lifted the edge of the rug. Underneath was a trapdoor. He lifted it, exposing a wooden ladder that led below. "The workshop is down here," he said flatly.

"You have a cellar?"

"No, I just like confusing people, so I built a false door in the floor," responded the old man dryly. With a word, he created a globe of light that hovered above his head and began to descend the ladder. As he went, he waved at Will. "Follow."

Will twisted the corner of his mouth up for a second, then answered with obvious sarcasm, "I can't. You said you don't have a cellar."

"Don't be a smartass, William."

Will followed. "I can't believe you told me that. You're the king of smartasses."

"I have a gift. It would be a shame not to share it," said his mentor. "You, on the other hand, should cultivate your own strengths."

When they reached the bottom of the ladder, his grandfather made an odd gesture with his fingers, and the magical light split into four parts and flew to the corners of the room where they took up residence in small glass globes mounted on the ceiling. The cellar looked to be as large as both of the upper rooms put together, with stone walls and a tiled floor. Two long, heavy tables, laden with glassware and other oddments, spanned either side of the room.

Unable to restrain himself, Will finally asked, "Just what are my strengths, in your opinion?"

"Gullibility and vapid stares," answered his grandfather immediately. "Thank you for asking."

Will groaned.

"None of that," said the old man, wagging his finger. "You proved the first trait by asking, and you're putting on a great show of empty-headed goggling at the room as we speak."

Will closed his mouth and crossed his arms, refusing to respond, primarily because he couldn't think of anything to say that wouldn't lead to more teasing. After waiting for a few seconds, his grandfather spoke. "Since you're unable to formulate a question, I'll explain. Most of the equipment you see here is for alchemical purposes. Since you're useless for other training, I thought I'd use this week to teach you a little about alchemy."

"Are you going to show me how to make essential oils?" asked Will, remembering a conversation with his mother from years before.

Arrogan's brows shot up in surprise, then he shook his head. "Maybe later. First, I think it would be wise teaching you the basics, such as how to measure with a balance scale." The next half hour was spent in explanation of just that, and Will began to see why he had been forced to learn so many different names for measures. The room contained a number of tools for measuring things by both weight and volume.

His grandfather also spent an inordinate amount of time discussing safety and showing him where the protective gear was stored. Will learned that for many things he would be expected to wear leather gloves and an apron.

"Also," said Arrogan, "before we go any further, I should tell you that while the tables are wooden, they've been spelled against fire and caustic substances. Don't take that as a challenge, though. They'll still burn if you try hard enough."

Will gave him a look of innocent outrage. "What do you think I'm going to do?"

"I wouldn't put anything past you," said his grandfather. "And while we're on the subject of stupid things you might do, avoid using the emergency exit unless there's an actual emergency."

"Exit?" Will looked around but saw only the ladder and trapdoor they had come in through. "Is there a secret door?"

"Pay attention," said Arrogan. "Look closer, near the wall behind that workbench." He pointed to indicate which bench he was talking about.

Will saw it then, something like a shimmer in the air, though it wasn't really visible to his eyes. Walking closer, he moved around the table so he could stand in the spot. His grandfather grabbed the back of his shirt. "I said *don't* use it unless there's an emergency."

He realized then that it was another point of congruence, similar to the one he had accidentally used to travel to the fae realm. "I wasn't going to step through it," he protested, though in fact he hadn't been sure what it was at first. "Does it lead to the fae realm?"

The old man shook his head. "No, that one goes to Muskeglun, a thoroughly unpleasant place."

"Muskeglun? What's that?" asked Will.

"The poets used to call it the 'Land of the Hidden Mists,' but the name is misleading. A better name would have been 'the shithole.' While it is invariably foggy and misty there, the place is predominantly a swampy dump suitable only for trolls and other unpleasant denizens," explained his grandfather.

He frowned. "Then why did you pick it for your exit?"

"I didn't pick it. I found it when I excavated this cellar," said Arrogan. "You don't *make* congruencies; they simply exist. That being said, I've found this one rather handy, and if I did have to make a hasty retreat, it's not the sort of place most people would want to follow." After a moment he added, "It's also handy for getting troll piss."

"That really was troll urine?" said Will, gaping. "I didn't think trolls were real."

"Maybe I'll take you with me next time," said Arrogan, grinning. "I'll introduce you to Gleg. He's not bad, as trolls go, which is to say he's awful, but he's learned better than to try to eat me."

Thoroughly fascinated, Will asked, "How dangerous are they?"

"Depends on who you are," said the old man. "I find them to be much more dangerous than the fae, but that's mainly because they're stupid. Trolls are difficult to deal with because they're resistant to magic and they can recover from just about any injury. But I would say that if you were a soldier, or preferably, a bunch of soldiers, trolls would be preferable because at least you can fight them. The fae are impossible for most people to handle."

As his mentor lectured, Will found himself wondering about other myths and stories he had heard. "If fairies are real, and trolls are real, are other things from stories real? What about dragons, or dwarves?"

"A better question would be, are there any other worlds that meet ours at congruencies like this?" offered his teacher. "To which the answer is yes, though no one knows for sure how many there are. Some intersect with our world at thousands of different places, like the fae realm, while others have only one or two known crossing points. Those other worlds have hosts of creatures, known and unknown to us. The dwarves you mentioned live in our world, though they're seldom seen." Arrogan stopped then, holding up one hand. "Now you've got me digressing. Today I'm going to teach you something practical, one of the most important recipes known to man."

Nodding, Will waited patiently.

"Ink," began his grandfather, "is one of the keys that led us out of ignorance. I'll teach you two types, oak gall ink, and soot ink…"

Will groaned.

CHAPTER 20

Near the end of his two weeks of 'light duty,' Will went to visit his mother. He hadn't seen her in months, and while Erisa was still relatively young, he worried about her living alone. When he got to the front door he stopped, feeling strangely uncertain.

Do I knock? It was his home after all, but then again, he hadn't lived there for more than two years. Would he startle his mother if he just walked in? In the end, he knocked, feeling slightly foolish as he did.

His mother answered the door moments later, her face lighting up when she saw him. "Will! You didn't have to knock."

"I wasn't sure," he admitted sheepishly. "I didn't want to scare you."

"It would have been a surprise, but a pleasant one," she agreed. "Don't worry, though. I still get lots of visitors from the village, so I'm used to people showing up at odd hours. Come inside. I haven't cooked, but there's still leftovers from last night."

Grinning, he went in and wasted no time demolishing the bread and cold soup she placed in front of him. He had always loved his mother's cooking, but tasting it again after so long was a revelation. While her food was far better than what he could make, he was startled to realize that it was far from what his grandfather made. The only thing about it that was superior was the fact that she had included some ham in the soup. His grandfather didn't raise any animals other than a few chickens or visit the village, so his diet was almost exclusively vegetarian, aside from eggs and butter.

And I still don't know how he gets the butter, Will reminded himself, before being struck by a particularly disgusting thought. *What if he gets it from the trolls? Is there such a thing as troll-butter, and if so, what is it made from?*

"Is something wrong with the food?" asked his mother, a concerned look on her face.

Will waved his hands. "Oh! No, not at all. I just thought of something unpleasant, but it had nothing to do with the food."

"Worried about Lord Nerrow coming back?" she asked, misinterpreting his remark.

He *had* been wondering about that, and since he didn't want to explain the horrors of his imagination, he simply agreed, "It's been on my mind."

His mother nodded knowingly. "He sent a messenger last week. There's trouble brewing with Darrow, so he's too busy to visit personally. The offer is still open, though. You just have to present yourself at the college in Cerria."

Will was relieved to know that the nobleman wasn't coming back, as he still had no idea how to turn the man down. He had already made his decision, and his grandfather had sealed it by tearing up the letter of introduction. "You know how I feel," he replied.

Erisa smiled faintly. "I hope it's the right one. I trust your grandfather, though I worry you're passing up the chance for a better future. As a licensed wizard, you could become wealthy. You won't be able to use what you're learning now without approval from the king."

"I'm more interested in knowing why Lord Nerrow is so insistent," said Will, giving his mother a direct stare.

She looked away. "You saved his daughter's life. Men like him take their debts seriously."

"You know what I mean, Mom. Why did he come here to begin with?"

"I've already told you," answered Erisa, obviously dissembling.

Pushing his empty bowl away, Will looked at his hands. Her evasiveness made him angry, but he didn't know how to express it without hurting his mother. "If you don't want to tell me, just say so. I'd rather hear that than have to pretend I believe the story you've made up. I'm not a kid anymore."

His mother flinched at his words, and he regretted what he had said almost immediately. "I suppose I deserve that," she said.

"I'm sorry, Mom," he apologized. "I'm just being honest. I hate being kept in the dark."

Erisa studied her lap intently, though there was nothing there. "You'll be seventeen this winter. Another year and you'll be a man. I can't keep it from you any longer, but I fear knowing the truth won't bring you any happiness."

"Then?" Deep down, Will had always suspected, but he hadn't dared to face his suspicion in the light of day.

"Lord Nerrow is your father," said his mother without further preamble. "But he'll never acknowledge you publicly."

"And the girl that came with him…"

"Is your half-sister, though I'm sure she had no idea. Lord Nerrow has two daughters. The other is a few years younger. I've never seen her, but her name is Tabitha."

"What about the older girl that came with them, Selene?" asked Will.

His mother shook her head. "I'm not sure. She's from a noble family most likely, but whether she's a cousin or just a friend of theirs I couldn't say."

Will had always known he was a bastard. That had been a simple fact of life, but he hadn't known who his father was, not with any certainty. "How did...?" He wasn't sure how to phrase his question.

"I haven't told you much, but I ran away from home when I was sixteen," Erisa interjected quickly. "But things didn't happen the way most people assume. I was fighting with my mother, but when I got to Cerria, I didn't work as a prostitute, no matter what anyone tells you. I worked in a small tavern called The Brass Button. It was a lucky job for me, since most of the customers there were rich, upper-crust sorts. I wasn't hassled much, as happens frequently at many places where men gather to drink."

He was somewhat relieved to hear that. His mother's silence on the topic over the years had led him to believe something terrible had happened. As he had grown older, he had stopped asking about his father, fearing he might have been the product of rape. It didn't sound like her story was heading in that direction.

Erisa smiled. "Mark was very charming back then. I saw him several times before he even asked my name, and after that—well, I can only say I was young and naïve. He was handsome, kind, and I was utterly smitten."

"But you knew he was a nobleman—that he couldn't marry you," said Will, unable to keep from second-guessing her judgment.

His mother nodded. "He was the second son. He told me he wouldn't ever inherit. Call me a fool, but I believe he loved me. We met frequently, and it wasn't until later that things became serious. When I told him, I was pregnant, he promised to marry me..."

That obviously hadn't happened, so when she paused Will put in, "But?"

"His brother died during a border skirmish with Darrow," said Erisa, her tone becoming sad. "It wasn't even much of a battle, just an unfortunate event. They encountered a scouting party and although they quickly sent them running, a stray arrow struck him in the neck. After that, everything changed. Mark was suddenly heir to the barony, and his father took a hand in matters. They arranged a marriage for him with the king's third daughter, a lady named Arlen, and that was that."

"Didn't he tell them you were pregnant?" asked Will, outraged.

Erisa shook her head and waved her hands. "Heavens no! What do you think would have happened to me if he had?"

He was too angry to accept that reasoning. "Nothing! If he'd married you, they would have had to accept it."

"You know better than that, Will," said his mother calmly. "I know it's unfair, but I've had a lot of time to come to terms with it. Mark helped get me out of the city, and when I came back I lived with Ar—your grandfather. He kept me hidden until you were born, and I didn't go home until you were almost two. My father was already dead when I went back, and my brother had taken over the business. If it wasn't for your uncle, I'm not sure my mother would have let me stay."

Will barely remembered his grandmother, mainly because once his mother had moved out they had only rarely visited her. Now he understood why. "Why wouldn't she understand? It wasn't your fault."

Erisa chuckled, a soft and bitter sound. "I never gave her a chance. I was determined to keep Mark's secret, both for his sake, and for yours. I worried that the new baroness might seek to get rid of you if she found out. Since I refused to tell her what happened, or who your father was—well, she was always quick to judge. She assumed the worst."

It was unfair, unjust, and painful to think about. "But she was your mom," said Will at last. He couldn't imagine a circumstance that would make his own mother treat him so badly. "She should have trusted you."

Erisa's eyes were brimming even though her face was smooth. "And that's why I will *never* do the same to you, Will. No matter what happens. I will always be on your side, no matter what anyone says." She was on her feet and without thinking, Will stood and hugged her.

His eyes were burning as he told her, "I know, Mom. I'm almost grown now. I'll always take care of you, no matter what."

She cried some at that, and Will joined her, but their sadness was short lived. While it felt as though the foundation of the world had shifted beneath his feet now that he knew who his father was, nothing had really changed, and the events she had told him about were long ago. They moved on to simple talk after that.

When he left to go back to Arrogan's home that evening, he walked slowly, taking his time so he could mull over what she had told him. A lot of things made more sense to him now, but in the end his life was still the same.

CHAPTER 21

"Today I'm putting the spell-cage back on," Arrogan informed him. "You've had enough light duty. It's time to get back to work."

Will was relieved. No matter what the old man called it, his light duty had been a pain in the ass.

"Clamp down on your source," ordered his grandfather.

He did, and he was surprised at how easy it was. He had been worried that the two-week break might have caused him to regress, but that didn't seem to be the case. Will felt a wave of fatigue and light-headedness as his turyn shrank, but it passed after a few minutes. His body was already drawing in energy to replace the turyn that he was no longer producing.

His grandfather nodded, observing him closely. "That's good. How do you feel?"

"It was easier than I expected," admitted Will. "I felt tired for a minute, but it didn't last long."

Arrogan raised one brow. "Really?"

Will had the feeling the old man might be on the verge of giving him a compliment, so he seized the moment. "Did I surprise you?" he asked, grinning proudly.

The old man 'harrumphed' and his features turned sour. "In a way, I guess. You might not be as completely useless as I anticipated."

He felt a warm glow. For Arrogan, 'not completely useless' was as close to praise as anyone could expect. "Be careful, old man," warned Will. "If word gets out that you've gone soft, you'll have people lining up outside to be your apprentice."

175

Arrogan snorted. "If that happened, I could quit wasting food on the moron I've been training. I'm sure even a village idiot would be better than you," said his grandfather. Without warning, he conjured a new spell-cage, and in the space of a few seconds, had reapplied it to Will.

"We'll spar and work on your studies the rest of the day, to give you time to readjust. Tomorrow we'll see if your explosive breakthrough taught you anything," Arrogan informed him.

The next day found Will frustrated, but he did have some success. After an hour of false starts, he did manage to 'express' his turyn as Arrogan described it, but it was far from being what his teacher wanted. No sooner than he had pushed some of his turyn out, it faded, dissipating like steam on a cold day.

"The idea is to contain and control it," repeated his grandfather for perhaps the tenth time. "Don't just push it out and forget about it. Don't try to do magic like you're passing gas."

It was a week before he managed to create a well-contained outer layer of turyn around what his grandfather described as his 'personal' layer. The terms confused Will a little at first, though. "Shouldn't my personal turyn be the tiny amount trapped inside the spell-cage?" he asked. "The turyn outside it is what I'm absorbing from the environment."

"You won't have that spell-cage on you forever," Arrogan reminded him. "In this case, I refer to personal turyn as the energy that your body needs and uses to function normally. The fact that you aren't actually producing it yourself is beside the point. What you're learning now is to create a larger supply that you can use to do things without affecting yourself physically. Functionally, however, it's all the same once you've converted it into your own energy type."

Will frowned. "What's the difference between turyn that's been converted and turyn that hasn't? You've told me that my body is doing it automatically, but I still don't understand what it means."

"Hold out your arm," said his grandfather. "I'll show you."

Suspicious, he hesitated. "Is this going to hurt?"

"All the best lessons do," said Arrogan, grinning maliciously. "Do it."

Squinting and gritting his teeth, Will held out his arm.

The old man picked up a long stick from the ground. He used it to point at Will's sacrificial appendage. "For this example, think of your arm as your turyn. It represents the turyn you control, whether it's the inner personal turyn that fuels your actions, or the larger outer layer you've just learned to create. It's *yours*. You can make a fist with it, punch someone, pick things up. You can do whatever you want. It's a part of you." Then he lifted the stick and showed it to Will. "This stick represents turyn that isn't yours. It's external and beyond your immediate control. It isn't part of you, and it can easily hurt you."

Without warning, his grandfather whipped the stick across Will's forearm. "Like this, for example," finished Arrogan.

"Ow!" yelped Will, pulling his arm back and rubbing at the red welt that was rising on his skin. "You didn't have to do that! I understood you perfectly."

"Pain is an excellent teacher," said his grandfather. "If you live to be older than me, you'll still remember what I just did, even if it's just to cuss me.

"Spells are like the stick," continued Arrogan. "You create them from your turyn and you can use them to do all sorts of things, as long as you keep your hand on them. The bigger question is, what can you do the next time someone decides to whack you with a stick?"

Will looked around and picked another dead limb up from the ground. "Make my own stick." He made a pretense of fencing with his grandfather's smaller weapon.

His mentor nodded. "That's one solution, and it's often the best one, but not always. Sometimes the other person has a much better weapon than you do." Arrogan tossed his branch at Will's face, and when he flinched the old man stepped close and twisted the larger stick from his hand. "If your will is strong enough, and you have the skill, you can sometimes take the other person's stick away from them." Will's grandfather took the opportunity to whip the branch across the back of Will's legs.

Will jumped, yelling. "Hey! Ow! Stop that!"

Things devolved quickly as his grandfather began chasing him around the yard, smacking Will's backside whenever he got close enough. Running faster, Will was surprised to discover that he still couldn't get away from his tormentor. *Damn, he's quick for an old man!* he realized. Eventually, he gave up trying to escape and ran for his sparring staff. Snatching it up, he whirled around and prepared to defend himself.

Undaunted, Arrogan launched a series of lightning-fast attacks with his much smaller weapon. Will managed to fend them off, but his grandfather outsmarted him once again. Getting in close, Arrogan hooked one foot behind Will's ankle as he changed positions. A second later, Will was falling, and somewhere along the way his staff wound up in the old man's grasp.

Not content with his victory, Arrogan began cackling with wicked glee as he turned the staff on its previous wielder, and Will was sent scrambling across the ground as he tried to escape real bruises.

Knowing he couldn't outrun the old man, Will went for the other staff, and while he took several smart raps to his arms and legs, he finally got his hands on it. After that, the lesson essentially turned into one of their more usual staff-sparring sessions.

His mentor finally relented, after more than half an hour. Will stared at him, panting. "How do you move so fast? You shouldn't be able to outrun me at your age."

Arrogan didn't answer for a few seconds, but finally he responded, "What is your personal turyn for?"

Will thought about it, wondering if it was a trick question. "You told me it's what we use to function. Walking, breathing, etc…"

"So if you can control it, and even increase it, what does that mean?" added his mentor.

Will gaped at his teacher as the meaning became clear. "You're using magic to make yourself faster!"

"I'm teaching you to be a wizard," said Arrogan. "That doesn't just mean learning to cast spells. It means becoming a master of magic in all its forms, the turyn in your body, the turyn in your spells, and even that of your enemy.

"That being said, your body has a limit. You can use your turyn to make yourself faster and stronger, but not beyond the physical capacity of your muscles and bones. You can give yourself an advantage in a fight, but if you try to take on a master swordsman, you'll still be gutted because he's spent his life training to do something you're just dabbling at."

"If I can make myself faster and stronger than a normal swordsman, shouldn't I be able to beat him?" asked Will.

"Magic is life," his grandfather informed him. "Just because you don't see ordinary people casting spells doesn't mean they don't depend on it. Athletes, warriors, people that train themselves to be the best at what they do, they're doing something very similar with their turyn. And on top of that, they're building their physical capacity at the same time. You can use your magic in a large variety of ways, including to give yourself a physical advantage, but don't ever make the mistake of underestimating people who train hard at fighting, or you'll learn a painful and bloody lesson."

Disappointed, Will responded, "When you put it like that, it makes wizardry sound a lot less exciting."

"I just want you to have realistic expectations," said his teacher. "Wizardry is still far better than anything else you could learn. You might never be the best swordsman, or the strongest man, or the best climber, or dancer, whatever you name, but with conscious control over your turyn you can become much better at any of those things. Your power is much more versatile, and we're only discussing the enhancement of your physical abilities—there are far more amazing things that can be done when you consider real magic."

"Speaking of which," said Will, "when are you going to start teaching me magic? You said it would be after I finished learning to compress my source, so..."

"You've already started," observed Arrogan. "Creating an extended layer of turyn is the first step for much of what you'll do in the future."

"What's the next step then?" probed Will.

"Learning the runes," said his grandfather immediately. "But before I teach you that, you need to master what I've already shown you."

With a sigh, Will nodded and began to practice 'expressing' his turyn again.

CHAPTER 22

After two weeks of practicing what he had already learned, Will was good and sick of it. "If I have to express myself one more time, I'm going to lose my mind," he complained.

"Don't get married, then," said his grandfather.

"Huh? Why don't you ever make sense?"

The old man laughed. "It's a joke, but I suppose you're too young to understand."

As much as he didn't want to listen to yet another weird lecture from his teacher, he was desperate to distract the old man from the repetitive drills. "Explain it to me then," he said, choosing the lesser of two evils.

"For marriage you need patience, which is one lesson you'll have to learn, but more specifically, you have to communicate well. You have to learn to *express* yourself," explained Arrogan. "Now, let's try it again."

Disappointed that his grandfather had finished so quickly, Will decided to fish for more. "You don't seem like the marrying kind. How did you wind up getting married?"

Arrogan paused, as though caught in a memory. Frequently when that happened, his eventual response would be, 'none of your damned business,' but this time he answered, "My teacher was determined to make sure I learned this lesson, so she took it upon herself to make it her life's work."

"Your teacher was a woman?" asked Will, somewhat confused. Then his mind clicked, putting together what his grandfather had said. "Wait! You married your teacher?"

Arrogan nodded. "She didn't give me much choice, but then, she always knew my mind better than I did. Aislinn made that same silly joke about learning to express myself, then she spent more than a century reinforcing the lesson."

"Hmm," said Will. "All you ever do is swear and berate people. I don't think you learned it properly."

His grandfather growled, "I make my feelings known. That's the point. But I'll admit, I may have been a little different back then. You'll see one day. A good woman makes you want to put your best foot forward."

Will doubted his grandfather had a 'good' foot. As far as he could tell, Arrogan was sour and mean from back to front. Rather than point that out, he asked a different question, "Wasn't it a little unusual to marry your teacher?"

Arrogan shrugged. "Even in my day, wizards were uncommon. We didn't have many peers to pass judgement on us, and we were a good match, though she was a little older than me."

"How much is a little?"

"Forty-three years," said Arrogan, his lips curving into a faint smile as he waited for his grandson's reaction.

Stunned, Will almost shouted, "She was older than my mother!"

His grandfather broke into a grin. "I said forty-three years *older*. I was fifty-four on the day we married."

Putting his still new math skills to the test, Will added up the numbers mentally. "She was ninety-seven! You said you had two daughters, how—"

"Two daughters and one son," corrected his grandfather. "You neglect the possibility that I may have had more than one wife during my long life; however, in this case you're correct. I was only married once, to Aislinn."

He still wasn't convinced. "But at that age…"

"Physically, she was similar to a woman in her thirties," explained Arrogan. "No one that saw us could even notice the age difference. In fact, when we did start showing our age people often thought I was the older one. Forty years is a small difference for wizards."

Will considered it for a bit and decided that while his grandfather was almost certainly right, it was still strange. As he thought about it, he saw a look in the old man's eye that indicated he was about to call for a return to practice. Searching for another distraction, Will blurted out the first thing that came to mind: "Her parents must have known she'd be a wizard someday, since Aislinn is the goddess of magic and the wife of Elth—the fae lord that we met." He caught himself before saying the name, remembering his grandfather's previous warning.

Arrogan flinched, almost as if he had been slapped.

He knew he had said something wrong, but he wasn't sure what. "Your Aislinn and his Aislinn are different people, of course." His heart sank as he saw the look on his grandfather's face grow even darker. "Right?"

Arrogan stood and walked a few steps away, heading toward the entrance to the house. "I think you've had enough practice for today. Why don't you take the afternoon off?"

"I didn't mean to offend," began Will, but his grandfather closed the door before he could finish. He stared at it for several minutes, feeling bad and unsure how to apologize. After thinking it over, he gave up. The old man would only make him suffer if he insisted on talking to him. Better to let him cool off. "I'm going to go visit Eric," he called to the door, raising his voice in the hopes Arrogan would hear him.

There was no response, so after a short wait, he left.

As he tramped through the woods, he mulled the conversation over. Tailtiu was Arrogan's daughter, and from what his grandfather had said, Aislinn was her mother. His daughter was fae because she had been born and raised in that other realm. Could his grandfather's wife really be the same as the Aislinn from legend? And if so, why had she married Elthas?

Whatever the explanation, it was very likely the reason Arrogan harbored such a big grudge against the fae lord. Will shook his head, as if that would clear up his muddied thoughts. It didn't. In the end, he had more questions than answers, and he could think of no good way to ask his questions. *Still, it's wicked. My grandmother is the original Mistress of Magic,* he thought. Not that anyone would ever believe him.

He was so caught up in those thoughts that he failed to notice the sounds of a man on horseback ahead, and he almost stumbled upon the stranger before realizing it. Coming to a sudden halt, he peered through the brush.

The man was probably in his thirties, and he had dismounted to lead his horse along what amounted to a small game trail. That in itself was unusual; few riders would choose to leave the more-traveled roads and paths. As Will watched, the man took an oiled leather skin out of one of the saddlebags and unrolled it. Inside was a strange metal instrument he didn't recognize, but what caught his attention was the fact that he could see flows of turyn moving around the device.

What is that? thought Will, instantly curious. Turning his focus to the man's face, he studied his features, memorizing them the best he could. The rider was definitely a stranger. Will knew everyone that lived in Barrowden, as well as most of the usual traders that visited from time to time. Of course, he hadn't spent much time in the village over the past few years, so it was entirely possible the man was a new trader, or even a new resident, but Will didn't think that was the case. *A trader wouldn't be on a horse, alone.*

After a moment, the man packed his device away, carefully rolling it back up and returning it to the saddlebag. Whatever it was, it was obviously important to him. Leading his horse once more, Will followed behind him, confident that the noise of the horse and a little distance would be enough to hide his presence. He was wrong.

Just a few minutes after he began shadowing the stranger, he stepped on a particularly thick dead limb. Despite looking sturdy, it snapped, and the sound was loud enough that the stranger stopped and looked back. Will froze, then gave the man a hesitant smile.

"Hello!" called the stranger in a friendly manner. "Do you live around here?"

Embarrassed at being caught, Will hoped his cheeks weren't red as he tried to act nonchalant. "Yes, sir, in Barrowden."

"Excellent," said the man, seeming pleased. "Perhaps you can help me. Am I heading in the right direction? I left the road a while back thinking I could shorten my trip, and I've been regretting it ever since."

"It's not far," said Will. "If you keep heading in this direction, although it's a difficult path for a horse." Curious, he added, "Where are you from?"

"Branscombe," said the newcomer without hesitation. "I thought I'd see if I could find a farrier in Barrowden to re-shoe my horse."

The story didn't ring true. Having spent considerable time around his uncle, Will knew that Branscombe had a blacksmith as well as a farrier. That was where his uncle bought the metal fittings he needed, since Barrowden had neither. Anyone from Branscombe should have known as much. "You're out of luck, then," said Will. "We don't have a farrier. You'll have to keep traveling and see if the next village has one. Closer to Cerria you'll probably find one."

"Damn the luck," said the man, then he stuck out his hand. "Gavin Kern. Nice to meet you."

Suspicious, but not willing to show it, Will took the proffered hand, shaking it vigorously. "Will Cartwright."

"Cartwright, huh?" replied Gavin. "Your family in the business?"

"My uncle is."

"Is he handy with horses? I still have the shoe my horse threw. Maybe he can put it back on for me and save me the trouble. I don't think it will need an actual farrier," said the stranger.

Will nodded. "I can ask him."

The man gestured to the trail. "Go ahead. Let him know I'm coming. I'm sure you can get there a lot faster if you aren't waiting on me."

"Sure thing," said Will, flashing a smile. Moving around the man and his horse, he darted down the trail and broke into a jog. He ran the rest of the way to his uncle's house.

When he arrived, he ran into his aunt first. She had a large basket of washing in her arms, but she called out as soon as she spotted him, "Will! It's been too long since you came to see us."

Breathless, he took several deep breaths before answering, "Aunt Doreen. I just met a stranger in the woods on my way here."

His aunt frowned. "In the Glenwood? That's unusual. Why wasn't he on the road?"

"He said he was taking a shortcut, but his story didn't make sense," said Will.

"Come inside and tell us about it. Your uncle will want to hear this too," she replied, before leading the way to the house.

Once inside, he greeted Eric and Sammy, and within minutes most of the family had gathered to hear his tale. He related what the stranger had told him word for word, and everyone frowned at the story.

His uncle spoke first. "That story doesn't hold water. You said he told you to come ahead and let me know?"

Will nodded.

"We'll see if he shows up. I have a feeling he just wanted to get rid of you," said Johnathan Cartwright. "He's probably planning to circle the village and keep going."

"Why would he do that?" asked Eric.

"Because he's most likely a scout for Darrow," said Will's uncle, his face serious. "We should send a messenger to Cerria to warn the king."

"But we aren't at war with Darrow," said Will. "It doesn't make any sense."

His uncle nodded. "Not to you or me. War never really makes sense, but the Patriarch in Darrow is young. He wants to flex his muscle. And that's before you consider that damned prophecy of theirs."

Will didn't really understand the religion of the Highest. He knew the people in Darrow believed in a singular god, and that their government was controlled by the Patriarch, but beyond that he was clueless. "What does their prophecy say?"

Johnathan Cartwright grunted. "You'd have to ask one of them. From what I know, it basically boils down to uniting all the lands beneath the banner of their lonely god. Every generation or two, a new ruler takes his place and figures he's going to be the one to make it happen, and a lot of people have to bleed before they decide maybe the time of their prophecy isn't at hand yet."

Sammy looked anxious. "Are they going to come here?"

"I don't know," said Johnathan. "But if they are planning an overland campaign, this is the most direct route. Barrowden is between the two mountain passes they have to control to enter Terabinia. That's why they're sending scouts."

The tension in Will was rising fast. "I need to warn Mom."

"Relax," said his uncle. "It's good to prepare, but they won't come this year. It's too late in the season. Fall is almost here. They're most likely scouting in preparation for the spring. Once the snows melt, they'll come looking for trouble. They might even wait another year or two, it's impossible to say. That's for King Lognion to worry about."

Doreen put a hand on her husband's arm. "We need to figure out what to do before spring gets here."

Her husband nodded in agreement. "Most of the villagers will flee into Glenwood when the time comes, but I'd like to be better prepared. We should plan a route through the forest into the hills. If we start now, we can build a shelter in the hills before winter gets here. We can winter there and then wait to see what happens in the spring before we come back."

Will's body was almost vibrating with anxiety as he thought about his mother. His aunt noticed and gave him a reassuring smile. "Don't worry, Will. You and your mother will come with us. We're family, after all."

A wave of relief passed over him at her words.

"I want to fight," said Eric, suddenly. "I'm almost of age. Will and I could volunteer for the army."

"Absolutely not!" declared Doreen.

"All the more reason for us to move quickly," said Will's uncle. "If the king thinks Darrow might invade in the spring, it won't be long before the press gangs show up to collect every able-bodied man to increase the numbers of his soldiers."

Eric's younger brother, Dougie, the youngest of the Cartwright children at only ten years, piped up at last, "I want to fight too!"

"You're too young," said Eric immediately.

"That goes for you too," added their mother, who then glanced at Will. "I hope you have more sense than my sons."

Will didn't know what to say. Being a soldier had never really seemed attractive to him. He wasn't as heavily built as Eric, and meeting the scout had brought the danger of the situation home to him. The man had looked extremely capable. If all the soldiers in Darrow's army were similar, Will would feel like a child on the battlefield. *I can't even beat an old man with a staff,* he thought to himself. *I'd be lost in an army of real soldiers.*

"I need to tell Mom," said Will.

CHAPTER 23

Will walked back to Arrogan's house that evening full of nervous energy. His mother hadn't reacted with quite the level of alarm he had expected, which worried him. Then again, it might have been that she felt the need to stay calm to avoid making him any more excitable. He had been pretty wound up when he told her.

"We'll do as Johnathan says when the time comes," she had said calmly. "If anything comes up before then, I'll come find you at your grandfather's."

That had effectively been the end of the conversation, and Will couldn't help but think his mother wasn't taking it seriously enough. When he got back to his grandfather's house, he hoped the old man would have some insight.

After urgently explaining what had happened, his grandfather was equally unimpressed. "Just bring Erisa here. She can stay with us. This place is safe enough."

"What if the Patriarch's army comes through here?" asked Will, aghast at his grandfather's seeming aplomb.

"They'll never find this house," said Arrogan flatly. "And, even if they did, we always have my rabbit hole in the cellar. That's assuming I don't decide to do something nasty to them rather than hide."

"But…"

Arrogan held up a hand to silence him. "How many years do you think I've been living here? Those fools in Darrow decide to wage their holy war every few decades, and I'm always still here after it all blows over. My only regret is that I didn't put an end to their self-styled prophet before he ruined the common sense of the people living in Darrow."

"You knew the Prophet of the Highest?" asked Will, once again surprised by his grandfather's revelation.

His grandfather nodded. "I mentioned him before— my wayward student, Valmon. He always thought he was smarter than everyone else, and I suppose in the end he was, in a way. He certainly taught me a lesson."

"I thought you said you killed him?"

"I did," spat Arrogan. "That was the lesson. Kill a prophet, and suddenly he's a martyr. If I'd left him alive, he might have lived long enough for them to figure out what a needle-dicked bug-fucker he was. Instead, killing him just poured oil on the fire."

Will gaped. "Needle-dick—what?"

The old man winked at him. "Take notes. You'll want to remember that one. It's a keeper."

He shook his head. Just when he thought his grandfather couldn't get any weirder, the old man said something like that. "What about what my uncle said? Do you think they should hide in the hills?"

Arrogan nodded. "Your uncle is probably right on that point. Getting out of the village before the press gangs show up is an excellent idea, whether or not the Patriarch's soldiers show up in the spring or not. Knowing Lognion, he won't take chances. He's probably already getting ready for the war."

"So what do we do now?" asked Will.

"That's easy," said his grandfather. "I'm hungry, so you get to cook supper. Tomorrow I'll start you on the runes."

***

The next morning, after breakfast, his grandfather brought out an old and extremely worn leather-bound journal and laid it on the table. "This was my first study journal," he informed Will. Next to it he put a second book, though this one was considerably newer. "This is yours. As you learn, I'll expect you to copy everything into this one. It will be good practice for your abominable penmanship."

Will groaned. "I thought you were going to show me the runes."

"I am," said Arrogan. "Runes are the pieces and parts that spells are made of, but as you learn them you also have to know how they're transcribed on paper. You saw the books in my room. Many of them are full of old spells. The books aren't magic, but if you're to use them, you have to understand what they mean. Once you know each rune and what it represents, you'll be able to recreate the spells created by men who died long before you lived. Open up my study journal."

Will did, turning it past the first two pages, which were blank, until he found the first entry. His grandfather pointed at a large symbol written at the top of the page. Having become fairly good at reading, Will knew it wasn't any letter he had learned before; it consisted of a short horizontal line with a downward curve at the end.

"This is the rune 'bruman,'" said the old man. "Copy it into your book and memorize how it's written." He stared over Will's shoulder until he had done as he was told. "Now, watch me and I'll show you what bruman represents."

Will watched as Arrogan brought his hands together and pulled them apart again, leaving a glowing blue line in the air between them. When his mentor took his hands away, the line remained, hanging motionless in the air.

"That's it?" asked Will. "A line? What good is that?"

"A spell is like a plan that an architect uses to build a house," said his teacher. "Do you think an architect could draw up a building plan without using lines?"

Will wasn't sure. He knew his uncle had built the house that his cousin Eric lived in, and he doubted the man had used a written plan to do so. He wasn't really sure what an architect was, but he guessed it was some sort of builder or carpenter. "Umm, maybe?"

"Don't be stupid," chastised Arrogan before sighing. "I didn't ask if he could build something simple. I asked if he could *draw* a plan without using lines. Can you draw without making lines?"

"I guess not," admitted Will.

"Now. Try to imitate what I did," ordered his teacher.

He tried, but succeeded only in creating a wide, blurry streak of turyn in the air that dissolved almost as soon as it had formed. Will was actually surprised that he did that much. He had never tried to do anything that precise before.

"What the hell was that?" asked his grandfather.

"It was a line," said Will defensively.

"Drawn by a drunken toddler," replied the old man. "And where is it now? It has to persist. Otherwise it will be gone before you manage to construct anything. Do it again."

Will tried several more times but could never satisfy his teacher's expectations. Frustrated, he asked, "What good is a line anyway?"

"You need it to cast almost any spell you can think of," said Arrogan. "Such as this one." Lifting one finger, Will's teacher pointed at one of the journals on the table. A blur of turyn streaked from his finger, invisible to normal sight, and settled over the book, which began to float away from the table a second later.

Will frowned. "You didn't make any lines."

Arrogan smiled. "I'll do it slower for you. Pay attention." This time, an intricate three-dimensional figure appeared in the air in front of him, constructed of a multitude of tiny lines and curving shapes. It floated across the intervening space and then expanded to cover the other book before dissolving into it. The second journal began to float as well.

Will was torn between amazement and frustration. There was no way he would ever be able to produce something so complex and intricate. "I can't do that!" he complained.

"Not yet," said Arrogan. "Which is why you have to learn the runes first, one by one. Practice and repetition. Even a pig could learn this if it had the capability and enough time. I imagine for you it will only take twice as long."

The weeks that followed were long and boring, so much so that Will began to look forward to the portions of each day devoted to reading and even math. He began to dread the practical portion of his training. After two weeks, he was still working on the first rune and the old man seemed to delight in finding new ways to tease him about his lack of progress.

"This is hopeless!" Will declared one afternoon, thoroughly sick of the entire thing. "I just can't do it!"

"That's the spirit!" said his grandfather, cheering him on. "Accept your own incompetence and you'll never be disappointed."

Will wanted to strangle the old man, and his eyes said as much. "Shouldn't you be encouraging me?"

"Where's the fun in that?" asked Arrogan, his eyes twinkling with mirth.

That's the light of pure evil in his eyes, thought Will. "How long did it take you to learn this?" he asked.

"You shouldn't compare yourself to others," said his grandfather. "It's never productive, and you'll only discourage yourself."

"Why?"

The old man spent a few seconds digging something out of his ear before examining his finger. When he finally answered, his tone was flat. "Because it only took me a day to learn this rune."

Unable to take it, Will blurted out, "That's bullshit!"

"I was something of a prodigy," said his mentor. "Which is probably why Aislinn found me irresistible. If I had been an idiot like yourself, you probably wouldn't be here to complain."

"You are such an asshole," observed Will with acid on his tongue. "Don't you think I'd learn faster if you were just a little bit nicer?"

"I was kind to Valmon—look how that turned out," Arrogan informed him. "I'm not doing this to make you like me. I'm doing it because I think you have potential, and whether it takes a month or ten years for you to learn this matters little in the long run. I've got time. Now, if you're done wasting my time jacking your jaw, start again."

Whether it was because of his anger or simply a result of repetition, Will succeeded on his next try, or so he thought. "Look!" he cried exultantly.

His grandfather sighed. "That's *lun* not bruman. It's turned the wrong way."

"It's a line, isn't it?" said Will, outraged.

"Orientation is important," said Arrogan. "Bruman is horizontal and parallel to your chest. Lun is horizontal and perpendicular to the chest of the caster."

Maintaining his proud little line, Will walked around to one side of it. "There, now it's bruman."

His grandfather arched one brow and merely stared for several long seconds, then he burst into laughter. It was a minute or two before he could collect himself enough to speak. "Fine, we'll count it, *this* time. From now on remember, it's defined by the perspective of the caster at the time of creation—all spells are. Otherwise, without an accepted reference point, none of them would make sense."

Will's frustration had vanished, replaced by a feeling of relief and accomplishment. Without waiting to be told, he tried to repeat his feat and succeeded after only two attempts. This time his line was oriented properly. Smiling, he did it the way he had the first time. "There, bruman and lun, I've learned two in one day."

"It gets much easier after the first one," said Arrogan. "It's just a matter of honing your skill at shaping, as well as memorizing the forms. The later runes are more complicated, but you're over the worst hurdle."

His mood was too good to think about what would come next. There was only one thing on Will's mind now. "What are you making for supper?"

His mentor chuckled. "You're spoiled! You think every time you accomplish something, I'll do the cooking?"

Will nodded. "I bow before your mastery of the pan. Please have mercy on this supplicant and grace the table with your divine art."

His grandfather's face showed disgust. "You're going to make me sick with that flowery crap." When his grandson continued to beg, he finally threw up his hands. "Fine! I suppose you've earned a small reward. I can't stand another day of your cooking anyway."

He almost clapped at the announcement. The old man's cooking was no joke. Over the past two years, he had learned that even with only simple ingredients,

Arrogan could produce something surprising, and on occasion he would bring out fresh additions that Will still didn't know the source of, such as butter, flour, or a variety of spices. He had stopped fretting over the mystery of their origin and now only hoped there would be some special additions.

They were headed into the house when a breathless voice called to them from the forest. "Will! It's me, Sammy."

Looking back, Will saw his younger cousin standing at the edge of the clearing, her cheeks red and her hair wild. She had obviously been running. "What's wrong?" he asked, his heart speeding up.

She was bent over, hands on her knees as she panted, trying to get her wind back. "They took Eric…"

"What? Who?"

"The king's men," said Sammy at last. "A group came to Barrowden this morning. They rounded up all the men and older boys. Dad and Eric were both taken to join the army."

"They took Uncle Johnathan too? How do they expect people to survive?" asked Will, aghast at the news.

"They gave Mom fifteen silvers, ten for Dad and five for Eric. Supposedly they'll be able to send their pay home in a few months, but they could be gone for years!" she informed him.

That was quite a bit of money to Will, but he knew his uncle earned at least two or three times that in a year. He had a family to support, after all. Hopefully his aunt had money saved; otherwise they'd be living in poverty within a year. Remembering the gold crown he had given them for the cot, he hoped she still had it.

"Where are they now?" asked Will. "Maybe we can sneak them out."

Arrogan spoke up behind him, "And do what? Hide them in the forest? Have your uncle become an outlaw? And that's assuming you don't get gutted by the king's men."

He looked at his grandfather hopefully. "You could do something."

His mentor gave him a sour look. "I could, but I won't. You still haven't thought the consequences through. It would only make things worse for your cousins. You also haven't considered the fact that the first thing they'll do when they see you is truss you up and haul you back to join the king's recruits."

"I can't just let them take him," said Will stubbornly.

"Eric wanted to go," announced Sammy. "Mother wasn't happy about it, and Father certainly wasn't either, but Eric was glad to go."

"There, you see," said the old man. "He's happy to serve his country. It's dangerous, true, but it could be worse."

Will was still conflicted. Deep down, part of him wanted to join as well, although the idea also scared him. But the fact that they had been conscripted bothered him.

"Mom wanted me to tell you to stay here," said Sammy. "Your mother said you were in Branscombe. As long as you don't go home, everything will be fine. If you show up now, they'll just take you."

Showing a warmth and generosity that Will hadn't known he possessed, his grandfather asked, "Have you had supper?"

Sammy shook her head. "In all the excitement and confusion, Momma hasn't had a chance to cook."

"I was about to make a Darrowan red stew," said Arrogan. "You can eat with us and take some home to your mother and younger brother."

Not having heard of that dish before, Will couldn't help but wonder what it would be like. "What's in it?"

"Beef, red wine, carrots—you'll see," said his grandfather. "It's a dish fit for a king."

Beef? Wine? Where did he get beef? Will shook his head. He knew better than to ask. The old man had steadfastly refused to give up his secrets in the past.

"Give me a hand, Will," added his grandfather. "We don't have meat often. This is an opportunity for you to learn the art of braising."

CHAPTER 24

The following week was annoyingly mundane. Despite the excitement and consternation created by Sammy's news, Will's life remained the same. Worse, there was no hope of relief from his routine; his grandfather had expressly forbidden him from visiting the village or his mother for fear he might be picked up by a press gang.

Fortunately, his training wasn't as frustrating as before. Having managed his first two runes, Will found that ones that followed were more complex, but he was able to produce them each within a day or two now that he could express his power with a modicum of control. His grandfather still found things to complain about, though.

"Damn it, pick a scale and stick with it!" swore the old man.

Confused, Will just stared at him. "Scale?"

"A size, lackwit," snapped his teacher. "You can make them bigger or smaller, but they all have to match, otherwise you won't be able to reproduce a written spell—nothing will fit together."

"Oh!" said Will, understanding at last. "You mean relative size, like a ratio."

"Exactly, oh lord of the obvious," agreed the cantankerous old man. "If your bruman rune is roughly an inch in length, then all the others have to follow suit. It's best to practice with them all at a certain size. Later, when you try adjusting them, it will be easier to scale them."

"That makes sense," admitted Will, beginning again.

Arrogan growled. "Everything I say makes sense. Eventually you'll figure that out, although I despair of you doing it in my lifetime."

Ignoring his grandfather's dour remark, Will asked, "How many runes are there?"

His teacher replied without hesitation, "A hundred and twenty-three."

"Ugh," groaned Will. "It's going to take forever to learn them all."

The old man laughed. "You'll have them down in a month."

"Then you'll teach me some real magic?" said Will hopefully.

"Hah!" said Arrogan. "You'll *know* them in a month, but after that you have to learn to connect them and produce persistent spell structures. It will be at least a year or two before you're ready to start practicing spells. Another ten or twenty years after that, I might even consider you proficient."

"I'll be *old* by then!" complained Will.

"Stop whining," said his grandfather. "You've already gained an incredible boon. Ten years is a drop in the bucket for you now. You probably won't even get grey hair until you're over a hundred. Spells aside, you've built the foundation for true mastery by learning to control your own turyn before bothering with the more superficial stuff."

Will's mind went blank for a moment. *Over a hundred?* He had figured out that his grandfather's training would make him live longer, but he hadn't considered just *how* long that might be. "How long am I going to live?"

"Knowing you, you'll trip over your own feet and break your neck, but barring accidents and your innate stupidity..." The old man looked off into the distance as he did a mental calculation. "Somewhere between five hundred and six hundred and fifty years; it's hard to say for sure. Your turyn source is producing roughly one-eighth the normal amount, so you take the years you expect to live, subtract the years you lived before learning to control your source, and then multiply the result by eight to get an estimate."

Stunned, he stumbled and almost fell down. To prevent a fall, he quickly sat on the ground. "By all the gods!"

"Don't thank me just yet," his teacher informed him. "It's not as wonderful as it sounds. It's as much a curse as a blessing, maybe more. You'll watch all your friends and family grow old and die, including your future wife and children, unless you train them as well. In my day, wizards often taught their families for that reason, but it isn't easy. Most fail to learn.

"Because of that, a lot of wizards committed suicide before getting past their second century, and some refused to teach anyone, which is partly how we wound up where we are today."

Uncertain of his meaning, Will asked, "Where are we today?"

"You and I are the only ones left," said Arrogan flatly. "As far as I know, anyway. Those two-bit dabblers at Wurthaven aren't even worthy of wiping the asses of the wizards from my day."

The more Will thought about it, the more it seemed that his grandfather's bitterness and isolation were the real cause of the problem. "Why don't you teach them?" he suggested. "If you're so much better, do something about it."

"Because I don't give two shits for what happens in this world anymore," said Arrogan. "Besides, they're too old. Training to control your source needs to happen when you're young, and most importantly, before you start expressing your turyn to perform magic. If you want to try and change the world, that's your business. I'm done with it."

"Then why did you decide to teach me?" asked Will pointedly.

His grandfather made a sour face. "Trust me, I ask myself that very question every day when you cook." The old man looked past Will's shoulder at the sky. "That's not good."

Turning around, Will saw a dark smudge rising above the trees. "Is that smoke?"

"Shit," observed Arrogan.

The village is in that direction, thought Will. *Did someone's house catch fire?* He started in that direction. "I should see if anyone needs help. Something must have happened."

His grandfather put a hand on his shoulder. "Let's go inside. You don't want to see that."

"See what? What happened?" asked Will. "Shouldn't we be going to find out?"

"Think about it," said his grandfather. "Rumors of war, press gangs, and there's smoke over the village. The most likely possibility is that the Patriarch decided on a surprise attack in a season when no one expected it. You don't want to see what's down there. Believe me, Will. You can't forget such things once you've seen them."

His heart began to race when he understood. "My aunt is in the village. Sammy and Doug are still there!"

Arrogan's face was dark. "By the time you see the smoke, it's too late."

"To hell with that!" yelled Will. His grandfather started to grab for him, but he ducked the old man's hand

and took off running. He knew the old man could outrun him, or paralyze him with a spell, but nothing happened. When he glanced over his shoulder, Arrogan was nowhere to be seen.

Putting those thoughts aside, Will focused on running. During their daily training sessions, he had started learning to increase his strength and speed, but only for brief periods. His grandfather insisted it was more important to learn to change the rhythm of his fighting than try to fight at top speed the entire time. Surprising an opponent with a sudden increase was often more useful than wasting resources trying to become a constantly furious fighting machine.

That wasn't what he needed now, though. He needed to run faster than normal, and he needed to maintain it until he reached the village. *I also need to avoid breaking my neck on the way,* he thought ruefully as he narrowly avoided tripping over a heavy limb.

To that end, he expanded and increased his turyn, something he had gotten good at over the previous month, then he took the excess energy and tried to focus it on his legs, heart, and lungs. Rather than try to exceed his best pace, he strove to maintain it for the long haul. His breathing was deep and steady as his legs pounded out a powerful beat beneath him.

He reached the outskirts of Barrowden in half the time it should have taken, and what he saw was pure chaos. Nearly every building was on fire, and people were running in the streets. The only order to be found was in the armed soldiers that stood between the buildings. They moved in small groups of four and five, cutting down anyone that came close, which was often, since the smoke obscured much of the scene.

Will ran through the smoke, slowing his breathing to avoid being choked by the noxious air. The grey clouds obscured a lot, but he could see the turyn of the soldiers and villagers. Dodging around and past them all, he ran straight for his aunt and uncle's home on the other side of town. Cries went up from some of the soldiers as he ran past, but none of them came close to catching him, and he was soon lost to them in the smoke.

The air cleared as he got closer to Eric's house. That end of the village was apparently the last to be torched and the flames were just beginning to rise from the houses there. A group of four men stood outside the Cartwright house, laughing as it began to burn. Two of them stood by the door, and Will saw one go inside as he ran toward them. The other two were entertaining themselves by toying with little Doug, who had come out to face them. One kicked the boy's feet from under him, and the other began mercilessly kicking the child as he lay on the ground.

All of them were easily fifty pounds heavier than Will. If he'd had any reason left, he would have run and hid, but his rational mind had taken a holiday. They hadn't seen him yet, since their backs were to him, and when he had closed the distance he reached for the sheathed sword of the man on the left.

Moving faster than he had ever believed possible, Will ripped the short sword from its scabbard and whipped it sideways, cutting deeply into the soldier's companion, nearly severing his arm. The man screamed, blood spurting from the wound while the man whose sword he had stolen looked at him in surprise. Will brought the sword around to capitalize on his advantage, but the warrior recovered faster than he expected. The man stepped away and avoided his swing.

"Not bad, kid," said the enemy soldier, "but you cut the wrong man. Jenson was worthless, and you're ten years too young to have a chance with me." Pulling out a long dagger, he grinned, licking his lips.

The man at the door turned, as if to help, but Will's opponent warned him off. "Stay out of it, Ed. Let me have my fun."

The soldier he had wounded sank to the ground, weak from loss of blood, and Will knew the unfortunate fellow would be dead soon if someone didn't treat him, so he kept his attention on the man with the knife. *He's big, but I've got a longer reach with this sword,* he told himself. *I should have an advantage.*

He quickly discovered otherwise. The dagger-wielding soldier was quick, and he knew what he was about, nearly gutting Will on their first clash of blades. Backstepping, Will tried to put some space between them, but the man stayed close, grinning all the while.

His speed was insufficient. The soldier was nearly as quick, and the long dagger was always just an inch from finding a home in Will's stomach. Within seconds he had two long, shallow cuts, one across his left arm and another down the outside of his right leg. Giving up his offense, Will let his body slow and focused on defense.

"Already worn out?" sneered the soldier. "Enthusiasm only gets you so far, boy."

Panting, Will glared at him. "I'm just waiting for you to make a mistake."

The older man laughed. "Is that so?" Then he leapt forward aggressively, shouting. Startled, Will jumped back and stumbled, tripping over the now-unconscious man he had wounded. Scrambling back, he kept his short sword up, assuming that his enemy was about to try and finish him.

The soldier used the opportunity to bend down and retrieve the sword from his dying friend's belt. Straightening up, he winked. "Now you're fucked." Shifting the dagger to his left hand and leading with the sword in his right, he advanced.

Will retreated, but the soldier's aggressive onslaught was too much for him to avoid it entirely. Beating away attacks, he knew he was only moments from a messy death. A scream from the direction of the house cut through the air, piercing his heart. It was Sammy. The man who had gone in was emerging, dragging Will's cousin by her hair.

"Distractions will get you killed, pup," warned Will's opponent, continuing to press his attack.

Will was practically running backward now, trying to avoid an early death. He wanted to circle around, to get to Sammy, but the man intent on killing him wasn't about to allow that.

The door to the house opened again, and from the corner of his eye, Will saw his aunt emerge. Her face was red, and one eye was swollen shut, but she held his uncle's crossbow in her hands. "Let her go!" she yelled at the man dragging her daughter away.

The other soldier waiting by the door drew his sword and thrust it toward her, but Doreen fired before he could strike, hitting the man holding Sammy. The quarrel buried itself in the soldier's chest with a heavy thump, followed by a gurgling sound as the man began to drown in his own blood.

That got Will's opponent's attention. Worried, he looked to the side to see what had happened to his friends. *Now!* In an instant, Will changed direction, renewing his focus on speed. He blurred forward and planted the tip of his sword in the swordsman's throat. The man stared at him in surprise for a second before falling backward.

Wasting no time, Will sprinted toward his aunt, but it was already too late. She was on the ground, a sword through her belly as she held onto her killer's arm, refusing to let go. The man struck her with his free hand, once, twice, and then again, driving her head into the dirt. His arm came back for a fourth blow, but it stopped as Will's sword went through his lower back.

Crying with rage, Will pulled it out and stabbed again, then again, tears running down dirty cheeks. He could think of nothing else, until he heard a voice behind him.

"Momma? Momma! No!" It was Sammy.

Will stared at her in shock and grief, and the look on her face was something he knew he would never forget. It probably mirrored his own. "Sammy, I tried," he cried. "I couldn't get to him in time."

She fell to her knees beside her mother, crying inconsolably, and Will might have done the same, but then he remembered her brother. Running back, he found the boy still lying in the dirt, dead. One of the soldier's kicks had killed him, and Will realized he had probably been dead the entire time he was fighting. A wave of dark despair washed over him. What was the point of fighting, when everyone he cared about died anyway?

No, not everyone, he reminded himself. *Sammy is still alive.* Turning back, he went to her. "We have to go. More of them will find us any minute now," he told her, but she didn't listen. Sammy was too caught up in her grief to listen.

He shoved the sword through the rope belt at his waist and gathered her in his arms. Lifting her up, he carried her around the house and into the woods behind it, away from the village. Away from their loss.

She continued to cry as he walked, and his own tears joined hers, falling from numb cheeks to land on her head.

CHAPTER 25

Will walked for several minutes, trying to put as much distance between them and the village as possible, but as he went, he began to worry about his mother. His home was outside of Barrowden, but not far enough to reassure him. Since the house was just off the main road from Branscombe, he figured the Darrowan soldiers would almost certainly get there soon, if they hadn't already. He began circling around through the wood to head in that direction.

"I can walk," said Sammy, her voice ragged and worn. "Put me down."

He did as she asked, and as soon as her feet were on the ground his cousin turned and wrapped her arms tightly around his chest. She didn't cry; that had stopped at some point while he was carrying her. After a few seconds, she released him, but she kept a firm grip on his hand as they walked.

Traveling through the underbrush would have been easier with both hands free, but Will didn't complain. Sammy was squeezing his hand so hard it hurt, and when he glanced down he could see that her knuckles were white. Even so, he wasn't sure who was comforting whom. It felt like the world had come to an end and they were cast adrift with nothing solid to cling to but each other.

They walked for ten minutes before Sammy spoke again. "Where are we going, your house?"

He nodded, not trusting himself to speak.

"Think it's safe?" she asked.

"I…" He stopped, unable to finish the sentence as his throat threatened to close up. *I hope so.*

He started to pull his hand free from hers, but she held on desperately. "Don't leave me, Will. Please, you're all I have left."

He wanted to reassure her, but when he started to answer, he felt his emotions swell, as though they would overwhelm him. Instead, he wrapped his arms around her and pulled her head against his chest. He couldn't breathe, and when he attempted to draw air his chest grew tight. Opening his mouth, a wrenching sob escaped before he clenched his jaw shut. Eventually he managed a hoarse whisper, "I won't."

It was a few minutes before they both continued on their way. Will guessed he could get home within about ten minutes from where they were currently, but walking hand in hand would take a little longer.

They were getting close when they began to hear the characteristic sounds of men and horses. "I hear them," said his cousin softly.

Will nodded. "The road isn't far from here."

"Your house is on the other side of it," she remarked. "How are we going to cross?"

"We'll have to wait," he replied. *And hope they aren't already burning it down.*

Not daring to get closer to the road, they stayed where they were, listening to the jingle of metal and the sounds of marching feet. It went on for an eternity, at least to Will. *How many are there?* he wondered. Judging by his ears, more men had passed than all the people he had ever met in his admittedly short life.

"Is that their entire army going by?" asked Sammy. "Shouldn't they still be in Barrowden?"

"Our village is probably insignificant to them," guessed Will. "They probably rode straight through and left the ones we saw to burn out everything behind them."

Eventually the sounds faded, and they were left with only the relative quiet of the forest. Creeping forward, they risked a look and saw that the road was clear. They snuck to the very edge and looked once more before crossing, in case there were others coming, but they saw no one, so they ran across to the safety of the forest on the other side.

They were very near to the small turn off that led to Will's house, but they didn't hear anything that would indicate the soldiers had gone to explore it. *Please let Mom be safe,* prayed Will.

Since the road was clear, they followed it, staying on the relatively clear verge, but they discovered something strange when they got to the place where the turn off should have been. The entire beginning of the path was covered in strange, swirling flows of turyn.

"It's gone!" gasped Sammy. "I don't understand. The path was here just a few days ago."

Will could see the trees and brush, but the magic rippling across the area made him doubt his eyes. "I think it's been hidden by some kind of magic," he told his cousin.

"Why would they do that?"

"It's our grandfather," said Will, and as he said it he realized that he could recognize the feel of his teacher's turyn.

Sammy gave him a strange look. "You know he isn't really your grandfather, don't you? Dad was very firm about that."

"He's actually a wizard," explained Will, "a very old one. Your Dad is right, he isn't our grandfather, but our many times removed great-grandfather. He's been teaching me magic."

"You really have lost your mind," said Sammy, a sad note in her voice.

Grabbing her hand, Will pulled his cousin along until they reached the area where the turyn was thickest. Then he walked straight toward a large elm that was standing where the path should have been. Sammy struggled, but she grew still when she saw his body pass through the seemingly solid tree.

The next few seconds were confusing, since the illusion wasn't thin, and stretched on for twenty feet or so, but Will walked resolutely through until they emerged on the other side. The path was still there, clear in front of him. Now that they were past the magic, he could see his house sitting quietly where it always had. He felt a wave of relief when he saw that it wasn't on fire, nor were there any soldiers evident. "We're safe," he announced.

Sammy was staring behind them at the trees they had just walked through. "They aren't really there. That was magic?"

Will nodded.

"And that crazy old man did it?" she asked.

He nodded again. "I'm certain of it." He pulled at her. "Let's go find Mom."

Moments later, they were opening the door and Will felt the tension go out of him when he saw his mother and Arrogan arguing and packing in the front room. They looked up as the door opened, both their faces registering shock and relief at his and Sammy's entrance.

Erisa dropped the pot she was holding and ran toward him. "Are you all right? Oh my god, the blood! Take off your clothes!"

Will smiled. "It's all right, Mom. It's not mine. I fought with some soldiers. It's their blood." He looked down as he said it and realized his words weren't true. He had gotten some of the soldiers' blood on him, but his shirt and pants were now soaked. The cuts on his arm and leg had been bleeding slowly during their journey through the woods. "Oh," he said lamely. "That blood. Yeah, I think most of that is mine."

"Don't worry, Erisa," said Arrogan. "His body can afford to spare some blood. It doesn't need the blood it sends to his brain. He never uses it anyway."

Erisa never looked away. She was busy cutting the cloth away from his arm, so she could dress the wounds. "Shut up," she barked at the old man. Sammy let out a semi-hysterical giggle at their exchange.

"They look worse than they are," pronounced his mother after a moment. "I can stitch them up later. For now, we can make do with pressure dressings."

While his mother wrapped his arm and thigh with clean linen strips, Arrogan interrogated his student, demanding to know what he had seen and what route they had taken to get back to the house. Will had difficulty answering. He relayed the story up until the point where he reached his aunt and uncle's house, and then stopped. Taking a deep breath, he tried to tell them what he had seen. "Doug was in front of the house, trying to keep the soldiers away, but they were too big…"

"Little Dougie was braver than anyone," said Sammy, and then her voice broke and she began to cry again.

Haltingly, Will described his fight with the soldiers, though he struggled with telling them about Doreen's brutal murder. He could feel his mother's hands tense when he relayed that part, but she said nothing. It was easier explaining his escape with Sammy afterward.

When he had finished, his grandfather sighed. "I'd like to tell you how stupid what you did was," he said at last, "but I think you already realize that. At the very least you proved me wrong. You managed to get Sammy away safely, and that was no mean feat."

"He saved my life," said Will's cousin quietly.

"Oh, I doubt they'd have killed a girl your age," said Arrogan. "They'd have—"

"That's enough," snapped Erisa harshly.

For the first time Will could remember, his grandfather looked not just chastened, but embarrassed. "Anyway, it's a good thing you got her away from there," said the old man. Then he looked at Sammy. "Pardon my rough edges, Sammy. I'm not used to talking to people anymore. I've lived alone a long time."

"I've been staying with you for years now," reminded Will.

Arrogan waved a hand dismissively. "You barely count as *people*." Then he addressed Will's cousin once more. "As I was saying, I've been without *civilized* conversation for longer than I can remember."

"Why don't we stick to practical matters for now?" said Will's mother as she finished tying off the last bandage. "How long do you think we have to pack?"

"We should leave now," said Arrogan. "I know you want to bring some of your herbs, but they could find us at any time."

"They can't find the path here," said Sammy. "If I hadn't known the house was here, and Will hadn't dragged me through whatever it was you did, we wouldn't have found it."

"How long will the spell last?" asked Will.

His grandfather shrugged. "Hours. That isn't the problem. What did you see when you found my illusion?"

"Trees," said Will simply. "It looked real."

"Of course, you saw trees, dumbass!" barked his mentor. "What *else* did you see? You knew it wasn't real, didn't you?"

"Oh," said Will. "Yeah, I could see the magic swirling around it."

Sammy stared at him. "You can see magic?"

"I'm his apprentice," said Will proudly, trying to make the title sound more important than it felt.

Arrogan snapped his fingers in front of them. "Stay on track. If you saw the turyn flows, what makes you think someone else won't?"

"Only we can see them, right?" said Will.

"Wrong," replied Arrogan. "Any magic user can, and a few mostly normal folk too, though they might not understand what they were seeing. When that army marches down this road, it's almost certain that whatever sorcerers or wizards are with them will point my illusion out and then we're in trouble."

Sammy broke in, "They've already gone past it. We had to wait for them to go by before we could cross the road." Will nodded in agreement.

"That was probably just the lead element, the vanguard," said Arrogan. "I guarantee that army won't have crossed into Terabinia without having at least a few high-powered sorcerers with it. The main element could come by anytime, and when they do, someone is going to notice."

Worried, Will asked, "Can you beat their sorcerers?"

His grandfather laughed. "Without question, but that's not the problem. They'll have an army of soldiers with them. Remember what I said about trolls and the fae?"

Will shook his head.

"Although most would say the fae are more dangerous, for me it's the trolls, or in this case, the army of soldiers. I can deal with magic, but an arrow can put a hole in me just like anyone else," explained his mentor. "That's why we need to get out of here, and the sooner the better." Arrogan stopped, his features growing still, then he frowned. "Someone just took down my illusion."

"They've found us then," stated Will's mother. "We have to get out."

"If we go out the back door and head straight into the woods, they might not see us," suggested Will.

His grandfather nodded. "Go with Sammy and Erisa," he ordered his apprentice. "But give me a second to make sure they haven't surrounded us." Lifting his hands, he created a small spell construct in the space of a second and then released it. Will saw it expand and then vanish, sending a rippling wave of turyn outward in all directions.

"Whoever is leading them is smart," said the old man. "He waited until the soldiers were around the house before alerting me by breaking the illusion. There are five men behind the house already." Moving to the front door, he collected his staff from where it stood, leaning against the wall. He handed it to Will. "Take this. Don't bother trying to use that sword. You're outnumbered and inexperienced. A staff is a better weapon against the blades they're carrying anyway."

Since Arrogan was effectively unarmed, Will handed his newly acquired sword to him, but the old man handed it to Erisa. "You know what to do," he told her.

His mother nodded and pulled her winter cloak over her shoulders, concealing the sword beneath it. Then she gave Sammy a long knife from the kitchen. "Hide it," she told her niece. "Wait until one of them starts to grab you, then put in his groin, belly, whatever you can reach."

Confused, Will asked his grandfather, "What are you going to do?"

"I'll make sure the rest of them don't follow you," said the old man.

"But you don't have a weapon!" protested Will.

Arrogan smiled. "Remember the lesson with the sticks? I'll be fine. Take them to our house. I'll meet you there after I've taken care of this. All you have to do is get past those five in the back. Don't bother trying to kill them all, just do your best to get past them. Listen to your mother—she knows better what to do here than you do."

Will glanced at his mom's face. She looked tense but determined. *What sort of lessons did he teach her when she was learning herbalism?* he wondered. *I guess I'm about to find out.*

Erisa motioned at him and Sammy with one hand and led them to the back door. "You'll go out first," she told Will. "Don't go straight out. Cut to the left as soon as you get outside. Do your best to make them focus on you with that staff. Sammy and I will be right behind you. When we scream, ignore us. It's meant to distract them, not you."

Then she addressed her niece. "Hold the blade reversed, against your forearm. Here, like this." She took the knife from the girl and demonstrated before handing it back to her. "When we go out, act terrified. Run toward one of the men on the right, keeping the knife out of sight. As young and pretty as you are, he'll try to grab you, so don't be afraid of his sword. When he does, start stabbing. Don't think, just stab. You'll be too scared to think straight anyway."

Sammy looked plenty frightened already. "I don't think I can do this," she mumbled.

Erisa patted her head. "You've already got it down. Just let your instincts take over. All you have to do is remember the knife as he grabs you. You can do this."

His heart was pounding in his ears as Will listened to the door. "What if they're right outside?" he asked. "If they get their hands on me before I can get enough room, I won't—"

Erisa interrupted him. "They won't be. As soon as you hear them yelling, throw the door open and do as I told you."

Will frowned. "Why will they be yelling?" he asked, but as soon as the words left his lips he saw a streak of turyn flash by and pass through the door in front of him. His grandfather had cast some sort of spell. It was followed a second later by several yells and one distinctly embarrassing shriek from the men outside.

What the hell was that? he thought, but his mother was urging him forward. "Go, now!" she barked.

With his stomach in his throat, Will pulled the door open and charged out, nearly dropping the staff as it caught in the doorframe for a moment. Fortunately, the men outside were too busy recovering from whatever had frightened them, or they might have capitalized on his awkward exit. He could see the traces of magic fading away in front of him. *Some sort of illusion, maybe?* Taking the staff in both hands, he stepped toward the two soldiers to his left and swung at their legs.

One of them recovered quickly and leapt back, but the soldier's friend wasn't so lucky. Still slightly bewildered, the man took a hard blow from the thick wood staff, directly to his knee. He fell with a shout of pain.

Will heard his mother and Sammy emerge from behind him. "Please, don't hurt us!" said Erisa, her voice full of fear and desperation. The soldiers grinned at her obvious fear.

The man who had been in the center took a step toward Will to help his friend who was being steadily forced to retreat before the long heavy sweeps of his staff. That left only two on the right for Erisa and Sammy to deal with. As soon as they were out, Erisa screamed at her niece, "Run, Sammy! Run!"

Sammy didn't need much encouragement. She bolted like a frightened rabbit. In fact, she almost did her part too well, for she moved so quickly that the soldier on the far right nearly missed her, but his fingers caught the back of her tunic at the last second. The man jerked her back, catching her against his chest as she spun and tumbled into him.

Will thought she might have forgotten to use the knife for a second, for the man made no sound at first, but a few seconds later he began yelling and trying to push the girl from him. It was too late, of course. Sammy had been frantically stabbing for several seconds before his brain registered what had happened.

The dying man's companion started to go to his friend's aid, but the moment he took his eyes from Erisa and started toward them, she jumped toward him. Will's mother didn't even bother taking the sword out from under her cloak. She stabbed through it and into the man's side with all the force her slim body could put behind the weapon.

All that happened in a matter of seconds, during which Will was forced to retreat from his two opponents. His back was nearly against the house, and as a result his movements were becoming even more hampered. The two soldiers knew how to work together, and he knew he'd be spitted by one of their swords soon.

One of the two was forced to turn and deal with Will's mother, though, and once the pressure was off, Will was able to take the fight to his foe. He threatened the man with a wide sweep and then dropped the tip of his staff to the ground and pretended to stumble as the soldier came forward. Increasing his speed as much as possible, Will whipped the end of the staff up and drove it forward in a hard thrust into the soldier's belly.

If it had been a spear, the man would have died there, but the hardened leather protecting the soldier saved him from the worst of the blow. Even so, he fell backward and before he could rise, Will thumped him on the head. Looking to his right, Will could see his mother retreating from the other soldier.

He'd been surprised by his mother's strength and quick thinking, but she didn't have the skill or muscle to match the man bearing down on her. The element of surprise was gone, and while Sammy might have helped, Will's cousin was still in shock, her head down as she sat atop the man she had stabbed to death.

He started to go to his mother's aid, but the first soldier, the one he had crippled, grabbed Will's ankle and he was forced to club the man into unconsciousness. Several frantic seconds passed as he fought to free himself. He was in a near panic by the time he got loose, and in his mind's eye all he could see was the vision of his aunt, stabbed and then beaten to death.

It was with immense relief that he saw his mother was still alive and fighting. She had continued retreating, making sure to keep her opponent's back toward Will. Her eyes met her son's for a split second, but she otherwise gave no sign that he was coming.

The last man went down hard as Will put everything he had into a wide swing that ended against the side of the man's head. Erisa gave him a tight smile. "Good job." Then she turned and helped Sammy up. The girl seemed numb with shock.

As she stood, Will could see that Sammy's hands and the front of her tunic were covered in blood. Her face was white, but she wasn't crying.

"It's all right, Samantha," said Erisa gently. "Come with me. It will be safe at Arrogan's house."

He helped his mother lead his cousin away, but he stopped for a second, looking at the wounded and unconscious men. "Shouldn't we—make sure they can't come after us," he said uncertainly.

His mother's eyes were cold as she responded, "Already thirsty for more blood, William Cartwright? They won't be going anywhere. Our goal is to escape." Without another word, she headed into the forest, pulling Sammy along with her.

Will followed them, but after twenty yards he stopped. "What about Granddad?"

"He'll be fine," said his mother, but Will could see uncertainty hidden behind her eyes.

Still scared, Will clenched the staff in his hands as he made his decision. "I'm going back."

"He chose this, Will," said Erisa firmly. "Don't ruin his effort. If you go back and get yourself killed, where will that leave us? Think before you do something stupid."

"I'm sorry, Mom," he apologized, stepping back before she could grab him.

His cousin's response was anything but reserved. "No, Will! You promised me!" she yelled.

Will was shocked at the volume of sound that came from his cousin's diminutive form, but he kept going, jogging away as she yelled at his back.

CHAPTER 26

Will's fear grew stronger as he ran, and he wanted nothing more than to turn around and rejoin his mother and cousin. The voice at the back of his mind was firmly in favor of that idea. *You're just going to get yourself killed,* it told him. *Your mother was right. He made his own decision. The wise move is to do as he said.*

"Shut up," he told himself, coming to a stop at the back door of his house. For a moment he considered going around the outside, but he knew he would be spotted then. His fear quickly overruled that idea. Instead, he opened the door and went back through the house.

When he reached the front door, he could hear his grandfather outside, talking in a strong, clear voice. "I'm not going to warn you again," said the old man. "Take these ugly-ass soldiers and turn around. I don't like killing, but I'm not above improving the world by getting rid of fools."

He paused for a moment, debating what he should do. The door loomed in front of him. Should he open it? Terror gripped his heart at the thought of stepping out in front of so many soldiers, not to mention the sorcerer that must be with them. It was certain death, no matter how confident his grandfather sounded.

Ignoring those thoughts, he gripped the door handle and pulled.

Nothing happened. The door was stuck and refused to budge. Will stared at it dumbly for a second. He had used that door almost every day of his life, and he knew how much force was needed to open it. Then he noticed the magic that followed the edges of the door. His grandfather had used some sort of spell to keep it from opening.

Why? he wondered. *Did he know I'd come back, or is this part of some strange plan?* Shaking his head, Will went to the left and peeked out the front window.

He didn't like what he saw. At least twenty men were standing in the front yard, spread out in a broad line. Behind them stood an extremely plump man whose head was entirely bald. Will could tell it was the sorcerer at once, for the man was clad in gaudy orange robes, and if that weren't enough, a large flame hovered beside him, invisible to normal sight. Beside the sorcerer were four more soldiers armed with crossbows.

"You seem awfully bold for a man with no friends and very little power to back him up," said the bald sorcerer.

"Why don't you step up here and try me out if that's what you think, you hairless flesh-bag," sneered Arrogan. "I was dealing with scum like you long before your father paid your mother to sleep with him."

Will saw his teacher's turyn swell, growing noticeably over a span of seconds.

The sorcerer saw it as well and his eyes widened. "What are you doing?" Alarmed, he barked an order to the men beside him, "Shoot him!"

Arrogan snapped his fingers, and Will saw a blur as a spell-construct formed and just as quickly vanished. The air around his grandfather roared, whipping around him in a circular fashion, sweeping the crossbow bolts away before they could reach him.

The sorcerer seemed surprised. "Who are you?" hissed the plump man. "Are you a warlock? No wizard could spend his energy like that."

"I'll gladly tell you my name," said Will's grandfather, "but then I couldn't let you live. Last chance. Would you rather hear my name or keep breathing?"

The leader of the enemy soldiers laughed, but it sounded forced. "You've got some serious balls, fellow. Not that I care, but tell me your name anyway. It'll make the story more interesting when we're laughing about it in camp tonight."

"It's your funeral," said his mentor before spitting off the porch. "My name is Arrogan Leirendel, and I'm no warlock."

As one, the soldiers reacted with chuckles. Even the sorcerer laughed, this time more naturally. Straightening his back, he responded loudly, "You're either a fool or moon-touched if you expect us to believe that, or perhaps you think you think you're a jester?"

Stone-faced, Will's grandfather said nothing, but his turyn began to grow again.

"He thinks he's the Betrayer himself," sneered the sorcerer. "Kill him."

The soldiers advanced, swords drawn, but Arrogan didn't wait on them. Stepping off the porch, he walked toward them. When he was within a few feet of the center of the line, the three men closest to him froze in place. Reaching out, the old man took the sword from one of them, and before the ones farther away could react, he began coldly butchering the helpless soldiers.

Will couldn't help but feel some sympathy for them. He had been paralyzed too many times himself. He could imagine the sheer terror they must have felt, finding their bodies no longer obeyed them, while a madman killed them with their own weapons.

Those farther away moved to save their comrades, but Arrogan dispatched the first to come within his reach, his sword moving in a blinding display of swordsmanship. Even Will was surprised, and for the first time he realized the old man had been going easy on him during their training.

But no amount of skill would suffice against so many. The invaders surrounded Arrogan, and Will felt sure the old man would be gutted—but as they closed on him Arrogan's turyn exploded outward as he launched another spell.

It was the same one he had used to deflect the crossbow quarrels previously, but this time it was flesh and bone around him. The raging air turned red as arms, legs, and less recognizable pieces of Arrogan's attackers flew in every direction.

The violence of the spell was so shocking that in its bloody aftermath no one moved for a second. Most of the soldiers were dead or dying, save for three who had been fortunate enough to be farther away. The crossbowmen were also unscathed, but as they registered what their eyes had just seen, they began backing away in fear, along with the surviving swordsmen.

Only the sorcerer seemed unfazed. He had been waiting, and now that his opponent's magic was exhausted, he struck. Will saw raw power flowing from the elemental and into the bald man, then it emerged from his hands as a powerful blast of fire, which he hurled at Arrogan.

No! Desperate to help, Will opened the window and climbed out, though he knew by the time he could get to him, his grandfather would already be dead. When he looked up again, he was surprised to see his teacher still standing with swirling flows of incandescent fire circling him.

"Took you long enough, you craven bastard," swore Arrogan. "You thought your men could take your lumps for you and then you'd step in and clean up afterward, didn't you?"

The remaining soldiers routed, dropping their swords and running toward the road, followed closely by the crossbowmen. None of them made it. The flames surrounding Arrogan shot out in long streamers, roasting them each in turn.

Will wanted to cover his ears, for the screams of the burning men were too horrifying to bear. Unable to help himself, he watched as they fell to the ground, thrashing and rolling. It was almost a relief when the flames reached their lungs and silenced them.

The sorcerer stared at him, stunned by what had happened. "That's not possible," he muttered weakly. His eyes locked on Will's grandfather. "Who are you?"

"I already told you, you demented, putrescent ass-pimple," swore Arrogan, walking toward the man. He still held the sword he had taken from the first soldier, and he grinned as he showed it to the sorcerer. "They say fire is the worst way to die, but I think we should put it to the test. I'll carve you up first, then burn what's left. If I see you in hell later, be sure to let me know which was more painful."

In a panic, the sorcerer called out to his elemental. The creature appeared then, finally visible to mundane eyes, a roaring bonfire of flames that reached almost ten feet into the air. It interposed itself between Arrogan and its master, but Will's grandfather didn't even flinch. He walked straight through the ravenous flames, ignoring them.

The sorcerer turned to run, but Arrogan leapt forward, stabbing the sword into the heavy man's leg. His opponent fell, crying in pain. When he looked up at Arrogan, his terror was so great that Will thought the man might pass out, for his eyes were starting to roll back in his head.

The elemental turned and swept great fiery arms at Arrogan, but they fell apart as they passed through the space where he stood. Will could see the creature's turyn dissolving every time it touched the old man. *How is he doing that?*

Bending down, his grandfather put one hand on the sorcerer's chest. "Time to return what you've stolen." The bald man squirmed, trying to push himself back and away with his one good leg, but Arrogan wasn't having it. With his free hand he stabbed the sword into the sorcerer's hip, just above the man's good leg.

The sorcerer screamed, but when Will's grandfather put his hand on the man's chest again, his screaming changed, rising in pitch and fervor. Will saw something emerging, being pulled away as Arrogan tugged at the man's source of turyn. When it finally came into view, he could see a complex, glowing knot of turyn. He had no idea what it was, but he could see a faint line of power stretching from it to the massive fire elemental.

Arrogan plucked at it with his fingers, unraveling it while the sorcerer begged and pled for mercy, weeping all the while. Will's grandfather ignored him, and after a moment, the knot of magic dissolved. Then he stood and stepped away from his broken opponent. Looking at the elemental, he spoke directly to it. "You've suffered long enough, old friend."

The elemental towered over the old man, unmoving. Will watched, fascinated, unsure what would happen, and then he was amazed to see the elemental bowing before his grandfather. After it straightened up again, it reached for the sorcerer.

The man's screams cut off quickly, and in a very short time the sorcerer's body was reduced to a pile of smoldering greasy ashes. Then the elemental faded away. Will was glad to see it gone, but the smell of burnt flesh and hair that lingered after was something he would never forget.

Will climbed through the window, then stood on the porch, uncertain, trying to absorb everything he had seen and heard, but he snapped out of his reverie as his grandfather slowly sank to the ground. At first, he thought perhaps the old man was merely exhausted, but something about the way Arrogan cradled his stomach made him think otherwise.

Then he spotted one of the crossbowmen at the edge of the forest. The man had snuck back at some point and was kneeling with his weapon aimed at Arrogan. Before Will knew what he was doing, he began running at the crossbowman, waving his staff and shouting to try and distract him.

Startled by Will's mad charge, the crossbowman jerked and fired, then he raised his weapon to ward off a blow from Will's staff.

Will let him catch the first swing with the crossbow, then shifted his grip and thrust the staff's end into the man's face. That effectively ended the fight, but he bludgeoned the crossbowman several more times to make certain before running to his grandfather's side.

"I knew you didn't have the sense to stay out of it," said the old man, holding his stomach with one hand. Will could see the end of a crossbow quarrel sticking out between his fingers, and the front of his grandfather's tunic was soaked with blood.

"Lie down," said Will. "I'll get Mom's tools. We have to get that out and stitch you up."

Arrogan shook his head. "Don't bother. I'm dead already." He looked at the bodies around him and chuckled. "Those fools were too dumb to realize it. If they'd backed off and waited a bit, I wouldn't have been able to stop them."

Will was still numb from seeing his aunt and cousin die. It felt as though he had no tears left to cry. "You're still talking, so there's hope. I just wish I had seen the crossbowman sooner. This is my fault."

"Nah," said his grandfather. "This wasn't from him. He missed after you startled him. This was from the first volley. One of them shot before the command to fire. I wasn't ready."

Will started for the house. "Let me get Mom's kit."

Arrogan stopped him with a word. "It hit an artery, Will. I've been bleeding through the whole fight. My heart stopped before I killed that jackass over there." He jerked his thumb toward the still smoking remains of the sorcerer. "I'm dead. It's pure stubborn will and magic keeping my blood moving."

Will shook his head in denial. "That can't be. You're going to be fine," he insisted. "Don't joke about this."

"Shut up," said the old man. "I don't have time for this. Listen. The house is yours, but my room is locked. Give me your hand."

As his grandfather spoke, Will could see the old man's turyn shift, growing weaker. When he reached out, Arrogan took his hand and touched his palm. A shining pattern appeared in the air above it and then sank into the skin. It burned for a second before fading away. "Ow," said Will reflexively. "What was that?"

Arrogan ignored his question, focusing instead on Will's chest. He placed one shaking finger on Will's breast, just above his heart, and Will felt the spell-cage within him dissolve. "Almost forgot to take that off," said his grandfather with a weak grin. "You'd have been cussing me for years if I had left that there."

He's really dying, Will realized, and he felt his heart break all over again. In the span of less than an hour, he would have lost almost half the people he cared about. New tears began to well in his eyes. "This can't be happening," he whispered.

"Life's a bitch, William," said his grandfather. "Sorry I couldn't finish teaching you, but you have to…" His eyes closed, and his words trailed off.

"Nooo," moaned Will, his voice beginning to crack. "You can't do this."

Arrogan's eyes opened again. "The goddamn cat," he said softly.

"Yes?" responded Will, blinking to clear his eyes.

"Don't piss him off. Make sure to read my—"

His grandfather didn't finish his sentence, although Will waited several minutes, refusing to move. When he had finally given up hope, he lifted the old man's head and torso, squeezing them against his chest. It was the first time he had ever hugged his grandfather, and his chest burned, for he knew it was too late. The old man would never know how he felt.

Sometime later, Will pulled himself together and got to his feet. Staring down at his grandfather, he knew he couldn't bear to leave the old man there, so he bent down and tried to lift him. It was a stupid idea, for he knew he couldn't possibly carry him all the way back to his house, but he was beyond rational thought. He was surprised to find Arrogan much lighter than he had expected.

Was he always so frail? Will couldn't believe it. The old man had always been larger than life, both his personality and his actions. The body was still a significant burden, but he managed to get him into his arms and stand again. Then he began to walk.

Unfortunately, despite his initial success, carrying his grandfather turned out to be impossible. Will made it into the woods behind the house, but stumbled soon after, and in the end he was forced to drag the body. The best he could manage was holding his grandfather's chest and letting the feet drag as he went.

It was slow going, and it would be hours before he made it back to his grandfather's home.

CHAPTER 27

It was dusk by the time he finally made it to the house, and he found his mother and Sammy standing in the front yard, waiting for him.

"Put him down," said Erisa, and when he did, she bent and checked for a pulse.

"He's dead," said Will.

"I've been doing this most of my life," said his mother. "I had to be sure." Then she stood and stared into her son's eyes. Without warning, she slapped him, hard enough to sting his cheek.

As Will rubbed his face, she continued, "Do you have any idea how stupid that was? How worried we've been?"

"I couldn't leave him," said Will.

"But you *could* leave us?" she rebuked him. "Don't ever do that to me again, William. I thought I'd lost you for good."

He'd never seen such a look of fury and anger on his mother's face, but despite the intensity of her gaze, Will was numb. Too much had happened. His mother lectured him for several minutes, and he was grateful when his cousin tugged on her arm. "Please, Auntie, let him be. We're all tired."

"Why don't we go inside?" suggested Will, his tone soft.

His mother and cousin looked at one another, then at the house. Sammy spoke first, "Maybe you can talk to him."

Him? "Who do you mean, Sammy?" asked Will.

Erisa pointed at the porch. "That one."

It was then that Will finally noticed the cat grooming itself on the porch, directly in front of the door. "Oh. The goddamn cat," he intoned matter-of-factly.

"William!" reprimanded his mother.

"Sorry, Mom. That's what grandfather named him. Why didn't you just step over him?" he asked.

"Try it," suggested Sammy.

He did, and was alarmed when the cat stood up and hissed at his approach. Will had never really gotten along with the cat. During his years with Arrogan, the two of them had developed a truce of sorts, which was to say that Will fed the cat whenever he appeared, and for its part the goddamn cat ignored him the rest of the time.

Even so, it was just a cat. Will started to step over it, reaching for the door handle, but immediately changed his mind when the cat growled. Its hair was standing out in all directions, and it gave every sign that it was about to start a blood feud with him. "What the hell?" swore Will. "He's never been like this before."

The goddamn cat didn't back down. Instead it began advancing on him, fangs bared and back arched. He almost thought it might be rabid, but as soon as he stepped off the porch the cat relaxed, though it kept its eyes on him, wary for any sign that he might try to approach the door again.

"There's something wrong with that animal," cautioned Erisa. "He may be sick."

Will stared at the cat for a long minute, during which the animal never blinked. To all appearances, mundane and magical, it looked to be a normal cat, but he could see a deep intelligence behind its green eyes. "I think it knows he's dead," Will said over his shoulder.

"Well we aren't spending the night outside," said his mother. "One way or another we're going inside."

"Do you think he's sad that his master is dead?" asked Sammy.

Will shook his head. "Not exactly, maybe, I don't know. Let me see if I can convince him to let us stay."

"Convince him?" said Erisa, her voice tinged with disbelief. "It's a cat."

"Grandfather didn't think so. He always said the goddamn cat was our landlord. Wait here a minute," he told them.

"Where are you going?" asked Sammy.

"To get an egg." Will went around the side of the house and through the garden, a trip he had made hundreds of times before. Moments later, he returned with a fresh egg in hand. He had no idea if he was doing the right thing, but he decided to trust his instincts. In his mind he could still hear his grandfather's last words, *"Don't piss him off."*

Sammy and his mother watched him with odd looks on their faces as he dragged Arrogan's body until it was at the edge of the porch. The goddamn cat perked up at that and stepped forward to investigate. As they looked on, it sniffed Arrogan's head and then licked it once before returning to the porch. It lay down there, crossing its front paws and staring at Will.

He could almost imagine its words. *Your move, human.* Approaching cautiously, he got down on his knees at the edge of the porch and held out one hand to the cat. "I know you had an agreement with him. He's gone now, but I'll do my best to honor it, if you let me," he said, keeping his voice neutral.

The grey tom blinked, once, then sat up.

I hope that's a good sign, thought Will. Reaching out with the other hand, he showed the egg to the goddamn cat. "Let me in and I'll get a bowl to put this in for you—ow!"

The cat's claws had flashed out and torn a deep scratch across the back of his hand, causing him to drop the egg.

Standing up, Will sighed and looked at the broken egg. It had fallen on the ground, where it began to seep into the dry dirt. He turned to the others. "I guess I was wrong."

Sammy pointed at his feet. "Look!"

Glancing down, Will saw that the goddamn cat had moved. It sat beside his leg, cleaning the blood from its foot. It finished and then stood, circling his feet once and brushing up against his trousers before walking to the front door.

"I think he's telling you that you can go in now," said Sammy, amazement in her voice.

Testing the theory, Will walked to the front door. The grey tom ignored him, but as soon as Erisa and Sammy started to follow him, it stood and hissed, arching its back once more. "They're with me," Will told it.

The goddamn cat let them by after that.

Once they were inside, Will's mother wasted no time cleaning the scratches on his hand. "I can't believe we had to negotiate with a cat," she muttered.

"Maybe he's magic," put in Sammy. "This is a wizard's house, after all."

Will wasn't so sure about that. He'd seen no sign of magic around the cat, or any other strangeness, other than its behavior. "I don't know," he admitted. "But before he died, Grandad warned me not to upset the cat. He made that point to me several times while I lived with him."

"Knowing him, that crotchety old man probably did it just to have a laugh. He's probably looking down on us now, laughing at us for believing him," said Will's mother. She wiped at her eyes with one sleeve. "He was always doing odd things when he taught me. I never knew what to think."

Sammy stared at her aunt. "You're a wizard too?"

Erisa shook her head. "No. He taught me herbs and midwifery. He always said he'd never take another apprentice." She glanced at her son. "Until Will convinced him somehow."

Will had no answer to that. "I should cook something," he told them.

"What about…" Sammy looked toward the door and they all understood her meaning. Arrogan's body was still out there, in front of the porch.

"We'll bury him in the morning," said Erisa. "Is there something we can wrap him in overnight?" she asked Will. "I don't want anything taking a bite out of him while we sleep."

Will gave her one of his blankets, and while she attended to the body, he went to fetch fresh vegetables from the garden. Following his old routine seemed natural and helped him keep his mind clear. The last thing he wanted to do was remember the things he had seen that day.

His mother complimented his cooking, seeming surprised at his skill even though it was simple fare that he served them. After that, he tested the door to Arrogan's room and found it opened at his touch. In the past it had always been locked by magic. *Maybe the spell he put on my hand was a key of some sort,* he mused.

Thinking about it caused the spell to itch, and when Will looked at his hand, the spell rose from his skin to float above his palm. He studied it for a moment, noting how similar it was to the heart-stone enchantment that Arrogan had pulled from the sorcerer's chest. It was connected to something, but he couldn't be sure what that might be. There was definitely not an elemental nearby. He would have to think about the matter later, and as soon as he pushed his question aside the spell vanished, sinking back into his skin.

"His room hasn't changed much over the years." The voice startled him, and he turned to find his mother staring over his shoulder.

"You've seen it before?" he asked.

Erisa nodded. "Quite a few times, though he only let me in when we were using the workshop. Is it still beneath the house?"

"Yeah," answered Will. "He's been teaching me the basics of alchemy."

His mother's brows went up in surprise. "How far have you gotten?"

"Not far," he admitted. He put up his hands and began ticking off what he had learned. "So far I've learned inks, soap making, how to differentiate acids and bases, simple distillation, steam fractioning, and the basics of tinctures, elixirs, and suspensions." Then he sighed. "None of it involves magic, though."

Erisa smiled. "That alone could make you wealthy if you have the right equipment." She walked over to the bookshelves and glanced over them until she found the section that held medicinal recipes and chemical preparations. "If you understand measurement and titration, you can use the knowledge stored in these books to prepare any number of valuable substances."

It was apparent that his mother was familiar with some of the books already. "Why didn't you teach me to read?" he asked.

She stood still for a moment, lost in thought. "After everything I went through, I was resentful. Mark gave me hope that I shouldn't have had, a view of a world I could never be a part of. Then the old man—he taught me more than I needed. When I eventually returned to the village, I thought maybe things would be different. But there was no need for what I had learned. Learning and letters had no place in that world. I thought I was doing you a favor. If you didn't learn about such things, you couldn't yearn for things you would never be able to have."

Will considered that for a moment, then asked, "And what about now? Do you still think that was the right choice?"

Erisa sighed. "Probably not. I started to have doubts when Mark offered to send you to Wurthaven." She paused. "Do you resent me for it?"

He shrugged. "I've gotten pretty good at it now, so it doesn't really matter. The more I learn, the more I realize we all make mistakes." Then he gestured at the bed. "I still have my cot. Do you think you and Sammy will be comfortable in that giant bed?"

Sammy had slipped past them and had been staring at the room in awe. She focused on the giant four-poster when he asked his question. "It's huge! What if we get lost?"

Will's mother walked over to it, then carefully lifted the frilly, embroidered pillow that Arrogan had so adamantly insisted that Will shouldn't touch. Moving to the end of the bed, she opened the chest that held Arrogan's blankets and extra bedding and placed it inside. "He's gone, but I think as long as we don't sleep on this he won't mind."

Will looked curiously at his mother. "Do you know why he was so particular about it?"

"I guess he never told you," said Erisa. "It was Aislinn's."

He remembered the name. "His wife? Do you know what happened to her? He was awful touchy about it. How did she die?"

238

It was Erisa's turn to shrug then. "He didn't tell me much either. I don't know how or when she died, but I don't think that's what he was upset about. From what I gathered, she left him, though I don't know why."

Will pondered that for a while. He knew Aislinn had also been his grandfather's teacher, so she had been a wizard. *Does that mean she could still be alive somewhere?* His grandfather had said she was older by some forty years, but then again, Arrogan hadn't seemed as though he was close to dying of natural causes.

Whatever the answers were, it was unlikely he would ever know the full story. *And I've got more important things to worry about anyway,* he decided. Barrowden was full of Darrowan soldiers, half his family was now dead, and he had to figure out how to keep his mother and Sammy safe.

And he was still two weeks away from turning seventeen. It didn't seem right to have so much weight on his shoulders. The world didn't seem to care, though. Little Dougie had only been ten and he'd been beaten to death trying to defend his family. "And Aunt Doreen," he whispered to himself, seeing her dying moments all over again. He could still hear the sound of the soldier's fist beating her head into the ground.

Without realizing how he had gotten there, he found himself crouched down on the floor, swept away by tears of grief and rage. His mother and Sammy had encircled him with their arms. This time it was Sammy who comforted him, for her own eyes were dry.

"You should sleep in the bed with us," said his mother. "None of us should be alone tonight."

"But…"

"I don't care if you're sixteen or thirty," said Erisa. "Besides, you're not the only one that needs comfort."

Will swallowed, unable to speak because of the lump in his throat, then he nodded.

That night his mother occupied the center of the bed, with Will on one side and Sammy on the other. Even with the chill of winter setting in, the presence of three bodies made them almost uncomfortably warm, and although they slept with but a light blanket over them, Will could tell his mother was sweating. But she didn't complain, and every time he tried to move farther away her arm tightened around his head, pulling him closer.

CHAPTER 28

"William Cartwright."

His eyes opened at the sound of his name. It had been a woman's voice, but not that of his mother or Sammy. Confused, Will lifted his head and looked around the dark room. With no candle or lamp lit, it was pitch black. He couldn't have seen his own hand in front of his face. Had he imagined the voice?

"William Cartwright, I call thee."

He heard it clearly then, as though the speaker's mouth was next to his ear, and he recognized the voice. She had been the subject of a number of embarrassing and often erotic dreams since their previous meeting. Tailtiu.

Will sat up in the bed, straining his eyes. Was she in the room? Maybe he had dreamed it.

"Will, are you all right?" asked his mother, half-asleep.

"I have to pee. Go back to sleep," he told her before rising and searching the floor for his boots.

"William Cartwright—thrice named and thrice called. I seek your counsel."

Will froze, waiting to see if the sound of Tailtiu's voice would wake his mother. After a few seconds he relaxed, for she gave no sign of having heard anything. Finding his boots at last, he gathered them up and stumbled out of the room. Once he was in the front room, he realized he knew where he needed to go. Within his mind, he could feel the direction of her pull. He was familiar enough with the surrounding area to know the spot she was calling from.

He hadn't realized there was a congruency there, between his world and hers, but that was to be expected, for the weak places between worlds were hard to notice, even with his relatively newfound sight.

Opening the outer door, he went out into the night, grateful for the full moon overhead. It was only then that he paused. *Should I answer her call?* Since his first disastrous meeting with Tailtiu, he had memorized the rules. He wasn't required to answer, and given all the things his grandfather had told him it would probably be wiser not to do so. The fae were dangerous beyond belief, and he had very little experience dealing with them.

And if something went wrong, his grandfather wouldn't be there to bail him out this time. Highlighting that point was the grey bundle on the porch, Arrogan's body, wrapped and waiting for burial.

Will squeezed his eyes shut and then opened them again as he took a deep breath. Then he began walking. *No one has experience dealing with the fae in the beginning,* he told himself. *This is how you learn.* Despite his internal encouragement, he couldn't help but wonder if he was about to learn more than he bargained for.

It was a fifteen-minute walk through dense forest and undergrowth, but despite the relative lack of light, Will didn't worry about losing his way. The place she was waiting for him was a beacon, invisible yet impossible to miss. When he finally drew close, he saw streamers of turyn in the air, and a moment later he heard her voice, purring to him from the shadows, "You came."

The forest cover was too dense there; he still couldn't see her, just the traces of her magic as it lingered. Will's mouth went dry as he realized how close she must be. "I was curious," he answered finally. "What did you call me for?"

"Can you see in the dark?"

"Is that what you wanted?" he returned. "We haven't discussed terms."

Another voice found his ears, smooth, feminine, and mature. The hairs on the back of Will's neck stood up as a fresh surge of adrenaline shot through him. "You've learned well. You do your teacher credit." A light blue glow filled the air, illuminating the area where he stood within the trees. Two figures became visible, Tailtiu, wild and naked as he remembered, and another woman with white, flowing hair.

Although neither of them showed any signs of aging, the white-haired woman emanated a feeling of age and maturity. Like Tailtiu she was bare-chested, but her hair draped artfully over her shoulders, obscuring the places his eyes went to first. Unlike Arrogan's daughter, she also wore a light ephemeral gown that seemed to be held up by little more than hopes and dreams. It draped from her shoulders, detoured away from her breasts, and then circled her waist.

For a fae, she was practically modest.

Fear helped him keep his thoughts in line. After his previous adventure in the fae realm, his grandfather had insisted he read a book detailing the fae and their customs, and while he hadn't finished it, he had learned quite a bit. He ignored the stranger, returning his eyes to Tailtiu's face. "I'll ask again. What did you call me for, Tailtiu?"

The red-haired fae girl pouted. "I thought we were friends."

"We are," said Will. "But we have to make the rules of our exchange clear before we can speak freely."

The stranger laughed, and Tailtiu's lips curled into a smirk, then she answered, "Mother wanted to speak with you."

Mother? If she's her mother, then that would make her... Will's mind stopped dead in its tracks, refusing to go further. His mouth opened and he heard himself say, "Grandmother?"

"Ware your words, William," said the fae lady. "Don't let surprise be your undoing."

Her warning was enough to snap his thoughts back into focus. Addressing Tailtiu, he asked, "What will you give if I speak with your mother?"

Tailtiu drew closer, a hungry look on her features. "What would you like?"

She's hundreds of years old, and she's my aunt, Will repeated to himself, not that his body seemed to care. "One hour," he said firmly. "For one hour you'll answer any questions without deception. In return I'll do the same."

The fae girl smiled. "Done."

"And what of me?" asked Tailtiu's mother.

"I can offer you the same terms," said Will.

The older fae seemed to think for a moment, then replied. "Not quite good enough. What if you decide to answer my questions and then kill me afterward to prevent me from using the knowledge I gain?"

It was a ridiculous suggestion on the face of it. Either of the two women could easily overpower or kill him, but it reminded him of something he had forgotten. "For one hour I'll freely and honestly answer your questions while you do the same. At the end of that time we end our discussion under an oath of peace. I will offer you no harm and you will do none to me." As he finished, a new thought occurred to him. *She's helping me.* That didn't fit with anything he had learned about the fae.

His chain of thought was broken when Tailtiu eased forward and brought her lips to his. The rush of pleasure shocked him into stillness. Her hands went up to brace his head as she leaned into him, and Will could feel his turyn draining away by the second. Somewhere deep down, a rational voice commented, *I'm dying.* But even as it warned him, his arms circled her waist.

"Stop," ordered Tailtiu's mother, and somewhat reluctantly, the fae girl pulled herself away.

Feeling faint, Will's legs gave out and he collapsed into a sitting position. "That wasn't part of our bargain," he gasped when he could finally speak again. Unlike the first time he had met Tailtiu, his turyn was recovering rapidly.

"I owe you another favor," said Tailtiu, without an ounce of repentance in her voice.

"An unbounded favor," clarified Will. "That makes three now. Two from last time, and this one." He had learned the term from his studies. An unbounded favor was rare, as it meant he could ask for anything. Such favors were almost never given in a negotiation, but were a penalty for a debt that accrued through accident or foul play. Such things were the main reason one had to be careful to set terms before asking questions of the fae.

Yet she indebted herself, thought Will. *That wasn't an accident. She knows the rules better than I do. They're part of her blood.* First her mother had helped him set his terms, now this. It couldn't be coincidence.

"What did you want to know?" he asked.

Since the hour had started, Tailtiu jumped into the conversation. "Can you see in the dark? You came without a light."

"No," admitted Will.

"Why didn't you make a light? You're a wizard after all," she continued.

Her mother interrupted. "He hasn't learned to use his magic yet. Have you, William?"

He shook his head. "I'm not really a wizard. Grandfather was just beginning to teach me."

Something passed across their faces, but whatever emotion it represented was too subtle for Will to guess. "Arrogan was the reason I had my daughter call you, William. I felt his death. Would you tell me what happened?"

The shift in the conversation caused Will's throat to tighten. Unsure what to say, he took a moment to collect his thoughts.

Taking his hesitation for reluctance, she added, "Do you know who I am?"

"I'm not sure," he answered, "but if you're Tailtiu's mother—doesn't that mean you're my grandmother, Aislinn?"

The elder fae studied him. Her face was inscrutable as she responded, "He was my husband once, but the woman who loved him died long ago. Don't make the mistake of ascribing human traits to the fae, William. There is no relation between us. Humans have souls; the fae do not. We are creatures of pure magic, without morals or true emotion. The closest thing we have is hunger and passion, bound by the rules of the power that sustains us. The only thing I share with the woman who was your grandmother is her memories and her name, Aislinn."

Her words matched what the book had told him, but he still couldn't believe it. "You've changed, but you're still the same person..."

"Do you know why they caution mortals not to partake of food or drink in the fae realm, William?" asked Aislinn. When he didn't answer, she continued, "Because it grows inside you." Stepping closer, she held up one finger then put it into her mouth, when she withdrew it a small cut was on the tip, bleeding. "A drop is all it takes." She lifted

246

the injured finger to his lips, letting it hover there an inch away. "The fae realm is immortal, as is everything within it. This is true of my flesh and blood as well. Your body is mortal, William, perishable. Any part of me or the realm I come from, if taken into you, would eventually replace your mortal husk.

"Even a drop of my blood would end your humanity, though it might take years. You would slowly begin to feel the call, drawing you to our realm, and you would heed it or perish here. In the fae realm it would grow, gradually replacing your mortal flesh, until all that remained of you would be a fae creature with your memories, and eventually even those would be lost to the mists of time," she finished.

Will stared back at her. Though she had finished speaking, Aislinn still held her fingertip in front of him, almost touching his lips. He could smell a faintly floral scent coming from her skin, or perhaps it was her blood. Growing up, he had seen blood many times, so it didn't bother him, but this time he felt a strange urge. He wanted it.

Aislinn's eyes grew dark. "Take it and your suffering will be over."

His mouth was watering and Will licked his lips involuntarily. Closing his eyes, he remembered his grandfather. *What would the old man say if he was here now?* Then he asked, "Did you offer this to him too?"

His grandmother flinched, then withdrew her finger. "Never."

"Why not?"

She sighed. "In the early days, I still loved him, and his hatred of my husband was always too great."

"Why did you marry Elth—?" Will stopped, for Aislinn had placed her uninjured hand over his mouth.

247

"Don't say his name or even my skills will not suffice to hide this meeting place from him," warned his grandmother. He nodded and she withdrew her hand. "I did it to save his life." Then she glanced at Tailtiu. "Though if I had known of the unborn life in my womb, I might have chosen differently."

According to the myths Will had grown up hearing, Aislinn was the goddess of magic. While it was obvious that those stories weren't strictly true, it made him wonder. He had seen his grandfather face down Elthas in the fae-lord's own realm. If she had been Arrogan's teacher, could she be any less powerful? "Do you fear him?" asked Will.

Aislinn laughed. "Not his power. The fae are bound by rules. I fear my oath. To save your grandfather's life, I pledged my service to the Lord of the Hunt. I cannot disobey him.

"I was naïve in thinking all he would take was my life. After I accepted his bargain, he took me as his wife. Knowing the dangers of the fae realm, I refused to eat, but it was not food or blood that he used to change me. For years he tortured me with pleasures too great for human flesh to endure. It was a relief when my heart finally disappeared and even my memories could no longer bring me pain."

As Will listened, the implications of her story began to sink in, rendering him speechless. *No wonder the old man hated Elthas so much.* Arrogan's wife had given everything to save her husband, and he had probably blamed himself for what happened to her. *And now he's dead.*

Aislinn watched his face carefully, as though she might read his thoughts. "Don't pity me. I am beyond sorrow now. Let my tale be a warning to you, William Cartwright, as you deal with the fae—as you deal with *me*. Make a mistake and I could do the same to you."

"No," said Will, meeting her eyes evenly. "You've already helped me. My mistake with the bargain earlier, Tailtiu's kiss, both of those things were done on purpose. You're not the same as Elt—as him."

"Such thoughts will lead to your doom," said Aislinn. "Now, I have answered some of your questions, spoken and unspoken. Answer mine. Did you see how he died?"

Casting his eyes downward, Will nodded. "He saved me, as well as my mother and my cousin. Soldiers came to my house, along with a sorcerer." He went on to explain everything he had seen, but he stopped short when it came to his grandfather's final moment, telling her only that the old man had removed the spell-cage within him.

"Did he give you something else?" asked his grandmother, her eyes boring into him.

Unsure what to say, Will looked away. He still didn't know what the spell was that his grandfather had given him, but it felt like a secret he shouldn't share.

"He did," declared Aislinn. "You passed the trials. He wouldn't have died without giving it to you."

"I'm not sure what you mean," said Will, stumbling over his words. "He was only beginning to teach me. I've only just learned the runes. I can't even cast a spell yet."

"Careful, William. Honest answers, remember? Break our bargain and no hidden sentiment will prevent me from extracting a penalty from you—a penalty you do not want to pay," she warned him. "I know the way he taught you, because I was the one who taught him. If he taught you the runes then you had already passed the trials. Show me the seal."

"I don't even know what it is," admitted Will, "or how to show it to you."

Grabbing his right hand, she pulled it toward her in a grip that seemed made of iron. "I cannot take it from you unwillingly," said his grandmother. "I can only examine it. Think of it and it will appear."

As soon as she suggested it, the spell-construct rose from his palm.

"He never changed it," said Aislinn, her voice dropping to a whisper. If Will hadn't known better, he might have thought he heard a hint of sadness in her words.

"What is it?" asked Will.

"Something you don't need," she answered, her tone grave. "A worthless relic from our time, long forgotten in this age of degenerate mages and indolent sorcerers. It is called a limnthal, the mark of a true wizard."

"Why did you say it hasn't changed?"

Aislinn smiled sadly. "Each one is unique, given by a master to his or her student when they feel the time is appropriate. Usually that comes after an apprenticeship has been completed, but Arrogan couldn't afford to wait. This is the mark I gave your grandfather when he satisfied my requirements. Ordinarily he should have created a new one for you, but since he was dying, he gave you his own, the one I made for him."

Will's eyes began to water, but he was shocked from his sorrow by her next statement.

"Give it to me," ordered the elder fae.

Without thinking, he answered, "No."

"It will do you no good," said his grandmother. "It grants no power or ability. It is little more than a symbol of achievement, something no one will even recognize, and if anyone did, it would bring you only misfortune."

"Then why do you want it?"

"Because it is mine. It means nothing to you. Give it to me and I will grant any wish you can imagine," she told him, her eyes shifting colors from blue to lavender as she spoke.

Will closed his hand into a fist, and the limnthal vanished from sight. "It isn't for sale. Useful or not, it's the last thing he gave me."

Aislinn seemed to relax. "Very well, Grandson. I will respect his discernment in deciding to give it to you, but you have chosen a hard road for yourself."

His face showed surprise at the word 'grandson,' and Aislinn laughed.

"Don't think too much on my acknowledgment," said his grandmother. "The fact remains that I will not hesitate to take everything you have if you make a mistake, William. Never forget that."

For a moment he could feel a sense of alien malice radiating from her, but rather than creating fear, it engendered a feeling of sadness in him. How terrible it would be, to have once been a woman who loved and was loved, only to be consumed by a magic that rendered you incapable of anything but hunger and cold logic. Aislinn must have seen the emotion on his face, for she looked away then, unwilling to meet the pity in his eyes.

"I only have one thing more to ask of you, William," she said. "Bring me his body if you have it."

"What do you want it for?" he asked suspiciously.

His grandmother laughed. "Nothing malign. I only wish to say my farewells, to bury him in the place where we first met."

It seemed fitting, but though it went against his human decency, he asked, "What will you give me in exchange?"

Aislinn smiled. "He would be proud of you. What do you wish?"

"My mother and cousin are living in his house, but there are soldiers from Darrow in the village. Can you protect them?"

"I will not go near the house," said his grandmother. "The creature that owns it and the land it sits upon is not kindly disposed toward the fae, but I can ensure that no enemy finds it. Will that suffice?"

She's afraid of the goddamn cat? thought Will. *How can that be?* "That will be good enough," he told her. "Do you know what the cat is?"

"It is a cat, of the worst kind," she answered. "It is not my place to speak of it."

CHAPTER 29

The sky was beginning to lighten when Will returned to the old shack. His grandfather's body was still on the porch, but as he started to drag it away a thought occurred to him. Going inside, he returned to the bedroom and opened the blanket chest at the foot of the bed and removed Aislinn's pillow.

"William?" It was his mother. She lifted her head groggily. "What are you doing?"

"I'll explain at breakfast. I'm going to cook something nice," he told her. "Go back to sleep. It isn't even dawn yet."

Erisa's head flopped back down and she closed her eyes. "That's nice," she mumbled.

Outside again, he tucked the pillow under one arm and lifted Arrogan by his shoulders so he could drag him into the forest. His grandfather felt heavier than he had the day before, and he was grateful when Aislinn and Tailtiu appeared after he had gone only a hundred yards. Aislinn's expression was unreadable as she stared down on the man who had once been her husband, then she noticed the pillow under Will's arm.

"Is that…"

He handed the embroidered pillow to her. "I think you should have this. He wouldn't let anyone else use it."

The fae woman accepted it so carefully it seemed as though she feared it would fall apart at a touch. "I can't believe it still exists," she muttered. "It should have rotted away by now."

He didn't know what to say to that. Whether Arrogan had used magic to preserve it he had no way of knowing. "The needlework is very fine. You must have put a lot of time into it."

She shook her head. "You're mistaken. This was his present to me."

His jaw dropped. "Grandfather made it?" He struggled to reconcile the lace and fine embroidery with his memory of the cranky old man.

"He was a tailor's apprentice when I found him," said Aislinn softly.

Feeling awkward, Will didn't know what to say, so he stood silently for a while. Looking down on his grandfather's bundled form, he made a quiet goodbye. *I hope this is what you'd have wanted.* Eventually he nodded to them and began to turn away. "I should go."

"Wait," said Aislinn firmly. "There has been no payment for this." She lifted the pillow in her hands.

"It's a gift," said Will.

"Then I must give you a gift in return," she replied. "Hold out your hand."

He shook his head. "That's not how gifts work."

Tailtiu spoke for the first time in almost an hour. "The nature of our existence requires it."

Aislinn took his hand and held it up, placing the palm of her own right hand beside it. Another limnthal appeared in the air above her skin. "Call your mark forth, William, so I can make the exchange."

He did, and a second later he felt something pass between the two spells, as though some energy had transferred from one to the other. "What did you do?"

"You returned his first gift to me, so I have given you the second gift that he gave me," she answered. "You may find it useful someday."

Curious and frustrated, he asked again, "But what is it?"

"A small thing," said his grandmother. "Once you learn to use your magic, you'll understand."

His jaw clenched. "But I'll never learn. I don't have a teacher."

Aislinn laughed, long and hard, as though he had said the most humorous thing she had ever heard. "The limnthal you bear is the first to have been granted since Valmon received his over four hundred years ago. You will live a very long life, William Cartwright, if you can keep from getting killed. You will have many teachers, and before your fate is done you will change the world." Leaning forward, she kissed his forehead before he could react. Unlike before, when Tailtiu had kissed him, he didn't grow weak. Instead he felt a faint tingling on his skin. "This is my blessing, invisible to most, but the fae will recognize it. If you deal with others of my kind it may save you from a foolish bargain."

Turning away, she gestured at Arrogan's body, and a spell ran from her fingers to touch his cold flesh. The body floated up from the ground and followed her as she and her daughter retreated deeper into the forest. Will watched them go, rubbing at his forehead, which itched strangely. He didn't know what to think of what had happened, so after a few moments, he turned back toward the shack that was now his only home.

***

"This is incredible," said Sammy, shoving her mouth full of egg toast. "How did you make it taste like this? Even Momma's isn't this..." Her voice stopped suddenly, and her face wrinkled as she fought back tears.

Erisa started talking, keeping her voice even. "Will's teacher was a very good cook. I learned a lot when I stayed with him before Will was born, even though he didn't let me cook very often."

That struck Will as odd, since he had been forced to cook the majority of the time. "Why didn't he let you cook more?"

His mother scrunched up her face. "He said I'd poison my unborn child, among other things, most of which are too rude to say in front of Samantha."

That made them laugh, a laugh that grew louder than it needed to be. Will stopped himself as he felt his emotions begin to swing out of control. "I always thought you were a great cook, Mom, until the old man let me try his food." He tried to laugh again, but his eyes were already wet.

None of them could speak for a while after that. Will began sniffling, and soon Sammy was sobbing. The food grew cold before they finished consoling one another. When they finally regained their composure, Will spoke up, "I have to tell you something about last night."

"Did you go somewhere?" asked Erisa. "I remember you getting up very early."

"I took Grandfather's body away," said Will.

Sammy's eyes went wide. "Did you bury it by yourself?"

It occurred to him that telling her that would be a far easier explanation, but he knew his mother would never believe it. Even with a shovel, burying a body would take much more work than he could have accomplished by himself in such a short time. "I gave it to his next of kin."

Erisa looked confused. "Who?"

"His wife and daughter visited last night."

"Aislinn is alive?" said his mother in amazement. "I suppose if she was like him, I should have known it was possible, but—" She stopped, changing her question, "Where has she been all this time?"

"She isn't like him," corrected Will. "Neither is his daughter. They're fae."

Sammy was watching both of them, trying to make sense of the conversation, then her eyes lit up. "Aislinn? His wife was the Goddess of Magic? Really? What about Elth—"

Reacting quickly, Will snatched up the toast from her plate and shoved it into Sammy's open mouth. "Don't say his name. Both of them can hear you when you say their names."

His cousin bit off a large piece of toast and began chewing furiously before swallowing it down. "Was he really our great-great-grandfather? Does that mean we have god-blood in us?"

He shook his head. "His wife was human once, but something happened to her before she had her last child."

Erisa added, "He really was your great-great-great-great-grandfather, though I don't know how many 'greats' to put there."

"So he was fae too?" asked Sammy.

"No," said Will.

"He was some kind of wizard," said Erisa. "Different than the ones we have today. I think he knew some secret that gave him great longevity."

"How old was he?" exclaimed Sammy.

Will's mother shrugged. "I'm not sure, but I know he fought against Darrow in the Terabinian War for Independence. He was very bitter about it. I think he had a grudge against their prophet."

"Valmon," put in Will. "The Prophet was his last student. He told me he killed him."

Erisa covered her mouth. "Did he say why?"

"No. He rarely talked about his past," said Will.

"Wasn't the War for Independence over four hundred years ago?" asked Sammy, her voice full of wonder.

"A little more than that, I think," corrected Erisa.

Sammy's eyes locked onto Will. "He was teaching you magic, wasn't he?" Her mouth went wide, and she stuffed her fist into it before mumbling around it, "Are you going to be a sorcerer?"

He couldn't help but chuckle. "Grandfather would have lost his mind if he heard you say that."

"He hated sorcerers," explained Erisa.

"And the fae," added Will.

"And deer," said his mother, beginning to smirk.

"And fools," said Will.

"Don't forget the king," said Erisa.

"The nobility," added Will.

"And most people in general," finished his mother, grinning. Then her face turned serious. "Except you, William. He pretended otherwise, but I could tell. He was very fond of you." As quickly as that, their tears returned and the conversation ended.

A while later, his mother decided to take an inventory of what was in the house, to see what they had and what they might need in the near future. Will took the opportunity to make an excuse. "It's cold and getting colder. I'll need to bring in some more firewood," he lied. His mother hadn't yet seen the large supply of wood that was already laid in on one side of the house.

"Don't go near the village, William," cautioned his mother.

He nodded. "I know, Mom." Stepping outside, he gathered his staff and set off in a direction that would take him away from Barrowden, but once he was out of sight he circled around. He needed to find out what else had happened.

CHAPTER 30

Will knew his decision to return to the village was dangerous at best, but he knew the area well and he was confident in his ability to sneak close without being seen. The thing he most wanted to know was whether the enemy soldiers had moved on after destroying Barrowden, or whether they still remained. If they were gone, there might be a lot they could salvage. *I'll be careful,* he told himself. *Mom will just have to forgive me.*

To avoid detection, he stayed away from the road, approaching the town from the north, where the forest was closest and the terrain the most difficult. He moved slowly, pausing for longer and longer periods the closer he got to ensure there were no lookouts that might spot him, but even so he nearly gave himself away.

He was less than a hundred yards from the northern edge of town, where the trees began to grow more sparsely, and he could already tell that Barrowden was still occupied. The collapsed building still smoldered, giving off smoke, but on the eastern end of town he could see tents and banners in the open field that the road passed through. The town itself seemed empty, though.

He had been getting increasingly more anxious the closer he got, though he couldn't put his finger on precisely why. His nervousness made him wait even longer before moving, though. He remembered what his grandfather had done with the illusory trees, so he examined the area before him carefully, in case the enemy had used similar magic.

There was no sign of magic, but something still felt wrong. He had almost convinced himself he was being overcautious when he realized what was bothering him, and he studied the terrain again. There was nothing unusual to be seen with what he considered his 'normal' sight, but the faint flows of turyn that he had grown used to seeing since his journey to the fae realm were different. It wasn't deliberate magic; that would've been much more obvious.

Sentries, he decided. In several places, the streamers of turyn were moving strangely, as though disturbed by something, like water flowing around a rock in a stream. It was something he had gotten used to seeing around his cousin, his mother, even Arrogan. Humans, like other living things, possessed their own turyn, but it was strongly bound to their bodies, causing the ambient turyn to be displaced near them. Trees and plants did the same thing, of course, but with animals the effect was more pronounced.

There were two trees and a large rock that all displayed an unusual displacement of turyn, as though someone was hidden behind them. It wasn't magic. The soldiers of Darrow were simply very good at hiding, much better than his childhood playmates had been. *And I almost walked right into them.*

So much for getting closer. Will settled down to watch. After a few minutes he noticed something that should have come to his attention sooner—the sound of axes. He had been overly distracted watching a group of soldiers digging a mass grave, but on the other side of town they were felling trees. *They're planning to settle in for the winter.*

Idiots, observed his internal voice, sounding much like his grandfather. *If they were planning to dig in, they*

260

should have left the buildings intact. He waited another quarter of an hour and then began to carefully ease away. His mother was probably in a panic by now.

As he made the difficult trek back, he felt his conviction begin to firm up. Something had to be done; otherwise his remaining family and friends would never be able to go home. It would take an army to drive them out, and he was beginning to see the conscription crew that had come to his village before in a different light.

***

"William Cartwright! Are you trying to drive me to an early death?"

They were standing in the dirt yard in front of the house. He had expected his mother to yell, but seeing the stark fear in her face made him feel incredibly guilty.

"If you're going to keep doing things like this, I'd just as soon kill you myself and get it over with! Do you have any idea the kind of things that went through my mind when we realized you had run off? They could have killed you! Worse, they could have tortured you to find out where we were hiding and then come to kill us as well. What would happen to Sammy if they found us here? Did that ever occur to you?"

Will's head was down, and he kept his eyes on the ground. "I'm sorry, Mom, but I had to find out what was happening."

Staring at her shadow, he saw her arm rise, as though she would strike him, but then his mother sat down suddenly, covering her face with her hands. "How strong do you think I am?" she asked, her voice breaking. "It's hard enough just to survive without worrying about you constantly."

"I'm sorry," he began again, but Sammy interrupted, putting her hand on Erisa's arm.

"It's all right, Auntie. He came back safe," said his cousin.

Realizing her outburst was upsetting her niece, Erisa wiped her face and stood up again. "What's done is done. Since you risked your fool neck, you might as well tell us what you saw."

Will explained what he had done, leaving out the part where he had nearly walked into the sentries. "They're burying the dead, but they're also cutting trees. They've set up camp on the east side of town. I think they're planning to spend the winter."

"I guess it's about what we should have expected," said his mother.

"Shouldn't they keep going?" asked Sammy. "If they're invading the kingdom, they shouldn't stop here."

His mother shook her head. "Attacking this late in the year was a surprise in and of itself. Winter is just beginning, and the passes will be snowed under in a few weeks. They're hoping that it's too late for Lognion to assemble a force to drive them out. In the spring, the Patriarch's army can cross and they'll have a good place to begin a full campaign."

"But the king will stop them, right?" asked Sammy, her voice full of both hope and fear. "Dad's in the army now. He won't let them take Barrowden."

"I'm sure Lord Fulstrom would like to drive them out immediately," said Erisa. "He's gathered his men in Branscombe. But the Lord has to obey his king. King Lognion will probably want to concentrate his forces before he responds, and that means they aren't likely to come until spring."

"What about us?" asked Will. "If they stay there all winter—"

"We'll have to get out," said his mother. "While they're fortifying the area, they'll also be sending out groups to scour the forest and hills, looking for survivors, food, and anything they can use. Eventually they'll find us."

"They won't," said Will firmly.

"Why do you say that?" asked Erisa.

"Aislinn promised me," he answered. "She said she would make sure that no enemy found this place."

His mother sighed. "She's fae. Do you believe her?"

He nodded. "They can't lie or break their bargains. They can twist the truth, but they can't break their word."

"If it was a bargain, what did you give her?" asked his mother, worry written on her features.

"Grandfather's body," he replied. "I know she's dangerous, but I think she really wants to help. They won't find us here."

"What about food?" asked Sammy.

Erisa took a deep breath. "There's enough stored to keep us until spring, but it won't be pleasant. It's mainly turnips, parsnips, carrots, and dried peas. Without meat we'll get sick of those pretty quickly."

"We've got eggs," suggested Sammy.

"The hens have already almost stopped laying," said Erisa. "I suppose we could eat a couple of them, but then we'll be in bad shape when spring arrives."

Will wished he knew how the old man had been getting butter and other necessities, but it was too late to ask him. "At least we won't starve," he said at last.

"We're wasting heat standing out here," said his mother. "Let's go inside. William, bring in some more wood."

They had a simple meal that evening, though Will still managed to earn high praise from both his mother and Sammy for his cooking. He wondered if they'd still feel the same after several months of eating the same food every day. Without much else to do, they talked and played chess with a gameboard and pieces that Erisa had found in Arrogan's room. She had to teach them the rules, so Will and Sammy lost every game, but it was fun anyway.

When they got ready to sleep, Will retired to his cot, leaving the bed to them. He claimed it was because he was too old to sleep with his mother, and while that was partly true, his main reason was that he needed time alone to think.

I'm seventeen now, he realized. In all the commotion of the past few days, his birthday had passed unnoticed. In a year he would be considered a man, though he hardly felt like it. *Eric was still sixteen when they took him. I'm certainly old enough.*

Although it had never been something he considered before, he felt a strong need to join the King's Army. It wasn't something he wanted, but seeing the soldiers of Darrow occupying Barrowden after their slaughter had changed something in him. Losing his aunt and little Dougie had shocked and hurt him, but it had also created a newfound determination. Without the old man around to learn from, he had no reason to stay. His main concern was finding a way to ensure that his mother and Sammy would be safe.

Aislinn's promise was reassuring, but he still worried. Food might not be an absolute problem, since there were plenty of vegetables, but he didn't like the thought of them spending the entire winter trying to subsist on just those things.

Unfortunately, other than the ability to sneak and hide, he had few practical woodland skills. He knew enough to make simple snares for small game like rabbits and squirrels, but those were unlikely to catch anything in the winter. He didn't have a bow, but even if he did, he didn't know how to use one, much less stalk deer or other large game. He could make a fire with simple tools, find edible plants, and move quietly. That was the extent of his usefulness.

Oh, and I can make funny shapes out of turyn that no one can see, he reminded himself. He knew the runes of power, but he hadn't the faintest idea how to use them. He couldn't even create a light. *I'm just another mouth to feed.*

He couldn't justify leaving them based on that, though. He needed to *do* something, and joining the army seemed to be the only way he could do anyone any good. But he couldn't leave unless he knew they would be safe.

His thoughts twisted back and forth along those paths for a long time before he finally gave in to sleep, but even his dreams were troubled.

CHAPTER 31

Will woke just as the sun was beginning to crest the horizon and went out to see if he might get lucky and find an egg. The hens hadn't produced many over the past week, but there was always the chance that they might lay one more before they closed up shop for the winter. He stopped when he stepped onto the porch, taking in a view that was unexpected for more than one reason.

The first snow had come, blanketing the world in a sheet of white—a blanket that was stained with crimson streaks. On the ground in front of the house was a large doe, a very dead doe. *Arrogan would have been thrilled,* was the first thought that came to him when he got over the shock.

There were claw marks along the doe's flanks, but that hadn't been what killed her. Something had bitten through the back of her neck, close to her skull, killing her almost instantly. Will jumped three feet backward when something brushed up against his leg.

It was the goddamn cat, his paws and muzzle stained dark with drying blood. Will stared at the feline with undisguised horror. "Did you do this?" he asked aloud.

There's no way this cat could have done this, he told himself silently.

The goddamn cat coughed and began to retch. After a moment he coughed up what Will thought might be a hairball, but on closer inspection turned out to be a piece of bone. The cat looked up at Will and bared his teeth in what might have been a smile, or a warning. Either way, with the blood all over his face the expression was terrifying. Then the cat walked around him, rubbing against his leg once more before walking over to sit beside the deer carcass.

"Is this for us?" asked Will. *I've gone mad,* he thought immediately after. *Now I'm talking to the cat too.*

The grey tom stared at him for a long moment, then blinked slowly before walking away, heading back into the wilderness. "This is unbelievable," Will muttered to himself before turning to the door and yelling, "Mom!"

Erisa took the news more pragmatically than he expected. Rather than ask questions, she instructed him to gut the beast quickly and then showed him how to hang it so she could bleed the body. "She's still warm," said his mother. "We want to do it before the meat freezes."

Will had never cleaned anything larger than a rabbit or chicken, but his mother had apparently had some experience and she walked him through the process. The gutting was essentially the same, but skinning the animal afterward was considerably more work. It turned out that hanging the deer was essential for that as well.

"When did you learn to do this?" he asked his mother when they were almost done.

Erisa smiled, as though remembering something pleasant. "When I was young. My father, your grandfather, loved to hunt. Mom wasn't very fond of cleaning game, so my father always had to do it. When I was old enough, he let me help him."

It didn't sound like a very pleasant memory, but he could tell from the look in her eye that she felt differently. He wondered how many more things there were about her past that he didn't know. People were full of mysteries. That thought brought him around to Arrogan, and he realized the old man had had hundreds of years' worth of experiences he knew nothing about—that he would never know about. Once again, he was almost overwhelmed by the sense of how much he had lost.

He was brought back from his reverie when he realized his mother had asked a question. "Sorry. What did you say?"

"I asked if you knew what killed the doe," said Erisa.

Will couldn't begin to come up with a lie big enough to cover this, so he simply answered, "I think it was the cat."

She laughed. "I could almost believe it of that strange cat, but the claw marks on the hind quarters were too big."

He held her eyes with his. "I'm pretty sure it was the cat."

She frowned. "You're suggesting it can transform or some such?"

"I have no idea. I don't know what the goddamn cat can do, but he's no ordinary cat," he told her. "I'm just glad he seems to be on our side. Aislinn said the fae won't come near the house because of him."

Erisa looked worried. "That would've suited your grandfather just fine, but how can we be sure it's safe?"

Will shrugged. "It's just a feeling, but I think he'll protect this place. Between him, and Aislinn hiding the house from the soldiers, I doubt there's a safer place in the entire kingdom."

His mother nodded. "I suppose there was a reason Arrogan chose to stay here for so long."

The next few days passed quietly as they settled into a simple, yet boring routine. With snow on the ground there was nothing to do but cook and sleep. Will continued his math and reading practice even though he had pretty much mastered the material he had. He also spent some time drilling with the runes. He knew them all by heart now, but it was recent knowledge. He worried he would begin to forget them if he didn't go over them every once in a while. *Not that it matters,* he thought sourly. *I can't do anything with them.*

"You will have many teachers," Aislinn had told him, and he believed her. Perhaps someday he would have an opportunity to learn enough to use them.

Such thoughts did nothing to cure him of his desperate desire to do something *now*. Aside from cooking, he had little to offer Sammy and his mother, and even that was becoming a topic of contention. His mother seemed to think the best way to cook anything, including venison, was simply to stew it. While that was fine now and then, he preferred to have a little variety, and his effort to teach his mother seemed to set her teeth on edge.

And they had only been cooped up together for four days. How bad would it be in a month?

If I'm going to join the army I need to leave soon, he thought. The western pass that led to Branscombe was easier, and wouldn't close as soon as the eastern pass to Darrow, but it *would* become impassable if he waited too long.

But he couldn't imagine telling his mother that he planned to go. She wouldn't accept it. Even if they had an army of soldiers and retainers to protect the house and see to their every need, it wouldn't have mattered. It wasn't her safety she was concerned with, it was his, and joining the army was too dangerous.

The next night, after his mother and Sammy went to bed, he rose quietly and began packing his meager belongings. There wasn't much, since he only had two sets of clothes. He added Arrogan's winter cloak to them and wrapped up enough food to last him three days. He didn't have any portable pans so he wouldn't have many options when it came to cooking the meat, but he could simply roast it he decided. The carrots he could eat raw.

Before he left, he got out his writing materials and penned a short note:

> *Mom,*
> *I know you'll be angry, but I have to do this. I'm going to Branscombe to join the King's Army there. I also hope to find Uncle Johnathan and Eric to let them know you and Sammy are safe.*
> *Will*

He stared at the note. It was very short, and he knew there were many more things he could say, but none of them would matter. He left the page on the table and put on the cloak before going out the door. The goddamn cat was sitting on the porch, as though waiting for him.

"I'm leaving," he told the cat. "I'm going to join the army to help liberate Barrowden."

The grey tom began cleaning himself, starting with his balls, as if to show his opinion of that course of action.

Will couldn't help but chuckle. "Granddad would have likely thought the same." After a few seconds, he added, "Thank you for the deer. I hope you'll watch over them until I get back."

The cat sat up, his ears snapping forward as all of his attention came to rest on Will. Then he walked forward until he was in front of the young man's boots. Unsure what to do, Will bent down and held his hand out, offering to scratch the feline's chin. With no warning, the goddamn cat's paw lashed out, leaving a bloody groove on the back of Will's hand.

"Ow!" exclaimed Will, snatching his hand back. "What was that for?"

The tom sniffed his paw, smelling the blood there, then walked to the front door and stretched up to catch the wood with his claws. Pulling down, he left scratches in the wood, then he turned and looked at Will again. He blinked once, slowly, then curled up in front of the door.

Was that his way of sealing a bargain? he wondered. It didn't seem entirely fair. *I should get to scratch him back.* He grinned to himself at the thought.

The sky was grey to the east and still almost black to the west. Dawn was close, and he knew his mother would be waking in an hour or so. It was time to go, so he stepped off the porch and began to march west. In the summer, when the road was dry and the pass was free of snow, the journey to Branscombe took a little less than three days, but Will knew better than to attempt the road. There were bound to be Darrowan scouts watching it.

He would have to stay in the forest as much as possible, until it thinned out as the land rose into the mountains. He would only approach the road itself when he got close to the narrow part of the pass, where there simply wasn't another option. If the Darrowans had placed sentries there, he'd have to figure out how to get past them when the time came.

Given that he wouldn't be using the road, his travel would take twice as long, at least until he cleared the pass, and even after that, the snow would slow him down. His best guess was that it would take him a week to reach Branscombe, and he only had enough food to last about three days.

It was also cold and would be colder still in the pass itself. A normal trip to Branscombe involved three days of travel and two nights camping on the road, but he didn't have the gear for camping in cold weather. He'd probably freeze to death if he tried.

The solution to both his food problem and the problem of camping was simple: he wouldn't camp. There would be a half-moon that night, and it was waxing, so it would continue to grow for another week. With clear skies, he should have enough light. He'd travel through the day and continue at night. With luck he would reach the narrow part of the pass at night, making it easier to avoid whatever sentries might be there. By not resting he could keep himself warm and cut his travel time nearly in half. It was the perfect plan, or so he thought.

Will only had a small amount of uncertainty, which, as always, spoke with his grandfather's voice, *Only a fucking idiot would try crossing the mountains at night during the winter.*

"Which is why they'll never expect it," said Will, arguing with himself.

His inner doubt didn't reply, but he could sense it quietly cussing in the background. The years with Arrogan had left their mark on him. He'd probably never be normal, but hopefully he could conceal his oddness from others when he joined the army.

The journey through the Glenwood was harder than he had expected. The new snow concealed the ground, causing him to trip over unseen limbs and other detritus. It also made it harder to spot low spots and holes that became more common as he got into rockier terrain. His staff quickly became indispensable as he used it to maintain his balance and check the ground ahead.

In the late afternoon, things got easier. The sun warmed his back, making him almost uncomfortably warm. He was forced to remove the heavy cloak to avoid sweating and making his clothes damp. The forest thinned out, and the terrain became easier to traverse. The snow was thin here, so he increased his speed to a jog. He was already beginning to tire, but his training had given him tools to deal with that. Will first expanded his turyn, drawing in more from the air around him, then contracted it, concentrating it in his lungs and the muscles of his legs to increase his stamina and endurance.

He knew from past experience that he could run for a long time using tricks like that, but he'd never done so for more than a half an hour before. There would probably be a price to pay when he stopped, but that was all right. He could rest when he reached Branscombe.

Thirty minutes into his jog, he stepped into a hole and nearly twisted his ankle. The reflexes he had developed from a lifetime of playing in the forest saved him, taking his weight off the foot that had nothing beneath it and bending his knee before it hit bottom. After he had regained his footing and moved on, he glanced back. "Anyone else would have been in serious trouble," he said, congratulating himself.

Fool's luck, warned his inner voice.

"Shut up," he told himself, resuming his journey, though he stopped jogging.

He was moving steadily uphill now, so his fatigue grew quickly, and his muscles began to feel heavy. The thinning air didn't help. Will increased the turyn in his lungs, but they still burned from taking in so much cold air.

Night fell as he entered the mountains. He stopped to eat a carrot, for his hunger was so great he thought he might be starving to death. It didn't do much to satisfy him, so he made a brief attempt at starting a fire.

Though his body was warm, his hands were cold and clumsy. The wood he found was coated with snow and ice. It didn't take him long to realize he wouldn't succeed. *Making a fire in these conditions is a skill, one you don't have—moron,* said his inner voice.

Ignoring the voice, Will took out his waterskin and took a drink. He was surprised to find that it was empty after only a couple of swallows. Had he been drinking that much? He knew better than to try eating snow, though it was tempting, so he spent some time packing snow in the small opening of his waterskin. It seemed to take forever, but hopefully it would melt while he traveled.

He was only getting colder, so he got back on his feet and started walking again, which was harder than he expected. After the short rest, his legs had gotten stiff and they now felt as though they were made of lead. At a guess he had been traveling for about fourteen hours. How bad would it be the next day?

His fatigue made the tricky terrain even more dangerous, so he began moving closer to the road, where it was more even. It was less than a quarter-mile from where he was, and wasn't even truly a road anymore, so much as a relatively clear and well-traveled path. The snow made it hard to even tell exactly where the road was, and he fell several times when his feet encountered unexpected rocks.

He focused his turyn once more, strengthening his legs and lungs, but it took longer this time. Even his turyn seemed sluggish, unwilling to respond, though he wasn't sure why. *Fatigue eats away at your will even faster than performing magic,* said his inner advisor. Was that something his grandfather had told him before, or was his imagination working overtime?

Gritting his teeth, Will kept moving. "I don't need your advice," he told himself.

If stubbornness was the same as 'will' you'd have nothing to fear, boy, but it isn't, said his grandfather's voice in his mind.

"You should know," answered Will, his voice raw from the freezing air.

You'll die if you don't find shelter.

"If you cared then you shouldn't have left me alone." He tried to spit to clear his mouth, but it was too dry.

Sometime after midnight he drew close to the crest, the high point of the path between mountain peaks. His thirst was intense, but when he tried to get water from the skin he carried he discovered it felt like a rock was inside. The snow had melted at some point and then hardened into a solid piece of ice. Ignoring his better judgment, he scooped up some snow from the ground and put it into his mouth.

It didn't help much with his thirst, but he felt better anyway. He ate some more and then decided he should take a short rest. His body was so tired that a nap sounded like a perfect remedy. He wasn't that cold anyway. He found a rock jutting up from the snow and sat down, putting his back against it. His eyes closed almost immediately.

Wake up, dumbass!

"Leave me alone."

You'll be as dead as that frozen lump of fat you call a brain if you don't get up, said his grandfather.

Will smiled. "You used to have better insults."

That's because I'm a delusion. You're too stupid to come up with a decent impression of me, said Arrogan. *Get up!*

Despite thinking it was a bad idea, Will tried. His eyes wouldn't open, and it took him a moment to realize they had frozen shut. He rubbed at them with his hands, but that didn't seem to work, so he gave up on it. He struggled to get to his feet but promptly fell over. "I can't," he mumbled into the warm snow.

Then call her!

"Who?" asked Will.

Who do you think? Never mind, just forget it. You're doing the world a favor by removing your stupidity from it.

Will giggled. "I was just teasing. I know you meant Tailtiu."

Say it again.

"Tailtiu," he whispered. "Your daughter is really beautiful, even if she's my aunt."

Once more.

"I've had some really naughty dreams about her. You'd be so mad if I told you," said Will.

Say it, you demented half-wit!

"Tail—" he began before drifting into a warm darkness.

CHAPTER 32

The first thing Will became aware of was a red glow that seemed to suffuse everything around him. In fact, it was the only thing around him. When he opened his eyes, nothing changed; there were no shapes or anything else, other than the red glow.

"You called, yet you say nothing when I appear," said a soft, feminine voice.

It sounded like Tailtiu, but Will wasn't sure. He might be dreaming. As far as he could tell, he no longer had a body.

"If you won't speak, I'll leave," she warned. "This is boring."

Will tried to answer, but the only sound that came out was, "Grhk." That answered the question about his body, though. He must still have one if he could make sounds.

"You're awake," she said, sounding surprised.

"Helphh," he managed. The words got easier as he moved his lips more.

"Why don't you look at me?" asked the fae. The light grew brighter for a moment. "Oh. Your eyelids are frozen shut. Why would you do that?" A warm wind caressed his face, and after a few minutes he felt his lashes come unstuck.

The red glow made more sense after he cracked his eyes open. A bright light hovered in the air above Tailtiu's head, but it had seemed red as it filtered through the lids of his eyes. "I'm dying," he told her, his voice thick but intelligible at last.

The fae woman cocked her head to one side, reminding him of a curious dog. "You've been dying since you were born. Is this a riddle?"

"Too cold," he said. "I need help."

Tailtiu frowned. "Why don't you just use your magic to warm yourself?"

Will groaned. "I don't know how."

Arrogan's daughter laughed as though he had told a joke. "That's ridiculous. Father could do it. You're just like him; you should be able to do the same."

Even exhausted, Will found her tone irritating. "Tell me how then."

His aunt shrugged. "I don't know how human magic works. Mother does, but you called me. Besides, that sounds like a favor, doesn't it? We haven't made a bargain. I could warm you myself if you like. Would you like to use one of the unbounded favors to ask that of me?"

As foggy as his thoughts were, Will still knew that was an unbalanced bargain. "Service for three days," he declared, although it came out as more of a mumble. "One favor."

Tailtiu smiled slyly. "Service? What sort of service do you require?"

Will felt a faint tugging lower down. He struggled to lift his head and managed to catch a glimpse of her hand unfastening his trousers. "Not that," he insisted. "Any service. Warm me up, help me travel."

She paused. "*Any* service should include sex, though."

He wanted to shout at the stupid fae, but that was beyond his capacity. "It does, but I don't intend to ask for that."

"It's gone," said Tailtiu, staring at his lower body. "Oh, there it is. Oh dear, how sad."

"Three days' service," he repeated. "In exchange for one favor."

"Shouldn't it be one favor for each day?" she countered.

Since the favor was unbounded there were no strict limits—Will knew that much. "Would you prefer three years for one favor?"

Her face went sour. "Three days then. Deal?"

"Deal," he answered. "Can you warm me up?"

Tailtiu exhaled, and a warm rush of air flooded over him, but unlike normal breath it lingered, wrapping itself around him and lifting his body from the icy ground. It felt as though he was in the softest bed imaginable. The warmth sank into him, and soon he began to feel uncomfortably hot. His arms and legs began to tingle and burn as though he had put them too close to a fire. "You're burning me," Will complained.

"You'll have to bear it," said his aunt. "The air is still cold."

Will tried to refasten his trousers, but his fingers refused to work. "Can you help me with this?" he asked at last.

"You humans and your fixation with clothing," said Tailtiu. She closed up his trousers and retied the laces, then fixed his belt. "Although, in your case I suppose I can understand. It's so small. It must be embarrassing for you."

He would have blushed if his cheeks weren't still so cold. "I was freezing to death," he insisted. "What do you expect?" It was then that he noticed the fae woman was nude, as usual. "Aren't you cold?" he asked. She didn't even have shoes.

"Hot, cold, it's all the same for us," she told him as she examined his hands. "These don't look good. You might lose them. Your feet are probably just as bad." Then she reached up and touched his cheek. "The cheeks too. You're going to be very ugly if you don't die."

"Can you heal me?"

Tailtiu appeared to give it serious thought, then responded, "The easiest way would be if you ate some of my flesh."

"Not blood?"

"That would be too slow. You need something more substantial." She held up her hand, wiggling her fingers. "Like this, or a foot." When she saw the look of revulsion on his face, she moved her hand across her chest. "Or perhaps you would prefer something softer?"

The very thought made him want to vomit. "I don't want to become like you," he said after he had wrestled his stomach back under control.

"How rude," remarked Tailtiu, then after a minute her look of outrage melted away and she began to laugh. "Mother said I shouldn't tease you too much." He could see turyn flowing around her, growing brighter and more concentrated around her hands. "I can heal your injuries, but as bad as they are it will probably be very painful."

Will didn't like the sound of that, but he didn't have much choice. He nodded to indicate his willingness.

But Tailtiu wasn't done with her warnings. "There are men on the mountain not far from here. If you scream, they'll hear us. Were you trying to hide from them?"

He was almost certain the ones she was referring to would be Darrowan scouts. "I don't think they're friendly. Why didn't they see your light then?"

"We are hidden by my magic to all but the closest observers."

"Couldn't you hide the sound of my yells?"

She shook her head. "My magic is good at helping one remain hidden, or to move without sound, but if you scream it won't be effective. Mother could do it with some of the human magic she knows, but I have never learned such things." Leaning close, she added, "I can put you into a deep slumber, where perhaps the pain cannot reach you."

"All right," said Will, and then he felt her turyn begin to move, sinking into his body. Seconds passed into minutes, and while he felt a number of strange sensations, he remained wide awake.

Tailtiu frowned. "Don't fight it."

"I'm not."

"Yes, you are," she insisted. "You're eating my magic."

Eating it? What did that mean? Perhaps his body was converting her turyn into his own as soon as it entered his body. Concentrating, he tried drawing his turyn inward, compressing it around his tiny source and leaving most of his body empty. When that failed to help, he expanded it once more and tried releasing his hold on his source, allowing it to return to what had once been a normal level of turyn production.

That seemed to work, and he began to grow drowsy, though it still took several minutes before her magic pushed him into unconsciousness. The world darkened, and he sank into oblivion. How long he remained that way he couldn't have guessed, but a searing pain brought him back. It felt as though flames enveloped his entire being.

He fought the flames for some period before his consciousness returned. He had a vague memory of wrestling with the power that was tormenting him, but he wasn't entirely sure what had happened. It wasn't until he heard Tailtiu's screams that he finally awoke fully, and his eyes snapped open.

The ground was ice cold beneath him, as he was no longer floating. Sitting up, he saw his aunt writhing in the snow nearby, her body marked by ugly black lines that covered her from head to toe in a jagged pattern. As he looked, the turyn connecting them disappeared; her movements slowed, and the screams tapered off into a soft groaning.

"What happened?" he asked as he moved closer. He reached out toward her, but she scrambled back, a terrified look in her eyes.

"You nearly killed me," she accused, keeping her distance. Her breathing was returning to normal, but the flesh near the black lines on her skin was becoming red. In some places she seemed to be bleeding as well. A fresh spasm of pain shook her, and she curled into a ball.

"How? I was unconscious." Even as he said it, though, he remembered fighting with something before he had awoken. As he spoke, he noticed his hand, which was no longer blue and purple. The skin was a fresh pink, and although it felt tender and sensitive there was no sign of the damage it had possessed earlier.

He heard a shout in the distance. The Darrowan scouts were beginning to search, having heard Tailtiu's cries. He glanced around. The magic Tailtiu had been using to hide them was gone, along with her light. They were in a slight depression beside the same rock he had collapsed against earlier, but otherwise they were completely exposed. Only the night hid them, and with a half-moon above that wasn't nearly enough.

"We have to move, or hide," he told her, but his aunt didn't respond. Will shook her, trying to get her attention, but her body was limp and her skin was as cold as the snow beneath her. *Is she dead?* he wondered. *Did I kill her somehow?* According to his grandfather, that wasn't supposed to be possible. The fae were immortal. Even if you cut one of them into a dozen pieces, those pieces would survive until they were reunited. Smaller wounds would simply regenerate.

The voices were getting closer, and Will could just make out dark shapes moving against the grey-white of the moonlit mountain slope. A surge of panic rose within him, causing his mind to go blank. Before he knew what he was doing, he began to kick snow over Tailtiu's body to conceal it.

An idea came to him then, and he stopped. Brushing the snow away from her, he moved her slightly so she would be more easily visible. Then he moved to the other side of the boulder to hide. Once there, he removed his cloak and scooped as much new-fallen snow over it as he could manage, and then he eased into a low crouch beside the rock and pulled the snow-covered cloak gently up and over himself. Some of the snow fell away, but he thought enough remained to disguise him as a snow drift in the poor light. He clutched his staff in his right hand and touched the sheath on his belt to make sure his knife was still there. Then he waited.

Despite their nearness, it took much longer for the scouts to reach Tailtiu's body than he had expected, and Will's hand began to burn with the cold where it gripped his staff. His entire body felt extraordinarily sensitive, and it was a struggle to remain still, much less contain his shivers.

There were two men approaching and one of them held a lantern. Both were wrapped in heavy cloaks, and neither seemed to be expecting an ambush despite the strange sounds they had heard. Will bowed his head and closed his eyes to preserve his night vision. His ears would tell him when they were close.

The crunching sound of boots in fresh snow grew louder, and then a man's voice called out. "There's someone here."

"Where?" answered the man's companion.

"Over there, near that big rock."

The steps came closer, and Will heard the sound of blades being drawn from scabbards. That wasn't something he'd wanted to hear. *It was a stupid plan,* he told himself. *Of course they would draw their weapons.* He doubted he'd have much chance against two armed and wary soldiers.

It was too late to do things differently, however, so he remained still. The steps got louder and then stopped. "It's a woman," said the first man. "She's naked!"

"Huh?"

"I think she's dead," said the first soldier. "Someone must have killed her and stripped the body."

"Be careful, it might be a trap," said the second.

"She's cold as ice. She has to be dead," said the first, then he hissed. "She's been tortured! Look at this!"

The second man wasn't having it, though. "Make sure she's dead first."

"How?"

"Stick your blade in her. Then we'll know for sure."

"You're an idiot," said the first soldier. "Look, someone's burned black lines into her. Her skin is charred. Damn, she's beautiful—or was. Who would do something like this?"

"We would," said the second man dryly. "Didn't you see what some of us did back at that village?"

"Don't remind me. I haven't slept well since." The first man added, "This isn't normal, though. It had to be magic. There's no sign of a fire, and these lines go all over her body."

"Let's get out of here. If there's a sorcerer, I don't want to meet him. What are you doing?"

"We have to take her with us," said the first soldier. "If it starts snowing, we might not be able to find her later."

"Don't be daft! Leave her there. You heard about the group that got murdered by that old man claiming to be the Betrayer himself. What if he's up here?"

"Someone has to bury her. It wouldn't be right otherwise."

As he listened, Will found himself agreeing with the first speaker. Neither of the Darrowans sounded particularly bad, and the first one seemed downright decent. He wanted to stay hidden—to let them leave and then sneak away—but he couldn't let them take Tailtiu. He waited as the first picked her up and struggled to find a comfortable way to carry the girl.

Lifting his head, he saw that they had sheathed their swords and the first man had settled on an over-the-shoulder carry. As they turned away, he leapt forward, using his left hand to sweep his cloak up and throwing it over the unencumbered soldier's head.

Taking the staff in both hands, he swept the legs out from under the one with the cloak over his head, then turned and rammed the end into the head of the one carrying Tailtiu—or rather he tried.

Both men were wearing heavily padded gambesons and steel caps. It was an excellent choice for winter, as the padding protected them well from cuts and blows and kept them warm in the cold weather. The end of Will's staff struck the man's steel cap and slid to one side, knocking him off balance but doing little real harm.

The other was scrambling to regain his feet and throw off the cloak, so Will devoted the next few strikes to beating him senseless. Again, his efforts met limited success. The padding made many of his blows ineffective, and the soldier instinctively covered his head with his arms, preventing Will from getting a clean blow to his face or neck.

The first had dropped Tailtiu by then, and Will heard his footsteps in the snow as he ran toward Will's undefended back.

Moving forward, Will jumped over the man he had been attacking and turned, making a wide swing with his staff to keep his attacker from closing. The first soldier stepped back reflexively and tripped as one of his feet caught on his injured friend.

Seizing his advantage, Will began pummeling both men, preventing them from rising. As before, most of his attacks had little lasting effect against their padded coats, but he made up for the lack of quality with an abundant quantity of blows.

It seemed to go on forever, and Will's stomach turned as their efforts to defend themselves grew weaker. He could imagine the pain they felt when his staff struck against their arms and legs. He winced as he heard the sharp snap of a bone breaking.

But he couldn't stop. As sick as it made him, his fear was greater. He had to make sure they couldn't follow him or report back to their camp. One of the men was no longer moving, and the other began to beg. "I surrender. Please stop. Don't kill me, mister!"

Will hit him again, and the man cried out in pain.

"We didn't do nothing to you! Have mercy!" The soldier's words were slurred due to the damage to his mouth and jaw.

Will hit him again, and the man rolled onto his belly, trying to crawl away. *Why won't he just pass out?* In the stories told by the bards, the villains always collapsed after a single blow, but it was quite obvious to Will that he wasn't in some hero's saga. Clenching his jaw, he moved to one side and aimed for the space just below the man's helmet, where the soldier's neck met the base of the skull. There was padding there as well, so he brought the staff down as hard as he could manage, closing his eyes at the last second.

The man stopped moving, and when Will knelt and felt for a pulse, he realized the soldier was dead. He nearly threw up then, but though his stomach heaved once, there was nothing in it. He was racked by guilt, something he hadn't felt after rescuing Sammy in Barrowden. That fight had been quicker, and he'd done it in the heat of the moment. The shock of losing his cousin and aunt had overshadowed the remorse he might have felt at killing them.

But this—this was murder, cold and cruel. He couldn't even hate them for what had happened in Barrowden, for from what they had said they probably hadn't participated directly. It had sickened them too.

After several moments, Will got his emotions under control, or at least managed to bury them deeply enough that he could function. When he checked the other soldier, he was relieved to find the man was still breathing. A short inspection showed him that the man's arm and jaw were broken, but aside from that he didn't seem to have any serious injuries.

Returning to the dead man, he began stripping the body, which took nearly half an hour, during which time he worried constantly that more soldiers would come. He wrapped the surviving soldier in his dead friend's cloak, thinking it might keep him warm enough to survive until he woke. Then he put on the dead man's gambeson and steel cap, which made him feel a lot warmer.

It did nothing for the cold, dead place in his heart, though.

The sky was beginning to brighten as he strapped on the dead man's sword belt. Will wrapped Tailtiu in his cloak and lifted her in his arms, then began retracing his path down the mountain. It was obvious to him now that he couldn't get through the pass, certainly not while carrying a body.

He jerked with surprise when he heard Tailtiu mumble against his chest. "Next time, once they're helpless, take one of their swords to finish them off. It's a lot quicker than beating them to death."

CHAPTER 33

Will walked downhill all morning, and if there was any pursuit, he saw no sign of it. He felt a profound sense of relief when he finally got back into the Glenwood. Tailtiu still hadn't moved, but she had remained awake. "Put me down," she said once they had entered the denser undergrowth.

He laid her carefully on the ground. "Are you starting to recover?"

She shook her head.

"I thought you were immortal?"

"In the fae realm," she whispered without opening her eyes. "Here the connection is too weak. You shredded my insides and exhausted my power. If I don't go back, I'll die."

Something occurred to him then. "Would it help if I gave you some of my turyn? Like before—?"

"I'm too weak. It would only make me sicker," she answered.

The only entrances to the fae realm that Will knew about were in the vicinity of his grandfather's house. It would take the rest of the day to reach either of those— longer since he had to avoid the road. "It will take a while to get you back," he told her. "How long can you last?"

"There's a place close to here," she replied softly. Tailtiu lifted her arm to point toward the south, and Will couldn't help but notice the tremor in her muscles. "That way."

Lifting her again, Will began walking. He began to wonder at his own stamina. He had been at the end of his rope the night before and he still hadn't eaten or had a proper rest, yet he felt no hunger. His body was tired, but when he drew in more turyn and focused it, the fatigue in his arms and legs all but vanished. He could only think that Tailtiu's healing had done more than cure his frostbite.

As the sun rose toward the middle of the sky, he noticed that his vision seemed better as well. In the past, things at a distance had always been slightly blurry, but everything was razor-sharp now. He could see the flows of turyn more easily as well, though his grandfather had told him that that would improve naturally over time.

"Did you do something to my eyes?" he asked as he went.

"You asked me to heal you," answered his aunt, her voice sounding raspy and faint.

"There wasn't anything wrong with my eyes."

"They weren't quite round enough," she responded.

Will wasn't sure why that mattered. He thought about what she had said for several minutes, then asked, "So you fixed everything you *thought* was wrong?"

She smiled faintly in his arms. "Who knew humans had so many flaws? I fixed as much as I could—before you tried to kill me."

The first thing that came to mind was his cheek. The scar there had bothered him for years, though he rarely admitted it. "What about my face?" he asked, since his hands were full and he couldn't check.

"You went berserk before I could," said Tailtiu. "Besides, it isn't so bad. It makes you look a little sinister."

Will didn't really agree with that assessment, but there was no point in arguing. It was then that he noticed a strange movement in the turyn flows ahead. Coming

289

closer, he realized it must be the congruence she had been referring to. It was definitely easier for him to spot them now. He wondered if there was a connection between his physical sight and his magical sight. Could one have improved the other, or were the two entirely separate?

He stopped next to the congruence and Tailtiu spoke before he could ask. "You'll have to take me across," she said.

Will started to, but she shook her head. "Wait. The place this touches is dangerous for you. It's very close to the Lord of the Hunt's home. Leave me there and return as quickly as you can. I will find you once I am recovered."

He shook his head. "You don't have to do that. I feel bad already for what happened to you."

"Three days, William," she responded, her voice firm. "My service isn't done."

Will nodded, then moved forward. Standing in the right spot, he could see both worlds at once in a sort of double vision. Moving sideways in that odd way that he had done once before, he took them to Faerie.

As before, the other side was very similar to his own world, though the colors seemed brighter and the turyn in the air was much more concentrated. Taking a couple of steps, he knelt and eased Tailtiu to the ground.

"Who are you?"

Will froze at the sound of the stranger's voice, then slowly turned his head. A man stood not far away, though perhaps the term 'man' was a bit generous. The fae had small horns sprouting from his skull, and though he wore no armor he carried a long, deadly-looking spear in his hands. It didn't have a metal point, but the tip was carved bone or horn of some sort.

The man pointed it at him with the confidence of someone who knows what he's about, and the abundance of muscles in the fae man's arms and chest only served to underscore the danger. Will and the stranger stared at each other for several long seconds without saying anything.

The guardian's eyes fell on Tailtiu and he hissed. "What did you do to her?"

What do I do? Will had no idea, but past experience had given him one role model. He straightened up slowly, keeping his hands relaxed and away from his weapon. There was no need to tempt fate. Grinning slowly, he made sure to angle his face so the stranger could see the scar on his cheek. *Maybe looking sinister will help.* "She displeased me," he said coldly.

The fae soldier's eyes narrowed angrily. "You dare?" When Will took a step toward the congruence, the fae threatened him with the spear. "Don't move."

Keeping his eyes cool, Will responded, "Don't interfere with our bargain, or your fate will be worse."

The horned man studied Will's face, focusing on a point just above his eyes. "You've been marked." His features showed uncertainty. "Who are you?" he challenged, regaining his resolve.

"Abelund, don't," warned Tailtiu from her position on the ground. "He'll destroy you."

"My name is not for your lips," said Will arrogantly, warming up to his role. "You need only know that I am Arrogan's student. If that name means nothing to you, I will be glad to teach you one of his...*lessons.*"

The fae soldier took a step back, and before he could say anything else Will stepped into the congruence and shifted back to his own world. Once there, he drew his sword and waited. If one of the fae followed, he would see just how effective iron really was against them.

A quarter of an hour passed before he relaxed. The adrenaline had worn off, and his body began to shake as the stress of all that he had been through sank into him. *I never should have left home,* he thought. *Mom was right.* A few seconds later, he chuckled nervously. *Damn, I was cool, though. Even Grandfather would have been impressed.*

In his mind he could almost hear the old man's reply. *Yeah, I was always impressed—by what a witless dumbass you are.*

It was late afternoon already, and Will's need for rest was starting to make itself known to him again, but he didn't want to sleep near the congruence point, so he headed north again. After thirty minutes he stopped and decided to make a fire. The forest was thick enough that there were still plenty of areas that hadn't received much snow beneath the boughs, and he was able to find enough dry grass and small twigs to kindle a flame.

He was far enough from Barrowden that he hoped whatever smoke rose from the trees wouldn't be noticeable. Even so, he stuck to using deadwood and avoided fuel that would tend to smoke a lot, such as leaves or greenwood. Once he had a good bed of coals, he used a spit to roast the meat he had brought. It wasn't until the first bite that he understood just how hungry he really was. His appetite came flooding back to him, and he wound up roasting the rest of the meat and two carrots before he felt full. All he had left now was dried peas.

He regretted the peas. Without a pot or a container of some sort he couldn't make porridge with them. Since they were his only remaining food, he would have to eat them dry the next day. The past two days had shown him just how little he really knew about surviving in the wilderness.

Belly full, he began to grow sleepy. The padded gambeson was sufficiently warm, so he removed his cloak and hung it by the fire. Melting snow had gradually soaked it, and while it still felt dry, the wool was many times heavier than normal. That was one of the nice things about wool. It could absorb a great deal of moisture before it felt wet. He hoped the fire would dry it out somewhat while he slept.

Leaning back against a tree, he let his eyes close.

Sometime later he woke. The darkness was thick and suffocating. His fire had burned out long ago, and the moonlight couldn't reach beneath the canopy of the trees. Will's body felt cold and sore. And he was hungry again—of course.

With a groan, he got to his feet and checked his cloak. If it had dried by an appreciable amount, he couldn't tell. It still felt as though it was made of lead.

Unable to see the sky, he had no idea what time it was, or which direction was which. Rather than stumble through the dark, he took down the cloak and wrapped it around himself. Then he tried to find a more comfortable position to sleep in.

It didn't feel like he slept any, but the sun surprised him, tickling his eyes as it danced between the shadows of leaves on his face. When he opened them, he was startled out of his wits, for just a few inches away were two green eyes staring back at him.

Tailtiu laughed as he yelped, jumped, and then tripped over a heavy branch. "It's a wonder your race has survived this long," she commented. "Your kind slumbers so heavily anyone could kill you in your sleep."

Will didn't reply as he gathered his thoughts. Tailtiu's face seemed normal, but he could see silver lines criss-crossing her features. "Are you better?" he asked at last.

"Mostly," she answered.

Reaching out, he touched her arm, tracing the lines there. "Will these…"

She grinned. "I haven't decided yet. Novelty is prized when you live forever. I may keep them for a while. Do you think I should color them? Red would look wicked, wouldn't it?"

"I'd rather you didn't," admitted Will. "I feel bad when I see them."

"So, I should remove my stripes to make you feel better?" she asked. "Is this part of my service?"

He shook his head. "That's up to you." Then he added, "You only have one day left, then you're free to do as you please."

She held up two fingers. "Two days. My time recovering doesn't count."

That didn't seem fair, but he didn't feel like arguing. Either way it hardly mattered. He couldn't cross the pass and he was nearly out of food. His only option was to return home and accept his punishment. "You may as well return home. There's nothing else I need."

She turned her head to the side once more, curious. "What was it you wanted to accomplish? Were you trying to freeze to death?"

Resting his elbows on his knees, he stared at the leaf litter on the ground. "I was trying to reach Branscombe, but that doesn't seem possible."

"Is that where Branscombe lies? It never seemed so mountainous."

"No. It's to the west, on the other side of the mountains. Don't you know where anything is?" he asked, somewhat surprised.

Tailtiu laughed again. "Not in this world. When my people wish to go somewhere in your world, we use whatever congruence is closest to our destination. Traveling through your world is too unpleasant."

Will stared at her, then asked, "Can you take me there?"

"It would be dangerous from here. The place you took me yesterday is a long way from the point that connects to Branscombe. You should have called me before you started your journey. There's a spot behind Father's house that comes out very close to a place in Faerie that connects to Branscombe," she explained.

"Behind Father's house," Will muttered, comprehension dawning on him. "You mean Arrogan—"

She nodded, her eyes crinkling at the corners. "The place where you live."

Leaning sideways, he began lightly banging his head against the tree he had slept beside, though the steel cap and padding robbed the action of much of its impact. Will had rarely felt so stupid, even back when Arrogan had been there to remind him daily. "Butter, cheese, beef, spices," he chanted quietly, listing all the mysterious items his grandfather had shown up with over the years.

Tailtiu studied him with a look of concern.

"I thought he chose to live there so he could be close to his descendants," said Will, still talking to himself. *But he was hundreds of years old. He probably had grandchildren all over the kingdom.* Now he understood. The old man had hated everyone. The place he had chosen was half an hour's walk from one of the most remote villages on the edge of Terabinia. He had picked it for solitude and easy access to a town market. Will and Erisa living nearby had merely been a coincidence. "Wow."

"Are you all right?"

"Yeah," answered Will. "Just amazed at all the things that never occurred to me before. Can you show me the spot?"

His aunt frowned. "I'd rather not. There's a creature there that doesn't take kindly to my kind. If you wish, I can meet you on the fae side."

"The goddamn cat."

He might have imagined it, but Tailtiu seemed to pale slightly. "Is that what you call it?"

"What do you call it then?"

His aunt shook her head, pressing her lips firmly together before answering, "It can hear its name when spoken, much like my people."

Will sighed. "Can you describe the spot to me then?"

"It is easy to find, just beyond the garden behind your house. Look for the largest tree, an oak. There's an opening amidst the roots. I should be able to get there before you."

He remembered the tree she was describing, though he hadn't noticed anything odd about it before. Of course, he didn't think he'd ever examined it after his sight had been awakened. Rising to his feet once more, he gauged the sun's position and started northward. "I'll meet you there," he said. Tailtiu was already gone when he looked back.

# CHAPTER 34

The journey back home took most of the day, and Will was forced to stop and hide twice when he heard the sounds of men and horses. It seemed the Darrowans were taking the job of patrolling the area around Barrowden seriously. Then again, it was also possible that word of what had happened to a couple of their sentries in the pass had already been reported. Will assumed that they probably thought someone had attacked the sentries while sneaking *into* the area around Barrowden.

He grew nervous when he got to the area near Arrogan's house. For some reason being caught by his mother was more terrifying to him than being caught by the enemy. He gave the house a wide berth, circling around it to approach the tree that Tailtiu had mentioned from the far side.

The congruence point was right where she had mentioned, and as Will stepped up to it he noticed a set of claw marks on the ground. Something big had scored the earth as well as the bark on that side of the tree. *The goddamn cat,* he guessed. Glancing around, he felt as though something was watching him, but he saw no sign of the feline. He suppressed a shiver and shifted himself to Faerie.

It was dark on the other side, for he had appeared within a small cave. Light entered from an entrance some ten feet away, but the area around him was too dark for him to make out much. He froze when a deep rumbling vibrated through the air, making the hair on his neck stand up.

Could the goddamn cat cross between worlds? Was it making the sound he heard? *Please let that be the cat,* he begged silently. "It's just me," he said aloud.

Something was behind him, and he felt its breath on his neck. Whatever it was sniffed at the air, and Will clenched his eyes shut. The rumbling vanished, and so did the presence he felt. Cracking one eye, he turned his head, but he saw nothing.

Unsure what to do, Will stumbled forward awkwardly. "Thank you," he said to the empty air, feeling foolish.

The area outside was different than the other places he had seen in Faerie, rather than a forest it was a wide field interrupted only by large stones that cropped up here and there. The sun was bright, the wind was cool but not chilly, and other than the strangeness he felt everywhere in the fae realm, it seemed entirely pleasant. He stepped out under the sunshine and nearly tripped over a large branch on the ground.

Except it wasn't a branch. As his eyes focused on the thing, he realized it was an enormous femur, sticky with blood and drying bits of flesh. The rest of the carcass lay scattered around him. Will hastened to put some distance between himself and the remains, noting the numerous other old bones hidden in the grass.

A movement in the distance caught his eye, and he saw Tailtiu across the field, some hundred yards distant, waving her arm to get his attention. She stood beside a massive rock formation that jutted at least twenty feet into the air. Will wasted no time crossing the distance to meet her. She looked nervous when he drew closer.

"How long did you have to wait for me?" he asked.

"Too long," she answered. "This is as close as my people dare approach, and even this is risky." She pushed something into his hand, and when Will glanced at it he saw a piece of paper.

"What's this?"

"You keep asking its name."

Unfolding the scrap, he started to sound out what was written there, a habit he had picked up while learning to read. *Cath Bawlg.*

His aunt clapped her hand over his mouth. "Don't say it, and that goes double in Faerie."

"So the goddamn cat is a native of the fae realm?" asked Will.

Tailtiu shook her head. "It lives wherever it wants. For the past century or so, it has lived here."

Will frowned. "I saw the remains of a lot of kills back there. If something eats here, doesn't it become part of your realm?"

"Not if that thing is already immortal," said Tailtiu. Her voice dropped to a whisper, "And whatever it eats does not return; its prey remains dead—forever—including us."

That was certainly ominous, but it bordered on a topic he had been wondering about. If even the plants and animals of Faerie were immortal, and Elthas was the Lord of the Hunt, what happened to the things he hunted and killed? From what she had just said, it sounded as though they eventually regenerated or returned to life in some fashion. It also made it abundantly clear why the fae feared the Cath Bawlg. *And I've been feeding it an egg every now and then,* thought Will. The more he learned, the more he realized that nothing surrounding his grandfather had been even remotely normal.

Looking around, he saw a distinctive shimmer on one side of the rock formation. "Is that the crossing point?"

His aunt nodded. "It leads to a small spring close to Branscombe. The town is to the south after you cross over."

Will offered her his hand, and together they crossed over, where he found himself once more surrounded by moderately dense forest. The spring was something of a disappointment, for it was little more than a damp place on some rocks that fed a trickle heading eastward through the forest. He supposed it must eventually meet other such flows and become a river, but at this point it wasn't even enough that he would want to try drinking it.

Following a small game trail, they went south, and after just a few tens of yards, Will saw the underbrush open up. There was a road ahead, following an east-west course. Looking out, he could see a wooden wall to the west. Branscombe was within shouting distance.

"You can go home now," said Will. "This is all I needed you to do."

"The bargain was for three days," insisted Tailtiu.

"I don't need you for another day," he said, giving her a hard stare.

She stared back at him unflinchingly. "Then you shouldn't have bargained for three."

There was no way he could enter Branscombe with a naked fae girl beside him. "I thought it would take me three days to get here, or longer," he explained. "They'll arrest me if I try to walk through the gate with you. Humans don't take well to naked girls gallivanting about."

Tailtiu turned away. "They'll arrest you anyway. Mark my words." Then she began walking back toward the hidden spring. "Call me when you need me. I still owe you one more day."

That settled, he walked briskly down the road. An older man with a cart reached the gate just ahead of him, and the two guards there ushered the man through without a word.

Will started to follow the cart through, but one of the men called out to him, "Stop! Who are you, trying to sneak into Branscombe?"

Will drew himself up and straightened his shoulders. "I wasn't trying to sneak."

The other guard broke in, "You were hiding behind that man's cart."

"Walking behind it—in plain view," insisted Will. "You didn't tell that man to stop," he added, pointing to the cart as it pulled away.

The first guard, a man with an impressively bushy mustache, gestured at Will's belt. "You can't bring a sword into town."

"You have swords," returned Will, but then as he looked at the two men he realized they actually didn't. They were equipped with spears and knives. "Well, you have spears anyway."

The mustached guard glanced at his companion. "Ned and I are constables, smartass. The weapons are part of our job. What are you anyway? You're dressed up like a soldier."

"A Darrowan soldier," said Ned as Will handed him his sword and belt. "That's the Prophet's crest on the boy's coat."

Will glanced down at his gambeson and mentally cursed himself for not thinking to remove the embroidered sun on his chest. "I'm not a boy, I'm seventeen. I'm here to join the King's Army."

The guard with the mustache leaned in, fixing Will with a suspicious glare. "Are you a spy, boy?"

Will's jaw dropped. "I'm not a spy. I'm from Barrowden. This isn't even my coat."

The two constables exchanged glances, then Ned said, "Where'd you get the armor from then?"

"They burned my village," answered Will, trying to project honesty. "I crossed the pass to get here. I took this from one of their sentries." When that failed to convince them, he added, "Would a Darrowan try to sneak into Branscombe wearing this?" He pointed at the sun crest.

Mustache rolled his eyes. "Exactly what a Darrowan spy would say. Hand over the belt knife too." As Will did so, the guard went on, "You expect us to believe you killed a soldier and took that gambeson?"

Will nodded his head vigorously. "I caught him by surprise. Look!" He held his staff out for them to inspect. "That's his blood on the wood there."

"You'll have to give up the staff too," ordered Ned, who then handed it to Mustache. "This is probably a murder weapon. Hold out your hands, boy. You're under arrest."

Will didn't resist, holding out his hands while they began tying his wrists tightly together. "I came to enlist," he protested. "If I was from Darrow would I surrender like this?"

Mustache snorted. "Probably trying to trick us into letting our guard down. You won't be fooling us, boy." Taking the other end of Will's rope, he tied a loop in it and tossed it over a nearby post that looked to have been put there for just that purpose.

"Isn't there someone else I can talk to?" asked Will, trying to sound reasonable.

"Sure," said Ned. "You can talk to the magister in the morning. For now, you'll be staying here until the wagon comes to pick you up and take you to the lockup." The two men returned to their posts and resumed staring down the road.

"You didn't even ask my name," said Will. "Shouldn't you do that at least?"

Mustache glanced sideways at him, clearly unconcerned. "What's your name then?"

"William Cartwright."

"Good for you," the guard replied, then looked away.

Will had a moment of inspiration. "There are people in town who can vouch for me."

Mustache sighed. "Oh really? Who?"

"My uncle and cousin, Johnathan and Eric Cartwright. They both joined the army last week. Have someone ask them," said Will.

Ned became animated and hopped as though he was preparing to run somewhere. "Why didn't you say so before? Greg, I'm going to run over to the camp and ask around. I'm sure everyone knows Johnathan and Eric Cartwright!"

Greg began snickering, and then Ned continued, "Is that what you thought we'd say?" The look he gave William spoke volumes. Ned tapped his temple with two fingers. "People always think we're stupid. Being a constable takes a lot more brains than you think, boy. The first thing you learn is never to abandon your post. You'll stay right there and if you have something worth saying, say it to the magister in the morning."

Will shut up. It was obvious he wasn't going to get anywhere. After a few minutes, his body began reminding him of its needs. "Can I have some water?"

"They'll feed and water you at the lockup this evening," said Greg.

"What if I need to pee?" asked Will.

"All the more reason not to give you any water until then," answered Greg, chuckling.

CHAPTER 35

The rest of Will's day was miserable, and the evening proved to be even worse. The lockup proved to be a small, stone room in what was the town's main headquarters for the Branscombe Constabulary. The building itself was two stories tall, with a front receiving desk and a few rooms on the second floor that were used by the constables themselves. Will didn't get to see the second level. He was ushered into the holding cell, which was barely ten feet square.

There were no benches or other furniture, and to make matters worse, the room was already occupied by three other men. There was a large clay pot in one corner, presumably for when they had to relieve themselves. The lid that should have contained the smell of what was within it was broken, and Will's nose notified him that it had already been well used.

The idea of undoing his trousers in such confined quarters with three strangers would have been daunting enough, but their appearances made him even more nervous. One of them was relatively young and slender, with a patchy beard covering a sharp chin. The look in his eyes was threatening.

The second was an older man, slightly soft around the middle, with a grizzled appearance and a mostly bald head. He didn't look quite as mean, but the smell of him was formidable. Apparently, he had been picked up for public intoxication.

The third man was enormous. His head nearly reached the low ceiling, which meant he was probably close to seven feet in height. The man's height wasn't the only thing that was prodigious, for he had broad shoulders and thick arms and legs. There was some fat around his middle, but it was deceptive, for the big man was heavily muscled. Will tried not to look at him, though he wondered how much the man weighed. *He'd probably give a black bear an even fight in a wrestling match,* Will observed silently.

Each of the men had taken a different corner to maximize the space between them, which left only one corner for Will—the corner where the chamber pot was located. Rather than sit there, Will remained by the door, which put him squarely between the skinny man and the giant.

"What are you, some kinda deserter from Darrow?" asked the skinny man, his tone hostile.

"I'm from Barrowden," said Will. "They burned our village, so I came here. The coat is from a Darrowan soldier I killed while I was escaping."

The slender man laughed, but the sound didn't lighten the mood. "You expect me to believe a kid like you killed a soldier? Look me in the eye when you lie."

Will met his gaze, hoping he looked confident as he did. "You can believe me or not. They killed my aunt and cousin. I caught one by surprise and beat him to death with my staff when I was crossing the pass. I would have frozen to death without this coat." He left out the other three men he had killed, since he knew that would be too much for anyone to believe. *Possibly five, if that last one wasn't found before he froze,* he reminded himself.

"My, my, my!" exclaimed the stranger. "That just about makes you a fucking hero, doesn't it? I'm sure that's why they locked you up in here with us undesirables."

Desperate to shift the focus of the conversation, Will asked the only thing he could think of, "What are you in here for?"

"Me?" said the lanky man. "I was lifting someone's purse and got caught." He mimed drawing a knife with one hand. "I cut the bastard and I would have killed him if the guards hadn't jumped on me." He gave Will a sloppy grin, as though he should be congratulated for what he had done.

Hoping to shift the conversation further, Will turned to the big man on his other side. "And what did they put you in here for?"

The big man's lips parted, and he started to reply, "I was—"

The skinny man interrupted. "The big fat one don't speak. Do you, fat boy?"

The big man closed his mouth.

"Want to see something funny, kid?" asked the slender man. When Will didn't reply, he stepped forward and slapped the big man so hard it rocked his head to one side. "This one's as gentle as a lamb. You could piss on him and he wouldn't do anything, would you, fat boy?" He slapped the big man again.

Will straightened up, squaring his shoulders. "Don't do that."

The skinny man slapped the big guy again. "Why, kid? Does it bother you? You should mind your own business. This is the only fun to be had in here."

Something about the cutpurse terrified Will, but he couldn't ignore what was happening. "I said leave him alone."

The thief grinned, stepping back. "Fine, kid. I wouldn't want you to be uncomfortable." He seemed as though he was about to return to his corner of the room, but in a flash he turned and slammed his fist into Will's gut.

The air left Will's lungs with an audible whoosh and he doubled over, unable to breathe. A moment later a boot slammed into the side of his head, knocking him sideways. The padding probably saved him from serious injury, but he was stunned, nonetheless. An idle thought passed through Will's mind, *I wonder if this is how the soldiers felt when I attacked them.* Another kick sent shivers of pain through his side.

The drunk in the opposite corner started yelling to alert the guards, but no more blows came. Will heard some scuffling, followed by a wheezing sound, and when he managed to look up he saw that the giant had pinned the thief against the opposite wall, his massive hand around the slender man's throat. The cutpurse's face was red and shading toward purple, his eyes bulged as he beat feebly at the giant's arm. Then he went limp.

A few minutes later, one of the constables entered the other room and looked at them through the barred window in the door. "What's going on?"

"They're killing one another in here!" screamed the drunk.

It was another ten minutes before the door opened, and Will could see that the other room was full of men. Five constables stood together with small wooden shields and heavy clubs. "Up against the walls!" one of them ordered.

Will complied and soon found himself pressed painfully against the wall. The small cell was crammed full when the rest of the guards entered. "What happened?"

One of them called out, "He's just unconscious."

"That guy attacked us," said Will. "The big man was just defending himself."

"Let's go, John," said the lead guard, addressing the giant. "You know the rules about fighting."

"That other guy is the one that started it," protested Will.

One of the constables laughed. "Looks like he already got what he deserved then." They led the big man out of the cell and shut the door again. A few minutes later he heard the crack of a whip and the sound of a man grunting in pain. Will couldn't help but flinch as it the punishment continued. Fortunately, the whipping stopped after three strokes.

The big man's shirt was bloody when he returned a short while later, and he sank into his corner to lean sideways against the wall. The sight of his obvious pain filled Will with a helpless anger at the injustice of it. When the cutpurse began to rouse, groaning and rolling his eyes, Will walked over to address him.

"Hey," said Will, suppressing the urge to kick the dazed thief.

The cutpurse focused bleary eyes on him. "Fuck off," he replied reflexively.

"What's your name?" asked Will, fighting to keep his voice even.

The slender man's eyes finally focused, and he seemed to take note of the crazed look in Will's eyes. "Dave," he said finally.

"The next time you decide to make an ass of yourself, Dave, I'm going to break something. And next time there won't be anyone screaming for the guards to save your stupid ass." Will glanced at the drunk in the other corner. "Right?"

The drunkard looked uneasy, but he nodded. "Sure."

The thief glared up at Will. "You don't scare me. I've already kicked your ass once."

"Catch me off-guard and maybe you will. But you won't manage both of us, and the big man here has already proved he can wring your scrawny neck as easily as a chicken's before a holiday dinner."

Dave's eyes burned with hate, giving Will ample warning this time. The man surged up from the floor, only to catch Will's boot in his chest. He fell back, and his head slammed into the stone wall so hard he lost his bearings for a moment. Then Will felt something heavy on his shoulder. Turning his head, he saw the big man behind him, a hand on his shoulder.

Dave stared at the two of them for a moment as he recovered, and then his tone changed. "Hey, kid, I was just testing you. No reason we can't be friends. Right?"

Will ignored him and walked back to the other corner before asking the big man, "What did they say your name was?"

The big man answered slowly in a deep baritone, "John, but my friends call me Tiny."

"Mind if I look at your back, John?" said Will. "I know a thing or two about cuts and bruises."

John hesitated, then nodded, resuming his place beside the wall and turning his back toward Will. "Call me Tiny."

Tiny's back was better than Will had expected. Two of the strikes had only left angry red welts, but one had broken the skin. It might leave a scar, but it would probably heal on its own. He would have liked to clean it, but without water or clean cloth, anything he did would just make it worse. He pulled Tiny's shirt back down.

"If they bring us some water later, we can wash it, but I think it will be all right," he told the man. "My name is Will, by the way. William Cartwright."

"I'm Sven," said the now mostly sober drunkard from the other side of the room. "If anybody cares."

"Nice to meet you, Sven," said Will.

The next morning was a disappointment, since it turned out the town magister wouldn't be seeing anyone until the next day. Aside from being allowed out briefly to empty the chamber pot, the only thing to break the monotony was the two meals they were served.

Calling the stuff in the bowls they received a 'meal' was being generous. *Grandfather would have been fine until now, then he'd have probably burned the place down,* thought Will. He almost gagged on the first bite. Whoever the cook was, he seemed to think that the best way to cook oats was to boil them until they disintegrated into a gelatinous goo. The cook also probably didn't know about salt or any other seasonings.

Still, Will was hungry, so he forced down about half of what was in the bowl before he stopped. He just couldn't make himself eat any more of it. When he noticed Tiny eyeing it, he offered the big man the rest of his portion. Tiny lifted the bowl and finished it in two large gulps.

"Thanks," said the big man.

The second morning they were taken out and lined up outside of one of the rooms on the second floor. The magistrate had them brought in one at a time. "Name?" asked the rather severe-looking man when Will's turn came.

"William Cartwright."

The magistrate gave him a bored look. "Care to explain how you came to be at the town gate wearing a Darrowan arming jacket?"

Will repeated the abbreviated story he had given the guards at the gate, mentioning nothing of the men he had fought in Barrowden or the help he had received from his faery aunt.

"You expect me to believe you crossed the pass from Barrowden while it was being defended by Darrowan soldiers?" asked the magistrate. When Will nodded he continued, "And that you slew one of their scouts and stole his armor and weapons?"

"It was dark and snowing, sir," said Will, trying to clarify.

The constable beside him growled. "Address the magistrate as 'Your Honor.'"

"Your Honor."

"You seem to be of age. Why haven't you been taken into the army already?"

"I wasn't in Barrowden when the press g—when the king's men came," said Will. "I came to Branscombe to volunteer."

The magistrate frowned. "Is there anyone who can vouchsafe your stated identity?"

Will nodded eagerly. "Yes, Your Honor. My uncle and cousin were taken into the King's Army a little over a week ago. If they're in Branscombe, they can prove I'm from Barrowden."

The magistrate glanced at the clerk who was seated beside him. "Have a messenger sent to Captain Levan. He can check the rolls. Mister Cartwright, if you will wait over there, we will come back to you once we've heard from the captain."

Will sat on the bench indicated and watched while his three cell-mates had their own moment in front of the magistrate. It turned out that Sven had been picked up for being out after curfew. His wife had locked him out from coming home drunk. Tiny had simply had the misfortune of trying to buy some staples for his father's farm. The town constables had decided that given his size he had to be a deserter, but the truth was that the big man had simply been unaware of current events. His father's farm was rather isolated.

Dave was the only one that Will had no sympathy for. As he had stated, the cutpurse had been caught stealing and then nearly murdered someone when his victim had protested. The magistrate made it clear that under normal circumstances he would have had Dave locked in the stocks for a week and then had him branded as a thief. Given the current state of war, he simply ordered the thief be forced to serve in the King's Army.

That hardly seemed fair to Will, since it was the same sentence given to both Sven and Tiny, even though neither had committed any real crime. Will had the sense to keep his mouth shut, though. *The constabulary might as well be another press gang,* thought Will. *All they do is round people up and then send them to the army anyway.*

It was almost an hour before the messenger returned with a note confirming Will's identity. Even so, he was surprised when the magistrate told him he was free to go. "You can pick up your weapons at the town gate when you leave, Mister Cartwright. Have a good day." Finished with his work, the magistrate stood as though he would leave.

Will gaped. "But..."

"Yes, Mister Cartwright?"

"You sentenced everyone else to serve in the army."

The magistrate gave him a severe look. "I know it may seem as though the local constabulary is simply a— what did you almost call them?—a press gang, but that is not the case. My job is to enforce the law. You have broken none that I am aware of, and your age is below that required to serve in the military, no matter what the king's agents say when they scour villages for able bodies. If you really do intend to enlist, the minimum age for that is sixteen, but that is entirely your business."

"Oh," said Will. "Thank you, Your Honor."

"A word of advice," added the magistrate. "Remove the Prophet's crest from that coat before you show up to enlist. I doubt the king's officers would take kindly to you if they see it."

A few minutes later, Will found himself on the street in front of the constabulary building, holding his steel cap in his hands. He put it on and buckled the strap since it seemed silly to just carry it. He was hungry, but what he wanted most was a bath.

The guard outside was kind enough to answer some questions, and he soon learned that Branscombe had a public bath, but it cost a penny to use. Unfortunately, he had no money, so that was out of the question, as was buying a meal. Without other options he decided he might as well go and present himself at the military camp, so he asked for directions to it.

"Head back out of town," said the constable. "The camp is a quarter-mile northwest. You can't miss it."

Will took the man's advice, marveling at the size of Branscombe as he walked down the cobbled street. It was several times larger than Barrowden and perfectly fit what he had always imagined a city would look like, yet the locals called it a town. *If this is just a town, what is a real city like Cerria like?* he wondered.

At the gate he recognized one of the constables from his previous arrival. "I told you I wasn't a spy," said Will sourly.

Ned grinned at him. "You still look like one to me." He wandered over to the guard post and opened a large wooden box. "I guess you want your things back."

"If you don't mind," said Will stiffly.

Ned sifted through the contents before withdrawing the sword and belt and handing them to the other guard. "One falchion of questionable origin," he said aloud.

The second guard handed it to Will.

"One belt knife, with sheath," added Ned. Will accepted that as well.

"One murder weapon," said Ned with a snicker, producing Will's staff.

With a sigh of long-suffering, Will took his staff and left without replying. As soon as he had put a little distance between himself and the gate, he took out his knife and spent some time picking loose the stitches of the embroidered crest on his gambeson. *At least I learned one thing,* thought Will. *Never show up at a gate with the enemy's crest on your armor.*

In the back of his head he imagined his grandfather's mocking laughter. *I could have told you that, idiot.*

CHAPTER 36

"You're here to enlist in the King's Army?" asked the officer sitting at the desk in front of Will. The officer's official title was lieutenant, though Will had no idea what that meant, and his name was James Stanton. The soldier outside the tent had told him to address the man as Lieutenant Stanton.

"Yes, Lieutenant Stanton," Will responded nervously. The office he stood in was actually a tent with a small table and several stools to sit upon. A clerk of some sort sat at another table on one side with several books and a tall stack of papers on it.

The officer sighed. "You don't have to say that every time you answer. A simple 'yes, lieutenant' or even a 'yes, sir' will be sufficient."

Will nodded, which caused the lieutenant to frown, bringing his dark brows together in a steep 'v' that went perfectly with his sharp mustache. "Nods and casual replies aren't acceptable, however."

"Yes, sir," he said hurriedly.

"Name?"

"William Cartwright, sir." The questions went on for a couple of minutes as the clerk recorded his name, date of birth, and where he was from.

When the main questions had been answered, Lieutenant Stanton jerked his head toward the clerk. "Do you have all that? Please add Mister Cartwright to the rolls." Then he looked back at Will. "Since you've volunteered and brought some of your own arms and armor, you will be listed as a voluntary enlistee. This entitles you to a slightly higher pay than the regular conscripts. You'll receive five silver clima per week and we won't be taking a fee for armor or sword, though you will still be required to pay for your shield and spear. Do you understand?"

Will was confused, which he quickly admitted. "Soldiers pay for their equipment, sir?"

"Conscripts don't," said the lieutenant, "though they are still required to pay for their food and drink, which comes to three clima per week."

"Would it be all right if I was listed as a conscript then, sir?" asked Will.

The lieutenant gave him a cold smile. "We could do that, but conscripts are only paid four clima per week. After expenses they only net one clima. Are you sure you'd like to do that?"

For the first time, Will was glad that he had learned to do simple sums in his head. If the conscripts only received one clima a week then they'd barely make five gold crowns in an entire year, whereas an enlistee would get a little more than ten crowns. "How much is the cost of the spear and shield, Lieutenant?"

"Five clima each," said the officer immediately.

Doing the math, Will realized it would take him five weeks to pay for the equipment, at a cost of one crown, leaving him nine crowns for the year, or four crowns more than a conscript would receive. From the point at which he had finished paying for the shield and spear, he would be making double what the conscripts made. "I think I would prefer to be an enlistee then, sir," said Will.

Lieutenant Stanton smiled again, and this time it reached his eyes. He gestured toward the clerk. "Enlistees need to sign the contract roll, but you can simply make a mark and Sergeant Kavanaugh will witness it."

The sergeant handed him a quill pen and turned a large book around to face him. It appeared to contain page after page of names with an x marked beside them, though occasionally he saw places where someone had written their own name. Curious, Will closed the book and opened it to the first page, which turned out to be a contract for his term of service. He could read it, though he didn't understand some of the meaning. "Five years, sir?" he asked.

The lieutenant and sergeant glanced at each other, mild surprise showing on their faces. "Five years is the standard term for a private soldier. I should have mentioned that. Another difference between enlistees and conscripts is that conscripts are discharged from service as soon as the Royal Marshall decides they are no longer needed." He paused, then asked, "You can read?"

Will nodded, then after a second he hurriedly added, "Yes, sir. I can write too."

"What other skills do you have, Mister Cartwright? We should list those since you may be eligible for other posts after your training period," said Lieutenant Stanton. Meanwhile the sergeant was muttering to himself and thumbing through a separate stack of papers.

"Cartwright, Cartwright, that name rings a bell for some reason," said the sergeant as he searched.

Will answered the lieutenant's question, "I can count and do sums. I'm well versed in fractions, ratios, geometry and stoichiometry. My mother was a midwife, so I've learned a lot about plants and treating wounds and illnesses."

The officer stared at him, his face blank. "Stoichi—what? Were you an accountant or something?"

"It's a type of math used for alchemy, sir. My grandfather was teaching me before he died," explained Will.

The lieutenant nodded. "You'll need to spell that for us when Sergeant Kavanaugh lists your skills. Is there anything else?"

"I'm a fair cook," said Will. "I'm not sure if that matters, though."

Lieutenant Stanton looked thoughtful. "Ever cook for large numbers of m—"

"Found it!" interrupted the sergeant. "Sir, Mister Carwright is listed on the service exceptions roll." He held up another small ledger, pointing at one of the entries.

Lieutenant Stanton's expression changed to one of annoyance. "Is there something you should have told us already, Mister Cartwright? Why are you here today?"

"Sir?" said Will, puzzled. "I came to enlist."

"Then why did someone pay for an exemption for you?" The lieutenant glanced at the sergeant. "Who paid the fee?"

"Baron Nerrow, sir."

Lieutenant Stanton studied Will for a while, his eyes full of questions. Eventually Will felt compelled to say something. "I've met him a couple of times, sir." The lieutenant continued to stare, so Will pointed at his cheek. "I got this from his carriage driver. I saw Lord Nerrow's daughter reach down to pick up a snake and pushed her away. His servant took after me with the coachwhip, thinking I was trying to do her harm."

Lieutenant Stanton shook his head in disbelief. "You're telling me that you were whipped by mistake after saving the baron's daughter?"

Will nodded, forgetting to answer properly.

"And that the good baron decided to buy an exemption for you because of that?"

"That's the only thing I can think of, sir," said Will with a shrug. It was a lie, of course, but he didn't want to admit to being a nobleman's bastard son. He went over to look at the service exemption ledger. As before, he found a short contract statement at the beginning of the book, and he started reading it.

"You may as well put that down and leave," said Lieutenant Stanton. "You've wasted enough of our time."

"I still want to enlist, sir," said Will firmly. "It says here the fee can be refunded if the named individual takes service later." Then he whistled as he saw the cost. Apparently, his father had paid ten crowns to keep him out of the war.

"Mister Cartwright, I don't keep gold here, nor do I intend to fill out the forms to make such a request for you," began the lieutenant.

Will was struck by a sudden inspiration. "My uncle! You don't need to give me a refund. Just mark it in the roll and put my uncle down for the exemption. He's lost most of his family. If I take his place, he could take care of his daughter and sister."

What followed was a long argument that showcased how stubborn Will could be. When it became apparent that he wouldn't win by logic, Lieutenant Stanton tried authority. "Mister Cartwright, I don't think you appreciate your position," he said. "I could have you whipped for insubordination."

Will shook his head. "I'm a private citizen, sir. You'll have to let me enlist before you have me punished."

Lieutenant Stanton turned red at that, and Will wondered if the man might explode, but the sergeant tapped the officer's arm and took him aside for a moment. The two began talking quietly to one another, and although Will's hearing had become slightly better after Tailtiu's healing, he still couldn't quite understand them. He did catch a couple of words, though, 'Nerrow' and 'bastard.'

He clenched his jaw, since it wouldn't do him any good to start a fight over that.

A moment later the lieutenant returned. "Very well, Mister Cartwright. I'll allow you to enlist and we'll release your uncle from his conscription. Are you happy now?"

"Yes, sir," said Will, trying not to smile.

"You can have the rest of the day to explain the situation to your uncle and see him off. I'll expect you back here in the morning to be sworn in. I sincerely hope you aren't assigned to my company, Mister Cartwright," said the officer. "Both for your sake and for my peace of mind."

***

"Will?"

Johnathan Cartwright was surprised, to say the least, when he was brought out to meet his nephew. As happy as Will was to see his uncle, he was momentarily overwhelmed by the thought of the things he would have to tell him. "Uncle Johnathan," said Will, stepping forward to hug the heavyset man.

As soon as they broke apart his uncle asked, "We heard the news about Barrowden. What happened? Are Doreen and the kids safe? Did they get out in time?"

"Let's talk after we get a little farther away," said Will, looking back at the camp. The anxiety in his uncle's voice made it hard for him to reply calmly.

Will's deflection undid the older man and Johnathan's face crumpled. "They're dead, aren't they?"

"Sammy is safe," said Will, his eyes downcast. "Aunt Doreen got her out in time. She shot one of the men after Sammy with your crossbow before—" He couldn't finish the sentence. "She saved Sammy," he said at last.

His uncle's breath was coming in great, heaving gasps, and his next question was almost unintelligible. "And little Doug?"

Will could barely see his own feet, his eyes were so blurry. "He was really brave. He tried to protect them."

"He was only ten," whispered his uncle. "What kind of monsters would kill a child?" Will's uncle sank to his knees.

A quarter of an hour passed before Johnathan Cartwright was able to stand, and when he did he started back toward the camp.

"Where are you going?" asked Will.

"I'm going to kill those bastards," said Johnathan. "I can't do it alone. The army is the best way I can think of."

"Sammy needs you," said Will. "Mom needs you. I left them alone back there."

"They didn't come here with you?"

Will shook his head. "They're living at the old hermit's cottage."

"That's not safe!" said his uncle, his voice rising. "The Darrowans will sweep the whole valley."

"I need to tell you some things, Uncle Johnathan," said Will, glancing around to see if anyone was nearby. "But not here. Come with me. Please?"

His uncle hesitated briefly, then nodded his head and followed Will away from the camp and down the road that led toward the mountain pass. They were almost to the spot that was closest to the spring when his uncle stopped. "How far do we need to go?"

Will met his eyes evenly. "I can take you to them."

"How? It's too late to cross the pass. There will be soldiers guarding it."

"Magic," answered Will. "Can you trust me?"

His uncle's face wavered between fear and anger. "I knew it. That old man really was a warlock, wasn't he? I don't want anything to do with demons or black magic."

"He wasn't a warlock," insisted Will. "He was a wizard, and he did teach me a little. I know enough magic to get you back. It's a shorter walk than the one from your house to my mom's if you'll let me show you."

"What did you sell for your power?" asked his uncle.

After everything he had been through, Will was beginning to lose patience. He wondered if that was why Arrogan had always been so grumpy. Every day that passed, he felt like he understood the old man better. "I didn't sell anything. One of the fae helped me."

"The fae?"

"Do you want to see Sammy and Mom or not?" asked Will, exasperated. "I'm not a warlock. I haven't sold my soul, and even if I did do something stupid like that it wouldn't have anything to do with you." Angry, he stalked away from the road, heading toward the spring. After a moment he heard his uncle start to follow.

When they reached the spring, Will stopped. "There's a door here. I'm going to take your hand and—"

"I don't see a door," protested his uncle.

"That's why I have to take your hand," said Will. "I'll take you with me."

"Where are we going?"

"We'll be in a field. From there I'll lead you across the field to a cave. Inside the cave is another door that you won't be able to see. When we cross again, we'll be back in our world, near the old man's house," Will explained.

"You've lost your mind," said Johnathan.

Tired of explaining himself, Will grabbed his uncle's hand and wrenched them both sideways into Faerie. He was rewarded by the sight of his uncle's jaw going slack as the older man stared around him at the sun-drenched field.

"How did…" began his uncle.

"Come on," urged Will, starting forward. "It's not entirely safe here. The sooner we cross back the better." When they entered the cave, he once again felt as though something was watching him. "It's me," he announced. "This is my uncle. I'm taking him to stay with Mom and Sammy."

His uncle was uneasy, but he couldn't help but ask, "Who are you talking to?" He froze when he heard the deep rumbling coming from all around them.

"Just stay calm," said Will. "He just wants to make sure we are who we say we are—I think."

Again, Will heard the sound of something large sniffing the air, and then the presence vanished. Wasting no time, he pulled his uncle forward and twisted them back, and they appeared next to the tree behind Arrogan's garden. He felt some of the tension release from his shoulders.

"Past all those brambles and bushes is the old hermit's house. Mom and Sammy are there," said Will, pointing out the way for his uncle.

"Aren't you coming with me?"

Will shook his head. "Mom will throw a fit if she sees me. I kind of left without telling her. Tell her I'm sorry."

His uncle started to grab his wrist, but Will twisted through the congruence, taking himself away. He had no intention of getting caught up in that conversation. *He'll tell Mom I'm safe. That's enough,* he told himself.

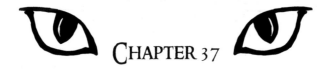

CHAPTER 37

Not having a place to sleep, Will wound up reporting that evening instead of the next morning, and after briefly being sworn into the king's service, he found himself in a large tent that was one of many. At a guess there were nearly twenty men inside, and while they were all strangers what really bothered him was the fact that there wasn't a bed in sight.

The sergeant that had led him in handed him a bedroll. "There's some space over there. You'll be assigned to a squad tomorrow, but for tonight you'll stay here."

"Will I get a regular bed then?" asked Will.

The sergeant let loose an evil laugh. "Soldier, ain't none of us got beds around here. Why would you be any different?" When he saw the look on Will's face he continued, "There's nearly eight hundred men in this camp. If this was a garrison there'd be beds, but not here. Get used to it. Whenever we eventually have to move, it'll be worse."

The bedroll turned out to be a piece of oilskin with a heavy wool liner sewn to one side and a separate blanket rolled up within. It also had extra strips of leather along the edges that seemed to serve no purpose. There was no pillow.

Glancing around, he saw that some of the others had a bag of some sort that they used to rest their heads on, so he asked the man next to him about it.

"That's a kit bag. They'll give you one tomorrow. You keep your necessaries in it, but it makes a shitty pillow too." The soldier laughed after he said it, though Will didn't see the humor.

The next morning Will woke with a sore neck, shoulders, and back. The sergeant was yelling for everyone to muster in front, and he had no sooner put on his boots on and run out than he was told to return and roll up his bedding. That turned out to be indicative of his day as a whole. One of the officers appeared and began calling out names and listing assignments.

Most of it meant nothing to him, so he waited patiently until he heard his name called. "William Cartwright, Company B, Fifth Platoon, report to Sergeant Nash."

As he had seen the last man do, he stepped forward and headed to the left, only to be quickly corrected and sent in the opposite direction. He felt awkward and foolish until he finally found the correct sergeant to line up behind. Sergeant Nash turned out to be a relatively short, clean-shaven man with broad, square shoulders and deep-set, serious eyes. Unlike most of the trainees and soldiers that Will had seen thus far, the sergeant wore a metal breastplate over his gambeson and thick leather vambraces on his forearms. Will was the only one lined up behind him, while the other sergeants had three or four new recruits each.

Fifteen minutes later the assignments were finished, and Sergeant Nash led him away without a word. After a short walk, he stopped in front of a large tent. "This is Barrentine's Fifth. You're in Sixth Squad. Corporal Taylor will handle you from here," said the sergeant.

"Thank you, sir," answered Will, but he paused before entering. "Is that all?"

Sergeant Nash's eyes focused on him then, as though he hadn't really seen Will before then at all. He looked up and down, then stared straight into Will's eyes. "Did you expect a welcoming party, trainee?"

"No, sir, I just——," Will stopped, unsure what he meant to say.

The sergeant gave him a sterile smile, displaying a flat line of teeth that did nothing to warm up the chill in his eyes. "Fine, here's my advice, trainee. Don't fuck up. Embarrass me in front of Captain Barrentine or the lieutenant and I'll flay the hide off your bones. Dismissed."

"Yes, sir," said Will. He remained still, uncertain what to do.

"That means get your ass inside and find Corporal Taylor," barked the sergeant, then he turned and walked away.

Will did as he was told, ducking through the front flap of the tent. Inside were several dozen men, all of whom turned their eyes to him as he entered, making him feel entirely too conspicuous. His ears picked up a few words from the background chatter, primarily 'fresh meat' and 'another kid.' A heavily muscled man who looked only a year or two older than Will called out to him, "Which squad?"

"Uh, Sixth, I think. Are you Corporal Taylor?" asked Will.

"Shit squat," someone muttered, but Will ignored them as the man that had addressed him answered, "I'm Corporal Grim of First Squad. Sixth beds down in the back corner over there on the right. Taylor is the skinny guy sitting next to the giant."

Will followed the other man's eyes and spotted a familiar figure, Tiny, sitting on a bedroll in the rear of the tent. He nodded to Corporal Grim. "Thank you, sir."

"Save the 'sirs' for the sergeants and officers," said Grim. "If a corporal tells you to do something, you do it or get your ass kicked. Other than that, you don't need to kiss ass."

"Um, thanks," said Will. He started for the back, eager to say hello to Tiny.

One of the other soldiers stood up and stepped in front of him as he made his way down the center. The man had a receding hairline and stubble so dense it was on the verge of becoming a beard. "You a private contract?" asked the stranger, his tone slightly belligerent.

Will nodded. "I enlisted yesterday. My name is Will, Will Cartwright."

"You a merchant's son or something?" asked the man.

Will shook his head. "No, why?"

"You must have money if you bought that gear," said the soldier.

"He took it off a Darrowan soldier he killed," said Tiny, stepping up behind Will.

The soldier snorted. "Probably looted it from a corpse." Then he glared at Tiny. "I ain't afraid of you, big man."

"Bickler, sit the fuck down," growled another man standing up nearby. "I'm sick of your shit. Private or conscript, we all bleed the same." Will noticed that the man speaking had a black stripe painted across one arm of his coat, identical to the one that Corporal Grim had.

"All right, Bradshaw," said Bickler. "I was just introducing myself. No need to get pissy." Bickler returned to his spot and sat back down, muttering to himself, "Fucking rich kids."

Will followed Tiny to the back of the tent, and the skinny man that had been pointed out stood and offered his hand. "I'm Corporal Taylor. Welcome to Sixth Squad. Since you already seem to know John Shaw, let me introduce you to the rest of the squad." He waved his arm toward two other men, both of whom Will recognized. "This is Dave Wilson and Sven Fausk."

"We met already, sir," said Will.

"We was locked up together," snickered Dave. "We're old friends now, ain't we, Cartwright?"

Will grimaced. "I wouldn't go that far." Sven started laughing when he heard Will's reply.

"All four of you were locked up?" asked Corporal Taylor. "No matter, we're all on the same team now." The corporal seemed slightly anxious, and Will wondered how long the man had been in the King's Army. He wasn't about to ask, though.

A horn sounded outside, and everyone got hurriedly to their feet. Taylor glanced at Will. "Just drop your bedroll and kit bag over there. It's time for muster." Then he paused. "Where's your kit bag? Never mind, we'll get that sorted out this evening."

Will had hoped that breakfast would be first, but he was disappointed to find out that wouldn't be for another hour yet. He was even more disappointed when he learned why someone had called Sixth the 'shit squad.' Their first duty for the day was digging new latrines and filling in old ones with ash and soil.

Corporal Taylor provided useful information as they went about their task. "Since this is a long-term camp, we dig the trench five feet deep so it will last a week, hopefully. Today is the worst since we're digging a new one and filling the old, but tomorrow we won't have to do much aside from add some ash to keep the smell down. When we're in the field, we only dig them a half a foot deep and we fill them back in each day before we move."

"Do the squads rotate latrine duty?" asked Will hopefully.

The corporal chuckled ruefully. "Afraid not. It's not as bad as you think, though. The other squads aren't resting on their laurels, they're busy digging and hauling for earthworks. We only have to dig this hard one day a week."

"At least they don't have to smell shit while they work," complained Dave.

The trench they were digging was almost six feet in length, which made it a considerable task since it would also be five feet deep. Will stared at the other five latrines nearby. "Do we have to do all of these?"

"No," answered the corporal. "Each company digs its own. Those belong to the other platoons in Company B."

"Why aren't they out here digging theirs then?" asked Dave.

"Each platoon does theirs on a different day, so we don't get in each other's way. Usually we use our own, but if one fills up too quick there's always a new one just in case," explained the corporal. Then he added, "Make sure it's five feet deep or deeper, though. The worst fights are often over latrines if one of the platoons starts slacking."

It took them a little more than an hour to complete the job, so they were one of the last squads to line up for breakfast. The food was much better than Will had gotten in the constable's lockup, being a pottage of peas, carrots, and ham. The ham was present in spirit only, being noticeable only by its flavor and the occasional bit of fat or gristle. They were also given a large portion of boiled cabbage and turnips. His grandfather would have probably had a much more severe opinion, but Will was simply grateful to finally have a full belly.

He felt a little guilty when he saw Tiny staring forlornly at his empty bowl just a few minutes after they had started eating. The big man probably needed more food, but the servers didn't make allowances for size when they scooped out the portions. He resolved to try and save a little for Tiny at the next meal.

The rest of the morning was taken up by a demonstration and then practice taking down and then putting up the platoon tent. They were also instructed in how to load the same into a wagon.

Sergeant Nash was quick to disabuse them of the notion they would be taking their own tent with them. "If and when we actually get the order to move, don't think you'll be sleeping in such luxury. We only bring large tents like this for the mess and similar things. On campaign you'll be sleeping in smaller, five-man tents. Do any of you have questions?"

Will held up his hand and heard several men nearby groan quietly, 'idiot.'

"Trainee, you don't need to hold up your hand. This isn't a school. If I ask for questions just speak up," said the sergeant. "What's your name?"

"Will Cartwright, sir. Where are the smaller tents? I haven't seen any."

Sergeant Nash's face lit up with obvious enthusiasm. "I'm glad you asked!" Turning, he waved his arm at another wagon, covered with a heavy tarp. "Over here behind me you will find thirty of those self-same tents, enough for every squad in the company. Next we will go over how to properly set up camp with those tents. When we're done, you'll be able to unload a wagon and set up in less than fifteen minutes."

Will received a number of dirty looks from the soldiers nearest to him. *It's obvious we'd have been doing this anyway,* he observed silently. He resolved to refrain from asking too many questions in future, though. He figured it probably wasn't a good idea to stand out.

After lunch they spent the afternoon learning drills. The main goal seemed to be to teach them how to move in a line without getting separated, which turned out to be harder than he thought. Learning the commands was easy, but learning what to expect from the men on either side of him was where the difficulty came in.

To make matters worse, Sergeant Nash kept pointing him out, though whether it was because the sergeant liked him or because he simply didn't know the names of the other soldiers, he wasn't sure.

"Stop!" yelled Sergeant Nash once again. "No! Don't anyone move. Stay where you are. I want everyone to take note of what a sloppy bunch of fuckwits you are!" He walked along the front line, stopping in front of Will.

"See this man here? He's where he should be. Look at your positions. Some of you are in line; some of you are so stupid you probably don't have any idea what the word 'line' means." The sergeant pointed at Dave, who was to Will's right. "You! What's your name?"

"Dave Wilson, sir."

"Trainee Wilson, does your mother know what a sorry excuse for a soldier you are? Straighten up! Square your shoulders and get that shield in line! By all the gods, your daddy's dick was probably limp by the time you were conceived, judging by your lazy ass! In fact, it's probably a goddamn miracle you didn't dribble down your momma's leg and end up as a stain on the bedsheets."

Someone laughed, and the sergeant turned on Tiny, who was standing on the other side of Sven. "What's your name, trainee?"

"John Shaw, sir, but most call me Tiny," said the big man.

Sergeant Nash responded instantly, "Why? Is your dick that small, soldier?"

Tiny seemed stunned, but he answered anyway. "No, sir."

The sergeant let out a dramatic exhale. "Well Mister Shaw, I am sure that is a relief to sheep everywhere. Did you find what I was saying to Trainee Wilson to be funny?"

If the insult bothered Tiny, he didn't show it, since he smirked faintly. "Yes, sir."

"Why you would find that funny is a mystery, Trainee Shaw, since by the look of you I expect your mother shat you out one day rather than give birth," said the sergeant.

Tiny didn't answer, but his face hardened and his ears turned red.

"Did that make you angry, Mister Shaw?"

"No, sir," said Tiny.

"Really? I find that surprising, Mister Shaw, since from the look in your eye I would strongly suspect you'd like to stick that spear in my gut. Isn't that true, Mister Shaw?"

Tiny shook his head. "No, sir."

"Perhaps you're worried about being whipped. I'm sure you know that striking a superior is a mandatory flogging. Wounding one is punishable by death," said the sergeant, his voice growing calmer. "In your case, though, I'll give you permission. Would you like to hit me now?"

"No, sir."

"Corporal Grim!" shouted the sergeant. The corporal hastily responded with a 'yes, sir.' Sergeant Nash went on, "Corporal, please make note that I'm giving Trainee Shaw permission to take a swing at me." Then he turned back to Tiny. "Mister Shaw, would it surprise you to learn that the reason you're so fucking big is because your mother was in fact the biggest sow on—"

The sergeant never finished his sentence, because Tiny dropped his spear and unleashed a wild haymaker. Sergeant Nash was expecting it, though. The sergeant leaned back and tilted his head, letting Tiny's fist glance off the top of his helm, then he stepped forward, putting one hand on the back of Tiny's arm and shoving while he kicked the big man's leading foot out from under him.

Tiny fell like a ponderous oak, and the men behind him tripped over one another as they hurried to get out of the way. Meanwhile the sergeant caught Tiny's spear as it started to fall and whipped it around with one hand. The point stopped just below Tiny's chin. Sergeant Nash stood over him with a look of malicious glee in his eyes.

"I would dearly love to put this through your ugly neck, Mister Shaw, but until this war is over you are the property of Lord Fulstrom, and he needs your fat ass to help fulfill his duty to the king."

Will couldn't stand it any longer. "Sergeant—"

Quick as a whip, Sergeant Nash turned and focused his attention on Will. "I did not give you permission to speak, Mister Cartwright, but seeing as I respect your opinion, I will let it go this time. Did you have something to say?"

All eyes were on Will, and he suddenly felt uncertain. Swallowing nervously, he answered, "I just don't think you should goad him about his mother, sir."

The sergeant took a moment and seemed to fall into deep reflection before saying, "Is that so?" Then he looked down at Tiny. "Mister Shaw, according to Mister Cartwright I owe you an apology. Did it hurt your feelings when I suggested that the reason you're such a colossal turd is because your mother was a farm animal?"

Facing the sharp end of a spear had caused Tiny to calm down quickly, but he still answered honestly, "A little bit, sir."

Sergeant Nash planted the butt end of the spear in the ground and offered his other hand to the fallen soldier. "Then I apologize, Mister Shaw. Let me help you up." Once Tiny was back on his feet, the sergeant addressed the company again, "I hope you all learned a lesson in courtesy from Mister Cartwright here."

Will's shoulders itched as he felt everyone's eyes on him.

# CHAPTER 38

That evening Will managed to save a few extra bites for Tiny, but it was an exercise of willpower for him. The long day's labor had given him a tremendous appetite. *But if I'm this hungry, how bad is it for him?* he asked himself.

Dave glanced up at them. "Ain't that cute. Will's got himself a girlfriend."

They ignored the remark, but Corporal Taylor took notice, staring at Tiny for a second as though he had just remembered something. Finally, he said, "They want you lean, Tiny, but given your size you probably need a little more." He offered the big man the last portion of his pottage. "I'll talk to the mess sergeant later and see if they can give you a little more from now on."

Tiny seemed embarrassed, and he stared at his knees. "Thanks, Corporal."

Dave spoke up again. "Sergeant Nash really seemed to love you, Cartwright."

Before Will could reply, Sven jumped in. "Just his bad luck. They always single someone out like that."

Corporal Taylor nodded in agreement, but Will was confused. "What do you mean?"

Sven waved his spoon as he talked to emphasize his point. "This ain't my first time in the army. I served five years as an enlisted soldier when I was a lot younger. They always pick someone and praise them like that. They try to make the others jealous. If he's a good instructor he'll switch to someone else in a few days, before the men get so mad they start laying for you at night. He'll probably turn you into his problem child just to fuck with your head."

Will didn't like the sound of that. Either way, it seemed like he was in trouble. Either the sergeant would start picking on him, or the other men would start trying to catch him alone. Pushing that thought aside, he asked, "What about Tiny? Why'd he go after him like that?"

"He was the best example, given his size," answered Corporal Taylor.

"Example?" Will was confused.

Sven pointed at Tiny with his spoon. "Look at him, he's huge. Probably the biggest guy in the whole cohort. The sergeant needed someone to teach the hotheads in the company a lesson. Otherwise someone might decide to take a shot at him when he isn't looking."

"At who?" asked Will.

"At the sergeant, dumbass," said Sven. "Everyone hates them, or at least they will by the time they get through breaking us in. So what they do is pick out someone that looks big, or maybe someone who seems especially tough. They push 'em until they have no choice, and when the poor guy snaps they put him down fast so nobody else will get the same idea."

"That's stupid," said Dave, spitting out a piece of gristle.

"Would you take a shot at the sergeant then?" asked Sven.

Dave huffed. "I'm not afraid of him, but I guess I'd think twice about it after today."

"I've made my point," said Sven smugly. "You're exactly the sort of asshole that demonstration was meant for."

Dave started to jump up, but Corporal Taylor grabbed his arm. "Simmer down, Wilson. You're gonna have to grow a thicker skin if you want to survive around here."

Dave glared at the corporal and then relaxed. Picking up his bowl, he turned it up and swallowed the last of his food before leaving by himself. Corporal Taylor watched him go, uncertainty written on his face.

Sven was the first to speak, glancing at Will. "He won't last long at this rate. He got into two fights the day before you got here."

"Didn't they punish him for that?" asked Will.

"Only if an officer or sergeant sees it," said Sven. "Most guys try to avoid that, even if they get their ass kicked, and if you snitch the other guys will do worse to you."

"That doesn't seem right."

Sven shrugged. "Fights happen when you cram this many men into one place. The sergeants know that. They prefer it this way. If they started paying close attention, they'd have to have half the men whipped before they even finished training. They'll turn a blind eye unless someone gets hurt bad."

The next days were similar to the first, except that the men spent more time digging trenches and creating long rolling mounds of soil for the earthworks. The idea was to create a wide, sloping trench and pile the earth on one side, effectively creating a wall they could shelter behind. It wasn't too good against arrows, but for that reason they would erect a small timber wall at the top once the earthen portion was finished. Even without the wall, any enemy charging at them would be forced to first run down into the trench and then up the sloping earth, putting them at a serious disadvantage.

They spent the afternoons drilling, marching, and occasionally sparring. During most of the breaks, one of the sergeants would lecture them on the importance of this or that. Will was particularly interested in a demonstration given by Sergeant Eckels from the Third Platoon.

Eckels was a burly man with an exceptionally thick beard. He stepped out in front of them while they were resting after a particularly long drill session. "I'm going to talk to you about the drills we've been doing and why we do them."

No one said anything.

"You may wonder why we spend more time practicing holding lines and using the spear and shield when you have a perfectly good sword at your side. The main reason for that is because we fight as a team, not as individuals. The sword is a backup weapon for when you've either lost your spear, or the enemy has gotten too close for you to use it effectively. We don't spend as much time on sparring because if you do wind up that close to the enemy you won't be sparring. There's no fancy swordplay involved when you're shoulder-to-shoulder and face-to-face. The only effective thing you can do at that point is thrust, and we'll make sure you get plenty of practice at that. Any questions so far?"

Again, no one spoke.

The sergeant gestured to two men standing off to one side. They carried a large, weighted pell onto the field. While most of the practice pells they had seen before were wrapped with leather and padding, this one was different in that a standard padded linen gambeson had been placed over it and tied in place.

"Do any of you know why the padded jack is the one piece of armor we issue to every soldier?" asked the sergeant.

A voice from the back answered, "Because they're cheap." A ripple of laughter followed.

"That's true," said Sergeant Eckels, "but it isn't the only reason. Anyone else?"

"They're warm," said someone else.

"Also a good point," said the sergeant amiably, "but we use them even in summer. Why do you think that is?" He waited a long minute before continuing. "The main reason is because it is the single most effective piece of armor you or I will ever wear. Short of something solid, such as a breastplate or helm, it is the only thing that will protect you from blunt impact."

"I'd rather have the breastplate," said a bolder voice in the crowd.

The sergeant tapped his own highly polished breastplate. "As would I, but you don't wear one of these without first putting on an arming jacket or similar padding. The same is doubly true of mail. A thick gambeson will stop most cuts, lessen the impact of a sword blow, and sometimes even save you from more dangerous things. The biggest danger to you while wearing it is a thrust, or an arrow." He pointed at one of the men sitting close to the front. "Lend me your sword, trainee."

The man unsheathed his weapon, which was standard for most of them, a short falchion with a blade no more than two feet long. The sergeant inspected the edge with his thumb and then whipped the sword across in a fast cut that hit the pell so solidly that it rocked back despite its weighted base. The gambeson had only a shallow cut in it.

"The falchion is one of the most effective types of cutting swords, but as you can see, it wouldn't have gotten through. In an actual fight, it probably would have been even less effective, because men don't generally stand still when you swing at them. That's one reason we will be teaching you how to effectively sharpen them. These swords need a very sharp edge if you're to have any hope of cutting through padding."

Sergeant Eckels returned the sword to its owner and unsheathed his own weapon, which appeared identical. He repeated his slash, but this time the sword cut through the gambeson entirely, though it only lightly scored the leather underneath. "With a very sharp blade and good technique, it is possible to cut the man wearing a padded jack, but it still isn't much of a wound most of the time." Then the sergeant stepped in and stabbed the pell, causing his sword to sink deeply into the pell. "As you can see, a thrust is much more effective, whether your sword is sharp or not.

"The enemies we will face are all wearing similar armor to what you have on now, and the most effective weapon you have for getting to them is the spear you carry, or failing that, a sword thrust," finished the sergeant. "Questions?"

"What if they're wearing mail?"

Sergeant Eckels nodded. "Good question. Mail does give a man better protection, so long as there's padding beneath it. The principle is the same. If he's got mail, a cut won't work. Ever. Your best bet is still the spear. A solid thrust can pierce mail, though you probably won't get as deep as you would otherwise. Failing that, your best bet is to hit them with something heavy enough to break the man under the armor. Anyone else?"

"If they're using spears, and we're using spears, and everyone is stabbing, what's the point of wearing padding?" asked a man somewhere in the middle.

"In the middle of a battle, you may get hit several times, but most of those hits won't be good ones. With a padded jack, your chances of getting wounded are much lower, but the gambeson isn't your only protection." He gestured to one of his other assistants, who carried a shield over to him. "This is your first and best line of protection, a shield. Given the choice between no shield and the best armor, or a shield and no armor, you'll usually want the shield."

He went on for some time after that, emphasizing the importance of prioritizing the placement of the shield depending on whether one was in the front, second, or third row of a battle line.

Once their rest was over, they did in fact practice sparring for a while, despite what the sergeant had just told them about its relative importance. Will learned how to make effective cuts and thrusts and watched practical demonstrations regarding when he should consider switching to the sword or continue using his spear.

In the last hour before the evening meal, they were shown how to sharpen their swords to a fine edge as well as how to maintain their other gear. Will was exhausted by the time they were finally released to go eat.

As they sat in the mess hall, he noticed that Dave's cheek was swollen on one side. "What happened to you?" asked Will.

Dave grinned. "Hah. You should ask about the other guy."

Sven shook his head in disgust. "That shit's going to come back to haunt you."

"I'm the one *they* should be looking out for," bragged Dave.

Will couldn't help but agree with Sven, but he stayed silent. He knew from experience that Dave wasn't one to take advice, especially if it was *good* advice.

Through the rest of the week Will began to get used to the routine, though it still left him bone-tired at the end of every day. Latrine duty, breakfast, and then digging for the earthworks took up the mornings. After lunch, the entire company would practice marching and formation drills for a couple of hours before moving on to either sparring or learning yet another procedure. Some days it was learning to set up and repack their camp before or after a march, other days it was maintenance of their equipment and weapons.

Through it all Will was constantly hungry—hungry for sleep, and hungry for food. He had never had much fat on him, but what little had been there started to melt away. He was pretty sure he had lost weight, but when he looked at his arms, they definitely seemed more muscular. Then again, maybe it was his imagination.

The changes in Tiny were more noticeable. The big man had definitely been a little chubby, but he was losing weight quickly, revealing the incredible muscle that had been necessary to move him around in day-to-day life. Tiny was still massive, but he lost the almost baby-like roundness to his face and began to look positively dangerous.

Will still thought they would all be gaunt and skeletal by the time spring arrived, however. His belly continually reminded him he wasn't getting enough food for all the labor that was expected of him. He began to have dreams about the meals at his grandfather's house, especially the ones that the old man had made personally.

He doubted he would ever have the chance to learn any more about magic, but he kept the source of his turyn tightly compressed, and he occasionally practiced the runes his grandfather had taught him. He did it in secret at first, until he realized no one could see the runes besides him. To the others in his tent, it just looked as though he was sitting quietly. He gained a reputation for being quiet and introspective.

It was almost two weeks after Sven's warning that he found out what the old soldier had been scolding Dave about. Will heard a strange scuffling that roused him from his sleep. The tent was dark, so he wasn't sure what time it was, but he could see dark shapes moving nearby. It looked as though someone had been wrapped in something and was struggling.

Will sat up. The back wall of the tent had been unpegged, and several dark shapes were dragging a figure wrapped in a blanket out through it.

"Don't get up. He ain't worth it," advised Sven's voice quietly.

"Who?" whispered Will.

"Wilson," answered the old soldier. "Looks like some of them got tired of his bullshit."

"What are they going to do?"

"Probably just beat the shit out of him. Depends how much they hate him. Sometimes people get a little too excited," said Sven. "Go back to sleep."

Will kicked off his blanket and began crawling toward the now-loose tent wall.

"Where are you going?" hissed Sven.

"He's in our squad," said Will, unable to think of another reason.

He heard Sven spit in the darkness. "That jackass deserves it. He even beat you up in the lockup. You think you're the only one that heard them drag him out? You ain't. Nobody else is going to go after them. Don't make trouble for yourself."

"What would your excuse be if it was me?" asked Will, but he didn't wait for a reply. Lifting the edge of the tent, he slipped out and followed the men dragging Dave's squirming body away from the camp.

The men taking Dave weren't gentle as they hauled him along between them. They'd gone barely twenty feet before one of them dropped one end of the bundle, and they angrily kicked their victim several times before lifting him back up. *They probably want to take him far enough away that no one will hear,* thought Will. *So, if I'm going to do anything, I better do it now.*

Too scared to think any further, Will charged forward, tackling the man holding Dave's legs from behind, knocking him prone. Jumping up quickly, he swung at one of the men on the left and felt his fist connect with something. Someone was cursing, and Will got several more punches in before something hard hit the side of his head. As he fell, he realized that there were more of them than he had thought. *Eight, nine? I'm screwed.* Hands caught him as he struggled to rise, and someone slugged him in the gut hard enough to take the fight out of him.

They let go of him then, and Will fell to his knees, expecting more blows, but when he looked up, he saw two more people had joined the fight. One was of an average size, but the other was too big to be anyone but Tiny. The two were outnumbered, but Dave's abductors weren't prepared to deal with a giant.

Tiny picked one of them up with one arm and threw him into a tree before wading into the rest of them. The big man took a lot of blows, but nothing seemed to faze him, and with every swing he sent someone else to the ground. The man with him was no stranger to brawls either, and as Will got to his feet he realized it was Sven. By the time Will rejoined them, it was almost over.

And then they heard the sound of whistles, and Will saw several lanterns approaching.

"Run for it," yelled Sven. "They can't see who we are yet."

"What about Dave?" asked Will as everyone began to scatter.

Sven pulled him along. "He's tied up, it ain't like they're gonna think he did it to himself."

The tent wasn't far, and as they reached it Tiny bent down and held the side up for them to enter. Will and Sven shimmied under it, but a voice yelled out before Tiny could follow. "You! Stop, right there!" Tiny dropped the tent flap, and Will and Sven could only listen from their bedrolls as he was taken away.

Looking around the tent, Will doubted anyone was actually asleep, but everyone was making a good show of it. Sven whispered to him, "They'll come in here in a minute. Just pretend to be asleep. Ain't nobody gonna say otherwise."

Will frowned. "How do you know?"

"Trust me. Soldiers hate snitches more than anybody. Remember that when they start asking questions," answered the older man.

Sven's prediction turned out to be accurate. Moments later, men with lanterns men with lanterns threw open the front flaps of the tent and walked down the center, checking to see who was present and who wasn't. They woke the corporals first and then dragged everyone outside for a roll call.

Amazingly, everyone had somehow managed to sleep through the entire event without hearing a thing, even Corporal Taylor. Will felt a strange mixture of awe and surprise as the normally honest corporal lied with a perfectly straight face about what he had seen. Will did his best to emulate the corporal's example when they got to him.

"What's that on the side of your face, trainee? A bruise?" asked Lieutenant Latimer.

"Yes, sir," said Will.

"And you still say you weren't involved in a fight?"

Will shook his head. "I got it during the drills earlier. I moved wrong and caught a shield with the side of my head."

The lieutenant looked at Corporal Taylor. "Is that so, Corporal?"

"Yes, sir. It didn't seem serious, so I didn't report it," lied the corporal.

The questioning didn't go on much longer after that. Dave was released, and ironically, he was the only one who truly hadn't seen anyone, although from the look he gave Will it was obvious he knew who had come after him. Tiny refused to say who had helped him, claiming it had been too dark, and naturally none of the abductors identified themselves.

It was then that Will discovered how quick military justice could be. The men took Tiny to one of the training pells and tied his hands together on the other side of it. They brought out a whip and he was given two lashes. According to the lieutenant, that was leniency on his part. The appropriate punishment was three, but he deducted one lash since Tiny had been acting on behalf of a squad mate.

Will still felt it was unfair, and he felt guilty that night as he watched the big man struggle to find a comfortable sleeping position.

CHAPTER 39

The next morning Will examined Tiny's back. The big man had a scar from his previous time before the whip, and it appeared he would get another from the previous night's punishment. Since he didn't have any freshly boiled water to clean the wound, he accompanied Tiny to the chirurgeon's tent to make sure it was well taken care of.

As they were about to enter, Will caught the sound of a woman's voice and paused. He and Tiny exchanged puzzled glances, as neither of them had seen or heard of a woman in the camp before that moment.

"What is he thinking?" protested the woman. She sounded young. "He should at least send Nerrow's men here. They're going to need more men to hold the pass. Doesn't he realize we have no magical support either?"

"My apologies, milady," answered a deep male voice. "You know I agree with you, but it isn't my place to second-guess His Majesty's judgment." Will thought the man's voice sounded familiar, but he couldn't place it. "I have two teams scaling the mountains via separate routes. They're experienced mountaineers and scouts. We should know more about Darrow's disposition in Barrowden soon."

"It won't matter much if he sends the entire army to Thornton. Even a modest force will be too much for us here," argued the woman. "Eighty-percent of the troops here are green, and our numbers are pitiful."

"At least we have you, milady," said the man. "He wouldn't risk you here if he didn't believe the intelligence regarding Thornton to be extremely credible. It's highly probable that Darrow's incursion into Barrowden is just a diversion."

"That diversion may well roll over us and sack Branscombe," countered the woman. "If he won't send men he could at least send a few sorcerers."

"At least Baron Fulstrom will be with us."

"Fulstrom is old, and his elemental is minor. If the Patriarch sends one of his cardinals, or even a couple of his more modest clergy, we will be entirely outclassed."

Afraid they would be discovered eavesdropping, Will decided to make some noise before entering. "Don't worry, Tiny. They'll fix you up better than new." The conversation inside ceased, and after a count of ten Will opened the tent flap.

A man wearing a full mail byrnie, as well as a breastplate and greaves, exited the tent. Will had never seen the man close up, but he recognized him immediately as Sir Kyle Barrentine. Sir Kyle was one of Baron Fulstrom's knights and the captain of Company B. Will and Tiny both snapped to attention and saluted, placing a fist over their hearts.

"At ease, men," said the captain. He left without looking back, and Will and Tiny waited a moment before entering the tent.

Will's eyes went wide with surprise when he stepped inside, and he stumbled deliberately, hoping to cover his reaction. The woman in the tent was a sorcerer, as evidenced by the two elementals hovering invisibly over her shoulders, one of water and the other of earth. Her hair was tied back and hidden beneath a simple yet elegant wimple, but despite the covering, Will spotted a small, black wisp of hair sneaking out beside one temple.

Two startling sapphire eyes locked on Will as he straightened up from his mock fall. "Are you all right?" she asked. "Is it your leg?"

Will chuckled nervously. "No, I'm just clumsy. It's my friend." He gestured at Tiny.

She indicated a low bench beside a table. "If you'll sit here. What's your name, soldier?"

Tiny sat. "John Shaw, if it please you, milady."

The woman waved her hand dismissively. "None of that, Mister Shaw. I'm just a nurse. You'll get me in trouble if someone hears you treating me like nobility. I'm afraid Doctor Guerin is away today so it's just me here. Are you the poor fellow who was punished last night?"

Will stood by quietly, watching as she lifted Tiny's tunic and examined his back. *She's obviously lying, but why?* The woman seemed familiar to him, but he couldn't place where he had seen her before. With the gown and wimple, he couldn't see much aside from her face, but that alone was striking enough that he didn't think he could have forgotten such a beauty.

Tearing his eyes away from her, he looked around the interior of the tent, noting several empty cots. To one side was a portable, wood-framed screen, and at the base he saw a shadow cast by someone's feet. Looking closer, he caught a glimpse of mail sabatons. Will lifted his eyes and caught the woman staring at him. "Uh, is there someone…" he began to ask.

She smiled. "It's just a patient. I put the screen there to give him some privacy."

More like a bodyguard, thought Will. *Who is she?*

The nurse went back to cleaning Tiny's wound, keeping up a continuous, light banter to set the big man at ease while she worked. Will didn't pay much attention to it. He was too busy studying her without being caught staring. Then he heard something that brought his mind back to the present. "You haven't told me your friend's name," she said to Tiny.

Will met her eyes again. "William," he said simply.

"Mine is Isabel," she replied, then her lips turned down slightly as she frowned. "What happened to your cheek?"

He covered his cheek self-consciously with one hand. "Nothing much. Just an accident when I was small."

"Looks like it was pretty bad, judging by the scar. What were you doing, trying to impress a girl?" she asked.

"Uh, no. It was just a fall…" he lied, "…caused by my own stupidity really."

Her eyes twinkled mischievously. "That's very modest of you. Most would brag about something foolish, or claim they got it saving a damsel in distress."

Will shook his head, but her attention was already back on Tiny. "I think this needs a few stitches. Can you bear a little pain for me Mister Shaw?" she asked. Tiny nodded, and she looked up at Will. "Would you mind helping? I need someone to hold the edges together."

He nodded and moved forward while she brought out a curved needle and thread. Just before she started, Will pinched the skin gently together.

Isabel smiled. "Yes, exactly there. You must have read my mind, William. Have you stitched someone up before?"

"No," he lied. "It just seemed like the best place to start."

Tiny was a good patient; he flinched slightly when the needle passed through his skin, but otherwise held still. Isabel's fingers moved quickly, and she deftly closed the cut on the big man's back with tight, neat stitches. Will moved his hand as she finished each stitch to make it easier for the next.

When she was done, Isabel tied the last knot and clipped the end of the thread. Then she stood and stretched. "You did well, William. You didn't seem squeamish at all. Most people get nervous when they see blood or needles."

Will shrugged. "It's never really bothered me."

Isabel wrapped a long strip of linen around Tiny's torso several times before instructing him to put his tunic back on. "Be sure to come back in the morning so someone can check it and change the bandage."

Tiny thanked her and they started to leave, but she put a hand on Will's arm at the last moment. "What company did you say you were in?" asked Isabel. Then she added, "I have to report on everyone that receives treatment and what unit they're in."

A horn sounded and Will darted outside, pulling Tiny along. "Sorry, we're late for breakfast!"

Tiny looked at him strangely as they hurried along. "I think she liked you."

"Don't be ridiculous," said Will, glancing back at the medic tent. Isabel had finally gone back inside. "Go on to the mess tent. I'll be there in a few minutes."

The big man seemed reluctant, but after a moment he relented and went on by himself. Will took a different route, and once he no longer in sight of the medic tent, he circled around to approach it from the back side. He stopped once he could hear Isabel's voice. His hearing had gotten substantially better since Tailtiu had healed him. At fifteen yards, it wouldn't be obvious to anyone watching that he was eavesdropping.

"Danner," said Isabel, her voice firm.

"Yes, milady," answered a male voice that Will presumed was that of her bodyguard.

"Find Lieutenant Stanton. I want to know that soldier's full name and how he got here," she ordered.

"The big one, milady?"

"No, the other one," she replied.

"Begging your pardon, milady, but William is a common name. Without knowing what town he comes from or his company, it will be difficult," said Danner.

"He's from Barrowden," said Isabel confidently. "I can't remember his surname, but he's probably in the same company as the man I stitched up. I believe he said his name was John Shaw."

"May I ask why you're interested in him?"

Isabel paused before answering. "He isn't supposed to be here. After you find out his name, tell the lieutenant I want to see him. In person."

Will left after that, rather than risk being seen if her bodyguard stepped out too quickly. His head was swirling with questions that had no clear answers. Why was a noblewoman posing as a nurse? How did she know he was from Barrowden? The thing that bothered him most was wondering why she seemed so interested in him. Had she seen something unusual when she looked at him?

He vividly remembered his grandfather's warnings about being caught as an unlicensed wizard. They'd accuse him of being a warlock. It hardly seemed fair, since he hadn't the faintest idea how to do anything useful with his magic.

He found his place in the mess hall and ate with mechanical efficiency, lost in thought. Sven and the others tried to draw him out, but he remained quiet through breakfast. Once or twice he looked up and saw Tiny watching him, but the big man didn't say anything.

Later that morning he received another surprise when someone from the company digging near their section recognized him. "Will!"

He knew the voice. He ran up the mound of earth and saw his cousin standing near the top. "Eric!" The two embraced.

"What are you doing here? I heard Dad was given an exemption, but I didn't know you were here," said Eric.

The others from his squad were staring at him, and Will saw Corporal Taylor frown. He had too much to say to simply blurt it all out. "We need to talk," he told his cousin. "Can we meet later? After supper?"

"Where?"

"How about by Company B's latrine?" suggested Will. It wasn't an ideal spot, but it was one of the few places he was allowed to go on his own during his severely limited free time.

Eric understood. "Sure. See you there tonight."

They parted and Will returned to digging. Corporal Taylor walked over to him. "Who was that?"

"My cousin," he answered. "I haven't seen him since before Barrowden was burned."

"I bet you're glad to see him," said the corporal amiably.

Will stared at the earth. "Yeah, but I have a lot of bad news to give him."

"Take your time when you see him then. If anyone asks why you're gone so long, I'll tell them you have the piles," offered the corporal helpfully.

"Thanks," said Will wryly.

That evening he rushed over to the latrines as soon as he was free, though his feet felt heavy as he did. Eric was there ahead of him, waiting. His cousin waved when he spotted him. They hugged once more and then Eric pushed him out to arm's length. "We heard about Barrowden a few weeks ago. How bad is it?"

The food in Will's stomach felt like a rock. "Really bad. They burned the whole village."

"What about Mom, Doug, and Sammy? They got out, right?" There was desperation in Eric's eyes, though he was doing his best to control it.

"Sammy is safe," said Will. "I didn't get there fast enough to help the others."

Eric's face was dark, his eyes swelling. "Then Mom, and Dougie?"

"They died trying to protect each other," said Will. "Your mom got one of the raiders with your dad's crossbow."

His cousin crouched, putting his hands on the ground as though to steady himself and hanging his head. "How much did you see?"

"It was mostly over before I got there. There was smoke everywhere. It was hard to see, but it looked like they died quickly without much pain. I grabbed Sammy and ran to my house."

"And your mom?"

"We got out before the soldiers got there, but the old man died trying to keep them from following us."

The two cousins remained together for half an hour, but most of their time was spent in silence as Eric was no longer able to speak clearly. Will sat beside him, feeling numb and dead inside. The only comfort he could offer was an arm around Eric's shoulders.

When Will finally returned to the tent, the first person to approach him was the last one he wanted to speak to. Dave grinned at him. "I saw you with your girlfriend over by the latrines. When will the happy day—" The thief stopped when he saw the expression on Will's face.

Will's fists were balled up so tightly that his knuckles had turned white. Deep down, he hoped Dave would go on so he could vent his anger on the man, but the ex-cutpurse surprised him.

"Whoa, sorry. I didn't realize it was something important." That said, the other man backed away and went to his bedroll. Corporal Taylor walked over and began whispering into Dave's ear, explaining what he knew of the situation.

Everyone left him alone until lights out.

CHAPTER 40

The next couple of months went by slowly for a couple of reasons, the first being that Will was anxious to get back to Barrowden. Aside from Eric's family, there were a lot of people he was worried about, like the Tanners—or Annabelle Withy. He tried to be rational. Chances were most of them were dead, but it ate at him not knowing.

The other reason time moved so slowly was that he was miserable. The constant drills and training had taught him new things about fatigue and exhaustion. His body had adapted, so it wasn't as bad anymore, but the constant supervision and lack of freedom was beginning to drive him slightly mad.

Once his first eight weeks were finished, he was told he was no longer a trainee, though he didn't feel any different. He had paid off his debt for the spear and shield and had six silver clima in his purse, more money than he had ever personally possessed in his entire life. Unless one counted that time when he had briefly held the gold crown that he had used to pay his aunt.

Since he was no longer a trainee, he was entitled to one day of recreation every two weeks, which seemed rather pointless since he didn't know anyone in Branscombe. Free days were arranged by squad, which meant he could go into town with Tiny, but Eric was in an entirely different company, so their days would never line up.

The first time he had the opportunity, he declined Corporal Taylor's offer to go into Branscombe together. He could tell his decision disappointed Tiny, but Will had one thing to do that came before everything else. Starting early, he visited the town's market and bought everything he thought Sammy and his mother were probably missing: salt, sausages, cabbage, lard, flour, dried beans. He even bought certain perishables, like milk and butter.

No matter how long he thought about it, he felt certain there were things he probably hadn't considered, but he did the best he could, and when he was finished his purse was empty. Heavily laden, he left town, keeping a close eye on the road behind him. It wouldn't do for any of his fellow soldiers to wonder about his destination. Then he went home.

The journey was short and unremarkable, taking only a matter of minutes, but when he reached his grandfather's house he hesitated. *Maybe I should just try and leave everything on the porch,* he thought, dreading the idea of facing his mother.

He nearly jumped out of his armor when he heard Sammy scream from the direction of the garden. Turning around, he barely managed to angle the hilt of his sword away so it wouldn't hit her in the stomach before she slammed into him at a full charge. She was slightly taller than he remembered, but that hardly mattered as she clung to him, repeating his name over and over. "Will, Will, Will… Do you know how worried we were? How could you do that? I thought you'd be dead for sure! Then Dad came back and we knew you weren't dead, but I was still mad! And your mom! Aunt Erisa nearly lost her mind. What's all this stuff?"

He had dropped his bags to catch her.

"Is that your shield? Your face looks so skinny. Why aren't they feeding you more? Is Eric all right? Dad said he hadn't seen him since they were conscripted. Is anyone picking on him?" The questions kept tumbling out of her at such a pace that Will couldn't hope to remember them all.

"William?" his mother's voice called tentatively from behind him.

Disentangling himself from Sammy, he turned to face her. She looked old, too old and fragile to be the woman who had raised him, and the expression on her face brought his guilt roaring to the surface. "Mom."

She took several hesitant steps toward him and he had to caution her, "Watch out. There's a clay jar full of milk in that bag. It was expensive—" Ignoring his advice, she stepped over the bag and put her arms around him.

Neither of them spoke for a while, but eventually she told him, "Make no mistake, I'm still furious with you. Especially so, since you brought Johnathan back and didn't even have the decency to let me see your face."

"I know, Mom. I'm sorry."

She stepped away and took note of the bags scattered around him. "Sammy, help me. We should take these things inside."

"Let me, Mom. I brought it."

"Nonsense. Go inside and take off that thing you're wearing. It reeks to high heaven. I've never smelled such a stench. You need a bath before anything else." The disgust on her face made it clear she thought his gambeson should be taken far away and burned.

There was nothing he could do but agree. He knew well how stubborn his mother could be. She and Sammy buzzed around him like flies, ushering him into the house and forcing him to strip down while they built up the fire to warm the front room. Sammy let out a gasp when he removed his padded armor and tunic—not because of his near-nakedness though; she had grown up with two brothers.

"Whoa! Look at your muscles!" she exclaimed.

Erisa intervened. "Sammy, take his clothes outside and wash them. Twice."

Two hours later, he was clean and sitting by the fire in one of his grandfather's old robes while his clothes were drying by the fire. His uncle had returned by then, and Will spent a considerable amount of time telling them about everything he had been through over the past couple of months.

His mother started to cook, but Will went over and told her to take a break. "You've been cooking for the three of you for the past few months. Let me."

She looked at him curiously. "You've hardly had a moment to yourself in ages with all the training. Wouldn't you like to rest?"

Being in his grandfather's house again had brought back quite a few memories. "I haven't been allowed to cook since I left. I miss it."

Erisa didn't argue any further, so Will set about his task. He had spent entirely too much on the pork tenderloin he had bought, partly because of his guilt, but he had also been imagining what he would do like to do with it. He cut the meat into four thick chops and melted some of the lard in the pan before adding them. "I saw some wood sorrel outside," he said without taking his attention from the pan.

His mother smiled and stepped out. She returned a few minutes later with several good handfuls of green sorrel leaves and stems. They looked a lot like clover, but Will knew from experience the taste was entirely different. Sorrel had a sour flavor that suited pork and fish.

While the meat finished, he bruised the leaves and put them in a bowl. Then he nodded at Sammy. "Mash them as much as you can, then add a little water and strain them through a piece of cloth."

As she started that, he took the meat out of the pan and sautéed some cabbage briefly before removing that as well. Then he added flour to the drippings and made a roux. "A little milk at the end and we have a nice cream gravy," he said, speaking to himself. Once the sauce was done, he added the cabbage back in and finished cooking it.

"There you have it," he told them as he divvied up the food. "Pork tenderloin with a sour sorrel sauce and creamed cabbage."

Everyone was smiling as they ate, and Sammy made no effort to hide her delight. "Is this magic?" she asked. "I've never had anything so good."

"The old man would have probably called it passable," said Will dryly. "If I had thought to bring some honey and mint, I could have made something even better. Of course, it's too early for mint."

"Actually, I've been growing some indoors," said his mother. "It's always handy."

Once the food was done Sammy cleaned up and the conversation returned to serious matters. "Have the reinforcements arrived yet?" asked his uncle.

Will scowled. "No, and from what I overheard there won't be any."

"That's insane," growled Johnathan. "Doesn't the king realize that won't be enough?"

"They seem to think the attack here is a diversion," said Will. "Lognion is sending the bulk of his army to Thornton to fend off an attack there. Supposedly the Darrowan fleet is going to make a landing somewhere near there."

Unable to contain himself, Will's uncle got to his feet and went to stand by the door. "The fool! I haven't risked getting close, but I've seen enough to know this isn't a diversion. There are several thousand men camped around Barrowden, and they've spent the winter clearing and widening the road. The Patriarch is obviously planning to march the rest of his army through here in the spring."

"Someone has to warn them," said Will, thinking aloud.

"Shouldn't that be you?" asked his mother. "You're going back this evening, aren't you?"

His uncle shook his head. "How? He can't just go up to one of the officers and tell them he used magic to get here and return. Even if they believed him, he could be arrested for being a warlock."

"I'm not a warlock," insisted Will.

"A sorcerer then," said Johnathan, waving one hand dismissively.

"I'm not that either," said Will. He was beginning to understand why his own questions had irritated his grandfather so much. "But you're right. I could be arrested as an unlicensed wizard." An idea came to him then. "I don't have to report it in person, though."

"What do you mean?" asked his mother.

Rising, Will headed for the door that led to the back room of the house. "I'll write a note. I think I know someone with enough power to get the information into the right hands." Opening the door, he was surprised to see that the room had changed. The bookcases were still there, heavily laden as before, but the top of Arrogan's desk was covered with clothes. "Where's the parchment and ink?"

It turned out that his mother had taken to using the desk as a worktable while mending their limited supply of clothing. "I put everything in the cabinet there," she said, indicating a cupboard built into a stand next to the bed. While Will brought out what he needed, she cleared away the top of the desk.

Will found the inkwell, several quills, blotting sand, and a small but valuable stack of parchment. Considering its cost, Arrogan had only let him practice his writing with actual parchment on a few occasions. Usually he had to make do with slate and chalk. He hoped the person who eventually saw his note wouldn't discredit it simply because of his poor penmanship.

On top of the parchment there was a large, leather-bound book. Unlike most of the books he had seen, there was nothing stamped on the cover or spine. He could also see a strange haze of magic hovering around it. Curious, he opened it. The first few pages were blank, but the fourth page seemed to be a title page, for written on it in large bold letters were the words, 'Journals Are Stupid.' The calligraphy was crude compared to what Will had seen in other books. *Almost as bad as my hand,* he thought with a smile.

He turned the page, and on the back close to the bottom, he saw something else. Studying it carefully, he realized it was another line, written so small as to be almost illegible without a magnifying glass: 'and so is Aislinn.' *Did Grandfather write this?* The lettering was far different from what he had seen in the past. Arrogan's penmanship was neat and precise, completely unlike the clumsy writing on the page. The next page held the first entry:

> *Y98 Earrach, Feabhra 10*
> *To whoever finds this, know that I am writing under duress. My teacher insists that writing is good for the soul, but that is in fact simply an excuse for her torture of this unfortunate prisoner. I have been encouraged to use this time to record notable events or lessons so that I can*

reflect on them in the future. Therefore, I will make this a record of my abuse at the hands of that cruel woman.

Feabhra 11

Nearly died last week (before starting this journal) but I decided I should make a mention of it here so I wouldn't forget. She (who should not be named) put me through a period of torment unlike anything ever experienced by man or woman. She claimed it was to prepare me for wizardry but that seems unlikely to me. Each morning I was put under a foul spell and forced to endure extreme pain for most of the day. Only at bedtime would she remove the spell and allow me to rest. I finally succeeded in escaping the pain only by twisting my soul into a perversely small knot. She claimed this was her goal all along, but I strongly suspect otherwise.

Feabhra 13

She refused to feed me today. What does cleaning floors have to do with magic? Answer, nothing. I already know she can clean them with a simple spell (which she refuses to teach me, along with anything else useful). Thus begins my slow starvation unto death.

Feabhra 14

After completing a hellish number of tasks, I was allowed food today, if what she prepared could credibly be called food. Once I had tasted it, I realized that deprivation might be a kindness.

"It's his journal," muttered Will. Year ninety-eight was nearly a hundred years after the War for Independence, which didn't make sense if Arrogan had fought in that war.

His mother's voice spoke from behind his shoulder, startling him. "I think the dates are in Darrowan years. Ninety-eight is around two hundred years before year one of the Terabinian calendar."

Will looked at his mother. "Have you read this?"

She nodded. "Not all of it yet. I found it after you left. From what I've seen, he wrote in it almost daily near the beginning, but later he started to skip weeks and months. Toward the middle he begins to skip entire years. In the later portion he skips decades, until you show up."

"Me?"

Erisa smiled. "You made a deep impression on him, I think."

Will thumbed through the pages in the latter half of the journal. His mother put her finger on the page when he reached the right spot. "Here," she told him.

> *Y770 Earrach, Marta 17*
> *Erisa's brat is just as stubborn as his mother. I'm still not certain why I agreed to help her. Maybe I'm starting to go senile. I can't have too many more years ahead of me, so it makes little sense for me to ruin them with such a burden, yet here I am. If I can teach the kid to hide his differences and avoid doing anything stupid he might live a normal life.*
>
> *Not sure why I care.*
> *Marta 20*
> *Will asked if he could call me Grandfather today and I didn't know what*

to say. The boy is obviously looking for a father figure of some sort, and I suppose I can't blame him since Mark Nerrow's biggest contribution to his life is making sure his wife's family didn't murder him in infancy. His mother did the same years ago, and I never had the heart to tell her that I didn't have a clue if we were related or not. After so many centuries it's possible I'm related to half the people in Terabinia, or none of them. I lost touch with the world for so long it's hard to say.

Why he would look to me is a mystery, I've certainly done him no favors. I definitely haven't been nice to him. Sometimes his innocence makes me angry, though in all honesty I'm probably angry with myself for all the mistakes I made back in the day. Having him around has brought up all sorts of things I would rather forget.

Y770 Fomhar, Lunasa 3

I dreamt about her again and woke up in a cold sweat. It's been decades since the nightmares bothered me. I was thinking about letting the boy sleep in my room during the winter, but if this continues it would only frighten him. Not sure why the dreams have returned. My first guess is that it's his terrible cooking. He and Aislinn could have competed for worst dish if there were contests for such things. Or it might be because he reminds me of myself back when I was his age, stupid and stubborn.

Fortunately, one of the other village brats brought a cot for him. At least I don't have to feel guilty about him sleeping on the floor anymore.

Lunasa 18

The little shit managed to get himself into serious trouble. Who eats strange plants? He claimed to be able to sense whether plants are edible or not, so he's definitely more sensitive than I thought. I may have been wrong to choose not to teach him. Either way, it's obvious the fae were hoping to trap him.

The only good thing about the day was scaring the shit out of Elthas again. I also saw Tailtiu, which hurt more than I thought it would after all this time. How long does it take for the heart to stop caring? Apparently four centuries isn't enough. Thankfully Aislinn wasn't there or I might have done something truly stupid.

Either way, I have to teach him now. I don't have the heart to abandon the boy.

Lunasa 21

He managed to reach the first order without dying. Not that I thought he wouldn't, but I used the later technique rather than the one Aislinn used with me. Doing it all in one day was far more traumatic, but at least it spared him from suffering for a full week as I did. Not sure if he would agree, though. The last half of it was rough, so I used a link to keep a close watch on him. Hurt like hell.

I almost gave up near the end before he finally got the hang of it. I don't know why I put myself through that. It isn't as though I like the kid, although he is pretty damn funny sometimes.

Y770 Fomhar, Deireadh 7

Nerrow showed up. The boy is still getting used to the second order. I followed him to make sure his noble father didn't attempt any jackassery. Surprisingly the pompous prick offered to send the boy to Wurthaven. Of course, the fools there would only ruin my work at this stage, but it might be useful for the kid later.

Y770 Geimhreadh, Noilag 19

He managed the third order and I don't think I've been this proud since Valmon made it. Hopefully he'll turn out better, but at my age I probably don't have to worry about living through it if he goes rotten. The kid has a good heart, far better than my last student, even if he's as dense as a rock sometimes. No less remarkable, his cooking has greatly improved (not that I'd tell him). Will has a tendency to experiment with edible wild plants, which often leads to surprisingly tasty results.

Not sure which is the better legacy, leaving the world with a great wizard or a great chef. It certainly doesn't lack for shitty food and mediocre magic these days.

Will had to stop for a minute to wipe his eyes. The most the old man had ever said about his food was that it was edible. "I'm on to you now," he mumbled to himself. Closing the book, he glanced up at his mother, who was still watching him. "I'll read more next time." It was getting late and he needed to write his note and return before lights out.

"Read the last entry before you put it away," advised his mother.

He looked askance at her, but Erisa didn't say anything. Opening the book again, he leafed to the end but discovered that the last quarter of the book was blank. He turned the pages back until he found the last one with writing on it.

> *Y771 Geimhreadh, Sauin 5*
>
> *He's making progress. Not the fastest I've seen, but certainly respectable. Will has a good head on his shoulders. If he can survive the ravages of stupidity that come with youth he'll be someone worth talking to someday. He's finished learning the runes, but his form is still rough. There are rumors of war and it seems that Darrow may invade in the spring. I should be able to start the boy on Clerides', Foundations of Spellcraft, this winter. Just learning the source-link spell would be enough to give him a powerful means of protecting himself should the need arise, especially since his staff-work is still a little clumsy. It won't help if he meets a skilled mage, but he's probably more at risk from ordinary soldiers at this point.*

His grandfather's handwriting stopped there. Source-link? Was that the evil green line his grandfather had so often used to paralyze him? He'd witnessed Arrogan using it against soldiers of Darrow right before he died.

Erisa tapped him on the shoulder. When he looked up, Will saw that she was holding a thin book. "I spent a few days looking for it after I read that," she said. The cover of the book was embossed with dark letters, *Foundations of Spellcraft*. "You should take it back with you."

Will shook his head. "I don't have anywhere to keep it. A book like this could probably get me in a lot of trouble if someone saw it." He took it from her hands and turned through the first few pages, which seemed to be an overly wordy introduction. Will's fingers stopped in the middle of the second chapter when he saw a diagram. The title above it read, 'A Simple Spell for Linking Turyn.'

"Lun, sarcat, kolbet," said Will, reading to himself. *It's just three runes.* The diagram showed them linked in what appeared to be an acute triangle. That was inevitable, of course, if they were drawn in that order and were all created from the caster's perspective. Arrogan had been insistent that runes should always be drawn in particular directions. He read the paragraph beneath the diagram:

An acceptable spell for beginner instruction, although care should be given to ensure students are not allowed to use it on one another in unsupervised circumstances. The structure is simple and only a small expression of turyn is required to activate. Dismissal occurs with cessation of concentration. Students should be cautioned against separating the target's will from their source as this is not only painful for the target, but the caster as well, due to the linkage. In extreme cases death can result. In general, the caster must have a far greater discipline of will than the target or the spell will fail.

He shut the book with regret. Will wanted to study it in detail, but there simply wasn't time. Perhaps on his next free day he could come back. He was fairly confident he could remember enough to try that one spell, however, if he had some time alone. Focusing on the task at hand, he wrote out a letter that he hoped would be sufficient to warn the army of what was happening in Barrowden.

> *Isabel,*
>
> *Darrow has moved large numbers of men into Barrowden, which I have seen with my own eyes. I don't have an accurate count, but their camp is many times the size of this one. I would guess that there are at least several thousand soldiers there. They have also been busy during their occupation of the area, primarily in building a fortified base to operate from and in widening and improving the road that leads to Darrow. I will let you draw your own conclusions on what this means for the spring, but it seems fairly obvious what they plan to do.*
>
> *Please forgive me for hiding my identity as well as the means with which I obtained this information, but do not discount this letter because of that.*
>
> *Sincerely,*
> *A friend of Terabinia*

With that accomplished he said goodbye to his mother, uncle, and cousin, and set out for Branscombe again.

# CHAPTER 41

Will made it back with half an hour to spare before lights out. Sven was already asleep, snoring loudly, and his nose informed him that the man had had quite a bit to drink. Dave was still awake, though the ex-thief was lying down as well. Dave's eyes tracked him blearily as Will sat down on his bedroll.

"Where've you been?" asked Dave.

"Out and about," said Will. "I did some hiking."

Dave stared at him incredulously. "Hiking? You've been cooped up in this stupid camp for two months and the first thing you wanted to do was go hiking? Don't we get enough exercise every damn day?"

"I just wanted to be alone. Being around people all the time feels oppressive," responded Will, hoping the other man would buy his explanation.

"You missed a good time," said Dave, smiling with his eyes closed.

Tiny entered then, giving Dave a conspicuous glare as he found his seat. When Dave started to speak again, Tiny growled. "Go to sleep."

"Fine, fine," mumbled Dave.

Will raised his brows. "Did you have fun, Tiny?"

The big man shook his head, then pointed first at Dave then Sven. "That one needs a leash, and this one had to be carried."

"Did you drink any?"

"I don't drink," Tiny said flatly.

"Why not?"

"People always want to fight. I have enough trouble already."

Will had wondered about Tiny's reluctance to fight before. "Why don't you like to fight? You seem like you're built for it."

Tiny shrugged. "Small men are always looking for someone big to fight, but for me, there's no winning."

"Huh?"

"If I fight and win, everyone hates me. 'Look, the big man is picking on everyone,' is what they say. If I fight and lose, I'm bruised and humiliated," said Tiny. "Usually I just refuse to hit back, but then people think I'm dumb."

Will remembered what had happened with Dave when they were all locked up together, and again during the first few days of their training with the army. He wondered how many times Tiny had been singled out for a fight simply because he was large. It was a perspective he had never considered. "I never thought about it like that." Remembering the past, he added, "I'm sorry. Because of me, you got dragged into two fights."

Tiny shrugged. "Don't apologize. Just think about it. You have a similar problem."

Frowning, Will asked, "What do you mean? I'm not big, I'm average at best."

The giant poked his arm. "Not out here." He shifted his finger and pointed at Will's chest. "In here. You have a big heart. Too big. It gets you into fights your body isn't big enough for."

"Like when they took Dave."

Tiny held a finger in front of his lips. "I don't know what you're talking about. That was just me." Then he smiled. "I worry about you. You aren't always where I can see you."

"It's not your job to take care of me," Will replied.

"You're my first friend."

Embarrassed, Will gestured at Sven and Dave.

"Squad mates, maybe brothers even," said Tiny. "But just like family, I don't necessarily like them." His eyes turned serious as he stared at Will. "Think about what you do. If that big heart of yours gets you into a fight, you might not be the only one bleeding at the end. Your friends might wind up bleeding for you." The big man lay back and closed his eyes.

Damn, thought Will. *I never realized he was a deep thinker.* Tiny's speech had made him feel bad on several different levels. The big man had been whipped because of Will not once, but twice, and on top of that, Will had been one of the people thinking that Tiny wasn't especially bright. *I'm a shitty friend,* he thought, but he promised himself he would do better.

Will stayed awake after the lanterns were put out. It was something of a struggle since his sleep habits had gotten quite rigid over the past few months. Hard labor, a fixed bedtime, and rising at dawn had set the pattern in his bones. He wished he could take a nap and wake in the middle of the night, but he knew if he let sleep set in he would be dead to the world until the sun rose. That was a simple statement of fact since he had joined the army.

Fortunately, that also applied to pretty much everyone else, aside from the men on night watch duty. Just an hour after lights out he could be pretty certain that the vast majority of the camp was asleep.

Easing up to a sitting position, he studied the dark interior of the tent. His eyes had had plenty of time to adjust to the dark, and though the only light was what filtered in from the gap in the tent flaps at the front, he could see well enough to navigate. Once again he had Tailtiu to thank for his better vision.

Slipping on his boots, he took the note he had written from his satchel. It was contained within a hand-folded envelope that he had sealed with wax. On the exterior was written one word: 'Isabel.' He hoped that would be enough to ensure that whoever found it first would give it to her rather than open it themselves. Given Isabel's poorly concealed status, Will suspected that anyone that worked near her would deliver it to her rather than risk reading a letter meant for such an important person.

He crept carefully to the entrance and looked outside. A pole in the center of Company B's tents held a lantern that provided some illumination, but the camp sentries weren't there. Each company had two men that walked the darker perimeter outside the circle of tents. Aside from the company sentries, Will knew there were also nighttime guards set in important places to guard the supplies, officers, and livestock. There were also general patrols that patrolled the perimeter of the entire cohort as well as sentries in fixed positions.

Will only had to worry about the sentries inside the general camp, meaning Company B's patrol and a few that might be positioned close to the medic tent. He waited patiently until he heard footsteps on the dark side of his platoon's tent. That meant the patroller was now at his closest, while his partner was presumably on the opposite side of Company B's perimeter. Will counted slowly to ten and then eased through the tent flaps before following the outside of his tent to the side hidden from the light.

He stopped again there, until his ears confirmed which direction the patroller had gone, then he followed the man. In the distance he could see light from the other companies' positions, and he used his memory of the layout to keep track of how far he had gone. Once he had moved a quarter of the way around the Company B camp, he set off at a right angle that should take him directly toward the medic tent.

After he had gone fifty yards, he knelt and waited again. He was in a nearly pitch-black pool of shadows that existed in the gaps between the various lantern poles. Though his night vision was good, the light from the lanterns regularly spoiled it and consequently he was nearly blind to what might be within the darkened area around him.

The various patrollers stayed primarily within the shadowed regions for an important reason. In the dark areas they preserved their night vision and could easily see anyone crossing through the lighted portions of the camp. Will did the same, but he would have to rely on his ears to warn him if one of the patrollers got close to his position.

Will's only advantages were his keener eyesight, better hearing, and the fact that he wasn't following a strict pattern with his movement. It also helped that he knew the patrollers were there, while they didn't know about him.

There were also the ever-present flows of turyn, and while they didn't provide much illumination, they helped slightly. At one point he was saved from walking straight into a guard holding a fixed position simply because he spotted the strange movement of turyn where the guard was standing.

He was almost to the medic tent when he heard approaching footsteps in the darkness to his rear. Glancing back, he saw two dark shapes faintly highlighted by a distant lantern behind them. Will froze, then got down on all fours. There was nothing close enough for him to use to hide, but if he stayed still and made no noise…

After several tense minutes they passed by after having come almost within ten feet of where he crouched. Will took a moment to let his heart calm down before continuing. He also took note of how cold his hands were. Though spring was almost upon them, it was still quite cold, and he hadn't worn his gambeson for fear it would make noise. *At least I'm not sweating,* he thought wryly.

Will was relieved to see that no guard stood outside the medic tent. Creeping close, he glanced within and saw a man and woman sleeping on two field cots. Seeing the cots made him jealous, for they seemed like an immense luxury after sleeping on a bedroll that was directly on the ground for months.

A sudden noise made him freeze in his tracks. It was the sound of metal and leather rubbing together. There was a guard nearby. It was a while before he heard it again, and his ears helped him gauge the direction. The noise came from somewhere behind the medic tent. Will debated whether he should leave his note and leave immediately or whether he should confirm the guard's position first.

It wasn't a patroller, or there would have been more noise. The sound had to be from someone standing guard in a fixed position. *I should see where he's at so I don't run into him by accident when I leave,* Will decided.

Moving slowly and carefully, he eased around the medic tent, stopping to wait and listen after every few feet. He could see something lighter than the darkness around him in the direction he was facing. Another tent, hidden by the shadow of the medic tent.

Will waited another ten minutes, until his eyes had adjusted enough that he could make out the dark form of the guard standing in front of the other tent. *Why would that tent have its own guard?* Will wondered. A guard meant something important. *Or someone important.*

Surely it wasn't possible. A noble lady should be housed in a room in the nearby town, or at the very least have her own tent near the camp commander and other officers. *Why would she stay here next to the medic tent?* It made no sense to him, since it wasn't necessary for her disguise, unless Lady Isabel really cared that much about treating the wounded.

Unable to contain his curiosity, Will began working his way in small increments around the tent, making sure to keep his distance from the guard. Once he was on the opposite side from the entrance, he crept up to the back wall. It was a relatively small tent compared to most of the others in the area, being only ten feet wide on each side. He listened patiently until his ears discerned what he thought might be the sound of someone breathing. It was such a soft sound that he wasn't sure if it was his imagination or not.

Imagined or not, there definitely wasn't anyone moving within the tent or he would have heard them. Will began feeling around for the bottom edge of the tent and discovered that it had been well secured, with stakes every four feet, keeping it tightly against the ground. He spent considerable time gently wiggling and pulling at two of them until the entire back side was free.

The corners still held it down, but there was enough give in the canvas that he could lift the bottom far enough to slip under. Easing the canvas up, he saw something that froze the breath in his lungs. A pattern of glowing lines covered the ground inside, snaking around the edges of the interior. *Some sort of protection or alarm?*

If an alarm went up, Will could probably run back to his tent in less than six or seven minutes. The odds were pretty good that as long as no one saw his face he wouldn't be caught. He considered simply sliding the letter across the ground toward the middle of the tent. She would definitely see it there in the morning.

Making up his mind, he whipped the envelope in a sideways motion, but as he did his hand brushed across the edge of one of the glowing lines. Magic rushed into him, and he felt a split-second of pain as a spell began to take hold, then it began to fade as his body absorbed the turyn, transforming it into his own. Once his panic subsided, Will smiled faintly. He might not be able to cast spells himself, but he had at least learned something useful from his grandfather's training.

His heart tried to jump into his throat when he looked at the ground once more and realized that the glowing lines were gone. He hadn't just nullified the spell's effect on himself, he had completely erased it. *She'll notice that in the morning for sure,* he observed.

Lying on the ground, he looked under the edge of the tent to see where his letter had gone. He had been in almost complete darkness long enough that his eyes were about as sensitive as they could get, but he still couldn't see it. All he knew for certain was that it hadn't landed in the middle of the room. *If it went under something, she might not find it,* he thought.

Lifting the edge of the tent, he began to slip under it. *I'm not doing this,* he thought, even as he slid all the way inside. *There's no way I'm stupid enough to do this.* Getting to his knees, he looked around.

The interior was a dark grey mixture of shapes. On one side was something that might be a desk or table, and beside it were several large, square things that might be chests. On the other side was a cot with an irregular shape on it, which he assumed was the occupant of the tent. It occurred to him then that he didn't know for sure that it was Isabel.

He needed some light to find the letter. Before he had destroyed the protective spell he had been able to see better, as its glow had helped. *I wonder if normal people would have seen that spell, or if it was invisible the way the runes I make are?* thought Will. *Wait, does that mean I can see better if I make a rune?*

It wasn't the proper use for them, of course, but they did glow. He had never tried making one in a place dark enough that it would matter. The light they produced probably wasn't enough to wake the person sleeping nearby. He hoped.

Trying to search without being able to see was probably riskier than making a small light, so Will tossed caution to the wind and produced a small lun rune in the air in front of him. Looking around, he thought he could see a little better, but the overall change in lighting wasn't enough to help substantially.

Dismissing the rune, he made another. This time he used pertos, which was essentially just a fat dot roughly the size of the end of his thumb. When he had first learned the runes, his grandfather had been insistent that he make them fixed, so that they wouldn't move. Apparently, that was important when crafting a spell so that all of them could be added without ruining the structure, but as a result of that practice he also knew quite well how to make them move, for that was what they did when he messed up.

Rather than make this pertos rune perfectly, he affixed it to the end of his left index finger. The light was still poor, but he could move his hand to bring it close to things he wanted to examine. Will was rather pleased with himself when it worked just as he had hoped.

Slowly working his way around the room, he found his letter had come to a stop against the bottom of one of the chests. He retrieved it and placed it neatly on top of the desk. He was about to leave when a cough and rustling from the direction of the cot stopped him cold.

The occupant had rolled over, but after a short time Will decided they must still be asleep. He moved closer, until he could definitely tell it was a woman. She had rolled onto her back, twisting the blankets until they exposed her left shoulder and one of her feet.

Taking a few more steps, Will reached the edge of the cot, and he lowered his finger so he could study her face. It was Isabel. The light was too dim to make out colors, but he knew from seeing her before that the smooth, full lips would be a soft pink color. A dark lock of hair had fallen across her cheek, and he fought a sudden urge to brush it aside. He stared at her for a minute, unable to take his eyes away.

Tailtiu came to his mind then, for the fae woman was flawlessly perfect in every detail. Isabel was not; from the faintest asymmetries in the shape of her face, to the pimple on her brow, she was profoundly human. *But I'll be damned if she isn't the most beautiful human woman I've ever seen,* thought Will. Unlike the alien beauty of the fae, Isabel's warmth seemed to call to him.

Breaking out of his reverie, Will went back to where he had come in and got down on the ground, extinguishing his makeshift light at the same time. Then he slid out and took his time putting the tent stakes back in place. He couldn't put the spell that he had destroyed back, but perhaps it wouldn't be a problem. At the very least there was no way they could figure out who had done it.

The journey back to his own tent took just as long, and he was grateful when he was finally able to take off his boots and close his eyes. The next day would be rough with only a half a night's sleep under his belt.

 CHAPTER 42

Will woke with a shock as horns blared outside, and Sergeant Nash yelled at them from the tent entrance. Sitting up, he pulled his boots back on and started to lift the gambeson so he could slide it over his head and shoulders. He was stopped when someone's hand fell on his shoulder. "William Cartwright?" said a deep voice.

Two soldiers he didn't recognize stood behind him. Both were clad in mail byrnies. "Yes?"

"On your feet, soldier!" barked the one who had spoken already. Will got up, and the two grabbed his arms and dragged him into the aisle, where they turned him around and bound his hands behind his back.

"What's going on?" asked Corporal Taylor.

"We're taking this man into custody at the order of Lord Fulstrom," said one of the two men holding Will's arms. Without another word, they shuffled him out of the tent and marched him across the yard. Once outside of Company B's campsite, they turned right and took him in the direction of the officers' tents. As they went, Will could see men hurrying back and forth. Sergeants were yelling, and patrols had formed to sweep the area outside the camp.

His stomach sank, and he realized that he was the most likely cause for the frenzy of activity.

They took him to a large tent he had never been in before, though he already knew who it belonged to. It was the Lord Commander's tent. He was being taken to Baron Fulstrom.

The interior was far different than any of the other tents he had been inside. It was partitioned, not with canvas, but with wooden screens decorated with intricate carvings of woodland creatures. Will's captors shoved him along until he reached an enclosed area at the far end of the tent where six people waited for him.

Four were guards, armed with swords and wearing mail. Will supposed they were probably from the baron's personal retinue, for they appeared to be in their thirties and all of them had the look of professional soldiers. The other two in the room were Baron Fulstrom and Isabel. Above Isabel's shoulders were the two elementals he had seen before, while above Fulstrom hovered a fire elemental. Will's letter was in Isabel's hand. *I'm so screwed,* he thought.

Everyone was standing, as there were no chairs. The baron walked over and studied Will's face for a moment. "Kneel," he commanded.

One of the guards kicked Will's legs from behind before he could do as ordered, and he fell to the ground. They hauled him up by his shoulders until he was on his knees. The baron stared coldly down at him. "You understand why you're here. Don't you, soldier?"

"No, sir," said Will.

One of the men holding him twisted his arm painfully. "You address the baron with 'milord' or 'Your Excellency.'"

"No, Your Excellency," said Will, hastily correcting himself.

Isabel stepped forward, the letter in her hand. "You placed this in my tent last night, didn't you?"

Will shook his head in vigorous denial. "No, milady."

Baron Fulstrom made eye contact with one of the guards and nodded. The world exploded into splinters of pain as a mailed fist slammed into Will's jaw with such force that he nearly blacked out. "Lie to me again and I'll have you whipped. Keep lying and your life will be extremely short."

"Fulstrom!" snapped Isabel, her voice firm with authority. "A word, please." The two of them stepped out of the room, and Will heard them speaking quietly on the other side of the partition, but he was too rattled to pay attention to their words.

When they returned, the baron pointed at the guards and snapped his fingers. "Outside." As the guards left, he looked at Isabel again. "Are you sure, Mistress Isabel?"

Isabel nodded, closing her eyes briefly. Will couldn't help but notice she didn't bother to answer properly. The baron followed his men out, and the two of them were left alone. As soon as everyone was out, Isabel went to Will and leaned close.

Will was startled, unsure of her intentions, until he realized she was examining his cheek. "It doesn't look as bad as it felt, I'll wager," she observed. "I was worried the mail might have split the skin."

His nose caught the scent of something floral. *Roses?* "Why am I here, milady?" asked Will, feigning ignorance.

Isabel straightened up and cocked her head. She held his letter in her hand. "I think you know why you're here."

"Did someone write something bad about me, milady?" asked Will. *I can do stupid,* he thought smugly, *as long as no one is beating my head against a wall.*

She frowned. "Don't play dumb. I know for a fact you were in my tent last night. You were seen."

Will adopted a confused look while he thought furiously. He knew no one had seen him. She might have some form of proof, but he was certain he hadn't been observed. He decided to call her bluff. "No one saw me..." he began.

"Then you admit you were there," said Isabel triumphantly.

"...because I wasn't there, milady," Will finished.

Isabel chewed her lip, while the tip of her tongue poked out on the other side of her mouth. It was obviously an expression of deep concentration, but Will couldn't help but watch her. *Damn, she's cute,* he observed. *If she doesn't have me flogged.*

Her expression became serious. "Please don't address me as 'milady,'" she told him. "I don't hold a rank worthy of such a title."

Will was starting to add things together in his head. It was obvious she didn't want to hurt him, otherwise she wouldn't have ordered the baron's men from the room, or checked his cheek afterward. *Why* she didn't want to hurt him, he didn't know, but that was one thing he knew. She was also clearly nobility, and of a rank superior to the baron. Those were his only two facts, however. *What would Grandfather do if he were in my shoes?* "The hell you don't!" swore Will.

Isabel flinched as though she had been slapped. "Excuse me? What did you say?"

Will elaborated, "I said there's no way in hell you aren't a lady." He paused, then added, "Milady."

"Explain why you think that."

"You called the Lord Commander by his name without an honorific, and he said nothing," answered Will.

"That doesn't mean..."

"And you had enough power to order him out of the room, despite the fact that it means you're alone with a supposedly dangerous man," added Will.

Isabel laughed. "Your hands are bound."

Will looked up at her with cold eyes. "My feet aren't, and I probably outweigh you by at least a hundred pounds.

If I *were* dangerous it wouldn't be wise for you to stand so close. The baron clearly thinks so, which means you had to have some serious authority to force him to leave us alone."

Her foot shifted slightly, as though she were about to take a step back, but Isabel held firm. "You're observant, I'll grant you that. But you've overestimated the danger you pose. You've forgotten that most nobles have magic."

He already knew that, but he decided to needle her a bit as he replied, "What, are you a wizard or something?"

"A sorceress," she corrected immediately, and the two elementals hovering above her shoulders shifted, becoming visible in the physical sense. One appeared as an intricate, silvery crystal, while the other was an amorphous, watery mass.

Will tried to look fearful as he leaned away from her. "Please don't hurt me."

"Stop that," snapped Isabel. "You aren't a bad liar, but your acting is terrible."

"I'm really afraid," insisted Will, scrunching up his face and keeping his eyes downward.

"That's really painful to watch," she observed dryly. "Please stop. I feel embarrassed just watching you."

Will gave up. Straightening up, he apologized, "Sorry."

"That's better," she said, and Will thought he saw a hint of a smile cross her face. "Now, tell me how you got into my tent."

"I didn't—"

"That's getting old," she said, interrupting him. "Would you like to see how I know you were there?"

He shrugged.

Isabel held up the letter with her left hand while an intricate construction of runes appeared in the air above her right hand. A second later it moved across to dissolve into the letter, then a strange mist appeared in the air above it. The mist swirled for a moment before resolving into four faces, all of whom he recognized; Arrogan, his mother, Isabel, and his own visage. Isabel pointed at his face, "Who does this look like to you?"

"I'm not sure," said Will. "It certainly resembles me a little." Then he asked, "How did you do that?"

"The spell identifies the residual turyn people leave behind when they handle objects, showing their faces to the caster. It only works if the user already knows the people being identified, though. Fortunately, I had already met you," explained Isabel. "Who are the other ones?" she asked, pointing at Erisa's and Arrogan's faces.

Will leaned forward, squinting. "A woman I've never seen before, an old man I don't recognize—" He pointed at Isabel's visage last. "This one, I'm not sure who it is, but I'm sure I would recognize a beauty like that if I had met her before."

Isabel blushed slightly, then scowled. "That's me, idiot." She studied him for a moment, then went on, "You've given yourself away. I know you're a mage of some sort now."

"No, I'm not," lied Will.

She smiled. "First, those images are completely invisible to non-mages. A regular person would have seen nothing. Second, you know all those faces. When I said the user had to already know the people shown, I didn't mention what they would look like if you didn't know them." She pointed at Arrogan's face. "For example, you said this one is an old man, but I couldn't even tell if it was a man or a woman. It's just a blur to me." She pointed at Erisa next. "This one I could see, but I don't remember meeting her. Who is she?"

Flummoxed, Will clamped his mouth shut. *Damn it!* He'd been outsmarted, mostly because of his inexperience, but he had to admire Isabel's cleverness. Then another thought came to him. *When would she have met Mom?*

"Are you determined not to answer?" she asked. "You realize my patience won't last forever, don't you? If you don't cooperate, I'll have the baron's men back in here. Is that what you want?"

He said nothing.

Isabel surprised him by getting down on her knees so she could meet him eye-to-eye. The expression on her face was full of emotion, though he couldn't have identified what moved her. "People like me can do anything we want to people like you. You realize that, don't you? We don't need proof or approval for our cruelty, either. Justice is irrelevant when you deal with nobility. Please talk to me."

Something in her eyes made his heart catch. "Why?"

Her eyes left his for a second, stopping on his scarred cheek, then they returned. "Because I don't approve of those who abuse their power. I want to help you."

"So, you have me arrested and threaten me?" said Will.

Isabel sighed. "Do you have any idea how disconcerting it is to wake up and discover that someone has broken into your quarters and rifled through your things? And I was there when you did it! It's the stuff of nightmares, especially for a woman. I had already raised the alarm when I found your identity with my spell. I regretted it when I realized it was you."

"I didn't rifle through your things," protested Will. "I just put the letter down and left." *And looked at you for a little bit,* he added mentally. *That's not weird, is it?*

"I need some answers if you expect me to help you get out of this without serious harm," said Isabel. "Trust me. I'm a friend of Terabinia too."

He released the air from his lungs in a long exhale. "What do you want to know?"

"How did you get that information about Barrowden?"

"Next question," he replied. When he saw the angry look in her eyes he added, "I really want to answer. Just ask me something different, please."

Isabel's eyes narrowed. "Who are the other people my spell showed?"

"My mother, my grandfather, and me," said Will.

"Are they in Branscombe?"

He shook his head. "My mother is hiding in the wilderness near Barrowden."

"Is the information in the letter accurate?"

"Yes," said Will emphatically.

"How did you remove the ward in my tent without waking me?"

Will frowned. "The what?"

Isabel's visage showed a curious expression, but she answered, "The ward. A ward is a protective spell. It was set around the boundaries of my tent. Anyone crossing it should have been paralyzed, not to mention it would have awakened me."

"Oh," said Will. "I don't know. It just vanished after I touched it."

"It just vanished," she repeated slowly. "You expect me to believe that?"

Will shrugged. "It's the truth."

Isabel didn't say anything for a while, then she asked, "Who trained you as a mage?"

"My grandfather," said Will. "But he's dead now. The Darrowans killed him. I didn't have a chance to learn much."

"Was he a sorcerer?"

If only you knew, he thought to himself dryly before shaking his head. "No. Just a wizard."

"Did he teach you a spell to remove wards? Such a thing might be valuable if you could share it with me." She looked hopeful.

"No. I don't actually know *any* spells. I can see turyn and that's about it." A sudden inspiration struck him then. "Oh, and sometimes spells fall apart when I touch them. Grandfather said it was some sort of 'spell anomaly.' It caused him a lot of frustration."

"Spell anomalies generally only happen when you first learn to express your turyn," explained Isabel. "I'm sure he was mistaken."

"I'm telling the truth," insisted Will, as he lied.

"I can find out if you're lying," she warned.

Will doubled down. "Please do."

A tiny spell construct appeared above her palm, and knowing what to look for, Will recognized it. *Lun, sarcat, kolbet, it's the same source-link spell that was in the book,* he noted. A green line shot from her hand to his chest and vanished as his body absorbed the turyn. Isabel frowned as her spell fizzled out. "That shouldn't happen."

"Told you."

She repeated the spell, and this time Will made a conscious effort not to absorb the turyn. The green line passed through his chest but just as it had the time his father had tried, it failed to connect to his source. He managed to suppress the smile that threatened to show on his lips.

"Are you doing something?" asked Isabel suspiciously.

"Not on purpose," said Will innocently. She tried twice more, and he practiced changing tactics, letting his body absorb the first and deliberately letting the second pass through him. He was glad to see that he could control his turyn absorption. He didn't know enough to be sure, but he suspected that being unable to stop absorbing turyn would probably be inconvenient in certain circumstances.

"That last one should have worked," muttered Isabel. "How long did your grandfather train you?"

"A couple of years," said Will truthfully.

"And you never learned a single spell?" she said incredulously.

"He always said he'd get to it later," answered Will. Then he added, "You have no idea how mean he was."

"I think he did you a terrible disservice," said Isabel. "Although, officially, I should say what he was doing was illegal. You should have been started on spell craft during the first year. The only thing I can think is that whatever exercises he was putting you through somehow helped you to develop a very strong will. Normally that spell doesn't fail unless it's attempted against a very experienced wizard or sorcerer."

Will shrugged. "He used to say I was as stubborn as a goat."

Isabel's features softened. "I'm sorry you lost him. Though I'm glad he isn't teaching you anymore. You need to go to Wurthaven. Otherwise you'll wind up in prison sooner or later."

"I'm a private contract," said Will. "I've got most of five years left to serve. Assuming I don't get hanged today."

She shook her head. "No. As soon as things are settled here, I'm taking you to Cerria. Unlicensed wizards can't be allowed to run amok."

"I'm not dangerous. I wouldn't do anything bad."

"Like sneaking into a young woman's bedroom?" said Isabel, raising one brow.

Throwing caution to the wind, he asked, "How old are you?"

"Just a few months older than you," she replied immediately.

"How do you know how old I am?"

"Oh," said Isabel, and her eyes darted to the side for a split second. "I saw your age in the contract book. I had Lieutenant Stanton look up the record while they were on their way to arrest you."

Will knew better, but he wasn't sure he wanted to confront her on the matter. He had already gotten himself in deep enough for one day. "What happens now?"

Isabel got to her feet and put her hands on his shoulders to steady him as he tried to rise. Will's knees were numb and stiff from kneeling so long, though, and with his hands tied behind his back he stumbled. Isabel stepped forward and caught him briefly, steadying him as his head landed on her shoulder. He could sense the muscles in her back as she kept him upright until he got his legs sorted out. *She's stronger than she looks.* Backing away, he apologized, "Sorry."

She ignored his remark and moved around him to untie his hands. "I should have done this a few minutes ago, when I was certain you were cooperating." Then she gave him a stern look. "Wait here. I'll go outside and explain to Lord Fulstrom that you were the victim of someone else's attempt to disguise the source of the letter. You'll be sent back to your company after that."

"Thank you."

She pointed a finger at him. "Only until we get reinforcements and the pass is secured. After that I'm taking you to Cerria to be properly trained."

Will's shoulders drooped slightly. "Fine."

"And if you need to speak to me again, come to the medic tent. I'll make certain Doctor Guerin knows to notify me if you show up. If I'm not there, find Sir Kyle, your captain. I'll give him the same instruction."

With that she was gone, and Will took a deep breath through his nose, trying to catch the faint scent of roses she left in her wake.

CHAPTER 43

Things returned to normal over the next few days. Will managed to dodge most of his squad mates' questions by simply saying he had been mistakenly accused. Dave had a great time teasing him about being a criminal, but he and Sven seemed to believe him. He wasn't as sure about Tiny though, and Will noticed the big man giving him odd looks now and then.

He couldn't help but keep thinking over the things Isabel had said, but nothing made sense. Was she a friend of Baron Nerrow's? If so, that might explain her willingness to help him. From what he had overheard her say previously, she had already known there was a paid exemption for him on the roll ledgers. Was his father more important than Baron Fulstrom? They were both barons, so he assumed they were of roughly equivalent rank, though admittedly he knew almost nothing of the inner workings of the nobility. If Isabel was acting on Nerrow's behalf, why was she being treated with so much deference?

On several occasions he was tempted to go to the medic tent and try to see her, but each time he talked himself out of it. All of his excuses seemed pointless or trite. Deep down he knew he just wanted to see her. *I'm such an idiot,* he told himself, and in the back of his mind he heard his grandfather's voice agreeing with him.

Almost a week passed before his next big shock. His platoon had just mustered for the morning roll call when Sergeant Nash called his name just before releasing the squads for their first duties of the day. "Cartwright.

You're relieved of duty this morning. See me for your assignment." Then the sergeant addressed them once more, "Dismissed."

Will waited, worried he was about to be punished for something else, though he couldn't think of anything he might have done—this time. The sergeant gave him an appraising look before speaking. "Go into Branscombe and see the armorer there. His name is Andrew Harless. He's expecting you."

"Sir?"

"Did I stutter, soldier?" barked the sergeant. "Get moving."

Doing as he was told, Will started to leave, but Sergeant Nash added one parting remark, "Cartwright, I don't care who your friends are, if you screw up or make trouble for my men, I *will* bust your ass."

Will stopped and saluted, thumping his fist over his heart. "Understood, sir!" Sergeant Nash stared at him for a few seconds longer then walked away. *What the hell is going on this time?* he wondered.

Half an hour later, he was standing in front of the smithy, feeling conspicuous. The man there sent him to a second building behind the main smithy, which apparently didn't deal directly with weapons and armor. The other building was open in the front with two small forges operating and a number of apprentices busy working on a variety of tasks. Harless turned out to be a short, heavy-set man with a pronounced lack of hair. Not only was he bald, but part of one of his eyebrows was missing due to a past scar.

"Who're you?" asked the master armorer, hardly bothering to glance up at him.

"William Cartwright, sir," said Will. "I was told to see you."

The smith cleared his throat and then spit on the ground before answering. "Oh, you." Straightening up, he called to one of his assistants, then directed Will to go with the man. "He'll take your measurements." A second later, the armorer returned to his work, apparently having banished Will from his awareness.

Will didn't move. "Excuse me, sir. What's all this about?"

The armorer sighed deeply, as though frustrated beyond all endurance. Will almost flinched when his eyes focused on him once more. "Fucking aristocrats," said the smith. "Not only do they want everything done yesterday, they want a nice chat as well. I'm not a goddamn tailor, and I certainly ain't a babysitter."

"I'm not an aristocrat," said Will.

"I know that, otherwise I'd be kissing your ass instead of cussing you, dumbass," spat the armorer. "Follow Jeremy and let him get your measurements. We need 'em if we're to make anything that fits you."

Will noticed the aforementioned Jeremy giving him a sympathetic look. Closing his mouth, he went with the apprentice, who promptly instructed him to strip. "Everything?" asked Will.

"Everything above the waist," said Jeremy. Will did as he was told. The apprentice looked over his gambeson carefully before setting it to one side and walking away. He returned a few minutes later with a similar coat, though this one was slit along the sides with laces to secure it. He helped Will put it on before pulling the laces tight and producing a long string with knots tied in it at regular intervals.

He measured Will's body in a bewildering number of places, his waist, torso, shoulders, biceps, forearms, and more. As he did, the apprentice armorer chalked his findings on a piece of grey slate. When he had finished, he helped Will remove the padded coat and gave him back his gambeson. "We'll send a note when it's ready, probably next week."

"When what is ready?" asked Will.

The apprentice gave him a strange look. "Your mail shirt."

"I didn't ask for one," stated Will. "How much does it cost?"

Jeremy shrugged. "Usually around twelve to fourteen gold, though we charge more for rush jobs like this. That's just a guess, mind you. I don't handle the money. You'd have to talk to Master Harless if he didn't give you a price yet."

Will goggled at the man. "I don't have that kind of coin." In fact, he had exactly no money whatsoever. He had spent it all buying good for his mother, and he hadn't yet been paid for the past week.

"Somebody does," said the apprentice. "Harless won't start things like this unless at least half is paid up front."

"Well, who paid?"

"Ask Master Harless," said Jeremy. "Whoever it was must have been important, otherwise you'd be waiting a few months. Yours is at the top of the list now. If you'll excuse me, I have to get back to work." With that, the young man left Will alone.

Will went back to stand in front of the master armorer. He waited without speaking for several minutes before the man looked up at him with obvious irritation. "What?"

"Master Harless, I don't have any money," said Will simply.

"So? It's already been paid," said the gruff armorer.

"Can I ask who commissioned it?"

Harless stared at him, lifting his partially missing brow. "Soldier, if you don't know who your friends are, you're dumber than I thought, and if the person who paid doesn't want you to know then I sure as hell ain't going to piss her off by telling you."

Her? Will bowed. "Thank you, Master Harless." The armorer's attention was already back on his work. He said nothing as Will left.

Back in camp, Will considered returning to his squad, but there were still several hours before lunchtime and he wasn't expected back before then, so he went to the medic tent instead. He figured he had a good enough excuse to see Isabel now.

Doctor Guerin glanced up from the man he was treating when Will entered the tent. "Are you hurt?"

"No, sir."

"What do you need? I'm a little busy at the moment," said the doctor amiably.

Unsure what to say, Will gave his name. "I'm William Cartwright. I was told…"

"She isn't here," said Doctor Guerin. "Left almost a week ago." Straightening up, the man wiped his hands on an already-stained apron. "One second." The doctor went to his desk on one side of the tent and rummaged around through his things. When he returned, he had a sealed envelope in one hand. "She left this for you."

Will accepted the note and went back outside, looking around carefully to make sure no one was nearby before he broke the seal and opened it. Inside he found a single neatly folded page. On it was a short letter, written in a precise, flowing script. It reminded him of his grandfather's later handwriting, but the letters were more elegant with long, flowing loops that made it distinctly feminine.

William,

I decided to act on the information I received and to that end I am traveling to the capital. If things go well, I should be back within two weeks with reinforcements. Be ready to travel when I return, for you'll be going to Cerria shortly thereafter. The army is no place for your talents.

I've made arrangements for a small present of sorts. Something to help keep you alive if my return is delayed.

Isabel

He read it twice before folding the letter and putting in his pouch. Will had mixed emotions about going to Wurthaven so soon. Part of him felt a sense of relief at leaving before war broke out. Deep down, his first taste of violence in Barrowden had left him terrified of the thought of facing a similar situation. Conflicting with that was his desire to avenge his family and friends who had died, not to mention fighting alongside the men he had been training with for the past few months.

Will was also confused about the wording. She had said '*you'll* be going to Cerria,' rather than '*we'll*.' Did that mean she would be staying behind to face the enemy? Granted, it wasn't as though he really knew her, or that he had any particular claim on her, but he had even less inclination to leave if he was going alone.

"And why in the hell is she wasting so much gold buying armor for someone like me?" he muttered aloud to no one in particular. It made no sense. *Unless she likes me,* he thought. "That's ridiculous. She's some sort of nobility, whereas I'm…" He stopped. What exactly was he? A commoner? The bastard son of a nobleman?

396

He could hear his grandfather's answer in the back of his head, *All of that comes second to the fact that you're a mentally challenged half-wit.*

Still, she had spent a considerable sum of money on him. Was she trying to buy his loyalty? Something his grandfather had said came back to him. *"Most of them spend their time bowing and scraping for the sorcerers, hoping to be given scraps."* Did she expect to train him as some sort of magical lackey?

It couldn't be any worse than cooking and cleaning for Arrogan was, thought Will. It wouldn't be a romantic partnership, though, and eventually he'd wind up serving her husband and family as well. As much as he appreciated her kindness and beauty, he didn't want to live his life that way. Better to be a hermit in the woods.

Putting those thoughts away, Will returned to the platoon tent, which was currently empty. He spent the last hour before lunch practicing the one spell he had learned. The runes were simple enough, but it took him some practice to reliably put them together quickly, and he was still nowhere as fast as Isabel had been, and far slower than his grandfather. The old man had produced the spell with such speed that he'd failed to even notice the spell construct at the beginning.

With no target, he sent green lines spearing outward to pass harmlessly through the tent walls while he practiced aiming. They vanished only seconds after appearing, since apparently they needed to connect to a living source to be sustained, but his first goal was simply to gain proficiency and accuracy.

When the bell rang for the midday meal, he went to meet his squad mates at the mess tent.

"Where the hell have you been?" demanded Dave as soon as he saw Will.

There wasn't much point hiding it, since it would be revealed when he received the mail, so Will answered honestly, "The armorer in Branscombe."

Dave and the others waited several seconds before the ex-thief prodded him, "And why would you go there?"

"Someone paid to have a mail shirt made for me," admitted Will.

"Liar!" exclaimed Dave. "I knew you were some rich merchant's brat."

"Is that true?" asked Sven.

Will shook his head. "No. You remember when they hauled me in to see Lord Fulstrom last week? I think someone took a liking to me, or maybe they felt bad for falsely accusing me."

"Bullshit," said Dave. "Noblemen don't give a shit about people like us. We aren't even human to them."

Will caught Tiny staring at him with a look that suggested he knew something, but the big man kept his thoughts to himself. The conversation returned to more usual topics after that, mainly complaints about the sergeants and officers. When lunch was over, Will caught Tiny's arm as they were filing out. "Can I talk to you later?"

The big man nodded. "Last hour, before lights out?"

"Sounds good," said Will.

CHAPTER 44

Tiny and Will walked out and stood near the company lantern pole, since it was too dark to go anywhere else. Plus standing in the light gave the added advantage of making it easy to see that no one was close enough to overhear them.

"It was her, wasn't it?" opined Tiny at the start.

Surprised, Will's eyes widened. He tried to deflect the other man's attention anyway, though. "Who?"

"The lady doctor," said the big man. "She was obviously important, and she took a lot of interest in you."

Sighing Will gave in and nodded. "Yeah, it was her."

"Why is she so interested in you?"

"I don't know all her reasons, but there's one I'm sure of, and that's what I wanted to talk to you about," said Will. "What do you think about magic?"

"I don't," answered Tiny. "It's all nonsense."

That was the last response Will expected. He'd listened to the villagers of Barrowden talk about it on many occasions, and their opinions had generally ranged from fascination to fear, but none of them had ever suggested they didn't believe in magic. Will showed his shock with an eloquent exclamation, "Huh?"

Tiny shrugged. "I don't believe in it. It's all just stories they tell farmers and townsfolk to keep them in line."

Flabbergasted, Will cast about for a counterargument. "What about the laws? Why would they have laws against warlocks and unlicensed wizards if magic wasn't real?"

"Old laws written by superstitious people," said Tiny. "Or worse, just another way of convincing people like you and me that it's real." Warming to his topic, Tiny went on, "Tell me this, Will, have *you* ever seen magic? Of course, you haven't. It's just like the stories of faeries who take milk from your doorstep and clean your shoes, or bogeymen who steal naughty children."

Waving his hands, Will protested, "But I have!"

"No, you didn't," said Tiny firmly. "You saw something you didn't understand and called it magic. Modern men don't need superstition to face the hard realities of the world. I'm a little disappointed you brought it up. I thought you were smarter than most."

"But…"

Tiny wagged his finger in Will's direction. "If magic was real, why aren't we using it for war?"

"It was used a lot in the last big war," argued Will. "And Lord Fulstrom is a sorcerer."

Tiny shrugged. "I've never seen him do any magic. It's just another excuse for them to claim power over regular people."

"I've seen his elemental," said Will, but he realized that argument wouldn't work either. All the sorcerers he had seen so far kept their elementals invisible to normal eyes most of the time. Frustrated, he changed directions. "I can do magic."

Disgusted, Tiny replied, "Show me then."

Tiny wouldn't be able to see the runes even if Will produced them, but what he really wanted was someone to practice his new spell with. "I can't show you here. If someone saw, I'd be put in irons."

"That's what they always say," said Tiny knowingly.

"In five days, we get another free day," Will told him. "Come with me and I'll show you. If you don't believe me, I'll buy you as much as you can eat."

"I can eat a lot," warned the big man.

Will chuckled. "Trust me, I know."

"Not just some lousy pottage either," added Tiny. "I want beef, or a ham."

"Whatever you want," said Will confidently. "We get paid tomorrow. I'll spend it all if you don't believe me."

Tiny's eyes narrowed suspiciously. "Don't try to get out of it by spending most of it before our day off."

***

On the day in question, Will led Tiny to the hidden spring by the congruence that led to Faerie. He didn't intend to use it to travel, but the place was free from prying eyes. Preparing himself, he gave Tiny a final warning, "I'm going to cast a spell. If it works, you'll be paralyzed. Don't panic. I promise I'll release you right away."

"Sure," said the big man, obviously not worried.

Will lifted his hands and constructed the spell in a matter of a four or five seconds. As before, a green line shot out as he invested a small amount of turyn in it, and this time it landed squarely in the center of his new target's chest and he felt it connect. The sensation was curious, as though he had two bodies. He was shocked to realize that he could feel everything that Tiny felt. "There," he announced proudly.

"What?" said Tiny, clearly unimpressed.

Will frowned. "You can talk?"

"Most people are surprised when they discover I can speak," said the big man, his voice laden with sarcasm.

Confused, Will made a suggestion, "Try to do something else."

Tiny shifted slightly to the side and farted so loudly that Will was surprised that the birds in the trees above them hadn't taken flight. The big man shrugged. "Don't blame me, it was your magic."

Stumped, Will tried to understand why the spell wasn't working as he had expected. Even now he could see the green line connecting them, and he could feel all sorts of strange sensations coming through it to him. Then a foul odor caused his nose to crinkle, and he began waving his hands to clear the air. "Ack, what did you eat?"

"Your magic is exceedingly potent," said Tiny dryly, trying not to crack a smile.

Perhaps he needed to do something. Sitting down, Will decided to try meditating to better understand the connection he had created. "Let me concentrate on this for a while," he told his friend.

Tiny shook his head. "Stop stalling. You've lost. Let's go eat. I'm hungry and you're paying."

Frustrated, Will stood up and dismissed the spell. "Give me your hand. I'll show you something else instead."

The big soldier studied his open hand as though it might be a trap of some sort. Finally, he took it, saying, "Fine. I love holding hands with fools and drunks."

Will twisted them sideways through the congruence, and the landscape changed, becoming the open grassland that surrounded Cath Bawlg's cave in Faerie. Then he looked over to see Tiny's reaction.

The big man remained utterly still, with only his eyes moving as they darted back and forth to study their surroundings. After thirty seconds or so, Tiny released Will's hand and turned around to look behind them. He stood there for a while, then his tanned cheeks began to pale and Tiny started to sway on his feet.

Shit! Will grabbed his friend's hand and shifted them back to the hidden spring. "Sit down," he cautioned Tiny. "If you fall there's no way I can catch you."

Tiny sat, and after a moment his color improved. The big man quietly studied the forest around them, then stared at the tiny spring for a while. "Where were we?" he said at last.

"That was part of Faerie," said Will. "It touches our world here beside this spring, and at other places. If I'm next to a spot where the two worlds come in contact, I can transport myself and others from one to the other."

"Faerie," said Tiny. "Does that mean faeries are real?"

Will nodded. "I've met several, but they're different from what you've probably heard about in stories. In general, it's probably best to avoid them."

"Does anyone else know about this?"

"Anyone that can see magic probably knows about the congruencies," he answered.

"Congruencies?"

"The places where different worlds touch."

Tiny continued staring into the distance, thinking deeply. "Worlds—does that mean there are others? If so, how many?"

"From what my grandfather said, a lot, but no one knows how many," answered Will. "There seem to be a lot more congruencies between our world and Faerie than other places. I think it's closer to our world than most of the others."

Tiny's head turned, and he fixed Will with a steady gaze. "I think you need to start from the beginning. Explain everything so I can understand this."

Feeling bad for the shock he had caused, Will asked, "Would you like to eat first? I'll still buy you whatever you want."

His friend's massive hand clamped onto his arm. "I need to understand this. Explain it for me. Food comes later."

And so Will did, beginning with his life with Arrogan. He abbreviated a lot of it, and he left out certain sensitive details, such as his bastard heritage, his grandfather's name, or the fact that he was related to a couple of the fae. He did mention the goddamn cat, but he left out its name.

"So, you're a wizard, but you can't use magic," said Tiny at the end, summarizing. "Your teacher is gone, and you know a few of the fae, but you don't trust them. The lady doctor is a sorcerer, but her elementals are invisible, so I can't see them."

"And I'm not sure why she's helping me," added Will. "I think she wants to make me into her wizard servant or something."

Tiny chuckled once, then twice, and after a moment he broke into semi-hysterical laughter while Will stared at him in confusion. When his friend finally stopped, he said, "None of that was funny."

"Sorry," said Tiny, wiping his eyes. "It just struck me that way. My entire world has been turned upside down and in the middle of it all you're telling me that you think the doctor wants to enslave you. I may have been blind, but you're dense, Will. Has anyone ever told you that?"

Will smirked. "Yes, all the time. My grandfather never let five minutes go without reminding me. And I never said 'enslave,' I said make me her servant. I don't think she's evil per se."

Tiny put a hand on Will's shoulder. "I won't pretend to know why she's helping you, but I can tell you this. She isn't out to gain anything from you. I went back for bandage changes for a week after that first day. Some days she was there, and others she wasn't, but on the days she was there I saw how she treated the other soldiers. If she really is a noblewoman, there's no reason why she had to do that job. She was doing it because she wanted to help others. She definitely isn't selfish, and if she does have a problem, it's the same one you have."

"What's that?"

The big man patted his chest. "Too much in here."

Will sighed. "I'd rather she didn't pity me." He shifted the subject. "So, now that you believe me, would you help me practice? I should be able to paralyze you with that spell."

"Depends."

"On what?" asked Will.

"Are you still paying for the food?"

Will laughed, and readily agreed. The two of them went back to town and sat down in a small eatery that was popular with the soldiers on their free days. The place was nearly empty since they arrived at an odd time of day.

Tiny made good on his previous boasts, eating enough to fill up at least three grown and very hungry men. Will finished while Tiny was still getting warmed up, so he spent his free time practicing as his friend ate.

Creating the spell was easy enough, and each time he felt that same strange sense of duality, as though he partly inhabited a second body. The trick was sorting out which was which, but eventually he figured it out. The main thing wasn't so much picking out Tiny, but identifying himself, since in the future the spell would be used on different people.

Once he could separate who was who within his perceptions, he simply had to force changes on the one that wasn't himself. Will remembered that sense of complete helplessness, when his grandfather had separated his conscious will from control of his body and turyn, and he used that as a guide.

Tiny had almost finished his last piece of ham when Will had his breakthrough. The big man's body seized up, causing the knife in his right hand to lightly stab into the meat of his thumb before he stopped moving.

"Ow!" exclaimed Will, feeling a sharp pain as it happened.

Tiny, of course, was unable to reply, but his eyes rolled back and forth wildly, and Will could feel his friend's panic building. Will released him quickly.

The big man gave him a hard look, then took a deep breath. "That was you?"

Will nodded. "Sorry."

"You couldn't wait to practice. Have you been trying the whole time we've been sitting here?"

Will glanced sheepishly down at his empty plate. "Only since I finished eating."

Tiny looked at his thumb, where a small drop of blood was beading up. He wiped it on his trousers and then took up his knife once more, spearing another piece of ham and putting it in his mouth. He talked as he chewed. "Wait until I'm done. We can go back to that spring in a few minutes. You can work your black magic there."

Will was surprised by Tiny's nonchalance. "It isn't black magic, but—thanks." While he waited for his friend to finish, Will thought about the pain he had felt. *Did that mean grandfather felt it when he killed those soldiers he had frozen?* He shuddered at the thought. Either Arrogan had been able to overcome unbelievable pain while he was fighting, or the old man had had some method for blocking the sensations from the people he linked with.

Either way, he was a badass, thought Will. He wasn't sure he could do the same.

Once Tiny had finished, they went back to the forest and Will practiced linking and paralyzing him over and over while Tiny sat in the grass. When he was sure he had a good feel for that, he made a new request. "Mind if I try something different?"

"Is it going to hurt?"

"It shouldn't," said Will. "I want to figure out a way to incapacitate someone without pain." He explained what had happened when Tiny had stabbed himself earlier, then continued, "I think if I draw some of your turyn into myself it should make you tired, or even faint."

"Turyn?"

"Magic," said Will. "The stuff everyone uses to move and do things, even normal people."

"Just promise you won't kill me," said his friend with remarkable equanimity.

Will promised. "Don't worry. I'm really good at manipulating turyn, even if I haven't learned much about spells yet." With that said, he cast the spell again, and this time he used the link to draw out some of Tiny's turyn, pulling it into himself. A faint wave of nausea passed through him before disappearing as his body converted the turyn, but Tiny's reaction was more pronounced. The big man's eyes drooped.

"Are you all right?" asked Will.

"Just tired."

"I'll replace it. Give me a second." Reversing the flow, he sent his own turyn back across the link, replacing what he had taken with some of his own turyn.

Tiny shot up into a sitting position, his eyes bulging wide and his face twisting. Leaning forward, he began to violently heave, expelling his stomach contents onto the ground. Will felt terrible as he watched his friend continue retching and heaving long after his stomach was empty. When it finally stopped, Tiny looked accusingly at him. The big man's face was damp with sweat and he looked haggard. "You poisoned me!"

Naturally, Will realized what he had done, remembering the time he had drunk the elixir of turyn that

Arrogan had given him. "Sorry, Tiny. I wasn't thinking. Your body isn't adapted to accept turyn from other people. When I gave you some of mine it caused that reaction."

Tiny was pulling up handfuls of grass to wipe his mouth with. "Well, I'm not tired any more, but please don't ever do that again. I think I'd rather die."

It was then that Will realized he hadn't felt the nausea himself. He had severed the link as soon as it had begun, but even before then it hadn't affected him. *That's probably the safest way for me to disable someone,* he decided. "I won't do it again," he said, "but I'd like to try—"

Tiny held up one hand. "No. I'm done. You'll have to find another test subject." Getting to his feet, he began making his way unsteadily back toward the road. Then he looked back, "Come on."

"Where are we going?"

"You owe me another meal."

Will gaped. "You can eat after that?"

"I damn sure will, if only to get even with you," said Tiny, spitting to clear his mouth.

"Aren't you still nauseous?"

Tiny gave him a malicious grin. "If I throw up, I will make *certain* to aim in your direction."

Will shuddered.

"Not to worry, though. I have the strongest stomach in Company B," Tiny assured him.

When the server at the eatery saw them returning, his jaw dropped. Glancing from Tiny to Will he asked, "You can't be serious?"

"I can pay," said Will.

The server scratched his head. "Money or not, if you keep coming back we'll run out of food and have to shut our doors."

CHAPTER 45

A week later Sergeant Nash informed Will that he was to return to the armorer. This time it was a bit less stressful, since he had been expecting the notification, and being given part of the day away from his normal duty was something of a treat.

Being in a good mood, Will smiled when he found Master Harless. The older man stared at him for a moment, then asked, "Is something wrong with your face?"

Will dropped the smile. "No, sir."

Harless nodded. "Off with your gambeson." He pointed at a pile of similar garments. "Drop it in the pile. We can use it for other things."

"Sir?"

The armorer sighed. "There's a new one with your mail. I don't do shoddy work. The new gambeson and mail should fit perfectly together."

Will did as he was told and soon one of the apprentices was helping him into a new, padded linen coat. The mail shirt went over that, and after a few claustrophobic minutes of shimmying back and forth Will felt it settle into place. It wasn't as heavy as he expected, but it still put a noticeable burden on his shoulders. He wondered what it would feel like after wearing it for most of a day.

The apprentice handed him a well-made leather belt. "This goes just above your hips. Be sure to cinch it tight. I'll mark a few extra holes in case your weight changes later."

Puzzled, Will asked, "What's this for? The shirt fits pretty well—"

Harless chuckled. "Damn right it fits well, but you'll still be miserable after a few hours without that belt. Trust me."

Will wrapped the belt around his waist and held it in place while the apprentice marked it. That done, the young man took it away to have the holes punched. When he returned a few minutes later, he returned it to Will who put it on. He noticed the difference immediately.

The mail shirt was long, reaching his mid-thigh, which coincided with the length of the new gambeson. The overall weight was probably close to twenty pounds, but with the belt on some of the weight was taken off of his shoulders. The belt transferred the strain from the lower portion to his hips, making the entire thing much more comfortable to wear.

The fact that the gambeson was sized to fit him was also an improvement. Overall, he was carrying some more weight, but it didn't seem like it would be too much of a burden. Harless walked around him in a slow circle, poking and prodding him now and then. Then he gave a grunt of approval. "If you don't die this year you should consider coming back." The armorer reached up and poked Will's throat. "This is where you're most likely to get a mortal wound. Remember that."

"What do you do about that?" asked Will.

"A padded coif and gorget, mail over that and sometimes a double layer of mail over the throat—or if you have enough coin, a new helm with a mail aventail, padded coif, and a gorget," said Harless.

"How much does that cost?"

"Doesn't matter," replied the armorer. "Your patron asked the same, but we're too busy with everything else right now. Things will be different once the war dies down."

Will thought for a moment, then asked, "How did you find enough time for this? Doesn't mail take a long time?"

The armorer nodded to his apprentice. "Show him what we're doing." Then he looked at Will. "Good luck, Cartwright. I hope you don't get killed. It's bad for business when people wearing my goods don't survive."

That was the end of their conversation, so Will followed the young apprentice. The man stopped along one wall and pointed to a large selection of mail that was hanging there. The pieces were of varying sizes and shapes. "We're up day and night making those. For a shirt like yours we take the sections already done and piece them together, adding just enough to fit your measurements. The gambesons are different, of course—we don't do those, but there are several seamstresses that work with us to make sure they fit the customer properly."

Will held up his arm and examined the armor. It was coated in oil that was already leaving gray stains on the linen underneath. Each ring was linked through four others, and there were tiny rivets holding them closed. "It must take forever to make this," he murmured.

The apprentice laughed. "You have no idea. I see those little rivets even in my sleep." He held a large leather bag out to Will.

"What's this for?"

"When you take it off," said the other man. "The leather is heavily oiled. It will help keep the mail from rusting."

"What if it rusts anyway?"

The apprentice smiled. "It will. Just put it in the bag and shake it. Or you can rub the mail against itself. Make sure to add oil to it now and then, including the bag. If something happens and it gets really bad, bring it back to us. We have a big sand tumbler we use for exceptionally rusty armor."

Will returned to camp feeling as though he had grown several feet taller. He definitely got a few extra looks from the camp guards, for not many of the soldiers wore mail aside from the sergeants and officers. Some of the veteran corporals had managed to save up enough for it, but they were few and far between.

When he rejoined his squad at lunchtime, Dave whistled. "Damn, that looks good! I'd kiss a lot of ass if I could get armor like that right now."

Will frowned. "Why?"

Corporal Taylor leaned in. "The orders came down just before noon. We move in two days."

"That soon?" asked Will. "I figured we had a few more weeks."

Sven broke in, "They don't pay us to think."

"They probably want to make sure we command the pass before Darrow tries to cross. There's been a rumor that the Patriarch might have a lot more men in Barrowden than we thought they did. If so, we might not be able to take Barrowden back. It might be all we can do to keep them out of Branscombe," explained the corporal.

"Easier to hold the pass than defend the town," agreed Tiny.

Unhappy with what he was hearing, Will protested, "We have to take Barrowden back. Won't the king be sending the rest of the army here?"

Corporal Taylor glanced around and lowered his voice. "They'd have been here already, which means they've probably been sent somewhere else, Cerria or Thornton maybe."

"Then someone screwed up!" swore Will, "Because Darrow is sending most of their army through Barrowden."

The others stared at him while Tiny closed his eyes and shook his head as if to say, 'idiot.' Hastily, Will added, "That's what I heard, anyway."

"You know something, don't you?" said the corporal with interest.

Will shook his head. "That's just what I heard the officers talking about when they arrested me last time," he improvised.

"Keep your voice down then," advised Corporal Taylor. "Or you'll be getting arrested again."

"Won't matter," snickered Dave. "He's better at getting arrested than I am."

They spent the next day packing wagons and double-checking lists while supply sergeants hurried back and forth, yelling at seemingly everyone. That evening the captain, Sir Kyle Barrentine, addressed the company personally, explaining that they would have the 'honor' of leading the vanguard.

That made little sense to Will, and he said as much as they gathered in the evening before lights out. Sven merely chuckled. "You'll see."

"What's that mean?" demanded Dave angrily. The ex-thief was no happier about being told they would be in the lead element than Will was. "Our company has the most inexperienced soldiers. Shouldn't they put the company with the most veterans up front?"

Sven shook his head. "First, this is just while we march, but I have no doubt they'll put us up front in the first battle as well. They put the green soldiers up front for a reason. If we get an easy fight and win, we build morale. If we don't, we soften up the enemy for the veterans to clean up after us. The veterans are less likely to run if things go ass-up too, and we can't run if they're behind us."

"Balls!" exclaimed Dave. "How do I get put in a veteran company? This sucks."

Tiny laughed. "That's easy. Live through the first few battles. After enough of us die, they'll probably reorganize us into different companies."

"Bullshit," said Dave. "We haven't had a real war in over fifty years. Who are they to say who's experienced and who isn't?"

"At least the veterans have fought bandits and whatnot before," said Sven. "That's more than we can say."

Something occurred to Will then. "Sven, you served a full contract before. Why didn't they put you in one of the veteran companies?"

"I'm a conscript now," replied the older man, "so I don't really count. More importantly, they don't make new companies out of nothing but green soldiers. They always mix in a few old timers to help the boys grow into soldiers."

"Who are you calling a boy?" asked Dave belligerently.

"You," said Sven pointedly. "You can't even have a drink without starting a fight or trying to steal something."

It seemed as though a fight was imminent, but Dave relaxed after a tense moment, then he replied, "I never drink when I'm stealing."

Maybe he's maturing, thought Will.

***

They woke up well before dawn on the day they left, and even as they were beginning to take down the tents, Will saw several groups of horsemen leave the camp. "Where are they going?" he asked Sven.

"Scouts," said the veteran. "They have to make sure the engineers don't get ambushed."

"Engineers?"

Sven laughed. "The ones who check the route and clear obstructions. The column can only march as wide as the narrowest point, otherwise everything goes to shit."

"I never thought it would be so complicated," observed Will.

"You haven't seen the half of it yet," said the old soldier. "First scouts, then engineers, then they'll send us. They'll send the companies out in intervals with some space between us in case there's an obstruction, so we don't all pile up. Behind the main body the wagons will follow, and then behind them the rearguard. We'll stop at the new camp before the rearguard even leaves this place."

"Huh? How does that make sense?" asked Will.

"You'll see," said Sven. "We'll be preparing the camp for a couple of hours before they reach us. We probably won't march more than five hours. And this is a *small* army. It gets even worse with a larger force."

Sven's words proved to be accurate. Company B led the column, marching five abreast through the morning. They stopped at noon and after a brief rest they were put to clearing brush and digging latrines. Men were also sent out to collect wood for the evening fires, and others began setting up tents and preparing food.

In the late afternoon the wagons started arriving, and the drivers and rearguard went to work unloading mules and caring for the horses. Once that was done, the evening meal was started and a variety of minor chores were begun. Watches were set, but most of the soldiers were in their bedrolls shortly after sundown.

Will was glad he hadn't been assigned to one of the night watches, for it seemed that almost as soon as he had put his head down Sergeant Nash was shouting for them to all rise and begin it all over again. Sitting up, he stared bleary-eyed, at the oiled bag that held his mail, wondering if he should put it on. The army had only covered ten miles the day before, but the march combined with all the labor had made the extra weight a misery.

I'll still have to carry it, whether I wear it or not, he told himself. *And if something does happen...* With a sigh, he removed it from the bag and began shrugging it over his head and shoulders.

CHAPTER 46

The second day's march was much like the first, except everyone was a little more tired. Will couldn't help but compare their travel to what it was like alone. A small group on foot could reach the top of the pass in a single day if they pushed themselves, though most would go slower and take two, but a large column took three days.

They had been on the march for three hours when something caught his eye. The road ahead was gradually rising, and the terrain on either side was increasingly rocky, but to the left a distant ravine caused it to slope downward. Trees and brush obscured everything in the distance until the next mountain rose up behind the tops of the trees. What held his attention was a spot where the turyn swirled in an unusual pattern, as though a person or large animal hid behind the thick brush.

Turning his head, he searched farther back and saw a few other similar places he hadn't noticed as they marched. Opening his mouth, he tried to catch Corporal Taylor's attention. "There are men hidden to our left."

The rest of the squad looked as they continued marching, but no one saw anything. "I don't see anything," said the corporal. "The scouts would have reported it if anyone was there."

"I saw them," insisted Will.

Sergeant Nash, who had been walking alongside the company, drew closer. "Dress the line! You're too slow!"

The corporal sped up, but he also responded, "Sergeant, one of my men saw something in the ravine to our left."

"We aren't stopping because some green recruit is jumping at shadows," barked the sergeant.

Will didn't like the way things were progressing, for the more he looked the more convinced he became that at least seven or eight men were hiding within thirty yards of the road. With the way the terrain dipped, there could easily be many more beyond them that were completely blocked from sight. He was afraid of the consequences, but after a moment he simply stopped in his tracks. "Sergeant, they're there. I can show you."

The men behind might have marched right over him, but Tiny stopped as well, and his sheer mass was far harder to ignore. Sergeant Nash began screaming, and the look on Corporal Taylor's face suggested he would have loved nothing more than to be able to vanish from the face of the earth. The entire company came to a halt and despite the shouting, Will heard the sound of hooves approaching as the captain rode up.

"Sergeant Nash! What the hell is going on?" demanded Sir Kyle.

"One of the new recruits is afraid of his own shadow," growled Sergeant Nash.

"Take him out of the line and have him whipped. Now, get these men moving," ordered the knight captain.

Will could see his chance of getting through to them quickly vanishing, so before the captain could ride on, he shouted, "I saw their helmets! Just over there!" He jumped and pointed to emphasize his point.

"I saw them too," lied Tiny, his deep voice booming.

Sergeant Nash hesitated then, and Sir Kyle rode closer. "Both of you saw this?"

"Yes, sir," answered Will and Tiny bobbed his head in agreement.

The captain lifted his arm and signaled to Lieutenant Latimer, who was riding farther back on the opposite side of the column, giving him the signal for a full halt even though they were already stopped. He leaned over in the saddle and gave Will a glare that could scour the rust from mail. "If we don't find anything, I'll have you both whipped." Then he began giving orders. "Send a runner back to let the other platoons know we are forming up to march on the left side of the road. They are to do likewise. Have Sergeant Moon send a runner from Second Platoon to inform Company D of our action."

In the span of a few minutes, Will saw the payoff for their months of drill practice as the entire company formed a line seventy-five men long and two ranks deep facing the left side of the road. Will and Tiny were in the front rank along with the rest of their squad. Sir Kyle and Lieutenant Latimer rode behind at either end of the formation.

The knight captain's voice boomed over their heads, "Company B, forward march!" and a hundred and fifty men began to advance in step with one another. "Shields up, ready arms! Sergeants, watch the line!"

The line shifted as they crossed the rugged terrain and were forced to accommodate obstacles like bushes and small trees, keeping the sergeants busy as they ranged back and forth behind them, shouting orders to keep the company in formation. Will started to get nervous as he saw that the strange flows of turyn no longer showed, indicating the watchers had withdrawn. At fifty yards, the company began to descend a steeper slope and there were still no enemies in sight.

Then a lone man broke from concealment behind an isolated boulder, running away from the shield wall. Shouts went up from the soldiers as they saw him, and the sergeants were busy once more keeping the men from speeding up to catch the stranger. "Hold the line, goddamn it!" shouted Sergeant Nash. "This isn't a fucking race!"

They reached the bottom of the shallow ravine and started up the other side when a long line of men just twenty yards away appeared, pushing aside the cut bushes they were using to conceal themselves and raising crossbows. Will ducked his head and felt something heavy strike his shield.

"Forward, double time! Stay together!" shouted one of the sergeants.

Will could see the head of a heavy bolt had come all the way through his shield and was now wedged there, halfway through, and from behind he heard someone cry out in pain. Looking over the top of his shield, he saw the crossbowmen fire again before turning tail and running. Something hard glanced off the top of his steel cap.

Even at a double-time march, they had no hope of catching up to the fleeing enemies, but Sir Kyle was firm in not letting the men charge. They followed the crossbowmen for several hundred yards before the knight gave the order to slow to a normal march, and they continued at that pace for another half a mile before he called a halt. Shortly thereafter, they returned to the road and assumed a defensive formation.

Sir Kyle was sending another runner back. "Tell them to get the chirurgeon up here. They can put him on a horse. I've got men bleeding to death here."

Will spotted Sergeant Nash and stepped toward him. "Sir, I have experience with wounds."

A few minutes later, he found himself with two or three other men, trying to treat those who had been hit by crossbow quarrels. Six men had been wounded: three had in and out wounds in their lower legs, which were fairly simple, but two of the others had bolts buried in their chests. The sixth was dying, and Will knew at a glance there was little hope for that soldier, for the head of the bolt had gone through just beneath his neck.

The leg wounds were already under control, with pressure being applied, so Will went to one of the men with a bolt in his chest. Someone had already cut the shaft down so only a few inches of wood protruded. Taking out his knife, Will carefully cut the soldier's padded gambeson away so he could see the wound itself.

The head had gone through the padding and sunk a full two inches into the unfortunate fellow's chest, just below the collarbone on his left side. Ignoring the man's screams, Will probed the wound, noting that only a trickle of blood emerged. *It missed the artery,* he thought with relief. If the head was barbed like the one that had gone through his shield, though, he couldn't safely draw it out. Removing it might hit the artery at worst, and at best would cause a lot more damage.

"I need some feathers," said Will, glancing up.

Sergeant Brummett was looking over his shoulder. "What?"

"Feathers," repeated Will. "Preferably large ones, like the sort you'd make a quill pen from." The sergeant went to see what he could find, and Will went to examine the other man with a chest wound.

The second chest wound was less serious, as it had only gone in far enough to bury the head of the bolt, and it was below the ribs. Will judged it could be removed safely, but he decided to wait on the feathers to minimize the damage it would do.

The company began marching again, while Will and the two other men who were experienced with wounds, Tims and Granthon, stayed with the wounded. Lieutenant Latimer rode up to them a minute later.

The lieutenant offered Will two quill pens he had scavenged from his writing kit. "This is the best I could find. The company will continue marching for another hour. After the chirurgeon gets here, follow the rest of the column and meet up with your squads. Doctor Guerin will have these men sent back to Branscombe."

The officer started to mount up again, but Will called out to him. "We need a pot to boil some water, sir."

Granthon spoke up. "I've got one in my pack."

The lieutenant left, and Tims watched as Will trimmed the points from the quills, leaving a blunt end with a large hole. "What are you doing?" asked the soldier.

"We're going to take the point out of him, but I don't want the barbs to tear him up," said Will. Using his knife, he cut the entry hole in the wounded soldier's chest a little wider. Then he inserted first one and then the other quill into the wound, slipping them over the barbed points.

"Start pulling on the shaft," said Will. "Slowly." Tims began pulling, while Will made sure each quill remained firmly over the tips of the barbs. Half a minute later, the head of the bolt was out, followed by a slightly stronger flow of blood. "Put pressure on it until we can clean it. I'll start on the other one."

Moving to the other man, he repeated the process with Granthon's help. Then he instructed them to start a fire while he started searching for herbs. "Bring it to a boil and put some of the linen we cut into the water while I'm looking," he told them.

He didn't have much hope of finding anything useful, such as yarrow. It was the wrong time of the year and the terrain didn't favor that plant, but he studied the grasses around them anyway. Eventually he settled on a coarse bush that grew in clumps not far from the road. In that strange way he had previously discovered, he could tell that the bush wasn't edible, but neither was it poisonous, and he got the sense that it might keep the wound from festering.

Will gathered several large handfuls of the leaves and then returned. Once the linen had been boiled, he removed two large squares and used them to make two small pouches, which he filled with leaves. Returning to the pot, he dipped them in the still-boiling water for a minute and then removed them.

He was hoping that the heat had softened the leaves sufficiently, and he used the pommel of his knife to crush them against the side of the pot to help bruise them further. That done, he waited for them to cool and then dressed the men's wounds with them before repeating the process all over again for the soldiers with leg wounds.

The sixth man had already passed away.

Together, the three of them waited with the injured soldiers until Doctor Guerin rode up an hour later. The chirurgeon examined the wounds carefully before addressing them, "Who did this?"

Tims and Granthon said nothing, so finally Will answered, "I guess you mean me, sir."

"Who told you to draw the bolts? These men could have died!" said the doctor angrily. "And what's in these poultices?"

Will explained what he had done, and after a few minutes the doctor was somewhat mollified. "You've had some training. Who told you about the trick with the feathers?"

"My mother, sir, she's a midwife in Barrowden," he answered.

"Hmmph!" said Doctor Guerin. "Well, I guess she knew what she was about, though I wouldn't expect a midwife to have known how to extract a barbed head. How about the plant you used?"

"I don't know the name of it, but I've seen her use it on wounds before," Will lied.

"I guess we'll leave it for now," said the doctor, "but I'll change it once the baggage carts get here. You men should return to your squads."

***

That evening all the talk was about their brief engagement. As Will and his squad mates sat on their bedrolls, Dave asked him, "How did you see those soldiers?"

"The sun reflected off of one of their helms, I think," said Will. "After that I just kept looking until I saw one of them pop his head up."

"You got lucky," said Corporal Taylor. "It was pretty cloudy today."

Sven piped up, "I'm more surprised one of them was foolish enough to stick his head up. They were good enough to fool the scouts."

"You must feel pretty stupid," groused Dave. "All it got us was five men wounded and one dead. We didn't kill a single one of them."

Sven glared at the ex-cutpurse. "Shut up. People wouldn't know what a damned idiot you were if you didn't talk."

"It's the truth!" protested Dave. "Actually, now that I look back, I wish I'd been wounded. Those guys get to take it easy back in Branscombe."

Corporal Taylor spoke up, "You should be glad he spotted them. Otherwise we might be going hungry soon. They weren't waiting for us. They were waiting for the supply wagons."

Will stood up. "How long do we have before lights out?"

"What lights?" asked Dave sarcastically. "All we have is a campfire."

"We stopped early today, so we still have an hour," said Corporal Taylor.

"I'm going to stretch my legs," said Will.

"I'll come with you," volunteered Tiny.

The corporal nodded. "Don't go outside the perimeter, otherwise the patrol guard will be all over my ass."

Will and Tiny walked until they were beyond the reach of the light from the campfires, then Will stopped. "I need to talk to someone. I wasn't expecting you to come."

"I can go back if you want," offered the big soldier.

"It's all right, just try not to be surprised," said Will. Under his breath he repeated a single word three times, 'Tailtiu.' Deep down he felt something, and he knew she had heard him.

Ten minutes passed in near silence before Tiny asked, "Is someone supposed to meet you?"

Will nodded. "She'll be here soon, I think. Thank you for today, by the way."

The big man shrugged. "I don't have many talents, but I know who to trust."

A voice purred at them from the darkness, "You have good taste then."

Will tried to reassure Tiny, who looked as though he was about to jump out of his skin. "Don't worry, it's my friend." It was then that a slender hand snaked up behind the big man and stroked Tiny's cheek and neck.

"W-wh-who are you?" said Tiny, his voice tremulous.

"Leave him be, Tailtiu," said Will sternly. "He's never met any fae before."

Tailtiu peered at him from around Tiny's shoulder. "Oh, I like them fresh." Then she moved around to the big soldier's front and gazed up at him hungrily. "And he looks delicious."

Tiny stood frozen in place, though whether it was from magic or fear, Will wasn't sure. His eyes moved down, taking in the fae woman's naked form. She was still covered in scars, though they were a dark green now, making her appearance even more feral. After a few seconds Tailtiu turned away and stepped toward Will. She opened her arms as though she would embrace him but almost immediately leaped back, hissing.

"Nasty!" she exclaimed. "What is that all over you? Iron? Why, William? Why would you do that?"

He chuckled. "I like breathing. This helps keep arrows out of me."

"Don't expect a kiss from me until you've taken it off and had a long bath," said Tailtiu with obvious disgust. Will saw one of Tiny's brows go up in surprise. The fae woman noticed as well and she gave the big man a sultry look. "Didn't you know? I'm his aunt, but don't let that fool you. We're very—close."

Alarmed, Will waved his hands at Tiny. "Don't listen to her. It isn't like that."

"Sure it is," said Tailtiu. "Would you like me to show you?"

Ignoring her remark, Will continued, "You still owe me another day."

Tailtiu sighed. "Always business with you. What do you want?"

"Can you move about without being seen?"

426

"Of course," answered his aunt, before glancing back at Tiny. She puffed her chest out slightly and formed her lips into a sly pout. "But I much prefer being seen."

Will's friend was turning red, and Will worried that Tiny might pass out from the strain of enduring Tailtiu's attention. "I want you to scout the mountain ahead of us. There may be soldiers in the area."

"Of course, there are," she said abruptly, waving her hand toward the camp. "I can smell hundreds of them over there, along with an unsavory amount of iron."

"That's our camp," said Will dryly.

His aunt smiled sweetly. "I knew that."

"How long will it take you?" he asked.

She pretended to think, putting one hand on her chin, then answered, "I don't know. I'll find you when I'm done."

Will had hoped it would be quick and easy, but he guessed that was just hopeful thinking. "We have to go back to the camp. I'll call you tomorrow—"

"It won't take that long, silly boy. Not to worry, I'll find you when I'm done."

"But we'll be in camp."

Tailtiu began walking away, fading into the darkness. "I can always find you, Will." She glanced back once, her eyes glowing ominously. "Remember that."

Once he was sure she was gone, Will nudged Tiny who seemed to have fallen into a trance, staring into the darkness. "Come on. Let's go back."

"Oh, right," said the big man. As they were walking, he asked a question, "So she's really your aunt?"

"Don't remind me," grumbled Will.

"And you—with her—you—?"

"No!"

They got back to their beds just in time, and while Dave was as talkative as usual, Tiny said not a word until after the fire was extinguished. Will was beginning to drift off to sleep when he heard the big man mutter to himself, "She's not *my* aunt, though."

 CHAPTER 47

In his sleep, Will found himself running through a forest, chased by a foe he couldn't see. Whenever he turned to look, all he saw behind him were golden cat's eyes, and no matter how he raced he couldn't escape the beast. Near the end he could feel its breath on his neck, until he turned a corner and found himself face to face with a dark-haired woman. It was Isabel. She put a finger to his lips to keep him silent, and he found himself sinking into her gaze. Like pools of clear water, her eyes threatened to swallow him, and he realized he couldn't breathe.

"William Cartwright," she whispered, and he found himself wondering how to answer. "William Cartwright, you will be mine."

Run, said a voice deep within. *Run before it's too late.*

"William Cartwright," she said again. "I've bought and paid for you. You will be the finest slave to serve me. Show me the limnthal."

"Thrice called," said another voice, and Will's eyes shot wide open. Tailtiu was leaning over him, her nose mere inches from his own. She had her hand over his mouth. "Shhh. Don't wake them."

Will turned his head, but quickly realized he couldn't even see the closest bedroll, aside from Tiny's, where the big man's body made a darker shadow against the mist that covered everything. "How?"

"No one will see me in this fog," said his aunt, "so long as you don't wake them."

"You did that?"

Her eyes crinkled into a smile and she nodded. "Of course. It made it much easier to search the pass without being seen."

"What did you find?"

"Men," she said simply. "Lots and lots of men, as far as my eyes could see. Were there always so many of your kind?"

"How many did you find?"

"As many as there are in your camp and half again more," she answered. "Most are on the other side of the pass, waiting just beyond the high point. A third are hidden in a camp in the rocks several miles south of here."

"Hidden?"

Tailtiu nodded. "No fires. They sleep clustered in small groups among the rocks that cluster along the side of the mountain to the south. Is that what you wished to know?"

"Yes. Thank you," said Will gratefully. "This resolves your debt for the favor."

She shook her head. "You still have another half day left, plus two more unbounded favors, but tonight could be free if you let me have the big one for an hour." Her eyes turned to focus on Tiny's sleeping form.

"No."

"Half an hour," she countered. "He'll thank you for it."

"No," said Will firmly. "Besides, he's his own man. I have no right to barter him."

Tailtiu's features showed surprise. "Oh, but you do! Or didn't you know?"

"Pardon?"

"The accord between Faerie and the mortal realm," she said matter-of-factly, "is held in trust by your kind. Or rather, it's held in trust by *you*, since you're the last one."

"The last what?"

"Wizard, silly," she answered. "Once you're gone, we can do as we please, for the accord will no longer hold force. Any humans that seek to deal with us will have to negotiate with their own strength—the strength of power—and from what I've seen, most of them have none. Didn't Father tell you?"

"I'm barely a wizard."

"But you're marked as one," said Tailtiu, "and that's all that counts. The limnthal proves it. It's a shame you didn't give it to Mother. Then I wouldn't have to ask." Her eyes flashed. "I could just take what I want."

"What about the wizards in Wurthaven?"

She cocked her head to one side. "Do they have it?" Tailtiu smiled. "I don't think so."

The simple, uncaring malice in her features made his mouth go dry. "I don't need anything else," he told her. "You should go."

"Very well. Take good care of yourself, nephew. When you're gone we will *devour* them." With those parting words, she disappeared into the mist.

Will lay quietly in his bed, but the warmth was gone, replaced by an empty coldness that chilled him to his bones. He tried to sleep, but his mind was spinning. If mankind was protected by some ancient accord, what did that mean exactly? The fae couldn't take humans without his permission? An evil thought came to him. *Does that mean I could offer the Darrowans to them in exchange for getting rid of the invading army?*

He shivered at the idea, and though he had no concrete knowledge, he suspected his grandfather would consider it a betrayal of the trust he had been given. Dealing with the fae was risky enough, but selling the life of a human to them was definitely an act of warlockry. Selling thousands was pure evil.

Will was unsure of the time. His body wanted him to return to sleep, but he still needed to figure out how to share the knowledge he had gained without getting himself into even more trouble. *Campfires,* he thought, *but it won't work after dawn.* Shrugging off his blanket, he rose from his bed and headed for the latrine.

On his way back he began to run, assuming an air of urgency. "Lights!" he told the camp watchmen. "There are lights to the south!"

That got their attention, but when they went to confirm none of the night watch could see anything. The perimeter patrol also reported having seen nothing, but Will persisted, claiming he had seen several lights in the darkness to the south. After some argument, they took him back to his platoon's tent and woke Sergeant Nash.

"Is it already time?" asked the sergeant groggily.

One of the patrollers spoke first. "One of your men is saying he saw lights to the south, but no one else can confirm his reporting."

Sergeant Nash sat up, irritation on his face. "Who's the jackass?"

"Me, sir," offered Will.

The sergeant stared at him until his eyes focused in the dim light, then he groaned. "Goddamn it, Cartwright, not you again."

"I really saw them, Sergeant," insisted Will. "They put them out after only a minute or two."

"What time is it?" Nash asked the guards who had come with Will.

"It's the middle of third watch, Sergeant. Roughly an hour before wake-up call."

The sergeant stared at Will, his expression unreadable. "Why should I believe you, Cartwright?"

"I have very good eyesight," said Will. "I swear there's an army out there. If we do nothing they'll be at our rear tomorrow."

"And yet none of the scouts found anyone to the south of us yesterday," grumbled Sergeant Nash.

"They didn't find the crossbowmen either, sir," Will reminded him.

The sergeant got to his feet. "We'll let the captain decide, but this is on you, Cartwright. If you're wrong, I'll make sure you wish you were never born."

Sir Kyle was none too pleased to be woken early, but the knight hid his annoyance better. "I'm not rousing the entire camp early on one man's word," he pronounced. Glancing at Lieutenant Latimer, he ordered, "Send four men, two to the south-southwest, two to the south-southeast. Cartwright, you'll go south on your own. Since you have such keen eyes, I'm sure you'll be fine, and if not, you'll be one less headache I have to deal with. Report back in an hour."

Shortly after that, Will found himself walking alone by the light of the stars. There was no moon, but the sky was clear and Tailtiu's mist had dispersed. Once his eyes had adjusted, he had enough light to walk without tripping, but the terrain ahead of him was just a mixture of blacks and grays. The turyn that flowed through the air helped slightly, and he hoped that by paying close attention to it he would be able to make out the positions of any guards that might lie ahead.

With only an hour to spend he did his best to make good time. From what Tailtiu had said, the enemy was three or four miles distant, an easy walk on level ground, but in the mountains, it was far harder. He had no way to track time, so he would have to guess at how long he had traveled.

After what he judged to be a half an hour, the landscape became more rugged and he doubted he had gone more than a mile. He saw no sign of the enemy, but he believed his aunt's report, so he continued on. He kept going, determined to vindicate himself.

The sky was beginning to brighten in the east, and he knew he had probably been gone more than an hour before he saw the telltale disturbances in the flows that indicated men hidden ahead. Most probably they were enemy sentries. Just as Tailtiu had said, the land dropped away behind them into a wide crevasse of some type. *They must be hidden down there.*

Turning west, he followed it for several hundred yards until he could see the land was smoothing out. He guessed that the enemy must enter the deep ravine from there. With two hours gone and dawn rapidly approaching, Will knew the army would begin to march soon, so he turned and began running back.

The light made it safer to run, but the rough terrain made it tiring, even without his mail. He began drawing turyn in and focusing it in his legs and lungs until his fatigue vanished. Once the land smoothed out it was easier, but as the army came into sight he could see they were already forming up to march.

"I told you one hour, Cartwright!" snapped Sir Kyle when Will was brought before him. "The others were back two hours ago. I'd given you up as a deserter."

"I found them," said Will, still struggling to catch his breath. He did his best to describe what he had seen.

Sergeant Eckels from Company B's Third Platoon stood close by. "A man will say anything to avoid a whipping."

"I'll still be whipped if they aren't there," argued Will.

"If they've got units behind us and a solid force at the top of the pass, we'll be hard put to survive," said Lieutenant Latimer.

"Which is why we scouted the area so thoroughly," growled Sir Kyle. "And they found nothing." He glared at Will. "Have you had any training as a scout?"

"No, sir," he admitted.

The knight captain's face was pensive, but after a minute he gave his orders, "Stop the march. Send runners to Lord Fulstrom and the other captains." That done, he glanced at Will. "Return to your squad."

Will did as he was told, donning his armor and waiting with the others while Lord Fulstrom and his knights decided on their course of action. Corporal Taylor watched him the entire time with eyes that seemed as though they would burn a hole through his armor. Tiny didn't ask him any questions, but Dave was far from reticent.

"What the hell did you do now? The entire camp is on standby. Why aren't we marching yet?" asked the ex-thief.

Will shrugged. "I saw some lights last night and Sir Kyle sent me out scouting afterward."

The horns sounded then and they had to fall in line. Three companies were sent directly south, while Company B and the other three were ordered to move a full mile west before also heading south. They remained in a standard marching formation until the shift south, at which time they were shifted into a combat line three ranks deep.

After a mile and a half, they reached the sloping entrance to the ravine that Will had found that morning. Companies A and C stood to the left and right respectively, their lines angling forward, while Company B took the center. When they within a hundred yards of the place where the walls of the ravine began to rise up, the officers called a halt and they began to wait.

Half an hour passed, and thick clouds of smoke appeared in the distance, coming from the ravine ahead of them. Horns blared, and the sounds of men shouting followed soon after, and then Will caught sight of the Darrowans emerging from the ravine. The enemy formation was anything but orderly, but the mob of soldiers began to form a line once they spotted the Terabinian troops waiting for them.

"Forward march double-time!" yelled Sir Kyle from behind, and the sergeants repeated his order. Company B began moving forward.

Will glanced at Tiny, who was on his right, and the big man nodded at him. "Keep your head down," said the big man, his lips tight.

The Darrowans were already in rough line when they finally made contact. Shouts went up, and the clash of spears against shields filled Will's ears. Something struck the top of his helm, and then his shield was nearly torn from his grasp as a more forceful blow struck it as well. A spear tip came through the gap as Will's shield shifted. It struck the right side of his belly, almost knocking the wind from him, but it didn't have enough power behind it to pierce his mail.

The enemy was getting the worst of it, and they might have broken, but their soldiers were desperate. They had nowhere to run. Companies A and C closed on the enemy flanks, and the Darrowan soldiers began to die in greater numbers.

As the enemy started to panic, they surged forward, threatening to overwhelm Company B's line. Will saw Sven fall on his left, and the enemy began to push forward, overwhelming Dave and the men farther down.

In seconds, Will knew their defensive line would break, and the fight would turn into a chaotic melee. Dropping his spear, Will did the only thing he could think of, casting the one spell he knew. A second later, a green line connected with one of the enemies and he pushed a generous amount of his turyn into the man before dismissing the spell. He repeated the spell as quickly as he could, and one after another the Darrowans nearest him began to collapse, vomiting onto the ground. Five, six, seven, Will kept going, though his head was beginning to spin. The first rank of Company B had collapsed, falling back while the second rank moved forward to take their place.

Will's knees started to buckle, but a strong hand caught him. Tiny pulled him up and braced him. "Don't stop," said the big man.

Rather than pushing turyn out, Will drained the next enemy he caught with his spell. His energy returned, along with a brief wave of nausea. Once he had recovered from that, he began repeating his previous actions, injecting his personal turyn into every Darrowan that came within fifteen feet of him.

Eventually he exhausted himself again, and this time he stumbled before Tiny could catch him. Will tried to rise, but a pain in his side made it difficult to get his feet back under him.

"Relax," said Tiny. "You're hurt. The others are coming up from behind them now. It's almost over."

Looking down, Will saw blood soaking the right side of his gambeson, though he couldn't find a hole in his mail. *How did that happen?* he wondered. Tired beyond belief, he sat down, and the next thing he knew he was opening his eyes to stare up into a blue sky. Somehow, he had wound up on his back.

Tiny was sitting next to him, so Will asked, "Did we win?"

The big man nodded. "We did. We took some losses, but fewer than they expected, given how many we faced."

"Really?"

"Yeah. You had a lot to do with that," said Tiny.

"I couldn't do much."

Tiny chuckled. "You took the wind out of their charge. I think you must have put at least twenty of them out of the fight." He glanced to one side, then back again. "Shhh, Sergeant Nash is coming."

"Is he dying?" asked Nash when he was close enough.

"I don't think so," said Tiny. "Something narrow went through his mail, but it wasn't deep. He's lost some blood. Where's the doctor?"

Sergeant Nash's face appeared above Will, blocking out the sun. "I'd love to know how you spotted their fires last night."

"Why?" asked Will, doing his best to concentrate on the sergeant's words.

"Because I heard from the companies that smoked them out that the Darrowans apparently kept a cold camp. There was no sign of campfires," said the sergeant, studying him suspiciously.

"Maybe they had a patrol with lanterns," said Will. "I definitely saw *something*."

"They'd have to be incredibly stupid to do something like that," said the sergeant before turning away. "I guess we should be grateful that the enemy is so inept."

# CHAPTER 48

Will's wound was even less serious than Tiny had first thought. The puncture in his side was fairly small, though it had bled a lot. He never discovered what had actually given him the wound, but the prevailing theory was that it had been a crossbow bolt with a bodkin point, since quite a few of them were found on the field after the battle, and several other men had been wounded by them.

The tips of such quarrels had a square cross-section that tapered to a long, slender point. Fired from close enough range, they sometimes split rings and went completely through mail, but Will had been more fortunate. His mail had held, and only the tip of the point had gone through far enough to pierce him. It had been pure dumb luck that it had nicked a small vein and caused him to bleed so much.

Sven admitted to some jealously. While Will's injury wasn't enough to get him sent back, it did free him from duty for the next couple of days. Will wasn't quite as enthusiastic, since Dave was also lightly injured and the two of them would be spending their time resting in close proximity. The ex-thief had fallen down when their line started to collapse, and he the rush of men had nearly trampled him. Dave had been fortunate to escape with nothing more than a few large bruises.

Lord Fulstrom had ordered their force to remain in camp for two days while the aftermath of the battle was taken care of. The wounded were sent back to Branscombe, and the dead were buried. The Darrowan force of some four hundred had been slaughtered nearly to a man, and the result was a mound of dead that was difficult to deal with.

In the end, the Terabinian army piled up the enemy corpses within the ravine and burned them, after stripping them of armor, weapons, and valuables. A few of the Terabinian soldiers were lucky enough to scavenge mail from the bodies that would fit them, though not many, because such armor was just as rare amongst the common soldiers of Darrow as it was amongst the Terabinians.

Sven was the first to return to the tent after the first day's hard labor disposing of bodies. He glanced at Will and Dave sourly. "Enjoying your holiday?"

Dave grinned. "Absolutely."

Will's expression was considerably less enthusiastic, and he looked in Dave's direction before meeting Sven's eyes. "Not so much," he answered. "How was your day?"

"Just the drab life of a grave digger," said Sven. "Things would have been a lot better if Lord Fulstrom hadn't been so bloodthirsty."

"What do you mean?" asked Will.

"I heard the sergeants talking about it," said Sven. "According to them, it was poor judgment not to allow the enemy to surrender, or even run if that wasn't practical."

Dave scowled. "It served them right. They should learn that death is the only payment for invading us."

Sven shook his head in disgust. "We lost more than a hundred men, most of them after the Darrowans started to rout."

"A hundred dead?" asked Will.

"No, maybe forty dead, but another sixty or so had injuries so severe they had to be sent back. For those of us here that's just as bad."

"What does that have to do with not letting them surrender?" asked Dave angrily.

"If you don't let the enemy flee, they keep fighting," said the older man. "Even the injured ones that can't run are still dangerous. They'll stab you from the ground, and the ones still on their feet will fight like the damned if they know they're about to be slaughtered."

The ex-thief still wasn't sympathetic. "It isn't as if we can afford to take that many prisoners."

"You still don't get it. We lost a hundred men, and three-fourths of those were hurt after we could have stopped fighting. Even if we had captured the entire Darrowan contingent, we could have escorted them back to Branscombe with only forty or fifty men to guard them, and there were far less of them by that point anyway. It's simple math. Let's say we had captured the last two hundred. Disarmed and put in a line, we could send twenty men to escort them back. If we had lost twenty-five of our own and then sent twenty with them, we'd only be down forty-five."

"And we're already short. They outnumber us," put in Will.

"Who says?" asked Dave.

"I do," said Will, feeling irritable. "There's twice as many waiting for us in the pass, and a lot more about to march up from Barrowden."

Sven stared at him intently. "How do you know that?"

Realizing he had said more than he should, Will looked away. "I don't know it. It's just a feeling."

"The same sort of feeling you had when you claimed to see helmets in the brush the other day, or lights at night, when no one else saw them?" asked the old soldier.

"Something like that," said Will.

Tiny ducked through the door of the tent, saving him from answering any more awkward questions. "Sergeant Nash said to get you."

Will got to his feet. Other than feeling slightly fatigued, he was none the worse for the previous day's injury. "What does he want?"

"Lord Fulstrom wants to talk to you," said Tiny.

Uh oh, thought Will, but he kept his concern to himself. Exiting the tent, he found two mailed armsmen waiting to escort him. They were obviously men from the baron's personal guard. Will didn't bother asking them questions while they walked. He recognized the one on his left; it was the same man who had bloodied his lip during his first meeting with the baron. *That's not a bad sign,* he told himself sarcastically.

Baron Fulstrom's personal tent was less impressive than the one he had occupied in Branscombe, but it was still the biggest in the camp, a modest pavilion some fifty feet wide on each side. Will bowed when he came into the Lord Commander's presence. Lieutenant Stanton sat nearby at a small table. "You asked for me, milord?"

The lord studied him quietly for a long minute, during which Will became increasingly uncomfortable. Eventually he spoke. "Have you had any training as a scout, Mister Cartwright?"

"No, Your Lordship."

"Then how is it that you have not once, but twice found what none of our scouts could find?" asked Fulstrom.

"My mother always said I had the sharpest ears and the keenest eyesight in the village, milord," Will prevaricated. "I also spent a lot of time in the forest as a boy, playing games of hide and seek with my friends."

"And do you think this has given you skills my scouts lack?"

"No, Your Lordship," said Will hastily.

Lord Fulstrom frowned. "False modesty will do you no favors here, young man. Twice you have demonstrated your skills, and twice you have succeeded. I am told your wound was not great. How is your injury?"

"I lost some blood, milord, but I think I fainted from exhaustion as much as from that," said Will.

"I would like you to ride with my scouts, tomorrow," announced the baron. "Are you capable enough for it?"

Will's mind raced as he considered his options. Refusal seemed impossible, and this was a chance to provide the army with the information he had already gained. Plus, he thought he might discover more on his own. Having other eyes beside him would only limit what he could claim to have seen. "I am, milord, but I would rather not."

The baron's eyes hardened. "I see."

"Begging your pardon, milord, I would rather go alone—or separately at least," Will hurried to add.

"Explain your reasoning."

"Men on horseback are easier to spot," said Will. "I believe I can get closer on foot."

"Men on horseback are also harder to catch," said the baron. "They are more likely to survive to give a report. You think you can avoid being seen?"

Will nodded. "Yes, milord."

"The scouts leave at dawn tomorrow," said Fulstrom. "I would like you to go as well. If you prefer to go alone rather than with them, I will allow it." The baron turned away, clearly dismissing him.

But Will wasn't done. "Excuse me, Your Lordship. I would prefer to leave in the evening."

Fulstrom turned back, curiosity on his face. "I intend to march the morning after tomorrow. Our best estimate is that we can reach the enemy camp in less than two hours. If you leave at night, your report will come too late to be of any use."

"I'll start before nightfall," said Will. "Once it is dark, I should be able to enter their camp. If they have any surprises planned, I can discover them."

Lieutenant Stanton spoke for the first time. "It will be too dark for you to see anything. Assuming you aren't caught."

Will shook his head. "The new moon begins to wax tonight. There should be a sliver in the sky. If we have clear weather, I will be able to see. I'll definitely see better than the enemy."

Stanton looked to the baron, who seemed lost in thought. Finally, Lord Fulstrom made his decision. "You seem sure of yourself, and I have little to lose gambling on your cocksure attitude. We march early that night so we can catch them at dawn. Be back two hours before then or any knowledge you gain will be wasted." The baron waved his hand. "You may leave. Stanton, give Sir Kyle my instructions."

***

The next day passed slowly. Will felt fine, but he was still off the duty roster, so he had little to do. He had spent part of the night focusing on the small wound in his side, trying to replicate something of what he had done for Joey. He wasn't really sure if it had made a difference or not, but the wound showed no sign of sickening and the skin had nearly closed. Given what he knew of such wounds, he thought it was healing faster than usual, but he couldn't say for sure that it wasn't his imagination.

He tried thinking about what he would do when he left that evening on his special assignment, but it wasn't possible to plan much. The whole point of scouting was to find new information, so he would have to rely on his judgment to decide what to do once he had seen the enemy force. Other than that, all he could think was 'be sneaky,' and his inner critic had nothing but sarcasm for that plan.

In the late afternoon the first scouts began to return, and Will was summoned to Lord Fulstrom's tent once more so that he could listen to what they said. Their reports matched what Tailtiu had told him previously, though the scouts gave a more detailed account of distances. Darrow's army was four miles distant, at the narrowest part of the pass. Their forward sentries were a half mile closer, and the scouts had been unable to confirm just how many men the Patriarch had waiting for them.

Will feared that the soldiers of Branscombe would be slaughtered if they followed Fulstrom's plan to engage the well-defended position, especially given the fact that they were almost certainly outnumbered, but without a good reason for the knowledge he had no hope of convincing the baron of that.

When he returned to his tent, he shed his mail armor. He considered keeping the gambeson, but even that was stiff and rustled more than he liked, so he removed it as well. Instead he wore his tunic and a heavy cloak, bringing only his sword for defense. He'd be somewhat cold, but the cloak would keep him well enough, and its dark gray color would be useful in the darkness.

His squad mates were still out, performing their duties, so he was spared the trouble of explaining his departure.

Setting out, he jogged through the camp and no one stopped him until he reached the perimeter guard, but they waved him on after he gave his name. His body felt light, almost ephemeral. He had been forced to wear the heavy gambeson for months and the mail shirt for the past few weeks. Without them it seemed as though he floated over the ground. Without shield or spear, his hands were free and felt he stronger that he ever had.

Enjoying the sensation of freedom, Will began to run, and even the slight incline and rough ground couldn't drag him down.

He covered two miles before he slowed to a walk. The sun had set behind him, and the sky was dimming rapidly. The Darrowan army's forward sentries were somewhere roughly a mile ahead, if the scouts had been correct. He came to a halt, waiting on full night to hide him, but he wasn't idle.

"Tailtiu," he called softly, repeating her name twice more. "Thrice called, come and render your service."

Half an hour passed before she appeared, walking slowly toward him from the north. It was almost completely dark, and the sliver of a moon had yet to rise, but even so he saw her by the light of the stars. He waved to her as she approached.

"Your eyes are much better now," she said happily.

"Are they?"

She nodded. "Before, you wouldn't have noticed me in this light until I was much closer."

Previously he had known his eyesight wasn't the best, but lately he had begun to wonder if it was now even better than the keenest eyes among the soldiers. "How close to you think I could get to someone else in this light without being seen?" he asked.

Tailtiu looked thoughtful. "It varies with your kind, but a safe guess would be less than half the distance I was at when you waved. Human eyes are not bad in the day, but at night they are exceptionally poor."

Wow, he thought. He judged that he had waved to her at roughly a hundred yards, but he had seen her well before that. If what she said was true, then his night vision was significantly better than he had realized. It was no wonder he had found it so easy to sneak around the army camp back at Branscombe.

"What did you need this time?" she asked, breaking his train of thought.

"I want to sneak into the enemy camp," he told her. "The mist you summoned the other night seemed useful. Do you think you could do it for me?"

"So long as I come with you," she answered. "If you intend to send me back, the mist will vanish not long after I am gone."

That wasn't what he'd been hoping for, but he could adjust his plan. "Then you'll have to come with me," he said after a moment. "But don't distract me. If they discover me, I'm dead."

Tailtiu's eyes focused sharply on him. "Remember what I said before. If you die, there will be consequences."

"Are you planning to give me away?"

His aunt took on an expression of great offense. "Please. You should know I am bound to aid you during this time of service. If you are seen, it will be because of your own clumsiness."

CHAPTER 49

"There's two men ahead," said Tailtiu, her hand on his elbow. "Less than fifty yards."

Will could see fine out to about twenty feet, but the mist obscured everything beyond that. "Can you see them? How?" he asked.

"My mist is no barrier to my sight," she told him. "Open your ears. You should be able to hear them talking."

He listened intently, and after a moment he caught the sound of voices. The sentries were deep in conversation, and while he couldn't make out the words, he was surprised he hadn't heard them before. A second later he realized that he had unconsciously focused his turyn on his ears. *If I can do that, couldn't I do the same for my vision?* "How do you see through the mist?" he asked quietly.

"How do you breathe?" she returned, answering his question with another question.

"Huh?"

She sighed. "Mother told me wizards could do the same, but they use a human spell. My magic doesn't work that way, though. It simply happens when I need it."

"Could I do that?" Will asked. "I was able to hear better by concentrating. Is this similar?"

"Fae magic is instinctive," said Tailtiu. "Faerie is swimming in turyn, so we learn to use it the same way you use your feet for walking. You could try, but I don't know if you'll succeed."

"Give me a minute," said Will. Turning his attention inward, he tried to focus more turyn around his eyes while

448

he stared intently at the fog. Nothing happened at first, but then the mist grew bright, almost blinding him. "That's worse," he complained.

"What did you see?" she asked.

"The mist got so bright I could hardly see at all," he answered.

His aunt smiled. "That's the starlight. It won't help you. It reflects off the mist and reduces the distance you can see."

Will was disappointed. "I guess this won't work then."

"You give up too quickly. If you were able to do that, you may be able to see the way I do. You just need to change what you're seeing," said Tailtiu. That statement confused Will, and it showed on his face. His aunt explained further, "Starlight is just like daylight or moonlight. It's wonderful when the sky is clear, but in fog or mist it's terrible. You need to focus on the heart-light."

"Heart-light? There's more than one kind of light?"

She nodded. "Is everything one color? Of course not. Heart-light is similar to red, but deeper. It's the light given off by warm things. You just need to focus on that instead."

He tried again, and while he did, she continued talking. "It's sort of like the way you focus your eyes normally. Every mist or fog is different, so your eyes have to adjust to see the right kind of heart-light. You'll know which is best as your distance vision improves or worsens."

At first his vision grew brighter, the way it had before, but as he concentrated it shifted and became dark, until he could hardly see at all. "This isn't working," he complained.

"Look at me," said Tailtiu patiently. "When you get close to the right kind of light, my body will start to glow brighter from its warmth."

He did, changing the turyn in his eyes all the while, and suddenly he caught a glimmer. Adjusting his turyn more, he saw his aunt's body begin to glow until she stood out as a white figure against a gray background. Looking away, he kept at it until the fog seemed to vanish and the world shifted into a strange, ghostly landscape. The ground and rocks were varying shades of grey, along with the occasional trees and brush, and the sky above was a pure black with no stars to be seen.

The enemy sentries stood out so clearly that he felt sure they must see him, and it took him a moment to get his heart rate to slow down. *They can't see me,* he told himself. "This is incredible," he whispered.

"I'll take that as a compliment," said Tailtiu. "This will be much easier now that I don't have to worry about leading you around like some blind worm."

Will found himself overwhelmed by a whole new world of possibilities, and a new level of responsibility. Being able to see while his enemies could not, did that mean he should try to do something to tip the scales in the favor of his allies? Did he dare? He thought about killing the sentries. He could probably get close enough to use the source-link spell, but could he stomach murdering them in cold blood?

If he did, it would give the Terabinian army another half mile before the enemy spotted their advance at dawn. That might make a large difference in how ready the Darrowans were for them. "And if I don't kill them, more of us will die than otherwise would," he muttered. Right and wrong had never seemed more confusing.

"Or you could let me do it," said Tailtiu eagerly. "I'm at your beck and call for the rest of the night. There's no need for you to bloody your hands."

For a moment he was tempted by her offer, but deep down he knew it didn't change anything. His enemies would still be dead, and it would have been done by his command. It also seemed like a violation of whatever treaty the ancient wizards had worked out with the fae to protect humankind. No, if anyone died, it would be by his hand.

Will shook his head. "No thanks. What time do you think it is?" His aunt looked up at the stars and he saw turyn flickering around her eyes. "What are you doing?"

"Changing my vision so I can see the stars," she said simply. Then she added, "It's close to midnight now."

If the Darrowans used a similar system, that meant the sentries, he was looking at were on the second watch. They would probably be changed out in a couple of hours when the third watch came on duty. Killing them would only alert the enemy. "Let's go see how far we can get into their camp," he suggested.

Circling the sentries at a sufficient distance to avoid being heard, they moved on, until the perimeter guard of the Darrowan army came into view. With the advantage of the mist and near-perfect vision, it was laughably simple to get past them. The Darrowans had done their best to erect an earthen defense similar to what Will had worked on near Branscombe, but the hard, rocky soil had limited what they could do. A shallow ditch no more than two feet deep was backed by a similarly short mound of rocks and dirt.

Keeping an eye on the patrols, Will and Tailtiu walked into the ditch and then back up the slope behind it without much trouble. They were in the enemy camp.

The layout seemed familiar, for the Darrowans used a similar layout to what Will had grown used to. Fifty yards past the earthworks lay the first tents, arranged in small circles at regular intervals. Each circle of tents had a lantern hanging near the center, providing light for any night-blind soldiers who needed to take watch or relieve themselves at the latrines during the night.

Will moved on, walking through the areas he thought would be darkest, if he had been using his normal eyesight. It was hard to judge while using the strange new vision Tailtiu had taught him. He began changing his vision back to what he considered normal every now and then, to help him plot a course that would keep them best hidden from the eyes of the nighttime guards.

There was nothing to be gained from examining the tents of the rank and file, so Will worked his way deeper. The officers' and commander's tents would likely be in either the center of the camp or to the rear, on the side farthest from danger of attack. Will knew that the Terabinians preferred to keep the supplies to the rear and command in the center, so he went toward the middle first.

Sure enough, he spotted what appeared to be the main command tent in the center of the encampment, surrounded by what were probably the tents of the higher-ranking officers. Unable to restrain his curiosity, Will dodged two patrols and went to the center tent. Two guards patrolled the entrance, yet another indicator that the camp commander was probably inside.

Will crept closer, until he was only twenty feet from the guards. At that distance he wasn't sure if the mist would completely conceal him, so he approached from the side, hoping the tent itself would block their view. He attempted the source-link spell but couldn't quite connect, so he was forced to get closer by crouching down and creeping forward, moving around the corner.

The second time he succeeded, and he quickly drew off the guard's turyn until the man collapsed. The soldier's companion tried to assist his comrade, but Will repeated the process and after a few seconds the second guard collapsed as well. Will kept pulling, trying to kill the second guard, but the man stubbornly continued to breathe.

"That won't work," Tailtiu whispered into his ear. "The body fights against death. The more you draw, the harder his source will burn to keep him alive. All you're doing is shortening his life by a few days."

"Oh," said Will, having learned something new. He stopped what he was doing. His body was already thrumming with too much turyn, so he spent a minute slowly expelling it until he felt normal again. Then he crept forward, toward the unconscious guards. Pulling one flap of the tent to the side, he glanced inside but saw no one in the front section of the pavilion.

"Aren't you going to kill them?" asked his aunt.

"How long do you think it will take them to wake up?" asked Will.

She shrugged. "An hour, perhaps longer. Everyone is different, but they will be exhausted for days."

"Then I don't need to kill them," decided Will, feeling an internal sense of relief.

"They're your enemy. Why not reduce their numbers while you have the chance?" argued Tailtiu.

He shook his head. "No. They're soldiers following orders. The Patriarch is my enemy. My goal is to stop him from invading my country, not to avenge myself on as many of his servants as possible."

"You're a fool, nephew."

Will ignored her remark. "Wait here. I'm going to look inside. If a patrol seems likely to find them, warn me." He ducked inside without waiting for her to respond.

The pavilion was partitioned, and the section he was inside appeared to be devoted to administration tasks. A wide table occupied the center, and two small camp desks were on either side. A pile of papers sat in the middle of the table, but Will saw nothing written on them. *Why are they blank?* He adjusted his vision back to normal and saw writing appear as if by magic, then he understood. *I can't see the ink with the heart-light.*

He still had no time to read them, so he rolled the entire stack into a tube before tying it with a strip of leather he found on one of the desks. That done, he stuffed the entire bundle into his tunic. It wasn't exactly comfortable, but at least he wouldn't risk losing the papers if he had to run.

Moving to the right, he went through the opening that led to the second portion of the pavilion. A large cot stood on the far side of the second partition, while a table and several chests stood near the walls. The cot was empty, and the area seemed unoccupied, but large quantities of turyn were flowing around the room, swirling and twisting like water in a river that had encountered shallow rocks. *What is this?*

A familiar green line speared into his chest, and Will felt his body seize up. Panic swept through him as he realized he had been caught. The only things he could move were his eyes, and as they darted from side to side, he saw the line of magic that had connected to his source. It emerged from his chest and angled downward, into the ground at the center of the tent. The rocky soil began to boil, as if it were liquid rather than solid, and a man slowly rose up from the earth itself.

The Darrowan commander was a lean man with a thin moustache and a receding hairline. He wore no armor, given the hour, but was instead clothed in a thick and heavily embroidered sleeping gown. "Fortunately, I'm a light sleeper," said the stranger. "What are you, an assassin?"

The man smiled when he saw that Will was unable to reply. "Next time, kill me first. The sound of you shuffling all those papers woke me. If you had found me sleeping, I doubt I would have survived. Perhaps you'll remember this wisdom in your next life."

The enemy commander began pulling at Will's turyn, draining him in the same manner that Will had with the guards outside. His paralyzed muscles went slack, and he sank to the ground. The other mage continued until Will was reduced to almost nothing, then released the source-link. The commander studied him for a moment, seemingly deep in thought.

Will watched his opponent the entire time, while doing his best to speed up the recovery of his turyn. Fortunately, the room was full of turyn, as he had already seen, which made the process faster. *Thirty seconds,* he thought. *That's all I need.* If the commander got close enough, he planned to draw his sword and stab the mage before he could be trapped again.

The enemy commander didn't get close, however. He studied Will warily. "Still conscious? How odd. What sort of assassin are you?"

He's not going to give me a chance by getting close, thought Will. The man was already suspicious. Will didn't dare wait any longer, so he shifted his plan. Forming the runes as quickly as he could, he attempted to link to the commander in the same manner as had been done to him.

But the stranger was faster. The mage leapt back several feet and caught Will with the source-link spell in the blink of an eye. "A wizard?"

Will focused all his attention on the link, and this time he caught his opponent as the man tried to separate him from his source. Pulling, Will tried to drain the other man's turyn, and a battle of wills ensued. Clenching his jaw, Will fought silently with the enemy commander, and as the seconds ticked by he felt his opponent begin to weaken.

"Damn," cursed the commander. "You're strong." Then he smiled. "But it won't matter. "Raiha, Selvaren, Trant, Laira, defend me!"

Will saw the turyn in the room shifting as four massive elementals began to answer the call of their master, coming from whatever strange place they were kept, but he ignored that. Keeping his will iron-hard, he drew his sword and lunged forward, driving the point through the sorcerer's chest.

He had missed the heart, but his sword must have hit something equally vital, for the commander's eyes glazed over almost immediately as the man slid into first unconsciousness and then death. "Next time you shouldn't forget that even a simple sword can kill." Then, just because he figured his grandfather would have appreciated it, he added, "Fucking sorcerers."

There were still other presences in the room, however, and when Will looked up he saw that he was surrounded by four elementals, two of earth and two of fire. They didn't attack, but remained quiet, watching him. Thin, almost invisible lines of turyn ran from them to the dead man, and as Will looked closer, he saw there was still magic glowing softly in the chest of the commander. *The heart-stone enchantments,* he realized.

Reaching down with his left hand, he felt something tug at him and four knots of intricately wound turyn rose from the sorcerer's chest. They looked very similar to the limnthal his grandfather had given him, and he summoned it just so he could compare them. But for a few minor differences, they were almost identical.

He was tempted to take them. Will could feel the magic seeking a new home, a new master, *him,* but he resisted the urge to take them. The elementals were still watching him, and he felt a sense of sadness emanating from them. He remembered what Arrogan had done when he defeated the sorcerer in Barrowden. Could he do the same?

Lightly touching the heart-stone enchantments, he thought he could feel the emotions of the primal spirits, but there were no distinct thoughts. *I am not a sorcerer,* Will thought, trying to project his intention through the enchantments. *I will free you instead. Will you do a favor for me before you go?*

As one, the four elementals bowed. Will decided that was as close to a 'yes' as he could hope for. Carefully, he began plucking at the knotted enchantments. *Once you are released, destroy the camp. These soldiers are trying to conquer my homeland. Help me keep my people free. Please.*

He continued teasing the knots apart until first one, then another fell apart. It took another couple of minutes before he had destroyed all four.

The two earth elementals sank into the ground, while the two fire elementals swelled, growing larger by the second. The tent caught fire as Will ran out, and he almost fell as the earth began to shake. Tailtiu waited outside with one hand on her hip.

"I knew you were a fool. That sorcerer nearly killed you, didn't he?" she accused. The tent exploded in a fireball as she spoke, but the fae woman ignored the conflagration.

"You knew I was fighting?"

"I heard everything," she answered.

Will glared at her. "Why didn't you help?"

"You told me to wait outside. Be careful what you say when I am bound by a bargain. I could not have set foot inside even if I had wanted." Then she glanced to one side. "Although honestly, it might have been more interesting if you had died."

The ground jumped beneath Will's feet, causing him to fall, and more fires erupted from nearby tents.

Everywhere he could hear men yelling, cursing, and sometimes screaming as they ran back and forth, uncertain where the source of the attack was.

Will looked up at Tailtiu, who was still on her feet, balancing on the heaving ground as easily as a captain on a ship at sea. "Unbelievable," he muttered.

"You set his elementals free?" asked Tailtiu. "Why not take their power for yourself?"

He sensed something behind her questions, a hidden meaning, but in the chaos, he didn't have time to think about it. "Because I'm not a fucking sorcerer," he spat. He might have doubted his grandfather's prejudice before, but he had felt the emotions within the elementals. Keeping them enslaved was wrong, he could feel it all the way down to his bones. Will got to his feet and promptly fell again when the earth bucked once more. "Can you help me? We need to escape."

His aunt smiled wickedly, then knelt in front of him. "Climb on my back. I can't carry you in my arms. I'll need them free."

Will gave her a suspicious look. He outweighed the fae woman by at least a hundred pounds, and though he knew she was strong, he couldn't imagine her carrying him piggyback.

"Hurry up," she urged.

He fell twice just trying to do that, but finally he got on, wrapping his legs around her waist and putting his arms over her shoulders. Tailtiu stood easily, then leaned back and purred, "That's a nice place for your hands. Please continue."

Will nearly fell off as he tried to rearrange his arms to avoid touching any of her more *interesting* regions. He nearly fell again as her body began to shift and change beneath him. Her skin sprouted fur, and her limbs elongated as her hands and feet changed into cloven hooves. Half a minute later he found himself sitting atop a doe nearly as large as a pony.

Tailtiu's long neck curved back as she fixed him with one eye. "Ever ridden a horse?" she asked.

"No," said Will, clutching at her neck so he wouldn't slide off her back.

"Good," she answered. "This is nothing like that." And then she leapt forward, causing him to cry out in alarm. The next few minutes were a nightmare. Not because of the carnage and chaos occurring behind him, but mostly because he was in constant fear of being thrown and falling to what he was sure would be a quick and painful death. The fae doe flew across the heaving ground as though she had wings rather than feet, and at points she soared through the air as she leapt over pickets and other obstacles.

In the beginning he tried wrapping his arms around her neck and keeping his body flat against her back, but that caused him to slam into her every time she jumped, so eventually, he shifted to sitting while just leaning as far forward as he could manage. When he looked over his shoulder, he saw more elementals in the camp, battling the ones he had freed. Apparently, the Darrowan army had more than one sorcerer with them.

Tailtiu ran on, her swift legs, carrying her effortlessly forward across the terrain like a mercurial breeze. They had passed the outer perimeter of the camp and were nearly to the place where the forward sentries should be when she came to a gentle stop. Her body shifted back to her normal form and Will found himself trying to disentangle himself from her without touching anything else that might cause her to tease him.

The fae woman's face flushed with excitement. "The dismount was almost as fun as the mounting," she said slyly.

It took Will a moment to get his thoughts under control. Then he asked, "Why did you stop?"

She winked at him. "If you ever let me start, you'll never have to ask that question." When Will refused to respond she began to pout. "You're no fun. My time is up. Unless you wish to invoke another of your favors I'm done. I have paid this one in full. Would you like to state your terms?"

Will shook his head. "No thanks. Do you know what time it is?"

Tailtiu glanced at the sky. "There's roughly an hour left until dawn."

"How long will the mist last after you leave?"

"A few minutes," she answered, "no more. Are you sure you don't wish to negotiate the terms of your next favor?"

Will bent his knees, then straightened them again, finding new appreciation for ground that didn't move underneath him. "No. I'll finish on my own." He regretted the wording immediately, but Tailtiu only snickered lightly before vanishing in the mist.

With an hour left he knew Fulstrom's army would be readying to march, but rather than slip past the sentries and return immediately he decided on another path. Slipping forward through the mist, he caught one of the sentries with his source-link spell and disabled him before doing the same to the man's companion. Once more he considered killing them, but he pushed the thought aside. *They won't be able to fight until this battle is long over.*

Expelling the turyn he had stolen, he moved on, targeting the next group of sentries fifty yards down the line. With luck he could get them all, giving the enemy army even less time to react when the Terabinian troops arrived.

CHAPTER 50

Will found the task of disabling the sentries so easy that by the time he got to the last pair he decided to experiment. He remembered seeing his grandfather catch three men at once, so he thought he would attempt to get both men at once. It turned out to be harder than he had anticipated, and he failed spectacularly.

One of the two spells fizzled immediately, and the second missed its target. The mist had already faded away, and one of the sentries caught a glimpse of his figure in the dark. The guard called out to his companion, and the two men lowered their spears in Will's direction.

Shit! He repeated his effort, aiming for just one man this time. When the line of his spell connected, he injected a healthy dose of his turyn into the man. It was far quicker than draining the sentry, and with the other soldier leaping to skewer him, time was at a premium. His target fell forward, vomiting, while Will tried to dodge right to keep from being impaled.

The tip of the spear tore through his left trouser leg, grazing the skin. Will tried to move closer, drawing his sword, but his opponent was too quick. The sentry backpedaled, bringing the point of the spear back in line for another thrust, and Will was forced to retreat. It was quickly becoming obvious that the instructors hadn't been lying—a sword was a lousy weapon against a spear in an open field. Making matters worse, he wasn't wearing any armor.

I'm about to die. Will took advantage of the distance between them to turn and run.

The sentry ran after him, but in the dark the sentry quickly lost sight of him. Will circled around, watching the guard stumble through the night, then he closed on the man from the rear. He had just gotten close enough when the man spotted him again, but it was too late. Will's spell connected with the sentry's source, and he sent a powerful pulse of turyn into the man. Before the soldier could recover, he ran forward and thrust his sword into the sentry's belly.

It was anything but a clean death. The soldier groaned and fell forward, vomiting onto Will as he stumbled and tried to stay on his feet. Will thrust again, this time higher, but his sword caught in the soldier's gambeson, merely grazing the man's ribs.

In the end it took him three more thrusts to finish the sentry off, and the man screamed repeatedly, begging him for mercy. Will felt cold tears running down hot cheeks as he tried to suppress his guilt. Then he looked around for the last remaining sentry.

The nauseated soldier had gotten to his feet and was running back toward the enemy encampment. Will went after him, catching up easily as the man fell and started retching again. What followed was simple murder. He felt a wave of nausea pass over him that had nothing to do with magic as he finished the man off, but he didn't vomit.

Closing his eyes tightly, Will spent several minutes getting himself under control. Then he bent and cleaned his sword on the dead man's gambeson before sheathing it. He set his feet on a westerly course, back toward his friends. He had a report to deliver.

***

The companies had already assembled into marching order when he arrived. The camp perimeter guard took him directly to Lord Fulstrom, who was still in his pavilion. The baron had just finished getting his breastplate on with the assistance of another man when Will came in. "You took long enough," said Lord Fulstrom. "Did you learn anything?"

Will wasted no time. "They have nearly twice as many men, but their camp is in chaos, milord."

"What does that mean?"

He pulled the bundle of papers out of his tunic. "I took these from the table in the commander's tent. They looked important."

Fulstrom thumbed through the papers quickly. "It's a mixture of logistics reports and other minutiae. Some of it may be important. Unfortunately, you took too long. We're about to march. These will have to wait until later." His gaze returned to Will and fixed him with an intense stare. "Did you say you got into their commander's tent?"

Will nodded. "I was caught after entering, Your Lordship. I killed the commander and ran. After that, everything went crazy. The earth started shaking and there was fire everywhere. If it hadn't been for all the confusion, I might not have gotten out."

"I can't even imagine how you got into the center of their camp. Didn't they have guards? How did you kill their commander? Wasn't he protected?" asked Fulstrom.

He knew he was treading on dangerous ground. He couldn't simply admit to using magic on the sentries. "There was some sort of commotion in the camp. I think two of the officers were arguing. When the fires started, the guards left their posts, so I ducked into the commander's tent. After I killed him, everything got worse. I think whatever magic he was using went out of control." Will was careful not to say the word 'elemental' since he hadn't learned it until after studying with Arrogan, and he didn't want to give away just how much he knew about sorcerers and their workings.

The baron rubbed his chin, muttering, "That makes no sense. Why would his elementals go out of control, and who would be fighting in their camp? Are you sure you've told me the truth?"

"To the best of my understanding, Your Lordship, which is limited. A lot of things happened that were incomprehensible to me," Will lied.

"Well, your account of their numbers squares with the rough estimates the other scouts gave. If their camp is in disarray, we had best not waste the opportunity," said Lord Fulstrom. "Find your armor and report back to your company. We march soon."

Grateful to be out from under the baron's suspicious gaze, Will returned to his tent. He had worried that it, along with his gear, might have been packed already, but it appeared that the army intended to return to the camp. His bedroll and kit bag were still where he had left them. Working quickly, he shrugged into his gambeson and mail and hurried to find Company B.

Dave gave him a strange look when he fell in with the others in his squad. "I thought you had deserted."

"I asked to help them scout," said Will.

Sven and Corporal Taylor glanced at each other while Tiny merely nodded. Then the big man spoke. "At least they're smart enough to listen to you now."

Sven grumbled. "Rule number one as a soldier, never volunteer. Don't say I didn't warn you."

"I'd volunteer to go the hell home if I thought they'd let me," said Dave. "I've got a bad feeling about today."

"They should let you rest," said Tiny. "You haven't slept since yesterday, have you?"

Corporal Taylor interrupted, "Fat chance of that. They know we're outnumbered. I heard the sergeants talking. They want every man that can walk on the field today."

"If anyone should be given a rest, it ought to be me," groused Dave. "I'm still covered in bruises."

"You look fine to me," offered Sven. "If anything, the swelling improved your ugly looks."

"It feels worse than you think," whined Dave. "I just want to make sure it doesn't turn into something more serious, like a spear in the gut."

"A spear would probably improve your conversation skills," observed Tiny.

Dave's eyes narrowed. "I couldn't talk. I'd be dead, idiot."

Tiny nodded in agreement. "Exactly."

Sergeant Nash yelled, "Silence in the ranks!" and moments later the orders to march went out. They did the first two miles in a column five men wide before switching to a combat formation that stretched out across most of the width of the pass. The main line was three ranks deep, though one unit, Company E, remained behind the lines with Lord Fulstrom.

The fact that they only had one company in reserve was a sad testimony to how undermanned they were. The shield wall passed over the now-conscious but still helpless sentries, and the men of Company E were tasked with rounding them up and putting them under a small guard. The main line was in sight of the small earthworks before a horn blast in the enemy camp announced their presence.

They marched on without pause, while in the distance Will could see the enemy scrambling to get their men into formation and prepare to receive them. *We caught them off-guard, but will it be enough?*

A chaotic mass of men ran toward their line. As they drew closer, Will could see that they were all young. The spears they carried were strange as well, with short, heavy shafts connected to a long, slender head that was more of a spike than a proper spearhead. Sergeant Nash yelled a warning from behind the line, "Skirmishers! Ready shields!"

"Skirmishers?" Will asked aloud, knowing no one besides Sven or Tiny could hear him.

"They won't engage," said Sven. "They'll just throw their spears and run back. Keep your shield up."

Just as the old soldier had predicted, the Darrowan skirmishers ran up until they were almost close enough for Will to skewer one, then they threw their spears and darted away. Each of the skirmishers carried two of the strange spears, and they threw the second one before they were out of range. Men up and down the line yelled out as a few of them were unlucky enough to be hit. Will saw one of the spears hit Tiny's shield, and the slender point went completely through the thin wood. The point had gone half a foot through the shield before it stopped, making it nearly impossible to remove.

Tiny struggled to keep his shield up properly with the long, wooden shaft throwing him off-balance. "Pull the shaft off!" yelled Sven. "It isn't attached."

That made little sense to Will, though he later learned the metal points were made that way to keep an enemy from picking them up and throwing them back. Even after Tiny had removed the wooden portion, he was still left with a sharp piece of steel pointing inward and threatening him every time his shield took another blow.

Glancing to one side, Will saw that one man had been much less fortunate. He'd had his shield braced against his shoulder, and one of the strange spears had gone completely through, pinning his shield to his chest. Will wanted to stop and help, but there was no time; the line kept moving.

Crossbow bolts began slamming into them then, and a few more men fell as they advanced. As the skirmishers fled the field, Will could see a shield wall topping the small, earthen ramp in front of them, and he realized they were about to march down into the ditch and then up again, all while the enemy was standing several feet above them. *Shit.* He was convinced he was about to die, and the urge to break and run was almost overwhelming.

But he couldn't abandon Tiny and Sven, and even if he were willing to do that, the second and third ranks were pushing them forward. Retreat simply wasn't an option. It was do or die. *Or more likely, do and die,* thought Will.

Working as quickly as he could, Will used the source-link spell and began pushing his turyn into the men directly ahead once they were in range. He managed to get one, two, three—and then the lines met, and everything went to hell. With his shield up, he couldn't see anything; he just kept pressing forward while blindly thrusting with his spear.

The men in the rank behind him could see, though, and they used their weapons to better effect. Most of the Terabinian line stalled in the trench, but the portion in the center, where Will was, managed to get up the earthen slope. Everywhere men were dying, screaming and bleeding, yet somehow Sergeant Nash's voice continued to cut through the cacophony. "Company B, wheel left!" The perpetually angry sergeant continued screaming, keeping order and somehow making what they had practiced in drill actually work.

Will and the men around him moved forward, swinging to the left while Company C went the opposite direction, opening a wide, clear area in the center of the enemy line which Fulstrom and the reserve company charged through.

Company B continued on, rolling up the enemy and destroying their cohesion, while Fulstrom's company moved on, wreaking havoc in the camp and scattering the Darrowan reserves who were still trying to form up.

Sven called out to Will from his left, "We might just win this th—" His words cut off suddenly. Will glanced over and saw a long, leaf-bladed spearhead pulling back—it had just gone through Sven's cheek and the back of his throat. The old soldier collapsed, blood pouring from his mouth.

Their formation had begun to disintegrate, and Will froze in horror as he watched soldiers of both armies trample Sven's dead body. A shadow caught his attention, and he saw a spear coming toward him. He had been too distracted, and now it was too late. Time slowed to a crawl as his heart sped up, but there was no way he could avoid the thrust.

A larger shadow eclipsed the sun as Tiny's massive form bulled forward, the edge of his shield knocking the spear away. Thrusting with his own weapon, Tiny impaled the Darrowan. Will saw the big man's face and was shocked by the rage he saw there. Snarling, Tiny lifted the man he had skewered and swung him sideways, hurling him off the spear and back into the enemy mob.

Tiny's spear had cracked under the weight of the man he had thrown, but he bent and snatched another from the ground and moved on. As he passed by, Will heard him scream, "Get up!"

Ashamed of his weakness, Will jumped up, lifting his shield and following his friend. He had lost his spear somewhere, but it wasn't his best weapon anyway. Staying close to the big man, he began using the source-link spell again, incapacitating as many of the enemy as he could. Together, he and Tiny destroyed the knot of rallying Darrowans, and Company B began surging forward once more.

Their line was gone. The enemy soldiers had lost all cohesion, and many of them began to run, followed by the Terabinian soldiers. Sergeants and lieutenants yelled continuously, trying to restore order to their own men, but the Terabinian army was hot on the heels of the routing Darrowans. Order was gone, and the battlefield devolved into a rioting melee in which it was hard to identify friend and foe.

Will stayed close to Tiny, and when he looked to his right, he saw Dave was still with them as well, though the man seemed to have gone mad. Spittle flew from Dave's mouth as he spat out a constant stream of incomprehensible curses. The ex-thief's voice had failed him at some point, but his mouth continued to open and close as he screamed and stabbed at anyone who got close to Tiny's right side.

Ahead, Lord Fulstrom and Company E ran rampant through the enemy camp, scattering the second half of the enemy force before they could form a cohesive force that might turn back the Terabinian army. As Will watched, the baron stood in his stirrups and began drawing power from his elemental, forming a large fireball above his raised hands. Before he could release it, though, streams of fire erupted from the enemy, coming at him from two different sides.

The baron was incinerated, and the massive ball of fire above his head exploded, devastating the men around him. In the span of a few seconds, half of Company E was gone. The world seemed to pause then, as soldiers on both sides stopped in horror to stare at the awful carnage. Will could feel the battle teetering on the edge of a blade. Given the slightest push, it might topple and fall either way.

For once, he was the first to recover. "For Terabinia!" he screamed, charging across the open ground in the direction of one of the two sorcerers who had slain Lord Fulstrom. Tiny and Dave went with him, and the Terabinian army began to move again, becoming a raging mob as they charged forward.

Will only had eyes for the dark-robed sorcerer. He feared to look elsewhere and lose sight of the man. He and his squad mates were ahead of the Terabinian charge, but he couldn't stop to worry about that. The sorcerer was surrounded by a small, protective guard composed of four men, but otherwise he was alone. His eyes met Will's, and Will saw them harden as the sorcerer gathered his power to destroy them.

They were less than twenty feet away when a massive ball of fire flew toward them. Acting almost on instinct, Will did what he had once seen his grandfather do. He expanded his will, creating a wide sphere around himself that was nearly devoid of turyn. During his practices, the purpose was to then fill that space with power for use in a spell, but now he merely hoped it would protect them.

As the ball of fiery power rushed toward them, his empty shell devoured the turyn, filling Will with burning energy. Meanwhile, Tiny had taken the lead in their three-man charge and he swept the sorcerer's guards aside like dolls with his shield. Dave was right behind him, and he dashed through the gap and buried his sword in the sorcerer's throat.

Will had fallen slightly behind. The burning power the sorcerer had thrown at them was almost more than he could handle. Running up to Tiny and Dave, he put his hands on their shoulders and tried to imagine them as part of himself. In his mind he created a small circle, a space within his power that had to be protected, and then he released the power he was holding. Flames burst outward, turning the enemies around them to ash and creating a burning circle of death forty feet wide around them.

"Fuck yeah!" Dave yelled, his hoarse voice barely rising above a whisper. "Die, you bastards, die!"

A wave of lightheadedness passed over Will, but he ignored it. He was empty, almost devoid of turyn, but his grandfather had trained him for that. He stayed on his feet by pure will alone, and gradually his vitality returned as his body drew in turyn from around him. Bending down, he pulled the heart-stone enchantment from the sorcerer's chest and began plucking it apart with his fingers. *Be free,* he told the elemental in his mind. *Help us if you can, but most of all, be free.*

Dave fell on his ass as the giant fire elemental materialized above them. "Holy shit." His eyes were wide with fear and awe. Then the fiery monster turned and moved away, wading into the Darrowan soldiers. Dave looked at Will. "What just happened?" he wheezed almost inaudibly.

Will straightened up. "There's still one more," he said, pointing in the direction of the remaining sorcerer.

The air was full of smoke and the stink of burning flesh. The Terabinian army had reached the remaining Darrowans, and the field had once again devolved into a chaotic mess. But the enemy sorcerer continued fighting, sending bursts of flame into any clumps of fighting soldiers that appeared to be mostly Terabinian.

The flames had almost died away, but those that were in their path winked out as Will began walking toward the last sorcerer with Tiny and Dave on either side of him. Despite the tumult around them, the few Darrowan soldiers who were in their way ran when they saw them approaching. The sorcerer watched them too, and he turned to flee, but made little headway through the mess. Will began to run after him, heedless of the pandemonium.

This time Will got there first, and he drove his sword into the sorcerer's back. The fighting continued to swirl around him, but Tiny and Dave stood over him while he extracted the heart-stone enchantment and released the sorcerer's elemental. This time he asked it to simply be on its way, as he worried that in the mixed melee it would harm as many Terabinians as enemy soldiers.

When he got back on his feet, he saw that the battle had moved past them. He and the remnants of Sixth Squad were standing on a torn field with nothing but the dead and dying around them. Dave was leaning on a broken spear he had found, and the ex-thief looked as though he might collapse from exhaustion at any moment.

"Should we go after them?" asked Tiny, his chest heaving as he tried to catch his breath.

Will understood their exhaustion. His mail felt as though it had turned to lead, but there was one more thing he needed to do. "Where's the baron's body?"

"Over there," panted Dave, pointing to a cluster of blackened corpses.

The three of them walked over, and Will bent down to free Lord Fulstrom's two elementals from their magical bonds. Again, he urged them to leave in peace, and he watched with a feeling of satisfaction as the elemental beings faded away.

"What did you do?" asked Dave. "I've never seen so much weird shit in all my life."

Will gave looked at the man, his face devoid of expression. "Nothing. I did nothing. We fought and killed the sorcerers and that's all."

Dave stared at him for several seconds. "Right..." Then he nodded vigorously, as though he had made up his mind. "Fuck it. You're right. If anyone asks, that's what I'll tell them." He held out his hand. "Brothers first."

He had never imagined saying such a thing to someone like Dave, but Will took the other man's hand. A second later Tiny put his massive hand atop theirs. "Brothers first."

Dave's legs gave out, and he sat down in a barely controlled fall. Will and Tiny sat beside him. All three of them were done. Then Dave said, "I'll never forget what happened to Sven, but at least we made them pay for it."

CHAPTER 51

It took more than two hours to restore order to what remained of the Terabinian army. They had lost more than half their numbers, and of those that survived, many were injured. Company E had taken the worst losses, having been nearly wiped out by first Lord Fulstrom's fiery death and then the reprisal that followed as the Darrowan mob surrounded them.

Corporal Taylor was found near the perimeter. He had died during the first clash, and Will hadn't even noticed. He felt badly for the man, but not guilty. He had too many other things to feel guilty about.

More than twelve hundred bodies littered the former Darrowan camp, two-thirds of them belonging to the enemy. At least seven or eight companies of Darrowans had routed, fleeing back toward Barrowden.

The Terabinians had won, but the cost had been terrible. Lieutenant Stanton assumed command of the remnants and tried to organize the survivors to clear the area and loot the bodies, but there were simply too few men in good enough shape to begin such an undertaking.

And then the bad news came. A mounted scout came galloping into the camp. Another of the Patriarch's armies had been spotted. Will was close enough to hear the man's words as he reported to Lieutenant Stanton. "There's at least five thousand soldiers on the road. They'll be here before evening."

"Goddamn," muttered Will.

Dave was close by and he leaned in with interest. "Did you hear what he said?"

"There's a huge army marching toward us from Barrowden."

Dave's eyes widened in disbelief and he swore, "That's not fair! Goddamn it! We won! It ain't fair!"

Shortly after that, new orders made their way through the tired army. They were to abandon their position and retreat to their own camp. Since they were too few—and too tired—to take the supplies left in the Darrowan encampment, they set fire to them and began to march. They left the dead behind, both theirs and the enemy's.

The sun had nearly set by the time they reached their tents, and Will felt grateful that they hadn't broken camp the day before. He didn't think he had the strength left to put up a tent. Supper was cold, as no one had the energy to cook. Despite his multitude of worries, he fell asleep almost instantly when he found his bedroll.

It seemed that no sooner than his eyes had closed, he woke to the sound of Sergeant Nash's familiar yelling. "Rise and shine, assholes!"

"I thought you died, Sergeant," said someone not far away.

"In your dreams, Corporal," said the indefatigable Sergeant Nash. "I was not given *permission* to die. Until I am, I will be here with your sorry ass. Now, get up!"

The sergeant continued until he got to where Will was rolling up his bedding. "Cartwright!"

"Yes, Sergeant!" said Will, jumping to his feet.

Nash held out a strip of linen that had been dyed black. "Since Corporal Taylor didn't make it back, you will be the new acting corporal for Sixth Squad."

Will started to protest, but after a second's thought he realized Sixth Squad now consisted solely of himself, Tiny, and Dave. He shrugged into his armor and Tiny helped him tie the black ribbon around the upper part of his left arm.

The sergeant continued, "Since Fifth Squad only has two men left, they'll be joining you in Sixth." Nash looked at the two men in question. "Mayhew, Wilkinson, did you hear that?"

"Yes, Sergeant!"

Will looked at the two men, then at Dave and Tiny. He felt awkward. What was he supposed to say? "Get your things together," he told them.

Will had thought that Stanton might have them retreat to the south. The mountainous terrain there would offer them a better defensive position, or maybe even a place to hide. But as he saw the supply and baggage wagons leaving, he realized why that hadn't been an option. They had slightly fewer than four hundred soldiers left, and only half of those were in any condition to fight.

They simply couldn't hide without abandoning the supply wagons and the wounded. That left them only one practical option. Retreating to Branscombe. With the men they had, the town wouldn't be defensible, but at least they could warn the inhabitants. The entire town might have to be abandoned, and that was their best-case scenario. There was still the significant threat that the Patriarch's forces would catch them as they withdrew.

Will found himself constantly looking over his shoulder as they marched. Sergeant Nash noticed his backward glances and slowed his pace until he was abreast of Sixth Squad. "Worried?" he asked.

"Yes, Sergeant."

"You should be. Our best hope is that they spend a day cleaning up the mess we left at the top of the pass, but they have enough men to spare that they could send some after us and still leave plenty behind to bury the dead," said the sergeant.

Some of the men farther ahead were looking back as well, and Will saw them staring at him. They looked away when he met their eyes, but he heard them muttering. With the noise of so many men on the march, he couldn't make out their conversation, but one word came to his ears repeatedly, 'warlock.'

There wasn't anything he could do about it, so he ignored them and focused on Sergeant Nash. "Isn't there anything we can do, Sergeant?" he asked.

"Yeah," said Nash. "March faster. We've done all we can. All the combat-ready soldiers are in the rear. If we see them coming up behind us, we'll have to turn and fight a delaying action."

Nash didn't say it, but Will could see in the old veteran's eyes just how he thought *that* would turn out. A tiny voice inside told him, *You don't have to die with them. Take off the armor and run. They'd never catch you, and after night falls, you could keep running.*

Shut up, he told his inner coward.

He marched on, but around midday their worst fears came true. A shout went up as someone saw the glint of sunlight on steel helmets behind them. Sir Kyle's voice rang out, "Company B, halt!" Similar commands came from the other captains and the small contingent of able-bodied soldiers came to a stop.

Dave glanced over at him anxiously. "We're all going to die. You know that, right?"

"Shut up," said Will.

"Yeah, I know. I hate myself sometimes," said the ex-thief. "If it's any comfort, the only reason I'm still here is you and the big guy, but if the two of you die before me, I'm going to run my scrawny ass off."

"That's all right," said Tiny. "I'm sure you'll bite it first."

More commands went out, and the men formed a shield wall. Their numbers were low, so it was only two ranks deep. They faced the oncoming Darrowans, and the words Will dreaded found his ears. "Forward march!" As one, the Terabinians began to march toward their end.

As had happened before, once the two armies were within fifty yards, a large mass of young men darted through the ranks of the Darrowan army and hurled spears at them. "Why don't we have any skirmishers?" complained Dave as they continued onward.

"Because most of us are conscripts," said Tiny. "They didn't have time to form any special units." Several men along the line screamed as the spears hit them. Then the enemy skirmishers withdrew, and a minute later, the two shield walls came together.

Fear and adrenaline had Will's heart racing, but his mind had found somewhere else to be. It was blank, empty of anything but the clarity of a man trying his best not to die. Without consciously deciding, he cast the source-link spell, and this time he caught two men simultaneously. He didn't have time to be amazed at his success, though. As soon as he had sent enough turyn into them to cause them to begin vomiting, he released the spell and caught two more. He didn't even bother trying to use his spear; Tiny and Dave were doing their best to take advantage of the holes that formed in the Darrowan line.

Thanks to his efforts, the center of the enemy line quickly gave way, but the Darrowan force was considerably larger than their own, and it was wrapping around their flanks. They pressed forward, and Will could see several reserve companies waiting to the rear of the shield wall they had just breached. They were doomed.

Horns sounded behind him, but he didn't have time to spare looking back. Will was determined to take as many of the enemy with him as he could before he died. Something hard knocked Dave back, and Will had the wind knocked out of him as something hard slammed into his stomach. He only saw the spear as it pulled back, but there was no blood on the point. Already exhausted, Will drained as much turyn from his attacker as he could and used the power to stay on his feet.

Then the Darrowans began to back away, and some of the Terabinians around him started cheering. Sergeant Nash yelled for the advance to halt, and their line firmed up. With the enemy pulling back, Will was finally free to look back, and for the first time that day he felt a surge of hope.

A huge army was advancing from their rear, and they bore the banner of Terabinia, a silver falcon against a blue background. Will saw a second banner beside it, quartered into red and black sections with gold oak leaves overlaying them. He wondered which lord the other banner belonged to.

The remnants of Lord Fulstrom's force waited, and soon the new arrivals passed by them and formed a new defensive line. Will counted the companies as they passed and tried to estimate their numbers. His best estimate was somewhere near two thousand soldiers. It was five times the size of the remnants of Fulstrom's army, but nowhere near large enough to retake the pass. *Is that all of them?* he wondered.

The Patriarch had at least three times that many that Will had seen, and there were potentially many more still in Barrowden.

The commanders of the new and old forces met, and soon Company B was on the march again, continuing their retreat to Branscombe since they were in no shape to stay on the field. It wasn't long before Dave resumed his usual commentary. "Look! They've got skirmishers—and archers. Aren't they fucking fancy? Cavalry too!"

"I'm just glad they're on our side," said Will.

"We could have won if we'd had all that fancy shit," said Dave sourly.

Tiny broke in, "Technically, we did win."

Dave agreed. "Damn right, we did! They're just the clean-up crew." The ever-energetic thief jumped up and pointed back the way they had come. "The shit's back there, boys! Go dig us a latrine!"

Will grabbed the slender man's shoulder, pulling him back into line. "Damn it, Dave! Don't get me in trouble. It's still my first day as a corporal."

Dave grinned at him, then gave an overly pompous salute. "Yes sir, mister Corporal, sir!"

Sergeant Nash had already noticed Dave's antics. "Corporal Cartwright! Put a leash on your idiot before I have to stop and build a stockade to put him in!"

***

They made it back to the camp outside of Branscombe in the afternoon of the second day. Will would have preferred to find a bed and vanish for a week, but of course the army didn't work that way. There was always more work to do. The only allowance made for their exhaustion was allowing them to retire as soon as their tents were pitched, but Sergeant Nash made it plain that they would be expanding the camp in the morning to make room for the reinforcements that were a day behind them.

Will couldn't just put his bedroll down and sleep, however. His curiosity was killing him. There was someone he wanted to see, so once his squad was settled, he left and headed for the medic tent.

He found several things had changed when he got there. A second, much larger pavilion had been set up in the open space in front of the usual medic tent. It was already filled with the most seriously wounded of Fulstrom's returning soldiers. Men were stretched out everywhere, some on cots and others on the ground.

If she's here, she's probably busy as hell, thought Will. *But why would she be here? She was only pretending.* A figure moved by in his peripheral vision, and when he looked, he saw Isabel. She was clad in a loose, woolen robe that had probably been a clean gray earlier in the day. Now it was marked with numerous blood-stains.

I shouldn't be here, he realized. He started to turn away when he heard her voice call out to him. "William!"

Turning back, he saw her face. She looked happy to see him. "Hello," he said, feeling stupid for having nothing better to say.

"Were you hurt anywhere?" she asked immediately, her expression shifting to one of concern. Her gaze searched him from head to toe.

"Uh, no," he answered. "I just came to see if I could help."

She stared at him curiously. "Do you know how to clean wounds, or sew stitches?"

He nodded.

Isabel frowned. "When did you learn to do that?" Then she paused, her face blank for a moment. "Oh, your mother. I should have realized."

Now it was his turn to be confused. "How'd you know about her?"

Something flickered across her features. Embarrassment? Then she replied, "You told me she was a midwife last time. When your big friend had to be stitched up."

Will thought about it. *No, I didn't.* He was certain she had lied, but he merely smiled. "Oh, sure."

Isabel shifted the topic smoothly. "Well, if you want to help, you'll need to take that off and wash up." She waved a hand at his armor.

He did as she asked, and a quarter of an hour later he was back. Most of the wounded in the tent had moderate injuries. Most of those who had serious wounds had died during the retreat, and those with minor injuries had already been bandaged before they arrived.

Those left had wounds that were too much for field medicine but not bad enough to kill them. Will assisted in cleaning wounds and stitching up deep cuts, and when he wasn't needed for that he boiled water, carried clean linens, and in one instance helped dilute a concentrated opium tincture down to something that could be given to those who were in pain.

Isabel walked up and touched his elbow. "When did you learn to use a scale?"

"Mom taught me," he answered. *A lie for a lie.* "What would you like me to do now?"

The hours had flown past, and it was now well after midnight. Isabel wiped her brow with her sleeve, leaving a red streak across her forehead without realizing it. "There's not much left to do now," she told him. "Watch and wait. You should go rest."

"What will you do?" he asked.

She smiled sadly. "I'll wait. One of the soldiers probably won't make it through the night. I'll stay with him, so he isn't alone."

"Let me do it," he offered.

"You can barely stand," said Isabel. "You've probably been up since before dawn. Go get some sleep."

"Speak for yourself," he shot back. "I can nap while he sleeps. You need to be free. There are dozens here asking for you every few minutes."

"Fine."

CHAPTER 52

The man's name turned out to be Tom Marcruse, a conscript from a farm outside of Branscombe. Isabel introduced them, and Will talked to the fellow briefly, but Tom kept drifting in and out of consciousness, partly because of the tincture of opium and partly because of his raging fever.

Will considered sleeping, but Tom kept groaning even as he slept. Tom's face was red and covered with sweat. He was a young man, and Will couldn't help but draw comparisons. *That could just as easily have been me.*

The soldier's wound had been a relatively minor one. A bodkin point had pierced his upper arm, but during the march back the wound had turned septic. By the time they had gotten back to Branscombe it had been too late. Even removing the arm wouldn't stop the infection in the soldier's blood.

Will's eyes drooped as he watched the man, and his thoughts drifted back to when he had seen a young boy suffering similarly. Joey Tanner hadn't been as far along, but the result would have been the same. *I don't have any herbs for this poor fellow, though,* thought Will.

But then, it hadn't been the herbs that had cured Joey. They had merely been the start. It had been his magic replicating what the herbs did that had saved the child. *Do I dare?* Tom would die anyway if he did nothing.

He scooted closer, so that he was right beside the fevered soldier, and he began studying the injured arm, trying to get a sense of the illness that had started there. Just as with plants, he could feel a certain sense of *wrongness*, but he couldn't simply push his turyn into the wound. That would only make the man worse. He needed a reference, something like the herbs he had used before.

Will examined the grasses growing around him, but none of them seemed right. A new idea came to him. *What about me?* He placed his hand beside the wounded man's flesh, comparing what his magical sense saw in him and in the other man. After a while, he began to get a feeling that he could tell the healthy tissue from the sick, but it needed to be more direct.

Unwrapping the bandage on Tom's arm, he looked at the putrefying flesh, then he took out his knife and made a cut in the meat of his own palm. The difference in his blood and the fevered man's blood was apparent to his eyes. Squeezing his hand into a fist, he dripped some of his blood onto the wound, then covered it with his hands, letting his turyn seep into the diseased flesh.

It needed to match Tom's native turyn, and it also needed to remove the sickness in the man's blood, making it similar to his own. Will spent several minutes tuning his turyn. The process was somewhat similar to what he had done with Tailtiu, when he had learned to give himself different kinds of night vision.

He felt the rightness of it when the turyn came into phase with what he desired, and then he began to *push,* forcing his power into the wounded man's arteries and veins until the flow of blood began to carry it throughout the man's body.

It took considerably more power than he thought he had spent on Joey, but he kept the flow of turyn slow, letting his body replenish his store from the environment so he wouldn't exhaust himself. Time passed at a rate unknown to him, so deep was his concentration. At some point he heard the rustle of grass behind him, as someone walked closer, but he never looked up.

Gradually, Tom's breathing smoothed, and his groaning stopped. The man's body cooled, and the redness of his skin returned to its normal color. When Will felt he had done enough, he stopped the flow of turyn. He needed to get up, to find a fresh bandage, but he stumbled as he started to rise.

Strong hands caught his arm, steadying him. Isabel was beside him, her face worried. Will gave her a weak smile. "Hi."

"What were you doing?" she asked. "That wasn't a spell."

"I didn't want him to die."

"Do you have any idea how much turyn you used? You were at it for hours," she said, disapproval in her voice.

"Enough," said Will. "I did just enough."

She turned him until he faced her, then put her hands on either side of his head. "Are you stupid? You aren't a sorcerer, Will. You probably used up a year of your life. Don't you realize how dangerous wild magic is?"

He stared into her eyes, the same eyes that had haunted his dream. "But you didn't stop me, did you?" *She's upset that I wasted her investment. A short-lived slave is worth less.* He started to say as much, but then he was falling.

***

Will knew something was wrong long before he opened his eyes. His surroundings didn't smell right. The tent he shared with his platoon had a distinctive odor that one learned to tolerate only through constant exposure, the smell of iron and sweat. Wherever he was now had none of that. The air was fresh, and when he inhaled through his nose he picked up a variety of scents that had no place in an army tent—clean linen, roses, and—something else.

His eyes flew open. He was in Isabel's tent. *What am I doing here?* Will felt a wave of panic wash over him. The last time he had been there, he had been arrested.

Remaining perfectly still, he turned his eyes to survey the rest of the room. It was much as he remembered it, except for the addition of a second cot in the center, a few feet away from the one he was lying on. The other cot was also occupied.

"Sweet holy Temarah, mother of kindness and mercy, save me from this calamity," he whispered to himself, repeating the prayer he had often heard his Aunt Doreen use. Isabel's sleeping form was almost within arm's reach, and the thick blanket she had wrapped herself in was tangled around her body. Her hair was loose and had fallen to one side, exposing the smooth curve of a naked shoulder. Farther down, one of her legs was entirely uncovered.

I'm dead, thought Will. *They'll have my balls for this.* Despite his anxiety, he didn't move. He watched her breathe, studying her nose and lips. Will knew that people were never one thing or another, but he couldn't reconcile the contradictory things he knew about Isabel.

She wasn't who she claimed. She was a noble, but she had none of the conceit he expected from those of her station. She was a sorceress, but despite the evil that was the source of her power, she seemed kind. How could someone so compassionate also live with the knowledge that they subsisted on the enslavement of innocent spirits? He was also nearly certain she intended to bind him to her in some way, though whether that entailed magic or simply mundane obligation he had no idea.

"Isabel?"

It was a woman's voice, coming from just outside the tent. Isabel's eyes shot wide, and for a second she and Will stared at one another in mutual horror. She sat bolt upright on her cot and her head whipped back and forth, searching for something. The neck of her gown drooped dangerously low as she did, but Will didn't dare warn her.

Isabel pointed at the desk on the other side of the tent, and Will answered with an expression that clearly said, 'who me?'

She nodded emphatically, pointing again at the space beneath the desk.

He shook his head—'no way.'

"I'm coming in," said the woman outside. "I better not find you hiding in there. If I do, I'll be very cross."

Isabel jumped up from her cot and grabbed Will by the shoulders. He was so stunned he didn't even think of fighting her as she shuffled him across the room and pushed him down under the desk. He pulled in his legs and folded his knees, but his mind was full of visions. He had seen things he was *not* supposed to see.

His hiding spot was far from perfect, though. The desk had four legs but no sides, leaving him clearly visible to anyone entering. To solve that problem, Isabel sat in the chair in front of him and threw her blanket over his head and her lap. She scooted the chair forward. "Come in!" Isabel called, answering the woman outside.

Will heard footsteps entering, but that fact was secondary to the reality of his current position. Isabel's knees were on either side of his shoulders. It was too dark under the blanket for him to see anything, but his mind had already mapped out a picture of where he was in relation to the rest of Isabel's legs—and her hips.

"So, you were in here. You should have answered sooner," said the other woman. "What were you doing?"

"I fell asleep at the desk," said Isabel.

Will couldn't breathe—or rather—he wasn't sure *how* to breathe. Through his mouth? His nose? What was the proper etiquette when one was trapped between a woman's thighs? Either choice seemed as though it would lead to his early demise. He exhaled slowly through his mouth and Isabel jumped slightly.

"You seem nervous," said the stranger. "Why is your face so red?"

"My leg went to sleep," said Isabel, pretending to stretch, which led to yet more interesting moments beneath the desk.

I'm a dead man, thought Will, even as something else occurred to him. What might he see if he used his night vision? *No, I'm not doing that,* he told himself firmly, then had to stifle a laugh, *but what would Tailtiu do?* He already knew what her answer would have been.

"What brings you here?" asked Isabel.

"What do you mean?" said the other woman. "I only came to this godforsaken place because you were here, but even though I arrived yesterday I still haven't seen you."

"I've had a lot of work."

The unknown woman scoffed at that. "What? Taking care of soldiers? There are others better suited to that. You shouldn't be working at all." She paused. "Why are there two cots?"

"I was using the other one to stack things on," said Isabel smoothly. "You still haven't said what you wanted."

"I want some company," said the other woman. Will thought she sounded young. "I've never been so bored in my life. Father won't even let me explore the town without an armed escort."

"It wouldn't be safe otherwise," said Isabel.

"You don't have a guard. That's an even bigger shock. Your father would have a fit," said the younger woman.

"I do."

"Where?"

"I sent him on an errand."

"Lucky," said the other woman. "I could never get away with that. Yours don't dare disobey you. Oh! I almost forgot."

"Forgot what?" asked Isabel.

"Father wanted me to ask if you knew where that peasant boy is. No one can find him. They said the last place he was seen was in the medic tent last night."

Isabel sighed. "He should be resting. Did you check the soldier's tents?"

"Of course not. Father wouldn't let me near them. Besides, he already sent someone to check for him there. They said you gave an order that he be given the day off."

"Well, he isn't here," lied Isabel. "Do you know why your father is looking for him?"

"No idea. Probably something to do with the rumor that he's a warlock," said the other woman.

"What? That isn't true!"

"I heard some of the knights reporting to Father," said the younger woman. "They say he killed at least three sorcerers, but that's not the strangest part." She paused.

"Spit it out."

The young woman's voice lowered to a conspiratorial whisper. "Their elementals were nowhere to be found. They just vanished! And that's not all. He was sent to scout the enemy camp, and when they marched on the enemy the next morning, they found all the sentries unconscious at their posts. Most of the blood had been drained from their bodies, leaving them too weak to fight."

Isabel laughed nervously. "That's just ridiculous."

"That's what they're saying."

"Well it sounds like jealous men trying to undermine the accomplishments of someone else to me."

"So, are you going to give me a tour of the town or not?" asked the younger woman, changing topics.

"Later," said Isabel. "Let me take care of a few things."

"Be sure to dress properly." The other woman stepped closer and Will felt her tug on Isabel's nightgown. "You were half out. If your father knew you were half naked in the middle of an armed camp, he'd cast you out for being a whore."

"Get out," ordered Isabel. "This is my tent. I'll dress however I like here."

Will heard footsteps retreating, and after a moment Isabel shoved her chair back and stood up. She started to speak, but Will put a finger to his lips, warning her to stay quiet. His ears had caught the sound of the other woman stopping not far away. Silently he mouthed the words, 'She's still outside.'

Will fanned himself. It had been hot beneath the blanket. As he stared at Isabel, he saw her face flush red. After a minute he heard more footsteps and he said, "She's gone."

"What did you do?" demanded Isabel.

"Nothing! I tried not to even breathe. It was your idea to shove me under the desk and—and—"

"Not that! What did you do to those sorcerers?" snapped Isabel. She was searching through a chest as she spoke. She found what she was searching for a moment later, and she slipped into a thick, quilted housecoat.

A little late for that, thought Will dryly, trying to hide his smirk. "I did what I had to," he said at last. "I killed them. They were trying to burn me alive, so I didn't have many options."

She noticed his faint smirk, and her face lit up with indignation. Isabel held up one finger imperiously. "First, you shouldn't have the power to kill a sorcerer—"

"There were hundreds of men on the field," he said, interrupting. "I wasn't alone, and just so you know, a sword works just as well on your kind as it does on anyone else."

490

"My *kind*?" spat Isabel. She shook her head as though trying to clear a bad taste from her mouth. "Never mind. If it was one sorcerer, I'd believe you, but three? No one gets that lucky."

"Well I did."

"And what about their elementals? Explain that for me," she demanded.

Will's temper was beginning to rise. She had finally shown her true colors. "That's what you really care about, isn't it?" he accused.

"Excuse me?"

"You heard me. All you people care about is collecting more power," said Will coldly.

Isabel's eyes were flashing with fury. "You have no idea who you're talking to, and after everything I've done for you!"

"I didn't ask you to do anything for me," Will shot back. "And one way or another I'll pay you for the armor. I don't intend to owe you anything. You can find some other wizard to kiss your feet."

"You ungrateful churl!"

"There it is," said Will acidly.

"If you don't explain what happened to those elementals, they're liable to execute you for warlockry."

"None of your damned business," ground out Will, heading for the exit. "And I'd rather be called a warlock than a goddamned sorcerer!"

"William!" she hissed, trying not to yell. "Get back here."

"I'm late for an execution," he said, stomping out of the tent.

Chapter 53

Will's temper cooled rapidly as he walked, leaving him feeling foolish before he had even reached Company B's campsite. *That was stupid,* he thought. Changing directions, he decided to circle the perimeter. He needed time to think.

"I'm about to be interrogated for black magic, and I just pissed off the one person with some power who might actually believe me," he muttered to himself.

He tried to figure out why he had gotten so angry. *It's her superior attitude,* he told himself, but he knew that wasn't true. Sure, she had called him a churl, but that had been after they started fighting. Was it because she was trying to make him into some sort of lapdog?

No, that wasn't it either. True or not, he found the idea intriguing. There were worse things in life than serving a beautiful lady of wealth and power. It was the sorcery.

When his grandfather had first told him about the magical slavery that gave sorcerers their power, it had been something distant from him. It had been unrelatable. But after freeing several elementals, it felt different. He knew for himself how repugnant the practice was. Arrogan had been right. They were worse than some warlocks. A warlock *might* only sell himself, though the really bad ones traded in other people's lives. But *every* sorcerer was a slave master.

Yet he had met several sorcerers without getting this angry. Why did it bother him so much that Isabel was one? The answer was simple. Because he wanted her to be better than that. She was seemingly perfect in every other way—and he liked her.

Will tried to clear his head. Isabel was not his main concern. His biggest problem was that he was about to be accused of a capital crime. There were only two practical solutions, run or stay. The congruence point that would take him home was only quarter of an hour's walk away. He could easily disappear.

Running would be the end of his effort to free Barrowden. It would be the end of his friendship with Tiny and Dave. Isabel's face drifted through his mind. *Leave me alone,* he thought.

Staying was potentially the end of his life. That fact should override all other considerations. Will stopped, turning in the direction of his freedom, but he couldn't take the first step. What if they didn't arrest him? What if he could convince them he was innocent? Even if they did put him in shackles, could they hold him? He was no longer the helpless young man he had once been. *If that happens, I could escape,* he told himself.

He turned around and began walking purposefully toward the center of the camp.

The commander's tent had a new banner beside the entrance, the same red-and-black quartered design with gold oak leaves that he had seen carried by the reinforcements. Two guards stood in front of the tent, and one went inside as soon as they spotted him. A moment later he was escorted in.

The man who sat at the center desk was known to him. It was the Baron Mark Nerrow, his father. Will could see several elementals hovering invisibly over the man, one each of fire, earth, and water. The baron looked at his guards. "Leave us."

They left, and Will found himself alone with his father for the first time in his life.

"Have a seat, William," said Lord Nerrow, gesturing to a chair that was probably meant for one of his aides.

Will sat. He hadn't expected this, though perhaps he should have. *Does this mean I have more hope, or less?* he wondered.

"Do you know who I am?" asked the nobleman.

He nodded. "You're Baron Nerrow. You visited our house last year." He wasn't sure what else to say, but then he remembered. "Milord."

The baron nodded. "You can drop the formalities since we're alone, William."

"Yes, sir."

Mark Nerrow leaned forward; his features stern. "I'm afraid to ask this, William, but I have to know. Forgive me if this causes you pain. I know you escaped Barrowden, but what of your mother? Is Erisa alive?"

"Yes, sir."

"Is she here, in Branscombe? Is she safe?" asked the baron.

Will stared at the man who was his father. The question made him feel defensive, or perhaps it was protectiveness. "She's safe."

Mark Nerrow paused, then replied, "You don't want to say where she is. Very well. Perhaps that is for the best." Rising from his chair, he went to a small chest on one side of the room and removed a bottle and two glasses. He filled each halfway and handed one to Will. "You've become a man, William. It seems I will have to entrust Erisa to you now."

Will held the glass but didn't drink. His reply shocked even himself. "She was always mine. You weren't there."

The baron sipped his wine, closing his eyes for a moment. "I can't deny that. Whether you believe me or not, all I can say is that I had my reasons."

Unsure what to say, Will took a drink from his glass. The taste was a shock. Was it really wine? The taste was a far cry from what he had drunk in the tavern.

"You say that she is safe," continued the baron. "If so, why are you here?"

"You called for me?"

"In the army, William. Why did you volunteer? You know I paid a hefty fee for your exemption."

"Oh," said Will, feeling foolish. He didn't have to think long about his answer. "They killed my aunt and one of my cousins."

"So, it was your uncle that you passed the exemption to?"

Will nodded. "Yes, sir."

"Did you make a deal, William? A deal to gain power, so you could avenge your family?" Nerrow's eyes were piercing as they bored into him.

His mouth went dry. Will knew his life probably depended on what answer he gave. Yet he wanted to be honest. The man in front of him was his father, and this was the first real conversation they had ever had. Nerrow was a sorcerer, but he wanted to believe the man wasn't evil, if that were somehow possible. "It wasn't that sort of deal. I didn't bargain for power."

"Who did you deal with?" asked the baron, his voice neutral. "And what did you gain?"

"One of the fae," said Will. "She helped me sneak into the enemy camp, but everything else was done with my own abilities."

"The fae?" Mark Nerrow's spine stiffened, and he nearly spilled his glass. "That isn't possible."

Will shrugged.

"The fae haven't dealt with humanity in centuries. They won't even speak to us. Any who cross into their realm are never seen again. How did this happen?"

"I crossed by accident, without knowing what I was doing," explained Will. "A girl there stole something from me, but I escaped. Afterward she told me she owed me a debt. The help she gave me was to repay that."

"And that's it?" asked his father. "You expect me to believe that?"

"It's the truth." Will took a second drink from his glass, hoping it would relieve his nerves.

The baron finished his glass and put it down. "I don't know whether to believe you or not, but I know others won't accept that as an answer. They're already whispering about you. When King Lognion arrives, I won't be able to stop them from beginning an investigation. Have you considered leaving?"

"Sir?"

Mark Nerrow leaned forward. "Running, William. You could run before the king's inquisitors take you."

Will had just been considering that very thing not long ago, but he had made his decision. "I thought about it," he admitted. "But I won't run."

His father's face changed subtly, showing an emotion that Will couldn't decipher. "Then you need an answer that won't get you hanged. You need power to prove you aren't a warlock." Getting up from his chair once more, Mark Nerrow left, heading into the private portion of the tent. When he returned, he was carrying a wooden box ornately carved with a depiction of waves. He held it out to Will. "Open it."

Inside was a glittering knot of magic, a heart-stone enchantment. Will had never seen one that wasn't attached to a person—or a corpse. He gasped.

"Take it, William," said the baron. "With that, you can explain your miraculous luck. All that is left is to explain what happened to the elementals of the sorcerers you slew. Do you know what became of them?"

Will was staring at the box in his lap. "No, sir."

"Then the most likely possibility is that the enemy claimed them after you left," said the baron. "I still don't understand why you didn't take them yourself. Do you have any idea how much power you left behind?"

Will felt his heart sink. For a moment, he had dared to hope. His next words would probably be his doom. "I do, sir. I didn't leave them behind. I freed them. If you give this to me, I'll do the same for the spirit trapped within."

Mark Nerrow's eyes seemed to bulge. "You—what? What did you say?"

He closed the box regretfully, feeling fresh guilt for not freeing the spirit within. *I can only do so much,* Will told himself. Then he stood and placed the box in his seat and finished the wine in his glass.

The baron was on his feet. "What are you doing? I haven't given you permission to leave!"

"Sorry, milord," said Will. He put his glass on the camp desk and headed for the door, but he turned back before he stepped outside. "I'm not a warlock, and I won't be made a sorcerer either, which is an even greater evil. I know you mean well, but you're wrong."

And then he left, while Lord Nerrow stared at his back as though he had grown two heads.

Thanks to Isabel he had the day off, which suited him just fine as he didn't want to face his squad mates—or anyone else for that matter. Plus, he had just pissed off the man in charge of the army in Branscombe. The last thing he wanted was to go somewhere he would be found and given new orders.

So, he went into Branscombe instead. He stopped at the armorer's shop first and found Jeremy, since that was the only apprentice whose name he knew. After a frustrating conversation, he finally convinced the man to look up how much Isabel had paid for the rush job on his mail shirt. He left in a state of shock. "Thirty-seven gold," he murmured to himself. There was no way he would ever be able to come up with that much money.

"Accept no debts," Arrogan had told him. He felt like he understood better now. The human world might not have the same black and white rules that Faerie operated under, but the wisdom of those words was still true.

With seven clima in his purse, Will went to the only place he could afford, a cheap pub that catered to soldiers. The sign in front had no letters, but the name was obvious from the garish painting—it was called the Red Goat. He went inside and ordered two ales. "Space them out for me," he told the barmaid.

Even drinking slowly, though, he finished them in less than an hour. Unwilling to spend more, he got up and left. The world had a slightly fuzzy feel to it now. *I'm starting to see why Sven liked his drink so much,* thought Will. As he started to step out into the street, he spied an unusual sight.

Four armored guards were escorting two women. One was a slender girl with brown hair and a round face. She seemed young, probably in her teens, and her dress was made of the finest material he had ever seen, dyed in shades of yellow and green. It had to be Lord Nerrow's daughter. *My half-sister,* he thought idly. Remembering the baron's visit to his mother's house the year before, he tried to remember her name but failed.

She was spoiled, though. That part of his memory was still clear.

The woman beside her almost missed his notice. She was taller and wore a subdued dress of dark gray material with no jewelry or other ornamentation. It was a match for her hair, which was darker still, almost black. When she turned to look at her younger companion, Will saw her face. *Isabel.*

He studied them for a moment. Isabel looked as though she was playing the part of the young noblewoman's handmaid. *Typical for her,* he observed. Why was she so protective of her identity?

Before he knew what he was doing, he began following them, keeping his distance. The younger woman seemed fascinated by the shops, but none of them held her interest for more than a few minutes. She looked bored, and Will could see her complaining to Isabel as they walked. He was close enough to hear their voices, but the noise of the street made it impossible to pick out what they were saying.

An old woman, obviously a beggar, approached them, and Will saw the guards begin to push her away, but Isabel ordered them to let her speak. Nerrow's daughter reached into her purse and pulled out several coins, but Isabel put her hand out to stop her. She spoke to the old woman for a moment, then they moved on without giving her anything.

So much for charity, he noted. He continued to follow them, until they stopped at a bakery where they bought several loaves of bread.

They almost saw him when they turned and headed back in his direction. Will was forced to duck into the closest shop and pretend to be interested in tallow candles until they had passed. He dropped the ruse and returned to the street after they passed by.

He didn't go far before he saw why they had bought the bread. Isabel was giving it to the old woman. *Goddamn it. Why can't she just be evil?* It would be much easier for him to understand her if she wasn't so complicated. Will started back toward the camp.

499

Sergeant Nash was waiting for him when he reached Company B's tents. "You're relieved of your duties, Cartwright," said the sergeant without preamble.

"I had the day off, Sergeant."

Nash sighed. "I know that. I mean you're permanently relieved. You aren't in Sixth Squad anymore."

Will gaped. "But—"

The sergeant held up one hand. "Let me finish. You're being assigned to Doctor Guerin, to assist with medical duties. Apparently, they think you'll do better there."

He could almost hear Sven's warning in his mind, *"Never volunteer."* One good deed and now he was being sent away from what he really wanted to do. "Shit."

Sergeant Nash looked almost sympathetic. "Grab your gear, Cartwright. The doctor will have a place for you to sleep. Give the armband to Shaw. He'll be the new corporal for Sixth Squad."

"Yes, Sergeant."

Will went inside. His squad mates were still out, laboring at whatever duty they had been given for the afternoon. He felt some relief at that. At least he would be spared any awkward goodbyes. Moving quickly, he rolled up his bedding, grabbed his kit bag, and hefted the oiled sack that held his mail.

As he walked toward the medic tent, he kept thinking about Isabel and the beggar. He had no illusions about his new duty. He wasn't being assigned to Doctor Guerin; he was being claimed by Isabel. He paused as the bread reminded him of something Sven had once said.

"An army marches on its stomach," Will repeated to himself. The biggest problem in the current war with Darrow was that they held Barrowden and the pass, making their supply line invulnerable to attack. Even if the king showed up soon enough to save Branscombe, it would be bloody. *Unless something happens to their supplies.*

Will began walking again, picking up his pace. He was almost to the tent when he heard Isabel's voice, talking to one of her patients. *Damn, she's back already.* He most definitely didn't want to see her. Skirting the tent, he went past the smaller tent that had originally been the main medic tent and found Isabel's. Even though she wasn't there, a guard stood by the door.

He walked up to the man and held out the oiled leather bag that held his mail. "I brought this for Isabel."

The man looked at it suspiciously but took the bag. "What is it?"

"Something I borrowed," said Will. "It belongs to her." He turned and started walking away.

"Who do I tell her left this?" asked the guard.

"Just tell her I'm sorry," said Will without stopping.

CHAPTER 54

Will was already on his way to the hidden spring when he heard hoofbeats on the road behind him. Looking back, he saw a rider galloping toward him.

Damn it! He started to run off the road when he felt the ground tremble. He turned in place and saw massive flows of turyn coming from the rider and entering the earth. Then his view was cut off as the soil at his feet erupted skyward. Within seconds, he was encased within an earthen dome with only a small amount of light coming in from a hole far above his head.

Several minutes ticked by, during which Will was painfully aware of how easily he could die by suffocation. A small change in the shape of his prison would cut him off from any source of air. The last time he had felt so helpless had been when his grandfather had paralyzed him while he was sure he was dying from the effects of the spell-cage around his source. "It doesn't speak well for my life thus far that I'm getting used to moments like this," he said to himself.

The opening above widened and the sides began to separate as the earth peeled back like a flower opening its petals to the sun. Isabel stood just beyond; her horse tethered to a bush not far away. She fixed him with an angry stare. With both hands, she lifted the bag that held the mail shirt. "What's this?"

Will crossed his arms, which he soon regretted. "I'm returning it."

With a heave of her shoulders, Isabel threw the bag. Arms crossed, he failed to catch the heavy bag before it struck him square in the face. The leather and mail together weighed nearly twenty pounds, and he fell backward to sprawl on the ground. "Ow!" Wiping his face, he found a red streak on the back of his hand. His nose was bleeding.

The look on her face said that she while she had acted on impulse, she hadn't intended to have quite that effect, but she said nothing. Will got carefully to his feet and then shook the bag at her using one hand. "What the hell was that?" he demanded.

"It's yours," she said stubbornly. "I was giving it back."

He drew back his arm as though he would throw it at her. "How about I return it the same way?"

Her eyes widened in alarm. "You wouldn't dare!"

"Try me," he growled, making as if he was about to do just that. Isabel turned and started to run, but he threw the heavy bag at her feet, causing her to trip and fall. Quick as a flash, he leapt after her before she could get back up. She beat at his hands where he held her dress, but he refused to let go. Shifting his grip, Will caught her shoulders and turned her over, pinning her down on the hard road.

She glared up at him, her eyes staring daggers of hate through him. Will froze. Their faces were only inches apart, and his anger was draining away. He could feel her breath against his lips, and he wanted to—a drop of blood dripped from his nose onto her cheek. Embarrassed, he sat up, pushing her away.

They studied each other silently for a minute, and then he noticed the scrapes on her arms. She had hurt herself during the fall. Will pointed with one finger. "Your arm—I'm sorry."

"Your nose is worse," she replied.

"No apology?"

Her expression was one of apology, but the words didn't come out. "I can't," she said at last. "I was raised not to."

Will used his sleeve to pinch his nose shut and tilted his head back. "Are you even human?" he asked with a nasal twang.

Isabel ignored his insult. "That's the first time anyone has ever laid hands on me. You could die for that alone. Do you realize that?"

"Add it to the list of my crimes."

She held up one hand, fingers outstretched, then began ticking them off, one by one. "Unlicensed wizardry, possible warlock, and assaulting a—" She paused briefly. "—a person of high station."

"You forgot one," said Will. "Aiding a fugitive."

"A fugitive?"

"My grandfather was a wizard too," he explained.

Isabel's eyes grew curious. "You never told me his name."

"No. I didn't," said Will, giving her a mock grin. "Just as you've never told me yours. Your *real* name."

"Fair enough," she replied. "Are you going to add desertion to the list?"

Will nodded. "I'm deserting Lord Nerrow, the army, and you. That's why I'm not keeping the armor." He noticed a fleeting look of pain as he said the last part. "But I'm not deserting Terabinia. I'm going back to do what I can, since it appears the country is about to deprive me of life and liberty anyway."

Isabel pulled up her knees and settled her arms over them. "Do you have a plan?"

"A vague one," he admitted.

"Where are you going?"

"Back to Barrowden."

The look on her face clearly spelled out how stupid she thought that was. "You can't get there. You're going to desert the army only to run into the arms of the Patriarch's forces. They'll kill you."

He didn't say anything.

Her expression turned hopeful. "I could protect you."

She's daft, thought Will, but when he spoke he took a more direct approach. "I'm not your servant. I never will be." *No matter how much I might want to be.*

"You're determined to do this?" He nodded. "And you have a way to get there, some secret you haven't shared?" He nodded again. "What will you do there?"

"Sneak into their camp and set fire to their supply warehouses."

"You couldn't get in," she challenged.

Will lifted his chin. "I got into their camp before and slew their commander. I can do it again."

"Another secret?" she asked. When he didn't answer, she went on. "If it's some trick of wild magic like you used on that dying man, there are some things you should know. For a wizard, your magic is your life. Keep using it as you have been, and you'll be dead in a few years."

"I know that," said Will. "But my grandfather was quite old. I think I'll survive a lot longer than you expect."

"You're a fool."

He nodded and got to his feet. Isabel did the same. "Wait," she told him. "I have a solution."

"What?"

Drawing herself up and straightening her back proudly, Isabel proclaimed, "William Cartwright, I order you to infiltrate the enemy camp and attempt to destroy their supply line. You are to leave in one hour." Then she relaxed. "If it's an order, you're a patriot, not a deserter."

He laughed. "I'm not your servant. I thought I made that clear, and besides, who are you to give orders to the army?"

Isabel's expression failed to conceal the mischief in her eyes. "Someone you shouldn't trifle with—as you did this morning."

"Trifle?" asked Will, confused.

"I felt you sniffing my leg," she accused.

Flabbergasted, he protested, "*You* shoved me under there! I was just trying to breathe. You nearly suffocated me!"

It was her turn to laugh then. After she had recovered, she told him, "Wait here. I'll go make this official. I'll be back in an hour with your escort."

"Escort?"

She nodded primly. "You're taking a sorcerer with you. You'll need some real power to make the most of this scheme of yours, even if you can sneak in there." Isabel untied her horse and leapt into the saddle with practiced ease. Then she stopped. "Do you need a mount?"

He shook his head. "I don't think it would be safe to bring a horse along the route I'm taking." He felt rather uncertain about her suggestion that he bring a sorcerer, but he had to admit that it would open up more possibilities. *Worst-case scenario they die, and I can free another elemental,* he told himself.

"How about supplies? You don't look like you brought much."

"I already have everything that I need waiting for me," he answered.

"What about for your escort?"

"There's plenty for him too," said Will.

"One hour," she reiterated, and then she was gone.

Will walked a little farther down while he waited, until he spotted the trail that led to the spring. Then he sat down in the grass beside the road. Mentally he reviewed their conversation, chuckling at parts of it. He wasn't sure how much he should believe. She had certainly showed considerable influence over Lord Fulstrom, but he wasn't sure if that would carry over to Lord Nerrow.

There was also a significant chance that she would fail. The next people he saw might be a contingent of soldiers sent to arrest him, but that didn't bother him too much. So long as he stayed alert, he could easily get to the spring and escape before they could lay a hand on him.

An hour and a bit more passed before he spotted a figure coming up the road toward him. The newcomer was hidden by a long, white cloak trimmed in fur. He goggled at it. *Is that arctic fox? How much would a thing like that cost?*

He judged the stranger to be of average height for a man, though he possessed a slight build. Had there been anyone like that in the camp? Surely, he would have remembered a thin, rich fop of a sorcerer if he had seen one. The stranger kept his head down, face hidden by the hood of his cloak until he came abreast of Will.

Will watched as the stranger threw back the hood of the cloak and flashed a smile at him. It was Isabel.

"Oh, hell no!" declared Will.

"I was the only sorcerer available," she told him proudly.

"I'm not taking you," he growled.

One of the elementals above her flashed, and turyn began to flow. The ground started to tremble. "I think you are," she said firmly. "But if you think you need more time in your cage to think things over, I can arrange that for you."

He bowed his head in defeat. "Fine, but only under protest."

Isabel pulled something from under her cloak and pushed it into his arms. "Here. I'm tired of carrying this. It's heavy." It was the bag with his mail.

Will pushed it back. "That's not mine."

"You're still a soldier," she insisted. "I gave you this free of obligation."

"I can accept no debts," said Will, then he remembered what she had said about apologies. "It's the way I was raised."

Frustrated, Isabel glared at him. "I'm not carrying this for the entire trip. How much money do you have?"

Will frowned. "Six silver clima."

She held out her hand. "Give it to me."

Fishing around in his coin purse he found the money and held it out. "What do you want with it?"

Isabel took the coins from his hand and dropped the bag at his feet. "Sold. It's yours now."

"You paid thirty-seven gold for that," argued Will. "You can't—"

"I can do whatever I please," she said, cutting him off. Her eyes drifted downward. "Are you going to leave that in the road? Should I add littering on the king's road to your list of crimes?"

Annoyed, Will exhaled. "You are the most irritating person I have ever had the displeasure of meeting." He bent and lifted the bag, settling its strap over his shoulder. "Come on." He began walking down the trail.

She followed. "Where are we going? Is there some secret tunnel that leads through the mountains?"

"You'll see."

And indeed, she did. When they stopped beside the spring, Isabel's eyes narrowed, studying the strange glimmer in the air. "That's a congruence," she said, speaking to herself. Her eyes went to his. "You don't intend to—"

Will took her hand and pulled her through. Isabel froze, her eyes roaming across the wide grassland they were suddenly standing in. "William," she said nervously. "Look at the flows. There's too much. We're in Faerie. Take us back!"

"Take yourself," he said heartlessly. "My route goes through there." He pointed at the cave in the rocks ahead.

She grabbed his arm. "You don't understand. They'll kill us. The fae hate outsiders. They hate *us*."

"Relax," he told her. "They won't come here." He began pulling her forward.

"Why? Why won't they come here?" she demanded, her voice pitching upward as she fought against her panic.

He kept pulling, dragging her onward. "Because they're afraid of the thing in that cave."

"Why would they be afraid?"

Will nodded at a pile of bones they were walking past. "Because it eats them. Don't worry, though. It won't eat us."

Isabel glared at him. "You *are* a warlock."

"I have bargained neither blood, body, nor soul. Not mine nor anyone else's."

"Then what did you trade?" she demanded.

"He likes chicken eggs," Will answered. "But that's just the rent."

"Rent?" she gaped. "You live here?"

"Not here," he said, shaking his head. "On the other side. You'll see."

He had to coax her when they got to the cave. Isabel's fear had become a palpable thing, and while he had rather enjoyed lording his familiarity with the dangerous area over her before, he began to feel slightly bad about it. "Just a little farther. We're almost to the other congruence."

Isabel's steps were short and halting as he pulled her into the cave. As before, the darkness surrounded them, and he felt an ominous presence. Isabel seized hold of him when the rumbling began, burying her face against his chest.

"You brought one of *them* with you?" said a deep, alien voice, thick with menace.

Will was shocked. He had never known the goddamn cat to speak before. "You can talk?" he asked in surprise.

"The fae hate her kind," said the Cath Bawlg, ignoring his question.

"And you hate the fae," returned Will. "Shouldn't that please you?"

"I hate her kind too. You tread on dangerous ground, wizard."

"She's not like the others," said Will. "I need her help."

A growl answered him, followed by a snuffling sound. "I have your scent now, sorcerer. Come here without him and I will suck the marrow from your bones. Betray us and I will hunt you unto the ends of the earth to extinguish your foul existence. Do you understand?"

"Y—yes," she said, stumbling over the simple answer.

"Go." And then the presence vanished.

Will led her to the congruence and took them across. Once they were in the Glenwood, Isabel took several steps before sinking to the ground, hugging her knees. She didn't speak for several minutes. When she had regained her composure, she asked, "What was that thing?"

"The goddamn cat," said Will.

"The what?"

"Grandfather called him that. He seems to like it."

Isabel looked up at him. "Do you know what it is?"

Will shrugged. "There's a lot I don't know. Are you feeling better?"

"Only if you don't have any more surprises like that in store for me."

He tried to smile reassuringly. "Just one, and it's a nice surprise." He held out his hand to her. "Come meet my family."

Isabel got to her feet and dusted her skirts off. Will led her around the brambles that guarded the garden and took her to the front of the house. He didn't see anyone outside, so he went to the door and knocked. His mother's voice responded as she opened the door, "Why are you knocking?" Her face lit with joy when she saw her son standing there. "William!" Erisa threw her arms around him.

She stiffened when she saw the woman standing behind him, and Erisa pushed him away. "You brought a visitor?" His mother began unconsciously combing her fingers through her hair.

Will stepped aside so they could see each other. "Mom, this is Isa—"

Erisa was already studying Isabel carefully, then she interrupted him, her face showing recognition. "Lady Selene?"

"Madame Cartwright," said Isabel, tilting her chin down almost imperceptibly. "I am surprised you remember me."

Erisa smiled. "You were only here—what? A year ago? You've grown! Please come in." The two women went inside, leaving Will standing bemused on the porch.

 **C**HAPTER 55

Will followed them in and glanced around, looking for his uncle and Sammy. Neither appeared to be present. His mother had already begun to busy herself putting a kettle on the stove for tea.

"So, tell me—Selene—if that really is your name," began Will, "You've met my mother before?"

Erisa glanced up. "Don't be rude, William. She came with Lord Nerrow and his daughter last year. Don't you remember?"

Everything came together in his mind, and Will's mouth dropped open. He stared at Selene with new eyes. He had met her twice before. Once, when his father had come to try and get him to go to Wurthaven, and once before, when he had nearly died from the emerald viper bite. He pointed at Selene. "You!"

Selene raised a hand to cover her smile. "Me." Erisa watched them from one side, unsure of what was transpiring between them.

Will turned to his mother. "Mom, do you know who this woman is?"

Erisa scowled, then crossed the room to cuff the back of his head. "Mind your manners, William. Lady Selene is our guest."

He refused to give up. "But do you know who she is?"

His mother flushed with embarrassment. "Please forgive him, Lady Selene. My son has always been thick headed."

Selene smirked. "I am well aware, Madame Cartwright."

"Please, call me Erisa, Lady Selene," said Will's mother.

"Only if you'll agree to call me Selene," said Will's companion in a tone so utterly charming that he wondered if she was the same woman he had recently fought with.

Erisa bowed her head politely. "You do me too much honor."

"Mom!" said Will, nearly shouting. "Who is she?"

His mother fixed him with a stare that threatened to peel the flesh from his bones. "She came as a lady-in-waiting with Lord Nerrow's daughter Laina. I don't know her pedigree, and it would be rude to ask, but you can be sure she's well above our station. Now, if you'd like dinner, you should sit down over there and shut your mouth before I sew it shut."

Selene tittered, and Will's eyes narrowed. Isabel didn't *titter*. She laughed, just like other people. "Stop it," he told her. "Don't try putting on airs with me."

Selene leaned across and whispered in his ear, "You're upsetting your mother, William. Remember, I am *well* above your station."

The door banged open, slamming into the wall as Sammy rushed into the room. "Is Will home? I saw a bag on the—" Her eyes lit on Will and she charged into him, knocking him off his stool. "Will! You're alive! Is the war over? Did we win? Is Eric all right? Were you injured?" She paused to take a breath, then put her hands on either side of his head. "More importantly, are you cooking tonight?"

Will struggled to disentangle himself, but Sammy was like a spider, clinging to him with a multitude of arms and legs. From the corner of his eye he saw Selene enjoying the scene with some amusement. "Eric is fine," he answered.

"Have you seen him?" asked Sammy anxiously.

"He's in a different company, but I know he wasn't wounded. The war is still on, though."

"Samantha," said Erisa coolly. "We have a visitor."

Sammy looked over, finally registering the presence of a stranger in the room. She looked Selene up and down critically, like a dog sizing up a rival that had entered its territory. "Who're you?" she asked finally.

"Samantha!" snapped Erisa. "This is Lady Selene. Introduce yourself properly before demanding someone's name."

Sammy held out her hand. "I'm Samantha." Selene took it and Sammy pumped it up and down, then she asked, "Why are you here?"

Selene laughed. "I'm here to help Will do something to drive the Patriarch's army away."

"Are you his girlfriend?"

Selene's cheeks colored immediately, and Will began coughing. Erisa was the first to speak, "Samantha Cartwright, do you need something unpleasant to occupy your attention?"

Sammy glared at her aunt. "But we have a guest. I haven't had anyone to talk to in ever so long."

"Then be polite."

Will's cousin turned back to Selene. "Have you tasted Will's food? It's marvelous!"

"I can't say that I have."

"Selene was raised on food far better than ours," said Will. "I doubt she'd be impressed."

Selene winked at him. "Why don't you make dinner and let me be the judge." Sammy began clapping.

Erisa frowned. "But he's tired. I was going to make dumplings with—"

"Please, Will!" begged Sammy. "If I have to eat Auntie's cooking one more day, I'll die. Look how skinny I've become." She leapt up and twirled.

Will's uncle showed up then, and a new round of introductions began. Once things calmed down, Will got to his feet and began searching to see what he had to work with. His mother frowned, but let him have his way.

There wasn't a lot to work with. There was no butter, but his mother had stored away some lard they had rendered from deer fat. There was also flour, carrots, parsnips, and green onions. He checked the spice cabinet and found they still had salt but no pepper. Then he went outside to check the garden.

Spring hadn't quite arrived so he didn't expect much, but in the worst case he could use some rosemary from the bush beside the house. He was pleased to see his mother had already gotten a patch of thyme started. *That will be perfect,* he thought. He collected some and went back inside.

He made dough for a pastry first, mixing some flour and a pinch of salt with the lard and rolling it out. Then he checked the stove to make sure it would be at the proper heat when he needed it. After adding a little wood, he returned to his ingredients and began chopping.

As he worked, he listened to the conversation in the room. His Uncle Johnathan didn't have much to say, and Erisa seemed to be playing referee while Samantha plied Selene for information. Will finished the chopping and put the vegetables in the pan to soften a little.

Samantha had been asking for stories about Will's time away from home, but she was shifting the subject back to their guest now. "Do you cook?"

"No, I've never learned," answered Selene.

Sammy tsked. "That's too bad. Will's the best cook in Barrowden. Maybe he'll teach you. What about sewing?"

"I know how to tat lace."

"Ever made a shirt or a dress?"

"No, but—"

Sammy patted Selene's knee as though she needed comforting. "Don't worry. Will isn't much with a needle, but he can sew buttons and mend tears. Aunt Erisa can teach you the hard stuff."

Will smiled to himself as he removed the vegetables and added some lard to the pan to melt. Once it was ready, he added some flour to make a thick roux. He continued to listen as his mother interrupted, "Samantha, where are you going with all these questions?"

"I just want to know a little about her, Auntie. We should know something if we're going to trust Will to her care," said Sammy.

Will fought to keep from laughing. His mother started to apologize, but Selene stopped her. "Please, Erisa, I don't mind. In fact, I agree with her."

He added water to the roux, making a thick gravy, then salted it and added the vegetables back to the pan along with the thyme. Will tasted it several times as he adjusted the salt in small portions. Sammy went on, "What sort of things do you like to do, or rather, what are you good at?"

"I've been working as a healer for the army," said Selene. "I've got some experience with injuries." She nodded deferentially to Erisa. "Though I'm sure I'm nowhere near as skilled as your aunt."

"Or Will," said Sammy confidently. "He's been learning since he was little. Auntie says he knows even more about herbs than she does now. A few years ago, he saved a boy who was dying."

Will could almost feel his mother glaring at Sammy behind his back, but Selene answered generously, "He helped a lot with the wounded soldiers back in Branscombe. I'm sure you must be very proud of him."

Johnathan broke in, "So what did you do before the war broke out?"

"I learned magic at Wurthaven for several years," answered Selene.

Will began adding the mixture he had created to the pastry, creating small pies. He brushed a wet finger along the edges and pinched them together before arranging them on a metal sheet meant for the oven. "So, you're a wizard?" asked Will's uncle.

"Actually, I'm a sorceress."

"Oh," said Erisa. The conversation stopped there, and an awkward silence filled the room.

Will slid the pan of pastries into the oven and turned around. "All done. Now we just need to wait a while."

Sammy leaned over and whispered to Erisa, "She doesn't look evil." Her voice was still loud enough for everyone in the room to overhear.

Erisa's cheeks flushed red with embarrassment, but Will intervened. "Mom, would you mind watching the oven for a while? I thought maybe Selene would like to take a walk."

"I'll come!" declared Sammy.

"Sit down," growled her aunt.

Selene rose to her feet. "I think I'd like that." Sammy was pouting as she and Will went outside. Once they were a short distance from the house, Selene observed, "Your cousin adores you."

Will snorted. "She's always been a pest."

"I think she's cute. She obviously wants to protect you."

He didn't answer.

"Your family doesn't think much of sorcerers, do they?"

Will shrugged. "My grandfather hated them. Mom probably heard his opinions on the matter when she was younger. I don't think Sammy and Uncle Johnathan have any definite thoughts about it, other than what I've said."

"But you hate them too, don't you?" asked Selene, fixing him with soft eyes.

Looking at her made his heart ache, but he wouldn't lie. "Yes."

"That's why you said those things before, when we argued," said Selene, then she laughed. "I've always been proud of it. I never thought I'd find myself in a place where people regarded me as something worse than a warlock."

"A warlock isn't necessarily evil," said Will. "Usually they are, but it depends on what they bargain with, and what they do with the power they gain. A sorcerer is evil no matter what they do, because their power comes from suffering."

She stopped, spinning around to face him directly. "Whose suffering?"

He glanced up at the elementals hovering protectively above her. "Theirs."

"They aren't human, William. They don't have souls."

"That's where you're wrong."

"I studied at Wurthaven for years. None of the teachers there would agree with you. My family has possessed elementals for centuries. I come from a long line of renowned sorcerers. None of them ever thought as you do. Don't you think it's a bit arrogant to presume you know better than the wisdom and experience of so many sorcerers and wizards?" she argued.

"Maybe," he admitted. "But my teacher thought that all those people you named were fools."

"And you believe his word over that of every other scholar of magic?"

"I wasn't sure at first, but over time I've seen the truth in everything he told me, even things I didn't understand at first."

They walked in silence for a while, the distance between them far greater than the foot or two that separated their bodies. Then she spoke again. "I heard about what you told Lord Nerrow. It didn't make sense before, but at least I know why you refused his gift. You alienated the one man with some cause to help you."

"I have other friends."

She sighed. "You think you can depend on me for everything?"

Her phrasing irritated him. "Not you. Friends who aren't noblemen. Wealth and power aren't everything."

Selene stopped, and when he looked at her, he realized he had gone too far; her eyes were red, and her hands were clenched into fists by her sides. "Am I not even a friend then?"

Without thinking, he threw his arms around her, pulling her close and squeezing tightly. She went rigid at first, but gradually she thawed. "I didn't mean it like that," said Will. "Forgive me." He relaxed and she pushed him back, turning her face away.

"I don't know why I put up with you," she said after a minute. "You've insulted me in more ways than I can count in just a few months of knowing you. In my entire life I never had to endure so much."

"No one would dare," he suggested, "since you were well above their station."

"I've spent a lot of time disguised as an unknown," countered Selene. "You still managed to outdo all the strangers I've met."

Will smiled. "It's a gift."

"Speaking of gifts, why are you so stubborn about accepting them?"

He had spent a lot of time thinking about that, and lately he had begun to develop some ideas. "It's a rule I was given, but I think I understand the reason now. It's the difference between a warlock and a wizard." She waited for him to explain, so he continued, "The simple definition is that a warlock bargains for power, but that doesn't really cover it. Warlocks bargain things that shouldn't be traded. In the best case they bargain their soul, and in the worst, they bargain someone else's, but either way they create a debt. A debt to whatever power is waiting to claim them, or a debt to the people they've stolen from.

"A wizard doesn't do that. A wizard trades honestly, and never trades himself."

"But a gift from a friend isn't the same," argued Selene.

Will shook his head. "It creates a debt of gratitude. That can be a problem for anyone, even ordinary people, but for someone with power it's more significant."

"Then friends shouldn't give one another gifts?"

"Friends should be equals. A great disparity in wealth or gift-giving poisons the relationship."

"What about married people? Should they also refrain from showing affection through presents?" she asked.

"That's different," he answered. "In marriage both partners have agreed to accept each other's strengths and weaknesses. They're united, in possessions and everything else. Since they don't own anything apart, they can't create that kind of debt."

Selene became thoughtful, and after a moment said, "What about love? Sometimes one loves another without receiving love in return."

Considering what had happened to his mother, Will had strong opinions on the topic, but all he said was, "I'm not sure."

"Love doesn't count," declared Selene confidently. "Because it's the one thing that becomes greater in the giving." Will didn't reply.

Selene began swinging her arms. "So, what I've concluded is that the only way for anyone to give you gifts is to marry you." She laughed when she saw the panic on his face. "Don't worry, I wasn't suggesting it. As I'm sure you've guessed, it wouldn't be possible."

He agreed, though perhaps not for the reason she thought. Arrogan and Aislinn had paid dearly for whatever mistake Arrogan had made, and they were both wizards. Applying the same logic, it occurred to him that a wizard had to be even more careful when considering marriage. Only a partner who could be trusted not to endanger the wizard with a debt or obligation that might be disastrous could be considered. By definition, a sorcerer would be a violation of that rule from the very beginning.

She had been watching him from the corner of one eye while he thought. Thinking she had made the mood awkward, she posed a new question, "How did you free those elementals? That was a lie, wasn't it?"

"Why would I lie?" he replied.

"To make him angrier," observed Selene. "You're spiteful like that. Do you have any idea how valuable his offer was?" When he just shrugged, she continued, "The king would probably have given you a title. After Lord Fulstrom's elementals were lost, his heir wouldn't be allowed to inherit. His family might even wind up on the streets. It's possible you might have been chosen to take his estate."

"I'm not his heir. That makes no sense. Can the king even do that?"

She nodded. "The nobles hold their lands in good faith, but it all belongs to him. He won't allow someone without power to inherit."

Will felt a slight pang of guilt over what might happen to Lord Fulstrom's family, but he shoved it aside.

It wasn't his fault. The entire system was flawed, built upon a foundation of suffering. "Well, what I said was the truth, regardless. Want me to prove it?" He held out his hand toward her chest as though he would pull the enchantments from her body.

She took a quick step back. "Only a master sorcerer could do that, and only for his own elementals."

Will looked at the ground, studying the dead sticks scattered around them. They reminded him of one of Arrogan's more painful lessons. "The heart-stone enchantment is just like a spell, only more complicated, and just like a spell it can be taken away from someone. Once you do that, you can pick it apart."

Selene frowned. "You can't take someone's spell away. Once turyn has been formalized into a spell, it can only be used by the owner of the spell."

"That's not what I was taught," said Will. Then he challenged, "Why don't we see who's right, my teacher or all those scholars of magic you're so proud of?"

"You don't even know any spells," she said dismissively.

"I've learned one," he said defensively, "but that's not the idea. You make a spell and hold it without releasing it. I'll see if I can take it away from you."

She gave him a smug look. "Would you like a simple spell or a complicated one? Not that it matters."

"Complicated. I don't want you saying it was too easy."

Selene held out her hands, and runes began to rapidly appear, too quickly for him to follow with his eyes. Over the span of a minute they built up into a complex spherical web above her palms. She gave him look of pride when the spell was complete.

"What does that do?" asked Will.

"It's a spell to clean a room."

His mind was boggled. "That's all it does? Why is it so complicated?"

"You're letting your ignorance show," she told him. "The most powerful magic isn't necessarily complicated, and sometimes a minor magic requires a lot of complexity to work properly. A cleaning spell has to have a lot of rules built into it; otherwise it will make a mess instead of doing what you want. It has to differentiate between dust and dirt and things that ought not be removed. Hard floors are not like rugs, and fabric can't be cleaned like dishes. This spell can handle all those things. Still think you can take it away from me?"

Will ignored the question. His mind was occupied by thoughts of all the hard labor he had done at his grandfather's request. *The old bastard could have cleaned it all in a minute,* he realized. He knew for a fact that the old man must have known the spell, for he had seen how clean Arrogan's bedroom had been.

He held out his hands, putting them on either side of her spell. A second later, the glow of the runes began to flicker, and Selene's eyes went wide. *No, that's not it,* Will told himself. *I don't want to absorb it; I want to take it.* He tried to remember the sensation he had felt when he drew the heart-stone enchantments out of the dead sorcerers' bodies.

Unlike those occasions, he felt a stiff resistance. Selene wasn't dead; she was very much alive and still holding onto the spell. What had his grandfather told him with the candle? He needed to change the color of the flame to regain control of his turyn. This was similar. He had to convert the turyn within the spell to his own type before the spell would be his.

Pushing aside his distractions, Will focused on the turyn within the spell. He didn't want to absorb it—he needed to change it. He felt his will tremble as something opposed his desire. Clenching his jaw, he bore down, refusing to accept the outcome.

And then it happened. The spell tore away from Selene, connecting itself to him instead. He took a step back, and the magical construct came with him, anchored between his palms. Selene's face was damp with sweat, and she stared at him as though he had grown a second nose.

Will began to speak in a nonchalant tone. "Now all that's left is to take it apart." With one hand he began plucking at the individual runes, tugging them out of position until the entire thing fell apart and dissolved.

"That's how you got rid of the ward around my tent," she sputtered. "It wasn't a spell anomaly."

Not exactly, thought Will. That had happened because he had accidentally absorbed the ward. What he had just done was much harder, but he didn't feel like being nit-picky about his victory. "It was similar."

Selene's expression was grave. "Listen to me, Will. What you just did—you can never do that again, not in front of anyone. The magisters at Wurthaven would kill to possess such an ability, and any sorcerer that knew you had it would stop at nothing to see you destroyed. Do you hear me? Every mage in the kingdom would become your enemy, for one reason or another, and they would turn the world upside down to either learn or destroy such knowledge."

He nodded. "I'll keep it a secret then."

"Teach me," she said sternly with a strange look in her eyes, a look that made him uncomfortable.

"I don't know if I can," said Will, waving one hand vaguely.

"Why not?"

"First you have to learn to control your source, then your body has to learn to absorb turyn from around you. I think that's where it starts," he explained. His grandfather's strange method of teaching began to make sense to him. While he had been busy complaining that the old man wasn't teaching him spells Arrogan had built a foundation in him to enable him to achieve greater control, not just of his own spells, but of others' spells as well.

She frowned. "Absorb turyn? Like I do from my elementals? It would make me sick to do that from other sources."

"Haven't you ever used the source-link spell to do that to someone else?" He thought about that for a second before realizing it wouldn't make sense. "Well, I guess you'd only do that if you were using it on an enemy."

"Supper's ready!" It was Sammy's voice, shouting from the house.

"We'd better go," said Will, but he could feel Selene's eyes on him as they walked back. He had a feeling their conversation wasn't over.

CHAPTER 56

The crust on the vegetable pies was light and flaky, though Will felt they could have been better. In his own opinion, he had overworked the dough ever so slightly. If Arrogan had been around, he would have had an earful. *Is this supposed to be pastry or leather?* The pies would also have been better with meat in them, but the last of the venison had spoiled as spring's proximity brought warmer temperatures.

"Oh!" said Selene as she took her first bite.

Probably thinking how poorly it compares to whatever they served in whatever palace she grew up in, thought Will. It was an uncharitable thought on his part, and he knew she was too tactful to ever suggest as much.

Sammy nibbled on one side of hers and then held it above her head as though she was making an offering. "The gods have blessed me with this heavenly food. Please grant my wish and chain William to the stove so that he will provide me with such treats for so long as I live." She yelped when a hot bit of gravy dripped onto her cheek.

Her father laughed. "Serves you right." Then he gave Will a nod. "Magic is a waste of your life, William. Your calling is obviously in the kitchen."

"Don't play with your food, Samantha," warned Erisa.

Selene smiled at the banter. "She's right. I've certainly thought of chaining him up as well." She winked at Will to remind him of when she had had her first long talk with him. The conversation at the table stopped as all eyes turned to her, and Selene's cheeks colored as she realized how her words had sounded. "No, no!" She waved her hands. "It was a joke. When we met at the camp, I nearly had him arrested for sneaking into…" Her words tapered off. After a second, she stared at the pie in her hands with sudden interest. "You know, I don't think I've ever eaten anything this good before."

Sammy leaned forward. "Sneaking into?"

Selene looked to Will's mother for help, but Erisa's attention was fully on her. Placing her pie down, she rested her chin on one hand. "I think I'd like to hear this story. What was he sneaking into?"

Will's eyes met Selene's as he considered whether he should rescue her from the situation. Then a look of malicious glee stole across his features. Selene began shaking her head 'no' in a silent plea. He ignored it and told them, "I was sneaking into her tent, while she was sleeping."

Sammy's eyes narrowed, and she began glaring daggers at Selene.

"Why are you glaring at me?" protested Selene. "I'm innocent." She pointed at Will. "He was the one trespassing!"

"Should I tell them what happened next?" asked Will with a grin.

Erisa barked at him, "William! Stop tormenting the girl and spit it out."

"Fine. I was delivering the note I wrote to warn them about the Darrowan army. I put it on a table and left. The next day, Miss Innocent over there used a spell and figured out it was me. They arrested me, and I was questioned about it. But—and I feel the need to stress this—at no point were there any chains."

"I'm starting to seriously reconsider it," stated Selene sourly. She took another bite of her food then added, "Especially after eating this. I can think of any number of kitchens you should be locked up in."

More explanations were needed, and Will and Selene were forced to elaborate on the story. After that, the conversation moved on to other topics, though it primarily revolved around the army and the battles with the Patriarch's forces. Will was glad when it finally shifted back to simpler topics, such as how his family had been getting along over the winter. Before long his mother noticed Sammy yawning.

"I think it's time we get some rest," said Erisa.

Johnathan stood up. "You can have Will's cot, Selene. I've been using it, but I can sleep elsewhere tonight."

Something occurred to Will then. He caught his mother's gaze, and then moved his eyes toward the door that led to the other room. Silently he mouthed the word 'books.'

"Bring it out here, Johnathan. She'll be warmer by the hearth," suggested Erisa.

"There's another room?" said Selene, puzzled. "Oh, there's a door. Why didn't I notice it before?"

Will's uncle wasn't as quick on the uptake. "Why don't I sleep out here with William? Selene can share the other room with you and Sammy."

Erisa gave her brother a pointed look. "She'll be more comfortable out here on the cot."

"Me too," said Will. "If I have to sleep on the floor, it will be warmer by the fire." His mother and uncle both gave him sharp looks.

"I don't mind," said Selene suddenly. "I trust him."

Erisa stared at the young woman for a moment, and something passed across her features. She nodded. "I understand. An unfamiliar place can be unsettling." She and Johnathan argued a little more after that, but Will's mother had made up her mind.

As his family left and closed the other door, he heard his uncle continuing the fight. "This is exactly how you wound up in trouble, Erisa."

"Shut up, Johnathan," said Will's mom.

They were alone, then. Will stared at Selene for a moment until she finally broke the silence. "I like your family."

She positioned the cot to one side of the hearth while he made pallet of blankets for himself on the other. "Don't worry," she told him. "I'll make sure you're warm."

He stared blankly at her for a moment.

"There's a spell," she hurried to add. "So the floor won't be cold." She held out her hands and formed a simple spell above them that consisted of just five runes.

"Wait," said Will. "Let me see that." He studied it for a moment, memorizing the structure. Then he attempted it for himself.

"Whoa!" she warned. "Smaller, much smaller. Make the lines thinner too. You'll make the floor so hot it will burn if you do it that way." He tried several more times, but she wasn't happy with any of them. "Let me do it," Selene said at last. "You need more practice."

When her spell was done, he saw a faint, rectangular area of turyn form around his sleeping pallet.

"The spell is timed," she explained. "It should last eight hours, and if you oversleep the cold will wake you."

"That's handy," he said enviously. "I wish I'd known about that before I tried to escape to Branscombe the first time. I nearly froze to death."

"You'll learn a lot more at Wurthaven. You'll see."

"Assuming we survive the next few days," he reminded her.

They bedded down, and thanks to his unforgiving schedule in the army, Will fell asleep almost immediately.

Something woke him later, though, and he lay quietly in his cot, listening until he heard a strange sound coming from Selene's direction. *Is she in pain?*

Opening his eyes just a crack, he looked in her direction. She was sitting up on the cot, clutching her chest with one hand. Through her fingers he could see a glow.

She stood abruptly, and he closed his eyes. He felt her approach, and it seemed as though she stopped beside him. A few seconds later, she moved on and he heard the distinct sound of the door opening and closing. *Where is she going?*

Rising quietly, he went to the door. She hadn't closed it fully, probably to avoid unnecessary noise. He pushed it further open and peeked out. The moon was hidden by the trees, so he adjusted his vision until he could see clearly. Then he spotted her.

She hadn't gone far, no more than thirty feet or so. She appeared to be talking to herself, so he adjusted his hearing as well.

"It wasn't planned," said Selene. "I had to improvise." She paused as though listening, but Will couldn't hear anyone else talking.

"I had my reasons," she said. "He's no ordinary mage. You'll understand when you meet him. I've seen him do things we were taught were impossible."

She listened some more, then responded, "No, that isn't it. I just thought it would be a shame to let him go to waste, but after I learned more, I realized he could be incredibly valuable to you."

She stopped then, bowing her head as though she had been scolded. When she lifted her head, her eyes were clear and her voice sincere. "My feelings have nothing to do with it. I have to win his trust. He's very suspicious of sorcerers. You'll always be first in my heart. Whatever I do, will always be with your interests foremost in my mind."

Son of a bitch! thought Will. *I knew it.*

"As you wish," said Selene, and it was apparent her conversation had ended. Will pulled the door back and hurried to his bed. When she entered, he kept his eyes tightly closed.

He heard light footsteps cross the room, and she stopped beside his pallet again. A soft rustling sound suggested she was doing something else, but she hadn't moved on. Then something tickled his face. Will opened his eyes and found her face just inches above his own. Her hair had given her away.

"What are you doing?" he asked calmly, though he already knew. *Making certain I was still asleep before she crawled back into bed.*

Selene jumped, nearly falling back into the fire. He caught her hand and pulled her back, watching her face all the while. Her eyes darted to one side as she tried to find a reasonable excuse. She came to a decision and answered, "This," and then she closed her eyes and leaned in, pressing her lips to his.

Her action filled him with fury, for he knew it was a lie. *She'd do anything to fool me.* Was a kiss the limit? Who knew how far she would go to gain his trust? For a split second, he was tempted to find out, but instead he gently pushed her away. Remembering Tailtiu, he said the first thing that came to mind. "I didn't give you permission to do that."

She flinched as though she had been slapped.

"If you were fae, I could demand an unbound favor for something like that," he added.

Selene was already climbing onto her cot. She rolled over and put her back toward him. "Is that how they work? What does an unbound favor entail?"

"Anything," said Will coldly. "I could even demand your life."

"Is that what you want?"

"Give me back my six clima," said Will suddenly.

Selene sat up violently, throwing back her blankets. He heard her bare feet slapping the wood floor as she stomped across the room to rummage through her things. She found her coin purse and extracted the coins, and he heard them scatter across the floor as she threw them in his direction. "There," she said venomously. "Was it worth it?"

"You tell me," he snapped. "You think your kiss is worth six silver?"

He heard her moving again, but he didn't open his eyes. She lay back down, and the floor began to grow cold beneath him. "Asshole," she muttered. "I hope you freeze to death."

Will got up, gathering his blankets, and moved to the other room. *Maybe the goddamn cat will come looking for his rent and eat her,* he thought ruefully.

***

He rose early, since his sleep had been restless after their argument, and by the time his family began emerging from the bedroom, breakfast was nearly ready.

"Where's Selene?" asked Sammy.

"Outside," said Will, before muttering under his breath, "probably trying to warm up her cold, dead heart."

His cousin went to find her, and soon they were all crowded around the little table. Sammy made noises of appreciation as she enjoyed the food, but Erisa and Johnathan had already noticed the chill in the air. They exchanged meaningful glances. "Told you it was a bad idea," said his uncle around a mouthful of food.

"Shut up, Johnathan," said Will's mother.

"Are you fighting?" asked Sammy innocently.

"No," Will said immediately.

His cousin pointed at Erisa and her father. "I meant them." Then she leaned closer to Will, squinting her eyes. "Something's fishy about you."

Erisa bent in her chair and retrieved something from the floor. "What's this?"

"Oh," said Will. "I dropped my coin purse yesterday."

"You need to be more careful with your money, William," his mother chided.

"Don't worry, Erisa. He never forgets what he's owed," said Selene, her voice thick with sarcasm.

"Well, that's good to hear," said his uncle. "What do you have planned for today?"

"We should start scouting, I would imagine," said Selene, filling her voice with false enthusiasm.

"Not in the daylight," said Will. "We'll go tonight."

"You can't be planning to go through the Glenwood at night," said his uncle.

Selene agreed. "If we create a magical light, it will give us away when we get close to the village. At least during the day we can—"

He cut her off, "I can see in the dark." Will got to his feet and headed for the door. "I hear really well too," he said over his shoulder.

"Where are you going?" asked his mother.

"To kill some time. I'll be back later." Looking back, he saw a worried look on Selene's face. Maybe it had been a bad idea to give away his hand, but he was feeling vindictive. *Good. Let her worry.*

CHAPTER 57

The Glenwood was a balm for his nerves. Throughout his life, Will had always retreated to it when anything bothered him. He didn't go far, though, since there was always the chance he'd run into a Darrowan patrol. Instead he wandered in the direction of the first congruence he had found, the one that had changed his life.

He stopped when he was close to it, but he had no intention of crossing. He did consider calling Tailtiu, but decided against it. There were still favors to collect, but he intended to take care of his problems on his own. The last thing he wanted was to have to deal with his sex-crazed fae aunt again.

"What would Tailtiu do?" he wondered aloud. The answer to that was always simple. Of course, in his situation last night, it might have been more practical than what he had done. Seduce the girl to keep her from getting suspicious—that would have been a wiser course. Play off his enemy's ignorance rather than give away what he had learned.

"That's easy," said Tailtiu, standing behind him. "You should know me better by now."

He was startled, but he did his best not to show it. "What are you doing here?"

"Looking for you. Mother wants to talk to you again."

"How did you know I was here?"

"I didn't. I crossed over to make it easier for you to find me when I called. Wait here."

She disappeared through the congruence and was gone for nearly a quarter of an hour before returning. Aislinn was with her when she reappeared. "Grandson," she addressed him.

He held up a hand. "Same terms as before? One hour, guarantee of peace afterward?"

Aislinn smiled. "That will do fine."

"What do you want?"

Arrogan's one-time wife narrowed her eyes. "You have the scent of a woman on you."

"I just saw Mom and Sammy—"

She held up a hand. "Not family, an outsider—a sorceress?"

He was impressed. "You can tell all that with your nose? Maybe I've been focusing on enhancing the wrong senses."

His grandmother nodded. "Tailtiu told me of your success with her type of magic. Who is the sorceress?"

Will knew not to trust the fae, even Aislinn, but he needed advice. Deep down he needed Arrogan, but that need sprung from a desire to find support from someone older and wiser. After hearing Selene's conversation the night before, he felt betrayed—and more importantly, alone. Starting from the beginning, he shared everything he knew about Selene with his grandmother, including his most recent discovery. He finished with a smile that failed to hide his pain. "Honestly and without deception. Was that an answer worthy of our bargain?"

Aislinn frowned. "It was far too much. If you deal with my kind like this in the future, you will surely die." Then her eyes softened. "But I'm feeling motherly today. Perhaps I won't use it against you. What would you like to know?"

Motherly? That bordered on a lie. She's pushing the limit today, thought Will, but it gave him an idea. "If you were still human," he began, "if you truly could feel motherly, what would you tell me? What would your advice be then?"

"Since you were so forthright, I will give you two answers, since I am not entirely sure what I would really do if I were human. First I'll tell you what I would advise as a fae, then I will guess at what my old self might have said."

"Fair enough."

"Kill her," said Aislinn, her eyes cold. "Her kind don't deserve to live under the best of circumstances, and she has betrayed you, so she is doubly damned. Or trade her to me, in exchange I will—"

Will interrupted, "I'm not going to do that, so let's move on to the second part."

His grandmother sighed, closing her eyes as if in deep meditation. "Give me a moment."

Is it that hard to remember being human? he wondered.

A few seconds later, she opened her eyes again and her entire demeanor changed. The alien stillness of her stance vanished, and her face showed such concern that he could almost believe it wasn't an act. "William, you've been hurt. Don't let your pain cloud your thinking. Do you have feelings for this girl?"

"What? No!"

Reaching down, she grabbed his ear, pulling him painfully to his feet. "Tell the truth."

"I think you're overdoing this human thing," he protested.

She glared at him. "Human does not mean *nice*. You should have listened better to what your grandfather told you about me." Then she twisted his ear. "Now, the truth."

"Ow, ow! Yes! Maybe? I don't know!" She released him then, and he could see Tailtiu laughing silently in the background.

"That's better," said Aislinn.

"So, you have feelings, and now you think she's using you. What you need to consider is—"

"Think? I know she's using me," corrected Will.

His grandmother's eyes narrowed. "Don't interrupt me again, William. I didn't misspeak. You *think* she's using you, and that may well be the truth. The words you overhead seem to indicate it, but they could have different interpretations. From this point forward you need to be cautious, but not stupid. Don't let your prejudice color your judgment. Stay in her good graces, discover the truth, but don't give away your heart until you know what that truth is."

Her human-like façade faded away after that, replaced by the cold, alien gaze of the fae. "I'm done," she said. "But also, I would like to add that you should kill her."

"You really are bloodthirsty, aren't you?" said Will dryly.

"The rise of sorcery and the war that followed have a lot to do with my current condition," said Aislinn. "Beyond that, the crimes they committed go far past my personal grievances."

"I need her help to destroy the Darrowan supplies in Barrowden," insisted Will.

"Easy enough," said Aislinn. "Trade her to me. In exchange, I will do everything she would have and ten times more."

"I already said no. I'm not a warlock."

His grandmother smiled. "You're beginning to think, learning lessons you haven't been taught yet."

Will was growing impatient. "You had some reason for wanting to talk to me. Thus far all we've done is discuss my problems."

"I have a gift for you."

Accept no debts. Will shook his head.

"But you will have to pay for it," added Aislinn, her lips curling into a faint smile.

"What is it?"

His grandmother waved a finger in front of him. "I will not tell you. I will only say that it is a thing of such vile knowledge and power as to cause weak men to faint and cry out in horror."

Tailtiu was standing behind her mother, nodding in agreement. "It really is. I can't wait to get rid of it."

"Silence!" snapped Aislinn.

"It doesn't sound like something I would want," said Will.

Aislinn shook her head. "It is something only *you* would want, as our prior conversation has already proven."

For the life of him, Will couldn't think of anything they had talked about that related to objects of vile power, but her statement that he would want it intrigued him. She couldn't lie directly, only mislead. "What is the price you want?"

"An elemental," she said immediately.

"I'm not a sorcerer either," said Will firmly.

"You don't have to deliver it. As a service to me, I ask that you free one elemental," she clarified.

Will thought back to his previous fights but failed to get an exact count. "I've already done that several times."

"Did we have an agreement then?"

He shook his head.

"Then don't pretend to be stupid, William. Free an elemental and call my daughter. I will give you my gift at that time."

"Well, if I don't get killed, I would probably do that anyway. So you have a deal," said Will. "Anything else?"

538

"Do you know the elements humans are composed of?"

Will was confused. "Do you mean like earth, wind, fire, and water?"

Aislinn shook her head. "No, they are made of three things, mind, soul, and flesh. All magic relates to those elements."

"Where is this going?" His grandmother was beginning to remind him of Arrogan, which irritated him. It also caused him to stop and think. "Wait. How do they relate to magic?"

"The mind represents the knowledge to create spells, the soul is responsible for the will that creates them, and flesh is the source of the turyn used for magic. When a person dies, these things become disconnected, but they are not necessarily destroyed. All mages are fundamentally the same, but they have their differences. Wizards focus more on knowledge than the amassing of power; warlocks deal mainly in things of the flesh to attain their goals."

"Why are you telling me this?" asked Will.

"Because riddles are the way that the fae coerce mortals into doing our bidding when they won't make a bargain. Teaching you to think is the only way you've left me to gain what I want. Think about what I've said." She turned away, walking back toward the congruence. "Think carefully. The answers to more than one question lie in what I have said."

Will stared after at the place she had vanished for several minutes after she had gone. As always, he felt that he had more questions than answers, but one thing in particular stood out to him. *She didn't say what sorcerers focus on. Is it the soul? The will?* Either way, it didn't make much sense. From what he had seen, he had a will at least as strong as most sorcerers.

Nearly all of Arrogan's strange training practices had focused on it, though he hadn't realized it at the time. In contrast, he was probably the most ignorant wizard in Terabinia.

"Stupid fae," he said. "Never a simple answer when you want one."

 CHAPTER 58

Back at the house, Will found Selene in the garden with his mother and uncle. Together they were breaking up the hard soil to prepare the ground for planting. Since Arrogan had lived alone there was only one hoe, so Erisa and Selene were using sharpened staves to help.

They hadn't heard him arrive, so he stood just beyond the gate that led through the brambles, watching and listening. There wasn't much to hear, though. The three of them didn't have much breath to spare on idle chatter.

What is she doing? Selene's earth elemental could have probably done the entire job in a matter of minutes, but there she was, bent over and sweating in the still-cold air of late winter. He couldn't imagine that she had ever done such labor before, and it wouldn't take long for blisters to form on her soft hands.

Then he noticed that Selene's hands were wrapped with linen strips. *Probably Mom's idea, since we don't have gloves.*

He didn't have a good reason to watch. He wasn't learning anything, but he didn't move. Quietly, he admired her strength and stamina, as she sweated and pounded the earth with her stake. There was something bewitching about watching her movements.

"Did you kiss her?" asked Sammy from beside him. Will nearly yelped with surprise. He had been so focused that he hadn't noticed her walk up. "Is that why she's so mad at you?"

The exact opposite, he thought. "No, it's nothing like that."

"I think she likes you," said Sammy. "Like a lot, a lot, a lot."

"She doesn't," said Will firmly. "And even if she did, she's nobility."

"They always find a way in the stories."

"Real life doesn't work that way. In real life the princess puts the hero in chains and forces him into slavery."

Sammy's eyes went wide. "Is she a princess?"

"No. Just a spoiled brat who wishes she was."

"She's working awfully hard for someone who's spoiled," noted his cousin.

"Don't let her fool you. She has magic that could do that entire job in a matter of minutes. She's just trying to make herself appear honest and sincere. It's all a façade."

"Maybe she's just being polite."

"Huh?"

"Well, if she just snapped her fingers and finished everything, how would it make us feel? I don't know about your mom, but my dad would probably feel kind of useless. He's always been very proud of what he could do with his hands," observed Sammy.

"Don't let your prejudice color your judgment," Aislinn had told him. Maybe he was being too harsh. Then again, maybe she was just trying to fool them. Will was surprised at the depth of his cousin's thought. He had always thought of her as a pest, and more lately as rambunctious and sometimes funny. Now he knew he hadn't been paying close attention to her. She was growing up.

And maybe I haven't paid close enough attention to Selene either. Turning away from the garden, he went into the house. "Come help me clean up so I can cook," he told Sammy.

The midday meal earned him overflowing praise from Sammy and a meager 'it's good' from Selene. He didn't blame her though. Whatever her deeper motivations were, he understood she was truly angry with him for what he had said the night before. He needed to find a way to get back in her good graces. *Otherwise I'll have no chance of ever figuring out the truth.*

As everyone was getting up from the table, he grabbed Selene's wrist, pulling her toward the door. "Come on."

She tried to pull away, but he held on. "I don't want to go anywhere with you."

He released her, mainly because his family were giving him disapproving looks. "We need to talk."

Silence reigned for an awkward span of time before she finally relented. "Fine. Let's go." Selene took the lead, striding out the door with the pride of a thoroughbred horse. Will followed, and they she stopped when they were around fifty yards from the house. She whirled to face him. "What would you like to say?"

"First, that I'm sorry. Not for rejecting you, but for how I did it," said Will.

"Apology accepted," she answered primly. "Are we done?"

Will frowned. "Don't you have anything to say?"

"I've already told you I don't apologize, and even if I did, do you think you deserve one?"

He waited, fixing her with an even stare while trying to keep his expression neutral. When she didn't say anything, he finally asked, "Don't you?" Selene still didn't reply, but he could see uncertainty in her eyes. A full minute passed, and he turned around to go back into the house.

"Yes!" she shouted at his back. Will turned back. Her face was red. "But I can't give you one."

"Why not?"

"You have your stupid rules about debts and whatnot, but so do we. Never apologize. It's been drilled into me since I was a girl."

"It's a good rule for sorcerers, I guess. Never apologize. They'd never be able to stop if they started."

He hadn't thought about what he was saying, but he realized immediately that his words could only make matters worse; yet Selene didn't look angry—there was something else in her eyes. "Is that why you were angry?" she asked. "Because you hate us so much?"

"No," he said flatly. "It's because you lied."

"I hadn't even said anything," she protested.

"The kiss was a lie. You were covering up what you were doing."

"You *did* hear then," she stated bluntly.

He nodded. "Care to explain?"

"I have obligations," she told him. "But they aren't sinister. I think you could do a lot of good if you're allowed to reach your potential."

"It sounded more like you were buying and selling horseflesh."

Selene stared at the ground. "I suppose it did, but I didn't intend for it to. The person I was speaking to is blunt and direct."

"Who was he?"

She didn't answer.

Will threw up his hands. "How am I supposed to trust you when I know almost nothing about you? You've lied about your name, kept your family a secret, and now I know you're on some secret mission to—I don't know what it is—enslave me?"

"To win you over, to recruit you," said Selene earnestly. "Not enslave you."

"Well you're doing a piss-poor job of it," he said sourly. "How do you expect me to trust you?"

She stepped closer. "I've never lied to you. I've hidden a lot—because I had to—but I've never lied, not in word or deed. I would never do anything to bring harm to you or your family."

Will sighed. He wanted to believe her. He really did. He wasn't even angry anymore, just tired. "Let's just do what we came to do. I'll trust you that far, but no farther, because you did lie and you're still refusing to admit it."

"How?"

He gave her the look Arrogan had often given him when he thought he was being particularly stupid. "The kiss." Then he turned and headed back to the house.

As he went, his sharp ears picked up a murmur from her lips. "But it wasn't…"

***

That evening as the sun began to set, they prepared to leave. It didn't take long, however, since they had little to carry. Will put on his gambeson and left his mail in its bag. As he was belting on his sword, Selene pointed to it. "Are we having this fight again?"

Will shrugged. "I'm not fighting with you. It's too noisy."

"There are plenty of soldiers in the enemy camp, many of them wearing similar armor. You'll fit right in," she told him.

"Where's yours then?" he pointed out. "You expect me to go armored while you walk around like an archery target? How about you wear it?"

"It's too big for me. At least one of us should wear it."

"It's still too noisy."

"I can fix that," she countered, wiggling her fingers at him in a pseudo-mystical fashion.

His mother stepped in. "You've got bigger problems," she said, looking Selene up and down carefully.

"Such as?" asked Selene.

Erisa stared at her chest. "Maybe they aren't too big. Come with me."

Selene blushed, and Will snickered as his mother shooed him away. "Go get your spare clothes from the other room," she ordered.

He did as he was told and then waited while the two of them worked on Selene's disguise. When they called him back, he took one look at Selene and began to laugh. His clothes hung on Selene like an empty sack thrown over a fence post. His trousers had the cuffs rolled up and were belted tightly at the waist. The only part that was snug was her derriere, which he found fascinating, since ordinarily it was better hidden by her skirts.

His mother gave him a sharp glance as she saw what he was studying. "William."

He reluctantly lifted his eyes. The shirt was almost as bad as the trousers, except it was loose everywhere. From the way it hung on Selene he guessed his mother had bound her breasts.

"What do you think?" asked his mother.

"From the neck down, she looks like a starving boy with an oversized b—"

"William," warned Erisa.

He stopped with a grin. "From the neck up..." Selene's hair had been tied up and was covered by a thick wool cap, but her slender neck, high cheekbones, and full lips were a dead giveaway. And her eyes—he stared into them for a moment as she stared back, and he felt his mouth go dry. Will felt his cheeks heat up, and he looked away. "Isn't there some way to ugly her up?"

His remark produced a smile on Selene's face that in her current attire could only be described as goofy. Erisa took note of the expression but said nothing. Instead she asked her brother, "Johnathan, we need an independent opinion. What do you think?"

His uncle studied her for a minute. "Will's right. If anyone looks at her close up, they'll know right away. Even at a distance, her walk will give her away."

"Because of her butt," Sammy declared gleefully, wiggling her hips.

"Samantha, would you like to do the wash a day early?" warned Erisa.

Sammy ran out the door. "Nope!"

Johnathan rubbed his beard. "There is one other option. There are some women in the camp. If we dress her like one of them, she might not seem out of place."

Erisa shook her head. "I still have a dress that would probably do, but trust me, even if they didn't suspect her, she would draw *far* too much attention that way."

"What women?" asked Will. He'd never seen any in the Terabinian camp, aside from Selene and Lord Nerrow's daughter.

There was a brief silence, then his uncle answered, "The comfort women."

"Comfort women? I don't think we had those at the camp I was in. What do they do?"

"That's because Branscombe was right there," said Johnathan.

"And how would you know that?" asked Erisa sharply.

His uncle held up his hands. "Don't look at me! I'm a married man. I'd never do that to Doreen." He stopped then, a look of pain on his face as he remembered he wasn't married any longer. "I'll go make sure Sammy isn't getting into trouble out there."

Will felt bad for asking. He'd figured out the general meaning from his uncle's remarks, but it was the reminder of who they had lost that made him guilty. Erisa patted his shoulder. "It's not your fault. These things just take time—a lot of time."

 CHAPTER 59

They left soon after that. Night was falling, and the sky dimmed rapidly after the sun dropped behind the mountains. Will was wearing his mail, and he stopped as soon as they were out of sight of the house.

"Don't stop," said Selene. "I won't be able to see my feet in a few minutes. We need to hurry before the light gives out and we're lost in these woods."

"I can see in the dark," Will reminded her.

"I thought you were bluffing. You know the spell?"

"There's a spell?"

Selene sighed. "Yes, but I don't know it."

"I thought you trained at Wurthaven for years," he replied, putting on a posh tone.

Selene hid a faint smile. "We don't sound like that. I told you your acting was terrible. And no, I don't know the spell, it's a complicated one. I'd have to study it a while."

"But you memorized the cleaning spell?"

She put her hands on her hips. "Which one do you think is used more often? I have yet to need a night vision spell, until today. Living in that army camp I needed the cleaning spell every day."

"What do you do in the dark then?" he asked.

Selene put one hand out, and a brief collection of runes rushed together. A second later a gently glowing ball of golden light replaced them. She extinguished it a second later. "A simple light spell, but we can't risk that tonight, can we?"

"Definitely not," he agreed. "But don't worry, as I said, I can see. I'll guide you. There's a game trail here, but the terrain is tricky."

"All right," she said after a second.

The path they took sloped downward—sharply in places—as it twisted and turned through brush and trees. Once the light had gone, Selene began to have trouble. She tripped several times and began to slide on particularly steep spots.

Will caught her wrist and anchored them by grabbing onto a scrubby bush. "Careful."

"Can't you teach me the trick to whatever you're doing?"

"You just concentrate some of your turyn around your eyes and then shift its phase until you can see properly," he told her.

She stared blankly at the spot she thought his face would be, though he was actually a few inches farther to the right. "How do you concentrate turyn in a particular part of your body?"

"The same way you do near your hand when you're forming runes for a spell."

"But…" She didn't finish her sentence. Instead she remained silent, and he could see a look of concentration on her face, though her turyn didn't seem to be moving. "I give up," she announced.

"You might have to go through all the other weird shit he put me through first before you can do it," Will theorized.

"Did he teach you that?"

"No. One of the fae did."

"Are you going to explain that?" she asked. "In fact, we still haven't talked about how we got here, or what that thing in the cave was."

"Are you going to tell me who you were talking to the other night?" Selene remained silent. "How about this, are you going to report anything I tell you to whoever that was?"

In the dark, he could see her biting her lip. "Yes."

"Then we're done talking about those other things, but thank you for being truthful—this time."

She growled, "I'd smack you if I could see where your face is."

"At least we're being honest with each other now," he said brightly. "I don't share any of my secrets, and you don't tell me a thing about yourself."

"You don't trust me at all, do you?"

Will helped her around several bushes. "Actually, I trust you a little—now that we're being honest—but I don't trust whoever is pulling your strings."

"You would trust him, if I could tell you."

"Then tell me!"

"I can't."

He wanted to shake her, but he restrained himself. They had a mission to accomplish, so he held his tongue and continued leading her down the game trail. A few minutes later she spoke again. "I can't tell you for two reasons. One, I'm bound by an oath, and two, once you know we won't be able to be friends anymore."

"You said I would trust him. Trusting and being friends goes hand in hand."

"Not where I come from."

He could see the lights from Barrowden beginning to show through the trees, though they were probably still too far away for Selene to see. Will stopped. "We're close. You said you could make my armor quiet, right?"

Golden runes appeared over her hand, flowing together into a spell composed of around fifteen parts.

Once they had connected, she reached out and pressed it against his chest, where it immediately fizzled out. As far as Will could tell, it hadn't done anything. "Can you please stop doing that?" asked Selene.

"Oh, sorry." He made a conscious effort to stop absorbing turyn. "Try again."

She repeated the spell, and this time it sank into his armor and clothing, spreading out over his body. "It will last about an hour," she told him. "During that time your clothing won't make any sound. That includes your boots but doesn't include your hands or any other part of your body that's exposed."

"Why not?"

"So you can talk, for one," she replied, "though I'm starting to doubt the wisdom of that part. It was the simplest way to make the spell practical, but the upshot is that if you break wind, sneeze, cough, or yell, it can be heard." She repeated the spell for her own clothing.

"Too bad we can still be seen," Will muttered. "Can you make a mist?"

"I can," she told him. "Syllannus, my water elemental, is good for that, but he can't cover the entire town, just a hundred yards or so. A mist that small would be suspicious, and any mages in the town will recognize the magic. Besides, we couldn't see through it."

Will grinned, an expression that was wasted since she couldn't see his face. "Make some mist. Just a little."

She gave him an odd look but did as he asked. Her elemental's mist was thicker than what Tailtiu had produced, blocking his sight of everything beyond a few feet. Will began adjusting his vision until he found the sweet spot, and the mist vanished. "That's enough," he told her.

"What was that about?" she asked.

"I can see through your mist. If things go wrong, make as much mist as you can and grab my hand. I'll be able to lead us out."

"A night vision spell won't do that. Is this more fae magic?"

Will shrugged. "I wouldn't call it fae magic. It's the same way they do it, but I think you would call it wild magic since I'm not fae."

They continued on until they were about fifty yards from the dimmest area of light that Will thought the patrollers could see in. He expected they would find the perimeter patrols about twenty yards or so closer in, but there were none in sight from where they were at the moment. He pulled Selene down to sit beside him. "We'll wait here."

"Why here?"

"You see the lanterns in town?" he said, pointing. "Closer to us from those is a dim region. The patrollers will be walking at the edge of that, where it's hard for them to be seen and where they won't spoil their night vision. Anyone that approaches without figuring out where the patrollers are will probably be caught, and once they're in the better-lit region, the patrollers can catch them easily. We wait here a while, and after I've got a feel for their timing, we can enter the town in between patrol sweeps."

"Shouldn't we find a higher point to observe from? We're in a dip here, aren't we?"

He nodded. "That would be nice, but they probably have sentries posted any place we would choose for that same reason. So we have to choose a shitty spot like this, where it's harder to see as well as to be seen. Fortunately, my eyes are good enough to make up for that."

"How long do you think we'll wait?"

"Until I see the same guards come by twice. Probably an hour or two."

Half an hour passed, and the cold began to eat at them since they weren't moving. Selene moved closer until their shoulders were touching. With little to do, Will began to think dark thoughts. "Hey, Selene."

"Yes."

"If something happens and I don't make it back, will you do me a favor?"

She gave him a sly look, though she couldn't see him well. "Wouldn't that put you in my debt?"

"I'd be dead, probably."

"Then you have to pay in advance. Your credit is no good."

"What do you want?" he asked.

"Tell me your favor first."

He sighed. "My cousin Eric is still in the army. I haven't thanked you properly, but this mail saved my life a couple of times. Could you do something similar for him?"

"I don't know," she said reluctantly. "That was a lot of coin, and you've made me regret spending it several times."

"Please?"

"Keep me warm."

"Huh?"

"That's my price," she explained. "Keep me warm until we can get this over with."

He stood and spread his cloak so she could slip inside it, then he eased back down into a sitting position so the two of them could huddle together. His arm was around her shoulders, and he didn't trust himself to speak.

After a while, she asked, "Are we friends?"

I would love to know the answer to that myself, thought Will ruefully. Over time he had become intensely attracted to her, but that wasn't friendship. It was lust. Friends should trust each other. There was some sort of warmth between them, both literally and figuratively, but he didn't trust her much. He decided to be truthful. "I honestly don't know."

"Oh." There was something sad in the way she said it.

"You have other friends, though," he told her cheerfully. "A peasant from Barrowden wouldn't be much to brag about."

She shook her head, tickling his ear with her hair. "No. I have family, that's it."

"What about Lord Nerrow's daughter, Laina?"

"Mark Nerrow and his two daughters are like family to me," she said. "In fact, he's been more of a father to me than my own father."

Will laughed bitterly. "Then he's been more of a father to you than he has to me."

She looked up, and he saw her eyes glittering in the darkness. "You knew?"

"Mom told me a while back."

"Don't judge him too harshly. He's one of the kindest men I know," said Selene. "I'm sure he never wanted things to turn out this way. That's why he keeps trying to help you."

"I don't know enough about him to have an opinion," said Will, "and while I haven't met my other half-sister, having met Laina doesn't give me much hope. She seems thoroughly rotten."

"She isn't as bad as you think," offered Selene. "She just hasn't seen enough of the world to learn more empathy yet. Her father has kept her sheltered."

"Yours certainly hasn't sheltered you."

"What do you mean?" she asked.

"You're obviously from an important family, but they let you run around loose in the world like this. It doesn't make sense. I was starting to think you were a princess for a while, but there's no way a king would let his daughter put herself in such dangerous situations."

"My family isn't like others."

"Do you have any siblings?" asked Will.

"Not anymore," she answered. "I had an older brother, but he died when I was small."

"I'm sorry."

She shook her head. "Don't be. He was much older. I hardly knew him."

"How did it happen?"

"An illness. They wouldn't let me see him, but that's what I was told."

Even without names, Will was learning more about her than he had discovered in all the time he had known her. "What about your mother?"

She shook her head. "She died giving birth to me. I have a step-mother, though."

Damn, thought Will. *She's had a tragic life.* "So, it's just you and your dad then."

"And the Nerrow family," she added. "I was fostered to their household when I was eight. It was much nicer than mine."

"Fostered?"

She chuckled. "It's something the nobility does. Most children are sent to live with a different family when they reach a certain age. It helps to create connections between families of power."

"But Nerrow didn't send Laina away," observed Will.

"He wouldn't. Not with me there," she answered.
"Besides, he's too soft. I don't think he could stand to be
parted either of his girls."

In the darkness, Will watched the first patrol he had
seen pass by for the second time. He had a good grasp
of the timing now. There were four groups of three men.
Each group completed a full circuit of the camp roughly
every twenty minutes. It would be six or seven minutes
before the next patrol came by. Since they were bundled
together, he held onto Selene, and they stood together.
"It's time."

They moved forward through the shadowy region beyond the lanterns of Barrowden, and soon they emerged into the light. It wasn't that late, so there were still a few people moving about, but since it was a military camp there were fewer than if it had still been a village.

"Shouldn't there be more guards?" Will muttered.

"I think since this region is so well protected by the pass they don't think there's much threat," suggested Selene.

As they walked, Will began to notice the difference in how much sound they made. Their feet were completely silent, and their clothes didn't rustle, but their voices were completely normal. As many times as he had had to sneak around thus far in his career, he figured he should insist that Selene teach him the spell after they were done.

Barrowden as he had known it was completely gone. The village homes and buildings had been razed, and whatever could be salvaged—along with a significant amount of new timber—had gone into constructing the new Darrowan base of operations.

Unlike the Terabinian army camp and the Darrowan camp in the pass, Barrowden's tents and new buildings had been arranged in a neat grid. Wide lanes separated the tents and intersected each other at ninety-degree angles. He supposed that the layout facilitated ease of movement and made everything easier to find.

The camp was also well lit, and though the lanterns weren't that bright there were very few truly dark regions within it. Again, that made it easier for people to move about after dark, but it also made it harder to hide. Will and Selene both tensed when a few soldiers passed them in the street, but the men barely glanced at them.

"This might be easier than I anticipated," Will observed.

Selene nodded. "Don't get too comfortable, though. Eventually we'll have to do something, and it won't be so easy anymore."

They continued on in a straight line, following the lane they had first entered on. Most of what they had passed thus far consisted of pavilion tents with short, temporary walls that rose four feet high along their margins to create semi-permanent dwellings. As far as Will could tell, they served as barracks, and they seemed to go on forever. The first section they went through was occupied, but the next was empty. *It must have belonged to the units that have already gone to the pass.* What worried him most was that there were obviously many more such sections, and soldiers still occupied many of them. The Patriarch's army was huge.

They went by much larger tents occasionally, and by the smell Will figured they were mess tents, but they found nothing resembling the centralized stores that they were looking for. Still, they had only walked through a small fraction of the enemy base so far.

Two men waited on one corner of an especially large intersection ahead that marked the center of the camp. Given the lighting, they had already seen Will and Selene, so there was no point in avoiding them, so they kept walking.

As soon as they were within twenty feet, one of the pair stepped out and challenged them, "Show your pass."

Will scratched his head. "I didn't realize it was that late. We'll head back to our unit." He made as if to turn back.

The guard wasn't going to let them off easily, however. "Stop. Which unit are you—"

Will had already connected his source-link spell to both men, and he began rapidly draining their turyn. Unaware of what he was doing, neither of them made the connection between their fatigue and the newcomers until it was too late, and both slowly collapsed to the ground.

Selene stared at him in surprise. "That would make me sick for hours, but there's a better way."

"Hey!" someone called from their left. Four more men were emerging from a small, wooden building that must serve as a guard station.

"Show me," muttered Will. "Or things are about to get ugly." He waved to the guards. "Give us a hand; something is wrong with these two!"

The newly arrived soldiers weren't buying his act, and they lowered short spears in his direction as they approached. The sword at Will's side felt woefully inadequate. He readied himself to cast his linking spell again, but he knew he could only get two. *Shit.*

From the corner of his eye, he saw a spell come together in Selene's hands. The runes had a light green color to them, and when she released it, the spell shot toward the men before expanding and slowly fading from his sight. All four collapsed to the ground.

"Damn!" said Will. "Are they dead?"

"Asleep. Let's get them off the street."

Make that two spells I want to learn from her, thought Will. *The silence spell and the sleeping spell.* Together they dragged the six unconscious soldiers back into the guard building, lining them up on the floor.

"How long will they sleep?" he asked.

"Hours, until the next watch shift comes and wakes them up."

"Or someone passes by and wonders why there's no one asking for passes," said Will. Stepping outside, he looked down each lane that led away from the intersection. The one to their left seemed much the same as the one they had walked down—more barracks—but the other two showed larger tents and buildings in the distance.

The sheer size of the base was daunting. From what they had seen, even if they found the stores and supplies, there would probably be far too many. Setting fire to one would raise the alarm, making it difficult to destroy the rest. "Even if we find the supply tents or warehouses, how are we going to destroy them all?" said Will.

Selene gave him a harsh look. "This was your plan."

A man emerged from a tent on the opposite side of the lane and walked toward him. The stranger wasn't dressed as a soldier though; he wore a black robe, and Will could see something like a black flame hovering above his shoulder. *A sorcerer.* "Stay inside," warned Will, hissing over his shoulder through the doorway behind him.

Will stepped out boldly. "Show your pass."

The man stopped, a look of surprise crossing his face, and Will worried that he'd made a mistake. A second later the stranger relaxed. "Certainly. Let me find it for you." The man lifted his hand, and the black flame pulsed. A spell formed above his palm.

Will snatched his sword from his sheath and ran forward, but he was too late. The sorcerer finished his spell, and a tangled web of black lines shot toward Will. It expanded when it reached him, and he felt a burning pain across his skin before the spell faded and fizzled out. The sorcerer looked at him in surprise, but before he could do anything else, something flashed across the lane and tore through him. Will saw a hole three inches across that went entirely through the man's body before he collapsed.

He turned back toward Selene. "What was that?"

"Will!" she yelled, trying to warn him.

Will looked back and saw the dead sorcerer's strange elemental just before it crashed into him. It seemed to be made of black, smoky flesh, and within it he saw claws and teeth. His sword found nothing when he tried to fend it off, and he found himself wrapped in powerful arms. Streamers of black turyn whipped around him, burning whenever they touched his skin, but they couldn't seem to do serious harm since they faded soon after touching him. It was the claws and teeth that scared him most. He felt powerful jaws latching onto him in several places, and though they didn't penetrate his mail he felt them begin to clamp down with bone-crushing force.

He was helpless.

Then something slammed into him from behind, knocking him free from the strange creature that had been trying to devour him. When he looked up from the ground, he saw a bizarre spectacle: Selene was battling the beast, her body covered in stone plates, while each of her hands held an incandescent blue blade.

Unlike his sword, hers worked to devastating effect, destroying whatever they touched. They ripped through the monster, and when they came in contact with other things, such as the ground, they tore through it, leaving deep grooves. Her first two attacks caused gouts of black blood to spray from the shadowy thing she fought.

Will watched in shock. *What kind of elemental has blood?*

Chapter 60

For a moment it seemed as though she would win easily, but the monster wasn't done yet. Slipping past her next swing, it fell upon her, wrapping itself around her body in the same way it had done with Will. With claws and teeth, it pried at the stone protecting her, and black mist began to seep into the cracks. He heard Selene shriek with pain and rage as the black substance touched her skin.

Her stone fists released the blue blades and they transformed, becoming broad, spinning circles that buzzed as they spun around her body, cutting and destroying anything they touched. Within seconds, they had shredded the beast clinging to her, sending bits of blood and gore all over the intersection. The black smoke slowly dissipated, leaving an odd assortment of arms, teeth, claws, and talons on the ground. Will didn't think it would have resembled any living creature he had ever seen, either before or after Selene had disassembled it.

She sank to her knees, and the stone plates crumbled to the ground, becoming dust, while the blue circles stopped moving and rediscovered gravity. They fell to the ground like ordinary water, soaking into the dry earth.

Will ran to her side. She seemed unhurt, but her face was red and sweat was dripping down her forehead. "What the hell kind of elemental was that?" he asked.

"Not an elemental," she panted, her breathing heavy and irregular. "A demon. He was a priest of Madrok." Then her eyes rolled back into her head and her body began to shake violently.

He spotted something dark on her shoulder, just beneath the collar of her shirt, and he pulled it open to reveal an ugly darkness that seemed to *boil* beneath the surface of her skin. *The black mist,* he realized. He clamped his hand over her shoulder and tried to draw it out, but had no success—it wasn't a spell. He decided to try something else, and a second later he cast the source-link spell, connecting himself with Selene.

As always, a sense of duality washed over him, and while he was able to separate his sense of self from his sense of Selene, he could feel the searing evil that was trying to destroy her from the inside out. Without any other options, he began drawing out her turyn, pulling it from her body faster than he had ever done with anyone before her.

The evil came with it, and because of his haste, his body couldn't change it quickly enough to protect him from the inevitable turyn sickness that came with foreign turyn. Yet this was far worse than the nausea that had he had experienced after drinking his grandfather's elixir of turyn. The same burning pain he had felt in Selene afflicted him for several minutes, until his body finished absorbing and converting it.

With his ordeal over, Will realized his eyes were closed, and he opened them. A sense of vertigo washed over him and he promptly vomited onto the lane. Off to one side, he saw Selene lying prone, her eyes open as she watched him. "Are you all right?" she asked, exhaustion plain in her voice.

Spitting to clear his mouth, he nodded. Selene sat up and began gingerly getting to her feet.

That surprised him. Normally after being drained of their turyn, people were helpless for hours. "How are you recovering so quickly?" he asked.

"The elementals," she said simply. "I can draw from them."

"It doesn't make you sick?"

She shook her head. "The heart-stone enchantment converts it for me." She gave him a worried look. "How about you? That was pure demonic turyn. It should have killed you."

564

Will got to his feet, doing his best not to stagger. "I guess my whole body is like the heart-stone enchantment. It converts anything I take in, just not as quickly." He walked over to the man they had killed. The black-robed stranger looked ordinary enough, but as he searched the body, he noticed a strange symbol tattooed on the man's chest. "What's this?"

"The symbol of Madrok," said Selene. "We need to move."

He had briefly considered moving the man's body into the guardhouse with the others, but there were shouts coming from several directions. It was too late. Selene grabbed his arm and slid it over her shoulder as a mist rose seemingly from nothing to surround them. Both of them had been through an ordeal, but she seemed to have recovered from it first.

She led him down a different lane, the one that headed to the right. Gradually, Will's balance returned, and he used his turyn to adjust his eyesight so he could see through the dense fog. He started to remove his arm, but Selene seized his torso, pressing her face into his chest. "I thought I was dying," she said into his shirt.

"We both would have died if you hadn't destroyed that thing," he replied, unsure what to do. Slowly, he relaxed, putting his arms around her. As the stress in his body began to drain away, he felt his arms begin to shake with a faint tremor. *That thing scared the shit out of me,* he realized. Things had happened so quickly before then that he hadn't had a chance to register how much it had shaken him.

Selene pushed him away, and her posture straightened as they began moving again. There were shouts in every direction now, and Will saw people running past them through the mist, heading toward the scene of their battle with the demon. He was forced to steer them toward the center of the lane as most of the responders ran along the sides.

"What did you do to that sorcerer?" he asked.

"Not a sorcerer," she corrected. "He was a priest of Madrok, a warlock."

"Oh."

"It was a water drill, a spinning vortex of water," she told him.

"And that thing with him was a demon?"

Selene nodded.

"Why didn't it vanish or go dormant after he died, the way elementals do?"

"A sorcerer controls an elemental through their heart-stone enchantment. When they die, the elemental becomes incapable of doing anything until someone new takes control. Demons are different—they're intelligent. The priests of Madrok sell their souls to him and he grants them a demon to assist them. The tattoo is a mark of that, but they aren't controlled like an elemental is. Once the warlock dies, they can do whatever they want," she explained. "What bothers me more is that there shouldn't be any priests of Madrok here. They come from the kingdom of Shimera. They're supposedly enemies of Darrow."

Will didn't like the sound of that, then he saw something that caught his attention. "What is that?"

"How should I know?" demanded Selene. "I can't see a damn thing."

On their right was a large, wooden building and Will could see several women standing along a railing that stretched the entire length of its front porch. They were staring out into the mist curiously, though he was sure they were just as blind as Selene. "There's several women standing in front of a building to our right."

"Just keep walking," urged Selene. "That's not our objective."

The women were only twenty feet from them as they passed the building, and Will stared intently at them. His mist-vision rendered everything in shades of gray, so he couldn't have said anything about their hair or eye color. If Selene had been standing among them, he might have had trouble identifying her, but one of the women seemed familiar somehow. He tugged on Selene's arm to stop her. "I think I know one of them," he said softly.

"You know what they are, right?" asked Selene.

He wasn't stupid. "Comfort women."

"Technically, the Darrowans call them 'merchant wives,'" whispered Selene.

"Wives? What the hell does that mean?"

"The Prophet's laws are weird," she explained. "Prostitution is illegal, but an unmarried man can sleep with another man's wife, so long as the husband gives permission."

"So they're selling their wives to other men?"

"Well, these are probably Terabinian girls. Women who are raised in Darrow are followers of the Prophet, so they have certain rights that foreign women don't. So when they took your village, some of the more enterprising soldiers married the women they captured so they could make a profit prostituting them to the others."

Will felt his eyes go wide. *Then these are my neighbors.* "We have to save them."

Selene shook him, hard. "How? Have you lost your mind?"

He was staring hard at the women, and he was pretty sure the one he recognized was Tracy Tanner. "I know that woman. I saved her son, Joey. She's a friend," he insisted.

"She's been here for months," said Selene calmly. "She's been remarried, beaten, raped repeatedly. They torture them, Will. She won't be in her right mind anymore. She's as likely to turn us over to her new 'husband' as she is to help us. And all that aside, how are we supposed to accomplish our mission if we stop and try to help a half-dozen women escape from the camp?"

Will looked down, meeting her gaze. "If it were you, would you want me to walk away and leave you?"

Her eyes were filled with uncertainty, but after moment she responded, "Yes. If it were me, I'd rather die than have someone I care about see what had become of me."

He stared at her for a moment. His heart was a confusing mess of emotions. "Well, too fucking bad. I'd drag your miserable ass out of hell if that's where you were and screw the consequences." Grabbing her hand, he pulled her toward the porch. "Keep your head down. You're a boy and I'm bringing you here to gain experience."

"What?" she exclaimed in a panicked whisper. "No!" But it was too late.

CHAPTER 61

Selene kept her head down as though in embarrassment as Will pulled her up to the front porch. He said the first thing that popped into his head, "My friend and I are here for some fun."

The women gathered around them like hens, clucking their encouragement. "Your friend seems shy," said the oldest, a middle-aged woman he didn't recognize.

Selene had her head bowed, her body facing Will, and she jumped as one of the younger ones ran a hand across her rump and gave it a firm squeeze. "Are you a virgin? I love how shy you are," said the woman.

It was Will's turn to be shocked. He had returned his vision to normal, and both the voice and his eyes confirmed the identity of the one who had grabbed Selene. It was Annabelle Withy. Their eyes met, and she stared at him in horror. His eyes darted sideways, and he saw Tracy Tanner staring at him as well. He gave her a smile full of false confidence. "You look ripe. How about you and your friend show us the ropes?" He nodded at Annabelle.

After a moment, Tracy broke out of her trance and smiled. "Of course! Anna, let's take care of these gentlemen." She was studying Selene's face, and Will thought she saw understanding there.

Tracy and Anna led them inside and positioned themselves to hide Selene from direct observation of the man who was seated there. He held out a hand to Will. "Six silver, three for each. You get one hour. If you want more, pay in advance."

He dug around in his coin purse, but it was empty. He'd never taken the time to recover his money from the floor at home. Unsure what to do, he continued to fumble until Selene shoved a gold crown into his hand. Will passed it to the man.

The man looked at it carefully. "A Terabinian crown?"

"Spoils of war," said Will with a nervous grin.

"Let me get your change," said the pimp. After a few seconds, he handed Will four unfamiliar silver coins of Darrowan currency. "You're lucky it's me," said the man with a wink. "You're supposed to turn in any Terabinian coin you find."

Tracy pulled on his arm. "Let's go upstairs," she said in a sultry voice he would never have imagined coming from her. He followed, and she led them up to a short hallway. There were four doors leading off from it. "Anna's room is over there," she said, pointing at the door across from hers, "but it will be more fun if we share mine." Opening the door, she let them in.

After the door closed, they were alone, and Annabelle latched on to Will's arm. "What are you doing here? Did you come for us?"

"Not exactly," answered Will, but Annabelle seized him a hug that nearly crushed the wind from his lungs.

"I never thought I'd see you again," she mumbled.

Selene was watching them with a face carefully composed to show no emotion. "We found you by accident," she said.

"It's dangerous for you to be here," said Tracy, her expression fearful. "They'll beat us if they find out we helped you."

"We're getting you out of here," declared Will. "How many of you are there?"

"It's just me and Tracy," said Annabelle, still holding him. "There's two other women here, but they're both from Darrow."

"And Stan," offered Tracy. "He's the one you met in the front room."

"That's it?" asked Will.

Tracy seemed angry. "That's all they need. Do you think we can just walk out of here?"

"I didn't mean it like that," said Will. It was then that he realized that Tracy Tanner was pregnant and just beginning to show.

"Do you know where the supplies are stored?" asked Selene, her voice cool and business-like.

Tracy gave Selene a suspicious look. "Who's she?"

Will stared at Selene a moment, unsure what to say. *I wish I knew.* Finally, he answered, "Her name is Isabel. She's a sorceress with the Terabinian army. We're here to burn the supply stores if possible."

"You're a fool, then," said Tracy. "They'll kill you and us too just for talking to you."

"Told you," said Selene coolly.

Will managed to disentangle himself from Annabelle. "We're leaving. It's up to you if you want to come with us."

Annabelle answered immediately, "I'm in. Tracy?" She looked questioningly at the older woman.

Tracy Tanner seemed uncertain, but then her jaw clenched, and her eyes shut tightly. "I'm only doing this for Joey," she said finally.

"Joey?" asked Selene.

Annabelle explained, "Her son."

Will was afraid to ask, but he did anyway. "Is he…"

"Dead," said Tracy, her voice cold and empty. "The warehouses take up most of the southeast quarter."

"What do they look like?" asked Selene.

"The only things in this town that aren't tents are the warehouses, the brothels, and the commander's residence," said Tracy. "The southeast quarter is nothing but large warehouses made of rough timber."

Will felt like laughing. They had entered through the southwestern quarter, narrowly missing the area of their objective. If they had just turned right before reaching the center lane, they would have found them almost immediately. "Let's get out of here," he said.

"How?" asked Annabelle. "They sounded an alarm not long ago. That's why we were all on the porch, trying to see what was going on." She glanced at Selene. "The mist, was that you?"

Selene nodded.

"How are we going to do this?" asked Tracy.

Will was full of anger over what the Darrowans had done to Annabelle and Tracy. He put his hand on the hilt of his sword. "I'll go down first and surprise Stan. Then Selene can re-summon the mist and we'll head for the warehouses."

"You'll have to kill the other girls too," said Tracy, her tone unforgiving. "The old hag would stick a knife in us as easily as breathing. Marcy is almost as bad."

That gave him pause. Could he kill Stan and then drain the girls? Selene gave him a glance that clearly said 'idiot.' Then she wiggled her fingers. *Oh, the sleep spell.* He nodded.

Selene led the way down the stairs, and before Will reached the ground floor, Stan and both of the other women were out cold. Annabelle began rummaging through Stan's clothes and held up a bag of coins triumphantly.

Selene gave will a sour look. "We aren't here to steal."

"It's our money anyway," said Tracy, before spitting on the floorboards. "Bastards."

Will shrugged, and Selene summoned her mist again. The four of them stepped outside. "I can't see anything," complained Annabelle, grabbing Will's hand. Will noticed a look on Selene's face that could have peeled paint from a wall.

Adjusting his vision again, Will told them, "We'll form a line. Annabelle, hold onto my belt. Tracy can hold onto you, and Isabel will take the rear."

"Good plan, hero," said Selene, her voice thick with sarcasm.

They left the porch and threaded their way down the lane, taking the first right they came to. At the next intersection of lanes Will saw a large group of soldiers, but he was able to lead them around it without problem. Further on he saw a massive wooden building looming, along with another large group of soldiers. As they got closer, he could see that the warehouse was nearly a hundred yards across on its nearest side. In the distance a similar building rose from the mist behind it. "How many warehouses are there?" he asked.

"Seven or eight?" said Annabelle uncertainly.

"Nine," answered Tracy. "They're all about the same size, built side by side. If you can see the closest one then there's two more to the left of it, and two more past it. They form three rows of three each."

"Damn," said Will. The first one was huge. He could only imagine how much grain and other foodstuffs might be stored in buildings of that size.

Someone called out from the group of soldiers, "They're approaching! That mist isn't natural."

Will focused on the source of the voice and saw a man with a burning flame above his shoulder. *Shit, a sorcerer,* he swore silently. He moved back along their line until he was close to Selene. "There's a group of soldiers in the intersection ahead and they have a sorcerer with them."

"What sort of elementals does he have?" she asked.

"Just one, fire."

She thought about it a minute before replying, "I could kill the soldiers, but the sorcerer will kill the rest of you. If I drop the mist so I can see him the soldiers will be all over us, but if I don't drop the mist, I can't use my water blades."

"You can't use them at the same time?"

"No," she said dryly. "And you wouldn't want me to anyway. Think about what would happen if I started whipping them around while blind. I'd be just as likely to kill you and your girlfriend as I would the enemy."

She's definitely jealous, thought Will, but there wasn't much he could do about it. "She isn't my girlfriend," he whispered.

"Say it a little louder," returned Selene. "She can't hear you."

Exasperated, Will replied, "Neither can the soldiers. Isn't that the point?" Selene said nothing, but her eyes were as hard as stone. "Can you set the warehouse on fire?"

"I don't have a fire elemental," she said, her tone implying he was stupid for asking.

"With a spell. Can't you just absorb some turyn from them and make a spell to blast it?"

"First, if I wanted to destroy something, ordinarily I'd just use one of my elementals, so I've never spent any time studying destructive spells. Second, most spells are small. Even at Wurthaven they don't teach things like that."

Will was dumbfounded. "Why not?"

"Because any wizard that attempted one would just wind up killing himself and no sorcerer would bother. Elementals are much better for that sort of thing."

Will had a feeling his grandfather would have disagreed, but it wasn't the time to argue. As he watched the soldiers, he realized the sorcerer had walked to one edge of the group, and Will had an idea. "I'm going to leave you for a moment. When you hear them start shouting, or me shouting, drop the mist and come save me." He walked away, letting the mist take him out of sight.

"Save you?" Selene hissed. "Will! Wait. What are you doing?"

He moved closer to the group of soldiers and shifted his vision back to normal so he could tell exactly how well he was obscured. Crouching low, he drew his sword and crept forward until he saw his first hint of a human figure, then he moved back a step and adjusted his vision until the mist vanished again. He was roughly ten feet from the soldiers. Any closer and they might spot him.

The sorcerer was talking steadily, trying to reassure the soldiers with him. "They're bound to be close, in the middle of this fog. Stay alert."

Will's hand was hurting, and when he looked at it, he realized he was gripping his sword too tightly. *Stay calm,* he told himself. Taking a deep breath, he exhaled slowly, then he expanded the outer boundary of his personal turyn, so that he would begin absorbing more to fill the emptiness around him. Inhaling sharply, he lunged forward.

The sorcerer saw him, and the man's eyes went wide with alarm, but it was too late. Will drove his sword into the man's chest and leapt away. Unfortunately, his sword didn't come with him. It had caught on something, and try as he might he couldn't pull it free. He was forced to leave it as the soldiers began to react.

The soldiers weren't behaving quite as he had hoped, either. None of them had shouted or called out. The fact that their sorcerer had been stabbed was still registering with those closest.

And the sorcerer was anything but dead. The man was gasping with pain, but the thrust hadn't been instantly fatal, as Will had hoped. The fire elemental swelled, and Will realized he was about to be roasted. "Selene!" he screamed. "Selene!"

The mist began moving, rushing inward as though a strong wind was blowing, and then everything was flames as the elemental's attack washed over him. Will shut his eyes, unsure if he would die or not, but after a second he realized he was still alive. He opened them again and saw that the mist was gone. Three soldiers with spears were charging toward him. *Shit.* He started running, heading away from his friends in case the sorcerer unleashed another blast of fire.

And then Selene was there, clad in stone and swinging blue blades of destruction. Men started screaming, and a severed arm flew past Will's head. He watched in fascination as she waded into the soldiers. Selene's swords didn't seem to cut metal, and he saw one man's sword almost pass through one of her blue blades before it was torn from the soldier's grasp and sent flying through the air. Their mail armor was similarly unaffected, but it didn't save them. Her weapons tore through padded gambesons and shredded the flesh beneath the armor. Men died in dozens, and Selene's swords turned red as blood mixed with the water.

The fire elemental rose up above them, a raging inferno, and Selene's swords melded to become an opaque disc that she used to shield herself as another searing blast of flame came down on her. The result was a blast of steam that exploded outward from her, scalding the last two soldiers that stood within her reach. But the shield was gone.

Will ran toward her as the sorcerer snarled and prepared a fresh attack. The man was on his knees twenty feet in front of her, sword still stuck in his chest. Ten soldiers were left beside him, but the sorcerer cautioned them, "Stay back. This will finish it."

Will reached Selene just as the next blast of flame came down on their heads. This time he felt the searing heat as his empty sphere reached capacity and he was forced to expand it even further as he tried to absorb everything the elemental threw at them. When the attack ended, he could feel his hair standing on end, and a globe of burning turyn surrounded him. He had reached his limit.

The power he was holding threatened to consume him, and there was only one thing left he could do. Thrusting his arms out, Will released it, and a wave of incendiary power washed over the sorcerer, his men, and the corner of the warehouse behind them.

The enemies' screams were brief as their lungs filled with flame, and moments later their bodies were just smoldering, black lumps of flesh as they fell to the ground.

Will looked at Selene first. "Are you all right?" She nodded, and then he glanced at Annabelle, who was huddled against the side of the tent on the opposite side of the square from the warehouse. Tracy was nowhere to be seen.

He spotted her a moment later, or rather, he saw what was left of her. At some point she had run forward and to the side. She had been caught in the edge of his blast. Will screamed, "No!"

The left side of Tracy's body was blackened, and half her face was gone, yet there was still some life in her. Her head turned as she tried to see the world with eyes that had burned away. Her arms and legs thrashed against the hard earth. "No, no, no," Will moaned, running to her side.

Tracy's mouth worked, opening and closing as she tried to speak with lungs that could no longer draw breath. "I'm so sorry," Will cried. "This isn't what was supposed to happen."

Mercifully, Tracy Tanner died a moment later, and her body grew still. Will felt Annabelle's arms around his shoulders. "It wasn't your fault," she said softly.

For some reason his first thought was of Sven, with a spear through his face. "Yeah it is," he said slowly. "The moment you pick up a weapon, it's your fault. It always is." He stood and shrugged off the embrace before going back to Selene.

"Can you make a new mist?"

Selene had dismissed her stone armor, and Will could see that the elementals hovering above her shoulders looked smaller. "No," she answered. "It will take a while before Syllannus recovers enough power. I've been using him steadily since we entered the camp, and that fire blast wiped out everything he had left."

He studied the elementals for a few seconds, seeing something he had never noticed before. The random wisps of turyn that floated through the air near them were being drawn in, sucked into the elementals. *They're absorbing ambient turyn—like me,* he noted. It seemed important, but he wasn't sure why. He filed the fact in the back of his mind for future consideration.

The warehouse in front of them was blazing merrily, but more needed to be done. Shouts were coming from every direction. Will found the sorcerer's corpse and quickly abandoned the idea of recovering his sword. The hilt was still too hot to touch, and the leather grip had burned completely away. Bending down, he held his palm above the sorcerer's chest and *pulled,* extracting the heart-stone enchantment.

As soon as he had it, he began plucking it apart.

"Don't!" exclaimed Selene. "William! You could use that to protect us! There are more soldiers coming. I can't do this alone."

He shook his head and finished, the enchantment dissolving in his hands. The fire elemental expanded, becoming visible and towering over them. *Please help us,* thought Will. *The warehouses need to be destroyed.*

He felt *something,* an emotion like gratitude, but he couldn't be certain. The elemental bowed and turned away, moving toward the other massive, timbered buildings. "You've killed us all," said Selene bitterly. "Was it worth it?"

Will began whispering to himself, "Tailtiu, Tailtiu, Tailtiu. Thrice called, come to me." He looked at Selene. "We just have to survive a little longer. Can your earth elemental keep the soldiers from reaching us?"

Selene's eyes were searching his face. "Maybe." A moment later, her earth elemental pulsed and walls of earth grew from the ground around them at a distance of twenty feet, creating walls fifteen feet high. "You're mad, you know that?"

"I prefer to think of it as purposeful stupidity," said Will.

"What happens now?" asked Annabelle. They could hear soldiers gathering just outside the walls, shouting back and forth to one another.

"In a few minutes one of their sorcerers will get here," said Selene calmly. "Whatever elemental he has will take my walls apart. After that we'll most likely die."

Will looked up at the sky. It was filled with smoke. "Will they be able to stop the fires?"

Selene shrugged. "I don't think so. Maybe if they have an elemental like my Syllannus, but water elementals are rare, and greater ones even more so. Fire or wind elementals will just make the blaze worse, and while an earth elemental might help put it out, the destruction would be just as bad."

"Greater?"

She nodded. "You didn't know? Both my elementals are considered major elementals. That's why they recover so quickly. Most elementals have a limited capacity before they need to rest for a long period." Something pulsed beneath her shirt, and Will saw a bright, golden glow radiate through her shirt.

"No!" said Selene sharply. "Not now! Please!"

"What is it?" asked Will. As he watched, power began to flow around Selene, rippling and shimmering.

She screamed, begging, "Please! Don't do this." Her form became indistinct. The last thing Will saw of her was her desperate look at him, and she broke her own rule. "I'm sorry, Will, so sorry." Then she was gone.

In shock, he stared at the place she had just been standing. "What the hell?" Panic set in as he realized she was truly gone, though whether his fear was for her or himself he couldn't be sure.

"Will?" said Annabelle timidly. "What's happening?"

Before he could answer, the northwestern portion of Selene's wall began to glow, turning red, then orange, before it began to slump and flow sluggishly to the ground. A wide hole formed, and then the entire wall on that side collapsed. Beyond it he could see another fire elemental, and behind that more soldiers. "Fuck," he said, to no one in particular.

CHAPTER 62

"Stay close to me," Will cautioned, pushing Annabelle behind him. He had no idea what to do, though. His last good idea had been waiting until Tailtiu could get to them, but that seemed unlikely to happen now.

Annabelle's arms went around his waist, and she squeezed him briefly. "I can't go back, Will. I can't. You don't know what it was like," she whispered. Then her arms released him, and he felt a tug at his belt.

Through the hole he saw a man lift a crossbow. "Stay behind me!" He never saw the man fire, but he felt something strike his chest like a hammer. A second blow staggered him as something slammed into his back, between his shoulder blades. He fell to one knee, and when he glanced up he saw Annabelle holding his belt knife.

She stared at the unbloodied blade in shock for a moment. "I tried, Will," she mumbled. "I wanted to save you too." Then she reversed the blade in her hands, holding it out from her chest. "Forgive me."

"No!" Will surged up from the ground and caught her hands before she could drive the blade into her heart. Annabelle struggled with him, desperation and fear lending her more strength than he would have believed possible.

"Let me go!" she shrieked. "I won't let them take me. Not again! Not again!" Tears were streaming down her cheeks as she fought to end her life.

Will felt two more hammer blows against his back and a sharp pain as something pierced his mail. Some of the soldiers were cheering the crossbowmen on as they reloaded. A shadow passed over him, and when Will looked up the largest owl he had ever seen dropped down and landed in front of him. It began to shift and change, and moments later Tailtiu was standing there, her hip cocked to one side with a hand resting on it.

With a sly smile, she asked, "Want me to kill them?"

Yes! he thought desperately, but something stopped him. "No! Get us out of here."

A quarrel appeared, sticking out of his aunt's chest. She glanced at it in disgust, then pulled it free and studied it. The blood covering the iron head bubbled and smoked, burning away. "They really need killing." His aunt lifted one hand, and vines shot up from the ground, forming a tight wall of greenery across the breach in Selene's earthen wall. "Who's the trollop?" she asked with a sneer, gazing at Annabelle.

Annabelle, for her part, had stopped struggling. With numb fingers, she released the knife and Will quickly put it back in his sheath. Beyond the wall of thorns, Will heard one of the men shouting orders. "Stand back! It's one of the fae!"

Tailtiu moved forward, studying Will. "Have you been having fun, sweetling?" Leaning close, she sniffed him, then her nose crinkled, and a look of disappointment showed on her face. "Apparently not. You still reek of virginity."

"She's a friend," said Will quickly. "Can you fly us out of here?"

Tailtiu appraised them for a moment. "You're too heavy."

"What about Annabelle?"

"Too heavy," said his aunt dismissively. She pointed a finger at the impromptu barrier. "The sorcerer is about to do something." Then she looked at Annabelle. "You're a pretty little thing, aren't you?" She ran a finger along Annabelle's jawline, and the girl shivered.

Will moved to stand just inside the green wall. "Leave her alone," he warned over his shoulder, then he expanded his turyn, creating another empty shell. He hoped it would work again. *What happens if it isn't fire?*

An intense wave of flames burst through the wall, incinerating it in a flash. Will caught it immediately, focusing his will to draw the turyn into himself. It felt as though he was getting better at it, but he didn't have time to waste with self-congratulations. Holding out his hands, he sent a gout of fire back at the sorcerer and the soldiers with him.

Acrid smoke and steam filled the air. The stench of death was palpable. As it cleared, he could see the sorcerer and twenty or so of the soldiers were down, never to rise again. He glared at the ones farther away and lifted his hands again. It was a bluff of course—he was empty—but they broke and ran nonetheless. Remembering his grandfather, he said, "About time I got some goddamned respect!" A laugh tinged with hysteria began to bubble up in his chest. *I'm losing it.*

Moving forward, he found the sorcerer's body and released the elemental, giving it one final instruction. *Burn everything.* He watched with morbid fascination as it went toward the pavilions opposite the warehouses. They caught fire with amazing rapidity. Looking to his left, he saw that all the warehouses were up in flames.

Soon the entire camp would be engulfed by the inferno.

A thin mist was rising from the ground, and when he looked back, he saw Tailtiu had become the massive doe he had seen once before. She knelt so Annabelle could climb onto her back. Will went to join them.

His aunt backed away as he drew close. "Want me to save you?" she asked.

Will groaned. "Really?"

"You have two favors left," his aunt said evenly.

Thinking quickly, Will said, "I completed Aislinn's task. You have to take me to her. That was part of her bargain."

Tailtiu studied him with one large doe eye. "You are so adorable when you say things like that. It makes me want you even more. Take off the iron, though. It stinks."

"No," said Will in flat denial. "You'll have to bear it." He began climbing onto her, getting into position behind Annabelle. Smoke rose from Tailtiu's hide whenever the mail came into contact. He did his best to hike up the bottom to keep it away from her, and he put his arms around Annabelle's waist. "You're going to have to hold onto her for both of us," he told his childhood friend.

Tailtiu began moving, gradually building up speed. "I really am going to kill you, William. One of these days you'll make a mistake, and I'll be waiting to make sure you enjoy it."

The fae woman maintained a brisk pace, but she didn't run, to avoid the risk of losing her passengers. Between her mist and the smoke, the visibility was almost as it had been with Selene's fog. Will adjusted his vision with difficulty as he discovered that the fires produced an incredible glare. It took him a moment to find a comfortable medium that allowed him to see without being blinded by it.

Tailtiu trotted on, occasionally passing so close to soldiers that they stopped to stare at them in amazement. No one tried to stop them. The soldiers of Darrow had better things to do, and the camp was in complete chaos by then. The glow grew brighter behind them, and when Will glanced back it appeared as though the entire world had caught fire. For a moment he wondered how many people would die in the blaze. *Most of those soldiers were ordinary men, like me, just doing what they were told.* Then he thought about the women trapped in the other brothels. How many innocents would die because of his actions?

He closed his eyes briefly and tried to push the thoughts aside. *I only did what I had to do,* he told himself.

But a nagging doubt spoke from within, *Did you? You suggested this. The entire thing was your idea.*

And what had happened to Selene? He kept remembering the desperation on her face. *"I'm sorry."* What could have made her break her rule? He didn't think she was dead. His impression had been that she was being taken away against her will.

They passed beyond the edge of the camp and crossed the empty region around it. The Patriarch's army had harvested most of the nearby timber. Will hoped it would be enough to prevent the fire from turning the entire valley into a bonfire. His own family would be in danger if that happened.

Tailtiu angled up as they started into the hills, then she reared, dumping Will onto the ground while Annabelle clung desperately to her neck. "That's enough," she said with an air of finality. "You'll have to walk the rest of the way if you won't take off that damned iron shirt."

Will was tired. His fatigue was far deeper than he had been aware of until then. He should have expected it, though. Fighting, even for brief periods, was exhausting, and what he had been doing with the fire elementals' attacks hadn't been easy either. Taking off the mail shirt was logical, but when he put his hand on it he couldn't bear to remove it.

Selene had fought long and hard to get him to wear it. Now that she was gone, it felt more precious than gold. "I'll walk."

Tailtiu continued carrying Annabelle as he traipsed along behind them. Something felt odd in Will's back, so he reached behind himself and his fingers found a wooden shaft. He tugged at it and discovered a crossbow bolt when he looked at his hand. It had a bodkin point, and there was blood on the head of it. *Hopefully I can find the money to get Harless to fix my mail,* he thought idly.

It took them most of an hour to reach the congruence point where he had met Aislinn before, and Will was beginning to feel faint. His vision kept narrowing, as though he was walking through a tunnel. It was a relief when his grandmother appeared before him.

"I did as you asked," he told her, his words slurring slightly.

Aislinn smiled. "You never choose the easy road, do you, William?" She held out her hand. In her palm was a golden ring with a white stone set in the center. As he looked at it, he realized that rather than a gem there was a tooth mounted on it, a human molar.

"This is the object of unspeakably vile knowledge and power?" he asked mildly. He saw no sign of magic around the ring.

"You'll understand soon," said Aislinn.

Tailtiu cleared her throat. "Please take it away before you bleed to death."

"Huh?" Will didn't understand. The world began to spin, and the ground rushed up to meet him. His last thought, as darkness closed over him, was that the rocks pillowing his head seemed much softer than he had expected.

***

Something tickled his nose, and when Will opened his lids, he found two green eyes staring down at him. He was surrounded by a halo of coppery curls. "Auntie! He's awake!" yelled Sammy, directly into his face.

His cousin hugged him, squeezing the life out of him, then she leapt up and bounced away. "You have no idea how worried I was, Will. Your mom said you were fine, but I was sure you were going to die."

He tried to sit up, and the world began moving in unexpected ways, so he lay back down again. He was on Arrogan's massive bed. His mother came in a moment later and sat on the edge beside him. "How do you feel?"

"Tired, sore, and when I try to sit up everything spins," he told her.

Erisa nodded. "You lost a great deal of blood."

"How did I get here?" Will shifted a little and the movement of the sheets told him that he was naked beneath the covers.

"Annabelle came. She was in quite a state. Nearly scared me half to death. She was convinced you were dead. Your Uncle Johnathan went with her and carried you back to the house."

Will peeked under the covers to confirm his suspicions. Worriedly, he looked at his mother, "Who undressed me?"

"Johnathan got the armor off you. The gambeson was soaked with blood. I washed it as best I could, but I'm afraid there will always be a stain," said Erisa.

"And my trousers?"

"Annabelle helped me clean you up."

Will grabbed an extra pillow and pulled it over his face in embarrassment. "Kill me now," he moaned. "At least it wasn't Sammy."

"I wouldn't worry about it, William. Annabelle's been through a lot. She's seen far worse," said his mother.

587

"Is she all right?"

"Physically? Yes. She won't talk about what happened to her, but I fear she'll be haunted by it for the rest of her life."

"She hasn't said anything about it?"

Erisa shook her head. "All she talks about is you. The story she told us is hard to believe. She said you were throwing fire with your hands."

"Only a couple of times," muttered Will. "What about the camp?"

"Johnathan got as close as he could, but there are soldiers all over the valley. He said that from the smoke it looks like the entire thing may have burned to the ground," said Erisa. Then she reached into her apron pocket and pulled something out. It was the ring. "What's this?"

Alarmed, Will snatched it out of her hand. "You shouldn't touch that."

His mother lifted her eyebrows.

"It's a gift from Aislinn," he explained. "I think it's dangerous, but I don't know how."

"There's a human tooth set in it," said his mother disapprovingly. "You should get rid of it."

He frowned. "Not until I know what it does." To change the subject, he asked, "Where was I bleeding from?"

Erisa helped him turn onto his side and guided his hand back to feel the bandage she had put there. It felt as though it was just a few inches above his right kidney. "It wasn't deep," she told him, "but all the moving you did kept it bleeding freely. Another inch or two down, though, and you might not be here now. Are you thirsty?"

The worry on his mother's face made him feel terrible. "I've never been so thirsty in my life."

She filled a wooden cup from a pitcher on the nightstand and handed it to him. He gulped it down and held the cup out for more. After his third cup, his mother asked, "What happened to Selene?"

"Didn't Annabelle tell you?"

"It didn't make sense," said Erisa. "What do you think happened?"

"I really don't know," he admitted. "It seemed like she was being taken by something. She didn't want to go." He described what he had seen, including Selene's last words.

Erisa pursed her lips. "I liked her. What else is there? You seem like you're hiding something."

Will tried to look innocent, but his mother scowled. "Spit it out, William. I don't know how to help you if you won't talk to me."

With a sigh, he told her the rest. It felt good to get it off his chest and he found himself telling his mother everything, from their first meeting up until he had overheard her speaking to the unknown stranger outside their house. When he finished his mother looked perplexed. "Well, what do you think?" he asked.

Erisa threw up her hands. "I lied. I don't know how to help you."

"Thanks, Mom," he said dryly.

"I know one thing, though," she said after moment. "That girl is in love with you."

"Mom, please! You heard what I told you. She was just trying to gain our trust," said Will, but he doubted his words even as he said them.

Erisa shook her head. "I saw the way she watched you while she was here. A woman only observes a man that closely if she's in love."

"Or if the man is her target," countered Will.

"You're wrong," said Erisa. "But even if you believed me, you shouldn't trust her. From what you've said, she

589

owes allegiance to someone else, and I don't think she's the kind that will let her feelings override her obligations."

"We agree about that, at least," said Will, "the obligations part."

"By the way, Annabelle has been watching you the same way," warned his mother. "Be careful with her."

Will groaned and put the pillow back over his face.

# CHAPTER 63

The rest of the week passed peacefully while Will recovered his strength. He was somewhat surprised at how long it took. Aside from his bruises and the small wound in his back, he hadn't really been too badly hurt, but his fatigue seemed to be bone deep. It was days before he was able to walk on his own safely, and even then, he found himself out of breath after only traveling a short distance.

"Your body is short of blood," his mother explained. "It takes time to replace it." All he could do was accept her words, for his body agreed with her.

Another deer appeared on the porch, courtesy of the goddamn cat, and Will was able to enjoy meat with his meals again. Erisa certainly seemed pleased, for she said it would help him replace the blood he had lost.

The only thing that bothered him was Annabelle. While he was bed-bound, she spent most of her time with him, and once he was moving again, she followed him everywhere. Even when she was busy doing something else, her eyes were always on him. Her devotion made Sammy seem like a welcome diversion, and he found himself seeking out his cousin's company as often as possible to avoid being alone with his childhood friend.

"I think she's crazy," said Sammy one day as they were weeding the garden. "She stares at you like she's going to eat you."

"You'll protect me, though, won't you, Sammy?" said Will, only half-joking.

She punched his arm. "Don't worry. I won't let anyone eat you but—" She stopped, rethinking her phrasing. "You know what I mean."

Will laughed with a smile. "Don't worry." The older his cousin got, the more he appreciated her energy and optimism. Everything else in his life seemed impossibly dark. He lightly punched her shoulder in return. "Cousins for life."

Sammy grinned and leapt to her feet, twirling and brandishing an imaginary sword. "Cousins against the world!" She looked back at him. "Next time you go on an adventure, you should take me with you. We'll show them what two Cartwrights can do!"

Will laughed again, but it tapered off quickly as he remembered Tracy Tanner. He still remembered her ruined face whenever he closed his eyes. Will tried to smile up at Sammy, but his vision was becoming blurry. "Maybe not, Sammy. I don't think that's a good idea…"

She saw the tears begin to spill from his eyes and knelt down to embrace him, pressing his face into her hair. "It's all right, Will. You're home now. It's all over. You won't have to do any of those things ever again. I'm here. We're all here."

It took him a minute to get himself back under control, and before he was ready, he heard Annabelle calling from the front of the house. "Will! Come help me hang up the wash!"

He shared a glance with Sammy, and she looked at her hands, which were covered in dirt. "Don't worry, I'll wash my hands and be right there," she assured him. "I'll stand in between you."

***

A few days after that, when he had almost completely recovered, he woke suddenly in the night. That had become a frequent occurrence, as his dreams were often bad, but this time it was for another reason.

He had taken to sleeping in the front room with his uncle, so the three women could share the bedroom. His uncle slept on Will's cot while he slept on the floor near the hearth.

His eyes opened with a start. Annabelle was lying beside him, her face next to his own. Her hand was under the blanket. Will wore only a long shirt while sleeping, and her hand had found its way under that as well, where it was urgently kneading something with expert fingers.

He started to open his mouth, but she covered it with her own, kissing him. Then she drew back. "This is just a good dream, Will. I know you've had it before, but this time it will be better." Her hand continued moving, and she shifted her body, preparing to straddle him. "You're ready now," she whispered.

He was definitely ready. He was so ready he wasn't sure he would last until she had mounted him. He froze for a moment. It would be easy to let her do what she wanted, what he wanted. *But it isn't what I want,* he shouted to himself. *Not this, not her!* He caught her shoulder with his hand, pushing her off to one side. Again, the first words that came from his lips were, "I didn't give you permission to kiss me." *Why do I keep saying that?* he thought angrily.

Annabelle frowned, but remained determined. "You're not objecting to this, though, are you?" Her hand continued to move in slow, sure motions.

"Stop it," he ordered.

"There's another trick I could show you," she said, beginning to scoot farther down.

"No, Annabelle," he insisted, finally finding the will-power to grab her wrists and stop the pleasant torture. "I don't want this, and neither do you."

"You do. Everyone does."

"Goddamn it. Get out of my bed," he hissed, trying not to wake his uncle.

The fury in his eyes finally convinced her, and Annabelle got to her feet. She stood in front of him, stark naked. A second later she reclaimed her nightgown from the table and slid it over her head. She looked hurt, but as she left, she made one final declaration. "You'll change your mind." Then she went to the door and returned to the main bedroom.

Will saw his uncle's eyes open, noting the girl leaving the room, but Will closed his own, pretending to be asleep. The last thing he wanted was another conversation.

***

The next morning, he made his announcement. It was time to return. He didn't expect the reaction he got, as everyone seemed universally against the idea.

"You've done enough," said his mother. "The army will be fine without you."

"But Eric is still there…"

"And if I could keep him here, I would bring him back in an instant," declared his uncle.

"Please don't go," pleaded Sammy.

Will glanced at Annabelle, and she mouthed the words 'don't go,' and that settled it for him. *I definitely have to go,* he told himself. "I'm sorry," he said. "I signed a contract for five years. I don't want to be a deserter."

His mother glared at him. "You didn't have a choice!"

"I did have a choice, Mom. I chose to get Uncle Johnathan out. I have to go back. Selene trusted me."

"She's dead," said Annabelle coldly.

"No, she's not," declared Will. "I don't know where she is, but I'm sure she's waiting for me to keep my word."

The argument continued for a while after that, but his mother could see the determination in his eyes, and when she gave up the others followed suit. Will apologized for his decision, but he was packing as he did so.

Dressing in his freshly washed though still-stained gambeson, he shimmied into the mail shirt and put on his belt. He no longer had his sword, which gave him a moment of chagrin when he realized he would be forced to pay for it when he returned. Thankfully, he had left his shield and spear back in Branscombe.

He held the gold ring in his palm for a moment, trying to decide what to do with it. It seemed too ostentatious to wear. That much gold in plain sight was an invitation to robbery or accusations of theft. Only a nobleman would dare wear so much wealth in plain sight. Still, he hadn't put it on even once since receiving it. *I'll just wear it until I get close to the camp,* he told himself, slipping it onto the ring finger of his right hand.

Nothing happened. He felt no overwhelming urge to do evil things, and there were no voices whispering wicked advice in his ear. Will was almost disappointed. Holding up his hand, he saw a glimmer of turyn around it, the first sign of magic he had noticed around it thus far. *I guess Aislinn didn't cheat me,* he thought. *It must do something.*

He shrugged and said his goodbyes, hugging everyone again. Annabelle followed him out the door. "I'll wait for you," she told him earnestly.

"Don't," said Will. "There's no guarantee I'll be back, and even if I do…"

"She's dead, Will," said Annabelle without a trace of remorse. A hint of madness danced behind her eyes.

"She's not. No matter what happened to her. I'll find her." Turning his back, he walked away, though he could feel Annabelle's eyes following him until he disappeared around the side of the house.

His trip back to Branscombe was unremarkable. The goddamn cat declined to speak when he passed through the cave, though he spent several minutes trying to convince the creature to converse with him. With a shrug, he resumed walking, and soon he was back at the hidden spring.

He recognized the guard at the town gate. It was Ned. The constable called out to him as he turned right to head toward the military camp, "I don't see your murder weapon. Did you leave it at the scene this time?" Ned began to laugh at his own joke.

Will just waved and kept going. *Actually, I did,* he realized.

The camp guards asked for his name when he reached the perimeter, so he answered, "William Cartwright, returning from extended duty away."

"Which unit are you with?" asked one of the two soldiers.

"Company B, Fifth Platoon," said Will.

"Extended duty?" asked the other.

Uncertain, Will rephrased his words, "Detached duty? Get Sergeant Nash. He'll confirm it for you."

"One moment."

One guard stepped away a minute, and a runner was sent. Will was forced to wait at the perimeter for nearly twenty minutes before Lieutenant Stanton appeared, flanked by no fewer than six men in mail. The look on his face was not welcoming. "Take him into custody."

Will's head went from side to side as the men maneuvered around him and grabbed his arms. "Wait. What? I had orders! Ask Selene, she'll tell you."

"Who?" The lieutenant raised one brow curiously.

"Isabel," he said, correcting himself. "Ask Isabel! She said she'd arranged the orders for us."

Stanton stared at him for a moment, disappointment written on his features. "I'm sorry to disillusion you Mister Cartwright, but the lady you're referring to is no longer at this camp. I would also like to remind you that she is not part of the military command structure. Was any part of that unclear to you?"

"No, sir," said Will reflexively. "I mean, yes, sir! She was part of the command, wasn't she?" His eyes were full of confusion.

"Bring him."

The men quickly marched Will to the command tent, but rather than taking him inside, they shackled his wrists together and attached the chain to a metal loop on a pole that stood nearby. The loop was above his head, so he was forced to stand with his arms in the air. "Could I talk to Lord Nerrow please?" he asked.

Lieutenant Stanton gave him a look that almost seemed sympathetic. "Lord Nerrow is no longer in charge of this army. The Royal Marshal has taken command." He started to walk away.

"But can I see him anyway?"

"He's returned to his estate. The king saw fit to put him to other duties." With that, the lieutenant left.

Will stood alone, while the occasional soldier walked by and gave him an amused look. "Goddamn it," he swore. Once again, he heard Sven's voice in his head, *"Never volunteer."* He promised himself he would never disregard the old man's advice again. He hoped he wouldn't have to wait for long.

An hour passed, and he began to wish they had taken off his armor before chaining him up. He was getting tired, but he couldn't sit down to rest. He tried bending his legs and letting his wrists take his weight, but the iron shackles cut into his wrists.

The afternoon passed slowly, and at some point, he realized he was still wearing the ring. He hadn't been armed, so the guards had only divested him of his belt knife. He admired their integrity in not taking such an obviously valuable ring. *Maybe there is still some good in this world,* he told himself.

A horn blew, announcing that mess had begun, and Will's well-trained stomach rumbled in response. He looked at his belly. "You're a better soldier than I am." He supposed he should be grateful he hadn't needed to pee. He'd been standing in the sun so long that the sweat soaking into his gambeson had dehydrated him and saved him from the need.

Supper ended, and soldiers went by, returning to their tents, but Will didn't bother to watch. He kept his head down, trying not to think of the meal he had missed. A shadow fell across him, and when he looked up Tiny and Dave were standing there.

"You look like shit," said Dave cheerfully, but Tiny held up a waterskin, offering it to him to drink.

After several long swallows, Will asked, "Are you going to get in trouble for giving me water?"

Tiny shook his head. "I don't think so. There's no rule saying you can't have water."

"Then why hasn't anyone else given me water?" said Will.

Dave grinned. "Probably because they don't give a damn. Makes you think though, doesn't it?"

"About what?"

"That maybe you shouldn't have deserted, asshole," said the ex-thief.

"I didn't desert," protested Will. "I had orders. Sele—Isabel said she would fix it."

Tiny shook his head again, this time sadly. Then he fixed Will with sorrowful eyes. "I warned you, Will." He patted his chest. "This is gonna get you in trouble every time."

"It's true! Where is she?"

Dave chuckled. "I feel for you. I really do. She hasn't been seen since you left." He stepped forward to pat Will's back comfortingly. "Which means you, my friend, are well and truly fucked."

"You might be better off not mentioning her," suggested Tiny. "She seemed important. If she ran off with you and you're back without her, it might be better to just take the whip for being a deserter."

They gave him some more water, but eventually they had to leave. Dave waved as they left. "Good luck, Will. I'll toast you with my first drink every holiday."

Will wanted to swear, but he didn't bother. Instead he did what he did best. Stand by his post. He chuckled ruefully. *Apparently, I'm here because I didn't stay at my post. Now I don't have a choice.*

A short while later, another familiar voice called his name. "Will?"

It was Eric. "Evening," said Will with forced cheer. "How'd you know I was here?"

"Some of the guys from Company B passed me the message. Did you really desert?"

"I vehemently deny that accusation."

"Then tell me what happened."

So he did, giving Eric an abbreviated version that left out most of the interesting details regarding Selene and his dealings with the fae. He made sure to include everything about Annabelle Withy, though he left out what had happened to Tracy Tanner. When he finished, Eric looked at him in disbelief.

"It sounds like they should be giving you a medal, not chaining you up. Is that all the truth?" asked Eric.

"I'd swear it on my life."

"Have you told them?" He nodded in the direction of the command tent.

"I haven't had a chance. They staked me here as soon as I got back."

There was a noise from behind, and Eric started to back away. "I think they're coming for you. Good luck. Try to think of a more believable story. They're never going to buy the one you told me." Then he was gone.

"It was the truth!" Will shouted after his cousin. *Why won't anyone believe me?* Twisting his head, he saw four more guards approaching.

CHAPTER 64

Will was on his knees in the same place he had once met his father, Lord Nerrow. The atmosphere was considerably chillier this time. A guard stood on either side of him, presumably in case he decided to act up. Lieutenant Stanton sat at a small wooden desk on the right side of the room, along with a clerk that Will didn't recognize.

The figure that dominated the room was the Royal Marshal, Duke Vincent Arenata. Stanton had taken him aside before the interrogation began in order to make sure Will knew that the man who would be asking the questions was in charge of the entire army of Terabinia. Duke Arenata stood second only to King Lognion himself. Two elementals hovered over the duke's shoulders, one of fire and the other of air.

How lucky am I? thought Will.

"Do you have anything to say for yourself?" said Lord Arenata. Apparently, the man thought that was a good way to start a long conversation, though Will felt there were dozens of better questions to start with.

"Yes, Your Lordship—" One of the guards kicked him before he could finish, knocking him onto his side.

Lieutenant Stanton spoke firmly, "You do not address the marshal as 'Your Lordship.' He is to be referred to as either 'Your Grace' or simply as 'Marshal Arenata.'"

Will started again, still lying on his side. "First, let me say that I'm incredibly honored to be interviewed personally by such an important personage as yourself, Your Grace."

Marshal Arenata glared, then nodded at one of the guards, who promptly kicked him again. "Please get to the facts Mister Cartwright. It's been a busy day and I don't have time for this. If it weren't for the fact that you claimed to have received orders from a certain woman, you would already be strung up for the whip. Talking to deserters is not a normal part of my day."

"Yes, Your Grace," said Will immediately. "She gave me orders to slip behind enemy lines and destroy their supplies in Barrowden. Lady Isabel told me that she had given orders to that effect. That I wouldn't be a deserter."

The marshal leapt out of his chair, his eyes giving Lieutenant Stanton an accusing stare. "Am I supposed to believe this tripe? I've never heard such utter nonsense in my life!"

Stanton held out his hands placatingly. "If it please you, Marshal Arenata, there have been numerous exceptional circumstances around Mister Cartwright. I have good reason to believe that at least this part of his story is true."

You haven't even heard my story, asshole, thought Will. Then a second thought came to him. *Wait, is he trying to help me?*

The marshal wagged a finger at Lieutenant Stanton. "Come with me." The two men left the room.

While they were gone Will looked up at the guards. "Is it all right if I get back to my knees? The floor is very nice, and I am tired, but it seems like it would be more appropriate."

The guard that had kicked him twice merely growled, but the second one grabbed his shoulder and helped him back upright.

The marshal returned a few minutes later, and he and Stanton reclaimed their seats. "The lieutenant gave me some details regarding your previous service to

Terabinia," said the marshal. "It seems he even believes you killed several sorcerers and the enemy commander at the Darrowan camp in the pass."

Will nodded. "Yes, sir." That earned him another kick, but the second guard braced him this time, so he didn't fall. "Yes, Your Grace," he amended.

The marshal continued, "So, given your remarkable abilities as a scout, you would have me believe that Lady Isabel ordered you to take on this highly improbable mission."

"Yes, Your Grace." Will hesitated a moment, then added, "And she came with me."

Marshal Arenata's face colored for a moment, but he held his tongue. "Very well. Explain what occurred during this most secret and highly dangerous mission you undertook almost singlehandedly." His voice dripped with sarcasm.

Will did his best, leaving out everything about his method of reaching Barrowden, as well as excluding any mention of his family. In the tale he told, they managed to sneak past the Darrowan army at night and went directly to their main camp in Barrowden. His story from that point stayed close to the truth, although he gave Selene credit for most of the feats of derring-do. No one would have believed his own contributions. He ended by telling them that they had escaped together during the confusion, and that Selene had disappeared shortly thereafter. After that he had camped a while, recovering his strength before making the difficult trek back.

The only mistake he made was when he slipped and reverted from calling her Isabel and began using her presumably real name in the middle of the story.

The marshal stared at him, pure malice in his eyes. "Your story is so improbable that it makes me want to laugh, but for one fact. You slipped up and gave yourself away when you called her Selene."

Uncertain, Will asked, "Is that a bad thing, Your Grace?"

"It means you knew very well what her true identity was. It also gives you an excellent motive for kidnapping or murder. Whichever is the case, you'll hang for treason against the crown." He paused for a moment, then addressed the lieutenant. "Wait, that doesn't sound right. What's the punishment for treason against the crown?"

"Death by flogging," answered the lieutenant.

"But I told the truth!" shouted Will. "You can check for yourself. Their entire camp is destroyed. They're probably already starving!"

The previously somewhat friendly guard kicked him this time, so hard that his head rattled when it hit the ground. Will mumbled into the dirt, "Your Grace."

The Marshall was on his feet, and he stared down at Will. "You make me sick. You lured Selene Maligant from the safety of this camp and kidnapped her. Beyond that it's impossible to say, but I would not doubt for a second that you either raped and murdered her or sold her to the Patriarch's men."

"But I'm innocent," said Will desperately. "She said she left orders." *Maligant? She's the king's daughter!* At last he understood how well and truly damned he had become.

"There were no orders!" screamed the marshal, spittle flying from his lips. "For the love of all that is holy, the only thing I don't understand is why you thought you could come back here! I'd kill you myself if it were allowed."

"Lock him in the stockade," said the marshal.

One of the guards smiled and the marshal turned back. "Don't touch him. The king will want him in perfect condition so he can see justice done himself."

Will wanted to cry as they dragged him away, but the hysteria rising up within him had different ideas. "We have a stockade now? That's new." He almost welcomed the blow that followed. *I kidnapped a princess—fuck me!* Then he thought about the night she had kissed him. *And I told her off for kissing me. Gods above, I'm the biggest idiot in the world.*

The next morning, he was loaded into a wagon, and the journey to Cerria began. Since there was an honest-to-goodness paved road and the weather was good, they made the trip in four days. Along the way, one of his guards informed him he was lucky it was treason he was charged with, otherwise he'd have already been executed by the military.

Small blessings, thought Will wryly. He was too glum to appreciate the high stone arches and soaring towers of Cerria as they rolled into the capital city of Terabinia. The city was a marvel of stonework and artisanship. It predated Terabinia itself, having been one of the two greatest cities of Greater Darrow before the war for independence.

But Will counted himself fortunate. He would get to experience the city from a vantage point few ever saw, the inside of the royal dungeons. He hoped the food would be better than what they served in the lockup in Branscombe, otherwise death might be preferable. He snickered to himself, wishing he could have told Arrogan his joke.

It turned out he was wrong, however. After they marched him down the long, winding stairs he was pushed into a tiny, damp cell and chained to a wall. When the door shut, moments later, there was no light to be seen. Days of absolute darkness without food or water taught him that there were indeed things worse than the food in the Branscombe lockup.

EPILOGUE

The door to his cell opened, and the rush of light that entered brought tears to his eyes. Two men, ordinary servants by the look of them, entered and unchained him from the wall. They grunted when they pulled him to his feet.

"This is a shame," said one of them. "They should have taken it off him."

Will clutched his right hand, trying desperately to hide his ring, but a second later he realized they were talking about his mail. Looking down, he could see that it had gone brown with rust. One of the men lifted his arms, and they carefully helped him out of the armor. Then they carried him along, helping him with the stairs, for his legs had gone wobbly.

"How long was I in there?" he asked.

"Three days," said one of the men.

"Am I to be whipped to death now?" asked Will, almost hopeful. Anything had to be better than the endless, gnawing darkness he had endured.

The other man chuckled, "Not until you meet the king."

Will squeezed his eyes shut. "That'll be nice," he droned sarcastically.

From there he was taken for a bath. His clothing was taken, and he heard one of the servants instructing the other to have it burned. He wanted to ask about his mail. It still meant something to him, but he supposed that since he was about to die, he would have to let it go. As before, no one mentioned the ring on his finger, but he was past wondering about it by then.

Scrubbed and washed, he was toweled dry by several older women who seemed used to the task. They combed his hair, and one of them produced a pair of scissors to trim it for him. *At least I'll die clean,* thought Will. They dressed him in the finest tunic and trousers he had ever worn.

They were dyed in shades of red and gray. "What are these made of?" Will asked, marveling at the softness of the fabric.

"Linen," one of the women told him. He didn't believe her, though. Linen couldn't be that soft and fine. He knew better.

He was given warm wool socks and cloth shoes were put on his feet. Will liked the feel of them, but they weren't very practical. One step outdoors and they would be quickly ruined. He said as much, but no one was listening to him.

Next they fed him and offered him his choice of either small beer or water. He chose the water, since he was so thirsty, he felt sure he was about to die, and he didn't think his stomach could have tolerated much else. After a small meal a guard led him into a sumptuous room with cushioned chairs and left him to his own devices.

The chairs were more comfortable than anything he had ever sat upon, but he was tired, so he curled up on the rug and within moments, he was asleep. After an unknown period, he heard a sound, and when he opened his eyes, he saw a man standing over him.

The man was dressed in a similar fashion to Will, though his clothing had embroidery around the edges and a massive gold chain hung around his neck. His hair and beard were a glossy brown, and when he smiled Will couldn't help but think he had rarely seen someone so good looking, of either gender.

Except Selene.

"Hello," Will said muzzily.

"Are you comfortable?" asked the man. "Should I get you a pillow?"

"No, I'm fine," said Will. "This rug is more comfortable than you might think."

The man began to laugh, long and loud, his voice resonant and hearty. "Might I ask why you are on the floor?"

Will's brain was beginning to work properly, thanks to the food he had eaten, but he wasn't ready to give up hope. "I'm waiting on the king," he answered.

"And is this how one waits on his king?"

Will nodded slowly. "If one is very tired." Inside, he was beginning to feel a sense of panic. *It's him. It's King Lognion, and I'm lying on his floor.*

Graciously, the king bent and held out his hands. Will took them, and the monarch helped him to his feet, then gestured to one of the chairs. "Please, sit. When we're done, I can offer you something much better to sleep upon."

Will struggled to think. "Is it—is it, a coffin, Your Majesty?"

The king laughed again. "Certainly not!"

"I don't mind, honestly," said Will. "The past few days have been…difficult, Your Majesty."

The king's eyes grew serious. "I only recently learned you were here. For that, I feel a sense of responsibility. The proper reports didn't reach me soon enough. You have endured a great deal because of that."

Will couldn't believe his ears. Why was the king being so courteous? "The Royal Marshall's report?"

King Lognion nodded. "That one, among a few others. It seems the marshal was too hasty to judge you. Terabinia owes you a great deal for what you've done."

"Then I'm not to be executed, Your Majesty?"

Epilogue

The king smiled. "Not today, at any rate. I won't make any promises about the future, but it seems unlikely. I'd like you to tell me of your experiences, leaving nothing out."

Will started, and then started again when the king asked him to start farther back, beginning with his training in wizardry. Will grew more nervous then, for he wasn't sure how King Lognion knew to ask about that. It had to be Selene. He tried to remember how much he had told her. A mistake at this point might be disastrous.

He started with a brief description of his childhood, leaving out any mention of Lord Nerrow, then moved on to his apprenticeship with Arrogan, though he omitted his grandfather's name. The king stopped him at that point.

"You didn't give your grandfather's name."

"Bartholomew," said Will hastily. "I'm not entirely sure he's even my grandfather. That's just what he told me. None of my cousins believed it."

"Go on," said the king.

He did, though he left out the details of his training and moved on to his time in the Terabinian army. He described his exploits in the army and then moved on to how he had met Selene and how they had eventually left to destroy the Patriarch's supply line. When he glossed over the journey back to Barrowden, the king frowned.

"You left out any mention of the journey through Faerie," said King Lognion, his voice edging toward anger.

Fuck. Will retraced his steps, including the trip through the congruence point, explaining that the presence of the goddamn cat kept that part of the other realm safe from the fae. King Lognion laughed at Will's name for the beast, but he claimed ignorance of the creature's true name, chalking it up to yet another mystery his grandfather had left behind.

"And you say this thing hates sorcerers?" interrupted the king.

He hadn't said anything of the kind, but again Will knew Selene must have given her father that information. Will nodded. "Yes, Your Majesty, though I don't know why."

"That's a shame," said the monarch. "Such a shortcut would be immensely useful. I almost wonder if we could kill the beast, but that would render the path useless, wouldn't it? Since the fae would no longer need to avoid the area. Please, continue."

Will did, regretfully including the information that his family was living in seclusion. There was no way he could hide that fact, since Selene had obviously told her father everything. Lognion nodded, waving his hand to urge Will onward. He didn't seem interested.

He told the rest without much editing, except to say that he didn't fully understand how he had been able to turn the fire elementals' attacks back against their owners. He also omitted Tailtiu's assistance with his escape. Thus far he had said nothing about the fae, and he prayed that Selene hadn't mentioned his one remark about learning the trick to seeing in the dark from one of them.

He was relieved when King Lognion accepted his story and smiled, but his stomach dropped when the king spoke next. "You are a remarkably brazen liar, William Cartwright. Not many would have the balls to attempt to hide things from me, especially given the fact that you already know how good my information is."

Will grew perfectly still, and he and the king fell into a staring contest that he knew he was doomed to lose.

But he didn't. The king spoke first. "I know a lot more about your charming grandfather, *Bartholomew,* than you may realize. Is he truly dead?"

He felt as though the breath in his chest would explode, and Will exhaled loudly. "Yes, Your Majesty. He's dead. I buried him myself."

"More good news, then," said King Lognion. "Now, if you'll be patient, I'll list all the reasons I have for executing you."

Will shut his eyes in defeat. *I knew it.*

"Unlicensed wizardry, harboring and giving aid to a fugitive wanted by the Crown, possible warlockry, desertion of duty, insubordination and disrespect to your superior officer, kidnapping and trying to seduce my daughter—"

"I didn't!"

Lognion held up one finger, silencing him. "Perhaps, but you admit the rest, don't you?"

"Not warlockry," said Will stubbornly.

"Yet I can see their mark on you!" The king lifted his hand and prodded Will's forehead. "You wouldn't have received that without making a significant bargain."

"It wasn't warlockry," insisted Will. "I didn't bargain with anything that was not mine to give."

The king studied him for a moment. "Arrogan's lessons must have been thorough. Not many understand the difference. What am I going to do with you?"

Will lowered his eyes. "Something that doesn't involve being whipped to death, hopefully."

"Answer one more question," said the king. "You say you're not a warlock because you haven't bargained anything that doesn't belong to you, but many warlocks only sell their own souls. If they aren't bargaining with someone else's life, how is that evil?"

Will had been giving that considerable thought, and he hoped the answer he had was the right one. "Because the soul doesn't belong to anyone. It belongs to the universe. No one has the right to give or sell it."

King Lognion nodded. "Not how I would have worded it, but good enough. Based on that and what Selene has said, I don't believe you've prostituted your soul. I'm almost tempted to debate you on your arrogant claim that sorcery is evil, but your opinion means nothing to me on that matter. That leaves only one matter to be settled."

Will waited.

"You lied to me, William, not once, but several times during our conversation. As a ruler, I cannot abide lies." Will could see something akin to anticipation in Lognion's eyes.

"Forgive me—" he began to say, but Lognion leaned forward with unbelievable speed, and Will felt something slam into the side of his head. The force of the blow was so great that he flew backward, causing the chair to tip, spilling him onto the floor.

Will tried to focus his eyes, and he saw the king staring at his own fist. The skin across his knuckles had split, and blood was dripping from them, but the look on the man's face was one of contentment. Will shivered.

"That's better," said King Lognion, standing and offering Will his hand once more. "I didn't break your jaw, did I?"

"No, Your Majeshty," said Will, having difficulty forming the words.

"Excellent. Now that the air has been cleared, perhaps we can be friends. Just be sure to never lie to me again. The second lesson won't be so pleasant."

"Yes, Your Majeshty."

"You will be enrolled in Wurthaven's College of Wizardry. Something you should have done when your father first attempted to convince you to go there. This is my gift and my judgment for you. You must be trained properly if you are to serve me well," said Lognion.

Epilogue

The king's eyes twinkled as he looked at Will. "You didn't think I knew? Selene figured it out years ago. I would caution you to make sure no hint of it gets past your lips. If Duke Arenata discovered the fact, it I doubt even my protection could save you. He's very protective of his sister."

"His sister?"

"Mark Nerrow's wife, Agnes Arenata."

Will couldn't understand such vindictiveness. "Does it really matter so much if I'm his bastard son?"

King Lognion nodded. "Agnes has given him two daughters, Laina and Tabitha, but no sons. Your existence could endanger their inheritance." He moved closer and put his arm around Will's shoulder in an almost fatherly manner. "Don't worry, though. I won't tell him. I have great hopes for your usefulness in the future. I never waste good men."

"Uh, thank you, Your Majesty."

The king smiled. "That's it then. I'll keep you a few days. Feed you and fatten you up, then I'll send you off to Wurthaven. A servant will show you to your room. You look as though you could use some rest." He started to turn away.

Will had one more question, though. "Um, Your Majesty?"

Lognion paused. "Yes?"

"How is Selene? I've been worried about her since she vanished."

The king's eyes darkened. "I almost forgot. She's currently being reeducated after her recent mistakes. I don't think she'll be out in public for a while. I'm sure you'll eventually see her, but you need to understand your place when you do."

"Yes, Your Majesty."

Lognion leaned closer. "When you see her, you are to say one thing, and one thing only. Listen carefully."

Will waited patiently.

The king continued, speaking slowly and putting emphasis on each word, "I—know—who—you—are."

Will stared at Lognion in confusion.

"That's it," said the king. "I know who you are. Tell her that and she'll understand. If she says anything else, walk away. She's been doing this for years, assuming secret identities and learning about life in the kingdom. Usually she undertakes these tasks at my behest, but I've drilled into her the importance of one rule. No one must know who she is. If they learn, that's the end of it. It wouldn't do to have her growing attached to people beneath her station. Nor would it benefit *you* to think that you could mean anything to her."

Will nodded slowly.

"Those words are a little joke she and I have developed over the years. Once she hears you say them, she'll understand that your little friendship has come to an end," said the king.

His heart felt cold, but he answered, "Yes, Your Majesty."

The king started to leave again, but he looked back one more time and pointed at Will. "Don't forget! I know who you are." Then he left, humming a playful tune as he went out the door.

Will stared after him. In his mind he remembered something Selene had told him. *"Once you know, we won't be able to be friends anymore."* Was this what she had been referring to? How long had she lived like this? How many times had she heard those words? I know who you are. It was a cruel joke, and he wanted to weep for her.

He stared down at his hand where the gold ring still lay on his finger. It was the only thing the king hadn't noticed. The sole thing he had been able to hide. His mind was a confused jumble, and there were only two things he was sure of. The king terrified him, and the king was completely mad.

Coming in October of 2019:

Secrets and Spellcraft

Will's journey continues as he studies magic at Wurthaven.

Stay up to date with my releases by signing up for my newsletter at:

Magebornbooks.com

Books by Michael G. Manning

Mageborn Series:

The Blacksmith's Son
The Line of Illeniel
The Archmage Unbound
The God-Stone War
The Final Redemption

Embers of Illeniel (a prequel series):

The Mountains Rise
The Silent Tempest
Betrayer's Bane

Champions of the Dawning Dragons:

Thornbear
Centyr Dominance
Demonhome

The Riven Gates:

Mordecai
The Severed Realm
Transcendence and Rebellion

Standalone Novels:

Thomas

LONG LIVE THE ELF QUEEN

THE ELF QUEEN SERIES BOOK 2

J.M. KEARL

Long Live the Elf Queen

By J.M. Kearl
Copyright J.M. Kearl 2022

Cover design by: Janie Hannan Kearl

This book is dedicated to the readers who love our sassy gnome Tifapine.

CONTENTS

CONTENT NOTICE

Please note this book includes content that may not be suitable for all audiences. Content includes mild foul language, moderate sexual activity, violence, depictions of war, and death.

Name Pronunciation Guide

Adley- Ad-lee
Aldrich- All-drich
Alisara- Al-I-sar-uh
Anami- Uh-nom-ee
Atarah- Uh-tar-uh
Athayel- Ath-ā-el
Devane- Duh-vay-n
Drakonan- Druh-co-nan
Dramus- Draw-muss
Dregous- Dreg-us
Evalyn- Ev-uh-lynn
Fennan- Fen-en
Kail- Kay-l
Katmor- Cat-more
Layala- Lay-all-uh
Leif- Lay-ff
Lyndora- Lin-dor-uh
Nyrovia- Ny-rove-ee-uh

Rhegar- Ray-gar
Ronan- Ro-nan
Scarvan- Scar-van
Seraphina- Sera-feen-uh
Siegfried- Seeg-free-d
Tenebris- Ten-eh-briss
Valeen- Vuh-leen
Yoren- Yor-en
Zaurahel- Zar-uh-hel

Calladira- Cal-uh-deer-uh
Delfaria- Del-far-e-uh
Malock- Mal-ock
Palenor- Pal-eh-nor
Pridam- Pre-dam
Runevale- Roon-vayle
Rynvengaard- Riven-guard
Sederac- Sed-er-ack
Svenarum- Sven-are-um
Vessache- Vess-ach
Villhara- Vill-har-uh

Book 1 Recap

Layala trained in hiding her entire life to kill the elf
king, Tenebris, and his son, Prince Thane, for
executing her parents and the raids in search of her,
the last mage. Thane, her magic-bound mate from the
time they were children, waited for the day to reunite
with Layala but he couldn't do that until his evil father
was gone. After Thane thought he killed King Tenebris,
he went after Layala in her hometown of Briar Hollow
where she lived among the humans. The time limit on
their mate spell waned and he had to bring her to his
home so she could take her place as Queen of Palenor
beside him.

She had other plans, and after trying to take his life,
they reached an agreement: if she could break their
mate bond spell, they could part. She had eight weeks.
During those weeks she learned the enemy wanted to
use her to raise the Black Mage, the creator of the pale
ones. The twisted, cursed elves were drawn to her
magic and sought to take her captive.

She also found that Thane wasn't the wicked king she believed him to be and with time and much back and forth they began to fall in love.

In the end she found a way to break the bond between them and chose not to.

Instead, she chose Thane.

They planned to marry and finish the mate spell before they would be cursed to turn into pale ones, but Thane's father returned from the "dead" and his lackey, the dragon shifter Varlett, broke the mate bond and abandoned Thane to die in the cursed forest.

After, Layala was taken captive and with a broken heart, left wondering: was Thane alive and if so, could he save her?

CHAPTER 1

Rain pelted the stone tower, drumming the rooftop like tiny fairy feet dancing overhead. The aroma of drenched earth drifted inside the window, fresh and wild. Layala loved that smell. It used to fill her with peace and calm. But not that, nor the beauty of the moon's pale light breaking through the dark clouds could penetrate the pain anymore. The smile it used to draw was stolen by a dragon's hand shoved through the body of her lover. She rubbed her aching temples, then picked up her only comfort, a dirty cerulean pillow. It smelled like ages of dust, but she held it against her middle, hugging it for warmth. She ignored the straw poking through the scratchy, hole-ridden sheet beneath her. The irritation of it was a reminder she was still alive.

Come to me. I need you.

"Thane," she whimpered as that deep, soothing voice echoed in her mind again. Was it possible to hear him with their mate bond stolen and erased? Or was

her own mind playing cruel tricks? She didn't know, but it only prodded at the pain throbbing in her chest.

Come to me. Please.

"I can't," she whimpered, letting her face fall onto the pillow. Her teeth chattered with the chilly breeze and the spray of icy droplets hitting her skin through the single open window, dampened her clothes. This circular gray stone room became a prison, the miserable color as depressing as the autumn rains. The only ways out were the window with a seventy-foot drop, and the solid door, always locked from the outside. Always.

"Remember the colorful blossoms of summer on the darkest days of winter. Remember the smells of lavender and citrus, and sweet smiles, for they will get you through that endless night," Layala whispered to herself. Aunt Evalyn would say that whenever the hard days threatened to win. She didn't understand what it meant as a child, especially since Briar Hollow didn't have long or dark winters. But she wholly understood it now—this was an endless nightmare, one she desperately wanted to wake up from.

Tears slipped out of her dry eyes and over-chapped lips. She was surprised she had any tears left. How many days had it been? One sunrise melted into the next. Days and weeks became a blur. How much time had passed since Thane sent that note? *"I'm coming for you, Laya."* How many days had she gone without food or water? Was it weeks now? She couldn't remember.

I need you, came that whisper. Was his voice

taunting her now a hallucination—was he even real anymore?

The door creaked open. The same auburn-haired soldier who came each sunrise, afternoon, and after sunset, stepped inside. His sword swung at his side tonight, rather than ready to strike. They both knew she was too weak to attack him now, as she'd tried in the past. Whistling a morbidly cheerful tune, he walked across the creaky floorboards. Neither of them ever uttered a word. This was the only person she'd had contact with in weeks, and she didn't even know his name. He was tall, slender but stronger than her by a shameful margin and he had weapons he wasn't afraid to use.

Lying on her side, Layala didn't move as he jabbed the barb into her arm to keep her magic at bay. The clinking of the metal chamber pot as he touched it with his boot echoed like a gong within the domed ceiling. He grumbled a nonchalant "huh" and left it. She hadn't needed to use it in a couple days. There was nothing left in her. If she were human, she'd be dead.

The door clicked shut, the quiet scrape of the lock slid into place, and she sat up. She stared at the back of the dark wood, covered in thin scratches and gouges. She could almost hear the echoes of her own screams even now. Glancing down at her fingernails, Layala's chin quivered. They were broken, splintered, and dried blood covered her hands.

The physical pain, even the excruciating hunger and thirst, wasn't even the worst part; it was not

knowing where Thane was, not being able to *feel* him. Or not knowing what happened to Piper and Fennan and Tifapine. Did Tenebris burn Briar Hollow? Did he have Aunt Evalyn, and would he kill her?

Her only hope was that he would keep them alive so he could use them to manipulate Layala, and Thane would come before then. He must come...

"Remember the colorful blossoms of summer on the darkest days—" her voice broke, and her body shook in silent sobs. Hope? What was hope anymore? She touched her chest for that familiar, worn piece of paper she kept tucked in her bosom.

She shot up, panic suddenly raking her chest. She pawed at the cot, searching for the only proof she had that Thane was alive when they insisted he was dead. The half-moon's light shone in through the window just bright enough to see but the shadows were menacing.

"Where is it?" Her trembling hands left streaks of fresh blood the harder she scraped the fabric, searching.

She slid her feet to the floor and dropped to her knees to look under the four-inch gap the bed stood from the stone. *Where is it?!* Maybe seeing Thane dead broke her mind. Maker above, what if she imagined the note? She saw his crumbled, bloody body with a hole in his stomach... He didn't move. He didn't breathe...

She crawled to the window, pushing up to weak legs, until she latched onto the ledge. She groaned

under the pressure of pulling herself up. Her heart crashed until it ached. *I can't breathe. I can't breathe.* Finally breaching the opening in her stone cage, she lay her chest across the ledge, one arm hanging out the window to the seventy-foot drop below, the other clutching the inside stone. A blast of cold wind hit her face and icy droplets shocked her out of panic.

"Thane where are you?" she whispered, staring down at the guards walking the pristine paths below. Were they completely oblivious to her or did they not care their supposed savior was locked up in misery? At some point someone must have heard her screams.

She cupped her hands, hoping for enough rain to quench her parched throat. The sprinkles were enough to wet her skin, but nature was a tease. Still, she greedily licked the moisture from her palm.

With a shaky breath, she tilted her head to look back inside. The small, crumpled piece of paper, her small bit of hope, lay next to the foot post of the bed. Shoving away from the wall, she dove for it and held it to her chest. On her knees, she straightened it and read the beautiful script:

I'm coming for you, Laya.

~ Thane

She climbed into the bed, tucked the note back in her top and finally slept.

The creak of hinges penetrated Layala's slumber. Her crusted eyes opened to the hint of morning sunshine, bathing the room in warmth after a cold dark night. Light footsteps quickened her pulse. That

was not the gait of her usual guard. She didn't move, barely allowed herself to breathe. She curled in on herself more, holding the small blue pillow. She hated that she'd become this, cowering like a small child afraid of monsters, but even the effort to crawl to the window the night before left her weak.

She caught a glimpse of blond hair, and it felt like her stomach leapt into her throat. *No, not him. Not him.* Nightmares of King Tenebris's ghoulish face standing over the dead bloody bodies of her parents, looming over Thane, cackling like an old crone, flooded her dreams. He'd grip her by her hair, tearing strands from her scalp, and scream at her to look at them. "Face what you have done!" She watched herself from far away, eyes slammed shut, trembling in his grasp, sobbing, pleading for him to stop.

She dragged in a deep breath, *that's not real. Not real.*

"Layala." It was Aldrich's voice. Did he sound almost—sorrowful?

She opened one eye slowly, then the other to make sure it was him. His blond hair was tied back in a tight bun that made his face more severe. His pointed ears seemed sharper. How did she ever miss the resemblance to Tenebris? He looked just like him. His once wide, bright eyes looked heavy as they took in her appearance. His lips pressed together, and he reached toward her.

She mustered up enough strength to smack his hand away. "Don't," she snarled.

"You're going downstairs. Get up, please." He was too patient, too calm. She didn't trust his demeanor after he'd knocked her in the head with the hilt of a sword and kicked her in the ribs. The bruises and cut were long gone but the memory lingered.

"You've been invited to breakfast."

Breakfast... Her stomach cramped and her mouth watered at the thought of food of any kind. Potatoes, eggs, fruit. Water. She craved water more than anything. Her tongue felt like sand and her throat, gritty and aching. She blinked, confused. Why would he take her out of this room for breakfast? She rolled onto her side and put the pillow over her head. This was a trick. A trick she wouldn't fall for. A false kindness or worse, if she was invited to breakfast with the king that meant they wanted to move forward, that they had a plan for her...

"Layala," he chided, like she was a small child that didn't want to get up for schooling. "You must be thirsty and hungry. It's been twenty-eight days."

"No."

"Do you want to stay up here forever?"

What a stupid question. As if she'd asked to be here? The sound of sloshing liquid in a container was enough to make her turn back toward Aldrich. His off-white tunic was too crisp, too clean. Even his hands look softer holding a metal canteen. Clearly, he'd taken his time away from Thane and the Ravens to indulge in the luxuries his *father* offered.

A drop of water slid down the canteen onto the

11

cot. Her throat burned like sparking dry flint. She reached for it with a shaky arm. The sheer effort it took made her angry. He kept moving it just out of her range. Furious tears stung. *Bastard. Bastard. Bastard.* She chanted and let her arm fall back to the bed.

"You're that weak? Can you even sit up?" He wasn't mocking her, and he sounded genuinely concerned but it must be an act.

It was an effort to pull air into her lungs at this point.

He pushed his arm under her back, forcing her to sit up. She was too tired, too weak to fight him off. "Come on. Have a drink. Please."

She pressed her back into the stone wall, and he twisted off the top of the canteen. Cold metal touched her lips then water slid over her tongue. She moaned in relief. Nothing ever tasted so good. She drained the entire thing in seconds and then lifted her chin to level Aldrich with a blank stare.

"I've convinced my father to allow you to eat. Come downstairs."

"What's the point?"

"I'm trying to help you."

"Why do you care? I'm here because of you. Just let me die." She didn't care anymore.

His mouth formed a hard line. "You won't die. You're an elf, Layala. Your body will go into hibernation for survival, and you'll sleep. For months—years even."

She'd felt that soul-deep tiredness in every pump

of her heart as it slowed. A few more days might have pulled her into the sleep he spoke of. He slid his arm around her waist and dragged her up. She hooked her elbow behind his neck, and her legs swung with his strides as he carried most of her weight.

Crossing the threshold of the door made her feel oddly fearful. Leaving her prison to go to something unknown... to face the tyrant who kept her here. They descended the curving staircase and her bare feet scraped against the cold stone. Her muscles stung and burned but it felt good to use them for more than a few steps to the window.

"I'm going to warn you now," Aldrich said once they reached the bottom of the stairs. "There are *people* here to see you."

Why did "*people*" sound off? "Who? Aldrich, if it's my aunt—if you ever cared about me even in the smallest amount, get her out of here. Please." She always thought she was above begging but she would for Aunt Evalyn.

"It's not her. She was gone when the soldiers got there. It appears someone warned her my father would be coming."

She glanced over at him. "Someone?" Thane? Was that where he'd been? Had he made sure that her Aunt Evalyn and the rest of her hometown wouldn't be butchered? The thought brought a small curve to her mouth. That must be why he hadn't come yet... but then why was his voice in her head begging *her* to go to him?

A set of guards with the Palenor weapons sigil on their armored chests moved down the corridor toward them. The clink of their boots bounced off the walls in the otherwise serene space. They wore deep gray battle helmets, pointed at the center—unlike the Ravens' winged helmets—shin guards that reached past their knees; one carried a long dark wooden staff. The chatter quieted the closer they drew. Their advance slowed and they stared at Layala with pity. Maker, she never wanted anyone to look at her like that. One of them opened his mouth as if he might say something but a low growl from Aldrich was enough to keep them on their way. These guards used to smile at her, now they looked afraid.

"I never found your gnome," Aldrich said, continuing to half carry her toward their destination. "She might be safe."

Tif was alright? A bit of the heaviness on her shoulders eased. At least that was something positive.

It was a few minutes before Layala recognized the hall they ended up in. Her room, the Starlight room, next to Thane's chambers was around the corner. The suits of armor built into the alcoves, and the sprays of fresh wildflowers in silver vases set on stands were more familiar than anywhere else here. A place she would have called hers.

He stopped in front of her mahogany door, tugged the gold handle down, and pushed it open. "Reina and Pearl will be in to bathe and dress you in a couple minutes."

She pulled out of his grasp and stepped forward, a sudden wave of strength and energy filling her. This room brought her a modicum of comfort in the agony of the last few weeks.

"And the servants' entrance has been permanently disabled so don't get any ideas." His sympathetic stare made the hairs on the back of her neck raise. Like she was a bird with broken wings who'd never fly again. "I know you loved him." He paused, and his jaw muscles quivered. "But so did I."

Gulping down the pain, Layala said, "You don't know what love is. Love for him would have put you in prison, not at Tenebris's side."

With a downcast gaze, Aldrich closed the door, the sound of it snapping shut brought a chill to her skin. She didn't like closed doors anymore. She'd never been claustrophobic, but the creeping anxiety, filling her with dread, told her she was now. With a shake of her head, she brushed that feeling off as best she could, slid open the vanity drawer, and grinned at the round silver foil. "Thank you, Tifapine." She tore open the six wrappers and shoved the first chocolate truffle into her mouth. It melted over her tongue like honey, and she closed her eyes as the sugar filled her with new life. She ate the others too fast to truly savor the delicious treats.

A quiet knock startled her. Her nervous hand slapped against her chest, and her rapid heartbeat whispered in her ears. She quickly shoved the empty wrappers inside and closed the drawer, keeping her

hands tucked behind her back. She turned in time to see Reina and Pearl step inside. Her tense shoulders sagged, and tears sprang, blurring her vision. Reina put a hand to her chest and her chin trembled. Pearl rushed across the room and swept her into an embrace. Layala stiffened at first, then returned the hug, chest warming at their kindness. Theirs were the first friendly faces she'd seen in what felt like forever. Those tears she'd been holding back slid silently down her cheeks.

"Oh, my dear girl," Reina said, slowly stepping toward her. "I'm so sorry."

Reina ran and wrapped her arms tightly around Layala and Pearl. "We heard you were locked in that tower, and they hadn't been feeding you," Pearl said, her voice wavering. "So much has changed... I'm so sorry we couldn't help you."

Layala pulled away first, swiping her fingers over her wet cheeks. "There was nothing you could do."

"We're not supposed to give you anything, just bathe and ready you for breakfast with King Tenebris, but..." Reina pulled a white napkin out of her pocket. She lifted open the edges and inside a hunk of bread waited in her palm. She pushed it into Layala's hand with a nod. "Eat it. We'll draw you a bath."

A sob caught in her throat as she took the bread. "Thank you." Her voice sounded shattered, broken, so unlike before.

Layala sat on the soft, silky bed, eating the food slower than she had the chocolate. She touched the

green vines that framed and wrapped around the bedposts and instinctually looked up at Tif's hidden perch, hoping to see her there. It was dark and empty, like she felt inside.

Soon, Reina and Pearl guided her to a steaming bath. She didn't protest as they gently removed her clothes and helped her into the gold clawfoot tub. She eased into the hot water, the feel of it soothing against her dirty, sore skin. Reina lathered citrus and lavender soap into her hair, the smell of it reminding her of the words she chanted in that tower room. The note Thane sent must have been stuck to her skin, it soaked into the water and the ink began to fade. She snatched it up and the fragile paper melted across her fingertips. Maker, no. Her body trembled with silent sobs as the only thing left of it was his name.

"What was that paper?" Pearl asked.

Layala stared as the last bit of ink turned into blotches that stained her broken nails and cut fingers until Pearl took her hands. She didn't answer. Maybe it was a blessing that any evidence of Thane being alive wouldn't fall into the hands of the enemy.

"What happened to your fingers, sweet girl?"

Layala swallowed hard at the memory. "I wanted out. I wanted—" Thane, but she didn't say his name aloud.

Pearl swiped a strand of fire-orange hair out of her eyes, slowly shaking her head in sorrow. She dipped a sponge into the bubbly water and dabbed at Layala's hands. Her eyes unfocused as her maids cared for her

in a way she had never allowed before. Tears stung, how arrogant and rude she'd been toward them, yet they still doted on her.

"I told my son that we'd get to see you today. Sir Aldrich informed us last night," Reina said. "My boy has been asking about you."

"I didn't know you had a son," Layala said, wondering why she had never inquired before. "How old? What is his name?"

"Charlie is nine. It took many many years for us to be blessed with him."

Pearl smiled. "He's the sweetest little boy. He talks about how much he wants to meet you. You're his idol."

"Me?" Layala said surprised.

"Oh yes," Reina answered, grinning proudly as if he was standing there beside her. "He always wanted to be a mage, you see. And he has black hair and blue eyes just like you. He's a beautiful child, and he'll be handsome when he's grown."

"Well, tell him I'd love to meet him—someday." The "someday" lingered between them for long moments.

Reina cleared her throat. "When things get better —we must believe and have hope they will—you will meet him."

Only when the bath cooled did Layala rise, drying herself with a towel. She stared at her reflection in the full-length gold-trimmed mirror. She wasn't sure what she expected to see, maybe gaunt cheeks and

protruding ribs, but her full breasts remained, even if her collar bones were sharper. Her strong, powerful thighs appeared more defined with the loss of some fat. The definition of muscle in her shoulders may have diminished some but not much. Her waist whittled inward a little and the roundness of her hips wasn't quite as dominant as before but somehow, she kept her form as if her body refused to become thin and brittle. Perhaps some part of her magic was interwoven into every cell of her body and kept her strong.

She felt weak, but she didn't look it. Her skin lacked the same bronzed glow and gone was the fiery fierceness in her gaze. The girl staring back at her was sad and hollow. Even she could see that. Who was this girl? Certainly not the Layala Lightbringer who fought against pale ones and destroyed those who tortured and would have killed her mate.

Reina draped a silky blue robe around Layala's shoulders and sat her in a soft blue chair. She combed through the tangles of Layala's hip-length, jet-black hair while Pearl added color to her cheeks and lips. Birds chirped outside the window and muffled voices from those walking below drifted up. The silence wasn't uncomfortable, but there were many things Layala wanted to ask, and the chocolates and bread gave her enough energy to work up the nerve. "What is the High King saying happened to—" She glanced down at her wrist where the mate rune should be, where it had been all her life, only to stare at her

unmarked skin. "Thane." She hesitated to say his name out loud; it hurt too much.

Reina stopped combing her hair. Pearl's dark eyes lifted to her partner's. Whatever it was, it couldn't be good. Reina cleared her throat and spoke first, "That King—er, Prince Thane was to be executed for treason because he tried to have King Tenebris killed for the throne."

"That's a lie," Layala snapped. The fire she thought went out in her sparked if even just for a moment. "He did it because Tenebris wants to betray all of us to the Black Mage."

Pearl's eyes widened a little. "The Black Mage? You mentioned that when you first arrived... You still believe that is true?"

"I know it is."

"When King Tenebris came back, we were all so surprised," Reina started. "It happened the day the Ravens returned home from Doonafell. He came through the front doors wearing his crown, Sir Aldrich at his side. We were excited our High King was alive. Until he announced that Prince Thane tried to kill him. He started arresting those loyal to Prince Thane to question them. Then it went from questioning to executing them in the streets. Then we heard he was holding you in the tower. We're all scared to death we're next to lose our heads." Reina sighed, lowering her voice. "But worst of all, I almost believed King Tenebris, too."

Layala jumped out of her chair and whipped around to face Reina. "You don't?"

Reina fidgeted with her fingers. "I saw something I think I wasn't supposed to see."

"What?" Both Layala and Pearl demanded.

"There is a..." She gulped. "A stranger here. I caught a glimpse of his hand, white as snow and black-tipped fingers." Her voice wavered. "I think he might have seen me, too. He was covered in a cloak from head to toe, but he'd removed his glove. I fear he might be," she broke off and shook her head.

"A pale one," Layala finished.

Pearl gasped. "No, it can't be."

Reina looked around with wide worried eyes. "I don't understand why King Tenebris would allow a cursed one inside the castle. What is happening?"

Goosebumps trailed over Layala's skin. Her eyes flicked to the doorway leading to her bedroom. Mathekis, the leader of the pale ones... it must be. Thane said Tenebris made a deal with Mathekis long ago. Layala gripped Reina's arm. "Listen to me. Tenebris wants to give me to General Mathekis for my magic. You remember when I told you that my parents died to get me away from the High King? They knew Tenebris would use me for evil. You see it now, don't you? He wants the Black Mage to come back. I must get out of here."

Pearl choked on a sob, covering her mouth. Terror flashed in Reina's eyes, and she stumbled back a step as if even hearing his very name weakened her. "T-

they've blocked the servants' door. There is no other way out of this room other than the front and there are sure to be guards."

Those were the only ways out using *doors*. As if she could just waltz right out of here. Layala dashed to the window and shoved it open. The green vines draping around the window frame could be long enough to at least get close to the ground. From there she might be able to scale the brick or jump. It wasn't that far down. The most difficult part would be going unnoticed by the guards. They passed by at regular intervals.

Three heavy knocks sounded on the door. Shit. Layala whirled around and shoved a finger at the maids. "Don't answer it." She gulped, staring through the archway into her bedroom where someone waited on the other side. If Mathekis was here...

Pearl's cries echoed off the marble-floored bathroom. Reina wrapped her arms around herself, backing into the corner. "We must," Reina said. "King Tenebris will execute us if you leave. He'll think we've helped. He's already killed several personal servants of Prince Thane's."

Layala's mouth dropped. "Why would he kill Thane's servants?" The Ravens she could see but servants?

With the back of her hand, Pearl swiped at her red cheeks. "We don't know, but we're sure to be next."

"Because he questioned their loyalty as he will ours," Reina said.

A fist slammed on the door four times now, each

with increased intensity. "Layala, are you ready? The High King is waiting and I'm afraid he's not as patient as Thane was."

Layala looked at her maids, at how afraid they were. Clenching her teeth together, she said, "Get me a dress. Quickly."

CHAPTER 2

Layala's silver-heeled shoes tapped lightly as she stepped into the corridor and closed the door gently behind her, leaving her frightened maids inside to compose themselves. Allowing Aldrich to see them in their panicked state would set off warning bells in his head. He'd wonder why they were so worried.

The traitor's eyes traveled down her form, more in an inspection than desire but that heat was there, too. She wanted to gag at what thoughts he might have about her. The high-necked gold gown hugged her waist and several layers of fabric created a round volume from her hips to her toes. She didn't want to show any more skin or curve than absolutely necessary.

"You truly are beautiful. Fennan and I had a bet; he said you'd probably be of average looks, and I, that you'd outshine the stars. He gladly gave over the wager."

Layala glared, disgusted. After what he did, he was going to talk about her looks? And how could he even speak of Fennan now? "Save your compliments, snake. They won't do you any good."

He frowned and reached for her. With a disgusted grunt, she stepped away, tucking her arms behind her back. She may have accepted his aid before, but now that she'd eaten, and bathed, she would use every ounce of her strength to manage the walk on her own.

"Stubborn as ever. What's giving you this newfound burst of energy?" He arched a sleek brow. "You could barely walk before."

Layala swallowed hard, thinking of Reina and how she'd been told not to give Layala food. "A hot bath can do wonders." Though when she started forward again, she faked a stumble, and he grabbed hold of her arm to steady her. She reluctantly grabbed hold of his elbow so he wouldn't suspect her maids aided her more than they should have.

"Stubbornness can only get you so far. I only want to help you," Aldrich said. "It's not a trick."

"Help?" Layala scoffed. "You want to help me now? Where were you when I was starving? Where were you when I wanted out of that room? Where—" She broke off as her surroundings began to spin and her head felt too light and leaned on him more heavily. Maybe he was right about her stubbornness.

"There was nothing I could do, but despite what you may think, I care about you. I don't want to see you suffer."

Seething, Layala gripped his arm tighter, digging her broken fingernails into his forearm. She learned long ago people showed who they truly were, and their words might mean nothing. She believed bold action over pretty lies. "And what about Piper and Fennan? Do you want to see them suffer?" They went as fast as she could, which was significantly slower than she wanted. Her weak thighs burned with the effort as did her pride.

"Of course not." He ran an exasperated hand down his face. "They are my friends but sometimes sacrifices must be made for the greater good. They'll be freed as soon as you cooperate."

"Greater good? You think raising the Black Mage is for the greater good? And your *friends*? I highly doubt they'd call you the same anymore." She shook her head at the thought of them locked in a damp cell with nothing to eat or drink, cold and shivering. Or worse, beaten and tortured.

"Listen to me," Aldrich said, jerking her to a stop at the bottom of the stairs. Several pairs of guards in the grand foyer watched them. They didn't flinch from their positions by the front entrance or guarding hallways, but they observed. Aldrich glanced around, as aware of them as she was, then met Layala's angry stare. "If you don't want to go back to that room, you'll do what my father requires."

"I'd much rather fall into an endless sleep than use my magic for that prick."

Aldrich's eyes flashed wide, and he lowered his

voice so she could barely hear him. "He will never allow that. He'll find ways to get you to cooperate. That stint in the tower was to weaken you, break your will. There is much worse to come."

Pressing her lips into a hard line, Layala wondered why the hell he was telling her this. Was he pretending to be the good elf and his father the bad one? Playing mind games? He couldn't truly believe he was her friend anymore or that he could be redeemed. "He can try."

Aldrich sighed and dragged her along beside him, gripping her arm hard enough that she knew his fingers would bruise her flesh. "Mathekis is here. I doubt in your weakened state you can resist his power. It's even a challenge for me."

Layala gulped down the nervousness rising in her throat. Thane said Mathekis was the last person he wanted to face in a one-on-one fight, and he was the strongest elf she knew. "You're doing all this to one day be High King, but there won't be a Palenor left to rule. Don't you see that?"

"My father and I have binding deals with Mathekis. We get to keep the rule of Palenor and the attacks will stop. This is how I can save our land from furthering the curse. I know you don't see it that way, but it's my intention."

"Really? Has Tenebris even announced you as his new heir? Reina and Pearl called you Sir Aldrich not High *Prince*. And have the attacks stopped?"

"He will. He's waiting for the right time." He shook

his head. "And the attacks will stop after they get what they want."

"Maker above, Aldrich, how can you be so stupid? And you think once the Black Mage comes back, he won't take Palenor? He tried to take it before, but your ancestors weren't fools. Your grandfather died in the war to save this land, and your father is just going to give it to him."

"You're wrong. The High King knows exactly what he is doing."

"And that is?"

"The Black Mage will restore magic to our people. My father made a deal. You don't care because you're a mage, but the rest of the elves want their power back."

"You believe Mathekis can guarantee that? Think, Aldrich."

"*He* doesn't even want to be what he is."

It all sounded too good to be true. Tenebris didn't care if other elves had magic. He wanted it for himself. And why would the Black Mage stop the pale ones when he was the one to create them? More lies, more coercions. Was Aldrich tricked into believing all this or was it all a ruse to get her to cooperate?

They approached the dining hall and the doors with ornate carvings opened inward. A pair of guards dipped their chins in greeting. Layala's feet suddenly felt heavy, as if boulders kept her in place. What waited in this room...

Aldrich placed his hand on her upper back, urging her forward. With a deep breath, she took one step

then another. Each felt like walking to her doom. The elf who murdered her parents, and took Thane from her, wore a green, high-necked tunic with embroidered ivy leaves and gold buttons down his center. A gold crown with emeralds and diamonds sparkled on his straight blond hair; the color gave his alabaster skin a little warmth. His slender build and narrow shoulders were nothing like Thane's. But what bothered her most was the way he watched her, like a hungry wolf, waiting for a meal, hidden in fine clothes and the ethereal face of an elf.

Layala glanced around the rest of the room. She'd eaten here many times, but the decor had since changed, green tapestries over the wall of windows instead of blue, a new honey-oak table with fancy silver dishware, even the calming green plants had been swapped out for potted red roses, as if Tenebris wanted to clear away everything Thane touched. The artistic painting that had been on the wall was replaced with a life-size portrait of Tenebris in a gaudy gold frame. Worst of all, Tenebris sat at the head of the table where Thane once had. He gestured to the seat beside him. The same seat Thane said was for his betrothed. Maker, she wished he was here, that if she closed her eyes and opened them, he'd be there instead. But he wasn't and she wanted nothing more than to grab a knife off the table and ram it through Tenebris's heart.

A cold sensation trickled down the back of her neck, and she whirled around.

A pale one with skin and hair as white as sun-bleached bone, slid his black fingernail across her shoulder. "Hello, pretty," he purred. Mathekis's black eyes locked onto the lily's mark on her upper arm, peeking out from the fabric of her capped sleeves, and he licked his coal lips. "We finally meet."

She bristled at his touch, at his closeness, and leaned away from him.

"I won't bite," Mathekis said with a wicked grin, each tooth narrowed to a point, perfect for a predator. "Over the last few hundred years I've gained necessary control of my urges. Don't worry, my lord needs you alive and unharmed."

With a sneer, Tenebris stood and waved his arms over the table. "Have a seat." His command was clipped and forceful, and the pinch of his mouth looked like he'd sucked on a lime.

Mathekis strolled into the room, graceful like he glided on air, and his long black cloak flowed around him like a pool around his feet. He took his seat and picked up a glass full of dark red liquid. He swirled it around, and the thickness of it made her gulp. It wasn't wine.

"I said, have a seat," Tenebris snapped.

Layala didn't move. She rubbed sweaty palms across her dress. *Run run run*, her inner voice chanted. Her gaze drifted to the three exits. Could she make it? Even the open window letting in a warm breeze looked appealing. She was in no condition to fight a

pale one—a cannibal, cursed elf. Ravenous and lethal in nature.

Heart thundering, Layala backed toward the hallway, and bumped into Aldrich. The jittery feeling now rushing through her jolted energy in her once-weak legs. She could make it to the servants' passage, hide.

"Come forward. Sit." Mathekis's voice took on a different sound, a more melodic and rich tone with a slight echo. Layala found herself involuntarily advancing. *No, no I don't want to go forward,* she thought but kept moving. She slowly shook her head even as she was powerless to stop herself. Spiking fear made her hands tremble. She reached the chair and grabbed the back of it and lifted her chin.

Mathekis smiled. "My, my, we have a stubborn one. You won't be the first I've broken."

The High King's upper lip curled, and he shot Aldrich a harsh glare. "Don't just stand there. Do your job."

Aldrich grabbed her hips, steered her around to the seat, pushed her down in the chair and scooted her in. That bastard. She still felt the ghost of his palms on her and her face heated in disgust. But that bitterness was quickly stolen away by the bowl half filled with ripe purple berries and a plate holding a buttered roll and a turkey leg. She inhaled the rich scent of the meat, her mouthwatering, and stomach growling as if demanding she take a bite. For a moment she wondered why Mathekis didn't smell rotten like the

others she'd encountered. Maybe the food masked the scent.

"You're hungry," Tenebris said. "Eat, Layala."

There was no silverware within her reach. Nothing to use as a weapon. The king's knife was on his left and she, on his right. Layala kept her hands on her lap despite how ravenous she was. This felt wrong. They'd ripped her from Thane, and starved her to only have her sit down and dine with them like nothing happened?

Aldrich pulled out the chair next to her and sat. "When will the dragon arrive?"

The dragon? Memories flashed of Layala driving her dagger into the dragon shifter's chest, nearly hacking off her arm and finally to the black-taloned hand that sliced through Thane's gut. She closed her eyes, taking in a deep breath to calm the anxious energy spiking in her again. She couldn't panic, couldn't black out. Not here.

"Any moment now," Mathekis answered.

As if on command, the doors clicked open. Layala turned her head. The pearl-white gown dragging on the floor behind Varlett hugged the dragon's curves like it was painted on. She was beautiful with her vibrant brown skin and golden curls that fell like a waterfall around her, spilling to the apex of her hip bones.

"Mathekis, my dear," she cooed, her heels tapping loudly on the glossy stone floor. "It's been too long."

Even her voice made goosebumps rise along

Layala's spine. If there was one person she wanted dead more than Tenebris it was that wench. If it weren't for her, she would still be with Thane. They'd have escaped through the portal together. She could be holding him right now, kissing him, loving him.

"Varlett." Mathekis's eyes greedily roamed over her without an ounce of modesty. "You look delicious as ever."

Ew, gag me, she thought.

Tenebris stood, then lifted a hand toward the chair next to Mathekis. "Welcome, Varlett."

Layala wanted to puke at all the formalities like they weren't a bunch of disgusting creeps. *Oh yes, let us sit down and act civilized when they eat people.*

Varlett took the seat beside Mathekis, and tsked, looking Layala over from across the table. She pushed out her lower lip dramatically, "You look sad, poor thing," she purred. "I couldn't possibly imagine why." She giggled as if what she'd done to Thane was funny.

Heat flared in Layala's body. If she had use of her magic, she'd strangle the life from her, watch with pleasure as she gasped for breath. "Bitch."

Smiling as if she'd gotten the exact reaction she wanted, Varlett said, "Feisty. Feisty. And here I thought a stretch in the tower would tame that tongue."

Tenebris pushed his shoulders back. "I need to know if you did what I asked." His voice was snappy and harsh.

Varlett arched an eyebrow. Leaning forward, she

tapped her three-inch talons on the tabletop. *Click, click, click.* The sound made Layala's skin crawl. "I severed their bond. You can check her wrist if you'd like. I don't know why you haven't already. You've had her for weeks."

"I meant, is he dead? I told you to go back and make sure. I can't very well have him coming for my head. He already tried to kill me once, and I'm hearing... rumors."

Layala's heart stuttered. Rumors Thane was alive?

"First of all, you don't *tell* me anything." She rolled her eyes to Layala. "I left him bleeding out on the forest floor with a hole through his gut. I doubt even he survived that." Varlett turned back to Tenebris. "But I suppose it's possible he lived. He is—*unique* after all."

The harsh frown lines around Tenebris's mouth creased further. "I wanted a guarantee. I paid you enough."

"Should I have brought your son's head to you? I'm sure your naïve wife would have loved that." She let out a cackle. "I did you a favor so if he's alive, it's your problem now."

"My problem?" Tenebris snapped. "You think he wouldn't come for you, too?"

Her eyes flashed and she smiled. "I'd welcome the challenge. It's fun to toy with boys."

Layala's hands curled into fists. Maker, she wanted to fly over the table and strangle her. She found it odd they spoke about this in front of her like she was a part

of their scheming crew or as if she wasn't there at all, but then again, it spoke volumes. They didn't see her as a threat. They didn't fear she'd lose her temper and slaughter them all even though that's exactly what she wanted, but like them, she knew, in this state, she wasn't capable of it. Without weapons and magic and with little food, she was no threat. Those weeks in the tower were his strategy for a reason.

Aldrich touched Layala's arm. "It's alright to eat," he whispered. "I promise it hasn't been tampered with." The food practically beckoned her to indulge but she stubbornly shook her head.

"Eat," Mathekis commanded in that rich timbre that made her muscles move. "You'll need strength soon enough."

No longer able to resist, Layala lifted the turkey leg to her lips and tore off a piece of meat. The salt, fat, and protein were better than anything she could recall ever eating. She almost moaned as she swallowed a mouthful. Even though she wanted to fight this command, just to prove she could, it was easy to give in.

After several bites Layala looked up to Mathekis and Varlett watching her with unnerving, predatory closeness. Even though Varlett was in her human form, she appeared very much like a dragon who wanted an elf for a snack. Layala cleared her throat and took a long drink of water. Perhaps she should play a game herself. "So we're here because you want me to bring the Black Mage back. How would I do

that? My magic creates vines and flowers. What does that have to do with the Black Mage?"

"We'll worry about that when the time comes," Mathekis answered. "For now, eat your fill."

"Zaurahel said himself an elven mage with a lily's mark would be born to ensure his return when he... died." Varlett's hesitation on the last word made Layala wonder. "And then stand at his side."

Layala fumbled her turkey leg and it clanked loudly onto the glass plate in front of her. Standing at the side of the most evil mage to ever live? How could that be? A lie. It must be. Layala would never take his side. "He was a seer?"

"He was many things."

Why were they keeping the how of it a secret? Would it cost her life? No, it couldn't if they believed she'd side with him after. Would she somehow lose her free will, be enchanted by him? Or maybe... Layala picked the turkey leg back up. "Do you even know how to bring him back?"

Mathekis stared at Layala with unwavering coal eyes. "Zaurahel didn't leave it up to fate. Fate is for the gods."

Tenebris tapped his fingers on the tabletop. "You don't need to explain yourself to her. She'll do it one way or another."

"I was alive when the old gods walked this realm," Varlett said, cutting off Tenebris to brag, "I know more than you possibly ever could, Layala. You're a little naïve girl and don't forget it."

Layala wanted to hide her surprise, but both of her eyebrows shot up. Varlett had to be at least two thousand, perhaps even three thousand years old. Odd that she wanted to point that out. Maybe she didn't like sitting at a table with two others who challenged her. She *did* say that power was the one thing she coveted more than anything. Of course, she may simply want to put Layala down, steal any confidence she could have left. "If you're so old and knowledgeable, why is it that you need Zaurahel back? Why did you even need any of his magic in the first place? Or mine for that matter."

Varlett's mouth twitched. "It's called loyalty."

"You said he loved power more than you, and so you had a falling out."

Varlett's golden eyes narrowed, but a serpent's smile played at her lips. Laughing, she turned to Mathekis. "This girl has quite the mouth on her, doesn't she?" She suddenly sprang across the table, crashing over glasses and food, and pressed her long black talon against Layala's closed lips. "And if you don't shut up, I'll cut out your tongue and eat it."

Layala pressed herself back in the chair, resisting the urge to shove Varlett back. She wouldn't win in a fight against Varlett right now, maybe not ever.

Tenebris smiled, watching the two of them with great pleasure. "She might not need her tongue for our goals. I know she doesn't need her ears."

Varlett's black slit pupils dilated, and she inhaled. "You do smell good, and those dainty ears would make

a fine part of my collection. I could make them into a necklace along with the bones in your hand."

"Enough," Mathekis said casually. "She's not to be harmed."

It wasn't a magical command, but Varlett still backed off and slipped into her chair once more. But hatred burned in her eyes, fire hot, and if Layala didn't know better, it was personal.

Layala picked up her turkey leg again, trying to feign like she didn't almost just piss her pants.

"Now let's get to business," Tenebris said. "Here's a little taste of what's to come if you want to rebel. If you don't want to cooperate."

Aldrich shifted noisily in his chair. He and Layala exchanged a glance and there was something very worrisome about the growing fear on his face. Doors crashed open and a pair of guards carried a female between them. Her head hung low, and her feet dragged as if she was unconscious. Her filthy moss-green tunic was torn off at the shoulder on one side and her too-big trousers barely hung on her hips. The red hair that was once as vibrant as a ripe raspberry was dulled from dirt and grime. A hand grasped the crown of her head and jerked her face up. Bruises and several gashes on Piper's delicate face made Layala gasp.

Piper stared out of her one unswollen eye. "Don't you do it. You let them kill me first, Layala."

CHAPTER 3

A stream trickled quietly nearby, and the songs of swallows from the colorful trees overhead enchanted Thane enough to ignore the pain, if only for a moment. Breathing hard and muscles straining, his palms lay flat against the stone edge of the well, bracing most of his weight. With closed eyes, he listened to the calming serene sounds of nature, such a contrast to the agony mutilating his soul. He was desperate to go to Layala, but after three weeks he barely had enough strength to walk to the well outside Mage Vesstan's cottage. He'd never had an injury take this long to heal, but he'd never been so close to death before. It was the Maker's will he lived. Otherwise, he'd have died that day, and with the mate bond broken, Layala would have been safe. As much as it pained him to lose the connection to her, a small part of him was thankful. It meant she wouldn't have to die if he did.

He grabbed the rope dangling over the well and set

one hand over the other and tugged until the bucket rose from the darkness. The healing waters of Calladira washed down his throat and filled his stomach. A small blue and gold butterfly landed on the bare skin of his chest. Its little wings pulsed, and he briefly recalled the time he told Layala that butterflies brought good luck. He needed luck now.

Taking his tall, white wooden staff into hand, he leaned on it with each stride back toward the yellow cottage, fighting the twinge of pain in his torso. The pink, damaged flesh, shaped like a serrated eight-point star was sensitive to the touch. It was as big as his palm in both his front and back, a few inches above his belly button. He wasn't sure it would ever fully heal like his other injuries had.

Mage Vesstan rocked in a chair on the small wooden porch, basking in the sun. His hair and beard shone even whiter in this light, but he somehow looked younger in his joy. He didn't begrudge him for being at peace but wished he could be so relaxed. Thane drew close, and without opening his eyes, Vesstan said, "Now walk back again. Go on. Ten more times before you can rest. Tomorrow, I want you jogging. Picture her face at the end. You'll get there."

"You torment me, old mage," Thane said but smiled and turned around. This reminded him of his days as an adolescent when Vesstan made him run, dive, and roll through an obstacle course, training for hours physically before Thane would even be allowed to practice his magic. *"You must be able to fight through*

pain and discomfort, push your body to its breaking point to master your power," he'd said.

Taking in a deep breath and slowly releasing it, Thane put one foot in front of the other, counting each step to focus his mind off the stabbing sensation in his torso. One hundred and fifty-seven paces later he stopped at the well again, leaning heavily on the wooden staff. After Varlett shoved her hand through him, he spent much of the first week in a hazy fever. That day flashed through his mind; he felt as if his insides were on fire, blazing hot enough to consume his entire being. He could hardly draw breath, couldn't move. The screams of Layala as she attacked Varlett still haunted his nightmares. He desperately wanted to get up and help her but failed. He'd only had enough strength to reach out and touch his fingertips to the stone portal. *Take us both. Take Layala and me somewhere safe.* He couldn't speak it aloud, but the portal hummed to life. The ability to carry himself through vanished with his strength, but he still hoped somehow it could take them. As if a strong gust of wind swept under him, he lifted off the ground. *Layala,* he begged.

But a quiet voice whispered, "She's too far away."

He was in and out of consciousness until Vesstan's face hovered over him. "Tell Layala I'll come for her," were the last words he spoke before he lost sense of time and reality up until about a week ago. When he had enough sense to know day from night, he sent a message to Leif, his fierce, fire-haired warrior from the

East, to gather the Ravens deep inside Brightheart Forest and wait for him there. From what he heard, Piper, Fennan, and Aldrich, along with other Ravens were being held in prison. Maker above, how could he have abandoned his friends to be captured? Even if they stood their ground while telling him to run, he shouldn't have. It didn't save Layala. It did nothing but end in misery. What were they going through right now? The horrors his father was capable of... the near-constant nausea intensified.

"Briar Hollow was burned to the ground a few days ago," Vesstan called from the front porch.

Thane whirled around, a sudden energy snapping into him. "And you're just telling me this now?"

"I sent word soon after your arrival here telling Layala's aunt to leave. From what we've heard from the birds, she and the town were gone when the soldiers arrived. They still burned it of course, as they like to do."

Thane ground his teeth and started back, grunting, and swearing under his breath. Layala loved that town, it was her home, but at least her aunt and friends were alive. Maker above, at the very least that.

Birds chirped annoyingly loud in the canopy of autumn trees. Didn't they have better things to do like give him an update on Layala? A blue jay belted out a tune. He stared daggers at it.

"I wouldn't be surprised if she comes here," Vesstan said, rocking gently back and forth in his chair.

"Who?"

"Layala's aunt. You called her Evalyn. In your feverish fits you kept saying, 'tell Evalyn to run. Briar Hollow'. I sent a letter explaining what happened and told her where to find you. It's nice having a gnome around who can speak to birds."

Thane pressed on, slowly gaining strength rather than tiring as he thought he would. Maybe movement was what he needed. "Find me? Why would she trust me? She watched me steal Layala from their home at knifepoint." Why had he done that? It seemed foolish in hindsight, but then again Layala was a much different elf now than the one he had taken months before.

Vesstan lifted a shoulder. "A hunch. You're the only one who can save Layala from Castle Dredwich."

A tiny scream made Thane jump. He turned. And there was Tifapine running in from the woods with a fox right behind her. The fox's upper lip pulled up, bearing two rows of small sharp teeth, ready to devour a meal. This gnome would be his end. He swore it.

"Help!" Tif wailed. Her brown curls bounced as much as her little protruding belly on her foot tall frame.

Thane grunted. Dropping his staff, he broke into as fast of a limping run as he could manage. He cursed himself and the damn dragon for how slow he was compared to the elf he used to be. Waving his arms, he shouted, "Get back!" The fox stilled. Its big fluffy tail

poised in the air, but it kept its predatory gaze locked onto the gnome.

Tif's dress snagged on something, and she went down and disappeared among the rich green grass. The mischievous little fox started for her again. *That damn creature.* Thane stretched out his hand, focusing his energy into his magic. Tifapine lifted into sight and flew through the air. She squealed like a dying cat until she reached the cradle of his arm. He couldn't help but roll his eyes at the dramatics.

With her little body shaking, Tif clung to him, digging her sharp nails into his forearm. "I feel dizzy."

"Get!" Thane shouted at the fox and stomped his foot. The small furry beast turned and slinked back into the shadows until it disappeared.

Out of breath, Thane said, "Tifapine, what have I told you about going into the woods by yourself?"

Pushing out her bottom lip, she whimpered, "You said, 'stay in the clearing because the woods are dangerous.' But I was hungry, and the berries are just right on the other side of the tree line. Big, juicy, fat red ones. I've been eating them for days. Then that big ol' mean fox had to ruin everything."

The exertion it took to use his power and run after Tif left the pain in his abdomen burning and throbbing. Shaking his head, he sucked in shallow breaths and started back for the cottage. That little blue jay Thane saw earlier dropped down from the sky in front of him, frantically tweeting. Thane's eyebrows rose when Tifapine slapped a palm over her mouth,

nodding. What could it possibly be saying? He still found it odd that she could converse with birds.

"No!" she said through her fingers then dropped her hand. "Are you serious?"

Thane looked from the blue jay to Tif. "What?" The bird kept madly tweeting, and Tif kept up with her cryptic "nos" and "oh my goodnesses". Thane's patience was at its end, but the bird zipped away. With a sigh, Thane set his jaw and gave Tifapine a scowl.

"Oh, I sometimes forget you don't understand *tweet*." She cleared her throat. "He said they took Layala from the tower and the dragon lady is there and so is a pale one named Math-uh-whiss."

"Kis," Thane corrected.

"Kiss, you say?" Her brows shot up. "I mean, you're engaged to Layala, but I can spare a kiss on the cheek, I suppose."

"No." Thane rolled his eyes. "Math*ekis*. His name is Mathekis."

"Oh," she drawled with a blush. "Right. I swear I've heard that name before. It sounds creepy. Do we know him?"

Thane closed his eyes and pinched the bridge of his nose.

"Oh, and you know they haven't been feeding her, right? Did I tell you that?" Her already ruddy cheeks deepened in color, and she grew a sheepish grin.

Thane set Tif down and squeezed his hands into fists, digging his nails into his calloused palms. "No, you forgot to mention that *huge* detail," Thane

snapped. He marched even faster, ignoring the throbbing pain, mind whirling. He must get to her. Now. "And for one who never stops talking, I don't see how you didn't tell me. You'll go on and on about falling out of a tree when you tried to steal a bird egg but not about Layala *starving*." This gnome was absolutely infuriating. Perhaps he should call the fox back.

Tif frowned, running beside him to keep up. "Well, first of all, it wasn't just any bird, it was a Calladiran mockingbird, and I hate them. They are mean—one tried to peck my very eye out. They're only good for their eggs at breakfast. I like blue jays and sparrows best. Ravens creep me out a bit, not going to lie. And I only found out about Layala's dreadful circumstances five days ago. And it's not like you could have gotten out of bed to go help her anyway. I thought you needed to heal first, or you'd try to leave before you were ready. Believe me it was a hard secret to keep. I've never been good at keeping secrets. Especially from my High King."

If she didn't stop rambling... Thane groaned. "I could have found a way to send her food. And with no more notes or any sign from me in weeks, she probably thinks I've abandoned her or that I'm dead." He barely gained her trust fully. Who knew what was going through her mind.

Tif looked up at him, chin wobbling. "And I sure hope she doesn't think you've abandoned her. My poor Layala, cold and hungry and hopeless. The birds say she cries a lot. I should have gone with her but that

stupid portal sucked me in when it took you. I mean, I was next to you getting into my pouch for some healing leaves." She sighed. "I did try to send her a bag of berries, but my messenger birds keep dying. They get shot down. Ol' blue is my last trooper. None of the others will risk getting close to spy."

"Why *were* you next to me when the portal pulled you in?" Not that he completely disliked the gnome, but she was almost like tending to a child. An obligation he didn't need at the moment.

"I said I was getting healing leaves."

"I mean how did you catch up to us? You're as slow as a snail."

"Well, that's rude." She flipped her brown curls over her shoulder. "But anyway, when Layala said 'run', I ran after you two. Because of course she'd want me with her. When you ditched Phantom to go into the woods, I climbed up and we followed. Poor horsey, I wonder where he is now."

Pressing a firm hand against his injury, Thane carefully bent down to pick up his walking staff. Tifapine was right. He wasn't ready to invade the castle, but he must anyway. There was no telling what Mathekis or Varlett would do to Layala. His father had starved her for almost four weeks? As if that wasn't enough torture. Leaning on his staff, he made his way toward Vesstan. His feet crunched lightly over the thick grass, and he swatted at a bee that buzzed by his ear. He needed to change, get weapons, and pack a small bag of provisions. He stepped past Vesstan,

pushing open the white cottage door. "My father has removed Layala from the tower. Mathekis and Varlett are there. I must go."

With more vigor and swiftness than he'd seen Vesstan use in years, the old mage jumped up and marched after him. "You're in no condition to do so. You'll get yourself killed and then what good are you to her? To any of us?"

Thane rested his staff against the wall and left it behind. For good. The pain throbbing in his core was intense but he was used to it now. Even with the healing leaves and salves, the pain became an unceasing companion. If he didn't think about it, it seemed to dull some. Maybe getting out of here was what he needed. It would take his mind off what he'd endured in the last month. Being tortured in the cage in Newarden by Brunard and then having a dragon's fist shoved through him, but worst of all was losing Layala. Having their magical bond severed just when they knew they truly loved one another. When they accepted they would be eternal mates. Maker above, he loved that elf more than life. "I can't sit here any longer and do nothing." Thane grabbed a dark brown leather bag and started around the room to collect items he'd need for the road.

Vesstan followed close behind him. "Look how much jogging a few yards taxed your strength. And you expect to fight well-trained soldiers on your own? Fight Mathekis or the dragon shifter again? You barely survived, Thane. If it weren't for your lineage and the

aid of healing paste, you'd be dead. You know I'd love to help you more, but my magic isn't strong enough."

"My strength is returning. It will take me a day or so to reach the portal on foot in this condition and then more time to the castle. I hope it's not too late by then." He already started to formulate a plan. There were only two ways to the castle; over the bridge or repelling down the mountainside the castle was built into, which meant there was only one viable way.

"See reason. You need rest."

With a vicious glare, Thane turned. "I've *rested* for weeks while the love of my life has been starved and who knows what else was done to her! I will rest no longer."

Vesstan waited for a few beats before he said gently, "Thane, this is the first day you've been able to walk out of this cottage. You've never had to spend more than a day or two to heal and recover, but you won't make it to the portal in your condition."

"Yes. I. Will." With determination he could accomplish anything. He believed it was possible and so it was. It's how he'd done every difficult thing in the past. He shoved a change of clothes into the bag and a cloak. Before long, his weapons belt was on, his swords strapped to his back, and he was ready to walk out the door.

Vesstan lifted his chin and picked up his staff. "I'll be coming with you then."

Hardening his jaw, Thane stared at Vesstan. The old mage managed to get around this small meadow

fine but undertaking this mission was beyond him, and in this condition, Thane wouldn't be able to help. "Can you make it?"

"Oh, I'm not as weak as you perceive me to be."

Tif stood on the kitchen table, squealing loudly, and pointed out the window. "Elves! Two elves are coming! No, three!"

Thane and Vesstan exchanged a quick glance. Great. Now they would have to answer to the woodland elves and hope he wasn't recognized. Unless... Thane moved toward the window. "Who knows I'm here?"

"Only Leif and Evalyn. However, correspondence could have been intercepted."

Pulling the white curtain aside, Thane peeked out. It was two males adorned in russet brown cloaks with hoods up. They wore dark green tunics with leather arm bands over their wrists, black gloves, and charcoal-colored pants. Both were adorned with several weapons, swords, daggers. The one on the left had a small ax on his hip. A slighter figure, likely a female, wore a chocolate brown cloak and walked between them. He couldn't tell from the distance if they were friendly or foe.

CHAPTER 4

L ayala gaped at the bruises and cuts and how thin Piper was. Her cheeks were hollowed out and the clothes hung loosely off her body. *Oh, Piper.* She cried in the tower feeling sorry for herself when Piper had clearly endured much worse. Yet, she lifted her chin defiantly, prepared to die. A lump rose in Layala's throat, and she slowly stood. She desperately wanted to go to her friend but the knife resting against Piper's delicate neck held her back. "Please, release her. This has nothing to do with her."

"Her fate is entirely up to you," Tenebris said with a sneer. He twisted his narrow shoulders to get a better view of Piper and gave a quick nod to the guards holding her. The blade pressed harder, drawing a line of blood.

"No!" Layala pleaded. Her legs felt weak again. Despite Piper's wishes, she couldn't let this happen. *Think, Layala, think!*

Mathekis smiled, revealing the sharp points of his

teeth again. "Bleeding hearts are so easy to manipulate. So, you agree to do as you're told?"

Layala felt the food she just ate wanting to come back up. "Why are you doing this when you can just *tell* me to do it?" If she could stall for another day, she could find a way out of here.

Mathekis stared at her, pinning her with those wholly black eyes. "Why not?" He shifted in the chair, and it quietly creaked under his muscular frame. "I do have the time to break you if you'd rather sacrifice your friends than simply agree. I don't care which path you choose although this one is much more fun."

Break me? She didn't want to know what that might entail but bringing back the Black Mage would cost much more than Piper's life. Why hadn't Varlett called in the bargain she made? She glanced at the dragon shifter. Layala owed her a favor. She mentioned it in the woods just before she—shoved her hand through Thane. Those talons wrapped around the goblet of wine showed no signs of the damage she did. Where was her mother's willow necklace she stole? Was it destroyed for good?

King Tenebris groaned and shot to his feet. He slammed a hand on the table, shaking the glassware. With his palms flat against the white tablecloth, he leaned heavily forward inching toward Layala. She forced herself not to recoil. "I will throw you in a prison cart and kill every last person you know. Is that clear?"

Piper and Layala shared a look, and she gave a

slight shake of her head. Damn it. She couldn't let Piper sacrifice herself for this. There must be another way. If she agreed, she'd buy more time to figure something out.

Tenebris swiped his arm across the table, knocking down three goblets of wine. One fell to the floor and shattered. Layala jumped at the sound of glass breaking. The liquid spilling onto the floor was loud in the following silence. "Kill her!"

"Wait, wait," Layala pleaded. "I-I'll do it. Just don't kill her."

Further sagging in the guards' arms, Piper looked utterly defeated. Layala glanced over at Aldrich; even after his betrayal she still wanted him to help. *Look at Piper,* she silently pleaded. Aldrich only stared at the wine spilling onto the floor. Coward.

Varlett tapped her talons on the white, stained tablecloth. "Pity," she cooed. "I thought we'd at least get to drink the redhead's blood." Leaning back in her seat with a lazy grin, Varlett said to Mathekis, "I'll meet you downstairs. We have things to discuss in private." Her chair screeched on the stone as she pushed away from the table, and whisked from the room in a graceful, silent gait.

"This meeting is over." Mathekis stepped away from the table. "Remember what I said about hurting her, King." When the pale general was gone, Tenebris waved a hand at his guards to send Piper away.

"Don't do it, Layala," she shouted over her shoulder. "He will come for you!" One of the guards tied a

gag around her mouth and the door slammed behind them.

Still standing, Layala stepped back from the table and stood behind her chair. It felt safer to have a barrier between her and the king. The wine staining the tablecloth looked like blood and all she could think about was seeing Thane unmoving, scarlet liquid pooling around him. The agony on his face when Varlett tore her hand free of him. The gaping hole she felt in her own chest now—that missing part of him.

Warm breath washed over the back of her neck, and every part of her tensed. Tenebris roughly wrapped a hand under her chin and squeezed her cheeks, forcing her to look at him. Even with the hatred burning in her eyes all she thought was that his skin was soft, not that of a warrior. "This is only the beginning." His spittle landed on her face, and she closed her eyes. "If you think you've had it rough in the past month just wait. You'll suffer for causing me difficulty. You'll beg me to let you raise the Black Mage before we even allow it."

Layala gritted her teeth then spat in his face. The gob of saliva slowly slid down his cheek. His backhand was swift, and it knocked her to her hands and knees. Metallic liquid filled her mouth, and her now-split lip throbbed. She cursed herself for not wanting to get up, not wanting to fight. How many times had she been knocked down but always rose? How many times had the men in the training yard knocked her on her ass, but nothing kept her down? Certainly no backhand

from a weak elf. But lying on the cold stone and closing her eyes beckoned her. They said they would break her, but in many ways, they already had.

"High King," Aldrich said quietly. "Perhaps it's best we don't incur the wrath of our allies."

What did that mean? Staring at the ground, Layala's vision became unfocused. *Get up. Get up.* But her mind drifted to Thane on that forest floor. He didn't get up. She should have crawled to him. She should have fought harder. Tears spilled onto the smooth light-gray stone. All she wanted was to see him. To behold his beautiful face and cocky grin with her own eyes. To have his warm arms around her and whisper conceited, annoying things in her ear. She would laugh and tell him what an arrogant prick he was, and he would smile at that. Maker, how she longed to see his smile.

A heavy black boot crushed down on the fingers of her left hand. She bit back a wail, and tried to pull free of the king's weight, but was trapped between him and the stone. "Take her back to the tower."

He twisted his foot, grinding her bones. Holy Maker above, that hurt. She let out a quiet whimper, biting down until her jaw ached. She might not have the strength to fight back, but she wouldn't give him the satisfaction of showing her pain.

"High King," Aldrich said with more force this time.

His boot lifted off and Layala sighed, tucking her stinging hand to her chest. The king's quiet footsteps

petered out of the room and a door closed. Aldrich dropped into a squat in front of Layala, lightly grabbed her arms and pulled her to her feet. No offered sympathies came but he said, "You can sit and finish your meal." And that was even better.

ALDRICH OFFERED his arm as they stepped into the corridor outside the dining hall. Layala took a step away from him. It did not matter if he was nicer than the others. She wouldn't fall for it. She trusted him even less now that he was being kind.

A few feminine voices drifted from down the corridor. She stared past the paintings of previous royals on the walls, the many tall vases of fresh flowers and over the red running carpet down the center of the hall. The light footsteps drew closer, their giggles louder. Was it the princess? Was Talon in on this too or had she also been a victim? After all, Aldrich nearly impaled her with an arrow. Maybe he wanted to take out the other heir so there was no question.

Talon came around the corner wearing a bright-yellow gown with white gloves. Her brown hair was pulled high on her head bringing out her fair skin and blushed cheeks. Beside her, Vyra and another maiden Layala recognized from the Summer Solstice stopped and stared. Even Talon seemed to be at a loss for words. Did Layala look so horrible that they were aghast at her appearance?

"Come on," Aldrich said, tilting his head to the left.

Ignoring him, she took a step toward Talon, but she couldn't find anything to say. The only time she even somewhat trusted Talon led to her being shot with an arrow. What if Talon had been in on it to lure Layala out to the waterfall?

Talon's brows furrowed, and she pushed away from her friends. Her heels clicked loudly as she stamped toward them, glaring at Aldrich. "You said she was with Thane. Father said after he rescued them from Calladira that they left because Thane didn't want to give up his position as High King." She set those fierce green eyes on Layala. "And what happened to your face?"

Layala brought a hand to her lip, almost forgetting about the dull throbbing pain. Maker above, could Talon truly be this clueless? Or was it an act? Layala didn't see any reason for her to be fake about this. Typical Talon would be to rub her demise in her face.

Aldrich stepped in between them. "Don't ask questions you don't want answers to, Talon. Now run along with your friends like a good little daddy's girl." His hand gripped Layala's arm hard, and he started pulling her down the hall. Layala stumbled over her own feet with his force.

"Aldrich," Talon snapped. "Where is Thane? Where is my brother?"

"Go play," Aldrich said over his shoulder.

"They tried to murder him," Layala called. "Left

him for dead in that haunted forest. Please find him, Talon. Find Thane!"

Aldrich squeezed her arm until his nails pierced through her skin and Layala yelped. "Stop. You're hurting me."

"That's the point. Now keep your mouth shut before my father hears you and you'll have much worse than a split lip and broken fingers."

When he brought her back to her room, the door creaked open, and he gestured for her to go inside. Why was she here? The king said to bring her to the tower. As much as she wanted to go dive onto the soft bed she knew awaited, her feet wouldn't go forward.

"Go. The king can't let his cruelty get in the way of reason. Mathekis specifically said not to hurt you."

"I don't understand you."

"I'm not cruel, Laya. I don't want you to be hurt, but I made my decision and now this is the path we both must walk."

"Not cruel? You betrayed your friend—your *brother* —for a chance at the throne. What would you call that?"

"Ambition."

She turned away, unable to look at him for another moment without wanting to claw his eyes out. "Ugh, you disgust me. You're worse than Tenebris. At least he never pretended to be something he wasn't. Thane will never forgive you."

"He's dead. I don't need his forgiveness."

That statement momentarily stole the breath from

her lungs. "You and Tenebris keep saying that because you're afraid. Afraid of what he will do to you."

Aldrich grabbed her arm and dragged her inside the room. With both hands wrapped around her arms, he pinned her against the wall, chest heaving up and down. His fingers dug in and a fiery temper she'd never seen in his eyes blazed. "Even if Thane is alive, he can't win. The people, the army won't turn on their true king. He will be seen as the enemy. You get that right?" Droplets of his spit hit Layala's cheek. "Thane can't beat him. He is nothing but a fallen prince with no land and no *wife*."

Layala rammed her knee hard into Aldrich's groin, then shoved him in the chest. "Get your hands off me. I may have had a weak moment back in that dining hall, but it won't happen again."

Clutching between his legs, Aldrich moaned and stumbled back a few steps. "Damn it, Layala. I'm trying to help you. Can't you see that? Or are you so blind by your loss that you can't see reason?"

"If that were true, you'd help me escape. The only one of us blind is you. For a crown, you'd trade in the freedom of all."

His stare was full of hurt and chaotic storms as if he was unsure of everything. "You're wrong. I will bring magic back to the elves of Palenor and they will love me for it." On his way out, he looked back once then slammed the door behind him.

Layala groaned as the pain from Aldrich's tight grip, her crushed bloody hand, and her throbbing lip

set in. She made her way over to the bed and fell onto the soft, silky fabric. At least she wasn't back in the tower. There were only a few minutes to relax before a quiet knock sounded and the door popped open. Reina stepped inside, patting her hands down her apron, and then dipped into a bow.

As she lay on the bed, Reina cleaned and wrapped Layala's bloody, broken fingers and dabbed healing balm on her split lip. "I'm so sorry, my dear."

Layala simply closed her eyes, her mind lost in the conversation at the dining table. Why would Mathekis or the Black Mage care how she was treated? And he'd been gone for four hundred years but they still followed his orders like he was here. If she was his life-line, it made perfect sense they'd want her protected. The Black Mage was what gave them purpose. And what was time for them? Varlett had been alive for thousands of years. A few hundred wouldn't seem so long to her.

They'd waited for her to be born and then waited again for her to resurface. Varlett spoke of seeing her mother give over the willow tree necklace, which meant she allowed Evalyn to take her away. Had the dragon known where she was the entire time? Was she simply waiting for something? And why make a deal with Tenebris if she knew? Or was it only Mathekis who made the deal? That would mean that Varlett never told him where Layala was. Either the three of them didn't trust each other or some piece of this puzzle was missing.

Her maid pulled the lavender silk cover over her torso and stepped back, folding her hands in front of her. "Is there anything else I can get you?"

With her belly full, too full to the point she thought she might be sick, and her injuries attended to, aside from an escape plan... "No but thank you for asking."

Reina curtsied and started for the exit.

"Wait," Layala said. Even if her mind and body were tired and hurt, her instincts kept firing. That core drive of self-preservation screamed at her. "I need a knife."

"You can't be thinking of doing anything, Lady. You're in no condition and you're outnumbered two hundred to one."

Even if she didn't get the chance to use it, she wanted it. *Needed* something to feel safe again. "Get me a knife. One that I can conceal in my dress. Please."

CHAPTER 5

T hane slowly opened the cottage door. The hinges squealed quietly, and he stepped out into the warm balmy air. The pair of approaching elves pulled their hoods back to reveal lunar tattooed faces, one redhaired, the other a rich golden brown, styled with braids and twists, one of them had an eyepatch—not Fennan or Aldrich but friends, nonetheless. The female in the center kept her face hidden, however. Only a hint of brown skin showed. *And who might you be?* Thane thought.

The dirt path leading to the front entrance wasn't wide enough for the three of them shoulder to shoulder. Gunner and Leif glanced at each other, their pace picking up, pumping their arms in a speed walk. A race, of course. Predictably mischievous, Leif shoved Gunner over green, round-trimmed shrubbery. With a curse and a grunt, Gunner rolled and sprang back to his feet. Thane couldn't help but chuckle, then imme-

diately regretted it. He clutched his torso, wincing at the pain a simple laugh caused.

"Don't ruin my rhododendrons," Vesstan called and sighed, hobbling out from inside. "Bunch of brutes, the lot of you."

Leif gave an apologetic shrug, while Gunner carefully hopped back over the flowering bushes, adjusting his slinking black eyepatch. Thane didn't know how he truly lost his eye. He told a different story anytime he was asked.

It was good to see familiar faces. It felt like a lifetime ago that he'd fought beside them in Doonafell. Although he never questioned the Ravens' loyalty to him, the situation with his father and Thane's attempt to murder him would surely test it. Thane lifted a hand in greeting, and when the pair reached the patio, they both dropped to one knee. The mysterious female waited a few yards down the path with her hands folded in front of her.

"High King," Leif said, while Gunner said, "High Prince." The pair looked at each other, confused.

"He's our rightful High King, you idiot," Leif said. "He was crowned High King; therefore he is."

"I meant no disrespect. I only thought..." Gunner's tan cheeks flushed, and he cursed under his breath.

"Leif. Gunner. My Ravens, rise," Thane said, patting them both on the shoulders. They both stood with eager smiles. "Until I remove my father, there will be debate on who the High King is." Thane cleared his

throat, unsure where to take this conversation. Would they be willing to go to war with Tenebris and their fellow soldiers—their brothers in arms. "As you probably know, I did try to kill my father and then took his place as High King. Our laws state—"

Leif grinned, wrinkling the crescent moon tattoos on the corners of his eyes, and grabbed Thane's hand to pull him into a rough embrace. "We will follow you into any battle, against any foe, Thane." His rolling accent sounded thicker than ever. A big hand slapped hard on Thane's back, taking the air from his lungs. Pain shot down his spine from the impact. He grimaced but kept quiet. Maker above, would this injury ever heal? He didn't know if it was the dragon's poison that kept his body from recovering faster or if it was too large of a wound. "Oh, apologies, sire." Leif pulled back, gripping his shoulders and held him at arm's length. "Are you hurt?"

"It's nothing. I'm better now."

Leif's blue eyes, so bright against his bronzed brown skin, flicked to Gunner. "You never mentioned injuries in your letter. You only said we'd be targeted by Tenebris, and we should go into hiding. The Ravens are ready to be at your side, no matter the cost. We will fight to stop the Black Mage and put you back on the throne even if that means battling against King Tenebris."

Warmth blossomed in Thane's heart. Maker, it felt good to know he wasn't alone in this fight. But battle

against Tenebris would have to wait until Thane could wield a sword properly again.

"I appreciate that, but who is your friend?"

"Oh," Leif said, folding his arms and stepping aside to make way for the maiden. "She insisted on coming. Found her on the way here."

"And she is?"

The maiden pulled her hood back, and Thane's chest instantly tightened. He knew that face well even though he'd only seen her once. "Evalyn, I presume."

"You," she snapped with accusation.

Thane couldn't help but smirk. "Me."

"It was you in the pub that night. I should have known." Her brown eyes dragged down Thane's body then back up. "You've certainly grown since you were a boy."

"I suppose I would have."

"And what now, hmm? The letter said you and your father had a falling out over her. That you actually love her. Hard to believe but the only reason I'm not going to take advantage of your injured state and kill you right now is I need your help to get her back. And if you love her, you'll do it. Then she'll be coming home with me. You've done enough damage."

Leif and Thane exchanged a wary look. With a deep, hopefully calming, pull of air into his lungs, Thane cooled the tension building inside him. After he took Layala against her will, he expected this. "I do love her, and as far as who she's going to go home with, well, that will be up to her."

She scoffed. "Oh, you suddenly want to give her a choice, do you? You're not going to try to force her to stay with you? Use her?"

Now he knew where Layala got her attitude from. It was almost like he'd been transported back to the early days with Layala having the same arguments. "I said I loved her. What about that would make you think I'd use her in any way?" He snapped, the pain in his abdomen began to burn again. "Once I explained things, she was free to leave at any time."

"You expect me to believe you after your soldiers held me captive, threatened me, and gave her no choice but to go with you?" She lifted a hand and jabbed a crooked finger at him, "If you tried to force yourself on her—"

"You're crossing a line, Evalyn," Thane tried to keep the snarl out of his voice but couldn't. "I would never do that. Never. And I had no choice but to take her that day. The mate spell would have turned us into pale ones. Once she knew, she tried to find a way out of it, as did I."

Evalyn's eyebrows shot up in surprise. "The consequence of not fulfilling the mate spell..." she trailed off and rolled one of the berries on her twine necklace between her fingers.

Mage Vesstan half stepped in front of Thane. His shaky hand dragged over his mid-belly length, white beard. "Today is the first day in nearly a month he's been able to walk without collapsing. I understand you are frustrated but we all are."

Thane turned and glared. He didn't want the pity of Leif, Gunner, or Evalyn for that matter, when they had a mission to accomplish.

Leif blinked a few times. "You, sire?"

"Unfortunately."

Gunner folded his arms. "We heard rumors for weeks. Some said you were killed by Brunard, then your father announced that you were to be executed for treason. Guards reported that Piper and Fennan are in prison. The rest of us went into hiding as soon as Tenebris started having Ravens killed in the streets, claiming mutiny." Gunner had the same distinct accent as Leif. "Think you ought to know that Layala is rumored to be held in the tower. At first, rumors said it was because she conspired with Brunard to kill *you*. Of course, we knew that was false. The girl was clearly in love with you last I saw her. Nobody will forget the way she straddled you on your throne—"

Thane loudly cleared his throat, eyes darting to Evalyn.

Gunner snapped his mouth shut, opened it, scratched his head.

Leif jumped in to save the situation, "It was perfectly proper."

Evalyn's raised eyebrows said she didn't believe it. "Layala, straddling you? In front of a crowd no less. A bit unexpected from her."

Leif chortled nervously. "It was the wine, surely. It can make even the sweetest maidens a little promiscuous."

Thane shook his head, not wanting to carry on with what happened that night, and lifted his shirt, showing the massive scar on his abdomen. The sight of it should be enough to detract from furthering Layala's said promiscuity. "A dragon shifter is what almost did me in. I think her claws are poisonous. She's working with my father and took Layala."

The harsh lines on Evalyn's face softened a little and her hand slowly crept up to cover her mouth in surprise.

"Damn," Leif said, rubbing the back of his neck. "That descendent of the gods' blood must run strong."

Everyone found it hard to believe, even Thane himself, but he couldn't deny it. He often wondered why his mother and sister didn't have the ability to heal as he did if it came through her blood as they say, and neither were mages. Perhaps he was simply favored by the Maker. "But you were right. Layala didn't try to kill me. She saved me from Brunard. It's a long story." He tucked his shirt back into his trousers. "But we need to get her before it's too late."

"Too late, sire?" Leif asked.

"Yes," Evalyn said, still toying with her strand of slumber berries around her neck. He remembered those too. "What is it exactly your father wants with her?"

With a deep breath, Thane told them the truth. How he took Tenebris to the Void and meant to kill him. What his father planned to use Layala for and his

deal with Mathekis and the pale ones. Why he'd gone to Brunard in the first place. That his mate bond was now broken. "And after we get Layala, and any others who've been imprisoned, I will take back my throne."

"Our loyalty will always be with you, sire," Leif said, bowing his head.

Gunner scrunched his nose and let out a long breath. "I can't believe Aldrich is a traitor. He was close to you for years. A Raven. He swore fealty to you, to *us*, publicly."

Thane tilted his head, confused. A sudden heat crept up his neck spilling into his face. A traitor? "What do you mean?" He hadn't heard anything about Aldrich specifically. He assumed he was being held with Piper and Fennan.

Gunner pursed his lips and rubbed a hand over the smooth tan skin on his jawline. "Sire, Aldrich joined your father. Some are saying he is a bastard son. Your half-brother."

Gulping down the sick feeling rising in his throat, he shook his head. "No, that can't be." As they'd said, Aldrich had sworn fealty to Thane. Aldrich had been by his side every day since Thane saved his life on the battlefield years before. If it weren't for Thane, Aldrich would be a pale one or dead. And he would know if his father had another son, wouldn't he? How could Tenebris have kept that secret? Thane hadn't seen his father with any mistresses. For all his faults, he thought the one good quality his father had was

loyalty to his mother... but why else would Tenebris take any interest in Aldrich rather than imprison him?

Leif's mouth twisted, and he cleared his throat. "We don't know if he is your father's son for certain, there has been no announcement made, but we do know Aldrich has rarely left Tenebris's side."

It felt like a wall of bricks began to fall one by one all around Thane. Layala said she thought one of his friends was a traitor, and had reported their movements, but he wouldn't hear of it. He wouldn't even allow that thought to fester. His rough fingers glided across his sweaty forehead. His mind whirled around every memory with his friend and Layala and never once had there been a hint that he'd betrayed them, had there? "Aldrich might be pretending to be on my father's side. If we can get word to him, he might be able to help us free Layala and the Ravens being held."

"I don't think that is wise." Leif's mouth twisted into a frown. "Right now, we don't know whose side he is on. We can't trust him. He's had over three weeks to help Layala or any of the others and has done nothing but be Tenebris's lap dog. I have a couple friends on the inside giving me information. My cousin is a cook, and a lady friend of mine is a maid. We're to meet her at Adley's Apothecary at dusk."

If Aldrich was on his father's side... he felt sick that he'd been such a fool. He couldn't see it. "Then we need to leave now to make it in time. We can go through the stone portal."

Leif and Gunner grinned. "We hoped you would say that," Leif said. "It took us a week to get here."

"At least you know your stamina is up to par."

Leif let out a deep belly laugh. "You lot are soft in the north. We run miles each day in the east. We're used to it."

"Did you walk this whole way?" Thane asked Evalyn. She was a woman in her sixties, human, and although he was sure she could walk fine, it was a long way from Briar Hollow.

"I had a horse up until we reached the Calladira border. Gunner and Leif suggested I leave it to be less noticeable by woodland elf patrol."

"I trust they took care of you on the way."

Gunner and Leif both put their hands to their chests, mouths agape, as if offended he'd even have to ask. But they could be a sour pair, difficult to get used to for some. Although from the company he saw in the pub in Briar Hollow, she couldn't be too bothered.

"They were kind enough to bring me along and shared their food. Need their mouths washed out with soap but I can't complain too much." Her lips pressed tightly together, and she brushed her hand down the front of her cloak. He had a feeling there was something else she wanted to say. A moment later she met Thane's gaze. "You're different than I expected—your highness."

"You can call me Thane. You're Layala's only family." At least Evalyn wasn't as hard to convince as Layala was. But Leif and Gunner no doubt had a hand

in that, and it was clear to all that Thane and Tenebris were on opposing sides.

The clop of Vesstan's staff as he hobbled disrupted the chatter. He paused at the entrance of the cottage and looked back, "Let's all sit down for a chat so you can work out a proper plan or all you'll do is get yourselves killed."

CHAPTER 6

The portal hummed to life at Thane's touch. His legs were on the verge of giving out, but he was on a mission and that alone gave him the strength to continue. At the base of the round stone as ancient as the very mountains, bright colorful wildflowers bloomed. Their aroma filled the balmy forest air. Thane looked up searching for the woodpecker who smacked his beak into the trunk of a tree like a hammer.

"So, this stone circle will bring us to The Valley?" Evalyn asked, skeptically.

"It will," Thane answered. He and Evalyn argued about her coming along. This would be dangerous, and she'd be putting her life at risk. It was better if she stayed with Vesstan until he could bring Layala to her, but the woman was as stubborn as the she-elf he loved.

"Hello, again," the voices of the portal hissed. "You survived. We are happy." It was as if the stone was

many people and they stood all around them, some closer, some farther away, all unseen. Were they ghosts of past mages tied to this place?

"We need passage into Palenor." Thane took a deep breath, holding his injury tighter. The portal began to pull at his magic, his energy, and the ache intensified, throbbing with his pulse. Leif and Gunner both watched him warily, as if he was a fragile glass about to fall off a shelf. "Preferably on the outskirts of the Valley of the Sun. I'm not up for a walk through the unnamed forest when it's almost dark."

"As you wish."

The center of the stone circle swirled to life, like rippling blue water.

Gunner cleared his throat. "Uh, you've done this before, right?"

"Many times. Follow me." Thane dropped his hands to his sides, clenched his jaw and stepped through. He appeared on the grassy green lip of the Valley's edge, overlooking his city. The setting sun stained the sky pink, coral, and a deep red. The golden rooftops sparkled in the dying light; Maker it was marvelous. Any other day he might stand here and admire the beauty of mother nature. Listening to the bustle of the city below where people walked the cobblestone streets, children ran and played, and the gong rang every evening as the sunset; a tribute to those who died in the war against the pale ones. He might bask in the sun's warmth and study the way the bright orb radiated behind Castle Dredwich at this

hour. But this day, Thane's heart ached as he stared at the many peaks and towers built into the towering rock in the distance. Whipping wind moved the Palenor flag in giant waves like the rolling ocean. It wasn't long ago he'd laughed and enjoyed himself at the Summer Solstice for the first time since he was a child. Without his father's ominous presence, he'd been able to be himself. He didn't have to worry his father might get angry and give orders to cut off someone's head or scold him for being too friendly with the "common folk." That was one thing Tenebris was adamant about, "never show the people weakness by relating to them. You must always appear to be above them," he'd say. To be free of Tenebris, even if for a short while, let him discover who he was inside. He'd danced and laughed like he hadn't in years and allowed himself to truly fall for Laya. But a dark cloud loomed over the castle. His father ruled there now, and Layala was a prisoner inside those deep-gray stone walls. Caged, like his heart felt with her gone.

Leif appeared at his side and tilted his head. "This way, sire."

Running low on stamina, Thane took a deep breath. The pain in his gut throbbed like a fire licking at his flesh. It was difficult to focus on anything but that, and his heavy gear impeded him further. But at least he didn't bear the extra weight of a little gnome. Leif volunteered to carry Tifapine, although she couldn't weigh more than ten pounds. He closed his eyes for a moment, clenching his teeth together,

willing the throbbing to stop. Maker, it was like someone shoved a hot poker inside him and dug it around. A blinding white light filled his vision, and his ears rang with a high-pitched whine. He felt himself wobble and pressed his palm flat across the injury. The pressure eased the searing pain if only in a minuscule amount.

A gentle hand gripped under his elbow, steadying him. "I think you need rest, sire," Evalyn said. The concern lining her deep-brown eyes warmed his soul; she didn't completely hate him. He didn't know if he could stomach someone with blind loathing at this moment.

"I'll be fine," he wheezed, and winced at how out of breath he was.

"I don't presume to tell a High King of the Elves what he is or is not capable of, but if you can't stand on your own, you certainly can't infiltrate a castle. Mage Vesstan was correct. You need rest, your highness."

"Thane," he amended, drawing in shallow breaths.

She pursed her lips. "Alright then, Thane. I love her too and I want her back, but you need strength to do it."

"Once we're at the apothecary, I'll rest for the night. But we must not miss meeting the person with news of Layala. She might not stay around if we don't show on time."

"Can I help you keep your balance at least? I'm

afraid you're too large for me to be of much use for anything else."

He smiled through the pain, urging forward to push through the ache. "Thank you, Evalyn. Your kindness means more to me than you know."

WHEN THEY ENTERED the cobblestone streets teeming with elves, Thane pulled his hood up. He couldn't risk anyone recognizing him and getting into a fight with city guards. He didn't want to kill his own people, and walking at this point was a struggle.

They passed bookshops and smithies. A hammer clanked onto a horseshoe followed by sizzling hot metal in cool water when the elf male dropped it in. Leif gestured toward a poster nailed to a wooden pole. Thane paused for a moment.

WANTED: RAVEN WARRIORS
For crimes of Treason, Murder, and Mutiny.
All must be brought to justice for the safety of Palenor.
A REWARD of FIVE GOLD coins is offered for information
that leads to the capture and execution of any Raven or
known loyalists to the false traitor High King, Thane
Athayel.

A wave of heat flooded his body and Thane grumbled. So, he was the traitor now, not his father who would sell them to the pale ones for power. He glanced

around to see if the people watched him too closely or if he drew suspicion in his cloak and hood, but no one appeared to take interest.

"Come on, sire," Gunner said quietly, adjusting his eyepatch. "The poster holds no true meaning. You are not a traitor."

Thane shook his head, and they started off again. Leif nudged people aside to make way for Thane, but the streets thinned out as the sky began to darken. His stomach gurgled at the smell of roasting boar. It wasn't that Vesstan was a bad cook, but he only ate fruits, vegetables, nuts, and bread with honey and that's all Thane had too. Smoke rolled out of a beige stone chimney. A place named Effy's Bakery. In the windows, layered cakes on platters were on display, and trays of buttered rolls and swirling buns with glaze. A lady turned the *open* sign over to *closed* as they went by.

A shorter, stout elf bumped into Thane, sending tendrils of pain through his core. Thane clenched his fists and sucked in a sharp breath, unable to stop himself from bending slightly at the waist. He didn't want to admit his incapacity, but Thane was in no condition to be on a rescue mission.

It was one of his father's guards who stopped and said, "Apologies, sir. Are you alright?"

Thane quickly turned his face away, staring at the light-tan stone under his feet. He didn't dare speak or they'd recognize his voice. Preparing for the worst, he slid his hand to the thirteen-inch dagger at his hip.

Gunner grabbed Thane's arm, steadying him. "He's simply had too much to drink. I'll be sure to get him inside." It was a risky move drawing attention to himself like that. The Ravens were wanted elves. Thane watched the guards' boots shuffle closer, and slowly withdrew his dagger from the sheath, keeping it hidden under his cloak. Leif would be more recognizable with his red hair and close friendship with Thane. He wisely remained quiet.

"You from Pridam?" the guard asked.

"Malock," Gunner answered.

"I always liked the markings the elves from the east do on their skin. Yours are lunar phases. Does it mean anything?"

Thane quietly groaned, hoping it would be enough for Gunner to end this conversation. Too many questions. Too much time spent in one place.

"It's a family tradition, but I best get him inside before he retches." He pulled on Thane's arm, and they started off.

The guard called out, "Wait."

Letting out a huff, Thane bit down, gripping his dagger's handle tighter. He stood at his full height and glanced up at the sky. The last of the pink and blue faded, revealing the stars. With fewer people on the streets, they could possibly kill these two without drawing a crowd if it came to it.

"I think you dropped this."

Thane glanced back. The guard held a folded piece of parchment with a black Raven seal that would be

their unveiling. *Shit.* Thane's heart thundered. With narrowed eyes, the other guard snatched it, and pulled it open. *Damn it all.* Gunner's dark-brown eye flicked to Thane and his throat bobbed. If there was nothing important in it, they could claim it wasn't theirs and keep moving.

"What's in it?" Thane breathed.

"Locations, names," Gunner whispered. "We can't let them leave with it." The quiet *shing* of Gunner's dagger sliding from his sheath rang as he stepped forward and grabbed the parchment. "A letter from my grandmother. Thank you for letting me know. She's ill." He attempted to pull it, but the guard didn't let go.

"That is a Raven seal. Your grandmother a Raven?"

"My brother was. He died. Damn pale ones. She still uses the stamp to seal letters. She's sentimental." He pulled again and the two of them began a staring match both unwilling to let go of the parchment.

"How'd you lose that eye?"

"Stabbed by an intruder who broke into my home."

Another set of guards came around the corner, and Thane silently cursed.

"Orders, sire?" Leif whispered as he stepped beside Thane.

"Take Evalyn and the gnome and go ahead."

There was little choice now. In three strides, Thane was at the side of the guard, unwilling to let the parchment go, and shoved his dagger into his heart. The

guard let out a quiet breath, mouth gaping. The other went for his sword, and Gunner stuck him through the middle.

"The other two?" Gunner asked, guiding the guard he stabbed slowly to the ground. He touched his forehead and whispered a quiet prayer, "May you rest and find peace this world doesn't offer in the eternities."

The other soldiers ran at them with swords drawn. Gunner threw two knives, hitting both his marks directly in the chest. After a few staggered steps, they hit the ground. Blood pooled around their bodies, reflecting the moonlight.

"Leave them," Thane ordered, looking around. There were sure to be witnesses. They needed to move. Now. Gunner grabbed hold of Thane's arm again, offering assistance as they jogged down the street. The pain seemed to recede slightly from the rush of tense energy coursing through his veins.

"How far are we from the apothecary?" Thane asked, barely able to catch his breath.

"Two blocks," Leif answered, cutting into an alleyway. They splashed through a puddle and passed by windows with orange firelight. When they came out two streets over Thane sighed with relief; the sign read Adley's Apothecary. Not only could he rest but maybe she would have a remedy for him. The black spots appearing across his vision and the weakness in his limbs made it difficult to walk without stumbling. *Come on, keep going.*

Strong hands on either side, grabbed hold. "Steady

now," Leif said. He knocked four quick raps on the wood door. The hinges groaned, and a lady in a gray dress with dark hair piled on her head stood inside. The warm glow of candles and bottles of various ambers, reds, and blues behind her was inviting.

Her eyes widened when they landed on Thane's face. "High King," she gasped. "Get inside, quickly."

The black spots were larger now and as Thane's boots crossed the threshold, creaking on the wood floorboards, his legs gave out. Gunner stopped him from crashing into the ground hard, but once Thane's back lay on the warm wood, he closed his eyes and gave into the darkness.

Chapter 7

Fire crackled in the great stone hearth that connected Layala's room to Thane's. Or what was once Thane's room. It smelled of cedar and light smoke even if most of it went up into the chimney. She hadn't dared open the stone wall until she had the cover of darkness and a slumbering castle. The stars twinkled outside her window and crickets chirped merrily. She rose out of the soft bed, her heart beating faster with each step.

Layala took in a deep breath and pressed her hand on the white stone mantel over the fire. It was warm enough in this room a fire wasn't needed, but after many freezing nights in the tower, she'd insisted it be lit. Sweating was better than shivering.

Feeling along the top, the smooth stone had no blemishes. Was there a button or lever to open this thing? She dragged her hand along both sides and then stood with her arms folded, inspecting it. It looked ordinary, beautiful, and ornate with crown

molding, but there didn't appear to be any tricky switches. Did it only open from Thane's side? She grumbled and paced the room. The food from dinner gave her energy she hadn't had in weeks even though her swollen lip and hand throbbed from Tenebris's abuse.

Her gaze kept drifting to the mantel and then she froze. The fire pokers. There were three of them. More than necessary. With her breath quickening, she hurried across the room and wrapped her palm around the middle one. It pulled free. She grabbed the left, and it too came loose. Damn. Maybe she'd been wrong. She grabbed the right and tugged. It didn't come free. She pushed it back and the grinding of stone made her smile. The stone wall turned ninety degrees, leaving an opening on either side of the fire.

A masculine fragrance that smelled of forests and rivers and the wild hit her. Her throat tightened uncomfortably. The room smelled like him. She wrapped her arms around herself, and tears stung her eyes. She crawled onto the bed, pulling the soft fabric of his pillow to her nose, and inhaled deeply. Maker above, she missed him. She lay down, pulling the blankets up to her neck and tears spilled down her face until she had no more.

She rolled over and peered at the sheer white curtains over the glass doors. Could she slip off Thane's balcony and get away? If she managed to get to the ground, there was still the matter of getting past guards and over the bridge. But if she found a way to

escape, would Tenebris kill Piper, Fennan, Reina and Pearl? The guilt already nudged at her insides.

After basking in Thane's scent for a while and relaxing on his bed, she got up and wandered the room. Her feet quietly padded on the cool stone floor as she made her way to the large nine-drawer dresser. Running her fingers over the ivy etching, she smiled at the candlestick set on top. She'd once thrown it at Thane in her failed attempt to murder him. Maker, that seemed like a lifetime ago. A corner of a piece of parchment stuck out from his top-right drawer. *What is that?* Curiosity getting the better of her, she tugged it loose. It was folded into a square. Should she peek at his private things?

Her fingers deftly peeled the edge back, and she opened it. She spread it out fully on the top of the white dresser and a chill rolled over her skin. It was a charcoal sketch of—*her.* Capturing her solemn elven features perfectly, wide eyes lined with thick lashes, black hair spilling all around her like a mass of waves. She looked so sad. Was this how she was perceived? When had Thane drawn this? On the bottom in a charming scrawl, it read: *the maiden in my dreams.*

"I'm going to find you, Thane," she whispered, choking on a sob.

The fireplace scraped and churned and Layala jumped. She looked about the room frantically for a place to hide, and shoved the drawing into the dresser. She slowly backed up, her pulse drumming in her throat. It was too late to go for cover now.

Soft brown curls and a beautiful blue gown came through. Talon looked left then right and found Layala. "You need to go. Now." She jerked the fireplace closed and her heels tapped loudly, and her dress swished with each step as she marched for Layala. She held a glass bottle in her hand. "Here, drink this. It should give you enough energy to escape."

"What's going on?" Layala asked, pressing her back into the wall. She kept her hands at her sides, rather than take the bottle. She didn't trust Talon. This was the princess who lured her into the woods to be skewered with an arrow after all.

"You'll have to go out the window. Stay in the shadows. I'll try to stall him." Talon grabbed Layala's uninjured hand and shoved the bottle of light-blue liquid into it. "Come on. Hurry."

Layala shook her head. "I can't leave. What if your father kills Piper and Fennan?"

"He won't..." her wide green eyes showed real fear as if she hadn't thought about that. "He'll—He'll keep them as leverage for now." She glanced warily at the door. "I'm not as big of a fool as my father and Aldrich think I am. Oh, I might play the part well, but I know that wasn't exactly what happened. Thane wouldn't just walk away." She took a deep breath. "And right now, my *real* brother is hurting, and he needs *you*. You're a mage. You can help him. I heard that creepy lady talking about how she shoved her—hand *through* him. I know he can heal fast but—" she cupped her mouth, and a tear ran down her cheek. "Oh, Maker

above, what if he's dead? What if it's too late? If he was alive, he'd be here to get you. I know he would."

"He sent me a note. I don't know why he hasn't come but I believe he's alive," Layala said even though she wasn't entirely sure, but she had to believe. "Do you have any idea where he is? Or where he might hide? Your father's entire army will be searching for him."

She slowly shook her head. "I can't believe this is happening," Talon cried, pushing her hands into her hair. "My father has one of *them* here. Here inside my home. He's trying to hide it, but I *saw* him." She started to pace, her breath coming faster and faster. "My father is a bloody traitor and so is Aldrich."

There was much Talon didn't know. It would take too long to explain. Three loud knocks interrupted the silence. It took her a moment to realize it came from her room.

"Open the door! We're leaving!" She knew that malevolent voice too well for not having heard it much. King Tenebris was in the corridor with a host of guards no doubt.

"*Leaving?*" Panicky sweat prickled on her back. "Leaving where?"

"To the pale ones," Talon whispered. "All these years he's claimed he wanted to find you to destroy the Void but—but I think he means to sacrifice you to them somehow."

Sacrifice me? Holy shit. Maybe that was why they wouldn't say how she could bring the Black Mage

back. What if they had to sacrifice her life for his... "He doesn't want to destroy the Void. He—"

Another jarring knock. "Open the door this instant or I'll have it kicked down. You won't like what I do next."

"Go," Talon hissed, and shoved Layala. She bumped into one of the large wooden posts on Thane's bed then turned, tucked the small bottle to her chest, and ran. Throwing open the doors to a burst of cool night air, billowed her hair like stalks of wheat. Once at the balcony's stone edge, she pulled the stopper on the bottle and drained it in two big gulps. The fizzy liquid burned her eyes and nose, but the effects trickled out from her chest to her limbs with a zing of energy and strength. Even her mind was sharper. She gripped the stone railing and peered down. This was the second story; she could make it.

Quiet voices drifted up. Guards. She ducked and caught sight of a tall tree to the right. It was a luminor with star-shaped blue-and-silver-tipped leaves, its branches strong. Clouds covered the moon, blanketing the castle grounds in darkness. She said a silent "thank you" to the Maker for the coverage and climbed up on the balcony's edge. In a crouch, she held on as a gust of wind wobbled her. She cursed herself for not changing out of her dress. The heavy fabric around her legs would make this difficult. The tree was five—six feet away, but there was a branch she could grip; all she had to do was jump.

Loud booms and wood cracked as the door was

kicked in. "Where is she?!" Tenebris roared. "Find her now!"

Layala took a deep breath. *One. Two...* She pushed off and leapt, flying through the night air. Wrapping her hands around the branch, it bowed under her weight. She almost yelped at the stinging of her injured hand. The healing balm hadn't had enough time to work properly and with broken bones it might take days. She breathed through the pain and murmured to the branch, "If you snap, I swear..." Shimming sideways, she cursed Tenebris for crushing her hand every inch of the way, and quietly climbed down. Kneeling with one knee in the damp grass, hidden among the shadows behind the overgrown, thick bushes, she watched a pair of guards walk by, oblivious to her presence. The brick path leading around the castle was clear both ways. Ahead there was a large blooming poplar tree surrounded by round green shrubbery. There was a massive open space between that and the horse stables, the only other place to hide. The bridge over the river was at least half a mile from here. Steeling her breath, she lifted the bottom fabric of her dress and took off. Just as she crossed the path, the doors to Thane's balcony crashed open. Layala glanced back. King Tenebris and a host of guards flooded onto the terrace.

"Stop her! Sound the alarm! Do not let her cross that bridge!"

There was no point in hiding now. Her legs and lungs burned with the effort as she ran like the

galloping horses in the fields. Her eyes watered with the force of the wind. Heavy, armored footsteps thudded to the left. She veered to miss the guard as he reached out. He grasped the bottom of her dress and yanked. Layala pitched forward and crashed onto her hands and knees. "You bastard," she spit and rolled. He stood over her and she shoved her foot into his belly, sending him flying back onto his ass.

Jumping up, Layala ran. "I swear I will never wear a dress again after this," she mumbled, sprinting alongside the horse stable and pasture. On the other side of the fence, a huge black horse with a white star on his forehead fell into pace alongside her. His hooves pounded against the ground. "Midnight!" she sang. Another horse joined at his side. "Phantom!" *They're both here!*

She glanced back; seven guards were hot on her heels. Pumping her arms and legs harder, she set her sights on the bridge. Three guards were at the entrance, but two of them leaned against the stone arch with their backs to her and one was lying on the ground. If the king saw him, it would be "off with his head".

Layala smiled at the two horses when the fence came to an end, vowing to come back for them. But a loud crash and wood splintering made her jump. Phantom and Midnight broke through and raced up on either side of her. Taking the risk, she leapt and barely made it onto Midnight's back, and swung her leg over.

She grinned and a euphoric feeling swelled in her chest. *I'm going to make it!*

The guards behind her yelled obscenities and commands. The trio at the bridge finally took notice of the commotion and drew their weapons. She nudged Midnight's sides; they couldn't stop now. She'd seen Phantom run elves and pale ones down. That's the kind of energy she needed.

Clinking metal like the sound of a chain being dragged over rocks dropped her stomach. *No.* The lowering spiked gate was closing off her escape. Hot tears welled up. No! She had to get away. She must get to Thane. The gate slammed to the ground and Midnight reared up, neighing as guards surrounded them. Phantom nickered loudly and slammed his shoulder into a guard before coming to a stop. "Curse this king, curse this place!"

Layala slid down and ran to the cliff's edge. It was fifty feet, maybe more, to the river below and high cliffs on both sides. The waterfall roared like white thunder clouds and sprays of mist hit her face with the breeze coming up.

"Step away from the edge, Lady Lightbringer," a guard said, palms up like he was surrendering.

Could she survive the fall and swim in these currents? Where was the land low enough she could climb out? She looked to the other side, desperately hoping to see Thane in the shadows. *Please, Thane, please.* He'd come before when she was in trouble; was he there now? "Thane!" she cried searching the

swaying grass on the other side. *Please be here.* The longer she looked the heavier the pit in her stomach grew. She glanced over her shoulder to find King Tenebris and at least fifteen guards closed in. No one was within arm's reach, but they inched closer.

"Lady Lightbringer, we're not going to hurt you. Please step back."

She moved closer to the edge, rocks and crumbling earth dropped. Her stomach whirled taking in the distance. Risk the fall and water or go back to the evil king? With shaking hands, she took another step forward, more dirt and rocks spilled off the cliff's edge. *Jump!* She sucked in a deep breath and tipped forward. She expected to feel wind rushing all around, hear her own scream, as she plummeted into the icy waters below but instead, fingers dug at her scalp and with a fistful of her hair, she was wrenched backward. Clawing at the person's hand she tried to turn but he had such a close grip she couldn't, until the gap between her and the edge was filled by soldiers. She was so close to freedom, to being able to search for Thane. The hold released and she turned to Aldrich. That bastard! Rage shook her entire being. His apologetic frown enraged her further. She clawed at his face with a scream that burned her throat. Guards grabbed her from the sides, holding her back from reaching him. "Let me go!" she seethed, kicking and jerking, sounding more like a wild cat than an elf.

One of the guards squeezed her injured left hand,

grinding the already fractured bones. She bit down to keep from yelling out in pain. "Enough," he said.

"Pig," she murmured to the guard. "Only a low-life prick would use an injury against someone. I'll remember your face when I am queen."

The guard's smug expression paled, and he released her hand.

"Good boy," Layala said.

With his hands casually behind his back, Aldrich shook his head. "I couldn't let you jump," he said, full of bravado in front of his father. "You could have killed yourself. What were you thinking?"

Tenebris stepped in front of him, his long blond hair moving in the breeze. He lifted his chin, and the gold crown he always wore glittered in the moonlight. If he wasn't such a sick bastard, one could call him handsome. The evil smile on his face reminded her of a pale one moments before the kill. "You are a foolish girl. And you need to be taught a lesson, so you won't try anything like this again."

Layala straightened her spine. She'd take his blow and wouldn't go down this time no matter how hard he struck her. He wouldn't get the satisfaction of that.

The guards at her sides shifted apprehensively and glanced back and forth between each other. Tenebris raised a hand and curled his fingers. There was something cruel and sadistic in his expression that made her stomach clench.

"Clear the way," someone shouted from the back.

The host of guards parted to let in a pair of

soldiers, and in between them walked Reina. Her normally tight bun on top of her head was loose and disheveled. Her deep-brown eyes searched the faces all around her but stopped on Layala. Her chin trembled and her cheeks glistened with tears. The two guards grasped her upper arms tightly, keeping her trapped between them.

Stomach dropping, Layala looked to the king, ready to plead for her maid's life. Reina warned her this could happen. If he suspected Reina or Pearl's involvement in her attempted escape, he'd execute them. Struggling against the guards' hold, Layala said, "Wait, wait, this isn't her fault. It's mine. She didn't know."

Tenebris walked up to Reina. The glint of metal in his hand shone in the pale starlight, making Layala more frantic. "She has a child! Please don't! Please!"

He dragged a blade across her throat. A thin line of scarlet erupted and poured down her neck, spilling onto her chest. Layala gasped, blinking several times in disbelief, unable to accept what was happening before her very eyes. Reina choked on her own blood; the sound of it bubbling up and out of her mouth made Layala want to vomit. The red liquid dribbled over her chin dripping onto her dress. This couldn't be happening. This couldn't be real. It was a delusion, a nightmare.

"Reina, no," she whispered, and gulped down the rising bile. Who would take care of that little boy if she was gone? She must hurry and put her hand over

Reina's throat to stop the bleeding. But within moments, Reina's face was colorless, her head lolled to the side, and her body sagged in the arms of the guards.

The booming in Layala's ears from the rush of her blood drowned out the king's voice. His mouth moved yet she heard nothing he said. But the sneer on his face, the arrogant smirk—Layala kicked her leg out, dropping the soldier next to her, and slammed her elbow into the nose of the other and ripped the dagger from his waist.

"My blade!" he shouted. Another soldier moved in her path, reaching out to grab her. She slashed at him. He threw up his forearms to block her strike and she dragged the dagger's sharp edge across them and shoved her foot into his belly, sending him flying back. All she saw was Tenebris, the bastard who needed to die. He deserved to suffer and plead for his life, but she would have to make this quick. He slowly backed into guards, grabbing several to push in front of him.

"I need her alive."

Coward. She moved through them, stabbing and kicking and slicing. Ducking under blows and blades, taking them down with speed and precision. She didn't think; she moved like a storm taking down all in her wake. She thought all elves could move as quickly as her, but they were seconds behind her. Until a string of bodies lay behind her and she was in front of the coward king, his eyes wide with terror. With a roar like a wild beast that belonged in the cursed forest, she

swung down at him. Aiming for the soft flesh between his neck and shoulder.

"Stay that weapon, Layala!" Mathekis's command washed over her, freezing her muscles. The blade stopped a breath away from landing. His power pulsed through her, like her skin throbbed and invisible talons groped her flesh, pulling her back. *No!* He wouldn't take this moment from her. The one thing she'd wanted since she was a child, her sole obsession. She grunted, pushing with all her might, her arm shook with the effort, but her body wouldn't cooperate. Her gaze flicked to Mathekis, who stood among the soldiers, partially hidden under his hood but the strain on his face was noticeable. Was it only a battle of wills?

Tenebris smiled wickedly, the huge grin of a mad elf, and he started laughing. A dark, mocking chuckle.

"Now step away from the king," Mathekis commanded.

"No," she said through clenched teeth, muscles straining once more to force the strike. She broke through his persuasion and hacked down as Tenebris backed away. The blade slid across his tunic, but she didn't puncture his flesh. Several guards grabbed her arms and around the waist, and no matter how she jerked and kicked, she couldn't break free.

"You might be a warrior, Layala but you're no match for Mathekis's power," Tenebris said.

"You're dead already," Layala growled. "You just don't know it yet."

CHAPTER 8

Thane opened his eyes to a wood-planked ceiling above him. He sat up quickly, heart thundering. The soft ivory blanket covering his bare torso was unfamiliar as was this room. Dark curtains were drawn over the window, a small white table with a single burning candle gave off the only light, casting shadowed corners. *Where am I?* he thought, glancing around the strange room.

He set his bare feet on the wood floor and stood. The boards creaked under his weight no doubt giving away that he was awake. *And why am I only in under-wear?* He hadn't woken up almost nude in an unfamiliar place in a long time. His fingertips glided over a brown wrap tight around his middle. And it struck him that the pain was nearly gone. He hadn't even struggled to get out of the bed, hadn't felt the sharp twinge when he moved or had to grit his teeth at the aching throb. He tugged at the corner of the wrap and

began to unravel it until it dropped to the ground. The scar was still there but smaller and matched the color of his skin rather than an angry pink. His abdomen was slick with oils that smelled strongly of pine needles, mint, and something else he couldn't name.

He remembered now that he was to meet someone at an apothecary. Sensing he wasn't in danger, the muscles in his back and shoulders loosened. His clothes sat folded neatly on the trunk at the foot of the bed, and his weapons were laid next to them. He dressed quickly, smiling that it barely hurt every time he moved. Whoever was here knew a great deal more about healing than Vesstan did.

Pulling aside the window's dark-gray curtain, he spotted the bright pinks and blues of the morning sky. He'd been there all night then. He paused with his hand on the door handle and listened to the faint call of morning birds outside and the rumble of voices from somewhere below. Two males, two to three females were nearby. The door clicked when he opened it, and he stepped into a bright hallway. Stained-glass windows on the right overlooked the street and buildings from the second floor. At the end of the corridor was a set of stairs he silently descended. He peeked around the corner into the main apothecary. Weeping plants hung from the wood rafters and potted in colorful containers on tables and plant pillars. Tifapine sat on a bench set up against the large floor-to-ceiling window, swinging her little legs

as she looked outside. She giggled to herself. Leif and Gunner relaxed on brown leather couches in a small lounge area. They held white cups of steaming liquid in hand, and with them was a female with red roots flowing into blonde tips—Pearl. "Do you have news about Layala?"

The group turned to face him, and Leif and Gunner stood. "Sire," they both said. Pearl slowly rose, keeping her eyes down, and nervously fidgeted with the hem of her apron. This wasn't new behavior; she was always like this in his presence.

A lady with hip-length black, curly hair and light-tan skin stepped out from a door behind the countertop. She and Evalyn grinned and chatted like two old friends. "I find poppy oil best for deep injuries, but I'll have to give the rose oil a try next time," she said. "And what about fennel seed? Have you used that in your tonic?"

"I haven't," Evalyn's eyebrows raised. "Sounds like I should be."

Wisps of smoke from incense sticks swirled and moved along behind them. Just noticing him standing in the room, the healer started and then smiled. "Good morning, your highness. How do you feel? Is there anything I can get you?" She stopped next to the shelves of different colored bottles lined on the wall behind her. Some amber, others red or blue or green. All different shapes and sizes, from skinny, tall beakers to bulbous bottles with cork stoppers.

With one hand on his torso that was only lightly tender now, he cleared his throat and stepped out. "I feel much better. I think I owe you a thank-you." Not only for healing him but for keeping quiet when his presence here would put her life in danger.

She put a fist on her hip, and brown eyes trailed over him. "Works like a charm every time." She stepped forward and held out her hand. "I'm Madam Adley and this is my apothecary." She shook his hand with a firm grip that said she was confident in who she was, and nodded toward the four on the couches. "They didn't believe you'd be up this morning. But they don't know what I do."

"What did you use?"

She winked. "A little pine, a little frivalla, poppy oil for the base and a touch of magic."

Thane's brow furrowed. "You're a mage?" He supposed it was possible that others still existed or had never been tested. Especially after what people saw happen to Layala's parents; they might hide their children.

"That depends on your definition of mage. Was I born with innate magic? No, but there are other sources in this world. I lived among the dragon shifters for a time. They have tapped into a power that doesn't come from within. Since we elves rarely associate with other races, or more they won't associate with us, we can't learn from them."

Thane knew the power of dragon shifters all too

well. The humans and elves were lucky they preferred the mountains and the gold within rather than conquering lands below. "I hope to remedy that someday."

"I know you do. It's why I helped you, young king. Your father has lost his way. Many of us know what he has done, others will remain loyal to him. We need someone to lead and stop his madness."

"We do, but what news from Pearl? Is Layala alright?"

Leif's mouth twisted, not the reaction Thane wanted.

"Sire," Pearl started. "I was able to see Layala yesterday. She has been locked in the tower for nearly a month. They weren't feeding her or giving her water. I wanted to go to her, but there was no way I could make it without being seen—"

Holding up a hand, Thane said, "I don't blame you for that. Where is she now?"

Pearl tucked some stray hair behind her pointed ear. "We dressed her for breakfast with King Tenebris, Sir Aldrich and two others. One I fear is a pale one, and the other a woman, not elven. She had golden hair and brown skin, eyes like rich buttercups, her fingers end in black talons... I've never seen anything like it."

"Varlett," Thane murmured. That fire-breathing wench needed to die. Slow and painfully then he'd stand and watch as vultures stole her rotting flesh. "Where is she now?"

"She was taken to her room but... she was injured. A bruised, split lip, possibly broken bones in her hand. Reina told me just as I was leaving last evening. The lip will heal quickly but her hand..."

Angry heat flooded his body, flaming in his cheeks. Maker above, he regretted now more than ever he didn't shove his sword straight through his father's chest. It could have been a clean transition of power where he and Layala could rule together. Thane swore under his breath and turned to Leif. "We need to go get her."

With a frown, Leif cleared his throat. "We should wait for darkness. There is no way we can infiltrate the castle in daylight. Not without killing many and risking our own lives in the process. And we'll need more Ravens."

"If I have to kill every last castle guard to get to her, I will."

Leif folded his arms and looked to be on the verge of arguing.

"You're either with me," Thane shifted closer to Leif, "or you're with my father. Those are the only two choices."

"With you, sire. Always."

"There's more," Gunner said, stepping into the circle. The lump in his throat bobbed, and he pushed his fingers through his hair. He turned to Pearl and let out a long breath. "I didn't want to be the one to tell you..." his voice trailed off.

Pearl anxiously searched his face. "Tell me what?"

Gunner looked to Leif, who slowly shook his head. Thane growled and grew impatient. "If something happened to Layala. Tell me now."

The clinking of glass on the counter drew everyone's attention to Miss Adley. "Your friend Reina, the maid—the king slit her throat. As punishment to Layala when she tried to escape last night. I have a friend at the castle too."

Pearl's hand flew to her mouth and a moment later she dropped to her knees. "We told her." Pearl sobbed into her hands. "We told Layala what would happen!" She cried louder and curled into herself. Leif dropped to his knees before her, and she fell into his chest. "Reina was terrified. Terrified—and now she's dead!"

Her scream pierced Thane's heart, and he averted his gaze, finding his focus on the bottles on the wall. He'd seen so much death and despair in his life and it never seemed to get easier. How many had he watched suffer because of his father's brutality? Hundreds? Thousands?

"Leif, Gunner, I need ten more of my best Ravens here." Thane went to the window and peeked out. The shop owner across the street swept the entrance to his place. A couple guards stood on the corner. They'd be on high alert today. "We infiltrate the castle at dusk." He turned to Madam Adley. She polished a short stout glass with a white cloth. "If you don't have young children, I need you to come with us. We'll be in need of a good healer. You're the best I've ever seen."

She frowned and set the glass on the countertop.

"Your highness, I am honored by the request but respectfully, I do have a ten-year-old daughter and her father is no longer with us. And there are many in the community who regularly come to me for ailments." She gestured toward Evalyn. "But Evalyn is quite capable. I can give her a few bottles of my best remedies."

Evalyn nodded. "Seen many die in my day and saved as many. I might not know magic like Adley but I can help in a pinch."

Thane still wished she'd go home or even stay here where it was safe. The road ahead wasn't meant for an older human woman with likely ailing health, but he already knew she wouldn't leave until she saw Layala herself. "Can you fight, Evalyn?"

She picked up a teacup from the countertop and brought it to her lips. "That's what I have you around for."

WITH SWORDS IN EACH HAND, hanging at his sides, Thane, Tif, Evalyn, and his twelve Ravens gathered on the grassy hill near the long bridge that led to Castle Dredwich. The sun dipped behind the castle bringing a chill to the air but sweat beaded on his brow. The thought of killing his own soldiers made him queasy. Taking a deep breath in through his nose, he spied the two guards on the tower on the far side, with a large bell for signaling attacks. Two more on this side of the river and seven staggered on the bridge itself. He was

surprised his father didn't assign more to watch the front with Thane on the loose. Tilting his head side to side, he cracked his neck. His Raven helmet fit snuggly, and his charcoal, shiny armor glinted in the dying sunlight. Ready for war.

"The bridge guards will be easy to take. It's the inner guards that are a problem. We know there are at least a hundred on the grounds at all times. If we can silence the first ones before they ring the bell, we can follow the edges of the property and go relatively unseen." Thane pointed to the left side of his soldiers, "You six will go west to the prison dungeons and free our Ravens." He gestured to the right, "You six will be with me. We'll enter through the servants' door in the rear. Evalyn, you're with me as well. Stay close."

Siegfried, a slight, tall elf who moved like the night wind, and aptly called the Wraith, tapped his sword against his outer thigh. "And what if the alarm is sounded before we kill the bridge guards?"

"Then we'll fight our way in," Thane took a deep breath, "and today is not a day to be merciful. My father never is. But they know our armor. They will choose whose side they are on before we even approach."

He looked to the tower where she'd been kept and the darkness within the single window. *I'm coming, Laya.*

Each step down the hill made Thane's heart thud harder. His palms dampened, making him adjust his grip on his swords. The waterfall thundered louder

than usual, churning white splashes against the blue and gray rock face behind it. The caw of a raven flying overhead drew his gaze. It cast a shadow over them, gliding on the wind. The Maker was with them this day; ravens had always brought him luck. He swallowed, wetting his dry throat; he'd never killed his own people before. Many of these guards served under him when he ruled for a short time and most he'd known his entire life.

The two bridge guards on this side of the river stood taller when they caught sight of Thane and his Ravens. The one on the left turned and broke into a sprint on the bridge.

Gunner pulled back an arrow. "You will not take another step if you want to take another breath!"

He wisely froze. A hum, like a warm wave washing over Thane's chest and down his arms, calmed his pounding heart. His mind quieted, thoughts and worries flowing away on the breeze and his attention settled on the bell tower guards. With intense focus his power pushed out, an invisible force coiling around them, until they looked like statues, frozen in horror. "You will not touch that bell."

"Slowly turn," Gunner commanded the others on the bridge. "And come back this way." He nodded. "That's it. Good boy."

Thane approached the closest male, lifting the point of his right sword to the guard's throat. Sweat trickled down the side of his face and under the collar

of his shirt. The willowy dark-haired elf raised his palms.

Tifapine popped out from the small pack on Thane's back. "Better do what you're told, elfy or you might lose your little peter." She pointed a small knife at him. Thane rolled his eyes and shushed her; now she wanted to get brave? With a squeak, she ducked back inside. He had to remember he was carrying around this little creature for Layala's sake.

"High Prince, you're—alive." The bridge guard gulped. "I will not fight you."

"It's High King," Gunner barked. "The true king."

"The imposter king," the other guard spit. Leif kicked him in the side of the head and sent him flying into the stone of the bridge.

Thane lifted his chin slightly to the guard at the end of his sword. "Now then, will you kneel and swear allegiance to me? Or will you die here and now?"

The guard's eyes followed the shiny length of the blade until they stopped on Thane's face. Knees bending, he slowly went to the ground. "You have my loyalty, sire. I will follow your command until my last breath." He gulped. "King Tenebris has joined forces with the pale ones. He brought one here, inside our very walls. I cannot stand behind him any longer."

Thane lowered his weapon and checked on the two in the bell tower. They remained unnaturally still. "And how do the other guards feel? That I'm an imposter king? A traitor?"

"Somehow, they have—forgotten a pale one was

here. It must be dark magic or something. They will be loyal to your father. He told us you tried to have him killed to take his place."

Thane narrowed his eyes. "But *you* didn't *forget*?"

"When the pale one told us to forget we saw him and what he did after Lady Lightbringer tried to escape—everyone did. But I didn't. I don't know why." His blue eyes glanced down a moment. "Lady Lightbringer killed eleven guards last night... I'm afraid she made many enemies. Before it was just following orders; now it's personal."

Thane grumbled. "Well, you're holding her prisoner. What do you expect?" And most would never believe that their High King would associate with pale ones let alone invite them inside. So, Thane and Layala would be seen as the enemy and Tenebris the hero. Maker, how did Tenebris always have the upper hand?

"So, the others will fight me when I go inside to get Layala?"

"You don't need to. They're not here." He sounded out of breath. "The king took your mate and left last night. And they took your Ravens, too."

"Where?" he snarled.

Leaning back slightly, he answered, "I don't know, but they went south."

Leif stepped up beside Thane and put his hand on Thane's shoulder. "You don't think—he wouldn't take her to the Void."

The hairs on the back of Thane's neck stood on end. The dirt road that led up the valley's hillside was

beaten down with heavy tracks of hoofprints, boots and wagon wheels. He cursed under his breath for not seeing it sooner. A cold sweat broke out over his body, and he swallowed down the rising nausea. "I think that's exactly where he's taking her."

CHAPTER 9

Layala's backside grew numb hours before. The hard, wooden bench she sat on in the prison cart wasn't meant for comfort. She suddenly longed for the cushy carriage Thane had taken her in months before. At least that was soft. The small, barred windows she peered out of now provided enough fresh air, but this was a cage. The wagon creaked, swayed, and bounced over the uneven road. Layala stood, going to the back door and wrapped her hands around the bars. A buzzing noise around her ears made her twitch. The flies in this cursed wagon wouldn't leave her alone. The stench of the dried animal shit on the floor not only stung her nostrils but attracted pests. The bottom hem of her dress was filthy and reeked.

Dust billowed up from the horses and foot soldiers outside. One of them turned, heavy-lidded eyes found hers. There was sorrow there, but the elf beside him stared at her with utter hatred. She recognized him

from the night before when she lost it and went on a killing spree. She wanted to ask the one with kind eyes to set her free, to stand against the tyrant king, but that would only get this elf killed, and probably his family too. She couldn't ask him to risk everything for her. She couldn't ask any of them.

What lies might Tenebris have told them about their precious savior—destroyer of the Void? Did they think they were taking her to save them now? Or that she was a traitor who'd taken Thane's side and now was Tenebris's prisoner. Loyal soldiers followed the orders of their king. Maybe they didn't question what was happening at all, maybe they didn't dare. Maybe they simply believed he was doing what was best for Palenor.

It felt like a stone sank in her gut. For the first time since they'd taken her captive, she accepted that Thane couldn't come for her. She was on her own. Perhaps Thane's injuries were too much. Maybe the note was sent by someone else to torment her, give her false hope where there was none.

Flashes of crimson stained her mind. Death haunted her like howling winds in a winter storm. First her parents, Novak, then Reina... Thane. She pressed a hand to her chest, willing the pressure to ease the pain throbbing there. It didn't. With an aching heart, she leaned back and closed her eyes. She didn't want to sleep. The faces of the guards she killed, and her last moments with Thane would haunt her there, but the swaying of the wagon made her limbs

heavy, made her breaths become shallow and even, until the swish of horse tails and the steady march of the army lulled her to slumber...

COME TO ME. *I need you.* Layala turned at the sound of the voice. "Thane?" she called.

She stood on a stone pathway in a garden surrounded by tall exotic trees with blooms of lavender and blush. This place was familiar, but somehow, she knew it existed only in her dreams. The sweet, rich scent of jasmine drifted on warm air. She'd always loved that smell. It made her feel at home. Her fingers brushed the open petals of midnight lilies as she passed them in a slow gait. She looked up, stars winked above, and a full moon coated the garden in its pale light. It was so beautiful here. "Thane, where are you?" she had to see him, even if it wasn't real.

"Hello, love. I'm here."

He sounded slightly different than she remembered but it must be him. That deep voice sent chills down her spine, and she smiled, almost giddy. She turned, ready to throw her arms around him, but her surroundings shifted to a figure in a black cloak, not Thane. Some instinct deep inside told her to run. Picking up the long fabric of her scarlet dress, she took off, tearing through a now dark, haunting forest. Wolf howls and owl hoots and glowing yellow eyes seemed to follow her. The hooded figure laughed and laughed echoing all around the inky

blackness, surrounding her like a cloud. His footsteps slammed the ground trailing close behind her, too close.

The hooded figure appeared in front of her, and she skidded to a halt, stumbling backward. He advanced with slow, methodical steps. "Don't run. It's beneath you."

In her retreat, her back bumped into a tree, the sharp bark scraping her skin. This felt too real to be a dream. "Stay away."

His hand reached for her, tattoos of black lilies on vines trailed up his arm. Maker above, it was him—the Black Mage! Her chest heaved up and down, and she pressed harder into the tree. She wanted to shut her eyes, willing this nightmare to dissipate, but her stare was fixed. Warm fingers touched her cheek. "I am your destiny."

JOLTING AWAKE, Layala blinked rapidly. Her cart was at rest, no longer jostling her on the rough road. How long had they been stopped? The cool autumn night air whisked through the bars. She rubbed her arms to fight off the chill and sat up taller. That dream felt all too real. She could almost smell the jasmine and feel the ghost of those fingers caressing her cheek. With a shudder, she pushed to her feet making her way to the barred window. Torches outside crackled and burned brightly. Tents went up all around and chattering and laughing soldiers surrounded her. Having a wonderful

time by the sounds of things. *And I'm stuck in a cage,* she thought.

They were cooking, too. Her mouth watered at the savory aroma of roasting meats. Would she get a plate? After being starved for weeks even the scent of it made her ravenous. Clinking metal against the cart door made Layala jump. She hadn't heard anyone approach. The metal hinges squealed as it swung, revealing Aldrich and three other soldiers behind him. He clipped the key ring to his belt and waved. "Let's go."

"Where?" She didn't know exactly the final destination the king had in mind, but she had an idea. She recognized the large poppy fields she'd passed by before. They moved south toward Doonafell, toward the Void, and they weren't there yet. They had another day or two to go.

"Mathekis wishes to see you."

Aldrich held out his hand. Layala shoved it aside and dropped to the soft grass. The three soldiers kept a grip on their sword pommels and backed up several steps. She smiled at their wariness to cover her remorse. She'd never wanted the soldiers of Palenor to fear her, but things changed and there was no appearing weak. How many did she kill on her rampage to get to Tenebris the night before? Nine, ten? From the moment the knife slid across Reina's throat to when she held the sharp edge of a blade to Tenebris's neck was a blur.

Yet Aldrich wasn't afraid of her. If he thought she would hold back when it came to killing him, he was

woefully mistaken. He was as much to blame for what happened to her and Thane and the others, as Tenebris. When the opportunity came to end him, she would take it.

With her chin held high, she walked beside Aldrich with the three soldiers in tow several paces behind. "If you play your cards right, you'll get to go free soon."

"Well, I never was any good at cards," Layala drawled. "Your father will try to kill me as soon as he gets what he wants." Layala hissed at a sharp sting in her arm. She turned to Aldrich pulling a barb out of her.

"It's much easier for me if I don't have to fight you to give the katagas serum." He tucked the barb into the brown pouch at his hip. He half smiled. "You seemed to have gotten back your spirit. I thought my father might have broken you for good."

Break her for good? No, the embers of rage wouldn't be snuffed out until Tenebris was dead and buried.

He gestured toward her wrapped, injured hand. The bandages were dirty now, but it didn't hurt anymore. "We need to get that changed and looked at."

Layala tucked her hand behind her back. "It's fine." Though the throbbing ache told her otherwise. She made it worse when she attacked the guards and went after the king. She turned her head to the lights of the town below, the waves of golden wheat fields in the distance, shifting in the night wind. Luminor crickets

chirped, and their bodies glowed like tiny stars. This place brought back so many memories. It was near here she fought Aldrich surrounded by the Ravens, when they named her "Fightbringer", and for the first time in her life she had felt like she belonged. Maker, she missed them. All of them. She could hardly stomach looking at Aldrich knowing the vow of loyalty to Thane he'd taken to be a Raven, and how easily he broke it.

"This way," Aldrich said, tilting his head to the left.

After passing through the outer edges of the camp, likely to avoid attention, they came upon a large beige tent. The slit in the opening revealed bright light coming from the inside. Layala swallowed hard, knowing full well who waited inside. Aldrich pulled the tent flap aside and gestured for her to go in. Her stomach ached at the thought of Mathekis having such control over her. The way he, with a *command*, stopped her from hacking that blade into Tenebris's neck even with the level of desperation and fury fueling her. She couldn't imagine what he must have been like four hundred years ago at the peak of his power with the Black Mage. She couldn't imagine what the Black mage—Zaurahel Everhath was like if Mathekis bowed to him. Atarah said they worshiped him like a god before he became the most feared.

She stepped inside and stood by the entrance. A firm hand pushed her a little farther inside and the tent flap dropped shut behind her. Mathekis sat with his legs crossed in a large wooden chair. The oversized

robe he wore to cover his identity was draped over the chair's armrest. Who did the soldiers think he was? Did they notice him riding amongst them, feel the evil coming from him?

One long snow-white finger ending in a pointed black nail tapped against his temple, and his other arm casually lay across his lap. Onyx eyes trailed over her from head to toe and back up. "I often wondered what you would look like. It was strange waiting for you to be born. Sometimes I pondered if Zaurahel was wrong. But here we are just as he said."

"Are you going to kill me?" After what Talon said, she couldn't get it out of her head. What if they sacrificed her so the Black Mage could absorb her power somehow? The more she thought about it, the more likely it seemed.

His black eyebrows rose. "Zaurahel wants you very much alive. Together the things you'll do..." Disgusted, Layala jerked her gaze from his endless dark eyes and up to several bright-yellow orbs that hung in nets from the tent poles above. They looked like glowing rocks. "Magic," Mathekis said, sitting taller. "You could make them alight if you wanted to. I could show you. From what I've seen and heard, you've barely used your power. You don't even know what you're capable of yet."

"Might I remind you, I've had a steady stream of katagas serum in my body for weeks," she said calmly although, she wanted to scream.

He smiled, showing his pointed teeth. Layala took

an involuntary step back. "My appearance disturbs you?"

"Of course, it does. You're a beast that *eats* people."

Unphased by her comment, he said, "Once, I was beautiful like you, like all elves. Vibrant olive skin, green eyes like a forest, thick golden-brown hair." He stared up as if to gaze at the stars if only the tent fabric wasn't there. "My mother said I was as handsome as a warm spring day. And now I am an endless winter, cold, dark, taking life without remorse. Feeling nothing and loving no one. You are right to loathe me, for I have become death and nothing more."

For a moment, she was sad for the elf he once was. It was difficult to picture him described as a spring day. The creature sitting before her now was hideous and grotesque; black lips and charcoal shadows around his eyes, every tooth ending in a point, but it was the wholly onyx eyes that was most startling. "If the Black Mage cursed you to be this creature, why do you follow him? Why do you want him back?"

"He has the power to free me of this curse. I don't want to crave elven flesh. I don't want to have the urge to take you to the ground and tear a bite out of your pretty neck." He stood and Layala retreated, heart beating faster. She had no magic and no weapons to defend herself with. She knew he harbored those cravings, but with his claim the Black Mage didn't want her hurt, she'd grown a little too comfortable in his presence. This was an elf-eating beast as much as the rest of them and she couldn't let her guard down.

Mathekis stared at her, calculating, eyes narrowing. What did he see there? "And the only way he can free me is if you free him."

She found his choice of words odd. Free him, as if he wasn't dead at all but... trapped. "Were you his friend?"

"Yes."

"Then why would he allow you to become this in the first place? I would never curse a friend to become what you are. Not even my enemy."

Mathekis placed his hands behind his back and slowly paced in a horizontal line. "My bargain wasn't met. I knew the price. He asked me not to go through with the spell."

"Asked you not to? As if he couldn't control the punishment? He's the one who made the stipulations. You see that, don't you? He's the reason you're cursed. He's not your friend. He should be your enemy."

His black lips pressed firmly together.

With a sigh, Layala said, "If you knew the consequences then why would you do it?"

"Because I loved her—turns out she didn't love me."

"A mate bond?"

Silence stretched long between them.

"What makes you think he will free you once he's back?"

His footsteps were eerily silent as he paced, as was his breathing. The sizzling candles on the small cherry wood desk were louder. How simple it would be for

him to sneak up on someone. He was as quiet as a ghost, as if he weighed nothing and did not draw breath. Chills peppered Layala's skin.

"He promised me if I delivered you to him, he would."

"You're taking me inside the Void." It wasn't a question.

He stopped his pacing and leveled her with his eerie gaze. "Yes. You will not be harmed."

She gulped and inched back until the tent's fabric grazed her skin. She had to get away from these people. Feeling with her hand, she searched for the tent's opening. Once she caught the edge of the fabric, she gripped it, ready to twist and run.

"I know you fear the stories—fear Zaurahel," he paused, "but you don't need to. And I have a feeling eventually you won't."

"Everyone fears him."

"He will be in your debt."

He wouldn't because she wasn't going to bring him back. Layala took a deep breath, plotting out her path of escape in her mind. She could dash through the tall wheat fields relatively unseen and make for the town below. There would be somewhere to hide.

"Don't try to run." Mathekis still held his hands behind his back as he paced. His words weren't laced with power. It wasn't a magical command. "You won't get far and Tenebris will only hurt you more. He brought your friends. And I'm sure you remember what happened to the maid."

"What friends?" Had Tenebris found Aunt Evalyn, Forrest or Ren?

"The red-haired warrior girl, Piper, and your prince's right hand, Fennan. I know them well."

Layala released the fabric, and her shoulders sank. Leaving would be a death sentence for them... her eyes widened a little. But if they were here in this camp, she could find them. They could run together. "Is there a reason you called me here or can I leave?"

He turned his back to her. "You may go."

Layala slipped past the tent's flaps and stepped out to find Aldrich and those same three guards waiting. All of them straightened their spines and pushed their shoulders back.

"I'm to give you a meal." Aldrich moved the plate toward her. A meager roll and maybe an ounce of meat. "And escort you back to the cart."

She snatched the plate, and as they walked through the camp, she searched for another prison cart or a place they might be holding Piper and Fennan. Across burning fires, tents, and groups of soldiers, she spotted another cart with bars.

CHAPTER 10

Two days and nights passed. With the vast green hills on one side and thick trees on the other, they were close to Doonafell. She remembered racing through Fanvore Wood to get away from pale ones like it was the day before. Layala would never forget the rancid smell of burning flesh and dejection in the people's eyes as their city burned and their loved ones died. She would also forever remember this city as the place she fell in love with Thane.

The high, bright moon shining in through the barred windows gave away the midnight hour. With her hands behind her head, Layala lay on the hardwood bench, trying to ignore the ache in her back. An owl cooed nearby, the soothing sound of it made her eyelids heavy but the last two nights brought endless nightmares of her searching for Thane but finding the Black Mage instead. She didn't want to sleep even though her tired body called for it. It was so quiet with

only an occasional murmured voice or light footsteps of passing soldiers. Her stomach growled; they didn't bring her a plate of food tonight and the lingering scent of roasted meat made her hungrier.

"We need to talk." Varlett appeared on the other side of the back barred window.

Layala shot up, all traces of tiredness gone. "What do you want?"

"We will be in the Void tomorrow."

"And?"

She paused; her bright golden eyes were even more beast-like in the dark. "And I want to remind you of our bargain. You made a deal with me."

"I haven't forgotten."

"I am on your side, you know," she cooed, her tone was all saccharine and poison saying she was anything but on her side. "You can give me what I want. Therefore you're precious to me. My precious little mage."

Layala rolled her eyes with a scoff. And lay back down. The audacity of this lady. "You ripped my mate bond from me and tried to murder him, but somehow you're on my side?" Layala actively avoided thinking about the Black Mage or what they might do to get her to bring him back the last few days. It made her stomach hurt. She feared she wouldn't be able to stop Mathekis from controlling her. At least that was a better alternative to having her friends murdered until she broke.

Varlett ran her black taloned fingers through her golden hair, clicked her tongue, and a cruel smile grew.

"So, you want your mate bond back? I know your gallant prince will want to be bonded to you," her smile turned into a pout, "when I broke that bond, I felt it rush through me. The connection you both harbored—" she pulled a deep breath through her nose, "it was intoxicating. It vibrated my very bones, filled me with euphoria before it vanished. A bond like that is rare even with magic. To have that stolen away, he must be slowly dying inside."

Layala touched her chest; the ghost of the pain still lingered there. *He* must be. Not her.

"His bond to you was stronger than yours to him."

They weren't the same? She glanced down. It made sense since Thane always embraced their bond, and she hadn't until recently. The broken bond didn't physically hurt anymore but it was a cold loneliness, like an endless night, intensified by everything else.

"If you want a mate bond again Zaurahel will have to do it. That same spell can't be restored."

Layala gently took her lower lip between her teeth. She couldn't be mate bonded to Thane again? Was that even true? The spell was back in the castle library. She shook her head and pushed herself back up to stare at the dragon shifter. "I wouldn't make a deal with the Black Mage even for that."

Varlett slid her talon down the bar, scraping it quietly and licked her lips. "Thane would."

"You don't even know him."

"I know him better than even you."

Layala's skin flushed hot, cheeks burning. The

nerve. She'd never even met Thane until she tried to kill him. "Why are you even going through this negotiation when you could just call in your favor? To bring him back is clearly the reason you negotiated the deal in the first place."

The dragon's yellow eyes seemed to shimmer in the dark. She clicked her tongue. "You don't have all the pieces to this game of chess yet. My favor won't be to bring him back. It will come after. All will make sense when Zaurahel is with us again."

Layala narrowed her eyes. What could Varlett possibly want from her after the Black Mage was alive? She did say she craved power as much as he did, but how could Layala be involved with that? There must be another reason. "I don't understand."

"And you won't, until you bring him back."

More coercions. Layala rubbed her temples. Her magic had nothing to do with regeneration or giving life; none of this made sense. "Why is it me who can bring him back and not any other mage? And saying it's the mark on my arm isn't helpful because I don't know why I have that either."

Varlett clicked her talons on the metal bars. The pinging sound grated on Layala's nerves. "I can't tell you that."

"Why?"

"Even if I wanted to tell you—" she ground her teeth as if struggling to speak, "I couldn't. My tongue is tied."

Layala's brow furrowed, unable to speak the truth?

How? "As in, he somehow magically forbade you to speak of it?" That didn't make sense either.

"I can't say."

Layala groaned. "What can you say?" She'd wondered about her magic, about this mark on her all her life. And ever since Thane told her that the enemy wanted to use her, she couldn't fathom why it was her. Why did The Black Mage have an apparent fascination with black lilies? Atarah said he'd had them tattooed on his forearms, and then there was his chair in the mage's tower; the likeness of it to her magic was too uncanny to deny. Was it simply because he foresaw her coming birth? That she was his savior, so he worshiped her before she even existed? And if he could see into the future, couldn't he have prevented his own downfall?

"Look I just thought I'd come over here and chat so we could prevent killing your friends tomorrow to get you to cooperate. Although, a goblet of the redhead's blood would be delicious. One way or another we will force your hand. You won't stop this. He will come back. That isn't a hope. It's a fact. Only then will you know the truth."

"Piss off." But her mind started working. "The stone," she murmured, tapping a finger against her lips. She didn't need Varlett or the Black Mage to give her answers. The All Seeing Stone would hold the answers to every question she had about her bond, her connection with the Black Mage and how to destroy the curse on this land.

"Stone?" Varlett questioned tilting her head slightly. "You mean the All Seeing Stone."

Layala turned her head away. Damn it all. Why did she say that aloud?

"Even if you had it, it wouldn't change anything."

When Layala peeked over again Varlett was gone.

THE ACRID SCENT of something burning pierced Layala's senses. Woken from a light sleep, she quickly hurried to the back door of the cart. It was still dark, but morning light peeked over the horizon. It smelled of burning wood. Oh Maker, no. Not again. Doonafell couldn't take another attack from pale ones. They'd already suffered so much, just months before, and were still rebuilding. Layala kicked at the door, grunting as her foot slammed over and over. "Come on, you piece of shit."

Why wasn't the entire camp on high alert? Could no one else smell that? The few guards she spotted walking nearby were laughing. Aldrich emerged out of the tent closest to her and stretched his arms over his head with a big yawn. A slender brunette with big messy curls came out moments later and wrapped her arms around his waist. Layala stopped kicking, knowing he'd hear it. When he looked over at her, she stuck her arm between the bars and flipped her middle finger. "Stupid bastard," she murmured. She almost blurted out about the smell of smoke, but she clamped

her teeth together. If the pale ones attacked, that would be her way out of here.

With his arm slung around the maiden wearing only an oversized white tunic, Aldrich sauntered over. Layala grew a devious smirk when they approached the cart.

"You're smiling for once," Aldrich said.

"I was thinking about when I stab you in the back like you did to Thane and me, only I will be literally stabbing you in the back, and then I will stick your head on a pike after I cut it off, so all will know to never betray me... and that thought made me smile."

Aldrich pulled his arm from around the squirming maiden and tucked it to his side. "You know, for how much you hate my father, you sound exactly like him."

"Your father only wishes he is capable of what I will do. You chose the wrong side." She plastered on a huge fake grin. "Have a nice breakfast."

The female stepped behind Aldrich and after he stared at her long and hard, he walked away. Maybe he regretted what he did. There was some sorrow in that stare. But he could never be trusted again, never be redeemed after a betrayal of this magnitude. He'd only thought about himself, and his own power and Thane might be gone because of it. *I will bring magic back to the elves and they will love me for it.* Conceited, arrogant fool.*

She pulled the last hairpin from behind her ear and held it before her face. "Don't fail me." Then she reached down and wiggled the pin into the big metal

lock. She'd tried this every night for three days and broken six flimsy hairpins in the process.

She paused; a shadow passed in the dark forest ahead. The hairs on her arms raised before she lifted her chin. Were the pale ones here? She searched the tree line. Mossy vines hung from branches. Thick green foliage covering the forest floor and wide twisting trunks made it difficult to see deep inside. The horse attached to her prison, neighed, and shifted, moving the cart enough that Layala tipped sideways and lost her grip on the pin. She cursed, and reached for it again, praying it was still in the lock. Her fingers grasped the tiny metal bar, and she sighed in relief. Another shadow moved in the woods. *Get out. Get out. Get out*, she chanted in her head.

The crunch of metal and the dying groan of someone nearby made Layala work furiously at the lock. She twisted and pushed and prodded. *Please. Please work.* The metal pin snapped. "Damn it all," she snarled.

Another quiet moan and a body hitting the ground, drew her arm back inside. At least the pale ones couldn't get her in here, right? But they weren't usually sneaky like this were they? More of a brute force attack with shrilling wails and—a black-winged helmet caught her eye. *Holy shit.* "That is a Raven helmet," she murmured. That little spark of hope she'd held onto for weeks soared. Was he here? Had he finally come?

Snapping jaws and wholly black eyes on a

ravenous face popped up outside the window. Layala shrieked and fell back hard on her wrist. It ached as she scooted until she hit the wall. The pale one sniffed the air. "Mmm, you smell delicious." Chest rising up and down, she pressed harder into the wall as it circled to the side drawing closer. "You're the mage, aren't you? The one master says not to touch." His voice was rough, and he smelled like he died weeks ago, like his flesh rotted while he walked and breathed. "But one little lick wouldn't hurt."

Following him closely with her eyes, she swallowed hard. *He can't get in here. He can't get in here.*

He wrapped his white hands around the bars and pressed his face against the metal and stuck out his long black tongue. What she wouldn't do to have a weapon to slice that disgusting thing off. "Come here," he said in a sing-song voice. "Let us have a taste."

His eyes suddenly bulged, and he stiffened, and his mouth opened wide into a silent scream. Then he dropped, disappearing from view. That Raven winged helmet she saw earlier took the beast's place. "Lady Layala?" a male with an accent questioned.

Layala jumped up, and dove at the window, heart crashing like a thundergod's hammer. Bright red hair, tattooed moons on a beautiful, blue-eyed, and brown-skinned face. Layala beamed. "Leif," she nearly cried, and reached through the bars.

He took her hand and held it. "Fightbringer," he said with a smile. "It's good to see you. We've been worried."

"Where is he? Is he here?" She couldn't keep the desperation from her voice. She searched the darkness around them. Another Raven moved along the shadows of a nearby tent, but he didn't look large enough to be Thane.

"He's here for you."

Those words flooded her with relief and happy tears slid down her cheeks. "He's alive? Maker above," she breathed, smiling. "He's alive. He's *alive*." All that worry, that back and forth of wondering, finally put to rest. She wanted to shout his name, to see him come running, and behold his beautiful face. She couldn't wait.

Leif patted her hand. "He is. And he's come to get you. The Ravens are here for you, but not enough to defeat the king's guard. We must be quiet."

"The lock." Layala moved to the door. "Break the lock. Get me out."

Leif bent down to inspect it. "That's a big bastard. It will take a lot of force to break it. Which will be loud. I need to get Thane. He will be able to get you out with his magic."

He took a step away and Layala reached out. "Don't leave me. Please." Her breaths came faster now. She could picture him melting into the darkness and never seeing him again.

Offering a reassuring smile, he said, "You're not going anywhere, and I'll be right back with Thane. I promise. You're safe now."

She slowly nodded with threatening tears sting-

ing. In a stealthy run, he took off and disappeared among the trees. It wasn't but moments later a loud horn blew. Layala jumped and darted to the other side of the prison cart where the sound came from. Several groups of four to six soldiers made their way toward the blowing horn to the North, metal armor clinking as they dashed.

"Intruders!" a deep voice shouted. "Pale ones! And Ravens!" The voice was full of fear now. "We're under attack!"

"Don't let them get the mage!" someone bellowed. "They are here for her!"

A pale one walked around the side of the cart, and the sorrel horse attached to Layala's cart neighed loudly. "What do we have here? A scared little she-elf? Let's hear you scream." He slammed his fists over and over on the wood door, rattling it so loudly it hurt her ears. Layala clenched her teeth together and moved as far away as she could. "Come here." He reached through the bars and clawed at her. "Come here so I can have a little snack."

Layala stooped down and picked up a handful of round goat droppings. "Have a taste of this!" she shouted and threw it in his face.

With a sharp squeal, the pale one jerked back and with pure hatred in his black eyes, he dashed to the front of the cart, and sliced through the rope holding the horse to a post. He hit the hindquarters of the horse and shrieked at the poor creature until Layala

fought the urge to cover her ears. The horse lurched forward, sending Layala crashing into the back door.

No! No, she couldn't leave this spot.

The pale one laughed as the horse, wagon, and Layala ripped by. "Scream, little elf," the pale one said with a laugh.

Layala desperately reached for a hold on something as they slammed over bumps, sending her bouncing around like a toy doll inside. Her head smacked onto the floor of the cart and then again on the bench. Warm blood trickled down into her left eye. Damn it. She mopped it with her sleeve and pushed up, jumping for the bars. "Stop, horse!" she yelled. She didn't want to shout for help. The wrong hero might catch her.

Tents, fires, and trees whipped by so fast everything became a blur. The sound of swords clanging rang out over the squealing of the wheels and stamping horse hooves. This horse had to come to a stop sometime soon, right? It would get tired and then hopefully it would be Thane who found her. If only they still had their mate bond, he'd be led right to her.

The momentum suddenly shifted, and they careened downhill. Great. Layala peered out the bars; there was nothing and no one around. The city of Doonafell was in the opposite direction. At her back the camp's fire lights grew dim, and the sounds of fighting drifted away. The road they were on was so overgrown with grass that it could barely even be

called a path anymore. Had she been this way before? It didn't look familiar.

Just ahead a staked wooden sign came into view. She narrowed her eyes to read: "Warning: road ends. Cliff."

"Shit. A cliff! A blasted cliff?" She looked around the cart she'd rummaged through for days for something to use to break free. There was nothing and the reins to control the horse were way out of reach. "Stop! Halt, you damned horse!" *Doesn't it know commands?* "Halt! Whoa—Walk!" The stressed wheels squealed even louder.

She slammed her palm against the metal bars in frustration. She only had one hope left. "Thane!" she screamed and her throat burned. "Thane!" Her voice echoed off the hillside, and if that was the last word her lips ever uttered, at least it was his name.

CHAPTER 11

Thane crouched behind a stack of wine barrels and listened to the footsteps of passing guards. Breath shallow and silent, he peeked out. He stared at a tall and wide beige canvas, and the shadow of the figures inside. One male, one female. A strange vibration flowed through him, making his skin sensitive and prickly with anticipation, fury, calm. Tenebris burst from the opening, tossing aside the tent flap.

Thane expected a furious outrage to course through him. He'd imagined this moment, where he would run forward and end his father for good, but he was surprised when it felt like a weight lifted off his chest. And the tense coiling of his gut relaxed. Why did he still love him? Why couldn't he cling to hatred, and believe all the evil he was? Yet seeing his father's familiar stern face, the pale-blond hair, the way his spine was always rigid, flooded Thane with ease. Tenebris was truly alive. He knew that when he'd seen him at a distance

on the hillside near Castle Dredwich before everything went to hell, but now he was merely yards away, and it was indeed him. Not a delusion or a trick.

Adjusting his body armor at the neck, Tenebris lifted his chin. "She better be well guarded," he barked at one of the guards standing next to him. "How many are there?"

"Aldrich was left in charge of her. And I'm not sure, High King."

"Is my son among them?"

The guard was silent for a moment. He and the other three exchanged quick glances. "Prince Thane?"

"Of course, Prince Thane," Tenebris snapped.

"We don't know."

"Find him and bring him to me."

Thane's sweaty palm gripped tighter around the sword handle. His heart crashed wildly in his chest. He was here for Layala, not retribution, but his father was so close... and yet if he went to strike him down, could he do it? Maker, the regret that wracked him for weeks, haunted his dreams was all for nothing. Could he live with that a second time?

The four guards shifted nervously. "Bring him, sire? We thought he was dead."

"Do what you're told, or *you'll* be dead."

"But Prince Thane is—umm, dangerous. I don't know how we can—"

A swift backhand cracked across the guard's cheek. "I know what he is. I raised him, and he's no fool. I

have what he wants. He'll come willingly to see his father."

Tenebris wouldn't just give Layala over, so what sort of offer could his father possibly have? He thought for sure the order would be to kill on sight. After all that transpired between them, Tenebris was willing to talk face to face? Wasn't he worried Thane would kill him? And yet here Thane sat back on his heels, unmoving, when it would take minimal effort to take out those guards and have his father at the end of his sword. An easy, clean death. A twinge of pain in his center reminded him of the suffering both he and Layala endured these past few weeks on his father's account. About the beatings he took as a child, and the screams of innocents on this tyrant's account. He gritted his teeth and pushed up.

"Tenebris," the female inside the tent called. Thane stilled at his mother's voice, sinking back down into the shadows. "What's going on?"

"Go back inside, dear. There are pale ones close."

"I don't care about pale ones." Her voice was as sharp as a finely whittled pike. "Did you say Thane is here? Let's put this mess behind us and settle the misunderstanding. I want my son back."

"I don't know if the matter can be settled, Orlandia. He tried to have me killed."

She lifted her chin and put her hand on his arm. "I don't believe that. Thane would never. Not my darling boy. He's always protected you."

His face twisted into a sneer, and he said in a low, raspy voice, "I remember that day quite vividly."

"It's that lowly elf mage you bound him to. She twisted his mind. I'm sure of it. She's angry about the death of her parents, at your hand, need I remind you? Those feelings leached into our son." Orlandia brushed her fingers down Tenebris's cloak. "We can fix it."

Thane slammed his eyes shut at the bitter anger softening inside him. Could it be fixed? Did life give him and his family a second chance? When he was young, he wanted nothing more than for his father to love him. For him to voice it just once. He wanted to beg him to care for him for any other reason than his connection with Layala. And though he hated it, those old feelings lingered even still. He worked diligently to become lethal, an effective killing brute for his father to try to earn his love. He couldn't deny he was what he was today because of the elf king... and if he didn't repair this relationship, he could never face his mother again. She would never forgive Thane if he murdered Tenebris, not especially now that she had her beloved husband back. So, could Thane too forgive like his mother wanted?

No. Maker above, how could he be conflicted about this? His father sent the dragon to break his mate bond so he could kill Thane and steal his mate. Ripped them apart without remorse. As if they could all live together as one big family? As if he could ever ask Layala to sit at the same table as the king who had her

parents executed? This feud was about love and power and neither side would yield. He would not yield. He *could* not yield. Because Layala would make him choose and he could never pick anyone over her. He'd made that choice years before he ever even met her.

"Once we have our magic, everything can be settled. Thane can have his betrothed, and you can forgive what he tried to do to you. He'll need convincing after you stole his mate. I've heard the kind of agony that causes. You hurt my boy, Tenebris."

Tenebris pushed her hand away. "It's not that simple. There are things you don't know yet."

She stuck a finger near his face. "I forgave you for having a child with another, and even allowed him to become part of our family, allowed him to befriend *my* son. You can forgive this. Make it that simple."

Even his mother knew Aldrich was his half-brother and she never said anything? Why? Who was Aldrich's mother? And did Aldrich betray him all for a chance at the throne? One thing Thane knew for sure was that Orlandia would never accept a bastard son over Thane, but did he have a claim?

"Psst."

Thane tore his sight from his parents and glanced over his shoulder. Leif crept among the shadows of the gathered horses and then darted across the opening and kneeled beside Thane. "I found her. She's—"

"Thane!" Layala's shrill, desperate call struck him like an arrow through the chest. He shot to his full height, not caring if Tenebris, his mother or the guards

saw him. How far away was she? The way her scream echoed off the rising cliffs distorted it. Turning to the east where her distant voice came from, he searched the dark. A skirmish between his father's soldiers and pale ones raged on, but he couldn't find her among the flashing metal in the moonlight and the shadows that clashed. Why wasn't she guarded here in the camp?

He met his father's gaze, but his muscles tensed. *Run run run, get to her*, and so he ran. Not entirely sure where he was going but he trusted his instincts to find her.

"Thane, come back here!" Tenebris bellowed.

But the only call he cared about was hers. His feet glided over the grassy landscape like he wore winged boots. He jumped over a set of broken barrels, slammed his shoulder into a guard, knocking him to the ground. A pale one dared enter his path. With a thought he snapped the hideous thing's femurs and he buckled to the ground with a howl. *Hold on, I'm coming.*

"Thane!" Layala's cry was like claws digging into his chest and tightening around his heart.

He'd never heard her sound this distraught, and the pounding of his heart intensified. What was happening to her? Who attacked her? Maker, all he could see was her blood, the pain on her beautiful face.

The sword in Leif's hand glinted in the pale light as he caught up to Thane. "Damn it, I shouldn't have left her."

"You *left* her?" Thane snarled, as they flew over the

grassy terrain. Then he saw it, the runaway cart careening down a hill he knew ended in a massive cliff. The horse came loose and bolted in another direction. She wasn't being attacked or tortured; she was about to fall to her death. He could stop the momentum of small things but a raging cart? He pushed wind and imagined the cart's wheels stopping and though the metal on wood squealed, it didn't slow enough.

Shit. He pushed harder until his legs and lungs screamed with effort, until the muscles tore. "Laya!" *Come on, shift through space. Do something!* But he had no control over that part of himself.

One of her arms stuck out through the barred window, reaching for him. "Thane, help me!" Her voice was strangled and full of anguish. It hurt him to even hear. Magic warmed his palms and tingled through his fingertips again. He was close enough to see the lock and broke it with hardly more effort than he blinked. The door swung open, and she stood at the edge.

"Jump!" he roared and then snapped the back wheel with magic. The cart dropped into the dirt, pitching on its side but skidding toward the cliff feet away. She had seconds—a moment, but the grass ended and as if in slow motion like rain droplets slipping down a window, the cart disappeared over the edge with her in it. Her terrified scream pierced the night air. Thane's heart lurched into his throat, *no no no no.* She couldn't be gone. He was so close to her, so close! Her smiles, her laugh, the way she kissed him

the first time and then shoved a knife to his throat flashed in his mind. Even though she'd wanted him dead, he wouldn't ever forget the way a shot of energy pulsed into him when her lips met his.

The thud of his heart drummed in his ears. The pounding of his footsteps matched its pace, and without slowing, he leapt off the edge after her.

CHAPTER 12

Wind rushed past, blurring his eyes with tears, but she was there. Layala broke free of the cart and her skirts billowed out around her, her mass of wild black waves flowing freely like a flag torn to ribbons near a windy sea. She was close—inches. The wind was deafening, drowning out the roar of his own voice screaming her name. His fingers wiggled; his arm strained to reach her. *So close. Just grab her!*

Moments before her face had been twisted in fear, as if all hope dashed away. But as they stared at each other now, there was calm in the soft lines around her tear-streaked eyes, a slight part in her lips, almost smiling. Focused and relieved. As if she had every confidence in the world he would save her from breaking on the jagged rocks below. Hands grasped for one another, until finally flesh met flesh. Thane gripped her and jerked her into him, body flush against his and then he summoned every drop of

magic he possessed. Like the time he shifted through an impossible distance to get Layala to the mage tower, power hummed like wild drums beating against his skin. Wind rushed all around them in swirling jet streams, slowing their descent until they floated, suspended in air. Layala wrapped her thighs around his waist and hooked her elbows around the back of his neck. They both breathed heavily in sync, greedily dragging in air and relief.

When it seemed like many moments passed, she whispered, "Are we—flying? Or are we dead in the afterlife?"

Thane smiled, but when he looked down the pit in his stomach grew. The cart crashed with a boom, splintering on rough boulders below. They were seconds away from the same fate. Thane had never attempted to fly before, but his magic rose to his call, and it felt strange to say it, but he whispered, "I'd say we're floating," he paused thinking of how absurd it was, "and we're still in Palenor." He pressed one palm flat against her back and the other, he cupped her behind. "Hold on." A strong whoosh of wind brought them back up onto sturdy ground, and he moved away from the cliff's edge, holding her tight. He took in a few steadying breaths, thanking the Maker to be alive and to have the maiden he loved more than all the stars in the sky in his arms. He gently rubbed Layala's back, basking in what it was like to feel the warmth of her embrace again. After a couple moments ticked by

and she kept her vice-like hold, he said, "You can open your eyes now."

She pulled away enough to look him in the face. Her fingers dug into him with frantic strength. "Thane," she whispered and then her lips crashed into his. Frenzied and hungry, claiming a long-lost prize. He smiled against her lips, laughter almost bubbling up in his throat. It was euphoric. Maker above, he'd missed her. He'd imagined this moment for weeks now, and before that, for much of his life. And she was here, and she loved him. His mate, the beautiful maiden of his dreams.

With her thighs still tightly hooked around his torso, she took his face in her hands and pulled back, cheeks glistening. "It's really you. You're here. You're alive."

"It's really me."

Tears cascaded down her cheeks and she choked on a sob even though she was grinning from ear to ear. "I was terrified I lost you. I tried to stop her. I tried to get to you—"

Thane cut her off with a kiss, willing her to feel the ocean depths of how much he loved her. None of it was important; the only thing that mattered was that she was safe, and they were together. "I know."

"But... What happened? Varlett slammed me into a tree, and I hit my head. I tried to escape," she gulped in air, "to find you." Her voice was still rushed, fraught.

"Laya," he said calmly, brushing his fingers over

her cheek, wiping her tears. "I love you. And I am here now."

A loud throat clearing made them both turn their heads. Leif tapped one boot on the ground. "Uh, I hate to break up the reunion, but it won't be long before they come looking this way. Also, if you two could refrain from jumping off cliffs in the future that would be great. Even if you knew you could fly, I didn't." He put a hand to his chest. "I threw up a little."

Thane chuckled. "I didn't know. But I wasn't going to let her die."

"I asked you not to leave me," Layala said, and shot him a glare.

Rubbing the back of his neck, Leif said, "I am sorry. Trust I won't make a mistake like that again."

Layala slid down Thane's body to the ground and gripped his hand, intertwining her fingers with his. He brought her knuckles to his lips and gently kissed them. "He's right. My father saw me. They'll be on their way here with a formidable force, no doubt."

Taking off, they headed west toward the city of Doonafell. A place they fought so fiercely to protect from the enemy his father now freely rode with. He never quite understood how his father made a deal with Mathekis and yet the pale ones still attacked at regular intervals. Was that what his father wanted? Wouldn't he have made a deal to stop the attacks? Or maybe they would only stop if he delivered Layala to Mathekis. Or did Tenebris want the pale ones to attack Palenor so that he could keep the hold on his power?

One thing Tenebris had over the people was that he protected them, and he was great at it. That earned trust and allegiance.

Even Brunard taunted him about his father's ability to keep them at bay, but once Thane was in power, they overran a major elven city and killed hundreds. They'd never been capable of that before, or at least that's what he believed. He thought it was his own incompetence or that they pushed harder now that they knew where Layala was. Perhaps it was a combination of everything. Exactly how far did the depths of his father's betrayal of this kingdom go?

Once they drew closer to the city, Thane made sure to stick close to the well-beaten paths to avoid being tracked. He squeezed Layala's hand every once in a while, and looked over at her lovely face to reassure himself she was there and that this wasn't some delusion of his broken mind. The tangles in her usually shiny raven-wing hair, smudges of dirt on her cheeks, and her chapped, scabbed lips ignited a spark of anger. The fiery hatred he held for his father burned once more.

They quietly made their way around the outside stone wall of Doonafell where elves stacked stone on stone, slapping on globs of mud to repair the holes. The workers didn't bother to look up as the trio jogged by.

The white-stone mage's tower came into view. The ivy and climbing vines that overtook much of the weatherworn stone appeared even greener and thicker

than the last time he'd seen it, on account of the start of the autumn rains.

"Could we stop here and rest?" Layala panted. "I haven't seen anyone following us," she dragged in another breath, "and maybe Atarah could hide us."

Thane slowed to a halt, dragging his gaze over her. He was so used to her being able to run like wild horses. This showed how she was treated. In fact, the more he really analyzed her, he was surprised she wasn't thinner and more sallow. Her breasts, waist, and hips were smaller, but he would never have noticed if he hadn't thoroughly inspected her form on many occasions before. "We can't stop. It will put you in danger when my father looks here. Get on my back."

Without her usual do-it-herself attitude, she nodded. He bent his knees and she jumped onto him, latching her body around his. What a change from the elf he'd first met. She would have never willingly accepted his help in this way, at least not without a fight.

They arrived in Fanvore Wood, and after climbing over fallen logs and through thick vines and dodging snakes and critters, they found the designated gathering spot: a group of ruined statues of four old gods, standing at least nine feet tall. Thane didn't know their names or what they were said to be gods of; they'd been lost to history but three were male, one holding a broken sword at his side and another large ax raised above his head. His long hair was carved in waves to his chest. His chin and nose had been broken

off at some point but the fierceness in those stone eyes made him ponder about who he might have been.

The second male stood tall and erect, with his hands tucked behind his back. A smirk played at his lips, as if he knew something everyone else did not. The flowing cape was worn and chipped, and the sword pommel at his hip was intricate. The blade itself was broken like the other. It was a shame someone hadn't taken care of these rather than let them go to ruin.

The third statue's head was crumbled, and body so weathered it was difficult to make out more than the trident in his hand and the belt holding up his trousers. The pillar beside him was the only one left standing among fallen piles of boulders covered in foliage and debris.

"These are—beautiful," Layala said and brushed her bandaged hand over the goddesses' moss-covered knee. "Why didn't you take me here before?" It was the female any who saw marveled at. Hers was the most well-preserved. She sat on a throne, with deep carvings of snakes behind her and twisted around down her arms. A starburst behind her head almost looked like she wore a headpiece, her legs crossed, chin raised, long hair carved as if flowing in the wind. A deep vee neck down to her navel, revealed full, round breasts. This goddess was power and allure. He believed if she were real, he would no doubt kneel. There were said to be other statues scattered throughout Adalon but he'd never seen them.

Thane smiled and rubbed the back of his neck. "I didn't think about it and it's pretty far from where we camped."

"Who are they?"

"From the old world," Leif said. "My Nana told me stories about the old gods that her gran told her. This used to be a sanctum, I think. Not much left of it. Many would travel from all over to see this place."

The group of Ravens, silent as a graveyard, emerged from the shadows like wraiths. Thane's eye was immediately drawn to the pair with their arms slung over helpers. They wore fresh clothes, but their hair was dirty. A smile tugged at the corners of his mouth. "Piper. Fennan." In a few strides he was before them and he wanted nothing more than to squeeze them both in bone-crushing hugs but with Piper's bruised cheeks shining with healing salve, he resisted. She eased out of the grasp of the Raven holding her and pressed her head against Thane's chest. Thane gently hugged her, careful not to use too much pressure. Fennan's right arm was wrapped in a sling, but he walked over with ease to embrace his friend. "Get over here, Fightbringer," Fennan said. She smiled and joined in the group hug.

"It's so good to see you both." Thane grinned. He wanted to be angry with what they'd been put through, but relief dominated everything else. His best friends were alive.

"Layala?" Evalyn called stepping out from behind a pair of Ravens. "Is it really you?"

Layala pulled away from them, and her dirty hand flew to her mouth. She rushed forward, throwing her arms around her aunt. "He didn't tell me you were here!" She pushed back, searching her face. "How did you get here?" She looked at Thane. "Why didn't you tell me?"

"I thought it would be a nice surprise."

Evalyn hugged her tightly. "I missed you, my sweet child. Are you well? What can I do for you?"

"I'm fine now." Her smile revealed her pretty, white teeth and tears sparkled in her eyes. "How did you meet Thane? I'm just so surprised you're here."

"Well," Evalyn said. "I found him so I could find you." She brushed her hand over Layala's wild hair, flattening out the strays. "So, you can come home. Everyone misses you. Forrest and Ren have been positively bored without you. It took me convincing them every day to let you go and do what we always planned."

Layala gently tugged away from her aunt and looked at Thane. "You didn't tell her?"

"I told her enough."

Evalyn patted Layala's wrist. "Your mate bond is broken, and you are free to come home. He said he'd let you go if that's what you want, and it's what you want, isn't it?"

Everyone watched with rapt attention, Thane included. Would Layala choose to leave? He couldn't even fathom it but if that's what she chose... Maker, he

suddenly felt nauseous even thinking about it. He couldn't bear her opting to leave him a second time.

"I love him," Layala said. "And I will go where he is. As much as I love Briar Hollow and you, and the others, Thane is my home now." She looked at him. "He's my everything."

Fennan whistled and pushed Thane in the back. "Go on, give her a kiss after that." Deep chuckles from the Ravens standing all around brought a lovely blush to Layala's cheeks.

"Don't be shy on my account," Evalyn said, shaking her head but smirking. "I'm just a little taken aback given—everything."

"Now it's uncomfortable with all of you watching," Layala said, rolling her eyes and waving her hand in dismissal.

"Don't worry, I'll get that kiss later."

Leif slapped Thane on the shoulder. "Hopefully more than that after the rescue we just pulled, aye."

"Oh, Maker above," Layala crowed and folded her arms. "We're not even going to start a public discussion about what Thane and I do." She rolled her eyes then glanced around. "Does anyone know what happened to Tifapine?"

"Here I am!" Tifapine poked her head out of the saddle bag on Phantom among the trees nearby. She stuck her arm out and waved but kept the leather flap half covering her. "No need to worry about me."

Layala's hand pressed to her chest. "Tif, I'm relieved you're alright." Tif smiled but when many of

the Ravens turned to look at her, she quickly ducked back inside and slammed the flap closed. Layala shook her head slowly but smiled. Things hadn't changed with the little gnome.

Thane turned back to Piper and Fennan, beaten and bruised because of his incompetence. He should have seen Aldrich for the traitor he was sooner. Piper's swollen black eye made his chest hurt and he didn't know how serious Fennan's arm injury was. "I should have been able to get you all sooner. I am sorry I was not."

"Don't say that. We're just thankful you're alive," Fennan said, patting Thane's armored shoulder. "We heard many rumors. For a couple weeks we thought you were dead, and the only reason we were being kept alive was to be used against," his gaze shifted to Layala, "You."

"That *is* the only reason you were kept alive." Layala let her eyes drop and her perfect lips turned into a frown. "And it would have worked. I would have done it."

Thane ran his fingers from her shoulder to her wrist and gently wrapped his hand around hers. He wished he could feel her emotions and send her comfort. It was so strange he couldn't. A lifetime of feeling that gentle tug, that line of connection obliterated in a few moments. Would they ever get that back? Would she want to be mate bonded to him again? Now there was a choice.

"Sire, we shouldn't stay here long," Leif offered,

removing his helmet. He shook his long red hair and smoothed pieces of it down. "They will track us here."

"What's our next move?" Fennan asked.

"Head north." Thane released Layala's hand and folded his arms.

"We can't leave," Layala blurted out. "I promised your father death and I'm not leaving without making good on that." Her chin trembled slightly. "He slit Reina's throat. Did you know that? He starved me for weeks and locked me up in that tower. The bastard needs to die, and we know exactly where he is right now. This is the perfect time." Layala lifted her chin and met him with a hard stare. "And we can take Mathekis down while we're at it." Some of the Ravens murmured. She pinned them with a glare. "Are you afraid?"

Evalyn stepped to her side and held her hand, rubbing her back with the other. Such a motherly thing to do. "Honey, you need rest and healing."

Thane nodded in agreement with Evalyn, but he knew better than to try and tell her she couldn't do something unless he wanted a fight. "You are brave, and I admire that. But many have tried to kill Mathekis. He's nine hundred years old and no one has done it yet. And my father has two thousand soldiers or more at his disposal who won't hesitate to kill us. Even if I had all five hundred of my Ravens here it would be a very bloody battle that would take the lives of too many of my soldiers."

She tore her gaze away, muttering a curse. "Swear to me, I will get my revenge."

Evalyn looked at him too, waiting. Layala wasn't the only one who wanted Tenebris dead.

"I swear it. When the time is right."

"And I will be the one to end Mathekis." She licked her lips. "I'll find a way."

Thane smiled at her confidence, as did many of the others. She may very well be the one, but he didn't want to find out just yet. He hadn't come to a one-on-one fight with Mathekis before. Deep down both Thane and Mathekis avoided the conflict, even if not intentionally.

"Fightbringer," Leif said, crossing his arms, "We'd all love to see both dead and burned and as much faith as we have in your ability, no one has ever gotten close enough to Mathekis to do it. Our arrows miss him as if he's protected by some force. Not even Thane has been able to touch him with his magic."

A few murmured "yeses" and some shakes of the heads from the Ravens followed his statement. "The only way to kill Mathekis is to destroy the Void," Piper said, as she leaned against the goddess statue. "That's how this all ends, Layala. You destroy the Void, you get revenge."

That fact sat with everyone for a moment of silence before Thane said, "We'll need to split up to throw off our trail. Fennan, Piper, Leif, Gunner and Siegfried will come with me. The rest of you will take the old road north to Brightheart to meet with the

other Ravens and wait for us there. Steer clear of the main road."

"Where will you go?" Nash, one of the other Ravens asked.

"Lakeside road."

Everyone moved to their mounts, but Layala grabbed Thane's hand stopping him. Her beautiful blue eyes searched his face for a moment. "I need to tell you what Varlett said."

CHAPTER 13

Layala watched Thane bend his knees and hold out his palms for her to put her shoe into. The once-white slippers were stained in grime and dirt so thick she was embarrassed to touch him. Her filthy, ripped dress smelled like goat shit and sour sweat. And he'd have to ride with her pressed against him for hours? She hadn't thought about it when she was falling to her death and he held her against him but now, her life wasn't on the line. He might be a little sweaty and dirty but somehow, he still smelled good and looked as beautiful as ever.

He looked up at her expectantly. "What's the matter?"

Tif popped out of the saddlebag. "Yeah, what's the matter? Are you upset Thane didn't bring Midnight? I said, 'she's going to want her horse', when the bridge guard retrieved Phantom from the barns, but no one listened to the poor little gnome. I bet even Midnight is upset he got left behind."

Layala glanced around at the Ravens, mounted up and already on their way moving out. "It's not that... Are there any clean clothes for me to change into?"

"Midnight is fine in the barn. It was enough of a risk for the stable master to grab Phantom," Thane said to Tif. He turned to Layala, "And if you're worried anyone is judging your appearance, we're not. Besides, the grimy look is turning me on a little."

Leif and Fennan laughed, of course. Layala narrowed her eyes. "Only you."

"Don't worry, Layala," Tif said with a big toothy grin. "I will wash your dress as soon as we can. It will be as bright and shiny as new."

Layala fidgeted with her hands, scratching at the dirt under her nails. It sounded stupid when she thought about it, but she was the only one who smelled like animal droppings. The last thing she wanted was to be pressed up against Thane and have him revolted by her scent. This certainly wasn't how she imagined their reunion. If she had Midnight, she might let this go.

Horses knickered and danced impatiently as the remaining Ravens waited on their mounts. Even Aunt Evalyn looked to be growing impatient. "Layala, you look fine," Evalyn said. "Since when did you start caring about fashion?"

"I don't care what I look like." That was only a small lie.

"Go on ahead." Thane waved them off. "We'll catch up."

Without hesitation, the group vanished among the trees into the darkness, except Evalyn who waited a moment, as if afraid to leave them alone together, but she too gave her horse a nudge and moved on.

When she was gone, Thane hooked a thumb on the weapons belt around his hips. "Do I need to threaten to put you on the horse again, stubborn one?"

"Oooo this is going to be good." Tif rubbed her hands together with a wicked grin.

Layala lightly bit her lip to keep from smiling at Tif's comment and folded her arms. "Try it and see what happens. You couldn't even if you wanted to."

He laughed. "Maker above, I've missed you."

She no longer held back that smile as warmth blossomed in her chest. How she'd missed him too. "What happened after—" the rest of the sentence caught in her throat. It hurt to remember him bleeding out on the forest floor, and the gaping hole through his center.

"It's not a long story but it's one I'd love to tell you." He gestured toward Phantom. "On the way."

"I saved him," Tif blurted out and rubbed her nails on her dress in a show of taking credit. Thane tilted his head in a lazy glare at her. "What? I helped. Don't try to deny it, and if I didn't speak tweet, think of the mess we'd be in."

"Tif was with you?"

"As I said, on the way," he motioned toward the horse again. "Besides, I'm more worried about getting you something to eat than what you're wearing." He

reached into the bag and pulled out a brown cloth wrap. "It's not much but something."

"You're telling me you don't have any clothes in your bag?" She continued, stubbornly and snatched whatever was inside the cloth. She unwrapped it and bit into the hardened piece of bread.

"None that will fit you. But you can still take yours off. I won't mind."

Tif's eyes widened. "Should I plug my ears now? I think I should plug my ears." With her ruddy cheeks brightening she ducked into the bag again, closing the flap over her head.

Layala chuckled at both of them, but it was Thane she spoke to. "Oh, you'd have me ride naked? With your Ravens to see no less. I didn't think you were the sharing type."

"I'm not." He stepped forward and lightly ran his fingers over her cheek. The gesture made her flinch. It was the same thing the Black Mage did in her dreams.

His brows furrowed and he dropped his hand. "My father hit you." The growl in his voice brought chills to her skin. He took her bandaged hand into his. "And this?"

"He hurt me. Just like you told me he would." She didn't dare reveal her dreams and the real reason she flinched. She was disgusted with herself that she had any connection to the Black Mage at all.

Suddenly, the forest darkened like a cloud blocked out the morning sun and the tang of Thane's magic coated the air.

"I'm alright." She closed her eyes and wrapped her arms around his middle.

He hugged her close. "I'm so sorry I wasn't there for you."

"I know."

They stood like that for what felt like a long time, basking in the heat and closeness. The embrace had its own kind of healing that no salves or magic could ever compare to. Her home.

He ran his hands down her sides and stopped on her hips and inhaled. "You *do* smell bad. No wonder you were worried."

She jerked back and shoved him in the chest. "You had to ruin the moment." She grabbed hold of Phantom's saddle. "Just for that comment, you can smell me the whole way. I won't even bathe or change when we get a chance. We'll see if you're turned on by my grimy look then."

He smiled in that devastatingly handsome way that was difficult to be angry at, and dropped to one knee, holding open his palms. She stepped into his waiting hands, and he lifted her with ease. "You're too easy to rile up, Laya," he said. "But it worked."

When she settled in, he climbed up and sat behind her. The corners of her mouth curled as she felt the pressure of his strong, firm body like a wall behind her. Maker, she loved him. "What worked?"

"To get you on the horse. I've successfully used your stubbornness against you. One mark for Thane."

With her mouth agape, she looked over her shoul-

der. The nerve. "First of all, what sort of arrogant turd refers to himself in the third person, and this is the game you want to play? Alright then."

"I've been besting you at this game since we met, my dear." The timbre of his voice vibrated her skin.

She thrust her backside hard into his crotch and rubbed against him. There was nothing but cloth there, no armor to stop him from feeling her body. He sucked in a sharp breath and wrapped his arm tightly around her waist in reaction. "Mmm, don't do that."

She wiggled again with a growing smile. "What's the matter, Thane?"

He chuckled. "I can't very well hump you against those statues and have my father ride up and slit my throat then take you from me. Even though I thought about it a few times already. The humping part, obviously."

Grinning, she twisted to look at the statues. The idea was intriguing.

Thane caged his arms around her to grab hold of the reins. "I think that might be what kept me alive. Picturing you naked. Or maybe it was the thought of your plump, soft breasts in my—" she elbowed him in the gut, and he laughed again. He nudged Phantom's sides with his heels and the horse started on a slow walk. "Am I making you blush?"

Layala's cheeks were indeed warmer. She shifted in the saddle, as a pleasant heat built in her. But as he said, it's not as if they could get down and dirty when Tenebris and his minions could be nearby. "Hardly. A

minute ago you were telling me I stink, and you expect me to let you carry on with your bedroom talk?"

"You're blushing," he whispered in her ear. She shivered as his lips grazed her ear. "So, are you going to tell me what Varlett said or was that a ruse to get me alone?"

Layala snickered and leaned her back into him, something she would have avoided before. "She said our mate bond can't be restored. Do you think that's true?"

His gentle breath brushed against her ear. The quiet hoot of an owl echoed from a tree branch nearby, but he didn't speak. Layala's mouth twisted, and she patted Phantom's soft neck. After what felt like too long, she asked softly, "Did you hear me?"

"Yes." He cleared his throat. "I'm thinking."

"About?"

"Do you want that? To be mate bonded to me again?"

"Of course I do." She turned to look him in the face. But then it occurred to her that maybe his hesitation was that he didn't want to be bound to her. Her cheeks flushed. "Um, it's alright if you don't. I would understand." As they both well knew, they hadn't chosen that the first time. To be mate bonded through magic was the highest form of loyalty and commitment. It was a literal death sentence to be with someone else, and since their life force was tied to the other, it also meant they lived and died as one.

He brushed his fingers through her hair. His soft

touch sent a tingle through her. "I can hardly stand not being bonded to you. It's making me feel physically ill. But I don't want your life tied to mine like that again unless that's what you truly want. You have a choice now. I never wanted to take that from you. I've never wanted to force you into anything. I want you to choose me and even though you said you wanted to marry me, it was still me or turning into a pale one. That's not much of a choice."

"Varlett gave me the opportunity to break our mate bond with the necklace at her cottage. I chose you then. I chose you at that very moment." She swallowed hard. "It's even more cruel she took it away from us because of that."

"The spell is at the castle. We'll get it."

"She said only the Black Mage could create a mate bond in us again because that spell can't be reused."

"It's just a way for her to manipulate you."

"That was my exact thought except... She helped the Black Mage create the spell, and she knew about Novak dying because of the loyalty clause in the bond." Layala sighed. "What if she's not lying?"

Thane wrapped his arm around her waist and tugged her closer to him. "Let's not worry about that right now. We're together and you're safe and that's what matters most."

"I say we find the All Seeing Stone and ask, along with everything else we need to know."

"I like this plan, my dear betrothed."

She was a little sad he couldn't call her wife yet.

That too had been stolen away from them by Tenebris. One person seemed to ruin everything. She glanced down at the ring Thane gave her, poking through the bandages. The purple jewel and silver band needed washing to sparkle again, like her. With a war against Thane's father and the task of finding the All Seeing Stone, a wedding and a mate bond would have to wait.

THROUGHOUT THE NIGHT, a steady drizzle breached the canopy of branches and leaves above. It was a warm rain, and the forest air felt heavy, damp. Thane offered his cloak, but she liked the feel of nature's bath against her skin, rinsing away the dirt. Horse hooves splashed through creeks and padded over soft ground. The Ravens were eerily quiet in their travel. The toads and crickets made more noise. They rode for hours until morning birds began to sing, and first light peeked through the darkness. When they came to the edge of the forest, the sun pushed through rain clouds, to reveal waving fields of amber and blossoming pink crabapple trees. The wind carried a line of flowers around them on an airstream. Intermingled with them was a six pack of silver and purple pixies laughing and playing with the sweet-smelling blooms. It felt like a good omen from the Maker. A long, dark night to bring a gloriously warm day. She was finally free and reunited with Thane.

Thane held up a fist and the group came to a stop.

Layala glanced around for signs of Tenebris or his army, but no threat was on the horizon. Thane twisted to speak to the group. "We will head west and ride along the lake towns. It will take longer than the main road but it's the best way to avoid my father's army. He'll no doubt send trackers, but we'll deal with them if they catch up." He tugged the reins to the left and started them down a narrow dirt path. He said quietly to Layala, "And while we are in these towns, we can find out more about who might have the stone."

"You think whoever took it will have told anyone?"

"The funny thing about someone who gets an item like that, is they'll want to brag about it. Maybe even sell it. I mean, you read that note. 'I got it first.' That was practically a point-and-laugh moment. They'll have told someone. I have a friend in the next town who deals in rare items, artifacts, and underground information. If anyone has heard, it's him."

"You? Your highness." She turned to look at him. "Slumming with the underground crowd? I'm surprised."

He smiled. "The majority of the elves in Palenor have never seen me. They don't know what I look like. It's easy to slip amongst them unnoticed. My friend Kail knows who I am but most in his tavern don't."

"A tavern? Maybe I can get rip-roaring drunk and give you a little lap dance."

Aunt Evalyn gave her a disgusted scowl, and Layala lightly chewed on her lower lip. It was going to

take some time for her aunt to get used to her relationship with Thane, wasn't it?

Tif stuck her head out of the bag for the first time all night. "Oh, can I too? Get rip-roaring drunk that is, not the lap dance. Although, I mean, I could..." With a cocked eyebrow, Thane looked down at her. Layala couldn't stop herself from laughing. Tif cleared her throat. "Or not. That's inappropriate for a number of reasons." She giggled and wiped her sweaty brow. "Don't take much for me to get tipsy. A couple thimbles and I'll honor you with my yodeling instead of dancing, High King."

He took in a long breath. "Please don't make my life harder than it already is. Either of you."

CHAPTER 14

When they crested a hill, they overlooked a small lake town. One road led in between two rows of colorful homes and businesses. There might have been fifty structures. Some of the buildings were light blue, or yellow, others, various shades of pink. She found it a little odd, having never seen the style of bright colors like this before, but it was unique. At the edge of town, a white lighthouse stood on the sandy beach of the lake. A few white sailboats were docked, and a sign at the bottom of the hill read: Braxentown.

"This is a cute little place," Layala said.

"Don't let it fool you."

"What does that mean?"

Fennan rode up beside them, one hand on the reins, the other still held up by a sling. "Let's just say the quaintness is a cover for what really goes on."

Layala raised her eyebrows. "I'm intrigued."

"Any gambling?" Aunt Evalyn asked.

"It's a bad habit, Aunty," Layala teased.

"Plenty of gambling." Thane pointed out over the water. "It's the narrowest part of the lake. If you look far enough, you can see the human lands of Vessache on the other side. Trade happens with them here. And since this is a trading town, there are lots of human men, as well as other creatures."

Layala noted the many docked sailboats. "I'm surprised your father allows it since he hates humans."

"He doesn't allow it," Thane answered. "He just ignores it because he's busy with his obsession for more power."

"Another reason why you make an infinitely better king than he does," Layala said and patted his thigh.

Thane smiled and then swung his leg over Phantom's back and hit the ground. "We need to change out of our armor. Since Ravens are wanted criminals now."

Clinking metal and murmured talk among the group was quiet enough but Layala still kept watch from the back of Phantom. He grazed on the tall amber wheat, tail swishing at flies and ears twitching. She watched the forest behind them and the open fields as if the enemy might show up at any moment. The other group split off from them hours ago, hoping to draw Tenebris away from Thane and Layala.

"Where is everyone in Briar Hollow now? I heard it was burned down." She paused, thinking of all the

memories from that place. "Does that mean our home is gone?"

Aunt Evalyn shifted in her saddle. "It's gone, Layala. All of it." Her voice sounded thick and hoarse. "But we're rebuilding with the help of neighboring towns. Svenarum's royal investigators showed up, too. They don't dare start a fight with Tenebris. I think it's more fear of the pale ones than anything, but they gave us some supplies to rebuild."

Layala chewed on her bottom lip. She couldn't believe her childhood home was gone. "And the boys? And the new puppy?"

"The boys are fine, taking care of Dregous for me. He's gotten big already and sheds that white fur like crazy. I left a note and tied him to Ren's doorstep and snuck off in the night. Fortunately, Ren's and Forrest's homes didn't burn. It was the town square and our house that took the brunt of the damage. Some wheat fields as well."

"When things—go back to normal, I want them to come to see me at the castle. They'd love all the food and the pretty maidens."

Aunt Evalyn scoffed. "As if they'd be welcome there unless it was for slave labor."

"Any friend of Layala's will be welcome there when I am king, no labor required," Thane said, retying his wavy dark hair back. "It won't be like when you lived in the valley."

"You'd welcome humans as guests?" Aunt Evalyn sounded skeptical.

"Yes. And when there are no more pale ones, I expect many things to change."

"You believe that's a possibility?"

"I have to believe that."

When they started off again down the slope to the town below, the Ravens simply looked like a group of travelers in cloaks and various colored tunics and leathers.

Layala turned to Fennan, who rode a few paces behind them. His eyes were up, and alert. They shaved off his once-beautiful black curls, leaving his hair only a few inches from his scalp. He had some bruising around his mouth and on his right temple, but he didn't look as bad as Piper. It was her still-swollen eye, black, blue and yellowing against her light, freckled skin that looked incredibly painful. She sat behind Fennan, arms around his waist. Her unmarred cheek rested against his back, both eyes closed.

"What happened to your arm?" Layala asked.

He nudged his brown horse's sides and caught up beside them. "One of the prison guards broke a bone in my forearm. He swung at me with a staff, and I threw up my arm to block my face." His cinnamon eyes flicked down for a moment. "You know, it was shocking how quickly they turned on us. As if they never knew us at all. They've known Piper and me for years, and it meant nothing."

"They're scared," Piper murmured and slowly lifted her cheek away from Fennan's back. "You know Tenebris threatens any disloyalty with the execution

of their families. Remember Devane and what happened to his wife and sisters?"

"How could I forget?" Fennan said.

Layala peeked back at Thane to see his face. His blank expression gave nothing away. The far-off look in his eyes as he stared ahead, seemingly oblivious that Layala watched him made her wonder. What was he thinking and feeling at this moment? He'd had so much regret when he thought he'd sent his father in to be eaten by the pale ones. Would he kill him if given the chance a second time? Perhaps he couldn't and that was the real reason they wouldn't go after him and Mathekis now. "What happened to Devane?"

Piper cleared her throat. "He was a castle guard who worked closely with the king. Devane came to me one night, frantic. He said for three days he heard strange voices in the king's chambers. Whispers about the Black Mage and dark magic. He was terrified that Tenebris had seen him spying. I told him to go to Thane but before he could, he was dragged to the prison below the castle. His wife was hanged as were his two sisters the next morning, while he was forced to watch, and then he followed them. King Tenebris told the people in the square that they'd been traitors, feeding Calladira confidential information that would leave us exposed to an attack."

"When was this?" Layala asked.

"About a year ago," Piper answered.

Fennan ran his palm over his short black hair.

"There have been others before and since. He sets an example every so often. Obey or die."

"But you didn't rule by fear. Why does he feel he must?"

Thane blinked a few times as if coming out of a daze. "Because my father is not a dangerous elf so he thinks that is what he must do. And no, I didn't rule by fear but that doesn't mean they weren't afraid."

"Did you threaten them?" What were those first weeks of his rule like? Did everyone immediately fall in line with their new king? During the games and festival, the people showed nothing but admiration for him.

"I never had to. They all know what I am capable of."

A small smile pulled at the corners of her mouth. "Your place was earned on the battlefield among them. There are not many rulers who will go out and fight for the cause. They follow you out of respect, not fear."

He leaned in and kissed her cheek lightly. "I suppose so."

"I think you underestimate how many will back you when you publicly kill your father and take his place. Who would stop you? Who *could* even if it's against your laws?"

Thane sighed. "They couldn't stop me, but I don't want to have to kill any of my father's loyalists, forcing me to become like him. And I truly don't want to be

the first elf king to murder his own father to take his place on the throne."

"But that is not what you're doing," Fennan interrupted. "It's not for the throne. We're stopping him from destroying Palenor."

"But will the people see it that way?" He paused for a moment. "Will my mother?"

They came up the entrance to the main street of Braxentown. Several hitching posts and a red-painted, twenty-stall stable awaited them. The roof was made of thatched straw and the doors, sliding wood. Half the stalls were already full, and a few horses were attached to the posts. A man shoveled horse manure into a barrel, and another came off a stool. He wore a wide-brimmed dirty black hat and chewed on a piece of wheat. "What can I do for ye?" From his rounded ears, pot belly and rough voice, he was most definitely human.

"We'll need to keep our horses here for a night," Thane said.

His eyes glided along the group. "There are six horses. It will cost ye."

"We have the money." Thane reached back, Tif handed him a brown leather pouch before he could ask. Thane gave it a little shake, jiggling the coins around and then opened it. "I think a solid silver coin should do."

"That's more than generous, sir...?"

"Sir, is fine," Thane responded. He pressed two

silver coins into his palms. "One is for your service. The other is for your silence."

The man's dark eyebrows shot up. "Anyone asks about ye, I'm a mute."

"Good man," Thane said with his charming grin. "I'll give you another upon return if you make sure none of our belongings are touched."

"Sure as the sun will rise, sir." He tipped his head and took hold of Phantom's reins.

Layala carefully slid off the horse and dropped to the ground. She lifted the flap to the bag and waited for Tif to come out. She didn't move until Layala said, "Tif, come on. We're going."

"I'll stay."

"No, you won't. It might not be safe here."

"Ugh, fine." She stood up and held out her arms like a small child would. Layala grabbed Tif around her little body and when she set her on the ground the gnome squealed and stamped her foot. "Have you lost your mind? I can't very well walk this busy street. I'd be stepped on and squished like a grape." She set her large puppy dog eyes on Thane and her smile turned into a pout.

Looking between the two of them, Layala asked, "Has Thane been carrying you around?"

He stooped down and grabbed her by the back of her dress and slid her into the hood of his cloak. "Unfortunately, I've become a pack mule for the wretched creature."

Her mouth hung open as her stubby fingers

wrapped around the hem of the hood and she peeked out. "Wretched?" She glared at the back of his head. "He complains but I've grown on him. I know that because he saved me from being eaten by a fox not long ago and he could have let it chomp me right up. I mean, I was this close to being a goner." She held her pointer finger and thumb a sliver apart. "I'd have made a fine meal for that fox too." She patted her cheeks. "A little chub adds good flavor."

"I should have let it eat you," Thane said and winked at Layala.

Tif folded her arms and sunk into the fabric. "I won't say another word until I get an apology."

"Excellent."

"He's not the only one that's had to carry her around," Leif said. "The little thing acts like her legs are broken."

Her cheeks grew redder, and her eyes looked like they might pop out of her head if she didn't speak. "Ok fine one more thing: I got little legs, not broken legs, that means small strides. It's only obvious I couldn't keep up with jumbos."

"She's got a point," Aunt Evalyn said. "I like her."

"I knew you were my second favorite," Tif said, grinning and bobbing her stubby finger at Aunt Evalyn. "Layala will always be my number one. I'm her lady's maid, you know."

Aunt Evalyn smiled further, wrinkling the skin around her eyes and mouth. "You told me that at least three times over the last few days."

Tif tapped her finger against her lips and looked up to the clouds as if the memory might be there. "Did I?"

"And she's the best lady's maid too," Layala said.

"That's debatable," Thane murmured as Fennan and Piper approached. She wore a wide-brimmed black hat... was it the same one the horse hand wore? It must be and it hid her bruised face well.

"We're going to find a healer," Fennan said. "We'll meet you at Kail's place later."

Aunt Evalyn grabbed her bag off her horse saddle. "I'm going with them," Aunt Evalyn blurted. "My backside has never hurt so much. If I never ride a horse again, I'll be happy. And I set Fennan's arm, but I want to make sure they use the correct medicines on it. Piper's ribs are fractured as well. Afraid I'm out of the pain relief bottle Adley gave us."

Aunt Evalyn was always one to jump in and help but Layala had a feeling it had more to do with not wanting to be around Thane and Layala together. She couldn't be upset with her; it took time for Layala herself to appreciate Thane. There was always the chance she simply wanted to sneak off and gamble too, maybe a bit of both.

"I'll reserve rooms for you then," Thane said. "By the looks of things Kail's inn will be full soon."

Aunt Evalyn, Fennan, and Piper started down the dirt road, until it changed to cobblestone a few yards in. With a frown, she watched Aunt Evalyn waddle like she was in pain. Could it be more than from riding?

Even if Aunt Evalyn was always strong, this type of journey would be hard on any human.

"Do you think she'll be alright?" Layala asked Thane.

He watched her for a moment. "I think the last few weeks have taken more of a toll on her than she'll admit."

"She never was one for travel. She prefers staying inside and sending me to scavenge for plants for her for the last five years or so." Layala tugged her fingers through her tangled black tresses. "Has she been rude to you?"

He lifted a shoulder and then grew a slow smile. "Nothing compared to you, my dear. But I suspect it will take time for her to accept me as not an 'evil, maiden-sacrificing villain', and even longer for her to accept us."

"Well, whether she accepts us or not, I'm so thankful you brought her. I truly missed her."

With a nod, Thane grunted and folded his arms.

"What was that for?"

"Piper and Fennan. Notice anything?"

The two of them stood close together, hands brushing. Then Fennan slid his arm around her shoulder, pulling her to his side. *Hmm what's going on there?* Maybe when they were stuck in prison together, something changed. Even if it wasn't romantic, at least they had a bond. "You don't like them close?" She couldn't imagine why.

"It's not that," he said and picked at the callus on

his hand. Pieces of his dark-brown hair that almost looked black in this lighting fell over his face while he looked down. She had the urge to reach over and swipe it behind his ear.

"Looks like the three of us are with you then," Gunner interrupted, and put a hand on his hip. He puffed a breath to blow a brown curl off his forehead.

"No fighting." Thane gave him and Leif pointed looks. "I don't worry about Siegfried but you two..." Layala knew Leif was mischievous, but Gunner had always seemed mild-mannered, and she didn't know Siegfried well. She'd seen him around in Doonafell, but he didn't say much.

Leif put one hand over his heart like he was offended. "Me, get into a fight? Why, it's unheard of."

"Uh huh," Thane mumbled. "You start it," he moved his pointer finger to Gunner, "and he finishes it."

"Siegfried finishes it usually," Leif added and shoved him on the shoulder. "It's always the quiet ones that are scary." Siegfried rolled his eyes.

Hand in hand, Layala and Thane started down the cobblestone street. Down the center of the roadway, vendors inside canopies and tents offered goods and services. Cooking meats sizzled over fire pits, fish dangled from hooks, and large bunches of spices and plants stung her nostrils. Layala spotted the franzen leaf for healing, and a long string of fluffy green gaudrey's root. The poison she once thought of using on Thane could be for people or pests.

"Pottifer," Layala murmured, eyeing the bright-orange leaves in jars, used for enhanced speed. It was one of Aunt Evalyn's favorites to collect, although the downside of eating them was extreme tiredness later on.

As they moved farther down it was so crowded that Layala slid behind Thane to keep people from ramming into her shoulders. He was a tall, powerful-looking male and everyone moved for him. Leif kept a close few steps behind, watching her back like his own. They strolled by a tawny tent filled with bouquets of orange poppy flowers, bundles of bright tulips in glass vases and lovely bright-pink peonies tied with string.

"Pretty flowers for the pretty lady?" an old woman crooned in a crackly voice, holding out a bunch of closed midnight lilies. She stepped right in between Layala and Thane, bringing Layala to a jarring halt. "I think these suit you."

Leif put a hand on Layala's shoulder, letting her know he was there. "Keep going," he said.

But Layala stared at the bundle in her hand. Black lilies. She swallowed hard and searched the old woman's face. Her gray and silver hair was a mass of halo curls around her head. Her milky, crepey skin almost ashen. Cloudy-blue eyes seemed to stare right through her, and a missing front tooth made her speak with a slight impediment. "The lilies will bloom in the dark, just like you."

Bloom in the dark? Thane moved in like a shadow,

half stepping in front of Layala. "We don't want your flowers, witch."

"Mmm, why if it isn't the Prince of War. You are as delicious as ever." She cackled. Lowering the lilies, those cloudy eyes trailed over him then she shifted her attention to Layala. "I guess what the spirits say is true. I began to wonder. It's been an age since I've seen the likes of you."

Layala's brow pulled tighter. "What are you talking about?"

Thane grabbed her hand, pulling her attention from the woman. The fierceness in his gaze surprised her. "Let's go," he demanded. The trepidation in his expression made her quickly agree. Did this woman work for Tenebris? Perhaps it was best they didn't let her go. But when she glanced back the woman had vanished.

CHAPTER 15

With Thane's hand clamped around hers, Layala let him pull her through the crowds. She watched every person she passed with suspicion. How many spies did Tenebris have? Would she be recognized? Would Thane? Their only possible lead on the All Seeing Stone was a friend of Thane's and risky or not, this is where they must be.

Thane pulled Layala toward a cedar wood building with a hanging white painted sign that read: The Salty Gnome. It was the only business on the street that wasn't painted a bright lively color. Instead, large reddish-brown logs lined the walls. Grass grew out of the roof with sprays of tiny lavender flowers. Smoke roiled out a chimney that faintly smelled of pine.

Thane abruptly halted, and Layala bumped into him. Two men in dirty brown leathers, and shaggy hair stumbled out the swinging doors in front of them. One fell onto his side and rolled over onto his back,

laughing up at the sky. He was either drunk or wasn't entirely right in the mind. It was then she noticed curling black horns coming out of the crown of his head and a long, skinny tail covered in tawny fur with a tuft of black hair on the end. He flicked it like a cat would. She couldn't help but stare, having never seen anything like him before. She'd heard rumors that people like him existed but didn't believe it.

A burly man with a barrel chest crossed his arms in the doorway. "And stay out, you filthy dogs." A streak of gray went through the center of the doorman's full, dark beard. He turned brown eyes on Thane and then spied Layala behind him. "Not sure you want to bring a lady elf in here, sir. Been lots of trouble today. Something in the air."

"She can hold her own. We're here to see Kail."

With a grunt he shrugged. "As you wish." He held the door open to a billow of smoke and loud chatter. The rambunctious atmosphere and low lighting were a stark contrast to the sunny day outside. Nearly every table was full of elves, humans, a table of dwarves with beards that reached their belly buttons, and a pair of those horned men with antlers any prized elk would have. Sprites buzzed around swirling the clouds of smoke, carrying drinks and small baskets of food. A lady elf in a floor-length scarlet dress sang on a stage to the right. Her voice was smooth as red wine and haunting like a deserted forest. Layala spotted a table full of females in extravagant yet revealing gowns. One elf with beautiful golden-brown hair held a thin black

cigarette holder between her fingers. She took a deep pull of smoke and blew it out without ever taking her lavender eyes off Layala. She couldn't decide if the lady wanted to attack her or ask Layala to join them.

Layala fidgeted with her hands, remembering how filthy her dress was and that her hair must look like a tangled wet mop. Thane slipped his arm around her waist and leaned down to her ear. "He'll be at the corner booth."

Before Thane could pull them inside further, she asked, "Did you know that old witch?"

"No, but it was obvious she knew who you were. I didn't like it."

"And you. But it was odd though. She looked blind."

He grunted. "Some human witches have the gift of the other sight. To see and know the truth. Perhaps she did."

"What do you think she meant about the spirits? And do you think she works for your father?"

He lifted a shoulder. "She could be deranged for all we know. She certainly looked it. As far as working for my father, I doubt it. He might work with the dragon and Mathekis for his own gain, but some old human woman? Not likely."

They started moving around the tables. "We're going to get some drinks," Leif announced, and they made an escape for the bar top.

As Thane and Layala wound around the patrons and through the trails of smoke, many turned to stare

as they passed, as if sensing something about them. She leaned in and said quietly, "And what are those horned men with tails?"

Thane smiled, tightening his hold on her. "They call themselves fae. There aren't many in Adalon. From what I've heard they come from across the seas. A land they call Delfaria, I believe. Since they've never caused much trouble, I haven't worried about them."

They came upon the corner booth to a male elf sitting alone with a black top hat, and charcoal suit with a purple undervest perfectly tailored to his body. On the table before him was a stack of papers, an ink bottle with a quill, and a glass mug of amber liquid. He lifted his head and a big grin spread across his handsome face. "Well, I'll be damned. You're not dead. The Maker has blessed us. Sit down, friend." He shifted his attention to Layala. "You too, lovely."

Thane slid into the red leather seat and patted the spot next to him. With a little reluctance she scooted in beside him. Thane tilted his head toward her. "Kail, this is Laya. Laya, Kail."

"It's a pleasure," he said with a smile. "I assume you two need a room and something to eat."

"Yes, a few rooms, for some friends, and she needs fresh clothes."

"And I'd like a bath." Layala was still self-conscious that she smelled like goat turds.

Kail lifted a hand and curled his finger. "Of course. I'll have Alisara assist you. She has impeccable taste."

Layala didn't even have to turn to know exactly who Alisara was.

The brunette appeared at the table a few moments later, blowing a stream of sweet-smelling smoke at Layala. She arched a sleek eyebrow, looking from Layala, to Thane and then Kail. "Yes?" she said in a slow, melodic voice.

"Sister, Laya here needs some new attire. Would you be a peach and get her a few changes of clothes?" He turned back to Thane and Layala. "Will that be enough? How long do you plan to stay?"

"Not long. Perhaps for the night," Thane answered. "But a week's worth of clothes would be appreciated. Traveling attire preferably."

"Of course." She dipped her head. "Anything for you, Highness." Layala didn't like the way her seductive gaze lingered on Thane. But Alisara held out her arm to gesture for her to follow, and Layala stood. She needed that bath.

Thane grasped her wrist, offered a brief smile, and kissed her knuckles. "I'll be right here."

She nodded as a nervous pull tugged at her insides. Parting with him so soon even if it wasn't for long, reminded her of their mate bond being torn apart, leaving her with a gaping hole that still ached. Her stomach knotted the moment he dropped her hand.

Thane turned back to Kail. "Remember that thing I asked you to find me? Did you?"

"I did," Kail's voice drifted away as Layala followed behind Alisara. What did he ask him to find? She

glanced back once more, trying to ignore that incessant feeling not to leave Thane. His bright-green eyes watched her with predatory awareness. With a deep breath Layala pulled her gaze away focusing on where she walked. The tables full of leering males made her skin crawl.

"Don't worry, most of them are harmless," Alisara said over her shoulder, blowing another puff of smoke. "But you are fresh meat so don't begrudge them for looking."

"I'm afraid I'm not much to look at at the moment." She gestured to her dirty dress.

Alisara dragged her lavender gaze up and down Layala and she turned without a word.

Before she got to the other side of the hall, Thane appeared at her side. "I'm walking you to the room."

The relief that washed over her was like warm summer rain. She slipped her hand into his and bumped her cheek into his shoulder.

Alisara turned slightly but kept walking. "This is your mate, isn't it? The one you always told me you waited for."

"Yes," Thane answered. Layala absently touched her wrist where the mate mark had been all her life—gone now. She glanced between the two of them. Did Alisara have feelings for Thane? They had some sort of past if he'd told Alisara about her.

A not-so-genuine smile pulled up the corners of Alisara's mouth. "Congratulations."

They marched up a set of creaky wooden stairs

with crooked frames hanging on the walls, passed several doors on either side of the long hallway, and ended up at the last room on the right. A gold key ring jingled from her pocket, and she stuck a thick silver key into the lock. It clicked and she pushed through the door. It was a small, plain room holding a narrow bed with red velvet covers. What appeared to be a large silver trough with a metal pump of some kind sat in the corner with a small arched brick fireplace behind it.

"Pull the lever a few times and hot water will run. There should be some soap and oils on the tray next to the tub. I'll be back with some clothes in a little while." She hovered near the door. "You and I look to be about the same size so it shouldn't be difficult."

"Running water?" Layala asked, stepping across the room. She touched the metal handle and inspected the spout.

"Yes. My brother's invention. He'll have to speak with you about installing it in the castle."

Thane plopped down on the bed, sliding his hand over the top of the velvet blanket. "Perhaps when I'm not a wanted fugitive."

"I'd heard there was a bounty on your head. Be careful, Thane." She rested a hand on the door handle, popping out one of her hips. "Money corrupts and the amount your father is offering would be enough to make even the most loyal consider turning on you."

"And where does that leave us then?" Thane asked, giving her a hard stare Layala had only seen

him use a few times. Usually right before he was going to kill someone. The coldness of it sent a chill down Layala's back and it wasn't even directed at her.

She raised her chin slightly. "You know I have plenty of money, *Your Highness*."

"And yet you're never satisfied."

So these two did have a past. It's not that Layala believed Thane didn't have a life before her, but the tension between these two left her with a lot of questions. They clearly knew each other on a deeper basis than mere acquaintances.

"You've always been able to trust my brother and me." She closed the door gently behind her.

Layala walked to the metal trough and tugged on the waterspout handle a few times. Water indeed rushed out of the spout. Her fingers glided through the hot water, and she smiled. It would feel wondrous on her grimy skin and hair. She peeked over her shoulder at Thane, debating on asking him about his relationship with Alisara.

As the tub filled, she pushed at the fabric covering her shoulders but then stopped. It wasn't as if he hadn't seen every inch of her bare skin, but a nervous twinge in her gut made her turn. It had been weeks since they bared it all in the ruins and explored each other's bodies for the first time. "Do you think we are safe here?"

Thane's eyes pinned on her revealed shoulder. The heat in his stare made her heart beat faster. "For now.

Even if she betrayed us, Tenebris couldn't get enough soldiers here tonight to deal with us."

"Can she and her brother be trusted?"

He looked toward the small window that let in a ray of sunshine. "I don't trust anyone anymore." His throat bobbed. "Not after what Aldrich did."

She felt sick about Aldrich's betrayal, and she wasn't nearly as close to him as Thane. How disgusted he must be was a whole other level. She closed the distance between them and placed a gentle hand on his scruffy cheek. "You can trust me."

A half smile lifted his cheek, and he kissed her palm. "I do." He pointed behind her. "Your bath is going to spill over soon."

She whirled around and dashed across the floor to turn the water off. A few lagging drops of water splashed into the full tub. Out of the corner of her eye she noticed Thane watching her and her heart raced. They were very much alone, and the heat of his gaze intensified. Her thoughts trailed to his hands gliding over her body, to his lips pressing to intimate parts. He'd brought her pleasure she'd never known before, and she craved that again.

She didn't know why she was more nervous about being with him at this moment than the first time. Maybe it was because a great deal transpired between then and now. Their newfound relationship was still fresh when they'd been torn apart. She'd only begun to discover who Thane was and what his touch did to her.

He stood and stretched his arms overhead. "Your gnome has been awfully quiet," he said, filling in the tense silence. "I almost forgot she was with us." He tugged at the strings holding his cloak on and gently set it on the bed. He smirked, moving a fold of fabric aside. "She's asleep. I swear the creature wouldn't wake even through a hurricane."

Layala half smiled until his bright-green eyes found hers, and the muscles in his jaw rippled. After they stared for a moment, Layala's heart began to thunder. She couldn't feel his emotions through the mate bond anymore, but it didn't make the room any less charged with longing. Almost like a tension line went taut between them. Warmth and desire pooled in her core trailing lower. Maker above, he was beautiful.

There was something intimate simply in the way he stared. "Do you want me to leave you alone to bathe?" he asked quietly, never breaking eye contact. She knew that wasn't what he wanted. She smelt the sweet tinge of his arousal in the air, and heard his desire in his rapid heartbeat. Even his pupils dilated with his excitement. The fact that she knew he craved her too made her want him all the more.

She swallowed down the nervous lump in her throat, feeling breathless. "I'd much rather you stayed... and bathed with me."

He smiled, and prowled toward her. "I hoped you'd say that."

CHAPTER 16

L ayala's breath caught as his calloused hands slid under the collar of her dress, and he lightly kissed the hollow of her neck. She closed her eyes and bumps slithered across her skin.

"Would you like assistance with removing this?" he asked.

Breathless, she nodded.

He pushed one side of the fabric off her shoulder, then the other and the dress cascaded down her body into a pool around her feet, leaving her in a pair of undergarments that barely covered her behind and tied at her hips. His thumbs hooked around those too. "And these?"

Layala bit her lip and then smiled. "Help yourself, my king."

He slowly lowered into a crouch, his warm breath moved over her exposed breasts and then he bit the fabric, tugging her underwear down over her hip. She

groaned as his nose grazed her sensitive skin. "Thane," she almost pleaded until the fabric of her underwear fell to her ankles. Any ounce of resistance shattered, and she may as well have melted in his arms. How did he know exactly what to do to make her desire him all the more?

He stood and took a small step back. His breath quickened as his heavy-lidded eyes drank her in. They roamed over her breasts and down her stomach to her thighs. "Maker, Layala, you're beautiful. And the way you say my name, that alone can make me come undone."

Always thinking of her first, he took her hand and guided her into the tub. She stepped in and slowly sank into the steaming water. Sucking in a breath she dipped under and scrubbed at her scalp. It felt itchy and gross, and the hot water soothed. She blew out her breath and let the bubbles rise to the surface before she followed them up. After wiping water from her face, her vision focused on Thane stepping out of his boots. His belt jingled as he loosed the buckle, letting his pants drop to reveal his long, muscular legs. *Nice ass*, she thought, biting her lower lip.

He glanced over his shoulder at her, a sly smile on his lips. "Enjoying the show?"

"Immensely." She didn't know if it was the water temperature making her hotter or the sight of him, but her cheeks suddenly felt like bright embers. "And I'd enjoy it more if you turned around and came closer."

He was at the edge of the large metal tub in a breath, eyes sparkling with curiosity and laced with seduction. She rose to her feet; water rushed down her body, splashing quietly into the tub. A low growl of need escaped him as his gaze greedily roamed over her, and he reached toward her hips.

She smacked his hand away. "You got to have your fun undressing me. Now let me have mine."

He chuckled. "Fine."

Arching her eyebrow, she gripped the bottom of his tunic, letting her fingers brush his skin as she slowly raised it upward. His breathing became deeper and his smile less play and more carnal. He lifted his arms, and she slipped the dark fabric over his head and tossed it away. Unable to stop herself, she slid her fingers over his round muscular shoulders, and across his collarbone.

"So you can touch me but I can't touch you? Tease," he purred.

"Shhh," she said and pressed her fingertip to his lips. Maker above, he was perfect; his form as powerful and corded with muscle as before. She continued her inspection, dragging her hands down his chest, admiring every inch of his perfect skin until... "Holy Maker above, that scar. Thane." Even after all those cuts and stabs from within that cage in Calladira he didn't have a mark, but the dragon's claw left him torn.

Looking down, his fingers ran over the raised pink flesh on his abdomen. "It's better than it was."

Swallowing hard, she placed her palm over it, feeling the violent edges. It must have been excruciating. "Does it still hurt?"

He placed his hand over hers, stroking his thumb over the top of her skin. "Only sometimes. You don't need to worry, my love."

But she was worried. No wonder he couldn't get to her sooner. That dragon bitch needed to die. "I'm going to murder her. Slowly."

He stepped into the tub and brought her hand to his lips and kissed her knuckles then pulled her down with him, raising the water level up to her shoulders. She rose to her knees and grabbed the sponge off the side table and dipped it in. After lathering it with soap, she leaned forward, leaving only inches between them and slowly wiped it across the hard planes of his chest, admiring his powerful, defined pectorals and shoulders. "How did you— survive?" It pained her a little to even suggest he almost didn't.

He watched her face as she concentrated on the sponge, gliding over his warm ivory skin; if she looked him in the eye now, she didn't know if she could hold herself back. The pleasant heat blooming in her intensified and she pressed her lips to his wet shoulder gently. His skin was soft and smooth.

"Barely," he said, his voice vibrated through her touch. His fingertips danced on the outside of her hips, gliding up her waist. "With the help of Mage Vesstan and my healing ability. I couldn't walk for a few weeks.

The first week I think I was in and out of reality, hallucinating in a fever."

She hated to think about how many days and nights he suffered. And she'd pitied herself for not being able to drink or eat, wishing for him to rescue her while he was near death. She should have found a way to go to him. Moving the sponge down his throat and over his arm, elicited a low hum. "That feels good, Laya."

"You truly must be descended from the old gods to have survived this." She dipped her hand underwater and touched his scar again, mystified.

He smirked. "You must be, for I have never seen anyone as divine." His hands gripped her waist, and he pulled her against him. A heartbeat later his mouth claimed hers. It wasn't a soft, tentative kiss. There was surety, ownership. It left no doubt that he was hers. "Or delicious." He kissed her again. "Or sexy. You are a goddess of desire, drawing me in, infusing yourself into my every thought—I've never wanted anything more than you, Laya."

The sponge plopped into the water. Her hands gripped behind his neck. Hot water made his skin slick and warm. His rough palms cupped her backside, and she wrapped her legs around his hips. "Mmm," he hummed until full lips crashed into hers again and his tongue slid past her teeth, flicking against her own. "Maker, I've never craved anything so much," he murmured, fisting her hair. "Never needed something like this."

She moaned as she rubbed against his hardness, pushing her hands along his scalp, gripping him tighter with her thighs. Her nails slid across the muscles of his back, and he arched into her further. His breath came faster and moved strands of her hair like a gentle wind. His smell: sweet but heavy, her nose trailed along his shoulder and up his neck, cedar, mint soap and sweat. She tasted the salt of his skin on her lips and wanted more. "I love you," she whispered. "And oh, how I missed you."

His kisses trailed down her neck, to her collarbone, raising bumps along her skin, and then his tongue slid over her sensitive peaked breast. Her head lolled back until he grabbed her face between his hands, forcing her to meet his gaze. What she saw there, the longing and wild intensity made her shudder. "Do you want me, Laya?"

She rocked her hips against him quicker. "Yes," she could barely breathe, "I want you, all of you." Their bodies fully met, and she let out a quiet gasp, as did he. Every sensation intensified with his lips roaming over her flesh, his hips moving in sync with hers. Even without their mate bond she still swore their emotions mixed: need, want, demand—filling her soul deep. Magic brushed down her spine, through her, like its own featherlight caress, the whisper of a forbidden lover in a crowded room.

"Promise me forever, Thane," she said.

"Forever and always," he said against her lips. "I

will never stop loving you. I will never stop craving you."

She closed her eyes, letting their connection soar. His moan vibrated through her core; the sensations of him made her feel lighter and heavier all at once, intoxicated. He grabbed her chin again with one hand forcing her to meet his gaze. "I want to look into your eyes when you say my name, when you let yourself go."

"Thane," she breathed. He slid his hands down her body, gripping under her thighs. A moment later he rose to his knees, lifting her with him. That careful delicacy he seemed to have when he touched her vanished and his movements turned eager, rapid. She sucked in a sharp breath; she was a rose on the verge of blooming. "Thane." He shivered at his name on her lips, and she wrapped her body tighter around him in reaction.

"Let go, Laya," his voice low, carnal in her ear, "let go."

She could have been a shooting star, burning hotter and hotter, flashing brightest as it reached the crescendo of its final form before it slowly faded into darkness.

They held each other in heart-pounding silence, the fire crackling quietly in the background. She pushed wet hair off his forehead and then kissed his full lips gently.

"Damn," he murmured with a smirk. "That was better than I remembered." He sat back down in the

tub, pulling her on top of him and ran his fingertips over her spine, eliciting goosebumps at his touch. "I love you, Laya." He took hold of her hand and kissed the engagement ring he'd slid on her finger weeks before. "And one day soon, I will make it known to the world."

CHAPTER 17

Relaxing into Thane's chest, Layala closed her eyes while he massaged her scalp and dragged his fingers through her hair with sweet pea and citrus-scented oil. She sighed at the pressure of his fingertips circling across her head. A couple firm knocks on the door, and she groaned. It was probably Alisara bringing the clothing but thoroughly interrupting her slice of serenity.

She sat up but Thane wrapped his arm across her breasts. "Stay with me."

"Someone needs to get the door."

He smirked and said loudly, "Come in."

"Thane," Layala balked. They were both completely nude in the bath. She'd gotten somewhat used to her own maids seeing her naked but not others.

The door handle pushed down, and a sliver of the hallway light peeked through the crack. Thane's hold was relentless, so she relaxed against him once more,

glancing down to make sure his arm covered her breasts fully. He wrapped his other around her, and they were large and muscular enough to cover most of her torso. Alisara and another lady with a much less extravagant dress stepped inside. Alisara froze mid stride, looking utterly baffled for a moment, and then she jerked her head away. "I apologize for the intrusion. I wasn't aware you'd both be—indecent."

"It's fine," Thane said and nibbled Layala's earlobe. Layala shivered with the gentle touch. Maker above, he was devious. "Set the clothes on the bed. Thank you, ladies."

The other maiden hadn't even glanced their way. She purposefully kept her line of sight on the bed, set the clothes down, and her feet quietly clicked on the wood floor as she hurried out. Alisara's chest rose as she took a deep breath. Her jaw muscles visibly worked as she laid out the bundle in her arms. Once she was at the door, she paused, keeping her back to them. "Kail is downstairs waiting. But of course, take your time."

Once she was gone, Layala tugged out of Thane's arms, twisting around. "What was that?"

"What do you mean?"

She arched her eyebrow. He was playing dumb. "You did that on purpose. To make her angry, didn't you? What was she to you before?"

He sat up, shifting the warm water and stood. The droplets ran in streams over his divine body, distracting her. "She wasn't anything to me other than

someone I got information from. Like her brother." He grabbed a thick cotton cloth off the side table, stepped out, and wrapped it around his waist.

"Do you think I'm stupid?" He couldn't have been intimate with her or she'd be dead as per the mate bond's infidelity clause but there was something there. Maybe he had feelings for her once.

He chuckled, pushing his hands through his hair, dragging them through the ends that reached his chest. "You're about as far from stupid as one gets." She sat back, crossing one leg over the other, and waited for him to answer. "As I said, I come to this town when I need information, to learn the gossip, or need to find something rare. Alisara is good at those things as is her brother Kail. One night while Fennan... Aldrich and I were in here drinking. I had to take a piss and on my way out back, I overheard her talking to some friends. She said that she'd planned to get me to her bed that night so she could carry my child and secure her position as the future Queen of Palenor." Layala's eyes widened at the scandal. The harlot didn't know she'd have been dead, not queen. "I wanted to make sure she knew who my queen is and it's not her. So yes, I may have done that on purpose."

She smiled and laughed quietly, wading her hand through the water to splash it across her chest and neck. "Did I tell you I love you? Because I do. Very much."

"You did but I don't get tired of hearing it."

Thane's cloak on the bed moved and two little

arms poked out. Tif stretched and yawned and pushed the fabric aside. Her little red hat was sideways and her brown curls wild and frizzy. She rubbed her eyes and then looked around. "Oh, I see we have a room. What a wonderful nap. I mean, I was out like the dead. But I had this dream that I was flying with a baby dragon, and it kept making this strange moaning noise. I think it was his battle cry."

Layala nearly fell out of the tub laughing and Thane shook his head, but his deep chuckle permeated straight through her.

Kᴀɪʟ sʟɪᴅ two mugs of ale across the table, and a massive platter of cheeses, meats, sourdough bread and various fruits, and plopped down in the booth. Layala didn't hesitate to dig in, grabbing a square of cheese first and popping it into her mouth. The rich savory taste was exactly what she needed. She couldn't wait to get back to training and to eat enough to get her strength back. She still felt weak in her arms and legs from lack of nutrients.

"I like the outfit," Kail said, nodding toward Layala. "For some reason I think it suits you better than a dress." Alisara brought two dresses, but the other four outfits were pants and long-sleeved tunics perfect for traveling. Layala chose the black pants, thigh-high stone-gray boots and the turquoise top with bell sleeves. She'd buttoned a vest around her

waist that was cut just below her breasts. The black fabric filled around her back and strapped over her shoulders. It had slits on the sides for weapons too which she took advantage of by sliding in two short knives. A gown was the last thing she wanted to wear when they had enemies all around and she might have to fight at any moment. He continued on, "You're like a deadly assassin who's so beautiful your victim might happily lay down and die."

Thane laughed and took a slug of ale. "You're not entirely wrong in that analysis, Kail."

"I've been known to sneak into a chamber and stab someone." Layala took another bite of cheese then slathered a piece of bread in butter.

Thane laughed again, and Kail glanced between them. "I feel like I'm missing something."

"A story for another time," Thane said. "First things first. Did you bring what I asked?"

Kail smirked. "Course I did. Got it off a rich fool in a game of poker not too long ago. He was sad to see it go. Once I found out he had it, I made sure to show up at his card night." He pulled a sword from the bench beside him and gently laid it on the table. The silver blade shined in the candlelight, revealing etchings of what looked to be old elvish down the middle. "It's worth a fortune now."

"Wow," Layala said, inspecting the pommel made of ivory and inlaid with ivy-shaped jade stone. "It's remarkable."

"I'm glad you like it. It's yours."

Layala leaned back and looked at Kail then Thane. "Mine?"

Thane smiled and nodded. "It was made by your father about a hundred years ago. There aren't many swords forged by his hand left."

Tears stung her eyes at the thoughtfulness of the gift. She'd mentioned she wished she had something her father touched and now she did. How could he be so wonderful? "Truly? What does the inscription say?"

Thane looked at her for a long moment. "Light-bringer."

"But..." if it was a hundred years old then. "So, I'm named after a sword," Layala chuckled. "Thank you for this. Thank you very much."

"It's fitting, you being named after a sword." Thane picked up a metal mug of foamy ale. "Did you know my sister's name is Talon Fearsome? In a way it suits her. She may not be feared on the battlefield, but you bet your ass every single maiden in the kingdom is afraid of that girl."

"I was always jealous as a boy that the girls got unique second names while we had to take on our father's." Kail flicked a crumb off his chest. "I always wanted to be Kail Bravest of Them All."

Layala laughed. "It's a bit long, don't you think?"

"I really wasn't the smartest kid. What about you Thane? Any name you wanted?"

He sat quietly for a moment and took a long drink. With a wave of his hand, he said, "Nah."

"Oh, come on," Layala pressed. "You have to tell us."

An attractive light pink colored his cheeks, and he grabbed a piece of bread. "Shadowslayer."

"That's actually pretty good."

"A Lightbringer and a Shadowslayer. The perfect match," Kail said with a wink.

"Perfect," Layala echoed and wrapped her fingers around the sword's soft ivory handle. Lifting it, she tested its weight. Its symmetry and balance were unmatched. Its weight was not overbearing but heavy enough it would create quick and precise momentum. *My father made this*, she silently marveled. She gripped the handle tighter. *He once held this sword.* She imagined him placing it over hot flames and then hammering it into shape. She could almost hear the sound of metal cracking metal.

"How does it feel?" Thane asked.

"Incredible. I can't wait to swing it around. Up for a sparring match?"

"Always. You can get me flat on my back anytime."

"He's such a flirt, isn't he?" Kail drawled. "You don't know how many maidens, human, elf and Fae alike drool over him without even knowing who he is. Not a dry seat in the house."

"Maybe it should be Thane Heartbreaker." Layala cocked a challenging brow. *Speaking of heartbreak—* she glanced at Alisara. Her talk of rewards and betrayal hadn't left the back of Layala's mind.

"I can't help that I'm magnetic, my dear."

"Big head," she murmured. She slid her new sword into the empty scabbard on her back. The weight of it was comforting; she had a piece of her father with her now.

"Anyway," Thane said with an eye roll. "I need to know if you've heard anything about the All Seeing Stone. Someone took it and I need it."

"Interesting," Kail said, bringing his silver mug to his lips. "In fact, I have heard about it. About six weeks ago. A group of travelers was in here bragging about someone they knew having gotten the stone. I figured it was just talk but—"

"Who has it?"

Kail's eyes darted around the smoky room, and he shifted a little in his seat. Someone at a table nearby let out an ear-wrenching bellow. Sensing Kail's nervous energy, Layala made a point to check who was nearby. At a nearby table Alisara sat smoking with three other maidens. The closest booth held a group of four human men with pipes in their mouths and cards in their hands. A man on stage played a violin with a light toe-tapping medley. And their three Raven companions sat at a table with human women on each of their laps. The lady with Leif hand-fed him berries like he was a High King.

"You're not going to like the answer," Kail said.

"Like it or not, I need to know."

CHAPTER 18

Layala's eyebrows drew up. That meant someone they knew possessed the stone.

Kail set his mug down and tapped his fingers on the rim. "I know you don't like the woodland elves here in our land, but I don't kick anyone out of my tavern unless they cause trouble, and that's who I heard talking about it. They said their Lord Brunard has it."

"Brunard," Thane said flatly. Layala could almost hear his teeth grind. She was instantly transported to Thane bleeding from a hundred little slices all over his body, slumped over with his arms held up in chains, caged like an animal. Jeers and taunts from the crowd echoed in her mind even now, and the same rage that filled her once, burned in her chest.

"I heard about your—run-in with him recently," Kail said. "How you'll persuade him to give it to you will be interesting. I almost wish I could be there."

"When I cut off his head, he won't need any persuading."

Kail laughed. "You'll need to get him to talk first."

Layala took a swig of ale to wash down her food and cleared her throat. Before Thane went into a rage, cutting off heads, they needed to know more. Something substantive, more than chatter. Layala knew too well that rumors could be complete fabrications. "How do we know for certain he has it? They could be untrue claims."

Kail shrugged. "That's the only thing I've heard. I don't see why they'd make something like that up. And if you two know for certain it's no longer in the tomb, then someone has it."

Layala shifted toward Thane. "Do you believe Brunard could have gotten through the traps to get it?"

"Brunard is both clever and able. It's possible. I just don't know why he'd want it in the first place."

"He is the Lord of Calladira, enemy to you and Palenor," Layala said. "At the time, everyone thought your father was dead. He'd likely want it to know how to destroy you so he could take Palenor for himself."

Thane's mouth twisted into a frown. "He almost did." He drained his ale in a few seconds and slammed the mug down loudly on the table. "Of all people, that little prick. A bloody thorn in my side... and yet he knew what to use to poison me. Had the blade ready when I came. As if he already knew I would be there..." He tapped his fingers rhythmically on the wood. The tension lining his face was like a dark storm brewing.

"You're alive though. He didn't succeed."

Thane pushed his shoulders back. "Didn't he though? There are more ways than one to destroy a person. I have no kingdom, no crown. I had my mate bond ripped from me. And what am I now but a wanted criminal on the run from his father? I would say that High King Thane has thoroughly been destroyed, dead or not."

Layala placed a gentle hand on his bouncing leg. "We'll get your kingdom back. And all that has happened can't be because of Brunard. It was my fault you were there in the first place."

Kail's mug scraped on the table, drawing their attention. "If I may offer my input. From what I've read about the legend of the All Seeing Stone, it doesn't know the future because the future's not set in stone," he raised a finger with a smirk, "pun intended. So it's technically not *All Seeing*. Besides, I hear it takes a mage to make it work. Last I checked, he isn't one."

"So," Layala started. "It should be able to tell us how to end the curse of the Void and the pale ones right?"

He tilted his head to one side. "Yes, if it's even possible."

"Thank you, Kail," Thane said. He turned to Layala. "I guess we have no other choice than to go to Brunard and hope that he does have it."

"On a positive note." Layala took another drink. The ale began to go to her head now. A tingle through her limbs and a lightness in her chest. "We can get

payback for what he did to you. That prick has no idea what a mistake he made that day."

Thane smiled, showing off his pretty white teeth. "Vicious, she-elf."

Light picks on a guitar and a steady drum of the tambourine lifted her toes. Under the table, Layala tapped her boots, and slowly bobbed her head. Didn't she promise Thane a dance? A couple others in the room took to the floor; a male with curling ram horns and one of the maiden elves at Alisara's table circled and laughed below the stage. A single man clapped and stamped a foot. A very loud and boisterous man hopped up on his chair and started singing, "Oh the pretty lass with a fine ass," and most of the room started in. Layala giggled, having never heard the tune before.

"If this is your mate..."

Layala turned her attention back to the elf across from her. The hairs on the back of her neck rose. Could Alisara or Kail have already alerted someone? After Aldrich, it was difficult to trust.

Kail's eyes roamed across Layala with some trepidation. "Is she the reason you're on the run?"

Thane lifted a shoulder and took a piece of cheese off the plate. "We're on the run because I failed to kill my father properly months ago. A mistake I won't make a second time." He appeared calm enough but the way he bounced his leg under the table told her a different story.

Kail's eyebrows shot up. "You—it was you who

almost killed him? Now I'm curious how that went awry. I don't know anyone who's gone up against the Warrior King and lived to tell the tale."

Thane's piercing green eyes dropped to the table-top. Chest rising and falling in a sigh, he grabbed a handful of green grapes and shrugged.

"Will you dance with me?" Layala blurted out to distract Thane so he wouldn't have to relive the details. He'd once regretted he fed his father to pale ones and now, he regretted that it hadn't worked properly. Tenebris didn't have to say it for her to know that Mathekis must have stepped in after Thane sent him into the Void. Either that or he'd commanded that his minions didn't touch the elf king. An oversight Thane should have taken into consideration knowing that his father was in communication with the pale one's leader.

"How could I ever say no?"

They slid out of the booth, leaving Kail with a grin on his face. Layala held Thane's hand behind her back and led him through the rowdy, singing crowd. Mugs in hands crashed into each other, spilling over the sides onto the floor. Her boots traipsed over small puddles and the stench of fresh ale pierced her nose. She stifled a cough as the cloud of pipe smoke thick-ened in this area. She wasn't used to it anymore. In many ways this place reminded her of the Smoky Dragon in Briar Hollow. She just missed the good company her childhood home offered. They reached

the clearing for dancing below the stage and Layala spun on her heel and faced Thane. He smiled at her with soft eyes. He took hold of her wrists and tugged her flat against him. Gentle hands slid down her back.

He leaned down to her ear and gripped her hips. "I never got to dance with you in Doonafell that night."

"Well, maybe because you ignored me and danced with a host of other beautiful maidens. I was incredibly jealous. I'll have you know."

His deep, midnight chuckle sent shivers down her body. "Oh, I certainly know. I felt your raging jealousy. Like a wild boar ready to spear me. I'm surprised I survived the night."

"Don't act like you weren't jealous I gave that boy a kiss on the cheek."

"You used him like a pawn, naughty girl."

"And you didn't use the maidens? You knew exactly what you were doing." She pushed her hands up his chest, hooking them around his neck.

His smile could have lit up the room. "I would never do such a thing."

"Liar."

"I may have danced with them, but it is you that dominates my every thought. You are the fire that burns inside me and without it, I'd surely die."

"Silver tongue," Layala teased.

"It's this silver tongue that made you fall hard."

"Actually, it was your pretty words that made me wary, as much as your pretty face. If you remember, I

thought you made your lovers go mad and murdered young females."

He laughed. "Ah yes, the sacrificial use of beautiful young maidens, what a beast I am."

He slid his hand up the back of her arm, across her elbow and took her hand, then spun her around. Sweeping a hand behind her back, he dipped her low and then with a tug pulled her back up. "You say you don't know how to dance but you move like the wind."

"I have a wonderful partner." As they swayed and moved to the beat of the drum and the violin's wistful melody, she got lost in it. The crowd around them seemed to fade away and with it, the pain and sorrow of the past month. Right now, it was them and a song. She pressed her cheek against his chest and reveled in his woodsy masculine scent, an escape from the acrid smoke.

"Since we're intimate now, one of us should get a preventative tonic. A baby is the last thing I want to bring into this chaotic world of ours. I can't even imagine what your father would attempt to do."

Thane stroked her hair, twirling a piece of the black strands around his finger. "I've been drinking a tonic since Doonafell. You don't need to worry."

Layala looked up at him, one eyebrow arched. "Since Doonafell, huh?"

He laughed at her. "I'm prepared and since I'm irresistible I knew you'd give in to me eventually."

"There's that big ego of yours popping up again."

A hand gripped Layala's shoulder. "Mind if I cut in?"

The playful smile on Thane's face faded to dark thunderclouds and those brilliant-green eyes of his shadows and the object of nightmares. The human man standing beside them, with his hand still on Layala's shoulder, was tall, taller than even Thane, broad shouldered and had massive arms. He looked like he could lift a horse, and the low partially-unbuttoned beige shirt revealed a hairy, barrel chest. He had a patch over one eye but looked young, maybe in his late twenties.

"I do mind," Thane said, holding her a little tighter around the waist. The growing tension was palpable, and she knew exactly where this was headed if the man didn't back off.

"I don't want to dance," Layala said, pushing his hand off her. "Now run along and find someone else."

Completely ignoring her, he kept his gaze trained on Thane. "Come on, elf. There are only so many wenches in here, and I want this one."

Oh, here we go. A blanket of raw power coated the air around them so thick she could taste the bitter tang of it. Even the floorboards creaked as Thane's power leached out. To her it felt like a gentle caress of a lover against her skin, but fear flashed across the man's face. Yet he was either drunk or stupid because his feet didn't move. Layala stepped out from between them. No way was she about to get into the middle of this one. As soon as she was out of the way,

Thane's fist cracked the jaw of the man. His body went slack, his eyes rolled back and he hit the ground with a bang. The stillness of the man was a little unnerving. Layala wasn't sure he was even alive until he groaned.

"Damn," Layala murmured to herself. The music came to a screeching halt and the loud chatter quieted down almost as if someone had snapped their fingers for silence. Several men at tables stood.

"Hey!" one man yelled, rising to his feet. "That's my captain, elf!"

The scrape of many knives and swords being pulled from their scabbards lilted around the room. Layala's magic itched down her arms and tingled her fingertips. A swell of joy filled her chest. She had her power back and Maker above; it felt good. Not that she would use it here. Kail's place would be utterly destroyed if she let loose her destruction.

Thane's mouth quirked into a half smile, and he held out his arms. "Your captain was in need of a lesson in manners."

Maker above, I love him. Layala stepped to his side, bumping her shoulder into him. "Nice punch. We should call you the one-hit wonder."

Thane's smile only grew, and he announced to the room. "And I'll be happy to oblige anyone else who needs enlightenment."

"Are you trying to start a brawl?"

"Why not?" He rolled his shoulders back. "I'm feeling agitated."

"Oh, and here you told Leif and Gunner not to start a fight."

Chairs scraped and clattered to the ground as several men shoved away from their tables. At least twelve moved in with wicked grins as if they were going to enjoy this fight. Layala withdrew her dagger and pressed her back against Thane's ready for the first assailant. He didn't pull any weapons out, but he didn't need them.

Leif slid in front of Thane, rolling his red head side to side. "All you little petered humans better step back."

Gunner, Siegfried, and several other elves from around the room joined the line of defense.

"Your captain is scum and had no business even asking her to dance," Gunner said and shoved his finger into the chest of a man with mangy brown hair and yellowed teeth with bits of black in between.

"Take that back," the man barked.

Layala looked over her shoulder and glanced up at Thane. "Seems we have friends to take care of our light work."

"Not that we need them."

"Certainly not," she agreed. "I could take this whole room myself."

Thane slowly shook his head but laughed. "I wouldn't let you have all the fun on your own, but it would be entertaining to watch you take these bastards down."

A shove in the chest by one of the elves was all it

took for the room to explode into chaos. Splinters of wood flew through the air as chairs crashed over backs. Tables tipped and ale sloshed across the floor, splattering on Layala's boots. She flicked her ankle, kicking some of it off. Grunts and roars of anger, and filthy curses that even made Layala cringe, ground against her ears. Fists cracked against bone, and it seemed the weapons drawn were only for show. No one died yet. The elves were quicker and stronger, but these gruff human men fought dirty; clawed and bit and sucker punched.

Suddenly, a wailing sort of singing voice bellowed out from behind her. *What in the hell?* Layala turned to find Tifapine standing on a stool, arms spread wide, yodeling. Her high-pitched voice was like nails scraping on metal only adding to the chaos. "Get down!" Layala demanded and marched toward the stage. She slapped her palm against the raised platform. The tiny menace was supposed to stay in the room.

Tif only yodeled louder, tapping her foot, and pushing out her chest. How could anyone that small be ear-piercing? And where did her acute fear of jumbos go all of a sudden? She'd barely come out of the bag or Thane's hood, but she would take the stage in the middle of a brawl?

One of the men made it past the other elves and Thane popped him hard with an elbow.

"Shut that thing up!" someone shouted and tossed a half loaf of bread. It sailed right by Tif but with her

eyes closed and her mouth wide open she didn't even notice.

Layala groaned and hopped up on the stage, snatching Tif by the back of her dress and lifting her up. "What in the world are you doing? Are you blind and deaf?"

A blush spilled across her cheeks, and she adjusted her little red hat. "I wanted to sing." She pointed out at the fight still going on. "And I have an adoring crowd."

The room was in shambles at this point, with men and elves rolling on top of each other, tables cracked, chairs split in half, food, and drink everywhere. Alisara and her group of friends disappeared and Kail still sat in his booth, head resting on his fist watching everything with a miffed expression.

Layala rolled her eyes. "Yes, they look so adoring, don't they? I told you to stay upstairs."

"I may have gotten a few thimbles full of this juice that turned out to be wine and suddenly I got real brave." She pulled a tiny sword from under her skirts. "Let's get 'em."

The entrance door crashed open, and sunlight spilled inside. Palenor soldiers in navy uniforms stepped inside. At first there was only a couple, but they kept coming. Thane hopped up on stage, grabbed Layala's arm and started for a shadowed corridor. "Time to make our exit."

"You think they are here for us?"

He shrugged. "They could be. Or someone got help

from the street patrol for the fight. Either way, we need to go."

"I can take 'em!" Tif said, slashing her weapon through the air.

"We'll get our things and take the back door." They rounded the corner that led upstairs to over a dozen guards blocking their path.

CHAPTER 19

Thane glanced back, finding five more soldiers coming up behind them. All of them had their weapons drawn. He held Layala's arm a little firmer, ready to negotiate until blond hair and a cocky grin stepped through the soldiers, and then he only saw red.

Thane's sword was out and pressed against Aldrich's heart in a flash. "Before you do that," Aldrich said, raising his hands in surrender. "Know that we have Piper, Fennan and dearest Aunt Evalyn being held outside. If you go out there before I do, my soldiers have their orders to kill them."

"You piece of shit," Thane snapped, hand shaking with rage. It took every last bit of his restraint to not shove his sword straight through Aldrich's chest. His hand snapped out and he gripped a handful of Aldrich's hair, jerking him closer. "How dare you show your face to me. I am the reason you still draw breath. I

saved your ass over and over and this is how I am repaid?"

Aldrich had the nerve to allow the corner of his mouth to curve upward. "You made a critical mistake, Thane. You forget I know you. I knew you'd split the Ravens to throw us off your trail, but I was at your side for years. So my gut led me here. Alisara looks good, doesn't she?"

Thane shoved him into the line of Palenor soldiers and a low growl rumbled in his throat. "The mistake was yours, thinking you could come here, and I wouldn't tear your heart out of your chest with my bloody bare hands."

The soldiers around shifted nervously, their breaths shallow and quick. They knew how fiercely a male would protect his mate and they knew Thane's threats were real. He contemplated his odds of being able to take everyone here down and getting to his friends before the soldiers outside could hurt them.

"Thane, if he has—" Layala started, and Thane cut her off with a glare. She clamped her mouth shut and looked away.

"Well, that's a first," Aldrich drawled.

"Watch your filthy mouth."

Katmor, one of the high-ranking generals, stepped partially in front of Aldrich. A close acquaintance with his father who'd been around Thane since he was but a boy. "High Prince Thane, you must do the honorable thing and face the consequences of your actions. You

attempted to assassinate the High King of Palenor. There is to be a tribunal. The War Council has made this decision, not Tenebris."

Thane slowly shook his head. "I will not go with you."

"We want to hear your side. Are you going to run forever, hiding in shit holes like this?" He held out his arms gesturing around. "Being a coward who won't face the repercussions of laws he swore to uphold?"

Thane's arm twitched to raise his sword, but instead he gripped the handle tighter. It didn't bother him to be called a coward, he knew he wasn't, but he didn't like the way Katmor accused him of things he knew nothing about.

"Don't speak to him like that," Layala snapped. "Your High King is a war criminal and the one who should be subject to a tribunal, not blindly followed. He has aligned himself with Mathekis and he will be the fall of this kingdom."

Katmor turned his fiery gaze on Layala. "Hold your tongue when males are speaking."

Thane growled quietly. That was not the thing to say to Layala. Before Thane could say anything, Layala threw her hand out and a black vine shot from her palm, wrapping around Katmor's neck like a serpent.

"You want to say that again?" she snarled. "Males think they can rule over us because of physical strength, but guess who holds the power between me and you, pig?"

Tifapine clung to Layala's leg but held out her stubby middle finger. "Pig," she repeated.

"Poor choice of words, Katmor," Thane said. "You're the only one who needs to hold his tongue, or I might cut it out."

The clatter of Katmor's sword hitting the ground was loud in the quiet shock of the soldiers. He choked for air and clawed at the vine tightening around his neck. "Thane, please," he gasped.

"It's not me you should be asking mercy from."

Katmor's eyes shifted to Layala as if seeing her for the first time. "Lady Lightbringer," he wheezed. She must have eased her magic's hold because he said easier, "Please release me."

She raised her chin slightly. "I'll let you go if you get on your knees and ask for my forgiveness."

"Layala," Aldrich said slowly. "Remember whose fate rests in your hands."

Without uttering a word, Layala thrust out her other arm and vine shot forth, coiling around Aldrich's chest and neck like a boa constrictor. "*Your* fate by the looks of things."

One of the soldiers lifted his sword; Thane held up his hand. "*Don't.*" With wide eyes, and a back step, the soldier lowered his weapon. "What's it to be, boys?" Thane's smile couldn't have been broader. "Your future queen commands respect."

Katmor slowly lowered, one knee hitting the ground, then two. Aldrich's red face began to turn a dark shade of purple before he followed the general's

action. He looked up at her, his fingers dug into the vine strangling him and a white milky substance oozed around his nails. The satisfaction this brought Thane was beyond words.

"Please forgive my disrespect," Katmor said.

Aldrich pressed his lips together like a stubborn mule.

"You're both going to walk outside," Thane said, and lifted his finger, pointing down the hall, "and tell your soldiers to let them go." Neither of them moved.

Thane laughed. Katmor always was a stubborn bastard, and he likely believed that Thane would be more merciful than Tenebris. Aldrich knew better. When it came to Layala, mercy wasn't in his vocabulary. "Snap their necks if you wish."

"Wait—wait." Katmor crawled forward to clutch at Thane's pant leg, his ragged breath growing weaker. Aldrich's bloodshot eyes were fixed on Layala as if she might give him grace if he didn't break from his stare. He was in for a rude awakening.

The magical vines slowly twisted more until Katmor couldn't pull in a breath at all. "Thane," he wheezed. Her magic eased off. It appeared Layala wanted to give him a chance to live.

Layala shrieked and the vines went slack, falling to the ground. Thane whipped around to one of the soldiers with a handful of her hair and a sword pressed against her throat with enough pressure it indented her skin.

"Help the general!" the soldier shouted. "Save Aldrich."

It took a lot for Thane to truly lose his temper and a blade at her throat snapped what little patience he had left. His magic flared like a lightning strike through him, coursing through his limbs with a buzz of energy. He thought about breaking the bones in that soldier's hand, and not a moment later, a snap and sickening crunch followed. The soldier cried out in pain, his sword clanked to the ground and Layala shoved away from him. Shaking, the soldier held his wrist, eyes fixed on his fingers curling in the wrong directions, and Thane snapped his forearm, too. He screamed louder as his arm sagged. He stumbled back into the wall mouth agape in horror. The other soldiers backed off several steps, including Katmor and Aldrich scooting backward. "No one ever learns, do they? I put the word out long ago that I would kill anyone who touched her."

"Thane, wait," Katmor blurted, reaching for him like he could stop what was coming.

The soldier's head twisted with a quick jerk, and he collapsed, never to rise again.

With a snarl, Thane whirled around. The soldiers charged in attack, and blind with fury, he slashed his sword across the chest of the closest soldier. A chilling wail followed, and then another, and another. Warm blood arced through the air, splattering on his cheek. Screams barely pierced his senses. The ringing of metal on metal an all too familiar tune. His swords

hacked and slashed, finding their way through armor, crunching through bone. Not one of them would make it out of this corridor, alive.

Only when no one fought against him, and unmoving bodies in useless armor littered the floor, and his boot splashed in a puddle of scarlet liquid, did he notice Layala staring at him with wide, surprised blue eyes. She'd never witnessed him like this, never seen him lose himself to war up close. He'd hidden this side of himself from her, afraid she'd reject him.

He breathed heavily and pulled away from her stunned expression. Fear tugged at his insides. Would she run from him now, repulsed by his wicked side? It was strange he worried more about what she might think than what he did, slaughtering his own kind like they were nothing but hogs. But it was them or her, and it was no choice at all.

He moved a body with his foot, searching among them. When he didn't see that traitorous head of blond hair, he said, "Where the hell is Aldrich?"

"I—I," she stuttered, "I don't know." She shook her head, snapping out of her stare and looked down the hall. "He must have snuck away. Oh, shit!" Terror flashed across her face, and she took off in a sprint.

Thane took off after her, his heavy breath coming faster with each step until she burst through the door at the end and blinding sunlight lit up the windowless corridor. They stood side by side, looking up and down the congested street. There were no soldiers holding their friends captive. No soldiers at all. Drops of blood

led to the right and disappeared among the many people roaming from one seller's canopy to the next.

Some onlookers gave Thane confused stares. A woman grabbed her two children's arms and dragged them from him as quickly as possible. Thane grunted and swiped his hand down the side of his face; it came away covered in crimson.

"He was bluffing," Thane said with a snarl. "He never had them. And the little bastard got away."

THANE DIPPED his hands into a small basin of hot water and splashed his face. The scent of Layala's arousal still lingered in the air, refreshing and nostalgic like rain hitting the ground after a hot summer day. An involuntary shiver wracked his body as he rubbed water over his arms to wash away the still-wet blood.

Layala shoved clothes into a brown leather bag and looked up at him. He was afraid he'd see revulsion there, or maybe even fear after what he'd just done. He'd wiped out those soldiers—*his* soldiers swift and without remorse, no matter how they begged. But her soft gaze told a story of understanding—of knowing. "Where do you think the others are? And do you think it was Alisara who told Aldrich? He mentioned her by name."

He glanced out the window. A raven perched on the ledge, digging its beak into its wing feathers. It was strange and ironic the creatures seemed to follow

him wherever he went. "Maker only knows where the others went. I'm hoping word of the raid on this place will have spread and they're already at the stables or headed there. And no, I don't think Alisara did. She was in the room with us when the fight broke out. Aldrich was already on his way here. He only said that to get a rise out of us."

Tif hiccupped loudly, drawing his attention. She tipped a bottle of wine, pouring the maroon liquid into a thimble. Maker, that girl was going to be his undoing. She was as vexing as a toddler but with the capabilities of an adult. "Put that down."

She froze like she'd been caught stealing and grinned. "Just one teensy weensy sip? I need to drown out what I just witnessed, although I'm already drunk so I might not remember in the morning. Is it morning?"

"I think you've had enough *teensy weensy* sips." At least this wasn't the first encounter of violence Tif witnessed, or she might be even more dramatic. He snatched the bottle and set it on the other side of the room. "Aren't you supposed to be a lady's maid? You should be packing."

"Oh." She tipped her thimble back and sucked it down. "Right. Better get to my duty. Mama always said slackers better be good packers because they'll be packed up and moved out." She tapped a finger against her red bulbous nose. "You know, maybe that's why she kicked me out of the hole. I always thought it was because I wasn't a good baker. Although I do

make a mean lemon zest cookie. Even she can't deny that."

"I thought you left because you had dreams of being an elven lady's maid," Layala said, slipping the strap of the bag around her shoulder.

"I did. She said I was always dreaming and not working when she threw my bag out the front entrance and sent me right after." Tif shrugged. "Left —kicked out, same difference. Truthfully, I'm glad she did. Look at what I've got to do because of her."

Thane threw open the door. "Let's go."

They hurried down the creaky stairs. The bodies were still in piles on the floor, but someone had lined them up and put white sheets over them. It was a real prick move to start a fight and leave a bunch of bodies for his friend Kail to clean up. He stopped outside the doorway that led into the main dining area. An apology and a hefty payment were in order. But what he saw inside froze his momentum and he stepped back, pressing himself against the wall.

Layala's brows pulled closer. "What's wrong?"

He held a finger to his lips and pressed his arm across her chest to ease her against the wall behind him. Slowly, he slid until he could see inside. There were only two people in the room now. A scaled, taloned hand wrapped around Kail's neck. Varlett's golden hair was tied back and her usually brown skin was replaced by shiny black dragon scales. She was partially shifted, and a three-inch poisonous talon stroked under Kail's chin. *Shit*. In this form, Thane

didn't stand a chance of penetrating those scales with his sword. And if outside the woods weeks ago was any indication, she was impervious to his magical attacks or at the very least, she had a resilient shield. Layala's vines hadn't gotten through, and she'd escaped the thorny cage easily.

"I know they were here. I can smell them, even over the stench of this place. They were at this table. What did they want?"

"They left after the fight. And they only wanted a place to lay low." Kail's voice was shaky.

"I'm only going to ask one more time." Her talon pressed into the soft flesh just below his jaw. "What did they want? They could have gone anywhere yet they chose to come here."

Thane gripped the doorframe harder. *Don't tell her. Don't tell her.*

His throat bobbed and he sighed. "They wanted to know where to find the All Seeing Stone."

Her amber cat-like eyes narrowed. "Mmm of course. Who has it? I know a little worm like you has heard. And before you consider lying, know I can taste lies."

Kail closed his eyes, pausing a beat before answering. "Lord Brunard."

Varlett smiled. "What a good little boy." She patted his cheek lightly then her long nails scraped along the tabletop as she stood. "You've really let this place go, Kail." Her heeled boots clicked loudly on her way outside. The door slammed shut behind her

and Kail sagged into the booth and let out a long breath.

"She's going after the stone," Layala whispered beside him. "We need to get to it before she can. If we don't, we'll never find out how to get rid of the curse."

"That will be difficult considering she can fly."

CHAPTER 20

Evening crickets chirped in bunches of wildflowers and thick grasses. In the absence of the bustle of bartering and crowded streets, the pleasant sound of lake water lapped against the shore. To stay out of sight, they jogged along the lake's edge. Layala's calves and thighs burned against the resistance of the dark golden sand. Lifting a hand against the setting sun's harsh light reflecting off the water, she spotted boats with white sails bobbing in the lake not far off, and men and elves alike carried goods along the docks. No sign of soldiers anywhere. If Mathekis or any of the pale ones were close enough to sense her use of magic earlier, they weren't here yet.

After running for a few minutes, the stables at the end of Braxentown came into view. Thane crouched behind a huge gray rock and waved for her to follow. Layala dropped beside him and risked a look. The stablemaster they'd seen earlier whistled while he

pushed a wheelbarrow along a path around the back. A horse whinnied loudly, and the grasses and trees swished in the breeze. Not finding anything out of the ordinary, she asked, "Do you see something?"

"No, but I need to make certain there's no enemy waiting to ambush us." He pulled the hood of his cloak up. "I'll go alone to be safe. Wait for my signal." He plucked Tif out of his hood and set her on the ground beside Layala.

"Oh, I'm only good enough to go on covert missions when Layala isn't around?" Tif folded her arms and stuck out her lower lip.

Thane grunted. "Keep up the attitude and you can walk from now on." He slipped away with the ease and grace of an eagle.

"You've certainly gotten much braver when it comes to Thane. Maybe a little too much," Layala said with a half-smile. "Before, you would barely let him see you."

"Yes, well as it turns out, he doesn't want to squish me under his boot as I once thought." She brushed some crumbs off her bosom. "Most of the time anyway."

Whispering voices and the quiet clank of metal drifted from somewhere close. Of course Tifapine began whistling and bouncing on her toes, until Layala popped her in the back of the head and put a finger to her lips. After a hiccup, Tif slapped a hand over her mouth and ducked lower into the grass. Layala slowly rose from her crouch, gripping the rough

surface of the stone. Her gaze swept across the land; the road was empty. People roamed the streets of the town below, but they were too far off to be the source of the chatter. Like a ghost hand passed through her, she whirled around.

She gasped, slapping a hand to her chest, and sagged against the rock. "You scared the piss out of me. And thank the Maker you're alive and well. Aldrich said he held you captive."

Piper, Fennan and Aunt Evalyn stood with confused looks. "You saw Aldrich? Is he—dead?" Fennan asked with some trepidation.

Thankfully the swollen purple eye Piper once had was down to minor yellowish bruising now. Fennan's arm was no longer in a sling, and he seemed to move it easily.

"No, he got away. But Thane—" She thought "butchered" was the appropriate word, but said, "killed over a dozen Palenor soldiers including an elf named Katmor. He spoke about being on a War Council."

"Tenebris is going to be furious at that," Piper folded her arms. "Katmor was one of his closest allies."

"Even I know who Katmor is, and over a dozen soldiers?" Aunt Evalyn clutched the twine of dried berries around her neck. "This isn't good."

Fennan's wary cinnamon eyes glanced at the road. "We saw you and Thane run out of Kail's place. It was too easy to follow your footprints in the sand, so we should probably go."

Piper watched the nearby road warily. "Where are the others? We heard there was a brawl there. What happened?"

"Thane got pissy when a human man asked me to dance and wouldn't let it go."

"The whole place is trashed." Tif emerged from behind the rock. "I started singing to soothe the rebels down, but it didn't work too well. Oh, then the dragon lady showed up."

"Varlett is here too?" Piper and Fennan said at once.

"Dragon lady?" Aunt Evalyn said nervously.

"She was here," Layala groaned. "Now I'm afraid she's after our only chance of finding out what we need, and I have no idea how we'll get there first. Thane went to check the stables." She waved for them to follow as she started off. "Let's go."

Layala found Thane and the other Ravens inside the stables, saddling their horses, chatting away as if she hadn't been waiting for his signal. She rolled her eyes, and she shoved the huge door aside. "Evening."

Thane turned on a heel with a grin. "Laya, I was just about to come to get you."

"Uh-huh." She put a hand on her hip and the others stepped up behind her.

"Oh, good," Thane said. "We're all here."

The stable master came out of a nearby door with a yellowed scroll in hand. He brushed his hand over it, creating a dust cloud. "Afraid I haven't had much use of it since I never leave, but here it is."

He tugged on a latch and a wooden table came away from the wall, where he unrolled and smoothed out the scroll. Layala and the others circled around a map of Adalon. The edges had been chewed on by mice and there were several stains, but it was legible. With his pointer finger Thane pressed on Braxentown. "We're here and we must get all the way over to Calladira in three days at most."

"That's not possible," Leif said, rubbing his chin. "It's at least seven days' ride and that's if we could take the main road, which we can't. We're looking at ten days minimum."

"The dragon will be in Newarden at Brunard's place to get the stone in three days, maybe even less."

Siegfried cleared his throat and rested his hand on the pommel of a dagger at his left hip. "I know of a way."

Everyone turned to the one they called The Wraith, standing in the back of the group. "You do?" Thane asked.

"There is a stone portal on an island. It's about a half day's ride to the town where we'll need to take a boat."

Thane's eyebrows raised, wrinkling his forehead. "You know about the portals?"

"I know about the portals," he repeated with a smile. "No one uses it but given we have a mage." He glanced at Layala then at Thane. "Or two."

"You're certain," Thane said. "We cannot afford to lose time if it's not."

"It's there," he said.

"The Wraith always comes through in dire circumstances," Gunner said, slapping his back. Layala noticed a fat lower lip with red bruising around the corner of his mouth. He must have gotten popped hard during that brawl with the men.

"In my opinion, as the group healer," Aunt Evalyn started in a firm tone, "we should make camp and rest until morning. None of us have slept in two days. And I'm afraid even my special drinks for stamina won't keep us going without sleep."

Layala glanced at the map. She didn't see an island depicted anywhere, but none of the portals' locations were on this map.

Thane nodded. "We can do that as soon as we are clear of this town and know we've not been followed."

Siegfried looked troubled when he said, "There is one problem I need to warn you about."

Everyone's attention was on him again.

Thane tapped his fingers on the map's surface impatiently. "Well, go on."

"Its waters are guarded by deadly creatures."

LAYALA STARTLED awake to birds happily chirping with the first signs of morning light. She rubbed her forehead and swiped away the damp sweat. She had that dream of the Black Mage again, taunting her, chasing her through dark woods. Heard the charismatic voice

calling to her, asking her to come to him. She would swear on her parents' graves it was real and she knew now it was not Thane calling to her, and she had a sick feeling it was never him. She couldn't figure out why they spoke similarly, had the same cadence. Did her subconscious use a voice similar to Thane's for the Black Mage's to terrify her even more? Could he be truly reaching out to her somehow? She shuddered at the thought. She'd never given much thought to dreams but these... these were different.

Under the bright stars, some hours earlier, they'd gathered along the shoreline with a small fire in a hollowed-out dip in the sand. She blinked, rubbing the sleepiness from her eyes, and tried to shake off the unease from her nightmare.

A small sense of ease soothed her when she noticed the warmth of Thane's body against her back. She wasn't trapped in the tower. He wasn't gone. They were together again. She took a deep breath and wiggled even closer to him, thanking the Maker for this moment of peace. The water quietly lapped against the sand and tiny fireflies hung in the air around them with the last of the dark. The scent of roasting meat hit her senses and her mouth watered. A couple Ravens hunted down a few wild chickens, and the meal waited on skewers, half eaten over the dying flames. Layala moved a little and Thane's arm slid around her waist, curling entirely around her body and hugged her even closer.

"Stay," he said in a raspy morning voice.

She smiled. "I wasn't going anywhere."

He nuzzled his face against the nape of her neck. "I wish we could stay like this all day. Listening to the water, relaxing in the sand and sunshine. Just you and me."

"And what else would we do?" she teased.

"Mmmm," he growled and nipped her earlobe. "Don't get me started on that or we might have to sneak away."

"Sire," Fennan called.

Thane groaned and pushed himself up, leaving the cool air to rush against Layala's back "Yes?"

"A few of us are going to ride into town and see if we can secure a boat."

He rubbed his scruffy chin and nodded. "Thank you. We'll be right behind you."

Layala sat up and dug her bare toes into the cool sand and wrapped her arms around her knees. Thane's rough hand glided up her back then he bear-hugged her from behind. "Were you having a nightmare earlier?" He rested his chin on her shoulder and toyed with a lock of her midnight hair.

"Why do you ask?" She swallowed hard. She wanted to tell him but was afraid of what he might think knowing she shared a connection with the Black Mage—the reason for the curse on the land. It was bad enough the pale ones were drawn to her. Now this? Now he called to her, infected her dreams?

"Because you were breathing fast, and I heard your

heart racing." He placed his palm flat against her chest. "It still is."

Why did he have to call her out? He couldn't even feel her emotions anymore and he still knew. She smiled and kissed his cheek. "I think you're trying to find excuses to touch my chest."

He chuckled and gave her breast a squeeze. "They are my favorite."

"I did have a nightmare but it's nothing. Just a strange dream."

"If you need to talk, you can tell me. Sometimes the nightmares, the death, all the blood and screams of war," he paused to swallow. "It's heavy."

Her heart felt the weight of that statement. And he would know more than most. "Thank you," she said quietly, and debated on telling him the truth. Thane would understand, wouldn't he? Then her stomach growled loudly, and he chuckled.

"Make sure you get something to eat before we go." He kissed her briefly and made his way over to Phantom.

She would tell him later; it was probably nothing anyway and he had enough to worry about. Out of the corner of her eye, she noticed Evalyn standing on the shoreline with her shawl draped over her shoulders and a scowl directed at the steam rising out of the metal tea mug in her hand. What was she upset about? Layala knew Aunt Evalyn well enough to know even if she was cordial to Thane, she didn't like him. They'd

spent most of Layala's life despising the Athayel family. She could only imagine what it would be like watching her adopted daughter in love with the enemy. Sometime soon, she and Aunt Evalyn would get into it over Thane, but that would have to wait, for now.

Most of the others were up packing their belongings or sipping from canteens staring out at the lake. The island they were supposed to sail to looked like nothing more than a dark blot on the horizon.

"What happened to your eye?" Evalyn asked Gunner. "I apologize if it's rude to ask but I've wondered since I met you."

Gunner touched his eyepatch and then grew a smile. "Oh, it's not rude. I was fighting a massive pale one. He was in a small village, trying to eat some children." He stood and gestured above his head by at least a foot. "At least seven feet tall. He knocked me to the ground and his mace caught my eye, but I shoved my sword right through his middle. Killed the bastard dead."

"Very brave of you."

He stared down at the dying fire and his smile dropped. He glanced between Aunt Evalyn and Layala. "Actually, it happened when I was a boy. The fire I stoked popped and shot an ember into my eye. Nothing so brave."

Aunt Evalyn licked her lips. "It's brave to tell the truth when you don't want to."

He smiled at that.

A waft of cinnamon and freshly-baked bread

wafted to Layala's nose. She turned to find Tifapine dragging a sack along behind her, leaving a trail in the sand. Always good for a snack, that one. She grinned at Layala and lugged it in front of her. "I found a community of gnomes nearby. They gave me so many goodies." Tif tugged open her bag and plucked out a thick roll sprinkled with cinnamon and blueberries. They were smaller than the average elf or human baked goods, but when she took a bite, she decided gnome food was better. The savory sweet taste was like water to a desert, and she closed her eyes and relished in the taste.

"Thank you, Tif."

Her little lady's maid chomped into her chosen delight and with a full mouth said, "So I was talking to the gnomes, you know, like I do, and they said they gave me this food because I wouldn't survive the trip to the island. A little bit morbid if you ask me. Absolutely zero encouragement. Wonder what's out there?"

Layala swallowed down her food. Siegfried said there were rumors that creatures lived in the water that could be dangerous, but she didn't know details. They'd dealt with pale ones, dragons, and enemy elves. They could handle whatever it was. "We'll be fine, like always."

She shrugged, tearing off another piece. "They said people who go out there, don't come back. They get lost to the waters around the island. I can't swim, so if the boat goes down, you better grab me, or I'll sink like a rock straight to the bottom."

"The boat won't go down. Stop worrying. You have the best warriors in Palenor to protect you too."

"I don't doubt it but maybe we should let Varlett take the stone from Brunard and then steal it from her."

Layala shook her head. "That would be more difficult than taking it from Brunard. She almost killed Thane. And what if she hides it? I don't think she even wants it for herself. She just doesn't want us to have it." Then the stone would be lost once more and what hope did they have of finding out how Layala was connected to the Black Mage or destroying the enemy then?

Tif rocked back and forth from heel to toe, tapping a finger against her lips. "Good point. Alls I'm saying is the trip to the island might be worse than the dragon lady. Gnomes don't give food away easily. They didn't even want anything in return, which is unusual." She put her hands out as if they were balancing scales. "Sharp teeth and poisonous talons, possibly being eaten," she grimaced, tipping to one side more. "Eesh, maybe I'd rather drown."

THE HORSES' hooves clicked loudly on the wooden docks of this small fishing town. They'd all been restless and jumpy since they entered the streets which was uncommon for such well-trained animals. There were only about six buildings and a few scattered

farms in the distance. One of the white-painted buildings looked like an inn which must be where most of the fishermen ate. There were more boats than establishments. She counted twenty-one bobbing in the lake, of various sizes and crews. The Ravens who'd left earlier were gathered near the center of the docks. Thane pulled Phantom behind him as Layala rode. She patted the black horse's neck and glanced back at Tif poking her head out of the bag.

"People don't come back," she whispered, and started chewing on one of her nails.

"We'll be fine, Tif," Layala assured.

They approached their group. Many of them dipped their heads toward Thane. Fennan folded his arms. "No one is willing to take us."

"Why?" he asked and held a hand up to Layala. She grasped his palm and slid down.

"They say it's too dangerous," Piper answered. "They say that we'll be attacked by lake creatures and die."

Layala gulped. Perhaps Tifapine's worries were warranted. She placed her hand on her brow, blocking the sun's bright light. "What is out there?"

"Sounds like superstitious nonsense," Fennan said with a huff. "It's a lake. Other than large fish, what could there be?"

A young human woman with bright-red curls in a wide, black-brimmed hat with an eagle feather stuck in the fold, hopped down from the stone wall a few yards down. Her pale skin had a splash of freckles

across the nose, and her thigh-high boots tapped loudly as she swayed her way over. "They're certainly not fish."

Thane turned and his eyes gave her a once-over. "And who are you?"

"I'm Captain Fella." She stuck out her hand partially covered with black fingerless gloves. "I've been listening to your boys ask every captain but me for a ride to the island. But I'm guessing you're the one in charge."

Thane arched an eyebrow. "Perhaps they simply didn't realize you were a captain of a boat."

"Ship," she corrected. "Mine's the biggest one."

"Are you offering your services, Captain Fella?"

"Depends." She peered down at her nails and picked at the chipping onyx polish. "How much money you got, pointy ears?"

Many of the Ravens shifted; even Layala bristled at the insult. She'd been called that most of her life by humans and hated it.

"If you knew who you were speaking to, you'd show more respect," Piper said, stepping out from the group. "Besides we're in elven land. You should think twice about who you offend."

Fella smiled broadly and lightly picked up Piper's red braid. They almost had the same hair color, but Piper's was a couple shades lighter. "Sensitive. But seeing's how I'm the only one with a way out there, and that's where you need to go, I can pretty much say what I want, pointy ears."

Piper's hand struck out like a snake, and she gripped the woman by the throat.

"Enough, Piper," Thane said. Piper's teeth ground loudly enough for Layala to hear it, but she backed up. Captain Fella laughed as Piper's grip dropped.

"Actually," Fennan said over Thane's shoulder. "We didn't ask her because the others said she was mentally unstable. I think they're right."

Fella spit a large amount of saliva near Thane's boot, and snarled, "I ain't mental, but I'm the only one just crazy enough to get you to that rock out there and some of you might even survive if you do what I say."

Thane's eyes darkened and he held up a hand to silence everyone. Even Fella shut her mouth. "First of all, don't ever spit in my direction again, Captain. Secondly, I don't have time for bullshit. Name your price. I have money."

She looked him up and down. "Mmm, I bet you do; fancy clothes, nice boots, and that face is delicious. Bet you'd even be a great roll in the sack. I haven't had elf cock in a while."

Layala's skin prickled, and she growled quietly. "And you won't be getting any either, woman."

Fella snickered and pointed at Layala. "I bet she could tell me if you know how to hump hard and when to take it oh so slow."

Layala's hand twitched toward her dagger and her cheeks lit like a burning ember to dry grass. How could this woman be so irritating after only a few minutes?

Maker above, she couldn't even imagine what Thane would do if someone said that to her.

"Relax, lady, it's a compliment to your man—er—male. Never quite understood why you differentiate it that way. Got the same parts."

"It's because we're not men. Man is a word only associated with human males," Fennan said.

The grumbles and murmured comments among the others could be summed up as "disrespectful" and "no manners."

"Your price, Captain Fella," Thane urged.

Her eyes trailed down his body, stalled on his crotch and seemed to take an exorbitant amount of time to look away. Layala rolled her eyes.

Fella touched her hat, pushing it up slightly. "Well since the black-haired beauty will gut me if I ask to bed you—" She peeked around at the rest of the group, paused on Fennan, winked and then her gaze fell on Phantom. "That's a fine horse you got there."

"You can't have my horse."

"Alright." She crossed her arms. "Thirty gold pieces."

"Thirty?" Layala balked before Thane could even open his lips. She'd never had even a single gold coin in her life. Only the wealthiest had access to that kind of precious metal. Most dealt in nickel coins, occasionally silver. Thirty gold coins could buy a whole house and a nice one at that, and even if Thane could afford it, it was almost robbery. "Five, at most."

With a hand on her popped-out hip, she said, "I'm

putting my life at risk. I'm not willing to potentially die unless the reward is worth it. Twenty-five gold coins and that's my final offer."

"Twenty," Thane said.

"Done."

Layala clenched her teeth hard. They could have negotiated down further. And the gall of that woman to suggest Thane would bed her as payment. Thane opened his saddle bag and Tif handed him a sack of jingling coins. She stuck her tongue out at Captain Fella and ducked back inside.

Thane opened the bag, plucked out several pieces, stuck them in his pocket then handed the small sack to the Captain. "Count it if you wish."

"I certainly will." She snatched it from Thane like he might try to take it back. She poured it out on the flat top of the stone wall. Layala folded her arms and leaned her shoulder against Phantom. Everyone silently watched her as she moved the coins from one pile to another. Horse tails swished, and the air felt a little tense. Phantom nickered loudly and stomped his front hoof against the plank of wood.

When she shoved the gold back into the pouch, she looked up. "What did you say your name was?"

"I didn't say." Thane's voice held more edge to it this time. "Now take us to your ship."

CHAPTER 21

With the horses loaded in the holding area, and Tifapine secured below with them, Layala hopped onto the main deck. Captain Fella didn't lie when she said she captained the biggest ship in town. It was at least seventy-five feet long and held the horses and their group easily.

A human woman tugged ropes loose from the dock and tossed them onto the ship where another waited to collect. Was this an all-woman crew? She'd seen six so far and not a single male apart from her own people. "All aboard!" Captain Fella shouted from behind a huge round steering wheel.

Layala leaned toward Thane. "Can we seriously trust this woman?"

"According to the sailors I spoke with a few minutes ago, she's good, unhinged but good. None of them will go to the island and they said we're insane for even asking. She's our ride, like it or not."

The ship rocked and bobbed as it moved away from the dock. A woman with black skin and gold circlet jewelry on her wrists and adorned around her neck, pulled on a rope and big white sails fell open with a pop, catching the wind.

Seagulls called and circled above. With the rumors of how dangerous this small voyage could be, Layala's stomach was upset. She didn't know if it was just nerves or the rocking motions. Maker above, she hoped she wasn't the type to get seasick. It was the wind over this massive lake that created waves similar to a sea. The last thing she wanted to worry about was if she would be puking her guts up while trying to fight off potential dangers. What was out there anyway? No one said exactly what they might face. They actively avoided speaking about what lived in the water as if the gossip itself might draw them bad luck.

Layala rested her elbows on the wood railing, looking down at the splashing, white foamy water. Sprays of it moistened her skin and curled the fly-away pieces of hair around her face. The briny, algae scent was present but not overwhelming—if anything the air smelled fresh.

She glanced back at the others, gathered near the center of the ship. Some of them sat on barrels or crates in casual conversation. Leif held his arms wide in the telling of some dramatic tale. His wild orangish hair with braids and knots seriously needed combing. Layala even spotted a couple small sticks... *and is that a*

caterpillar or a fuzzy leaf? "My nana used to tell stories about beautiful women who would lure and enchant naughty boys into the water with their songs," Leif said. "Claimed she'd toss me to them if I acted a fool." He gave Fennan a light shove. "Fennan will be the first one they grab."

Thane was leaned up against one of the masts, arms crossed, and let out a deep-bellied laugh. A shiver tingled along her spine just hearing that sound, his laughter. Maker, he had no idea how beautiful he was.

"Hey," Fennan chuckled. "I'm a good boy. Never touched a tit in my life. Don't like to drink either."

Layala rolled her eyes. From what she'd heard Fennan was quite the lady tamer.

Aunt Evalyn appeared next to her. She looked even less enthused about the topic of the boys' conversation. "I worry for you." Her voice was low, purposefully so the others wouldn't hear.

"And I, for you. It's dangerous for you to be with us, being hunted."

"I feel you've already been caught in a trap, Laya, and you don't even know it." She tugged at the end of her sleeve. "It would be the perfect chess move, gaining your trust, your love, and then asking you to do the forbidden."

"You don't know him." There wasn't a shred of doubt in her mind.

"He's charming, quite attractive, and has the

charisma of one who's played the game at court for a long time. I don't blame you for not seeing it."

Layala ground her teeth. The time she spent doubting and distrusting him had long passed. He showed her nothing but loyalty and almost died for her. "He's been the most adamant against me bringing back the Black Mage, even more than I am myself. It will take time for you to see his true colors and not be blinded by hatred, trust me."

"You need time away from him to get your head clear. You need to come home even if just to think. See your friends."

"Look, I've been down this road. I attempted to kill him, and escape. It wasn't as if I saw him and instantly fell in love. You need to trust me."

"Layala," her voice took on that motherly sternness. "I've watched hurt, sorrowful girls like you fall for charm and good looks. My instincts tell me he is not as terrible as his father, but there is something there, in the way he moves, his predatory gaze. He watches you with unnerving closeness. And you, if you're not near him, I see the panic in your eyes. It's not healthy. Thane is dangerous and not the one for you."

"Because he's afraid something will happen to me and so what if I worry when he's not near me. I'm scared to death of losing him. I almost lost him once."

Aunt Evalyn went quiet. They both watched the blue-black water cutting against the ship for a while. "That's what scares me the most. When Novak died—

it broke my heart to see you go through that. I thought I might lose you. You weren't yourself ever again."

Layala brushed her fingers over her hair. Aunt Evalyn didn't know how Novak died. And the truth was, with Novak, it was guilt that nearly did her in, thinking she was responsible for his death. But if Thane died, her suffering wouldn't compare, for their love was as endless as the stars. "Novak died because of the mate spell between Thane and me. He and I slept together, and it killed him because he wasn't my mate. For a long time, I harbored guilt about that. I thought it was my magic, that I had killed Novak. I didn't know there was a loyalty clause in the mate spell."

Aunt Evalyn's eyes widened. She remained quiet for what felt like too long, rubbing her hands over the slick wood railing. "So again, Tenebris killed someone you loved. He's the reason you were mate bonded to Thane to begin with."

"Yes," Layala said.

"I am sorry you placed that burden on yourself. I wish you would have told me sooner so I could have at least bore it with you."

"I was afraid everyone would think I was an abomination—even you. Everyone adored Novak."

She pursed her lips. "Layala, you carry too much." She glanced at Thane. "If you love Thane, then I will trust you. I will give him a chance."

Layala smiled and pulled Aunt Evalyn into a hug. It meant more to Layala than Aunt Evalyn even knew.

"Thank you. I want to tell you all about him, and everything that has happened since he came for me." Layala looked down at the other side of the ship. The crew's demeanor was focused, wary, even a little fearful. Whatever was in the water that her friends joked about was no laughing matter to them. "But I'm afraid we'll have to talk more about that later."

With her hand gliding along the ship's slick railing, she made her way over to one of the crew. Silver-flecked gray eyes, so bright against her black skin, inspected Layala before she said, "Something I can help you with?" She reached up and touched one of her two thick, braids, dragging her hand over the length to the ends at her waist.

"What's in the water that has you all so nervous?"

She took a deep breath. "They've been called many things—temptress, evil, water nymphs—but we call them sirens."

She'd never heard the name. "And what are they exactly?" Surely Leif's story couldn't be true? Water women who called males with songs?

"Unfortunately, I'm sure you'll see for yourself soon enough. Your men folk should be a lot more nervous than they are."

The island was in close proximity now. It must be only a mile in length, but it was covered in trees and foliage, darkening the view of anything that might be inside.

"Get ready," the woman said and hurried over to a six-foot-long chest. The click and grinding of other

trunks opening all over the deck put Layala even more on edge. She gripped the railing for balance as the ship dipped sharply to one side. The crew didn't seem to notice the movement and tossed out ropes, clunking loudly to the deck. What were those for? To capture these sirens?

Captain Fella smiled down at them. "Time to tie up, boys. We're getting close."

Thane turned and found Layala, pinning her with a concerned stare from across the ship. Fennan chuckled when one of the women handed him a long thick rope.

"Around the metal loops on the floorboards," she said. "Quickly."

Thane hurried up the steps to the Captain and Layala dashed after him. "Tie up?" Thane demanded.

"Yes, darling," Captain Fella winked, gripping the wheel. "The sirens will take ya if you don't. It's the males they want. And their songs will call even the most resistant male to the depths of the lake. I've seen it many times. Men and elves who think they won't fall victim and splish splash." She waved. "Bye-bye."

"Is this a joke?" Thane asked.

A gust of wind blew Layala's hair wildly, and Fella put a hand on top of her hat. "You think all those men at the dock are simply cowards? I joke about many things but not this. It's why I run an all-woman crew. We're not subservient to the sirens. We hear them but it's nothing more than a lovely tune. Some-times we gotta fight the nasty wenches off but the

island holds precious plants we sell for a fortune and we're the only ones willing to go. Now strap down, handsome, or you won't live to hump your girl again."

Layala gripped Thane's forearm. He would without a doubt be able to break the rope, especially with his magic, and she had a sick feeling the only reason the chains held him in Calladira was because he'd been weakened by poison. How could they keep Thane restrained? "We need chains. Strong ones."

Thane leaned over the side of the railing. "All male Ravens, tie yourselves down. Piper, Evalyn, make sure none can get loose, or they'll die."

"You can't be serious," Fennan said, tossing the rope across his shoulder.

Piper and Aunt Evalyn both looked at each other then ran to pick up ropes off the deck. Not waiting for anyone, Leif dashed across the ship's wood planks and grabbed a rope himself. "Guess Nana didn't lie, and I'm no saint."

"Whatcha need chains for?" Fella narrowed her eyes. "These ropes will hold anyone."

"I *need* chains." Layala pointed at Thane's back. "For him." She hoped that would even be enough.

Fella lifted a shoulder, but interest flashed across her face. "I don't have any, lassy. The ropes will have to suffice. There's some in the chest over there." She tilted her head to the left where a huge reddish-brown chest with gold buckles and trim waited. "We have about ten minutes before we'll hear the sirens' songs."

She then shouted down to the main deck. "Prepare to be boarded!"

Layala shoved up the lid to the chest. "These sirens come *on* the ship?"

"With this many males?" Fella said with a crazed grin. "Certainly! They'll be in a frenzy. They exist to hunt and kill men. Don't know why. I hope you know how to fight with those daggers on your waist."

Layala jerked a long thick rope out of the trunk. "You've seen this?"

"They did it to my own father." Her grin turned almost sadistic. "A right nasty bitch took him down when I was fifteen. She gave me this when I tried to save him." Fella jerked up her sleeve to four long red rakes across the otherwise porcelain skin on her forearm. "I take joy in killing as many of the soul-sucking wenches as I can and today shall be glorious." She jerked her sword from her hip and raised it into the air. "To battle, ladies!"

"Hooza!" they shouted back in unison.

Maker above, this woman *was* unhinged. Thane's worried eyes searched Layala's face as he held out his wrists to her. "It will be alright. These will hold me. You know how to tie a good, strong knot?"

"I do." That was part of her training back in Briar Hollow. She'd never had use of the skill until now.

"Tie him to the mast or he'll scoot to the edge," Fella said over her shoulder, turning the helm slightly to the right.

How could this be happening? A song, a voice of

some creature would take Thane from her? Steal her Ravens? With hurried steps, they rushed to the upper deck mast. Thane pressed his back against it and wrapped his arms behind him around the pole. Breathing heavy, Layala tied his wrists, then wrapped the rope around his torso, down his legs and around his ankles and knotted it good and tight. She tugged on it several times, walking around him in a circle to make sure he couldn't slip the rope. "Alright, you should be secure."

"Did all of you women lose someone to the sirens?" Thane asked.

"Everyone but Keera," Fella said, hooking a loop around one of the helm's handles to steady it. "She just enjoys the fight and the spoils the island offers."

"Laya," Thane said gently but there was an edge to his tone. "Go make sure the rest of the Ravens are secure, please."

Her heart thundered like the dark storm cloud that brewed in the distance. A quiet boom of thunder and a streak of lightning stretched across the sky. This couldn't be a good sign. "I'm not leaving you. If you break through those ropes..." Would she even be capable of stopping him? His physical strength outmatched hers by a large margin.

One of the women from the lower deck shouted, "Siren spotted!"

Layala swallowed hard. What would the siren look like? Black eyes, scaly skin, jagged teeth like the pale ones? Talons like the dragon? Part of her didn't even

want to see what they looked like. Her heart thrummed harder when Fella let out what could only be a war cry. "Come on, you nasty wenches!" Water sprayed in a great white arch over the bow of the ship.

Layala stepped back and bumped into Thane. "Laya, you're equipped to handle any enemy. Your training will kick in no matter what you see."

She slowly nodded. Of course, he was right. With a deep breath, she scanned the deck's edge, waiting for something to pop up. Another boom of thunder and the howl of wind brought goosebumps to her flesh.

"Sirens!" another woman below bellowed. This time Layala dashed to the edge and peered down at the blue-black water. A ghostly, fin-tailed creature, she guessed to be eight feet long, zipped by and disappeared under the shadows of the ship. In the silence of waiting for an attack, her nausea intensified. She gripped the railing until her knuckles turned white.

It started with a single hauntingly beautiful voice. Like the whisperings of the wind in green, lush mountains. The sound of it brought a shiver down her spine. Then another voice joined in, and another, in different octaves and tones but so in sync they could have been one.

"They're here," Fella said, quieter now, almost reverent.

Layala backed from the edge and pulled out her new sword, Lightbringer, the one her father crafted. It almost seemed to hum with power in her grip. She turned to tell Thane what she saw but his eyes were

unfocused and staring, his expression slack and lost—transfixed. "Thane?" she whispered.

Nothing about his demeanor changed or even registered her at all. A *thump, thump, thump* sound drew Layala forward to the railing. She peered down over the main deck. The other's hands were tied behind their backs attached to metal hooks on the deck near the center. Gunner jerked and kicked wildly. It was terrifying to watch him fight so fiercely against his bonds. Maker above, was he going to break free? Layala noticed Fennan's hands moving slowly, twisting and tugging, trying to work them loose, rather than outright fighting them. Piper knelt beside Fennan, gripping his shoulders but he stared past her like she wasn't even there.

Down below, Aunt Evalyn held onto the stair railing with one hand and a short sword in the other.

"Come up here," Layala said.

Aunt Evalyn shook her head at Layala. "Your Ravens might need me to defend them down here. Catch this." She tossed a black barb covered in a shiny oil substance.

Layala caught it and her brow furrowed. "It's katagas serum." She knew it from the smell.

"If Thane is capable of what I think he is, you'll need it."

Layala didn't have time to wonder why Aunt Evalyn had this and ran to Thane. "Sorry," she murmured, jabbing the point of it through Thane's shirt and into his arm.

He was too dazed to even notice.

It wasn't but a moment later Leif yelled, "I need her!" Confused, Layala ran back to peer down at the lower deck. "Cut me loose!" Leif begged, wiggling his body on the ground. "I need to go to her."

"Yes, set us free!" Siegfried shouted in a booming voice so unlike him.

"They need us."

"She begs for me."

"We have to help!" Fennan roared.

"Don't listen to them," one of the women snarled at Piper and Aunt Evalyn. "It's a trick of the siren."

"Obviously!" Piper snapped back.

The sirens' lovely voices grew louder, drowning out the sounds of the water crashing against the boat and the rushing of the breeze, covering up the pleas from the males below. Layala nervously peeked at Thane again. She let out a long thankful breath, finding he wasn't fighting to break loose. In fact, he almost looked like he was on the verge of falling asleep. Maybe he was strong enough to fight the temptresses' call. Some of the knots in her gut loosened. He was the only one she was truly worried about breaking loose.

"On your left!" Fella bellowed.

Layala whipped around, a pale hand with pointed white nails slid over the ship's railing. A moment later a head of bright pink hair and a face as lovely as the sea itself, rose over the ship's edge. Her eyes were such a light blue they almost looked white. Layala had

expected a beast, something grotesque akin to a pale one but this creature was one of the loveliest beings she'd ever seen. She pulled herself up until her aquamarine-scaled breasts appeared. From her chest down she was covered in shimmering fish scales, and her large whimsical fin waved in the air behind her.

With her sights set on Thane, she curled a finger. "Come to me, my love." Her voice took on several octaves with whistle tones as well as a dark, lower register.

The allure the beautiful creature had shattered. She wanted the elf Layala loved—she wouldn't have him.

Thane twitched and thrust his hips, trying to loosen the ropes. No! Layala rushed forward, swinging her sword at the siren with a whoosh. The female ducked below the railing and hissed. Layala hacked down, splintering the wood, and chopping the siren's clinging fingers off. The siren wailed in such a high pitch, Layala wanted to slap her hands to her ears. She watched as the siren dropped into the water with a loud splash.

"Die, you cock-sucking wench!" Fella cried and swung her curved sword across a siren's neck, severing it completely. A green-haired head flopped onto the deck with aquamarine lips held open wide in an endless scream, and the body disappeared over the side of the ship. Disgusting.

A loud crack that sounded an awful lot like wood breaking sent a tendril of fear shooting through her

veins. Chest heaving up and down with wild breaths, she looked back to Thane jolting and wrenching against the ropes, and a very clear split ran up the mast almost to the top. Holy Maker above, the ropes held but the ship itself wouldn't.

"He's going to break my ship! Stop him!" Fella screeched and turned to another onboarding siren, creeping over the edge. "What the hell is he? No elf I've ever seen is that strong."

Layala shoved her sword into its scabbard and pressed her hands to Thane's chest. "Thane, it's me. It's Layala." He grunted in his struggle and his hard-set jaw didn't waver. "Those voices are sirens. Remember? They want to kill you. They want to take you from me." Another snap of splintering wood and she gripped his face, pulling his head down to look eye to eye. Though he stared at her, his bright green eyes had what appeared to be a white cloud over them. Could he even see her? He didn't focus on her; it was as if he was lost in a dream. "Stop fighting to get free. You must resist them! Please!"

With a flash of red hair, a black hat, and a *thunk*, the ropes loosened and fell to the ship deck. Layala gasped at Fella attempting to pull her sword loose from the wood mast; she'd cut Thane loose. Layala pressed her hands into Thane's chest harder; there was nothing to hold him back now but her. "What did you do?" Layala cried.

"If he destroys this ship, we'll all go down." Fella frowned, jerking her sword free. "I'm sorry."

Thane marched forward and his strong body slammed into Layala, nearly knocking her to the hard planks. She gritted her teeth and shoved him in the chest, driving her legs until they screamed, and her boots slid on the slick surface. He was like pushing against a mountain that wouldn't yield. "STOP!"

He kept going, shoving by her.

She gripped his shirt, jerking it so hard it tore the sleeve off, but his determination to get to the edge where another siren waited, smiling, curling her finger at him, was relentless.

Not seeing another choice, Layala jumped onto his back, sliding her arm under his chin and squeezed. *Come on, go to sleep, go to sleep!* Thank the Maker he didn't fight her. It was as if he didn't even know she existed and that might have been their only blessing in this moment. Even without his magic, Layala didn't believe she could beat him in a real fight and if he wanted to kill her to get to the sirens...

Shit shit shit. It's not working! With how hard she squeezed around his throat, he should be going down. Wrapping her legs tighter around him, she pulled her sword and knocked him upside the head. His skin split, and blood oozed down his face, but he didn't lose consciousness, didn't falter in his step. They were mere feet from the water, from the poisonous but beautiful creature beckoning him forward. Layala swung her leg out, and nailed the siren in the chin, sending her flying off. There was no way she was going to lose him now.

Magic whispered down her arms and a thick black vine appeared, first wrapping around Thane's knees and thighs then it snaked its way up his body to wrap and pin his arms to his sides. Layala adjusted her position to avoid being trapped herself but held on. The vines traveled down around his ankles, and he stumbled forward toward the opening in the ship that would take him straight into the water. Layala shoved her foot against the ship's railing and with one big jerk of her body, the momentum carried them both back. She braced herself for the impact and grunted when she slammed into the deck, stealing the breath from her lungs, and the full weight of him crushed her into it. A sharp pitch sent them both sliding toward the center until they hit the mast again.

As Thane bucked and squirmed, she wiggled free, got to her feet and shoved her boot onto his chest. The ship tilted, sending her off balance. Her arms circled around wildly trying to catch herself, and she stumbled into the railing where the sharp edge of it bit into her lower back.

A hiss from the water creature, then a quick jerk of her ponytail dragged Layala into a backbend, exposing her neck and chest. Sleek lavender hair and a razor-nailed hand poised above her. "Die!" the siren wailed.

Throwing her arms up, vines shot from her palms and punched straight through the siren's neck and chest. Cold blood splattered across Layala's face, into her eyes, and the metallic taste filled her mouth. "Ugh!" Layala spit in disgust. The vines lifted the

siren's wiggling body into the air until it swung her down into the depths of the lake and the vines went with her.

When she turned back, Fella stared, jaw dropped. "Alright, now I really need to know who you people are." The cries for freedom and the chaos of fighting from the lower deck made it difficult to hear but Layala understood.

"That is Thane Athayel, High King of the Elves of Palenor and I am his mate and future queen! Now help me keep him alive!"

Fella's eyes widened further. Her sword clattered to the deck, and she dove. Thane rolled toward the edge where, yet another siren held on, until Fella landed on top of him. He bucked and grunted, kicking his bound legs into the air. Layala jumped on his lower half, hoping their combined weight could keep him down.

"Let me out of these! I love her! I must go to her! My Layala is down there!" he roared, throwing them both off. The vines began to bow and snap. Holy shit, the sirens created hallucinations.

Trying to rise to her feet, Layala slipped on the wet deck, crashing to her hands and knees. Fella was used to the dipping of the ship, the dampness of its deck and scrambled up, and drew out her sword. Two sirens crawled toward them, teeth bared, long fingers digging into the wood.

"Give me him!" the purple-haired siren hissed. "He's mine."

Layala grabbed Lightbringer and rammed the tip of it straight into the siren's mouth. "No, he's mine." She kicked her free of the sword, and Fella smiled at her.

"You're badder than you look. But I got the other siren. You get him!" Fella bellowed then slashed her blade wildly through the air.

Layala dropped down onto Thane's chest, straddling him with her thighs then slapped him hard across the face. "I'm right here! Your Layala is right here!"

"Layala! I'm coming!" he shouted toward the water's edge.

It was like he couldn't even see her, as if she'd gone invisible to him. She gripped his hair, jerking him to look at her face inches from his. "It's me, you stupid prick."

His jaw tensed and he blinked several times, slowly shaking his head as if trying to clear away a fog. "Layala?"

All it took was calling him a prick huh? "Yes. I'm here."

"We're getting closer to the island," Fella said, slashing at the siren who hacked back with wicked claws. "The power of their call is fading but not gone yet. Not until we are close to shore."

"Layala, we need help!" Piper sounded hysterical. "They've got him! Help!"

Layala looked to Fella. "I can't go. You must."

"If I leave you, we might lose *him*. He's the High

King of the elves. He's more important than them, right?" Her blade sliced through the siren's forearm and the creature wailed, and dark-green blood sprayed across the deck.

"My arm! My arm!" she screeched and charged Fella, blue tailfin slapping against the deck, and face twisted in rage. The lake creature whirled around, sweeping out her fin and knocked Fella's legs from under her. Her clawed hand swung down at Fella's head. She brought her blade up just in time to slice off the arm and then kicked the siren hard enough to send her sliding across the deck and into the water.

Thane began struggling again. Whatever breakthrough Layala had with him was gone. More screams from below made Layala's heart ache. They needed her.

Fella spit, and swung her sword over her head and moved toward the ship's edge again to take on another siren climbing over the rail. "Sometimes hard decisions must be made, lass."

Wilder than ever Thane bucked and kicked. Layala forcefully pressed her palms against the vines wrapped around Thane's chest, making sure to keep him in place, but even her magic's hold began to strain, and the restraints snapped one by one. She conjured more to wrap around him, more to keep him bound.

"Layala!" Aunt Evalyn shouted. "There are too many! Help us!"

Her chin trembled and her heart ached for aban-

doning them but... Hard decisions. "I can't leave Thane!" Her voice broke on his name. Maker above, what if it was Fennan? Could she forgive herself?

Piper screamed and the agony of it tore a piece of Layala. "I'm sorry," she murmured, as her vision blurred from tears. Thane fought and roared and grunted. Her vines kept snapping and she kept creating them. She sobbed as Piper and Aunt Evalyn shouted for help and there was nothing she could do.

As quickly as it came, the sirens' song stopped, and Thane quit struggling. That far-off cloudy look in his eyes disappeared, and he focused on her poised over him. He looked down at the thick layers of vines wrapped around his body, then his eyes searched her face. "What happened? The last thing I remember is you tying me to the mast."

Layala swiped her hands across her wet cheeks. The better question was, who was now gone forever?

CHAPTER 22

Layala took a deep cleansing breath, trying to stop the tears from streaming down her face. Words wouldn't come from her achingly tight throat. How could she tell him she'd failed their Ravens? They were hers too. Shaking her head, she reached back and pulled her sword, Lightbringer, loose, then slid the sharp edge of the blade under the vines, careful not to slice into his flesh. He tensed as the cool metal slid along his torso.

"Layala," Thane urged, more forceful this time. "Did I hurt you? Why are you crying?"

"No." She continued cutting through the vines. She considered she might be able to dissolve her own magic, but she didn't have the mind to try anything new at the moment.

Fella's boots clopped loudly as she made her way over from the ship's railing. She stood over them with her mouth twisted into a frown. "You lost someone,

maybe more, King Thane. Me and my girls did what we could. We fought hard."

He shoved his arms out, snapping the vines down the center until he was completely free of his binds. "Who?"

Scooting off him, Layala sat and pulled her knees to her chest and wrapped her arms around her legs. She didn't want to know who she'd failed or how many. Was the All Seeing Stone even worth it? What if they didn't even make it in time and this was for nothing? They'd known it would be dangerous, yet she never expected to lose anyone. But the Ravens' battle prowess apparently meant nothing against the sirens and none of them anticipated that.

Thane pushed up, squared his shoulders, and the sound of his slow footfalls toward the edge of the upper deck, made her heart beat faster. She watched him acutely, as he gripped the railing and peered down. He turned back. His face ghostly white. Maker above, were they all gone? Her body trembled but Layala shoved to her feet on weak legs. She worried he might collapse but she could barely stand herself.

Was Piper dead too? Were Aunt Evalyn and Piper slaughtered and the boys dragged away? Was Piper's last scream not for someone else but for her own death?

The woman with silver eyes and gold jewelry appeared at the top of the steps. "One of the sirens got fully on deck and cut through his ropes. I'm sorry."

Layala's hand dropped. "Who?"

Thane's mouth twitched and he glanced down before saying, "Gunner is gone."

"Can we get him back?" Layala demanded.

Fella stood at the wheel again. "If you could breathe underwater, you ladies could go fight for him, sure. But you don't, so you can't. And it's been well over five minutes already. He's gone." Her chest rose and fell heavily. "If it helps, he believed he was with the love of his life and happy as can be as his lungs filled with water. You saw the way your king reacted to them. He thought it was you calling to him."

It didn't help.

"We're coming up to the dock," Fella said and gazed up at the dark clouds. "And I don't mean to be insensitive but a storm's coming and we'll need to hurry to unload your horses so we can get back."

Layala finally dared to look down at the others. Piper knelt at the edge of the ship, sitting back on her heels. Her arms hung loosely at her sides; her bloodied sword lay next to her. The others were being cut loose by the ship's crew. Aunt Evalyn attended to a wound on one of the ship crew's calf. Knowing her friend needed comfort, Layala quickly descended the stairs and knelt beside Piper. With a gentle hand on her shoulder, she said, "You did everything you could, Piper."

Red, tear-brimmed eyes still searched the water. "At first, he kept fighting to get away from me. Then the siren grabbed his leg, and he fell onto his back. But I had him, Laya. I held onto his arm, pulling as he was

273

being dragged to the edge. When he looked at me, he knew. Gunner KNEW. He gripped me back and kicked at the siren but another one of those *things* latched onto his other leg and he was—gone."

"I'm so sorry, Piper." Layala's throat was unbearably tense again and her voice came out weak and strained. "I'm so sorry. I heard you calling to me," a tear rolled down her cheek, "I failed you—failed him."

She sniffed and wiped the back of her hand across her wet cheek. "You had to protect Thane. I would have done the same thing. Gunner would understand that, too. But I had him. He was right there." She took in another deep breath and reached over to Gunner's eyepatch lying on the deck. It must have fallen off during the struggle. Piper clutched it to her chest. "He'd been with us since the beginning, since Thane formed the Ravens. He has a younger brother who wanted to join us at the proper age and Gunner always promised to watch his back."

There were no words to console her, no poems to heal the loss.

The ship jolted and scraped against the stone dock leading out from the shore of the island. Wide canopied green trees with leaves as large as her head covered most of the island. There was something haunting about the water cascading over the black rock from fifty feet high into the lake just down the shore. It wasn't the waterfall itself but the memories it raised, where she collapsed into darkness with an arrow through her.

Loud bird calls of all kinds singing from high branches snapped her out of her stupor.

"The island itself has never given us any troubles. You can rest easy about that at least." Fella stood behind Layala and Piper and gripped the brim of her hat, tilting it slightly. Her gaze lifted to the lush trees. "Hopefully the portal you're looking for is here, and you can make it work. We won't return for a week, and I'd hate to see you all lose any more of your people on a ride back."

GATHERED on the black sand shoreline of the island, the horses munched on the grass at the jungle's edge, and where an array of colorful wildflowers grew thick and full. There was no obvious path to take. It appeared as if they'd have to make their own and with the closeness of the tree trunks and twisted, curled, protruding roots, it would be slow going with the horses.

Holding onto two horses' reins, Fennan stared out at the water. "I can't believe he's gone. Just gone, not even a body to mourn."

Tifapine's chubby hands gripped the rim of the saddle bag. Her little chin trembled and her eyes glittered. She didn't have to witness anything while she hid below deck, thank the Maker. Her tender heart couldn't take it. And who knew if she would have survived the attack had she been exposed.

With stuttered breath and tears streaming down

her cheeks, Piper shook with silent sobs. This was the first time Layala had ever seen Piper cry. Not even when her own life was at stake did she shed a tear. There wasn't much emotion in her after the battle at Doonafell either, but this one hit her hard. Maybe watching as Gunner was ripped away was the final piece that snapped her usually stoic demeanor. It was difficult to see her face buried in the neck of her horse to hide her tears. Layala almost felt worse for her than for Gunner. Almost.

She turned her attention to Leif, who was Gunner's closest friend. Water lapped over his boots on the shoreline as if he contemplated diving in to retrieve his friend's lifeless body. "I didn't even get to say goodbye. I didn't even fight for him." He kicked, sending an arc of water soaring and let out a heart-breaking roar.

It hurt too much to watch them any longer. Layala turned away and gripped the saddle of what was Gunner's horse to keep from breaking down to her knees. She was their future queen. She must be strong. Thane didn't cry, didn't speak, his face hard as stone. Since he'd found out what happened, he wouldn't look at her. Maybe he wouldn't look at anyone directly, but it felt personal.

To get her mind on something other than loss or what Thane may or may not be thinking, she scanned up and down the shoreline. The island wasn't large. Perhaps a mile long. It shouldn't take them much time to find the stone circle but what could lurk inside

among the trees? It reminded her a bit of the unnamed forest with massive scorpions and giant one-eyed men. Although the energy around it didn't feel dark. It might be peaceful if not weighed down by sorrow.

"I know we're all hurting," Thane said, finally breaking his silence. "But we can't stay here. It's time to move." He turned to Siegfried. "Any idea where the portal is located?"

Siegfried brushed his palm along his horse's shoulder and then pointed toward the water cascading violently down the rockface a quarter mile away, "It should be near the waterfall."

"On top, behind, at its base?"

"Near the top."

"With me." Thane started down the sandy shore-line, tugging Phantom along behind him.

Layala hung back to give him some space and let the others go around her. Whether he blamed her, himself, or the world, sometimes people needed to be left alone. Heavy silence between the Ravens weighed like a stack of bricks, and then the thunder cracked above. The ever-darkening, inflated clouds seemed to be angry too at the death that infected the air. A raindrop hit her cheek. Layala groaned, and then another until a downpour rivaling the waterfall itself hit. It made the grass slick as they started their climb. Those in front hacked furiously at twisting roots the size of Layala's thigh and sliced through low-hanging branches to clear a path up the incline. It was an hour before they made it to the summit,

nearly dusk, but as Siegfried said, there the portal stood.

It was covered in moss, the edges chipped, the runes running along the top weather warn, and at its base, ivy and white calla lilies grew densely. Thane wasted no time in placing his palm flat against the stone. Everyone gathered in a half circle and waited. And waited. With the horses and elves shifting uneasily, Layala's grip on the leather reins in her hand tightened. Was his magic still suppressed by the katagas serum?

Although the rain had eased, droplets hung on her lashes and dripped from her nose. She swiped a hand over her face to clear the water. This couldn't be a good sign. The other portals had filled with warmth and life within moments.

With a frustrated sigh, Thane dropped his hand to his side and tilted his chin up. His shoulders rose and fell sharply. "Layala, come here please."

Everyone stared, except Thane. His back was still to them. Letting the horse's reins go, she quietly stepped forward and to his side. It took strength to look up at him. He kept his gaze narrowed on the stone. "Can you get it to work? I can barely feel my magic because of the serum."

She lifted a shoulder and with bated breath, touched her fingertips to it. It was cool, slick, and the energy that hummed from the others wasn't there. *You can't be serious.* She closed her eyes and flattened her hand, willing something to happen.

Come on, wake up... a moment passed... there was... something there. A spark of warmth barely discernible.

Hello? Layala silently called.

Nothing. She was about to let go when soft voices said, *"Hello."* She somehow knew that it was only in her head.

Can you take us to Newarden, Calladira?

Our power is weak. Long have we lay dormant.

You can have some of mine.

A long pause.

We sense sadness in you, mage.

Thane cleared his throat, and Layala opened one eye. "I'm—communicating."

"Communicating? What is it saying?"

She shut her eyes again. "It senses—sadness."

"Can we go through or not?"

Impatient, much? *Can we pass with my magic's strength?*

We need more.

"Thane, touch the stone. It seems my magic alone isn't enough."

"I don't have much to offer at the moment."

"We need to at least try."

She didn't look to see if he complied. A tugging sensation down her arm and through her hand was tell enough.

This is old magic... ancient, the wispy voices said. *Somehow familiar.*

Thane finally met her gaze. He must have found

that as strange as she did. Neither of them had ever been here.

How? Layala silently asked.

A pause. *We can't place it.*

It kept taking and taking. It was like trying to swim against a violent current that towed her back, until fatigue set in her legs, her shoulders sagged, and her arm felt like it was weighed down with sandbags.

"That's enough," Thane said sharply. Cool fingers wrapped around Layala's wrist, and he pulled her touch away from it.

The inside of the portal flickered, like a spark of two rocks clashing together then nothing happened.

We need more magic to regenerate fully.

"Then you'll have to wait," Thane murmured, seemingly out of breath himself. He peeked over his shoulder. "Set up camp. We'll rest here for now."

CHAPTER 23

Layala dropped to the soft, green forest floor and leaned her back against the stone circle. The quiet hum from within it warmed her skin but there was no pull or draining of her magic. She closed her eyes, breathing in steadily. The tremors in her hands and legs and weakness in her muscles brought up a rush of anxiety from her time in the tower. She could almost feel the straw from that disgusting bed poking into her, taste the dryness in her mouth, the sting of cracked lips, experience the ache and gnawing at her stomach from raw hunger. Reina's terrified face popped into her mind and the line of crimson that welled up when Tenebris drew a blade across her delicate neck. Piper's scream as Gunner was torn away, lost to the lake forever. Everything seemed to hit her all at once.

Thane wouldn't even look at her. He blamed her for the loss of Gunner, didn't he?

"Are you alright, Layala?" Aunt Evalyn asked gently.

Her heart began to pound and despite how weak she was, her eyes shot open, and she shoved to her feet. Worry lined Aunt Evalyn's face as she stared, as they all did.

She must run. She needed to feel free, to get away from those memories. The itch of her hot skin, the rushing of her breaths—if she didn't move, she would burst. Everything around her seemed hazy except those memories of death and despair.

Forcing one foot in front of the other, she started off slow, clutching a hand to her heaving chest. Then she sprinted, tearing through the trees at a wild pace. Her surroundings zipped by in a dark-green blur, low hanging branches snapped across her face, but she barely registered the pain.

"Layala!" Thane's voice sounded far away.

Run. Run. She couldn't stop. The ache in her body stole the anxious, repetitive thoughts that seemed to be on a wheel sliding through her mind. She wanted to grip her hair and scream but kept pumping her arms instead. Hot tears streamed down her face. She leapt over a fallen log and slammed down on the other side. Quiet feet flew over the dense foliage. She weaved around tree trunks until she broke free of the forest and came to the edge of the island. Wide open space was less claustrophobic. The lake glistened as the sun peeked out from the dark clouds above offering some sense of relief.

Layala collapsed to her knees, barely able to catch her breath, and tipped over onto her side in the ebony sand. Then she rolled flat on her back, and her sword jabbed into her, but she ignored it as she stared up at the sky. A drizzle of cool rain pitter-pattered on her face. Why did so many bad things happen? Why did people die when she was around? Did the Maker care about their suffering? Didn't he hear their pleas?

Come to me. I will help you, that now-familiar voice of the Black Mage whispered.

Layala slapped her hands on the sides of her head. *Stop it! Leave me alone.*

I feel your suffering. I will make the hurt go away. But I need you to find me.

No! She silently screamed in her head. Because that's where the voice was. Maker, maybe she was losing her mind.

I truly need you. I've waited so long.

A quiet rustle of bushes drew her attention. Layala tilted her head to see Thane emerging from the break in the tree line. For once he appeared to breathe heavily. She clenched her jaw and turned away, wanting to hate that he followed her but the tightness in her chest eased slightly.

Silently, he traipsed over the tall grass and lay beside her in the sand. In serene quiet, they both stared at the sky for a while. The deep pull of his lungs was almost a lullaby to calm her nerves. The rustle of wind in the treetops and chirps and songs of birds with the steady lull of the water, seemed to put her in

a trance. The tightness wound around her chest loosened some and the tears dried. She felt like she could breathe again.

"I forgot how fast you are," he said reverently, as if breaking the peace was a sin.

She pursed her lips and said nothing.

His hand brushed against hers, and then warm fingers gently nuzzled their way in between hers. "Why won't you look at me?"

"I could ask you the same question."

"I'm sorry," he said. They were quiet again as she waited for an answer rather than an apology. "I feel I've failed you. You had to fight me rather than help them."

"You think *you* failed *me*?" She sat up and tossed her arm toward the water. "You were not in control of yourself out there. I was. They begged me for help."

He pushed up to his feet and stared out over the water. "Gunner is dead because I commanded him to be here. He's dead because of me. Just like all the others I've lost but at least they died in a battle for something greater. To protect the lives of their families and the people they love." He did finally look at her, wild-eyed, face twisted into agonizing fury. "Gunner died for a stone we don't even know exists for certain. It's nothing more than rumors or hearsay. Maker above, I am weary of my people dying needlessly."

She unintentionally moved back at the wrath emanating from him like a blast of wind. She'd seen him angry a few times, but this was different. This was

—anguish. "I'm sorry this is your burden. And I'm sorry I couldn't save him."

"I'm not blaming you," he snapped. He smacked a palm to his chest. "It's on me."

Gritting her teeth, she stood up and matched his ferocity. "No, you don't get to do that." How many times had she blamed herself for all of this and he refused to let her? She'd even suggested if she wasn't alive, it would end this chaos, but he wouldn't allow her to speak of it. With flared nostrils he stared down at her but stood still. "This is on your father and the Black Mage. It's them, not us. There would be no war to fight, no Void to destroy. We would never be here if it wasn't for them." A long breath passed through her lips.

"My father," he murmured with a humorless laugh. "I was within my reach. I—could have killed him."

Layala swallowed hard. He had the opportunity and didn't take it? "What?"

He looked away as if reliving the memory. "He was feet from me. It was strange to see him near when I had mourned him and felt the guilt of killing him. He was conversing with my mother." His beautiful, soothing voice dropped lower. "They spoke about making—amends."

"Amends?" Layala balked, cheeks flaring hot with frustration. She balled her hands into fists at her sides. "Amends! Between you and him? They can't be serious." The shadows of confusion and doubt were

written all over his face. He ran his fingers across his loose dark-brown hair. "You're not..." Oh Maker above, he was. "You're thinking about that? Considering it?" She couldn't fathom it. After everything Tenebris did. The elf king was immoral, wicked, a fiend and deserved no sympathy, least of all from Layala or Thane.

"I," he paused, sliding his palms down his face. "I don't know. I want him gone but—I thought I fed him to pale ones, and a part of me is relieved he didn't suffer that way."

She remembered walking into his tent one night when he'd dreamed of the day he brought his father to the Void and the guilt that ate away at him. She *felt* it then. She didn't now, and maybe that was why her jaw still dropped, why she couldn't understand. Tenebris had a list of unforgivable offenses a mile long. *I can't believe this is happening.* Layala wanted Tenebris dead almost more than anything. She would take her revenge, the thing she'd been trained to do her entire life despite Thane's conflicted, twisted relationship with his father.

"He's the worst person imaginable, Thane! Release this guilt. It's unwarranted!"

"You don't understand because he's not your father."

That felt like a slap to the face. "I don't even have a father because of him!" she snarled. "You insensitive prick." She turned away, stalking down the beach, seething. She shoved her fingers into her hair, scraping

her nails over her scalp. He saw his father one time and suddenly changed his mind about this? How could they live in a world where the three of them existed? Tenebris who would use her, Thane who lived to protect her, and she, the source of conflict in between.

Large fingers wrapped around her bicep and spun her around. "Laya, stop. I'm sorry. I *am* an insensitive prick. I wasn't thinking."

"I'm never going to forgive him." She jerked out of his grasp, taking one step back, two. "Never. He's dead one way or another."

"I'm not asking you to forgive him. I never would." The storms in his very eyes were as dark as the booming sky above.

He reached for her, and she pushed his hand away. "But you're asking me to let him live, aren't you?"

"No," he said gently. The rain streaked down his face, and the sag of his shoulders looked to hold the weight of the world. "I'm asking you to understand. Understand why I couldn't kill him. And my mother was there and I—I couldn't."

She didn't know her parents but if Aunt Evalyn was evil, she didn't think she'd be able to kill her when it came down to it. Especially if she wanted to ask for forgiveness. Killing a stranger was much easier than a loved one. But would he stand by and watch as Layala did it? Would he try to stop her? This situation made the knots in her stomach worse.

She sighed, turning toward the forest. Would he hold it against her if she did kill him? Was she going to

have to choose between killing Tenebris and loving Thane? "You won't have to. I will. You can't rob me of this. He almost took you from me. For power, Thane. And you're defending him." She shook her head, thinking of Tenebris's boot smashing her hand in the dining hall, grinding her bones. She started to walk away again.

He stepped in front of her and took her face in between his hands. "I'm not going to fight with you, and you're not just going to walk away." Then he smashed his lips to hers.

She gripped his wrists, kissing him back. He was as infuriating as the day she met him, but she melted in his arms.

He pulled back and rested his forehead against hers. "I will always choose you, Laya." His voice was gravelly and full of emotion. "I want you to know that." And he had proved that time and again.

She looked up into his eyes. He tentatively lowered his lips closer to hers, a breath away, this time waiting. After a few beats she gave in again, kissing him deeply, wrapping her arms around his neck. The rain poured down, soaking through their clothes. She would normally be cold in this stormy weather, but his hot kisses trailed down her neck, warming her body. With frenzied desire building inside, Layala dragged him down on the wet grass. Callused hands slid around her waist, gliding under her top. She craved his touch like a drunk longed for booze, intoxicated in much the same way. "You promised," she breathed, while his

fingers inched below the hem of her pants at her waist and tugged them down, "to destroy anyone who hurt me."

"And I will." He dragged his hands roughly over her bare thighs. The thunder boomed with the ferocity of an angry god. With eager longing, Layala watched his deft fingers pull his belt loose. "I will," he swore.

A moment later, she pulled him on top of her, wanting, no, needing him. His kisses were intense, full of hunger and command, as was the way he moved against her. Everything in her felt a little hazy and heavy like the horizon dotted with mist and as she arched his thumb tugged down her bottom lip. His touch might have been embers igniting her flesh. Every kiss left its heated mark on her. Every sound she made, a call for more. As she watched the forked lightning streak across the stormy sky, it could have been her, crackling with blazing heat, illuminating the dark, and finally bursting into thunder where hot and cold collided.

THE SUN PEEKED out from behind the angry clouds, warm and soothing. She lay on Thane's chest, absently running her fingers over his bare skin. "Were you ever tempted to sleep with anyone else?"

"Is this a trap?"

She chuckled and lifted her head, propping her

chin on her folded hands. "No. I'm serious. Was it hard to wait for me?"

Bringing up his arms behind his head, he took a deep breath. "Well, I am an exceptionally attractive elf and there were many females groveling at my feet."

She lightly pinched his chest. "Arrogant pig."

He laughed, a deep rumble that seemed to move through her. "Of course it was hard. There was more than one occasion that I came into my room to find a mostly naked, if not fully nude, maiden there waiting on my bed."

Layala's mouth dropped. "Who?"

"So you can punish them?"

"No, I'm dying to know the juicy castle gossip. Pearl and..." She trailed off before saying Reina aloud. "They talked about maids trying to move up in status."

"Well, Vyra for one. I'm sure it was Talon who told the guards to let her in."

For show, Layala dramatically gasped at the scandal and twisted a piece of his long dark hair around her finger. "She did? What did you do?"

"You really want to know?" he asked and arched an eyebrow. She nodded. His chest heaved and dropped sharply. "I had been drinking wine, a little too much. I came into my room to find the fireplace already ablaze but that was usual. And there she was in nothing but a white, see-through nightgown. Don't know what the point of the fabric is. I saw every inch of her private parts."

"To stand completely bare in front of a male the

first time is nerve wracking, perhaps it was for her comfort. But I also imagine it would make a girl feel sexy."

"I can see you wearing something like that to show me you want me without saying it, but you could also strip down to nothing. I'm going to take it off anyway."

Layala smiled. "I'll keep that in mind. Go on with the story."

"Alright, well, Vyra practically mauled me. I stood there in shock for a moment." He laughed at the memory. "She was like a rabid badger. Jumped on me, wrapped her legs around my waist. The kisses—so wet." He shuddered.

"Wet?" Layala laughed.

"Yeah, like a slobbery dog." Layala cupped her hand over her mouth to stop from laughing more. He carried on. "But I got my wits about me and had to unlatch her. She didn't want to let go. She made sure to cop a feel of the goods too."

"She grabbed your..." her eyes flicked down.

"My cock and balls, you can say it. Or how about meat and two veg? Wait, no, rod and berries."

She shook her head but smiled. "What kind of berries? Aren't berries a little small?"

"Plums. Actually, let's go with grapefruits."

"Grapefruit?" She rolled her eyes.

"It's a figure of speech, my love."

"We're getting off track, so she grabbed your rod and *blue*berries."

"They're not blue anymore."

Layala burst out laughing.

"But yeah. She grabbed me painfully hard. The girl has no finesse. I'm sure she talked to some harlot for advice and went a little overboard. And then to be nice I sent her out the servants' passage with a blanket around her shoulders."

"I don't know how she showed her face after that. And you're way nicer than I ever would have been."

"So I hear. You gave a man a black eye for grabbing your ass. I heard your friends say it at the pub in Briar Hollow."

That was right when she'd walked in with Forrest and Ren, and she hadn't noticed him at all. "Bet that made you fall straight in love."

"Almost went right to my knees before you. But it was when you stuck a knife in my shoulder in my room that I knew you were the one for me. All I thought was that this lovely maiden is wild, and I love her."

"Maker above, are you ever going to let that go?"

"Never," he teased.

"When was it that you really fell for me? The truth."

He sat quietly, watching the clouds pass by above. She recalled many moments that whittled away at her heart.

"Hmm, I loved the idea of you most of my life. And you did truly dazzle me when you came into my room to assassinate me. I mean, the audacity alone." He

smiled. "But I knew what we had was real or what I felt was real, anyway, after the funerals and we stood out there in the rain and you slipped in the mud into my arms. You remember?"

"Yes."

"I looked down at you and it hit me like a slap to the face. It's why I had to ask you to forgive me, because I couldn't live with myself if you didn't. And Maker above, did I want to kiss you."

"I remember you almost did, but you pulled away. Why?"

He brushed his thumb over her lips, eyes focused on them, as if they were back in that moment. "I needed to know that's what you wanted before I ever kissed you again. And it was you who kissed me at the Celebration of Life."

She laid her head back down on his bare chest, watching the lake's shoreline. A pair of ducks waddled up onto the sand, quacking happily, then a set of tiny yellow babies appeared behind them. "Why does that seem so long ago and yet like it was yesterday?"

"It's strange, isn't it?" He stroked the top of her head, scrubbing his fingers into her scalp. "And what about you, Laya? When did you know you loved me?"

"If I'm being completely honest with myself," she wanted to say it was the night she left him alone in that mage's tower, but it was before that, "I think it was the moment I put on that flower crown. I wanted you to do something, to show me that what I felt was

real and I hadn't imagined it all. You didn't disappoint."

He chuckled. "Oh, you wanted me to toss that crown, carry you in my arms, and drag you onto my lap?"

Her finger drew little circles across his soft skin over the planes of his muscular chest. "Or maybe it was your reaction to the crown when I knew I loved you. I would have never told you about Novak otherwise."

"You can talk about him, you know. Did he treat you well? Was he respectful?"

Layala lifted her head and sat up. She reached for her top and slipped it on. "You think I would have tolerated less?"

Laughing, he shook his head and pushed up onto his elbows. "No, I suppose not."

"He was funny and had a sort of boyish charm. Slender, a little taller than me but not much. He liked to fish in the river. We'd do that together sometimes, but I hate gutting fish. It's too slimy and gross." She tugged the tie at the end of her hair loose and brushed her fingers through her long locks. "We'd been friends for so many years, and I'd loved him for a long time, but it was different than with you. I loved him like a friend. I think I knew he loved me long before anything ever happened. But I was never that physically attracted to him. He wasn't ugly but sort of plain, with a good heart."

"But you are drawn to me and my dashing good

looks," he teased. "And my charm, we mustn't forget the charm."

Although she could have come back with a snarky remark, she wanted him to know the truth. "You're the most beautiful person I've ever seen, Thane, on the inside too. I was a little smitten when I saw you even if your presence unnerved me."

"Please, do go on. About the smitten part."

Now she rolled her eyes and began to twist her hair into a braid. "The romance between Novak and I wasn't perfect. It seemed once we admitted our feelings, he was jealous. We argued more than we ever did before. He'd get angry when the men looked at me too long at the training yard. He started fights sometimes over lude comments. I finally made it a rule he couldn't go because they only did it more to rile him up. But he made me happy too. He baked the best cinnamon sugar cookies. And it was cute how nervous he was to even kiss me. He never wanted to take things further because I was mated to you. He said he didn't want to have me fully until I was free, until I could be his and not yours." She nibbled her lip, wondering if she would have let herself fall in love with Thane if Novak was alive. "We were together for a year and a half before our emotions got in the way of his vow not to bed me... anyway, it was a clumsy attempt. I don't think he had a Fennan to give him a book on pleasing a female." She giggled.

"So you never felt the peak of lovemaking before?"

She shook her head. "Not until the ruins with you."

"Well, I'm glad he was there for you when I couldn't be. Even if I'm jealous he was your first love." Thane grabbed her hand and kissed the top of it. "But I am all too thrilled to know I'm your exceptional *final* lover."

"A talent I am grateful for," she said with a slight blush. "Anyway, speaking of Fennan and lovemaking." Layala stood up and slipped on her pants. Either the time they'd spent laying on the wet grass had rejuvenated her strength, or the lovemaking did but the weakness in her limbs was gone.

"I'm not going to jump to conclusions but that sounds odd—"

"Piper," Layala said, exasperated. As if she'd ever think about herself and Fennan together. "You should ask him about Piper."

"Eh." He didn't sound enthused and got up to dress.

"Spill," Layala said. Why was he against them being more than friends?

"It worries me. I don't want to see her get hurt. Piper has been courted by a few Ravens, but she's never had her heart broken because she never loved them. She's always been waiting for Fennan to really notice her. And Fennan, as I'm sure you've heard, is a lover of many. He leaves broken hearts in his wake like a pixie trails dust."

They started back up the way they came. Through

the woods to reunite with their companions. Thane pushed aside a heavy branch to let Layala go by. "But he wouldn't do that to her," Layala said. "She's different. She's Piper."

"And he should know that. I don't think he'll take it anywhere unless something changed him in the dungeons."

When they drew closer to the encampment, the clinking of metal, grunting, and jeers sent Layala's heart racing. Were they under attack?

CHAPTER 24

Thane saw the alarm on Layala's face and grabbed her wrist before she went sprinting ahead in a panic. He'd recognize what was going on anywhere. He'd been doing the same thing most of his life. "It's alright. They're sparring. I'm sure they needed to get their minds off what happened. We don't like to sit around and mope. And it's not the first time we've lost a friend. The repeated loss numbs you after a while."

But Layala wouldn't be as used to watching companions die on a battlefield. Sadly, it was all too familiar to Thane and the sting of the loss of Gunner already faded away like the whirl of ash on a breeze. He almost wished the hurt lasted longer. As if his sadness would somehow honor Gunner's memory. It had only been half a day since Gunner was taken by the sirens, and Thane had already gotten lost in the pleasure of his lover when his Raven's heart would never beat again.

They broke through the tree line, into the clearing and sure enough, Piper was going rounds with Leif. She swung her sword down hard, clashing it against Leif's blade. He grunted and shoved back. *Clank, ping, crack!* It seemed their pain wasn't drifting away as fast as Thane's. And neither of them was going easy on the other. Leif's nose was bloodied, and Piper limped. He sighed, debating on stopping it, but Piper would be upset with him. She'd say he only stepped in because she was a female, but truthfully, she was barely on the mend as it was.

Tugging Layala to the base of a tree, he slid down to the mossy forest floor, bringing her with him. He wrapped his arms snuggly around her body, pulling her in close, and leaned his head back against the bark. His soldiers fought for what felt like hours. Sweat and anger and frustration permeated the air. They needed to get this out before they went into Brunard's city. Hot heads led to rash decisions, something they couldn't afford. He wouldn't lose anyone else so they must infiltrate Brunard's manner without raising his entire city guard.

There was no time to rally the entire Raven battalion to take the city or he'd bring them all simply to watch Brunard lose everything before he killed him.

At some point during the clashing of swords and banter, Thane's eyelids grew heavy. The warmth and comfort of Layala lying against his chest put him at ease and he dozed off.

. . .

CRIMSON LIQUID SMEARED his father's face. A gaping wound, entrails spilling out of his abdomen dragged on the grass as Tenebris limped toward Thane. "How could you do this to me?" His skin was ashen, lips, a blue gray. His pale blond hair was damp with dark red. "How could you murder your own father? I gave you life. All I wanted was your forgiveness, my son! Don't you remember how happy you were when I gave you your first sword? Or the day we went for a ride through the forest on your first hunt. I was so proud you shot your first stag."

Thane was a little boy again. Terrified and shaking. "I'm sorry, Father. I remember. I remember!" He dropped his face into his palms. He didn't want to look. Couldn't see the horrifying image.

"Look at me! Look at me!"

Thane was older now, dressed in his Raven armor. Chest heaving up and down, heart racing. He took a step back from the haunting, putrid Tenebris, but he couldn't stop staring at it, like magic beheld him and forced him to see, to watch his father's corpse walk toward him.

"You let her do this," he snarled. A decayed finger jabbed toward him. "You let her take my life. Your mate. Your disgusting, blood-thirsty mate. Your mother will never forgive you. And I will follow you for the rest of your miserable, traitorous life. Every time you close your eyes, I'll be here. Waiting."

· · ·

WITH A GASP, Thane's eyes shot open. His heart pounded like a drum and the breeze felt cool against his sweat-covered brow. His gaze darted around the forest clearing, searching for the nightmare, for the animated corpse of his father. *It's not real. It's not real.*

He swiped his arm across his forehead and tried to calm his anxious nerves that had his entire body charged, ready for a fight. Everyone slept around a small fire. The horses nibbled on the grass in a spot near the stone circle. Layala curled up on him with her head resting across his thighs. A cloak draped over her, and her quiet, even breath told him she still slept.

He leaned his head back against the tree trunk, and rubbed his temples. Maker, his father wasn't even dead and still haunted him. Would it ever stop? Some part deep down wanted Tenebris's forgiveness for taking him to the Void, for leaving him there to be eaten by pale ones. And the other part of him rationalized that in the end the tyrant must die. Too much blood spilled because of Tenebris, and much more would if he got his wish to bring back the Black Mage. How could the thought of magic give him such a sick compromise? It was difficult to believe that one person could be so selfish... but what if it wasn't entirely him? What if he'd been swayed, twisted into believing this is what he must do? Thane never considered it before, but could Mathekis have a hold over his father? Was it possible Mathekis sunk his claws into his father's mind so deep and for this long? *Or maybe this is all you trying to find an excuse for him.* He shook his head at his

own thoughts. Something Thane could never understand was why Mathekis needed his father in the first place. *Was it because he knew that I would be able to find her?* But for Tenebris to want a child with a lily's mark in the first place, he would have already been in touch with Mathekis. Which meant Mathekis somehow knew Layala would be born an elf in Tenebris's kingdom; he just didn't know when. And when she disappeared, Thane was the only link. He knew Thane would have to go to her before the twenty-fifth year. They just bided their time. Tenebris even gave them months to fall in love before he made it known he wasn't dead. He scrunched his nose. It felt like he'd played right into their hands.

The only missing puzzle piece was Varlett. She knew exactly how to break the mate bond, which would have freed them from the possibility of becoming pale ones, an outcome his father and Mathekis must not have wanted. She could have done it at any time, but she must not have gone to Tenebris until after Layala showed up in the mountains. But there was still something he couldn't see. Varlett had the ability to break the mate bond and take Layala herself, *unless* she needed something from Mathekis or Tenebris. But what?

A quiet yawn and rustling in the grass caused Thane to turn. A bright-red hat poked out of thick tall grass. Tifapine emerged with an arm full of white-capped mushrooms. "Oh, hello there. Didn't think

anyone was awake yet. But the birds are up, gossiping about us so I couldn't sleep."

"The birds gossip?"

"Certainly. A pair of gulls told me you and Layala were, ehem, getting busy on the lakeshore earlier." Tif wiggled her eyebrows.

"And that's the birds' business?"

"Well, it's not like they could avoid seeing it. You were out in the wide open."

Thane rested his palm on Layala's shoulder and wrinkled his nose. "They do it in the wide open."

Tif shoved a mushroom in her mouth. "True." The word was barely audible with her cheeks full. "But that's not gossip. That's life in the wild bird kingdom. They also said Fennan farts in his sleep, but I didn't hear nothin'."

"That's an outright lie." Fennan sat up, rubbing his eyes.

Thane chuckled. "How would you know? You're asleep."

"I know. Besides, it's the gnome who gets gassy. Probably all those mushrooms."

Tifapine dipped behind the mushroom tops, peaking out with one eye. No denial came.

Leif pushed up and patted down his tangled red hair. "Everyone rips in their sleep. It's natural."

With perfectly sleek hair, Piper rolled over to face the group. "Is this truly the conversation we're going to have first thing in the morning?"

"Pipe, you tear them off louder than anyone." Leif bellowed out a laugh. "I like that in a female."

Piper picked up her bundled cloak she used as a makeshift pillow and launched it at him. "Shut up. Or I'll kick your ass in sparring again."

"Oooo," Fennan jeered. "She did get you good last night. You have a shiner."

Reaching up to his right eye, Leif touched the slightly-swollen purplish flesh. "So I do. It feels a little sore this morning. Wanna kiss it all better, Pipe?"

"You wish."

Leif tossed her cloak back to her. "Come on, us redheads need to stick together so we can breed more redheads."

"You went from me kissing your eye better to *breeding* a little quick, Leif. At least get me flowers first."

The others snickered. Evalyn shook her head while stoking the fire's embers.

"Just a *little* quick? I can go slower. Real slow, and I'll pick you flowers anytime, beautiful."

"Alright," Fennan said, hands fisted at his sides. "Lay off her."

"Why, because you want to lay on her?" Leif challenged and it wasn't entirely playful. "You mad because you can stick your rod in every maiden but her?" Seems others noticed Fennan and Piper had gotten closer too. Piper stilled and dropped her gaze to the ground.

Thane felt the air shift. Seems Siegfried did too; he

changed positions to a crouch, ready to spring into action. Swiping up her teacup and shawl, Evalyn shuffled back a few feet. Thane knew Fennan better than anyone and the fiery look in his best friend's eyes, though subtle, was evident. He *did* want Piper.

"I feel like there's some love rivalry here," Tif loudly whispered into Thane's ear. "Juicy."

Fennan rolled his shoulders back. "Just because she's a female doesn't mean you can talk to her like that. It's disrespectful. She's a Raven, same as you."

Leif stood, as did Fennan. There were several feet between them, yet it wouldn't take but a few strides for them to clash. Thane contemplated getting up but he'd only step in if it got too bloody. Sometimes things like this needed to be worked out on their own. And males typically did it through fist fighting.

Clearing her throat, Piper stood, and stepped in between them. "It's just fun. No disrespect," she said to Fennan, then turned and looked at Leif, "right?"

"Course it is," Leif said and smiled. "I respect you as much as any Raven, Piper. You know I just like to tease. Never been a problem before." Leif gave Fennan a hard stare.

Fennan kept his face cold as stone, said nothing, and started packing up his belongings. There was a collective sigh among everyone present. Did Leif also like Piper or was he being a prick because he lost Gunner? With Leif it was difficult to know. He'd tried to grab Layala's ass the moment he saw her, more to rile Thane up than anything, but it wasn't as if his flir-

tations were anything new. Thane thought he was with Pearl. Maybe she was only a friend, or they were not committed.

With a turn, Layala looked up at Thane. Still lying on his lap, she placed her hands behind her head. She smiled as if simply seeing him made her happy. He loved that. "Good morning," Layala said. "I must say there is never a dull moment with this group."

THE STONE PORTAL hummed with energy even as they approached it. The birds chirped louder as if they knew something magical was about to happen; even the gray sky overhead drizzled heavier rain. Thane and Layala exchanged a quick glance. "Ready?" she asked.

"We have a solid plan," Thane said. "Ready."

With his palm flat on the large round archway, it warmed and buzzed. The worn inscriptions around the top gave off a subtle glow. *Hello, again,* the voice whispered.

"Can you take us just outside Newarden, Calladira?" Thane asked.

With more magic.

"Take it."

Layala placed her hand on it and then Thane felt the tug on his magic, like the wind whispering over his skin at first. The pull grew stronger, and the center of the portal flickered with light and then finally swirled like a pool of water, inviting them to take a plunge.

Safe travels.

Thane stepped through first, leading Phantom behind him. Morning sunlight sparkled off dewy blades of grass on the other side. The wide-trunked trees creaked and shifted quietly. Phantom dropped his head and jerked up a large chunk of grass, loudly munching. Thane inhaled deeply, basking in the smells of lilac with hints of spice and a touch of damp moss. It was always more peaceful here in Calladira. This land wasn't plagued with war and cursed creatures. It was quiet serenity, exactly how elven lands should be. As if to prove that, sheep bleated in a meadow clearing ahead. A farmstead with a small, thatched-roof cottage sat center. They must be on the outskirts of the capital city, Newarden.

The rest of the group filed in after him and Siegfried stepped to his side. "The city is east, about a mile from here. I recognize this place."

Thane nodded and turned around. "Remember what I said. We're here for the stone and Brunard's head, not a battle with the entire city guard of Newarden. Stealth and secrecy are the mission here." He smiled. "Even if we would win." Deep chuckles filled the wooded area. "Leave the horses. Let's move."

CHAPTER 25

Creeping ivy climbed along the back of Brunard's large, ivory stone manor and surrounded the one door. The chatter of the city in the distance and the birds singing happily in the trees greeted them. Layala peeked out from behind a thick blackberry bush with plump berries ripe for the picking.

"Mmm," Tif mumbled from the pack on Aunt Evalyn's back. The gnome snagged a luscious berry to plop in her mouth. The loud munching in Layala's ear made her turn and glare.

"Do you mind?" Layala hissed.

Tif grew a sheepish grin full of purple juices and seeds. "Thorry."

"Eat berries later."

Tif pulled out her little dagger and her chomping turned into a warrior's grimace. "Ready for battle, my queen."

"You're staying."

"Way to crush my dreams of being a warrior sidekick."

Layala rolled her eyes. The gnome was scared of everything. A warrior sidekick was the last thing she would ever be.

A set of guards looped around the back of the manor, chatting happily, and completely oblivious to the threat merely feet away. Seeing their green and brown garb, and the pearl-colored chest armor brought memories back to the day she hacked, slashed, and killed only Maker knows how many. It was a flash of red, of chaos, and screaming.

Sweat dampened her temples. She could only imagine what feelings this place brought up for Thane. She never asked how long he'd been tortured in that cage. He told everyone they weren't here for a battle but if she worried about anyone doing something rash, it was Thane.

A cool breath seemed to cascade down Layala's neck and she had the unmistakable feeling someone stood close. Whipping her head around, she reached back for her sword but dropped her hand. Siegfried seemed to have appeared out of nowhere and lowered to one knee behind Thane and Layala. All elves were light-footed but Siegfried was a ghost.

"No sign of the dragon or Brunard on my perimeter sweep," he said in a low voice. "The city appears to be doing business as usual."

"Alright, we go in then," Thane said.

The group waited in silence. Even their breaths

could barely be heard. Layala's own heart beat louder. She counted, *one, two, three, four... thirty-one.* Another set of guards came around the corner, different from the first. They waited again, counting the time between.

"We have about a thirty-second window to get through that door," Thane said. And there were at least two sets of guards in rotation, possibly more given the size of the building. "I'll go first to get it open."

"You?" Fennan balked. "No, if anyone goes first, it's one of us who are more disposable. I'll go and kick in the door."

"None of you are disposable," Thane snapped.

"Kicking it in will be way too loud," Piper hissed. "And the guards will notice a splintered door."

"Thane is right. This is a job for him," Leif said. "You broke the padlock on Layala's prison cart easily."

Thane sat quietly for a moment rubbing his scruffy chin. "Yes. There's a chance I might break the door handle as well, but I'll take it."

Layala stared at the large keyhole below the round gold handle. She'd done this before to free Thane. "I'll do it and there won't be noticeable damage."

"Your magic could alert pale ones if there are any close by," Aunt Evalyn said, beside Layala.

"They would likely have followed our trail to the lakeside towns. If there are any pale ones near it won't be many and the city guard will handle them. It would be a welcome distraction if anything."

"It's risky, Layala." Aunt Evalyn put a gentle hand on her shoulder. Aunt Evalyn knew the consequences of her magic as much as anyone. She'd almost died because of it once.

"We take the risk, or we prepare for a big battle and the possibility that Brunard will be alerted and get away."

The Ravens looked at each other. Another set of guards came into view. Everyone seemed to crouch lower at once. Thane twisted his mouth but nodded and once the guards were out of sight, he leaned closer. "I'll be right behind you. There will likely be guards inside that we need to silence immediately. Evalyn, you'll wait out here. If things get bloody, run back to the horses. You too, Tifapine."

"I'll whistle if anyone approaches," Fennan said.

With a deep breath, Layala nodded. They waited in tense silence for the next set of patrol to move by and disappear. Then Layala dashed out, her shirt snagged on a thorn of the blackberry bush and sliced through her sleeve and into her arm. She winced at the sting but didn't slow. At the door, she looked both ways to make sure it was still clear. *Come on, hurry hurry.* Heart hammering, she set her right palm against the lock and pushed out her magic. The breaking of metal quietly clicked and with her other hand she twisted the gold knob.

A whistle cut the air. Shit. Had it been thirty seconds already? Thane shoved the door open, grabbed her arm and dragged her into a dark corridor.

Her eyes adjusted to the change in lighting quickly; they were alone. Thank the Maker.

Thane eased the door shut. They waited in silence for shouting, an alarm, for a guard to burst inside. One beat, two, three—nothing.

"They didn't see us," Thane murmured. Both Thane and Layala stepped away to give the others room to file inside once the guards passed. While waiting, she glanced around. At the very end of the long corridor a single torch burned. Quiet clanking of what sounded like pots and pans came from somewhere nearby. It was warm in here, the kind of heat an oven might produce. And once she got past the musty damp smell, she picked up hints of cakes, or something equally sweet, baking.

The door clicked open and the other four dashed inside until they filled up the small space. Piper nudged Layala with her elbow. "Anything?"

"No sign of anyone yet."

"Do you know the layout of this place?" Fennan asked.

"What if he's not here?" Leif interjected. "What if the dragon got here first?"

Layala lifted a shoulder. "Then we'll find out soon enough, won't we?"

Thane moved through the group to stop in front. "I've never been to this part of the manor. When I was here, I was taken from the entry to a large—entertaining room. Stairs led to an upper level. There were

many doorways both up and on the main floor. He could be anywhere."

"Why don't we start by asking her," Siegfried said with his bow in hand and an arrow leveled on a female standing at the end of the hallway. She stood stark still, fists clenched at her sides. A white apron tied around her front and her blonde hair rested in a disheveled bun on top of her head.

"Don't scream or that arrow will find its mark," Piper said, marching toward her with a dagger in hand.

Leif moved a sweeping hand in front of Layala, allowing her to go first. She and Thane walked side by side. The elf's eyes were fixed on Thane despite Piper having her weapon out and Siegfried with an arrow ready to fly. Her chin trembled. Piper grabbed the maiden's arm and dragged her against the wall that was out of sight of the kitchen on the other side.

Thane stopped before her. "We won't hurt you if you stay quiet."

"You're—you're," her voice broke off.

"Thane Athayel, yes."

"You're here for L-Lord Brunard."

"Very astute," Thane said with a smirk. "Where is he?"

Her chest rose and fell faster, her breaths sharper. "He's up-up," she stuttered and swallowed, "Upstairs in his chambers."

"And which are his chambers?"

313

She slammed her eyes shut, squishing her face. "The ent-tire right side of the t-top level."

"Is there a servants' entry?"

She shook her head.

"Are you lying to me?"

"I—I—nnno." Layala wasn't sure if the maiden always had a stutter or if it was from her fear. "There a-are only the s-sets of stairs in the foyer to the up-upper level."

"How many kitchen staff are there right now?"

She held up her hand with four fingers. Thane nodded and turned to the Ravens. "Tie them up, gag them." Piper grabbed the maiden's arm and dragged her along with the tip of her dagger pressed against her side.

Silent as the dead, the others swept around the corner. Layala followed in the back and watched as they apprehended the three other cooks before a scream could be let out. One large wooden block dominated the center of the kitchen. On it were various bowls and platters, chopped vegetables, and an entire uncooked pig. The bright pink of its skin and wide-open black eyes were a little unnerving. She half expected it to jump up and start squealing. Other pots and pans hung from hooks above, flour was sprinkled on some parts of the squares of the brown stone floor and table.

A huge rack of wine stood against the far wall. Leif walked over and picked one up. "Don't mind if I do."

"Really?" Fennan drawled.

"To take with me, not to drink now, clearly."

Layala smiled but slowly shook her head. As if that was even slightly important at the moment.

"I mean, they do have the best wine," Thane said with a wink at Layala. "And Brunard's personal stock? It must be good."

Layala swiped a hand across her damp brow. The stone oven produced enough heat to cook them it seemed. Only one window about as tall as her upper half was open to let in a breeze... one small window. The guards might see them. She dashed across the room, practically diving for the white curtain tied off to the side. Voices drifted on the air. Gah—faces. She gasped and with a quick jerk, slid the curtain over.

"Hey," one of the guards said.

She waved wildly for everyone to take cover. They dragged the kitchen staff to an open pantry door. Layala slid her sword out, setting it down on the table before she pushed the blade flush against the wall so it wouldn't be seen. Then she snatched an apron on a nearby hook, threw it over her head, and just as she finished tying it behind her back, a hand grasped the curtain and moved it aside.

Layala picked up a bowl of flour and dunked her hand in, only to realize something wet and gooey was inside. A couple of eggs. "Hello," she said with a big smile. Probably too big. She relaxed her face some. "How are you today?"

His curly light-brown hair was half tied back, and

his smile wrinkled his eyes. "I've never seen you before. You new?"

His partner tapped his shoulder. "Come on, we can't stop to chat with pretty maidens." He started walking off.

Please, just go with him. Layala silently pleaded but kept her smile plastered on.

"Just started." She mashed the eggs into the flour.

"You're not from here, are you?" His eyes trailed over her face and down to her breasts. "And you haven't met Lord Brunard either, I assume?"

Layala's heart thundered. She laughed off her nervousness. "What makes you say that?"

He gestured toward her head. "As beautiful as you are, Lord Brunard wouldn't have you in the kitchens. He'd have..." His mouth twisted into a slight frown. "Other uses for you."

Other uses? By his tone and shift in demeanor it couldn't be a good use. What did he do to beautiful females? "You're right. I moved here not long ago from Quindar." She said the only other Calladiran town she knew of.

"Ah, nice town." His blue eyes darted around the room behind her. "Where is everyone else?"

That stopped the other guard. *Maker, no. Just go away.* She didn't want to have to kill them, the other set of guards would notice, and they'd be discovered. "Um, seems like a bout of the runs is going through the others. They had to find a toilet. You might want to stay away."

"Runs?"

The other guard turned on his heel and kept walking. He appeared to catch on quick.

Layala couldn't help the blush creeping up her neck. Was that not how they referred to loose stool sickness? Why didn't this elf get it?

Then the guard's eyes widened. "Oh." He took a step back. "Right. Well, I better be on my way. Just a warning to the new maiden, if Lord Brunard sees you, he'll invite you to be a part of his harem. He rewards the females well but—I don't know, you just seem too good for that."

With a flour-covered hand, she waved. "Thanks for the warning. Bye." And with that, he hurried to catch up with his partner. Layala's tense shoulders dropped, and she set the bowl down, and pulled the curtain closed again.

The Ravens crept out of the walk-in pantry. Layala tossed the apron overhead and onto the counter. "His harem? He has a harem of females for sex?" Maker, she was disgusted by the idea, and thankful Thane was nothing like the typical male in power.

Thane lifted a shoulder.

"A shrug? You're not appalled. That doesn't bother you?"

Thane pulled her into a hug and ran his hands up and down her arms. "It's not ideal but it's also none of our business. I saw them last time I was here so I'm not as surprised as you."

"Oh, and you still offered your sister to him as a wife?"

"It's complicated. I'm not offering her now, am I?"

"You know what a great idea would be," Leif said, tapping a finger against his chin. Layala didn't like the mischievous look on his face. "You and Piper go in, dressed as part of his harem. It would be easy for you two to get past the guards."

The harsh look on Piper's face made Layala laugh. She clearly wasn't enthused about the idea. "Why don't we put you in a skirt and add some rouge to *your* cheeks?"

He grinned. "If it would work, I'd do it. But I don't think Brunard wants someone with a tallywacker between his legs and hair on his face."

Deep chuckles bounced around the room. Fennan tapped his boot on the floor. "Actually, it's not a bad idea."

"Absolutely not," Thane said.

Leif threw up his hands. "There's no servants' entrance and only one way up and that's the stairs in the foyer. So unless you want us to start a battle..."

"Oh, I'm fine going on a killing spree rather than putting the girls at risk like that," Thane said with a growl. "I recognize some of these guards and I remember what they did to me."

"Then Brunard might sneak away," Layala said and nibbled on her bottom lip. If Brunard heard them coming, they could lose their chance at the stone. She couldn't believe she was going to say it but, "I'll do it."

Piper's mouth dropped. "Layala."

"No, you will not." Thane's jaw tensed and he shook his head. "For one, he might recognize you. I doubt he would forget the face of the elf who ripped apart his city with her magic."

"Then I'll go," Piper said. "He won't know me. I'll get him to tell me where the stone is."

"You going to screw him for that information?" Fennan asked, a slight edge to his tone. "You can't just ask him."

"You're a real prick sometimes," Piper snapped, with flushed cheeks. "There are other ways to persuade someone."

"You're not going by yourself," Layala said, folding her arms. "Even if Brunard thinks my face is familiar he will never suspect Layala Lightbringer, Thane's betrothed, to come into his room as a harem maiden. And if he does, well, then Piper and I will knock him unconscious."

"I'll go with them," Leif said. "Snag me a guard's uniform."

"First of all, you have tattoos all over your fore-head," Thane said. "No one in Calladira does that. And —" Thane's face was all shadows and fury. With a sharp huff, he said, "I'll be the one escorting you dressed as a guard. All we need to do is get to his room."

Some of the others grumbled. Fennan stepped forward. "If anyone will be recognized, it's you."

"Then I'll wear a hood. Some of them do."

With a grunt, Fennan waved a hand and turned away. "Do what you want. You always do."

AFTER ONE OF the cooks gave up the location of a changing room where the maiden's risqué outfits waited as well as spare male uniforms, Piper, Layala and Thane stood in front of a large floor-length mirror. Layala's lingerie could hardly be described as anything more than scraps of fabric. A sheet of white hung over her buttocks and front barely reaching the tops of her thighs, held up by a thin piece of string around her hips. The top wasn't more fabric than her bralette with floral lace, and for show, she tied a gold chain with moon and star symbols dangling around her waist. Piper's bodice was a deep purple, high cut over her hip bones and a plunging neckline that reached her navel. The straps over her shoulders were thinner than a finger and the back was left completely open except for a narrow crop of fabric over her behind.

Thane's eyes traveled greedily over Layala's form. "This should be—interesting. I think you might take that with you when we leave."

Piper folded her arms over her chest. "When the other guards mention something about our looks, and they no doubt will, keep your temper neutral. I know you won't like others touching or even looking at Layala."

Keeping his eyes trained carefully on Piper's face, he said, "I will stay perfectly calm."

"Uh huh," Piper murmured. "Remember, us finding the stone and not starting a massive battle depends on you staying in character."

Thane held up his palms in surrender. "I'll be a good boy."

"And you," Piper said, shooting a finger at Layala, "No throwing a tantrum if someone grabs your ass."

"We understand our roles." Layala put a hand on her chest. "Submissive harlot and," she gripped Thane's forearm, "Brunard's prick of a guard."

With a satisfactory half smile, Piper tugged open the door. On the other side waited a grand foyer, with gold trim around the doorways and floors, and ornate fixtures. Gaudy framed paintings and chandeliers gave the place an air of royalty. The crimson carpet running down the center of the room led to a set of stairs at the end.

Piper stepped out first and a guard immediately moved into her path. His gaze stuck to her like honey and then a smirk pulled up. "Well, hello there beautiful." With a sharp intake of breath and a dry throat, Layala glided up beside her. She didn't want Piper to feel alone while she was ogled. He shifted his attention, mostly to Layala's breasts which were quite a bit larger than Piper's. "Maker above, you two are as sweet and sultry as pixieberry pie. Mm, mm, mmm."

Thane brushed against the left side of Layala.

"Lord Brunard wanted the new maidens to be brought up."

With raised eyebrows, the dark-brown-eyed guard made a kissing noise with puckered lips at Layala. "I'm sure he did."

She gave Piper an annoyed sideways glance. This was going to be harder than she thought. She might very well kick someone else in the balls for that. Keeping in character, Piper kept her eyes low.

Another guard, this one with eyes blue as the sky, left his post from across the hall and sauntered over. "New recruits?" Blue Eyes asked.

"Looks that way," Brown Eyes replied.

Layala bit her lower lip to keep from blurting anything out. She figured the maidens would be quiet.

"Yes," Thane answered. "I'm sure he's eager to meet them."

"He is up with Lorabell, and we all know his number one girl doesn't like to share her bed time." Both guards laughed and Thane joined in as if he knew exactly why.

"Perhaps he'll have a new number one girl, or two," Piper said in such a seductive voice even Layala was surprised. "But we'll never know if we're kept down here waiting."

Brown Eyes slid his arm around Piper's rump and pulled her into him. "You know, what he doesn't know won't hurt him. We could take one of the rooms real quick."

His following wink was particularly atrocious.

Maker above, did he think he was charming?

Thane noticeably stiffened and let out a long but quiet breath. *Keep it together, Thane,* Layala thought.

With a giggle, Piper gently pushed his hand off her. "I came here for Lord Brunard but thank you for the offer."

He grabbed a handful of her ass and said, "He lets us indulge from time to time. If you want to, that is."

"But that decision is his, isn't it? And hers," Layala said, hoping to draw their attention away from Piper. "Not yours. So you shouldn't touch her like that unless she asks."

"We got a feisty one." Brown Eyes released Piper. "Bet you'd be a wild ride."

By some miracle Thane kept silent and only clamped his fists at his sides.

Blue Eyes tapped Brown Eyes' shoulder with the back of his hand. "She's right. I don't want to lose house privileges. Best leave them alone. Remember when you grabbed Grinella's tit in front of him and he almost cut your hand off?"

With a grumble, Brown Eyes backed off, opening a gap for them to pass. "How could I forget? Move along, ladies." Stepping quickly, they started for the stairs at the end of the foyer. "Hey, who are you anyway? I haven't seen you before."

"Keep walking," Thane whispered from behind them.

"Stop."

"Go on ahead," Thane said. "I'll catch up."

Layala felt the heat of his body from behind her disappear. She peeked over her shoulder to see Thane twist around to face them. Piper wrapped her hand around Layala's wrist and kept up her steady pace. "Let him handle it."

"They might recognize him," Layala hissed.

"Then I guess he'll get the fight he wanted." They made it to the first step and slowly began their ascent. Layala gripped the gold railing, unable to look away from Thane below.

"I'm from Quindar, same as the girls. They needed someone to escort them here and that's what I'm going to do."

Layala waited in moments of heart-pounding silence. Thane sounded so confident she didn't know how the guard would suspect anything else. The lie rolled off his tongue like the utmost truth. *Believe him. Your life depends on it, you stupid prick.*

The guard gave him a wary nod. "Right... well, put in a word with the redhead for me, will you?"

"I'd be happy to," Thane said.

By the time Layala and Piper reached the top level and stood in front of the double doors with twin rearing black bears burned into the wood on either side, Thane already hustled up the steps. He took them two at a time and before she knew it, his hand rested on her shoulder. Thankfully there no other guards on this level to deal with.

"Now for the really fun part," Piper said. "Let me do the talking."

CHAPTER 26

P iper pushed down on the flat, gold door handle. With a quiet click and a groan, the doors slowly swung inward. To the left was an unlit fireplace with a mantel made of iridescent blue stone the likes of which she'd never seen. Unlike the simplicity of Thane's room at Castle Dredwich, this chamber was filled with shelves of statues and vases full of blooms, and artwork depicting war but somehow in a beautiful way. As if the warriors were in a dance rather than a sword fight, with the light pastels and puffy white clouds and blue skies. A sofa and loveseat circled around a silver rectangle rug. On a table in the center were a plate and a half-empty glass of wine and an old book with loose pages sticking out. Airy white curtains to an open balcony shifted and danced in the breeze.

Why was it so quiet? And where was Brunard? The right side revealed an archway opening into another part of the chamber where she spotted the end of a

bed. The thick beige posts were etched with whorls and berries and leaves.

"Hello?" Piper called softly.

Layala almost jumped at the interruption of the silence. It felt like intruding on someone's private moments. But at least he wasn't in the middle of something intimate or they'd have heard *something*.

Thane moved across the wooden planks like a phantom, cautiously stepped out onto the balcony and disappeared behind the curtains. Floorboards creaked in the other room. Someone was in here. Layala and Piper both nodded at each other and made their way to the arch. Layala stepped across the threshold first and cold metal slid across her neck. She froze, barely registering the sting, careful not to breathe too heavily or risk pushing the blade further.

"Lord Brunard." Piper's wide eyes stared to the left of Layala. "We mean no harm. We're the new—"

"Female company in my chambers is by invitation only."

Layala could barely make out auburn hair and light skin out of the corner of her eye, but she didn't dare move. It would take minimal pressure for him to slit her throat. With hands raised, Piper stepped closer. Her eyes darted to the room behind, and she gave the slightest shake of her head.

"Lord." She lifted her hand toward him and licked her lips. He didn't flinch away or say a word the closer she drew, so Piper slid her fingers along the bare flesh of his arm. Layala dared turn her head in the slightest

to watch her companion's next move. Piper's fingers danced across his shoulder and then caressed down his back. She put her chin in the hollow of his neck and said softly in his ear, "Your guards thought we'd be a nice surprise. A gift."

"Mmm," he crooned. "Did they?" But he'd yet to remove his weapon. He glided fully in front of Layala. It took everything in her to not lean back or let her buzzing magic tear apart this room. This was the elf responsible for torturing Thane, after all. She expected him to be uglier or there to be some sign of his wickedness on his face, but he was as beautiful as most elves, more so than some. His dark eyes glittered as they trailed down her body. With care, he watched as he slid the dagger down her throat, across her collar bone and then pressed the tip gently above her left breast. "I can hear your heart beating. Are you nervous?"

"Yes," she answered.

"Are you afraid?"

Layala briefly looked at Piper. Her friend rubbed her hands down his chest and back up. "No."

"You've never done this before, have you? Offered yourself to a male you don't know."

Not even close, Layala thought. "You're correct, Lord." And why hadn't he taken his dagger away from her chest yet? And why wasn't Piper talking like she said she would?!

He tilted his head to kiss the top of Piper's hand as she rubbed his shoulders. They should have had a clearer plan. What was the blasted plan? Fennan said

she'd have to hump it out of him, but Piper said she had other ways of persuading, and truthfully, Layala came along for support. Her only thought was to tie the bastard to a chair and pull his fingernails off until he gave up the location. Maker, she was a brute in need of finesse.

Brunard scrutinized every inch of her face. She stared back at him, counting the beats of her heart to focus on something other than her itching magic or the pinch of Brunard's dagger. Did he recognize her? Long moments passed. He must know, mustn't he? Would he shove the blade straight through her heart?

Piper, say something!

"I love the innocent ones," he said and slid his other hand over her stomach, holding his fingers under the chain around her waist. Her skin prickled at the violation. "The ones who need me to teach them things."

What a disgusting prick. She could no longer stand the blade at her heart. Her hand wrapped around the sharp metal, and she pushed it back slightly. It cut into her palm, but she gladly took the sting. He didn't ease off. Did this elf have some sort of knife fetish? She thought seriously about slamming her knee into his crotch, twisting the dagger out of his hand, and using it on him. But she would give Piper more time to do whatever it was she had in mind. "Lord, please."

He smiled and eased the weapon off. "It was just so delicious watching you get more and more nervous. You're like a frightened doe and this is unusual for me.

Most of the maidens I get are experienced and eager to please."

He backed her against the wall and his palms hit on either side of her head. "Tell me, what do you want to do to me, precious?"

She swallowed hard. "Truthfully?"

His finger wrapped around a piece of her long hair and then he pulled on it enough to hurt. "I'd love to hear it." Before she could answer he leaned forward and fully kissed her on the mouth.

Holy shit.

She went stark still. Revulsion pulsed through her as the taste of wine on his tongue filled her mouth. Was he drunk? And holy Maker above, could Thane see this? She wanted to slam her hands into his chest. Where the hell was Piper? She glanced behind him and found Piper silently rifling through the trunk at the end of his bed. Layala of all people was Brunard's distraction?

Layala put her palms flat against him and pushed gently but enough to get his lips off her. "You know what I'd love to do to you, Lord Brunard?" *Cut out your wretched heart.*

"Tell me," he begged. "I love watching your lips move. They're so soft and plump." He leaned forward, moving in for another kiss.

From behind, Piper pulled his chin around to face her. "Come play with me. You're giving her all the attention." She slipped a full glass of wine into his hand. "Have some more, Lord."

She gave Layala an apologetic look and then took his hand, leading him toward the bed.

He tipped his head back and drank it down in seconds. "You're too kind, lovely." He grabbed a handful of her hair and pulled her to a stop. Bringing the locks to his nose, he inhaled. "I adore redheads. You don't feel as much pain."

Piper turned and grabbed between his legs. He lightly hissed. "You have red in your hair, so tell me, does that hurt or do you like it?"

"It hurts and for some reason I like it," he slurred.

Either that wine was hitting him hard or there was something else in it.

"I thought so," Piper crooned, then she grabbed his shoulders and pushed him back on the bed. "I heard you have the All Seeing Stone. Is that true, Lord?"

Layala almost groaned. She truly just came out with it? Maker above, it's not like he was simply going to hand it over.

But to her surprise, he nodded, tongue practically wagging as she climbed on him. "Yes. What do you want with the stone?"

"Where is it?"

His eyebrow ticked up and that seemed to sober him some. He snatched Piper around the throat, and she immediately grabbed his wrist with both hands. "Why are you asking me about the stone?"

Shit, Layala rubbed her face and found herself moving across the floor toward the pair. The wine wasn't hitting as hard as they thought.

"Don't hurt her. It was my idea."

"What was?" he snapped.

"To come in here and ask for the stone. I need it. It's important."

His glassy eyes narrowed but he only tightened his fingers more around Piper. Her wheezing sent a shot of panic through Layala.

"So you're not my gift."

"No."

He dropped his hand and Piper gasped for air and wrapped her hands around the front of her throat. He shoved her to the side and got up.

"Just for the fact that you had the guts and ability to slip by my guards and get in here, I'll hear you out. But if I think you're lying, I won't tell you where it is and trust me, you'll never find it." He looked Layala up and down. "And I have a soft spot for beautiful half-naked females, high elves or not."

How did he know?

He stepped around Layala, swaying a little as he walked to the room where they'd left Thane. She could hardly believe he hadn't stepped in already. Layala curled her fingers, nails biting into her palms. Had Thane found a place to hide? What would Thane do when they met? Threaten him with death? Something about Brunard told her, he'd rather die than give anything to Thane.

She waited for a shout, for Thane to start barking orders, or a fist to crack flesh and bone but the shirtless Brunard simply sauntered over to the loveseat and

picked up a glass of wine. "Why are you two still standing there? Come. Sit." He waved a lazy hand at the sofa across from him and leaned back, legs spread wide as if he had not a care in the world. At least he wore pants.

Layala glanced at Piper. *Where did Thane go?* There were no shelves or doors or shadows to hide in or behind. Her gaze drifted toward the balcony. Was he giving them a chance to talk to Brunard? He must believe it was a possibility to get the stone's location without torture and mayhem.

Layala gracefully lowered onto the soft navy-blue sofa and rested her hands on top of her bare thighs. She kept her spine rigid, not comfortable enough to lean back and relax. What story was she going to come up with to convince him to give her the stone?

Piper held the same posture beside her. On guard, waiting for Brunard to do something rash. The worn, silver book with pages falling out caught her attention. Under it was a drawing and from its peeking corner in black ink, she made out the outline of what might be a scepter of some kind. An ornate piece a king might hold.

Brunard leaned forward, gripped a white napkin from beside the book and wiggled it at Layala. "You're bleeding a little. Ever since your fallen prince escaped, I've wondered if he might come back to kill me. You'll understand if I'm cautious."

"Our fallen prince?"

"Oh, I know neither of you is a woodland elf. There are subtle differences in your features."

"Oh, of course," Layala said, and grasped the napkin, trying but failing to keep her hand from trembling a little. The rush of adrenaline, the urge to fight still surged through her veins. She forced herself not to look at the balcony again. Thane had to be out there, and if he heard that Brunard made her bleed? Maker above, she was shocked he hadn't blasted in here yet. With a deep breath, she pressed the crisp napkin to her throat. "But he's dead or hadn't you heard?"

With a smile, he leaned back in a casual manner. He took a sip of wine and then swirled the white liquid around. "I did hear that."

But he clearly didn't believe it. "So, the stone. Do you in fact have it?" Layala asked.

He tapped a nail against his glass. "There is something so familiar about you. I can't put my finger on it. I thought for sure when I kissed you the memory would return."

So he had been playing them? "I assure you we've never met. I'd remember," she said coolly and smiled. She'd remember the face of the elf who tortured her lover, no doubt about it. When she tore apart Newarden in her rampage, she never saw Brunard. She didn't even know what he looked like until now.

He let out a dark chuckle and sat forward, forearms rested on his thighs. "You know I thought the same thing. You're quite striking to look at but I know I've

seen you somewhere before, and remember I said I wanted the truth or no stone."

"Before we tell you anything, we need to know if you have it," Piper said.

"I do and I've told no one else where it's hidden."

Sweat beaded on Layala's back. What if he could detect lies? He seemed sure of himself, as if he'd know if she or Piper lied. "I have been here before. Once," Layala said. "To Newarden." She suddenly remembered seeing his auburn hair, screaming at the ledge of the fountain for his soldiers to attack the oncoming pale ones and to leave her. "I saw you near the fountain then. I'm sure we shared a look."

He stared into her eyes. Even if he was a little drunk, it was as if he could discern truth or lie. She could almost see the thoughts flying through his mind as if he were trying to recall the moment. The breeze from the balcony whisked into the room and the fresh air cooled the sweat glistening on her body.

Finally, he nodded. "Why do you want the stone?"

"I want to know the truth about who I am. Things have been—kept from me." She tried to tell the truth without giving anything away. And it was true. She wanted to know why she could bring the Black Mage back or if she was the one to destroy the curse of the pale ones.

Brunard leaned back again and tilted his glass of wine until it was gone. "I'm afraid it doesn't work on its own. Something I didn't discover until recently."

"What does that mean?" Piper asked.

"It means after I held the thing in my hands and tried everything I could imagine to get it to do something—anything, nothing happened. So I did some in-depth research. Turns out for it to work it has to connect with a scepter which was deliberately kept separate from the stone. And only two mages can get it to work even with both. This is a power the ancients didn't want us to have."

Layala glanced down at the book. A scepter was drawn there... Of course, fate wouldn't allow this to be simple. She wanted to use it for good. Why couldn't the Maker be on their side in this? "And who has the scepter?" Layala asked.

"The dragon king, according to my great grandfather's journal. A place I dare not venture. I'd rather not be eaten."

As in Varlett's king? Could things get any worse? Both Piper and Layala sat in stunned silence. To face even one dragon had led to disaster. How many dragon shifters could be in the dragon court? Would they be attacked there? Would they be allowed to enter? They stayed in their mountains and didn't associate with the rest of Adalon.

"I had a similar reaction."

"We'll risk going there," Piper said. "But we need the stone. What do you want for it?"

With a mischievous smile, he stared into his empty glass of wine then set it on the table. He lifted his gaze to Layala. "I want you, in my bed."

Layala's heart nearly jumped into her throat. "No."

"Then you can't have it."

"You can have me," Piper blurted out and stood.

Layala almost gasped. She stared wide-eyed at Piper. She couldn't possibly bed Brunard for the stone. Who's to say he would even give it over afterward?

"A most generous offer, lovely," Brunard said but his eyes flicked back to Layala. His stare was hard and uncomfortable as if he could undress her with a look, as if he saw her as nothing more than a vessel for pleasure. "But I want that pretty mouth wrapped around my cock and then I want to ride you until you scream my name—Lady Lightbringer. That's who you are, isn't it? I want Thane to hear us in the afterlife."

Holy shit, he knew. And he was trying to draw Thane out or testing to see if he was here. He must be, or at the very least, if he believed Thane to be dead, he wanted what he thought once belonged to his enemy. "If you know who I am, you know exactly what I am capable of, and I'll cut off your cock before it ever comes anywhere near me." Layala stood, fury surging through her. "And if you don't give me the stone, I'll make sure you suffer as much as Thane did before I kill you. It will be you screaming my name, begging me to stop the pain."

Piper was as still as a statue beside her. Brunard stared at Layala, but that lustful hunger shifted. She could almost smell the fear leeching out from him. He was trying to decide if she was serious or not, maybe debating on his chances of winning against her. It was rare for a female to have the power to kill and make

commands of a lord like Brunard, and she could see he didn't like it.

Faint screams from outside, drifting in from the balcony, broke their staring contest. Had her brief use of magic breaking the lock triggered a pale-one attack? The rising of shrills and shrieks and... loud snapping trees, intensified. *What is happening out there?* Pale ones couldn't tear apart trees.

With a puzzled look, Brunard stood, facing the balcony. Thane burst through the curtains, sword in hand and a ferocious scowl. With a wave of his hand Brunard flew and slammed into the wall, pinned there by an invisible force. The woodland Elf Lord wore an expression mixed with fury and surprise.

"What's going on?" Layala followed him as he stalked across the room.

"Varlett has arrived." He smiled wickedly at Brunard and slid his blade's edge to his throat. "Hello, old friend. Where is the stone?"

"Go lick donkey dick."

Thane smirked. "I was hoping you'd say something like that." With a quick jerk, he slid the blade across flesh and a well of blood bubbled up and spilled down to his collarbone. Brunard winced but that stubborn set to his jaw remained. "The next slice will kill you. I don't have time for your horseshit. Where is the stone?"

Screams and cries for help grew louder outside. Layala fidgeted nervously with the chain around her belly. She peeked over her shoulder—how long before

Varlett came flying in through the balcony? Or maybe she'd tear off the front doors of the place and kill everyone inside.

"You brought your army to slaughter innocent people?"

"No, you have a different threat to deal with. One with scales, and if you want to live to help them, you better talk."

Brunard stared hard into Thane's face. "Your word on your honor as High Prince that you won't kill me if I tell you."

The jaw muscles in Thane's face twitched. "Fine. I give you my word as High Prince."

"On your honor."

"On my honor," Thane said. Seriously? From what Layala had seen, Thane always kept his word. He was going to let Brunard go?

His head tilted toward his bedchamber. "At the end of my bed, under the chest there is a loose floorboard. It's there."

Piper was already pushing against the chest before he finished his sentence. Fingers dipped into a crack, and she pulled the wood plank, and then beheld a round object in brown cloth, tied with twine. She pulled the tie and it fell open, revealing a rough cut, milky-white stone.

The deep roar of Varlett's mighty dragon form shook the very floors they stood on. Dust dropped down from in between panels in the wood ceiling. Layala gulped and snapped her head toward the

windows. How close was she now? Could they fight her off? A vase slipped from a shelf and shattered on the floor.

"We have to go," Thane said and released his magical hold on Brunard and took a step back. Thane's gaze fell to her neck, on the spot Brunard had sliced her, and his serene calmness snapped, obliterated like the fragile glass of the vase now scattered on the floor. With a whoosh, his sword cut through the air, and he shoved his blade right through Brunard's chest.

Layala gasped and slapped her hand across her mouth.

Brunard's lips gaped open like a dying fish. "You promised. You gave your word," he wheezed.

"I lied, and my honor as a High Prince means nothing. I am no longer a High Prince," Thane growled. "You tricked me then tortured me in a cage. And I could have forgiven that, but I can't forgive you for hurting *them*. I heard everything you said. And you thought you could kiss my girl and walk away?" Thane shook his head slowly. "You knew this was coming. So long, old friend."

He slid his sword free. Brunard let out a quiet cry and slid down the wall. Blood oozed down his chest over his abdominals and pooled on his lap. The ragged sound he made as he struggled to pull air into his lungs made Layala's skin crawl. She couldn't look away, as his every breath rattled, and blood rushed out with each beat of his heart. Thane's cloak whirled out around him as he spun on his heel. He gave one last

look at the balcony then jerked the doors open into the main hall of the manor. "Move. Now, ladies."

Brunard choked until blood bubbled out of his mouth. Why did a small part of her feel sorry for him? This fallen ruler left dying in his own chambers while a dragon ripped apart his city. Even if his end was what he deserved, it surprised her that Thane went back on his word. She'd come to know him as the playful, flirty male she loved, who felt remorse, believed in sacrifice, duty, and honor, was adored by his people and those who knew him best. She let that overshadow the fact that Thane was also a ruthless killer when it came to protecting those he cared for. She'd seen a flash of that back at Kail's place, the empty look in his eyes when he cut down his own elven kind. It had startled her. Now she wondered what he would do when it came time to take down another ruler— Thane's own father. Would the merciless killer or the dutiful son win that battle?

Piper gripped Layala's arm and tugged her toward the door. "Come on. Thane will need our help. We're going to have to fight our way out of here now."

Layala pulled free and grabbed the journal off the table then ran out the exit.

CHAPTER 27

The soft red carpet brushed Layala's bare feet as she dashed down the stairs. Guards and the house staff ran in every direction, shouting orders or frantic for help. It was both terrible and a blessing; no one noticed them or cared about their presence. The front doors to the manor opened wide to the chaos outside of people screaming and crying. Acrid gray smoke made the town square hazy. Another great roar rattled the ground. How close was Varlett? Maker above, Layala was in a skimpy outfit with no weapons, and she might have to fight a dragon? She'd never felt so exposed in her life.

A slender guard raced up the stairs, shoving between Layala and Piper. "Lord Brunard!" he hollered.

She paused only to look back and see the guard disappear into Brunard's chambers. Not good. Not good at all. A beat later he yelled, "Lord Brunard has

been assassinated!" He stepped into the archway. "Stop them!"

Shit.

Taking two steps at a time, and half looking over her shoulder at the guard now racing after her, Layala crashed into the back of Thane. The ringing of metal hit her ears then a head plopped to the floor. *Did he always have to cut off heads?* She stared at the brown eyes looking back at her. *So barbaric.* With a tight grip on her arm, Thane dragged Layala beside him. Wood splintered as his foot collided with the door and sent it flying. It was the room they'd left their clothes in. "Dress. Quickly."

"If you hadn't kicked the door off its hinges, we could have shut it!" Layala hollered snatching up her shirt.

The other door, the one that led into the kitchen flew open and slammed against the wall. Leif and Fennan stood on the other side. "Time to go!" They both said in unison. Leif took in Layala and Piper's nearly-naked appearance and his eyes doubled in size. Fennan's jaw dropped as his eyes glided over Piper from head to toe.

With a scoff, Piper quickly threw her shirt on. "Are you going to stand there and ogle or help Thane?"

The dying groan of an elf jerked Layala's attention. Thane tore his blade free of another guard and his body crumbled to the floor. Three more blades came at Thane in rapid succession, the pinging of metal on metal sang throughout the high ceilings. His skill with

a sword was almost magical in itself. His talent beyond his years, as if wielding a weapon was what he was born to do.

Leif dashed to Thane's aide with sword raised high and a bellow. They both stepped out into the corridor to fight.

A dark blond head popped into the room. Siegfried didn't seem to care about the state she and Piper were in. "With me, quickly," he said.

With her top hanging from her teeth, Layala stepped into her pants. Another dragon roar rocked the manor. Much closer this time. How long could the guards hold her off? Or was she simply toying with them? Several minutes passed since they'd first heard her. She could be inside by now.

Layala slipped her shirt on, strapped on her sword, and said, "Let's go!"

Piper held out the stone to Layala and pushed it into her hand: "You should be the one to carry it."

The brown cloth covered the stone, but she half expected to feel something from it. No vibrations or humming like the portals. No sign it was magical at all. Did Brunard lie? Did he trick them, knowing Thane would kill him anyway? Layala unwrapped the stone and touched her fingertips to the surface of the rock no larger than her palm. It was cool and ordinary, but a sort of static spark zapped her. That was good right? She lifted her inspection to Thane. He stepped toward her with streaks of blood like raindrops sliding down his thunderous face. Maker, he looked like the god of

death, the reaper he'd promised to be. But his green eyes, bright and wild like an untouched forest, told a story of lament for what he must be, what they needed him to be to survive.

A deafening crash and then heeled boots on hard stone. Varlett must be inside. "Oh, Lord Brunard!" She sang in a sickly-sweet voice. "You have something I need."

Thane held his arms wide, herding them into the kitchens. "She hasn't seen us. Run."

A THICK CLOUD of dark smoke roiled up into the sky. Shouts for help and cries of agony drifted to Layala's ears even as they stood at a distance. The towns folk ran with buckets of water to put out the massive fire at the town's square. Bright-orange flames engulfed a huge oak tree surrounded by what was a white picket fence, now char and ash.

The Ravens ran alongside the town, hidden among many trees and foliage. Aunt Evalyn and Tif were nowhere in sight so they must have run back to the horses as they were directed to. At least, she hoped. Layala's lungs burned from their pace to get away and the smoke in the air, but she had to ask, "Does that tree mean something?"

"It's the sacred tree of Anami," Siegfried answered from her left side. He brushed the back of his hand over his forehead, the sadness in his eyes was

evident. Did he have ties to the woodland elves or was he simply sympathetic to what was sacred to them? "Every elf in Calladira goes through a trial of some kind. Finding a fresh well of spring water, bringing home a deer to feed the family, raising and caring for an animal from birth. They mark the tree when they pass and accomplish something for the community and a new leaf sprouts. Or at least, it did."

That pricked Layala's heart a little. Even through the flames its fullness was unmistakable. Why did Varlett have to be such a heartless wench? Tearing her eyes away from the burning tree, Layala followed behind the group as they solemnly made their way back to the horses.

It was only when they'd gotten far enough away that the crackling flames and the shouts couldn't be heard anymore. They slowed to a brisk walk. Layala took the stone from the pouch on her hip. Without an imminent threat, she could get a feel for it. She turned the white stone, about the size of a large duck egg, over in her hands. It was cool and rough-edged against her flesh, and if the thing beheld great power, it didn't feel like it. That one spark was the only sign it wasn't as plain as a sparkly rock plucked from a river.

"Doesn't look like a magic stone," Aunt Evalyn said, popping out from behind a tree. Tif clung to her back. Her little red hat and brown curls bouncing with each step Evalyn took. She had the biggest smile plastered on her face and there was no doubt in Layala's

mind that she was up to something or found something she was proud of.

Layala slowed to fall into step beside her aunt. Aunt Evalyn limped ever so slightly and the way her boots crunched over grass was comparable to a horse clop while the elves sounded hardly more than a butterfly landing on a flower. Layala almost forgot how much different humans were. Watching on with concern, Layala's eyebrows furrowed. Aunt Evalyn placed her hand over her chest and took in deep breaths. This journey was a hardship on her, maybe too much.

Layala tucked the stone back into the pouch. "According to Brunard it must be paired with a scepter that the dragon king has. And we won't know if it's real or fake until we do that."

Aunt Evayln's brows raised. "The dragon king?" Her gaze dropped and she went quiet for a moment, contemplative. "Layala, I'm too old for all this. I'm a plant collector. I like my naps and I like my home."

With a shocked expression, Tif patted Aunt Evalyn's black curls like she was a cat. "You're not old." She chewed on her lower lip for a moment. "Although, I sometimes forget humans don't live very long."

Layala swallowed hard. It was selfish to ask her to stay when it put her in so much danger, but she also worried about the risk it was on her own. Briar Hollow already burned once. Who's to say that they wouldn't come back a second time? "But we might need you. You're good at healing."

"I am more of a burden to all of you than a help. You've always been special, and I knew you'd do something great but Briar Hollow needs to be rebuilt. It's home. You don't need me anymore, my dear child. You haven't for years."

"No," Layala said, a spike of fear pushed her voice higher. "If you leave, you're in danger. Tenebris could capture you, or—"

They stopped and she gently took Layala's hand into hers. "He'll be busy trying to find you and Thane." Aunt Evalyn looked at Thane's back several yards ahead. He and Fennan led the group and appeared to be in deep conversation. "I am still somewhat wary about your relationship but it's obvious that he loves you. I didn't want to believe it, but anyone can see it. And in some ways, it makes me happy to see *you* so in love with him. After Novak, I worried you'd never smile again, that a dark cloud would follow you all your life. But you're glowing even with all this chaos. I haven't seen your pretty smile like this in years," Aunt Evalyn grinned and patted Layala's arm. "But elven wars and dragons are not for old human ladies like me. I can't fight and after the sirens came and took your friend Gunner... I want to go home."

"But..." Layala's vision blurred with tears. She knew she must let her go, and that Aunt Evalyn was right, and this wasn't a life for her, but she wanted her to stay for her own selfish reasons. Aunt Evalyn was the one constant she'd had all her life, the person she

went to for advice and reassurance... but that shifted, didn't it? Thane was that person now.

"Once we get to the portal you can send me back. Forrest and Ren are worried; everyone is. They need reassurance that you and I are alive and well."

"Alright. I will send you home."

Tifapine started blubbering and swiping at her tears. "I hate goodbyes. It's just so sad. I mean what if we never see you again, Evalyn?"

Reaching over her shoulder, Aunt Evalyn rubbed her head. "Me too, little one, but you will." Then she looked at Layala. "I expect updates regularly," she held up a finger, "and your wedding, if I'm not the first to receive an invitation I'll make you stand with your nose in a corner like when you were a child. Might even make you swish with bitter root."

Layala laughed. "Uh, that is the worst thing I've ever tasted."

"Serves you and Ren and Novak right for talking filthy."

Layala wrapped her arms around her aunt and hugged her tightly. She inhaled her cinnamon scent and smiled. "Thank you for everything you've done. Even the bitter root."

Aunt Evalyn patted her back gently. "Go and be the fierce warrior this world needs you to be."

CHAPTER 28

A great wall made of smooth, white-gray stone stood before them high enough Layala squinted to see the top. Wind rustled around the thick pine trees of the surrounding forest, and the river at their backs babbled, but no sounds of civilization, no chatter, or even smells of a city drifted over the wall. Were they in the right place? The portals hadn't made mistakes before so this must be where the dragon king resided... or once resided.

"It's so quiet," Piper said with a fist on her hip. "If I didn't know any better, I would think there was no one on the other side."

"Maybe they wait to come out until they're hungry," Fennan said with a smirk.

Leif and Siegfried both tossed pinecones at him, nailing him square in the face and chest. Tifapine shrieked from within the bag on Phantom that she'd remained hidden in since they stepped through the portal and said goodbye to Aunt Evalyn.

"Bad joke?"

"Yes, since I have a very real fear of being eaten," Leif said, "Nana's stories about the sirens were true. She said dragons love to eat elves and pick their teeth with our bones."

Although Layala put on long sleeves against a slight chill, it was surprisingly warm in this part of the Sederac Mountains. Surrounded by spruce, pine, and fir trees, it smelled fresh and untouched by people. Snow topped the tallest peaks in the distance but here in this valley, green grass swayed in the breeze and wildflowers blossomed.

"Doesn't look like there's an easy way in," Fennan said, shielding his eyes from the bright sun as he peered up. The wall was nearly seamless, and she didn't like the idea of trying to scale it with the use of her vines. It left them too vulnerable against beasts with wings.

Layala watched Thane for any signs of fear or nervousness. His stoic expression as he inspected the barrier before him gave nothing away. Was he not afraid of being ripped apart by dragons, especially after what Varlett did to him? The worry gnawing at the back of her mind was constant. She'd almost lost him to a dragon once. He was a valiant warrior and extraordinarily gifted but was he a match for these beasts? They couldn't even take down Varlett, and inside waited hundreds, maybe even thousands of vicious dragons like her. They would be at the mercy of

the dragon king, and they'd have to rely on intellect rather than brute strength this time.

With his fingers gliding along the stone, Thane walked to an area with a thin, straight line that ran up the entirety of the wall. Several feet over another crack in the stone ran from top to bottom. "I think this is a door."

"The grass around it hasn't been disturbed in a long time," Fennan pointed out. "It either opens inward or they don't use it."

"Why would they need to use it? They fly." Leif stepped back under the canopy of a nearby pine tree. He pulled a small brown sack from his hip pouch and dug his hand inside. He popped a handful of nuts into his mouth and chomped loudly. "Should we scout along the wall for a way in?"

Thane pressed his lips firmly together, looking toward the heavens. "It might be better to wait for them to come to us rather than sneak inside. I know if I found intruders stepping on the grounds of castle Dredwich I'd treat them as such."

"Wait to be eaten?" Leif said. "I'm not going out like that. Nah I'll die on a battlefield hopefully many years from now. I'm only seventy-three."

"Wait to be invited inside by their leader," Thane said, raising a challenging brow. "If I thought we'd all die coming here, I wouldn't have led you here. My gut tells me they'll talk to us before they attack, and well, if they attack first, we'll fight back."

"Something tells me they won't be as civilized as elves," Fennan said.

Piper folded her arms and laughed. "No shit, their alternate form is a dragon."

"Civilized is subjective," Thane said, leaning his back on the wall. "The woodland elves think we're barbaric."

Leif dropped to the base of a needled tree, leaned his head back, crossed his ankles, and closed his eyes. "Alert me when something exciting happens."

Thane smiled while shaking his head and started walking alongside the wall, inspecting it carefully. Maybe he thought he'd find a way to get the door open.

Fennan and Siegfried went to the river to fill canteens, and that left Piper and Layala alone. She'd wanted to talk to her for days without prying ears. Layala glanced at Leif resting against the tree trunk. He probably wasn't actually asleep and the topic she wanted to talk to Piper about involved him. She touched Piper's arm. "Let's go help Thane." On their walk, Layala asked, "So, what's going on with you, Fennan and Leif?"

Piper kept her gaze forward. "Nothing. Why?"

"You and Fennan seem closer, and everyone saw that Leif and Fennan were about to fight back on the island. They've never butted heads before."

Piper ran delicate fingers over the length of her thick braid. She cleared her throat, and they stopped beside Thane. He tapped his finger against an inscrip-

tion. The long curling and sweeping symbols were the only blemishes on the wall. It was unreadable to Layala, and she didn't think the others would know the language either.

Thane turned and leaned back against the wall, arms crossed, one boot heel behind him. So casual and cool as if they didn't wait at the base of a monumental wall built by fire-breathing beasts. "Yes, I'd like to know the answer to that as well, Piper. Why are Fennan and Leif fighting over you?" Thane asked. "Fennan hasn't said a word."

Piper rolled her eyes. "You two are nosey."

"As if you weren't on my ass every day when Layala and I didn't get along. Asking if we'd held hands, kissed, analyzing our interactions."

A bright-pink blush spread across her lightly-freckled cheeks. "That's different. You quite literally could have turned into a pale one if you two didn't love each other... But I might have been a little too involved."

"So you're not going to tell us what happened in the dungeons?" Thane said. "Because I know something happened, Piper. You and Fennan have been friends, but this is different." Thane turned back around, sliding his fingers over the carved symbols. "I wonder what this says," he murmured.

"Hell if I know. Probably: Beware, you'll be burned to a crisp if you enter here," Piper said and then she groaned. "And as far as Fennan and I, we were kept in cells next to each other. The guards came into mine to

beat me several times for information and each time Fennan provoked them, so they'd go beat him instead of me. I begged him to stop protecting me after they broke his arm. I thought they would kill him."

"But he didn't stop," Thane assumed.

"Of course he didn't. He's a pigheaded fool." Her eyes fell to the ground. "On the last night before we left, he was lying on the ground unable to get up. I was crying because I thought that was it. That he wouldn't get up ever again. It was dark and I could barely see his chest rising," her voice broke. "He said 'if we don't ever get out of here, I need you to know I love you, Piper. I've loved you since I was seventeen.'"

Thane's eyebrow popped up. "And you told him how you felt then too?"

"I tried but he lost consciousness after that. And then we were taken on the road in separate prison carts."

There was something she wasn't saying because there was a reason they weren't openly together. Layala folded her arms. "And you still haven't told him, have you?"

She swiped her fingers across her cheeks. "I'm scared he only said it because he thought he was dying, or he was delusional from fever. What if he didn't mean it? He hasn't said it again or talked about it. Not a word, not a move, not a kiss."

Thane sighed. "Maybe he hasn't brought it up because he thinks you don't feel the same. You should tell him. Or are you not sure anymore because of Leif?"

"Leif and I flirt, always have but it's just fun."

"I wouldn't be too sure about that on his part," Thane said, his green eyes drifting to where Leif sat at the base of the tree. "I've seen the way he looks at you, and so has Fennan, no doubt."

An earthshaking dragon's roar drew their eyes to the sky. Layala fought the urge to slap her hands over her ears. Three dragons flew out from behind the wall and circled high above them. Holy Maker above, Layala's heart crashed into her ribs. She wanted to run for cover. All she could think about was Varlett and how much destruction and power a single dragon had. Now there were three.

"Stay still," Thane ordered. "If we run, they'll see us as prey. We are not prey."

Under the cover of the trees the horses neighed and bucked, but thankfully they were secured. Layala wanted to run to grab Tifapine, but she was safer staying hidden.

The others dashed in, forming a circle of their own. Layala grabbed Thane's hand and squeezed tight to keep herself planted firmly in place because she very much felt like prey. Her magic wouldn't save her against three beasts who could burn her vines with fire breath and slice through the stalks with dagger-sharp claws. Her blade was useless against dragon scales. They were only weakened in human form, something she didn't think they'd risk. It seemed they were at the mercy of predators honed to tear through flesh with ease.

Three sleek forms darted toward them like a hawk might dive for a mouse. Layala's knees went weak. They dropped so fast that their huge bodies were hard to track. Her breath hitched when the trio crashed into the ground, *boom boom boom* one right after the other. The earth beneath the elves' feet rocked and shifted. Big yellow eyes with black slits stared back at her, a cat with a mouse. With a gulp, Layala took a step away but froze when a low growl rumbled behind her. Smoke rolled out of the nostrils of the colossal beast before them. Bright pearl scales shimmered in the sunlight like tiny jewels. Horns as tall as Layala grew out of a massive head with jaws wide enough to snap up even Thane in a single bite. The dragon was both beautiful and terrifying, like lightning that streaked too close across a night sky.

"Trespassers in our land get eaten." The deep masculine voice rumbled right through her core, but it wasn't the dragon in front of her. Layala whipped her head around to the left where the half-human, half-dragon giant of a male stood. Charcoal-gray scales covered where skin would be, great membranous wings spanning at least twelve feet wide spread behind his frame. Was he over seven feet tall? He towered over Thane by at least a head. Light-silver hair was tied back into a tight braid that reached the top of his thighs. He wore a red waistcoat perfectly formed to his muscular physique, with gold embroidered trim around the wrists and down his chest. Black trousers with knee-high boots. Layala was

surprised to find no weapons on him, at least none that she could see.

Thane held up his palms in a surrender gesture. "My name is Thane Athayel. I am—"

"The elf king." The half-shifted dragon cocked his head to the side, in an almost bird-like way. "Or traitor king, depending on who you ask. I'm aware."

Thane pursed his lips. "I ask for an audience with your king." He sounded calm and confident, nothing like Layala felt.

A hot puff of breath washed across Layala's back, billowing her hair and sending a wave of fear through her body. How close was the dragon now? She felt like he was inches from touching her. *Don't turn around, don't turn around.*

"On what grounds?"

"On the grounds that I am a king and what I have to say is for his ears only. But I will say it has to do with the Black Mage."

The dragon's eyes narrowed. "We have no obligations in your war."

"No one knows better than I that you'd rather hide in your mountains behind high walls like cowards than help us against a great enemy."

Layala almost choked in surprise. Maker above, did he truly say that? She wanted to smack him. The growl behind them made the ground shake, and yet the half-shifted dragon burst out laughing. Piper took a small step closer to Layala's side. Siegfried whispered something that sounded like a threat.

"I heard the great Thane Athayel had no fear. Usually rumors are but that." He smiled revealing white, human-looking teeth and took a step, and then another circling around them. His animal-like eyes spent a fair amount of time assessing Thane then his attention drifted to Layala. The corner of his mouth twitched, his slit pupils narrowed, and his nostrils flared. He lurched for Layala. In a flash, Thane's fingers cinched around the dragon's neck, and he stood between her and the threat. "Touch her and I'll rip your throat out," he snarled. "Don't think your dragon scales will save you from *me*."

CHAPTER 29

L ayala felt Thane's power hit her in a burst, a thick cloud coating everything nearby like an invisible damp mist. It pulsed in wave after wave, water lapping against a shore. Layala's ears began to ring; she'd never felt the severity of it like this before.

The two males stared at one another. Surprisingly, the two full dragons behind them didn't move, didn't make a sound. They must fear for their companion's life, assessing Thane as a true threat.

The Ravens tensed; Leif tugged Layala's shoulder, silently asking her to step back. She didn't move.

The half-shifted dragon took in a deep breath through his nose and clicked his tongue like he tasted the very air. "It's been a long time since I smelled the magic of the old gods."

He could *smell* Thane's magic, even more his lineage? She shouldn't be too surprised. Varlett tasted Layala's blood and knew what she feared about her

mate bond with Thane. The harsh sneer on Thane's face did not ease. With bared teeth, he stared down the taller dragon shifter.

"I only wanted to test if you were as valiant as they say. I won't touch your lady friend and I mean none of you harm."

After a few beats, Thane slowly drew his hand back and the tautness in Layala's every muscle eased some.

"I'm quite sure my father will be interested in speaking with you," he said, and with that his wings vanished, and the dragon scales turned to flesh, revealing pale skin with rosy cheeks. Those yellow eyes turned icy blue; the male looked like the human form of winter. With the drop of his protective scales the tense atmosphere shifted to one more open. "It's been what, four hundred years since we had the honor of meeting with a member of House Athayel?"

"Long before my time," Thane said.

The dragon prince nodded. "I'll allow *you*."

Thane shook his head. "I'm afraid that's not going to work. We all go."

"And these people are?"

"My personal guards. I'd never ask you to come into my castle without your,"—he looked at the other dragons—"escorts."

"Hmm, I suppose that is fair. I just have to ask, do you like wine? I have some really delicious wine."

Thane chuckled. "I do. We also stole a bottle from Calladira if you want to exchange."

"Stole? Well, that's a story I'd like to hear."

It was strange how quickly they went from nearly ripping each other's throats out to talking like old friends. Thane always seemed to be able to charm if he wanted to, and this dragon prince appeared equally schooled in the ways of the court, like Aunt Evalyn had once said.

With a big smile the dragon prince said, "Great, well it's settled then. You have my word as a Prince of House Drakonan. None of you will be imprisoned or killed if you are peaceful." He held out his hand to Piper. "My name is Ronan Drakonan."

Piper's hand stayed at her side for a few beats before she grasped his palm. The dragon shifter's hand dwarfed hers. "I'm Piper Fireheart."

"Fireheart? I think your parents were right to choose that for you." He kept hold of her hand, even though it was past time what Layala believed to be customary. His crystalline-blue eyes locked on to Piper without an ounce of pause. Did the dragon prince catch a fancy for the redheaded elven warrior? "It's tradition for elves to choose their female children's last name rather than inherit their father's or husband's, correct?"

"Yes," Piper answered, pulling her hand away and partially tucking it behind her back.

Layala tried not to smile. *Fennan will really enjoy this... another suitor for Piper.* She glanced at Fennan. He frowned and held onto his sword handle. Hopefully he didn't do anything rash.

Prince Ronan turned to Layala. "And you are?"

361

"I'm Layala Lightbringer."

"My betrothed," Thane added casually but the claim itself wasn't friendly. It was a warning.

With a smile and a nod, he said, "I thought so." He did not offer his hand but dipped his chin. Then he swept an arm toward the wall. "Well, the only way in is to fly, so you'll have to hop on. That's Dax," the pearl-colored dragon bobbed his massive head. "And Vaper," the giant bronze had a sleeker snout but a larger horn on the tip of his or her head.

"Greetings." A feminine voice came from Vaper.

"*My* personal guards," Ronan said. "Although we can carry more than one of you, I prefer that you each have your own escort. As I said, as a whole our people are not always open to outsiders." With a snap of his fingers, the bronze dragon named Vaper called in a deep trill, three times.

What did that mean? That they each needed their own dragon to protect them from others?

Without asking for the other's names, he said, "King Thane, I'll ask you to go with Vaper. Layala, with Dax." He turned to Piper. "Piper, you wouldn't mind riding me, would you?"

Even though there wasn't a speck of innuendo in his tone or expression, Layala bit her lower lip and turned away to keep from snickering.

With a low, almost inaudible growl, Fennan stepped up beside Piper, and though he didn't speak his action said enough. *Great, let's start a fight with the dragons already,* Layala thought, and clenched her

hands. Thane narrowed his eyes at Fennan and slowly shook his head.

Ronan looked between Piper and Fennan with an arrogant smirk. "Is that a problem?"

"No," Piper answered. "No problem, Prince Ronan. It would be an honor to be escorted by you." She turned to Fennan and gave him a small reassuring smile.

Wings shimmered into existence, protruding from his back. "I could carry you in my arms if you'd prefer that."

Leif grinned with delight, and patted Piper on the shoulder. "I think she would prefer that. Less intimidating. She's a delicate flower."

Piper smacked his hand away. "I'm no delicate flower."

Three more dragons came soaring over the wall and dropped to the ground, this time with such grace they barely made a sound. Two were smaller, though still massive, with cobalt scales, almost identical. They had sleeker, less square faces as well. Layala wondered if they were female. The third had a spiked tail and onyx scales much like Varlett but with two gold horns growing out of the crown of his head.

"The rest of you, pick your escort. I assure you, no harm will come to you. These are my most-trusted people."

"I don't know about this," Leif said, looking back to where the horses were tied up among the trees. "Maybe one of us needs to stay behind and guard our

belongings." The worry lines on his face were etched deeper than ever.

"The gnome will stay and watch out for the horses. You're coming. Quit messing around and let's get on with it," Thane said and walked to Vaper.

She didn't want to leave Tif unguarded in a forest with dragons and Maker only knew what else, but she was probably safer out here, and someone did need to stay with their horses. Tif was good at attending to them, at least making sure they had food and water. She poked her head out of Phantom's saddle bag and gave a thumbs-up. At least she was happy with the idea of being out here alone.

Thane looked back over his shoulder, staring down the big pearl dragon Layala had been assigned. "Be careful with her. She means more than you even know."

A puff of smoke burst out of his nose and the corners of his humongous mouth curled up revealing too many sharp teeth. Should they be trusting these beasts so quickly? There wasn't much of a choice if they wanted an audience with the king for the scepter. As Aunt Evalyn once told her, "There is never a great reward without great risk." It was worth it to find out the truth.

With a gulp, Layala started for Dax. Would it be shameful to ask if she could ride with Thane? *Come on Layala, now isn't the time to be a coward.* But those big yellow predatory eyes still followed her steps like she was a tasty snack. Even crouched, Dax's spiked spine

reached the treetops. She had no idea how she was meant to climb up there. Maybe a half-shifted dragon would be better after all, but then she'd be curled in the arms of a strange male and that was an even more uncomfortable thought.

"Hello," Layala said with a sheepish smile.

He winked and although she was terrified, something deep inside her trusted this dragon. His presence was somehow warm and welcoming although he looked intimidating and lethal. Maybe their initial thought of dragons was skewed by their encounters with Varlett. The prince seemed cordial enough.

A grunt escaped the dragon's throat then his massive paw lifted off the ground carrying with it pieces of grass and debris that dropped like rain. A shadow cast from above her and she backed up a step. That giant paw came down. She held in a scream— *He's going to scoop me up!* Long talons closed around her in a cage of scales. She clutched onto the thinnest talon, and even then she was barely able to fit her arms around it. *Holy shit. Holy shit!* Thane, and the others grew smaller; her stomach flip flopped. She slammed her eyes shut, and even wrapped her legs around the talon now. If she fell from this height, she'd splat like a bug under her shoe. The movement stopped and another grunt came from Dax. One eye peeled open, then the other. She hung from his finger, hovering a few inches above his back. Flushing, she let go and launched herself at the spike in front of her that was much like a talon but more rounded. This

was good. She could hold onto this while they flew. Oh holy Maker above, she was actually on the back of a dragon. And going to fly. She quickly sat, straddled the spike, and hugged it tightly.

The huge white membranous wings spread and with a *whoosh* they lifted off the ground. Layala screamed—partially from fear but also from delight. She didn't care if she sounded ridiculous or if the others would laugh at her. Pressure pushed her further into the dragon and then suddenly it was like she floated as they rose high above the wall and dropped into a glide. Wind whipping through her midnight hair, they leveled out with the bright yellow sun, and she let out a giddy laugh. Throwing her fist into the air she let out a wild howl. *Is this what it felt like to be totally free?* Riding a galloping horse felt like flying but soaring through the air made an uncontrollable laugh bubble up in her. Dax peeked back at her, and his body rumbled beneath her. *Was he laughing too?*

She dared peek down. It seemed impossible but yet she couldn't deny what she saw. Levels, upon levels of roads and homes and structures existed below. Cobblestone bridges without railings connected to towers or trees hundreds of feet off the ground. Exotic plants grew in pots in front of shops. Statues made in bronze of dragons, animals and human forms in various poses littered the bridges. Some sprayed water into shallow pools. Half-shifted dragons flew from one level to the next, shifters in human form walked along the bridges, full dragons

hung off what looked like giant bird nests with large sticks and fluffs of cotton poking out from perches on spirals and peaked buildings.

Roars and snarls from the left made her whip around. A pair of dragons fought mid-air, clawing, and snapping at each other. The white one had wide-open red gashes along its throat and chest, and the other, a golden-scaled beast had one bite mark near his shoulder. A high-pitched keening came from the white dragon. Layala held her hand over her mouth as his torn wings snapped on one side and he went down in a spiral. Not too far ahead another pair of shifters fought, but in the middle of the bridge and in human-scale form. Their fists cracked each other's faces over and over. Claws raked over scales, cutting into them. This place was... brutal. If they did this to each other, what might they do to outsider elves?

As they passed a nest with two eggs, one white with blue spots and the other a solid amber, Layala smiled. Dragon eggs were said to be rare, but they were right there out in the open. And did the color of the eggshell reflect the color of their dragon scales?

This city must have taken hundreds of years to build, Layala thought, inspecting the homes with massive doors and windows built into the tops of trees. The floating intersecting pathways, and crowds blocked any view of what lay at the ground floor.

"Wow," she breathed. "Do the bridges connect all the way down?"

A grunt and a nod. She figured that meant yes. "It's wonderful."

A sapphire dragon with a spike-tipped tail soared up beside them. As large as Dax but sleeker with no horns growing out of the top of her head, Layala assumed she was female. Her wide jaws snapped at Dax's shoulder, dangerously close to Layala. She tucked her leg up higher, and the warmth of her magic lit within her chest and trickled through her veins to her fingertips ready to unleash hell. So this was what the prince meant. Dax let out a barking growl, raising his lip to show all those teeth.

Maker above, they weren't about to fight, were they? Layala gripped the spike harder. Dax pitched sideways, knocking his shoulder into the sapphire dragon. The collision jolted Layala, and she squeaked, clawing desperately for a better hold. She conjured vines out of thin air until they wrapped behind her back and secured to the spike in front of her in a loop. *I'm not about to fall to my death. Nope.*

"No outsiders allowed in our city, Dax," Sapphire's voice was feminine and yet gravelly. "It is treason."

The rumble of his growl shook Layala. *Oh shit.* Out of the corner of her eye, Dax's pearl tail lashed out and slapped Sapphire's wing, sending her in a downward spin. She howled on her way down and slammed into the top-level bridge. Bits of it crumbled under her colossal weight. Other dragons leapt from perches below and soared up on either side. Layala glanced back, *where in the hell are Prince Ronan and Thane?* She

spotted them in the distance but too far back to intervene.

"Dax," a silver-and-black-striped dragon barked. "Hand over your passenger."

Didn't these two know Dax was the prince's personal guard? Or, *holy Maker above, what if they'd lied? What if he wasn't the prince? And why isn't Dax defending himself by explaining who I am?* Dax only snapped his jaws.

"I'm here under Prince Ronan's protection," Layala shouted over the wind and beating of massive wings. She opened her mouth to go on, but they dropped into a sudden dive, and a scream tore from Layala. Tears streamed down the sides of her face from the speed of the wind. With his wings pinned to his sides, Dax zipped down almost completely vertically with his tail straight up behind them. Weaving between houses, and trees, and bridges like it was an obstacle course. The ground level wasn't far below now, and he wasn't slowing. *I'm going to die! I'm going to die!*

CHAPTER 30

D ax's wings popped out with a snap and caught the air. Dragon and rider slowed, floating down like a feather, and with gentle ease, Dax's legs touched the ground with a rumbling clatter.

"Next time can you not try to kill me?" Layala said, finally letting go of the spike, her arms stiff and achy from the tight grip she held.

He grunted and shot steam from his nostrils. Layala watched him for a moment. Dax couldn't speak, could he? The other two male dragons landed lightly and shifted into their human forms. They each wore blue-gray robes tied at the waist and loose pants that reached mid-calf and brown sandals on their feet. With wings spread wide, a red dragon insignia was embroidered above the left breast. So dragons did possess magic. How else could they appear in clothes?

The sapphire female dragon who'd taken a nasty downturn shot at them like an arrow and just before

she impacted, she shifted into a human form and her boots hit the ground. "Where is Prince Ronan?" she demanded. Her hair was as blue as her dragon scales, tied back into a tight bun on top of her head, and her skin as white as Dax's pearl. She touched her hip and a sword appeared in her palm. Layala balked. It had somehow been veiled before.

A low rumble came from Dax but that was all. Sapphire put a hand on her hip then threw it into the air in frustration. "You will see punishment for this Dax. I don't care if Prince Ronan gave you permission to bring in an outsider. It must be cleared with *Crown* Prince Yoren, King Drake or Queen Nyrovia." So Ronan was a second-born prince perhaps? Third or fourth? How many children did dragons have? She held out her hand and curled her fingers. "Give her to me."

Dax rose up a little higher, pushing out his big chest and shook his head. At least he had Layala's back, or the word of his prince at least, however far down the line he may be.

"Utter fools," Sapphire turned to the male beside her, with salt-and-pepper hair. "You deal with Ronan today. I don't have the patience." She whirled around on her heel and stomped away. Layala's gaze followed her; the shifter marched toward a castle. Gold pillars wrapped around the front, holding up an overhanging balcony with creeping vines and flowers blooming along the railing. The beige color reminded her of sand. She looked up, and up and up. The castle seemed to go on forever until it reached the clouds. Dragons

flew in and out, from different balconies. Others sat tall and erect on perches, staring out over the rest of the city; sentinels, she presumed. At the base level, wooden doors large enough to fit a dragon as large as Dax, opened inward to allow the sapphire shifter to enter. In comparison, she looked no bigger than a pixie walking inside the average elf-sized doorway.

The sound of beating wings lifted Layala's sights to the sky, the bronze dragon carrying Thane landed gently beside them. And Prince Ronan, in his winged human form, dropped down with Piper in his arms. The others were close behind. Layala wasn't sure but she thought she saw Leif slapping at a sparrow diving at his head.

Ronan grinned at the salt-and-pepper-haired shifter standing with his arms tucked behind his back and an expression of clear annoyance. Ronan set Piper on her feet and strode ahead. "Where is my father? I have some exciting guests."

"Eating lunch with the queen and your brothers. Where you should be," he answered.

Ronan patted him hard on the shoulder. "No one expects me to eat every meal with them at my age. Almost six hundred years of the same old boring conversations. It's absurd."

"They do when it's your mother's birthday," the male clipped.

"Dragon's piss," Ronan murmured, rubbing his chin. He turned around and faced Dax. "Why didn't you remind me?" he waved a hand in a sign of

dismissal and pointed at Vaper. "You should have reminded me."

Thane slid down the dragon's shoulder, onto his elbow and then landed gracefully on his feet. Layala peeked over the edge. The distance to the ground made her feel a little woozy, but she slipped out of her vine and prepared herself to get down. Thane's dismount made it look simple. With a deep breath, Layala lifted her leg over and prepared to slide down. Without warning, the dragon's body vanished from underneath her and she was free falling. Layala clawed at the air reaching for something, *anything* to hold onto until she slammed into Dax's human arms. His smile told her he knew exactly what he did.

Layala smacked his chest. "You scared me on purpose. Prick." Her heart beat so loudly she had no doubt everyone could hear it.

Thane chuckled quietly beside them. He was seriously laughing? She looked around and they all were. Even the stiff guards broke their looks of annoyance. Maybe he'd done it to break the tension. Layala wiggled out of his arms and shoved him away from her when she was on solid ground again. "Some warning would be nice."

"I like her," Prince Ronan said. He clasped his hands together. "Let's go interrupt lunch, shall we? And wish mother dearest a very happy birthday."

Thane quietly cleared his throat. The sun beat down on him, bringing out the flecks of gold in his dark-brown hair. It was wind swept and falling loose

from the ponytail at the nape of his neck after the dragon ride. "I'd rather make a good impression, if you don't mind, Prince Ronan. Perhaps it would be better if we waited to be invited in by the king and queen."

"Well, you're no fun." In two strides he was before Layala. He wrapped his hand around hers and pulled her along beside him. "Fine, I'll just take your betrothed..."

What is he doing? Layala walked beside him but gave Thane a questioning look. His clenched jaw rippled, and the harshness set to his eyes reminded her of the fury of a gathering storm.

Ronan grinned. "I'll tell mother and father that she's *my* betrothed now."

Layala jerked her hand out of his grasp. "We're definitely not doing that." She was under the impression this prince was a troublemaker and she didn't want any part of it. Not to mention Thane looked like he was about to say some things they all might regret.

The guard with the gray-silver hair rolled his eyes. "Don't ruin the queen's day by telling them you're betrothed to an *elf*, Prince Ronan. You cause her enough strife."

"Oh, but she's much more than just an elf." He shoved his hand into the middle of Layala's back driving her toward the male. "Smell her."

Layala scoffed. *Smell me?* Could he scent her magic?

"That is improper, Ronan," he said sharply,

keeping his stiff posture. "And who are these people? Why have you brought them here?"

Layala rolled away from Prince Ronan, but he caught her waist and tugged her flush against his side. "This is Layala Lightbringer, betrothed to the... *disputed* King Thane of the elves of Palenor." He winked at Layala and turned to Thane with a sweeping arm. "Said king. And their companion Piper Fireheart, and the trio, we'll call them."

Fennan looked more than annoyed with the prince. His scowl was hot enough to burn.

"Then you should take your hands away from King Thane's betrothed before you start a war."

Ronan chuckled and flicked his wrist. "Oh, he knows it's just fun and games."

Did he though? And was it fun and games? They met Ronan not even an hour ago and knew absolutely nothing about him other than he was almost six hundred years old and forgot his mother's birthday. Layala shoved his hold off her waist and stepped to Thane's side. His magic radiated again but only a whisper of it. "If he touches you again, break his hand or I will." Then they'd really start a war, except Thane didn't have the backing of his father's military, but they didn't know that, did they?

"If you insist on propriety, Vaper and I will go tell them you're here. Dax will stay. The rest of you may go." He waved off the other dragons who escorted them in like they were children. "Dax won't say much. Poor Daxy lost his tongue about a century ago." Dax

lifted his middle finger at Ronan. The apparent universal sign for "piss off".

Salt-and-pepper sighed and started for the castle. "I will go inform your father. At least if it's from me, he won't think it's another one of your tales."

"I resent that comment," he said, stepping beside the shifter. "And you're not taking credit for my discovery." They disappeared into the massive doorway leaving the elves with Dax and another guard.

The guard in the blue-gray robe gestured to the left where a three-tiered fountain quietly trickled water over each golden lip into a bigger pool at its base. "You may have a seat over by the fountain while you wait."

Thane took hold of Layala's hand, intertwining his fingers between hers, and in a casual stroll they started for the fountain. Piper fell into step on Thane's other side. And *the trio* kept a close pace behind. The three Ravens looked around, eyes narrowed and bodies tense as if a threat might come at them at any moment. Layala felt much safer knowing they were around.

"Prince Ronan informed me he has a twin, Yoren," Piper said. "I have a feeling they are more rivals than close allies."

"Did he tell you anything else useful?" Thane asked. They came to the sand-colored stone edge of the pool and sat. Thane leaned forward with his elbows on his thighs waiting for Piper to answer. Layala placed her hand against his back and then slid

her fingers along the leather straps that held his swords. A large pine tree offered shade from the afternoon sun though it wasn't warm enough out here to need the coverage.

Piper nodded. "There is a ball tonight for his mother's birthday."

Layala's eyebrows furrowed. "So he didn't forget."

"Nope." Piper watched the entry of the castle acutely. "He asked me to be his date."

His date? Already? Layala turned to see Fennan's reaction. He kept chatting with Siegfried, acting like he didn't hear but she knew he did.

Thane sat up tall and ran his hand over his stubble. "What did you say?"

"I said that it would depend on a lot of things. Like us being invited, and not to be the main course. He thought that was funny."

"I'm sure the rumors that dragon shifters regularly eat elves and humans are exaggerated. We never see dragons in Palenor," he held up a finger, "with the exception of Varlett." Thane slid his hand around Layala's waist then lifted her onto his lap. He rested his chin on her shoulder and hugged her around her middle. His lips grazed her ear. "Just in case they forget you're mine." He lowered his voice. "It makes me crazy when other males touch you."

"I'm proud of you for not losing your temper," Layala said with a smile.

"I contemplated ripping the heart from his chest."

Piper looked over, bouncing her legs nervously.

"And then we'd all be dead. I estimated at least five thousand dragons in the city with the houses I could see from the air. We are at their mercy."

Thane grew an arrogant smirk. "You underestimate me, Piper."

She scoffed and shook her head. "Oh, so you think you can take on an entire legion of dragon shifters by yourself? Ones that are clearly capable of magic. Need I remind you Varlett nearly got the job done all on her own."

Ouch, even Layala winced at that one. Thane grunted and nuzzled his face into the nape of Layala's neck. The scruffy hairs on his chin tickled and she laughed, pushing him away. "Stop it. You're making me look like a lovesick teenager."

He nipped her earlobe. "Oh, you definitely have Thane-fever. Maybe I should take you somewhere to see if we can cure it." His wandering hands slid up and cupped her breasts.

"Thane." Layala pushed his hands back to her waist. "Now isn't the time to be thinking with your rod and berries."

Piper let out a loud "ha" then slapped her hand over her mouth. "The public display of affection is a little disgusting," Piper said, but she smiled through every word. "And yeah, keep the rod in check, would you? We have scheming to do."

"I'd think a lot more clearly if—" Thane pushed up, arms still firmly around Layala, bringing them both to their feet.

Prince Ronan appeared in the massive doorway, leading a host of guards, effectively cutting off Thane's statement. They all wore those same blue-gray robes, cropped pants and sandals. But these guards had their wings on display and spears in their hands. The prince held out his arms with a grin, rushing down the steps. "I hope you like to dance because you're cordially invited to attend the royal ball of House Drakonan. Special guests of King Drake, himself. You're going to need new attire."

CHAPTER 31

With damp hair from a bath and in only his undergarments, Thane stood on a raised sand-colored platform with his arms out to his sides. One male attendant held up a measuring stick, the wood point poked into Thane's armpit, another held up different scraps of fabric of various colors, contemplating each one carefully then tossing them aside. He'd been fitted like this before, but this attendant was much more particular than those he had at home. There was a pile of color scraps on the floor now. Not a single one sufficed?

Ronan lounged in a scarlet velvet high-backed chair, pulling bits of raw, red meat and tossing it to a silky black panther. The giant cat snatched the food out of the air and licked its wide jaws. Thane couldn't help but keep an eye on the predator. He'd never seen a panther before and couldn't believe how large it was, bigger than any dog, even wolf he'd encountered.

One of Ronan's legs hung lazily over the arm of the

chair. "So why are you here, Prince Thane? Are you finally desperate enough to ask for help against the cursed elves? What do you call them?"

"Pale ones."

The cat growled and swiped at his foot. "Be nice, Lyndora," he chided and tossed her more.

The attendant in front of Thane grinned. The smoky black cloth in his hand paired with an emerald green appeared to be a match. Although the colors looked like a dozen others he'd tossed aside.

Thane lifted a shoulder. "Is that something you'd consider?" It wasn't why he came but even if a handful of the dragons joined their cause, they'd have a better chance of defeating Tenebris and getting his throne back. His five hundred Ravens alone couldn't do it. Not even with Thane and Layala's magical power.

"My father? Never." He popped a piece of the raw meat into his own mouth. Thane wouldn't normally stare but then Ronan licked the blood running down his wrist. This certainly wasn't Palenor. "King Drake is in constant skirmishes with the other dragon tribes."

"Other tribes?" Thane was embarrassed to admit he knew almost nothing about the Dragon Kingdom. If he'd had more time, he would have gone to the mage's tower and studied the dragons.

Ronan practically purred; delight filled his features. "Well, this is a surprise. It's not often I get to teach someone about dragon courts. My father may call himself King of the Dragons but there are four major tribes. Ours is the largest. The other three can't

agree on anything, so they don't band together, thankfully or they'd overthrow us." He paused and stared out the window thoughtfully. "However." He hopped to his feet and set his meat on a small round corner table. The panther stood on her hind legs, took the leftovers into her mouth, and sauntered off. Ronan tucked his arms behind his back and squared his shoulders. "I might consider joining your cause."

As much as Thane wanted to believe this good news, there must be a catch. He'd barely met Ronan and he'd consider going to war? A war they'd always stayed out of. No one did anything for free, especially royals. So, what would he want in return? But there was a small chance, perhaps a small mercy of the Maker; Ronan wanted to make a name for himself, and fight for the elves. Or maybe he wanted to upset his parents. He was difficult to read.

It felt like everything was against him and Layala, even fate at this point.

The attendants stepped away with shallow bows to him and Ronan and disappeared into another room. Thane let his arms rest at his sides and stepped down from the dais. "As you know, my father and I are not on good terms. In fact, you could say we have become enemies. He has an agreement of sorts with Mathekis, the pale one general."

Ronan's light eyebrows shot up, wrinkling his otherwise smooth forehead. "Now that must be a fascinating tale. I wondered what happened between you two. We only heard you became king when your

father died in battle and then miraculously Tenebris returned. Though we haven't heard much after."

"It's fairly simple," Thane said, trying to keep his bitter feelings from showing in his tone. He looked out the window at the late afternoon sunlight streaming in on the miniature potted bonsai tree, picturing his father standing at the top of the hill with his army. A part of Thane was still angry he ran. "I tried to kill him so now I'm seen as the usurper king. It all comes down to him wanting more power. He wishes to be a mage and he'll bring back our enemy to do it. No one knows or believes that's what he wants. For most it's unfathomable that he'd want to bring back the Black Mage when he's spent his whole life in war against the pale ones."

"And he needs your girl to accomplish that," Ronan stated. He grew a slow smile, very pleased with himself. "I know who she is."

How could Ronan possibly know that Mathekis could use Layala to bring back the Black Mage? Thane only knew that because he'd spied on his father. It wasn't common knowledge. To everyone else she was the savior of Palenor, destroyer of the Void. Other than the fanatics who believed she was evil due to the sign at her birth. "What makes you think that?"

"General deductions. Your father has an obsession with this girl, enough to magically bind you to her as a child, and tear apart his kingdom to find her, and now he's formed an alliance with Mathekis. Obviously, she has some part to play." Ronan's boots tapped heavily

on the stone floor as he walked toward a sandstone shelf filled with books. "But you love her. She's not just your betrothed. You will protect her even against your own father. You have your Ravens, an elite force of elven warriors, but that's not enough to fight Tenebris and the pale ones. And you came to ask for our aide. Am I right so far?"

Ronan was smart and cunning, and seemingly had others fooled into thinking he was the fool. "In part," Thane lied. It never occurred to him to ask for their aid, simply because he worried they were another enemy, not a potential ally. Ronan, and the dragon court in general, was much different than he'd anticipated.

"If your father wanted magic, he could have come to us. We could have taught him nature's magic." He paused for a moment. "I understand what you do is an innate power within you, the same as my gift to shift into a dragon. But we learn simple enchantments and spells. Without it we'd all be walking about naked after shifting."

Thane chuckled. "I've seen little bits of the magic. How?"

"By using the energy of nature around us. It takes many years of practice but what is time to an elf?"

That might have been true in the past but not in Thane's life. "In Palenor, any moment could be your last. The once peaceful nature of elves is sullied by the horrors of war."

"It's a good thing you're not too peaceful or you'd

be eaten alive here in dragon territory. You don't want to look like prey to the predator."

Thane licked his dry lips and rubbed his arm absently. "I wasn't alive at the time, but many said you abandoned the elves when the pale ones arose. You've refused contact with us."

"I was young then, but we've always remained neutral. We didn't want to involve ourselves in the curse you brought upon Palenor. We feared losing ourselves to our beast forms as punishment." He tugged a blue, leatherbound book from the shelf. The gold lettering was in a language Thane didn't recognize. "Make no mistake, that's what it is. A punishment for upsetting the symmetry of nature. The high elves took and took, seeking to grow more powerful, the same as your father is now. Those who weren't mages sought to become mages. They asked for things not given to them. The Maker decides who is a magic bearer and who is not. It wasn't just the Black Mage's fault the curse came. He was but the conduit for your greed. The All Mother, the overseer of balance in all things, is not pleased with the elves."

Another chill ran down Thane's back. He'd never heard it described quite like that. He knew that the Maker took the elves' magic, but he always thought it was because of the Black Mage and the pale ones. He didn't like to think that the true villain of the elves might be themselves.

He'd never heard the term All Mother. Thane only dabbled in religious beliefs. He believed in a creator,

the Maker most referred to, but that was the extent of his thoughts on the matter. He supposed the zealots who built shrines in the name of his mate turned him away from it all. They praised her like a divine being, as they would him if they knew what he was capable of.

Ronan held out the book to Thane. "You might find this interesting."

The heaviness of it settled into his palm. It was at least a thousand pages and must weigh ten pounds. Thane flipped open the heavy cover. The title was unreadable to him. He flipped through the pages stopping at a drawing. Now *that* he could understand. Riders rode on the backs of dragons, clashing with one another among the clouds. Wings tore, wicked teeth sunk into dragon scales. The warriors on the backs of the dragons wore winged helmets much like his Ravens. He flipped through more pages, more drawings. Was this the history of Adalon? The sketches beheld great battles, kings' and queens' portraits, one name and face he recognized: his great-grandfather, High King Dramus. The crown on his head was the very same his father wore, gold and rubies and with etches of ivy. He ruled for a thousand years before stepping down to allow his son High King Scarvan to rule. Both ended up dying in battle against the Black Mage before Tenebris took the throne.

"Did dragons fight in the last war? I thought..."

"No," Ronan said. He walked over to the open window, leaned down to a silver-petaled rose, and

inhaled. "Those depictions are of the battles between the gods, long before the Black Mage. They were gods and goddesses from the Runevale realm. That war spilled over into this realm, Adalon." He paused, giving Thane a thoughtful look. "You're a descendant of one of the gods from Runevale. I can smell it in your magic, in your very blood."

Thane nodded, but it bothered him that he could *smell* it, and why was he so interested in his lineage? And the way he treated Layala, telling the others to smell her... he thought it might be because of her magic but what if there was more. "So I've been told. But if you can smell it, that would mean you've met one of these gods before." And if they no longer walked this realm, how was that possible?

"I have once, but that's a story for another time."

"You met an actual god and that's a story for another time?"

He chuckled. "He was a descendant, or so we thought."

How many realms were there? Thane flipped through the pages to find the one with the dragons in battle. "You'll have to forgive my ignorance. I don't know this language and our records of the past were destroyed or lost during the great elven war, and as you know, many died during the war, so we don't have a host of old elves who remember. The old gods are nothing but tales to my people now and I've never heard of other realms. I assume that means a place not of Adalon?"

"From what I've read, the realms align but don't immediately connect and there are those who can travel between them. Some of the gates were opened at one time. Dragon shifters came from Ryvengaard along with the faeries. Elves and humans have always lived in Adalon. Other creatures were brought over during the gods' battles or sometime long ago."

Thane's mind drifted to the unnamed forest with giants and wicked creatures that came out at night. Someone had trapped them for as long as anyone could remember. "Why did the gods and goddesses leave?"

He shrugged. "We believe they were called home."

Thane licked the tips of his fingers and turned the page and stilled. Drawn in color was an ornate, golden scepter with a rough-cut stone, like the sketch from the journal they took from Brunard. Maker above, if he could only read the text. He took a risk, tilting the book so that Ronan could see the page. "What is that?" He needed to make sure he was correct.

"The Scepter of Knowing." That's also what the journal said.

"What does it do?"

Ronan narrowed his eyes and stepped away from the window. "It's a powerful tool. The two pieces were separated, and it's forbidden to join them." His suspicion shifted to a smile. "We should see if your suit is ready for the ball."

If his words weren't clear enough, his demeanor was. The Scepter of Knowing paired with the All

Seeing Stone just as Brunard said. Thane shut the book with a snap and set it on the nearest table. Now he had to figure out how he was going to convince them to give him a scepter that was forbidden to join with the All Seeing Stone.

LIGHT STRING MUSIC played from the corner of the grand hall. The ceiling was at least a hundred feet tall and painted with stunning depictions of dragons flying among white puffy clouds in a blue sky. Golden vases lined the pearl-colored walls and overflowed with shiny gold coins and precious jewels, even spilling onto the white marble floor at the base. It was so vast and airy here. Huge open windows with ornate crown moldings let in a breeze. This hall made the one in Castle Dredwich look small. There was room for at least ten full-sized dragons to shift and fly in here.

The people walked around and stood in groups around food and drink tables. The females dripped jewelry from their necks, ears, wrists, and ankles. Huge, even obscene gold and silver pieces that must be heavy. Displays of wealth no one here lacked and not even Thane had ever seen. Thane's black suit was simple, tailored perfectly to his muscular form and the green undervest shimmered in silk. The only jewelry he wore was gold cufflinks with an emerald at the center.

He tapped his shoe on the floor by the grand hall's

entrance, waiting for Layala and Piper to be brought as promised. How long had it been? The ladies typically took more time to get ready, but he didn't like to be separated from them in a foreign place, no matter how cordial the people seemed so far.

Fennan stood beside him, arms folded, eyes roaming the place for danger. He wore gold hoops near the tips of his ears, something he only did for special occasions, and the ivory suit he wore made his black skin appear even richer. Their hosts graciously gave his three Ravens party attire as well, and Leif combed his hair for once. The tattoos on his forehead and temples made him stand out all the more. Siegfried looked utterly out of place in his black suit and shiny shoes. Thane suspected he wore his long dark-blond hair down to cover his ears and shield his face. He preferred armor over dress attire and the shadows over attention. And they were on display tonight.

A pair of ladies in white flowing gowns that brushed the glossy floor, with gold trim and white-blonde hair stopped in the entryway beside him. Their tan skin and violet eyes glimmered like jewels themselves. Identical faces tilted toward him. "Greetings," they said at once and strode forward with their hips swinging. "Have a wonderful time."

"Those must be the twin blues that brought us in," Leif said. "Cousins of the royals. I recognize their voices."

Siegfried nodded his agreement.

Many others passed by them, gawking and glaring.

Some whispered about their pointed ears and shorter stature. Although each of the elves was over six foot three, the dragons pushed seven feet or more, even the females were as tall or taller than Thane. Others talked about their beauty, for each elf was handsome in their own right. Thick braids along the sides of Thane's head swept the hair away from his face into a tie at the base of his skull where the majority of his locks flowed freely to his upper back putting his pointed ears on display. He had no reason to hide who he was. "Keep your guard up, no matter how friendly they seem. And don't drink more than a few sips of wine. We need our heads clear."

"Yes, sire," Leif said, watching the crowd with caution.

Lightly clearing his throat, Fennan leaned closer to Thane's side. "Should we scout the castle for the you-know-what while everyone is distracted?"

Ronan left a single guard, the mute, Dax, while he "attended to some business". The guard might not be able to talk but his eyes and ears were fine. He stood on the other side of the wide archway opening. At least he didn't hover. With a quick glance his way, Thane whispered, "Siegfried, go do what you do best." If anyone could find the secret hiding place of the scepter, it was him. As silent as the night sky, the Wraith vanished. "You two," Thane said to Leif and Fennan. "Mingle. Find out what you can about this place. Find a way out that doesn't require flying."

Leif stepped into the party without hesitation and

snagged a glass of wine off a table as he went by. It wasn't long before a pair of females approached him. Leif was a good talker, and an even better flirt.

Leaning forward, Fennan peeked inside the massive hall once again. The four colossal golden thrones sat empty. Even with his own rules, the two adjacent, four-tiered fountains trickling what appeared to be maroon wine called to his parched throat. He really needed to stick with water. "What's wrong, Fennan?" He hadn't moved yet.

He brushed his hand over his short black curls. "I—wanted to wait for Layala and Piper."

Thane rubbed his chin. Perhaps this was a good time to talk to Fen. Was he ready to give up all others for Piper? If not, Thane wouldn't approve. He couldn't dictate what they did but he'd make his opinion known. "She's Prince Ronan's date tonight."

He shoved his hands into his pockets and shifted his weight. "I know. I just want to make sure the girls are alright. Don't you think it's odd they're taking so long? I mean, my future queen could be in danger."

Trying to cover his worry for Piper with Layala? Why didn't he feel he could talk to Thane about this? They'd been friends forever, talked about everything. Thane knew of almost every romantic relationship he had, and it was Fennan who gave him advice with Layala. "She's proven she can handle her own. And you know it takes them longer to get ready."

"True." He averted his rich, red-brown eyes. He still didn't go anywhere.

"Are you and Piper..."

"No," he said quickly. "No, she's too good for me. And it would be odd, right? I've known her for years and I haven't exactly forgone other ladies."

"So, what if she dated Leif then?"

"Bloody hell, no. He's not good enough for her either."

"Maybe you should let her decide who is good enough." Thane nodded at a pair of ladies passing by. "I expect you to be on your best behavior while she's with Ronan. She's a big girl. She can do what she wants. That includes allowing Leif or Ronan or anyone else to flirt with her." There absolutely could not be another standoff like on the island here or it would risk their mission.

Fennan pressed his lips together, then he waved a hand and chuckled. "That was nothing. Don't worry. I'm always smooth at these types of things. I'll find our way out of here." He put on a smile, although it didn't appear genuine, and he faded into the crowded room.

A strange itch at the back of his head made him look over his shoulder, and he smiled. Layala glided alongside Piper, grinning back at him. Maker above, he didn't think he'd ever get used to how stunning she was. Everyone else seemed to fade away. Her silver-blue gown cinched at the waist, thin straps over her shoulders and a V-neck revealed the perfect amount of cleavage and collarbone. His stomach fluttered a little and he held out his hand to her. Her touch sent a heat pulse through him. "Hello, my dear."

"This is some place, isn't it?" Her blue eyes slid down his form. "I almost forgot how wonderful you look in a suit. You've been my dirty warrior for weeks."

He chuckled and kissed her jaw, right next to her ear. "I'd love to get dirty with you later." A slight blush pinked her cheeks. He loved that he had that effect on her.

Ronan cleared his throat. "Well, aren't you two precious." His arm was looped with Piper's, and the mischievous smirk he wore unsettled Thane's gut. Ronan wore a seven-peaked gold crown with round diamonds inlaid in each. "The king and queen shall arrive soon. But it would be rude to approach them. You'll need to dance, drink, eat, be merry, and perhaps after, they'll call an audience with you."

"Perfect," Thane said. "I'm starving."

"Luckily, we have more food than you could ever want. Dragons have a salacious appetite and beastly tempers. Beware." He brought Piper's hand to his mouth and kissed her knuckles. Surprisingly, Piper stared up at him almost mesmerized, eyes glittering in the sunlight cascading in from the windows. Thane arched an eyebrow. He had a feeling this prince had a salacious appetite for pretty maidens, and Piper was something new and unconquered.

"Oh, there's my brother. Shall we?" Ronan swept an arm to the right where tables filled with meats, fruits and bread waited, and a tall male with a rose-gold crown stood with a group of seven surrounding him. Prince Yoren differed from Ronan in almost every

aspect. His skin was dark brown, and his short black hair reminded Thane of strands of silk. He was taller than Ronan by at least three inches and lean whereas his brother was bulky and broad. Where Ronan appeared relaxed, Prince Yoren was stiff, and held a stern expression.

Thane held out his arm to Layala and she wrapped her hands around it. She leaned in close to his side and lowered her voice, "What do you think? Do we have a chance of getting the scepter?"

"The dragons have forbidden joining it with the stone so... we may have to steal it. We just need to find it and by the size of this city, that could take a while."

"How do you know this?" She smiled as they passed a group of five shifters that observed them with a little too much lip licking for Thane's liking. His jaw tightened. He didn't like to be looked at like a meal.

"I saw it in a book upstairs and asked Ronan about it. He doesn't know we want it, and I've not told him we have the stone."

"I don't know if it's wise to steal something from the people we want help from. Ronan told me you asked for his help to fight Tenebris."

Thane stopped and tilted his head. "I didn't ask. He assumed that's why we're here which is to our benefit. And we need the scepter more than him." He didn't like being a thief either but desperate times shoved people into the shadows of transgression.

CHAPTER 32

"Meet my new friends, Yoren," Ronan said, gesturing toward the three elves. "This is High King Thane of Palenor and Layala Lightbringer, his betrothed, and my lovely date, Piper Fireheart."

Prince Yoren dipped his head slightly. "Greetings. It's been a long time since we welcomed the high elves. I hope our court has treated you well so far."

"Quite well," Thane said. "I'm more than impressed with your palace and I haven't seen a spread to match this in years. I daresay the high elves must up their creativity."

Prince Yoren smiled. "You'll forgive our initial reaction to you and yours, I hope. We don't allow outsiders inside our city often, especially high elves." His golden eyes trailed over Layala, pausing on the lily's mark on her arm then he briefly inspected Piper. "Because of the curse on your land. You understand."

"I do," Thane said. "And I am grateful for your

hospitality. Had I known it was the queen's birthday, we wouldn't have crashed the party."

Ronan waved a dismissive hand. "She's had over a thousand now."

Prince Yoren turned a steely gaze on him. "Mother wishes to speak with you. I hope you have a gift for her."

He grew a serpentine smile. "*They* are my gift. The entire court is talking about them. Look at everyone watching us. She enjoys attention. Everyone will think she invited them to her party."

Thane peeked over his shoulder. Nearly every person here was fixated on them like a child with a new toy. Some starred with lust, others with curiosity, a few like they might shift into beast form and attack. The twins he saw earlier toyed with their hair, licked their lips, coy smiles all directed at him. Many of the males watched Layala and Piper with a hunger that raised the hair on the back of his neck. Unlike the elves, beauty wasn't inherent among the dragon shifters. They were similar to humans in how much their features differed, and the range from homely to stunning varied but most were neither. Some had large noses or eyes a little too close together, weak chins, or crooked teeth. Both princes were handsome in their own ways. Thane expected their mother would have been chosen for her beauty.

The music stopped and everyone who'd stood in the center of the room moved off to one side or the other, leaving a wide gap. The king and queen strolled

inside. The king wore a gold, foot-tall crown on his black hair and a navy-blue robe that pooled on the floor behind him. White fur trim around his neck and down his front. Prince Yoren inherited his bronzed-black skin and raven-colored hair from his father. The queen's complexion was white as milk, and her thick, silvery-blonde hair reached the floor in waterfall waves. Her ruby-red gown hugged each curve and the fabric dragged at least three feet behind her. The crown on her head was as tall as the king's, and sparkling rubies covered every inch of it. As Thane guessed, she was easily the most beautiful dragon in the room.

A guard tapped his staff on the shimmering marble floor three times. "Your king and queen."

Everyone dropped to one knee aside from the princes. Layala looked at Thane with wonder glittering in her eyes. He slowly shook his head and took hold of her hand, squeezing it gently. He did not kneel to monarchs, fallen king or not, and neither would she.

Whispers skittered around the room.

"They don't kneel?"

"Disrespect."

"Who are they?"

Thane drew in a deep breath and kept his shoulders back and chin high. The dragon king and queen glided by without sparing a glance. Ronan leaned his shoulder into Thane. "That thing between your legs must be big."

Thane cracked a smile. "It's quite small actually. Tiny even."

Chuckling, Ronan shook his head. "I didn't think you'd be funny. But let's hope mother dearest doesn't bite your head off for that. She has a temper hotter than the sun as do many dragons, although everyone will be on their best behavior with elven guests."

King and Queen Drakonan took their seats. The music resumed and everyone rose and chatted as before. King Drake's severe gaze landed on Thane, and he leaned over the thick gold armrest to his wife. She turned those wintery eyes on him and Layala then she looked away as if they weren't worth the attention.

"Why don't you two have some wine?" Prince Yoren said and gestured toward the nearby golden fountain trickling the blush liquid. "And help yourself to the food."

"We will, thank you," Layala said, and took Thane's hand to saunter over to a spread full of meat, consisting of different animals. From full boars, some cooked others raw with chunks taken out of it—that made his stomach turn a little—to venison, rabbit on a stick, and fully-roasted pheasants and chickens. The rich hors d'oeuvres and sweet desserts were but an afterthought.

Thane glanced at Piper; she slowly shook her head, and then patted Ronan's arm and continued her conversation with the prince. Nothing important from her either. It seemed they had their work cut out for them.

"Any ideas?" Layala asked, then tipped a full wine glass back.

Thane watched her down it a moment later and arched an eyebrow. "Thirsty?"

"A little," she said, sounding exhausted. "Ronan gave me a glass earlier. Have you tried it? It rivals Calladira's wine. And honestly this whole party is making me nervous."

"Well, slow down. Please. I have a feeling they want us drinking."

"Why would they?"

"Just trust me on that."

She looked at the swirling pink liquid. "This will be my last one."

"Right now, we need to fit into whatever mold they want us in. Be pleasant, smile a lot. We can't make them more suspicious than they already are. I already pissed them off by not bowing down." She started humming to the music and watching the dancers. With a frown he lightly touched her cheek, getting her attention. "They cannot know we want the scepter."

"I'm aware. Don't worry."

He smiled. "You look stunning. I can't help but stare."

"Stop," she said and giggled, bumping her shoulder into him. "You're trying to make me blush."

"If I wanted to make you blush," he said and slid his fingers down the back of her arm, "I'd tell you all about my dream the other night," he leaned closer, "and the sounds you made. I can't get them out of my

head. It's like a melody playing over and over." A light-pink shade colored her cheeks. "It's too easy."

She lifted her chin a little. "It's the wine, making me a little warm."

He laughed and wrapped his arm around her waist, pulling her in. "We'll have our own room tonight, I think."

She smiled coyly. "I made sure of it."

A group of seven shifters, three females and four males emerged from the crowd and surrounded them. Thane moved closer to Layala's side, placing a possessive hand on her lower back. One of the males, young, likely not over twenty couldn't seem to look away from Layala. Not that he blamed him. One of the ladies wore a five-emerald-piece necklace with so many diamonds it looked like an inverted tiara. She smiled and asked first, "How are you liking it here?" Followed quickly by a barrage of questions from the others.

"How old are the pair of you?"

"Have you ever seen dragons before?"

"What is it like in Palenor fighting against pale ones?"

Layala smiled and nodded, sipping her wine. Thane answered most of them. He knew she didn't like interacting with strangers like this. The last question was much deeper and harder to answer than the other fluff. He tried to keep it as light as possible given the context.

The music changed to a faster tune, and the same shifter who stared at Layala, held out his white-gloved

hand. "Oh, a favorite song of mine. Do you mind if I steal your beautiful betrothed for a dance? I'll bring her right back, promise."

Thane didn't blame him for being infatuated with her. But it grated on his nerves that he'd hardly taken his eyes off her since he'd approached. Thane ground his teeth and tried not to look like a jealous prick, but he was one. "What does the lady say?" If this party didn't require him to be on his best court behavior, he'd tell the bastard to piss off.

She set her empty wine glass on the nearby table. "Why not," she lifted her shoulder, and he immediately took her hand.

Thane watched to make sure he danced proper. One hand was high on her waist, the other clasped around her palm. The distance between them was... sufficient.

"Would you mind dancing with us then, Prince Thane?"

He turned to the icy-blonde twins he'd seen earlier. "Uh," he tugged on his collar. "Both of you?"

"One at a time, of course," the one on the left answered.

"Me first," said the other.

"Alright." Taking her hand, he led her onto the dance floor with the mass of other couples.

Layala looked and rolled her eyes over the shoulder of her dance partner. He tried not to laugh as he placed his hand on the twin's silky waist and took her other hand. She immediately stepped closer,

putting not even a finger's width between them. Thane cleared his throat and took a half step back and then moved into the dance. "So, what is your name?"

"I'm Devlyn and my sister's name is Destinee. We're friends of Prince Ronan's—second cousins on his mother's side. We flew in your friends."

"Ah, I thought you looked like the queen, and thank you for that."

"So, when's the wedding?"

"We haven't set a date yet," Thane said. *Unfortunately.*

She tilted her chin higher. "She's sweet, and Ronan says she's a mage, not to mention pretty, you should marry her before she gets away." Her tongue slid across her bottom lip. "Are you—hesitant to commit? I imagine as a future king you are rather picky on whom you will choose as your queen."

Thane sighed. He truly didn't want to have to put the queen's cousin in her place, but it looked like it was heading that way. "No, I'm not hesitant. We're at war in my land—it's complicated."

"You know, being engaged to be married isn't married." She slid her hand from his shoulder to his chest. "There's still time to... play."

Thane dropped both hands to his sides and dipped his head. "Thank you for the dance, Devlyn." He turned away to find Layala. This was a mistake. They should have given being cordial the middle finger and stayed together.

"I hope I didn't offend you," Devlyn stepped up

beside him. "You're so—beautiful." Her eyes dropped to her fidgeting fingers. "There's just something about you."

Unsure what to say, he kept searching for Layala among the couples still dancing around them. He spotted the one who'd asked her to dance, and she wasn't with him anymore. He scanned along the catering tables where they'd been before, and she wasn't there either. Leif, Fennan, and Piper all danced with partners so she was alone.

He turned to Devlyn with suspicion. Was this a play to get them apart?

"She's over there," Devlyn said, nodding toward the thrones. He finally spotted Layala standing off to the side, talking to Prince Yoren. Maker above, he was paranoid.

"Thank you," Thane said and moved across the room with hurried steps. When he reached her, he leaned down to her ear. "Are you alright?"

"I'm fine. Why?"

"I lost you for a moment."

"Oh," she smiled and rubbed his arm. "I was just talking to Prince Yoren about the music. This song is eight hundred years old. Fascinating." She giggled the way she did when she'd had a little too much wine. That nervous feeling he'd had all day intensified.

Prince Yoren nodded and took a glass of wine off the tray of a servant and handed it to Layala. Thane clenched his hands at his sides, tempted to snatch it away.

"It's my father's music, composed for my mother as a wedding gift." His eyes flicked to the queen still sitting stiffly on her throne, holding the hand of the king, but she smiled for the first time. "They only play it on her birthday now."

"It's nice. Will we get an audience with them?" Thane hardly noticed how much time had passed but the sun traded places with the moon. Massive torches on the walls lit up, candles bobbed above their heads, suspended in mid-air, bringing a hint of smoke and warm light. It was a wonder no wax dripped. The golden fountains of wine had thinned significantly, and the food tables dwindled to scraps.

"Appears that way," Prince Yoren answered.

Thane turned to the queen, curling her fingers in a "come here" motion.

"Don't fret. I'll keep an eye on your fiancée," Prince Yoren said, and turned to Layala. "How do you like the wine?"

Layala smiled. "It's the best."

With a deep breath, Thane ground his teeth again. They were trying to get her intoxicated. Wine tended to loosen the lips, but he couldn't ignore the queen's beckon, and against the tug in his gut, he left her. With a few long strides, he stood at the base of the queen's dais waiting to be addressed.

King Drake dipped his head. "Welcome to the court of dragons."

"Greetings, Princeling." The queen's pale-blue eyes

slid over him. She stood and glided down the steps. "I am Queen Nyrovia."

Thane bristled at the term "princeling" as if he was but a child. "Queen," Thane dipped his chin slightly.

She arched a sleek brow. "You do not bow?"

"No impudence but a High *King* of the Elves does not bow."

The cock of her brow and the downturn of her lips said she wasn't impressed. "*King*? I wasn't aware your father was dead."

"He's not."

She looked over her shoulder at King Drake. The corner of his mouth curled up and he said, "So the rumors are true. There is a discrepancy in leadership. Interesting."

"I'd like to introduce you to my betrothed, Layala Lightbringer." He glanced toward her, still beside Prince Yoren. She was laughing about something, though over the music and the chatter, he couldn't hear.

A smile spread across the queen's face. "Ah, yes. The stolen bride."

Stolen bride? How did the dragons know so much about them? Did Varlett have Queen Nyrovia's ear? He did a quick scan of the room to make sure she didn't hide in a corner somewhere, waiting for her moment to strike. If she was here, she wasn't in the open. Although, he didn't think it was possible for her to fly here so quickly.

The music changed to a wistful melody of flutes

and strings that brought people to the center for a dance.

Queen Nyrovia held out her hand to Thane. "Ask me to dance, Thane."

"It's King Thane," he corrected with a smile that had charmed many. "And would you like to dance, Queen Nyrovia?"

"How kind of you to ask."

Many watched and the dancing group cleared a circle as they stepped out onto the floor. Thane placed one hand on her hip and took the other in his grip. "What brings you to my court, King Thane?"

"I thought it was high time we rekindled the old friendship between dragons and elves. From the old stories, we were friendly once." He didn't know if that was true or not, everything he'd heard of dragons was they were ruthless and deadly, but it was worth a shot.

She smiled a saccharine smile. "Ah, and what do you have to offer in this new possible friendship?"

"Open communication with the elves, trade." He needed something to sweeten the deal, some reason that things would have changed over the last thousand years. Something that might tug at her heartstrings, make it more personal. "My betrothed is a mage, one of the last of her kind."

"And you're the descendent of a god. So?"

"We might help each other. You don't need to stay in the mountains forever."

"We like our mountains."

"There's nothing the elves have that you want? We

have gold." He smiled at that. If the overflowing vases of gold coins and precious jewels were any indication, they loved treasure.

"So do we."

"I'll be honest." He pressed his lips together a moment, considering the only thing he had left. "I'm here for selfish reasons. I want the maiden I love to be free from being hunted," Thane said. "I want to marry her and have babies with her and live in peace." If she agreed to help, maybe he could simply ask for the scepter. And every word he said was true. As much as he wanted Palenor to be safe, and for the war to end, and no more elves to turn, Layala changed everything. She was the real reason he was here.

She stared at him a moment, eyes glistening in the torchlight. Her grip on his shoulder tightened ever so slightly but then she tugged her gaze away and he felt her decision before she even spoke. "I do feel for you. I know what hunts her, but we will not join you in this plight nor open to trade. The risk is much too great." She tugged out of his grasp. "You're welcome to stay, dine, enjoy the luxuries we have to offer for as long as you like. Escape from the horrors of war for a while, make love to your betrothed without worrying someone will come for her, but there is no alliance between dragons and elves, *King*. We will not risk the curse being brought on our people to fight beside you." She lifted her chin and swept away with her crimson gown trailing behind her.

He sighed, standing alone in the middle of the

dance floor. They'd have to do things the hard way then.

Before Prince Yoren could get Layala to say something they all might regret, and that could truly be anything. She had the mouth of a front-line soldier, not a lady. He trudged across the floor, only to find her gone. Prince Yoren wasn't there either, Thane realized, and found him on the dance floor with a tall female wearing a diamond tiara.

Where was Layala then? He turned in a slow circle, heart beating a little faster the longer he looked and didn't find her. In the far corner, hidden partially by shadows, three males blocked someone in, someone in a silverish-blue gown. He swore under his breath and rammed his shoulders into several people on his way across the floor.

When he heard her say, "Don't touch me." He moved like shadows invading the land when the sun went down. His fingers dug into the shoulder of the shifter in the middle and jerked him back, sending him to the ground. The one on the right dropped her wrist and tucked his hands behind his back, like he could hide what he did. Thane grabbed him by the throat and slammed him into the wall.

"You messed with the wrong maiden." Thane slammed his head into the wall again but this time it cracked.

"I'm sorry," he wheezed.

"Hey, back off," a deep voice said behind him. "You

came to our party, elf. And you left your lady alone. That's fair game around here."

Heat flared in him like a lightning strike to dry grass. He dropped one offender and turned around with wild eyes. Before he could do anything, Layala threw her full glass of wine in his face and said, "Prick. I'm nobody's game."

The dragon shifter's backhand struck Layala in the face and knocked her into the wall. The thud of Thane's heart pounded in his ears. With a snarl, he stepped forward and shoved his hand straight into the dragon shifter's chest, through flesh, through bone, and gripped something soft, warm, and round. His skin shifted to shiny silver scales that might have saved him, and back to soft flesh several times within seconds. "Too late, dragon." His heart hit the ground with a wet plop, but no one screamed. Many in the room observed and whispered, and to Thane's surprise, the shifters kept sipping their wine and indulging in their company. His Ravens however, carefully made their way over.

Guards with scales covering their bodies rushed over and formed a half circle around them. Thane stood in front of Layala, body tense, hands curled into fists as the uncomfortable sensation of his magic biting to get free, pulsed with wave after wave. He had no swords, no arrows, but he never needed them. "Come at my mate, my people, or me, and you'll never see another sunrise."

The half dozen guards looked amongst each other, unsure, hesitant. They should be.

Prince Ronan pushed between a pair of guards and said, "I got to hand it to you, High King." He barely even glanced at the dead shifter on the ground. "You know how to liven up a party."

Thane's chest rose up and down with heavy breaths, he clenched his jaw and waited for what the dragon prince would do. Ronan nonchalantly tugged on his suit sleeve and then shooed at the guards. "Do something useful and get the body out of here. You act like this has never happened before." He turned and said loudly to the room, "The elf king just set the precedent. Don't trifle with him or his crew, and especially not his lady." He smiled at Thane. "I think we're going to have a lot of fun in the next few days."

Relieved he wouldn't have to fight a room full of dragon shifters, Thane wiped his bloody hand down the front of his suit then turned and scooped Layala into his arms. She held her red, already puffy cheek and leaned her head against his shoulder. In a world less cruel Thane might have been a saint, but this one required a monster.

CHAPTER 33

The fire crackled and popped in the hearth set in the sandstone wall. The open balcony doors let in a cool breeze through the bedroom Layala and Thane were given. After Thane killed someone, Layala thought for sure they'd have been tossed into a dungeon or at least outside the walls but instead, they'd been given a suite and room service. At the party she'd drunk too much and tried to leave to find somewhere to use the toilet. Those dragon shifters easily herded her into a corner and started interrogating her about the real reason she and the others were there. Bastards. She wasn't sure if they were sent by the royals, or if they had acted on their own. But it didn't matter now. Three days passed since the queen's birthday ball, and while the time since then was full of leisurely walks through gardens and exploring huge libraries, watching sanctioned fights in the courtyard with Prince Ronan as their escort, being in a foreign place left her worried and restless most

nights. The snarls of the fighting in the courtyard below went on for half the night. That was how the dragons settled disputes of any kind, with their claws and teeth, not usually to the death but she'd witnessed a few bodies dragged away, bloodied, and not breathing in the last couple of days. It was no wonder no one batted an eye when Thane tore out a heart. This place was unsettling, and she felt like she hadn't slept since they arrived.

Yet, the muffled deep voices of Thane and the others in the adjacent room soothed her already tired mind. She should be in there, talking with them about the plan they had in the works. But this bed was soft and the crackle of the fireplace, comforting. And with no fighting dragons in the courtyard, she tugged up the soft, silk blankets, turned on her side and let the night claim her...

CRICKETS CHIRPED and sweet jasmine swirled in the air. She walked in a lush garden gliding over a white cobblestone path. The silver gown she wore sparkled like the moonlight and stars above. It was so bright here she marveled up at the sky for a while. It took her a moment to notice but did the stars look different? Layala knew them well, it was the best way to navigate the land, but she couldn't find the three bright stars of the north shaped in a triangle... There were only two. *Odd*, she thought but kept walking. The fabric of her dress dragged lightly behind her until she spotted a

blooming night lily. She squatted down and grabbed hold, snapping its stem and then brought it to her nose. It reminded her of home, like this is what it should smell like. Although she and Aunt Evalyn tried to grow the flowers that only bloomed at night, they hadn't had much success.

"I've been waiting for you," said a deep voice.

A chill ran over Layala's skin, and she slowly lowered the lily. That wasn't Thane, though they sounded similar, a trick she'd decided. Layala blinked, suddenly aware that she was dreaming. She knew who waited there. She didn't want to run this time, didn't want to be afraid of the mage who tortured her sleep.

Standing, she turned to face him, chin raised high. The hooded, broad-shouldered male waited a yard away. His presence didn't seem as menacing this time, perhaps because she expected him.

"You're not running." He sounded surprised.

"No." Layala even took a step closer. A long dagger appeared in her hand. "But maybe you should be."

The sliver of light under his hood revealed a smile, a small scar across his chin, and a dimple. A breeze picked up pieces of her hair and made the fabric of his cloak float around his ankles. "You can't hurt me here."

"What do you want?"

"You must find me. I've waited a long time."

"That's not going to happen." In the back of her mind, she screamed at herself to wake up, to not speak to the Black Mage any longer. It felt wrong, felt like he was awake and alive in her dreamworld.

"It doesn't have to be this way. We don't have to be enemies." He waved his hand and the lily left Layala's fingertips and traveled to his. He looked at it as if it was special. "I can give you power."

"You're talking to the wrong person. I don't want power. I never have."

He was suddenly behind her, his fingers gliding along her upper back, down her arm. He grabbed a piece of her hair and brought it to his nose. She clenched her teeth but refused to show her disgust.

"Everyone wants power," he said and dropped her hair. His light steps circled around her. "You want vengeance. I will give you what your heart desires most."

She turned to watch him on her left. "I can get my own vengeance."

"Perhaps," he said. "But your enemies are vast, even more than you know, and much stronger than you are now. You are afraid of your own magic." He leaned close to her ear. "Afraid of what you truly are."

Bristling at his closeness, she turned to shove him, and he caught her wrists. She would have sworn he was physically there, gripping her as if his life depended on it. As she tried to wrench herself free, he began to laugh. "You can't even control your own mind. We're in your world, in your head. Come on, break free." She kicked out to sweep his legs and he vanished, appearing behind her. "Over here."

Whirling around with the dagger, she slashed, and he was gone again. She searched among the

bamboo and the exotic flora. A silver butterfly fluttered from one of the lilies and she watched it fly until it led her to him lying on a stone bench, with his hands behind his head. "You need me as much as I need you."

"You're wrong," she said, gripping her dagger tighter. "I have everyone I need already. And one day I will destroy you."

In a flash, he was in front of her, inches from her face. "Come and find me then," he hissed. "I dare you to try."

LAYALA SHOT UP IN BED, sweat soaking her hairline. She clutched the blanket and took in slow deep breaths through her nose. Maker, that was too real this time. Birds happily chirped with the morning sunrise. She could hardly believe the night came and went, when it felt like she barely closed her eyes. Thane's side of the bed appeared undisturbed. Had he stayed awake all night?

Setting her feet on the soft sheepskin rug, she slipped out of bed and peeked in the other room. Thane lay back in a huge beige armchair, staring up at the ceiling. Siegfried, Leif, and Fennan sat in a half circle around him. None of them slept? What had they been doing all night? That's when she saw the table between them all was full of silver and blue chips, playing cards and coins. The pile in front of Siegfried was the largest.

"You four stayed up all night playing poker? We have plans today."

In the middle of pulling his dark-blond hair back tight, Siegfried looked to Layala and stood. "Plans will continue." He gestured to the chair he'd been in and leaned against the wall.

She folded her arms against the morning chill, even the thick sweater she wore didn't defend from, and stepped into the room. Thane dropped his chin and smiled. "Hello, my dear. Did you get any sleep?"

She shrugged and sat in the soft, maroon armchair Siegfried had given up. "A little." Should she tell them about her dreams? About how this connection she had with the Black Mage seemed to be growing? "But I had a nightmare."

"Oh?" He cocked his head to the side. "Do you need me in there to chase them away?"

She rolled her eyes as the others laughed. "The Black Mage was in my dream. And—this wasn't the first time." She pawed at the tangles in her hair, thinking about the venom in his voice with the last words he said.

The four males looked back and forth between each other. Leif grumbled something about his Nana and prophetic visions but rested his chin on his fist and stared at her.

"What kind of dreams?" Thane's brows lowered and he sat forward, leaning on his thighs. His loose dark hair fell forward. She hadn't noticed it before, but it had gotten longer. It must reach his mid back now.

She thought about the first one he appeared in. "In the beginning, he would chase me through dark woods. And I was terrified." She chewed on her lower lip. "But this time... it felt real. Like it wasn't a nightmare at all but as if both of us were there, in the same garden together, talking."

Thane kept his face placid. "About what?"

"About waking him up, finding him. He said he could give me power."

Fennan shot to his feet and cursed. "You can't let him get in your head. What if it is real? What if he has found a way to get to you?"

"I'm not *letting* him in." She rubbed the back of her arms, shaking her head.

"But he has," Thane said slowly, eyes lined with concern. "He has gotten into your head. Is there more?"

Layala looked down, watching her bouncing toes. Angry tears stung. "I've heard his voice, calling to me even while awake."

"Why didn't you tell me this before?" Thane asked. He didn't sound angry but frustrated and worried.

"I thought it was you!" she stood and began to pace next to the low-burning fireplace. "When we were apart. *Come to me. I need you.* He sounded so similar to you and when I realized it wasn't, I didn't say anything because I was scared of what you would think." She shoved her hand toward Leif who looked more nervous than the rest. "You're afraid I'm like him, aren't you? Afraid that I'll go bad."

Leif shook his head, blinking rapidly. "No, Fight-bringer. You don't need to be afraid of that or what we think. You're good. I know you are. It's just disturbing that he's found his way to you. And I'm afraid for you. We need to stop him."

"How? He's dead and he still has more power than all of us."

Thane leaned back and his chest rose and fell. "You must find a way to keep him out. Is it every night?"

"No... just sometimes." This was the first time it had happened in days.

Thane stood and slid his hand around her waist and stopped her pacing. He wrapped his arms around her from behind and hugged her close. "It's your mind. You have the power there. You control it. Force him out."

"What if I can't?" she whispered.

"You can, Laya."

"Well, this just proves we need to get the scepter and fast," Fennan said. "We better pray to the Maker that today we have luck on our side. All the other days have been shit."

A knock at the door startled them all. Layala nibbled on her lower lip, hoping that whoever stood on the other side hadn't heard anything important.

Siegfried jerked his dagger loose and swept to the other side of the door, ready to get the jump on whoever it might be. Piper was the only one from their group not with them. Thane nodded to Siegfried, and he pushed down on the flat gold handle. The door

creaked open to reveal Prince Ronan and Piper. She looked so dainty next to him. At her five foot six and his over seven feet, his silver hair, and her bright red, they were quite the pair.

"Good morning, all," Ronan said cheerfully, and placing his hand on Piper's lower back, he escorted her in with him. He did a quick survey of the room and then his jaw dropped. "You didn't invite me to poker night? I'm offended."

Siegfried placed his dagger back and closed the door behind them, retaking his spot on the wall.

"You're more than welcome to join us tonight," Thane said.

"I think I will."

Layala noticed that his hand grazed Piper's, almost as if it was a request. She tucked her hand in her pocket but smiled up at him. Interesting.

"Anyway, we have a tour of the history museum this morning as requested. I'm intrigued that the elves are interested in dragon history."

Thane leaned his elbow on the fireplace mantel. "Ever since you showed me that book I've wanted to know more. Wars with gods, other realms, who wouldn't like to know more?"

Layala smiled. "It's fascinating." And it was, but so was the scepter.

CHAPTER 34

Thane marveled at two massive stone dragon sculptures overhanging the entrance to the museum. Their tails curled down wide pillars and their mouths were open to throw rainwater away from the building. The artist who carved the gray marble must have taken years with the detail from the teeth to thousands of divots for the shading of the scales. The massive dark wooden doors with a dragon wing etching on each side were pulled inward as they approached. If their suspicions were correct, the information they needed about the scepter would be here. The library held nothing of note, and what better place to keep the story of the scepter than here. With luck, it may very well lie in these walls.

They walked into an open area with a domed ceiling made of glass, letting in bright sunlight. "Wow, would you look at that," Leif said, pointing to the paintings on the left side of the wall. "It's Thane's grandfather, High King Dramus shaking hands with,"

he looked at Ronan, "is that..." he trailed off tapping a finger against his chin.

Ronan opened his mouth to speak but the lady on the right side of the door, sitting behind a massive cherry oak desk, blurted out, "It is King Drakonan. That depicts the last meeting with the high elves seven hundred and three years ago." She jumped to her feet, pushing her round, gold-rimmed glasses up her nose and strode out to meet them with her hands clasped together and a wide grin. "Greetings, Prince Ronan, and our elven guests. I am absolutely thrilled you want a tour." If she was any more excited, she'd start clapping. She gestured to the left. "Let's start here, shall we?"

Both sides of the walls were covered in paintings framed in pure gold by the looks of it. A small stone dragon fountain, no larger than a five-year-old child, sat in the center of the room, trickling water out of its mouth.

With his arm looped around Piper, Ronan looked back at the group. "Is there anything in particular you wish to see?"

All of them shook their heads and a chorus of nos echoed throughout the room. They didn't want to give away any suspicion of what they were after. Thane hung back as the group started the tour. The doorways to the left looked to hold statues, and to the right, shiny objects in glass cases. That's where he needed to go.

"This is called Winter's Dream," the lady began,

"and was painted in the year three twenty-two, by the marvelous Jonis Drevor. He's the oldest dragon alive in Adalon. He even remembers the great wars and our origin realm. This is one of the landscapes of his homeland."

Thane's light feet tapped over the glossy white floor and caught up to the group. The painting showed arches of blue ice and brushstrokes of white wind. A dragon perched on a cliff's edge, roaring up at the blush-pink sky where three moons of various sizes hung in the backdrop. This old dragon might be worth talking to.

"And here we have..."

Thane tapped Ronan's arm, and said quietly, "I'm going to take a piss."

He nodded and pointed to the doorway to the right. "Chambers are in there."

Excitement at the luck made him smile. This might finally be it. They could find the scepter and get their answers. "Thanks."

As he suspected, the room was full of precious objects along the walls, down the center, and even some hung from the ceiling in what he might call bird cages. Thane passed by gaudy goblets, small and life-size statues of people and animals made of solid gold. A cat with emerald eyes in a crouch had a wooden name plaque under its paws but it was a language he didn't know. A golden egg the size of Thane's torso sat on a perch of silver. Rubies and sapphires and emeralds were artistically placed like starbursts. The thing

must be worth a fortune. The voices of the others got quieter the further they moved away. It must be in here. He rushed from one treasure to the next and after he'd circled the entire room with no luck, he rubbed his hand through his hair. *Shit.*

"Something I can help you with?" asked a deep, rough voice.

Thane slowly turned to find a stout shifter with a black beard that reached his pot belly standing in the doorway. As with all the others he'd seen, he was tall, pushing seven feet and broad. His dark-brown eyes trailed Thane head to toe, sizing him up, assessing a threat.

"No. I was using the chambers."

"You ain't a thief are ya? One thing dragons hate more than anything are thieves. We covet our treasure, elf." He took a step into the room, his heavy boot like an anvil dropping.

Thane arched a dark brow, now assessing him as a threat. He didn't like the dragon's tone. "You think I don't have everything I could ever want. I'm a High King of Palenor. And treasure isn't something elves covet, dragon. I have more important things to worry about than shiny objects that don't kill my enemies."

The dragon took another step forward, looking around the room, seeing if everything was in its proper place. He cocked his head to the side in an almost bird-like way. "Best catch up with your friends, *High King.* You wouldn't want to miss out on the riveting tour now, would ya?"

The two watched each other closely as Thane stepped by him; he didn't turn his back until he was a ways clear of the treasure room. The others were moved onto the far wall now, gathered around a dark painting of bloodied, broken and tattered dragon wings on the back of a pale white, nude female. He couldn't quite say why but it made him sad. He'd seen more than his fair share of death in real life, but this captured the horror of war in a beautiful but haunting way. The nearly transparent, ghost of the female's face looking back at them was being pulled in wisps upward as if the wind stole her spirit.

Layala stared at it with wide eyes, the way a child marveled at something new. "Who is she?"

"This is another one by Sir Drevor," the tour guide said, folding her arms behind her back. "He titled it 'Taken Too Soon'. If she was real, we don't know who she is. Another tragic loss to war perhaps, a senseless murder. Dragons can be—temperamental. Some speculate it was his wife."

"If he's alive," Fennan said, "Why don't you ask?"

"His mind isn't what it once was," Prince Ronan answered. "He doesn't speak anymore, but he paints."

She stepped to the next painting. "This one is quite different from the others. It was done only twenty years ago, featuring our own Crown Prince Yoren."

Thane slipped his hand into Layala's and gave a shake of his head. She frowned and sighed. No luck today it would seem. When her jaw dropped open though he followed her gaze to the painting. It was

perhaps five feet high and three wide. The background was smudged and unclear almost like a fog was over it, like the artist couldn't see where Prince Yoren stood. The beige color vaguely resembled a wall or high building. But it wasn't the background or Prince Yoren himself that took him by surprise. Thane's gaze pinned to the gold chain and the piece that hung against Prince Yoren's chest. It was the Scepter of Knowing. There was no mistaking it. And when he thought back on it, he remembered seeing a gold chain around the prince's neck, but the end of it was always tucked under his clothes.

"This one is titled, 'The Guardian'."

"Who is that in the painting with him?" Piper asked.

At the bottom, the backs of two heads of dark hair were unfocused, smudged, and parallel to each other, maybe admiring him. Or even possibly standing against him. Prince Yoren held two swords at his sides.

"The anonymous artist left it against the museum door. So, we don't know."

Feeling it more than seeing it, Thane knew Ronan watched him, stared even, as if he suspected something. "The Guardian," Thane murmured. So Prince Yoren was the guardian of the scepter and Thane would have to take it.

It had taken another hour by the time they got through each painting, coveted treasure, and statue. The tour guide handed them each a small silver coin

with the image of the museum stamped on it on their way out the door. A souvenir.

Thane paused at the top of the steps to drop the coin in his pocket then looked up to Ronan staring again. The others were already halfway down the long set of stairs.

"You want the Scepter of Knowing. I can see it in your eyes. I saw it the moment you spotted it in the book."

And yet Ronan had handed him the book... Thane met his light-blue gaze. There was no anger or bitterness, no surprise or accusation. Thane didn't deny it. What was the point? Ronan knew.

"And if I did?"

"Well, then you have to battle the guardian for it. No one takes a dragon's treasure without a fight." A slow feline smile. "And the arena is filled with the skulls of those who've tried."

THE CHAIR LAYALA sat in felt cold, hard, and uncomfortable. The dim firelight cast long shadows across the room, over the dragon queen's face. Ronan escorted them directly here after the museum. The smirk on his face made Layala nervous, as if he knew something, she did not.

And whether the queen was furious or amused, Layala wasn't sure. The softness of her glossed red lips contrasted the narrowed glare. She sat on the edge of a

massive cherry oak desk. With her legs crossed, she bounced her top foot and stared at Layala like she might have the plague.

No one had said a word since they stepped into the room. Prince Yoren stood with his arms folded, legs spread wide in a stance not easily knocked off balance, and Prince Ronan sat with his feet up on his mother's desk behind her.

Layala turned slightly to look at Thane in the chair next to her. He didn't look at all worried or upset. In fact, he sat there with a serene if not smug half smirk to rival Ronan's. Maker, she wanted to punch him sometimes. Both of them acted like this was one big game.

"So you have something to ask me?" the queen drawled.

"We have the All Seeing Stone and you have the Scepter of Knowing," Thane said. "I need the scepter, so as you can see there is a little bit of a problem."

Her forehead wrinkled in surprise. "You don't even know what you're truly asking for."

"We need to end the curse, and we need to know how."

She glanced over at Layala for a moment. "Do you know what happened the last time they were joined?"

Thane and Layala glanced at each other. "Rhegar used the All Seeing Stone to find a way to defeat the Black Mage," he answered. "So it must give answers. And we need answers."

Pressing her lips together, Nyrovia went quiet for a

moment. Her harsh silver-blue eyes flicked over to Yoren. They exchanged some sort of silent communication. She could see it in the way he tilted his chin lower—an approval?

The dragon queen slid off the desk and stood tall. Her white silken evening dress shimmered in the sunlight pressing in from the high windows behind her. With her movements, the diamond-encrusted bracelets and rubies hanging from her earlobes glittered, too. "I've heard you're a great warrior, the best in Palenor, and Lady Lightbringer is quite powerful herself."

Shifting slightly in her chair, Layala turned to Thane; she didn't like where this might be headed. She wished Thane could communicate with her like he did with the mate bond spell intact, feeling out what he might be thinking. Nyrovia's heels clicked on the wood floor as she walked closer. "There is a story among our people. That the gods would send their own to Adalon once again, and lead the dragons back to our home realm, Ryvengaard, the place before they brought us here, and only they could use the scepter and stone properly."

Sweat slid down the back of Layala's neck. Why was it suddenly so hot in here? "What does that have to do with us?" she asked.

"We'll give you the opportunity to fight the guardian of the scepter."

Fighting a dragon? She was afraid to even ride one, let alone fight one. It made her sick to even consider it.

"You're offering a chance for us to put them together," Thane said quietly. "That means you think that this person chosen by the gods might be one of us."

"All of us can smell their magic in you *and* your betrothed. Their blood is infused in the scepter and the stone and you two smell of them. Both of you could be descendants of the gods and goddesses of the Runevale realm. They walked Adalon at one time and mated with the elves."

"Layala too." It was more of a confirmation than a question.

Me? A descendant of the gods? If that were true, why didn't she heal quickly like he did? But she noticed now more than ever, she moved faster, was stronger than the average female and obviously possessed magic. But did that make her a descendant of the gods?

"But they've been joined before," Thane stated. "This is how Rhegar knew how to kill the Black Mage. I'm assuming he didn't defeat Yoren unless there was a previous guardian."

"They were joined—by Rhegar *and* the Black Mage. It takes two, one to hold each piece." She cleared her throat. "We freely gave the scepter to Zaurahel Everhath and the elf warrior Rhegar. It killed Rhegar as well as the Black Mage," she paused. "And the Void was created."

Layala's jaw dropped. This story was entirely different from what she'd been taught. What every elf

and human she'd ever spoken to about it knew. "You're saying Rhegar didn't kill the Black Mage, he was helping him and it somehow backfired?" Layala pushed an annoying stray hair off her face. "And why would you willingly hand over such powerful tools to him?"

"We are neutral in your war, and Zaurahel brought no trouble for us. He offered an opportunity when he brought the stone that had been missing for thousands of years."

"That's not what my people say happened," Thane interjected. "Rhegar was the hero who killed the Black Mage."

"Your stories are wrong, elf king. I was there when Rhegar was at the Black Mage's side," Queen Nyrovia said, holding up a long thin finger. "One could argue that he somehow knew it would kill Zaurahel and that tempting him with this power was the only way to defeat him. But what happened when those two pieces joined isn't entirely known. We only know that Rhegar died with the stone in his hand and was found at the edges of the Void and the Black Mage was gone. After, the elves protected the stone, and we took back the scepter."

"What do the two pieces do?" Thane asked. "Have they ever been used successfully?"

"There are tales of its power passed down from generation to generation and age after age, but no one knows for certain. Some say the two pieces can open to new realms, others that it will give the user the knowl-

edge of the gods." She paused. "It would seem the Black Mage and Rhegar were found unworthy. It would seem," she repeated, "we gave the scepter too willingly."

Thane sat up taller in his wooden chair. "You believed the Black Mage was a descendant as well then?"

"Yes. With the power he possessed and his scent, we couldn't explain it any other way."

Thane's green eyes trailed over Layala. "Did the Black Mage have children or siblings?"

That heat she felt before flared up again. Why would he ask after looking at her like that? Did he think that *she* might be related to him? No, that couldn't be possible. There was no way she was related to the Black Mage...

Lifting a shoulder, Queen Nyrovia answered, "No known children, but a sister, I believe." She paused for a moment, analyzing his face. "You're worried you are from his bloodline? It's been long since I saw him, but there are similarities in your features. Although many elves look similar in my eyes."

Thane shook his head. "No, not me. I know my lineage well."

The dragon queen carefully inspected Layala now. "Her?"

Thane pursed his lips. Maker above, what Layala wouldn't give to be able to feel his emotions right then. Was he disgusted at the very idea as much as she? If it were true, would he want anything to do with

her? It would certainly explain a lot of things like the pale ones being drawn to her and them needing her to bring him back, if she was. Now she wanted to know why more than ever.

"There is only one way to know for sure." The queen gestured toward Prince Yoren. "No ordinary elf, not even a mage, could ever take it from my Yoren. He has killed hundreds who've tried. Those who thought they could be the chosen of the gods, noble warriors from all over. Dragons, elves, even some men. We give any who think they have a chance the opportunity, but you're the first since Zaurahel that has the scent of the god's magic in your blood."

"And what if Layala and I are cursed like the Black Mage and another Void is created, or we're killed?"

"Well, assuming you can take it, that's a risk for all of us."

CHAPTER 35

Layala and Thane stepped out into the hallway. His usual calm, even arrogant expression changed to one of worry. It made the nervous ache in her gut intensify.

You need to trust Thane. He'll figure something out. He always does. Layala wanted to believe that, but at the moment he looked as lost as she felt. He closed the door to the queen's office leaving them alone in a quiet, dimly-lit corridor.

"You know I love you, right?" he said and took hold of both her hands.

"Yes," she said skeptically.

"I'm going to fight Prince Yoren. Alone."

The shock of his statement had her blinking instead of speaking. Fight the dragon prince by himself? "What? No, that's an insane idea. We need to ask them for another way to prove ourselves."

"This is the only way. I'll get it."

"How could you possibly defeat him?"

His deep chuckle sent vibrations through her chest. "I'm glad to know you think so highly of me. I did kill a dragon shifter once already. It was easy."

She sighed. That's not how she meant it. "In his human form, I have no doubt you could beat him. But in his beast form, he'll be impossible. Dragon scales cannot be penetrated by weapons."

"Can't be penetrated by metal weapons. *Our* metal weapons."

"You think you can get to him with your magic? Or they have weapons that can?"

"I'm willing to bet my life on it. The guards here carry swords and spears. They wouldn't if they were useless."

"Alright, let's say they have a sword that can cut through dragon scales. If they'd even allow you to use it, he's still bigger than a house. I mean, their backs reached higher than the tops of the trees. His claws will be nearly as long as you are tall. A sword would merely be a scratch."

"Layala," he said gently. "I must do this, or we'll never get the scepter. I'm not going to spend the rest of our lives running from my father and Mathekis. It's not in me to run. I hate it." He paused. "And we need to know who you really are and why you can free him."

"I'll fight with you then. If it takes both of us to reunite the two pieces, then it's only fair."

He tore his gaze away and pursed his lips. "I don't want you to fight with me. It's too dangerous."

435

"Then if it can only be one of us, I'll fight him on my own."

His head snapped right back. "No."

"See how that feels."

"This is different."

"Why?"

"Because I could never live in a world without you, but you could go on without me."

Tears pricked and her vision blurred. If that wasn't a slap in the face... Did he truly think so little of her? Even Varlett had said something similar. "Why would you say that? You know I love you."

"You left me once. You could do it again. I'm not saying you love me less. I mean you're stronger than I am." He brushed his fingers across her collarbone. "My entire life has been to protect you, to love you, to make sure you were safe. If I didn't have you, what would I live for?"

She clenched her teeth. This line of talk scared her. "Stop it." Layala pulled away. She wanted to smack him upside the head. "You're acting like this is the end, that it's already over and you lost."

"I'm only preparing you for a possibility. Yoren is old, powerful and has never been defeated."

Her bottom lip trembled. "If you die, I die, remember? Bond or not." She whirled away from him, determined to go through that office door.

"Layala," he quietly called. His fingers brushed her arm, but she jerked away.

Even if the dragons scared the shit out of her, to

potentially watch the one she loved more than life die, frightened her even more. There was one way to get this done. She shoved through the door. "Thane *and* I accept the challenge."

Prince Yoren looked her up and down and then turned to the queen. She gave one slight nod. Prince Yoren's face lit up with a huge grin; he may as well have been clapping. Was this a huge mistake? Probably, but she didn't regret it.

She felt the breeze of Thane's presence just before his hand rested on her lower back. Yoren stopped in front of them. "I accept your challenge Lady Lightbringer and King Thane. I'll give you two days to prepare, and no one will blame you if you change your mind." His normally dark-brown eyes flashed yellow, and the round pupils turned to slits. "And make sure to prepare arrangements for where you want your bodies sent, just in case. We'll at least give you that for having the courage to try."

The door clicked shut in Layala's face. Thane glared daggers at the door before he turned that furious gaze on her. He could be angry all he wanted, she wouldn't back out, nothing he said would change her mind. She raised her chin and waited for whatever argument he wanted to have out.

Thane's nostrils flared and he opened his mouth only to be cut off by Ronan slipping out to meet them. He slow-clapped. "Bold move." He let out a giddy laugh and threw his arms around both of their shoulders, walking in between them down the empty hall.

437

"Let's go get you two ready, eh? If you want a chance at not dying, you'll need my help."

THE MORNING SUN hung level with the mountain range, staining the sky a vibrant pink. Layala stared at how the colors changed from light blue, to salmon, to pink. The wide, blue slow-moving river trickled serenely, and wind brushed through the needles of anciently-tall pine trees.

Things seemed more beautiful when life threats lurked around every corner. Although, she refused to die in two days' time. She had too many things left to do. Even if fate tried to deal her that hand, she'd pull an ace from up her sleeve and fight it. That dragon prince had no idea who he was dealing with. And Layala had a feeling they'd only seen the seedling of Thane's power of what could be a mighty oak. Like her, he didn't rely on his magic, didn't use it except when necessary. What would happen if he'd leaned into it fully? And now that she would be fighting beside him, he'd do anything to win. When it was only his life on the line, he seemed to allow death an option.

Prince Ronan gave them fire-resistant, bronze-colored armor that shimmered in the sunlight. She brushed her fingers over the coin-sized pieces, seamlessly melded together, dragon scales. Real ones. It was surprisingly pliable, considering its weight. She

was covered from neck to ankle and the pieces must add an extra twenty pounds to her frame. Thane tightened one of the buckles on her left, jerking it tighter than necessary. Layala rolled her eyes. "You can be pissy all you want. It's not going to change anything."

"I will be pissy. Thanks for your permission." He moved onto the next buckle and tugged on it like a brute would a saddle.

"I'm not a horse you know."

"Clearly. A horse would listen." He stepped back, fury smoldering. "Now I'll have to not only take on a dragon, but make certain you don't get hurt or killed while I'm at it."

"You've known since the day you met me that I don't follow orders like one of your servants." He reached for another loose strap on her side, and she smacked his hand away. "And you don't need to make sure of anything. You do what you need to do, and I'll do the same." Layala worked furiously on latching her own armor. "It will probably be me saving your ass."

Prince Ronan stood beside Piper with his arms crossed. "They always like this?"

"Half the time," Piper answered with one hand on her popped-out hip. "This isn't as bad as they used to be though. They've had some epic blowouts. I mean, she tried to murder him once in his sleep."

Prince Ronan laughed and slapped his thigh. "Oh, that's spectacular."

Thane rolled his shoulders and neck. "I would have

gotten out of that cage without you, you know. Those chains were close to breaking."

Oh, now he wanted to bring up what happened in Newarden? If she, Piper and Fennan hadn't come to save him, he would have been tortured to death. "Your ego is astounding." Layala picked up her sword. "And here I thought you were grateful we came."

"I am. I've already said thank you. All I'm saying is I'd have gotten free." He swung both his swords in figure eights in front of him. "And I'm not the only one of the two of us that's needed rescuing. If we're going to keep a tally I've got a couple marks on you, my dear."

Layala arched an eyebrow. "Do you? Shall we talk about the sirens?"

"How about," Piper said, stepping in between the two of them. "You work together rather than try to prove who has saved who more times. And please for the love of the Maker, stop arguing. You have two days to prepare to fight a dragon prince."

Ronan crossed his arms over his broad chest. "Your lives depend on you working together."

"Why are you helping us anyway?" Layala asked. "If we win, that means your brother is dead."

Ronan tsked. "Oh, sweet child, they'll never allow you to kill Yoren. Defeat him, possibly, but don't count on it. And look out for other obstacles."

Other obstacles? Like what? And how was that fair?

"We can't kill him, but he can kill us?" Thane

drawled. "And if he has to cheat to win, he shouldn't be the guardian of the scepter."

"You are on our land. You must play by our rules. No one ever said it would be fair. No one told you you had to fight him. The choice is yours." He looked at his fingernails.

Piper eyed him skeptically. "What do you stand to gain from this? Do you have no loyalty to your family? Or did your parents ask you to help prepare them?"

"Elves are so distrustful." He lifted a shoulder. "Look, I'm as curious about exploring other realms as anyone. If the legends are true and you two can get us to our original realm, I'm willing to help you get there. And if not, well, we get to watch you be slaughtered in the arena."

Ronan waved his hand and out of thin air two swords appeared and hovered beside him. With a push of magic, the swords floated over to Layala and Thane. "We give all competitors at least a fighting chance by allowing them our weapons. You'll need these. Your weapons will break on dragon scales. And even if he doesn't shift into his beast form, he'll certainly be armored with scales."

"I'm curious," Layala asked, sheathing her sword, and grasping the other. The handle was made from gold of course, with a red jewel in the pommel; the blade wide and shiny silver. "If it were up to you, would you have us fight your brother for the scepter?"

"All fight my brother for the scepter. It's the way."

Without saying anything, Thane swung his sword

at Layala. She brought her blade up and blocked his light chop. The ping of the weapons echoed in the forest clearing. Thane still used his own swords, to make sure he didn't accidentally hurt her, no doubt. The dragon blades could cut through dragon-scale armor. "It's been too long since either one of us sparred." He smacked her hard on the left shoulder. His sword bounced off her, but it stung, and she suppressed a wince. "A little rusty?" He teased and stepped to the side.

"Oh, you're asking for a beating." Layala swung at his thigh; he promptly blocked it.

"Don't threaten me with a good time." Their swords clashed over and over in quick succession.

"Keep being a naughty boy and see what happens."

"Will you threaten to slay me? I do so enjoy that." He parried her strike and somehow wrapped his arm around her torso from behind, tugging her hard against him. He slipped his sword to her throat and raised her chin. "Tonight, when those pretty thighs are wrapped around me," he purred, "I want you to be as feisty as you are now. You don't need to be shy."

Layala swallowed hard as heat flooded her body. She elbowed him in the gut and shoved his arm away, twisting out of his grasp. Now her blade point was at his throat, and she marched him backward into a tree. He grinned, thoroughly enjoying this. She didn't know how she ever resisted him for so long before. "And you're so certain you can have me tonight?"

442

"You're bewitching when you threaten me. My absolutely beautiful, enchanting, betrothed."

She lowered her sword. "I don't know if I've forgiven you yet for saying I could simply walk away and would survive your death so easily." Weapons clashed again, but both of them were relaxed. It felt good just to swing a sword and move her body again. She enjoyed the burn from pushing her long-ignored muscles.

"I'm sorry. Shall I get on my knees before you, so you'll forgive me? You're the only one I've ever gotten on my knees for." He struck harder and faster now, putting her on the defensive, pushing her back. Now she was the one pinned to a tree. He pressed his sword against her, resting the blade on her chest. Maker, she loved and hated how good he was with a sword, as if the ability was a gift the same as his natural means to heal quickly. "I'll start by kissing your thighs, beginning on the outer, then sliding my way to the soft inside. After you shudder with pleasure, I'll work my way just a little higher until I hear you moan, quiet at first." Her chest rose and fell rapidly, she felt out of breath. From the sparring or his seduction, she couldn't be sure. He leaned down and brushed his lips over her jawline. "Mm, you smell good when you're aroused."

"Thane, they can probably hear you," she whispered, cheeks burning, eyes darting to Piper and Prince Ronan who luckily were paying more attention to each other than them.

"Does it look like I care?" he asked and kissed her cheek. "Now if you want to hear the rest, you have to get through my defenses and strike a vital part of me. A nick on the forearm doesn't count."

"When I get through your defenses, you'll *show* me the rest." She slid her hand up his chest then shoved him away.

His answering grin warmed her to the core. "Alright, Lightbringer. Let's see if you got it. And not to brag but no one has landed what would be considered a critical blow in a sparring match since I was fourteen years old. However, I might still give you a consolation prize for the effort."

Laughing, Layala stepped around him. "I think you've forgotten how many times I've held a blade to your neck, Athayel."

"That has only happened when I allowed it."

Layala's eyebrow ticked upward. "You're still going with the story you let me in your room some months ago?"

"Oh, yes," he said. "You intrigued me then and even more now. I even heard your heart pounding from across the room."

She shook her head in disbelief and sliced her blade through the air with a *whoosh*. It clashed against Thane's left-handed blade with a *crack*. "Oh, she's bringing the heat. You must really want to know what else I plan to do to you."

Clack, clack clack, they hit swords again and again. It wasn't long before sweat beaded on her hairline.

They danced around each other, striking and blocking. But no one laid out any rules, did they? She let the itch of her power cascade through her body, and her magical black vine worked its way up Thane's ankle like a serpent. He went to step, and then looked down as it climbed up his thigh. Layala smiled and another vine climbed his other leg, effectively trapping him in one place. With a wave of her hand, she bound his wrists and cinched them together. He smiled even as he shook his head and dropped his arms down. Both his sword points fell into the dirt. Layala sauntered closer and pressed the tip of her blade over his heart. "Is this a critical strike?"

He was out of breath when he said, "I surrender."

Off to the side, Ronan clapped. "Bravo. It seems my brother will be outmatched in the sword. So, I'm certain he'll shift into his dragon form rather quickly. I suggest you don't play nice."

Layala heard him but her focus was on Thane and the primal gaze pinned on her. He would strip her bare right then and there if they didn't have an audience. She was certain of it. She slid her blade between Thane's wrists and cut him loose from her magical vines.

Thane easily stepped free of the ones wound around his legs and put his arm around her waist and tugged her flush against his chest. His fingertips slid over her mouth as if he was fascinated by them. He didn't look at Ronan when he said, "We're going to take a break from sparring."

CHAPTER 36

The door to the room clicked shut. Layala's heart thudded like a drum. Thane turned around and took her face between his palms, then kissed her. The intensity of it made her pull him in. His rough stubble lightly rubbed her skin. She grabbed and tore one of the buckles holding on Thane's armor, thankful he only had one on each side. Her body throbbed for him. She couldn't wait any longer to have him. They bumped into the dresser, lips trailing over exposed skin. Thane growled low and snapped the buckles on her top armor, Layala raised her arms up and he jerked it over her head in one swift motion. It fell to the floor with a thud. And the other pieces and clothes came off, dropping to the floor with clanks of metal on stone.

Thane's big hands clamped around her rump and lifted her up. "I'm supposed to be taking this slowly, kissing your thighs."

But she didn't want slow torture. Her body

demanded all of him right then. She slid onto the dresser top and pulled him in with her legs. "Not slowly," she said and dragged him to her mouth. "Don't make me wait."

Layala's backside bumped into the clutter on the dresser. Without looking, she reached back to clear it away, but her hand dipped into something sticky and warm. She looked down to see it covered in chocolate. A bowl of it with a tray of fruit waited beside her.

"Mmm," he murmured and took hold of her wrist and sucked the chocolate off her middle finger. "Tastier on you." Hot kisses pressed over her throat, and she shivered with pleasure. "Listen, my love, you must wait. I said I'd kiss your thighs first." He grinned knowing the torture he caused her. He pressed his lips to her outer thigh then drug his tongue over the top where chocolate dripped. His hands slid up to her hips and dug into the soft flesh. "And then here." He kissed the inside of her knee.

"Thane," she pleaded, sliding her chocolate-covered palm over his shoulder and across his chest.

"I'm not finished." He kissed higher, his breath whisking across her sensitive area. "I want to know how you taste."

Layala leaned back into the wall, closing her eyes. She didn't know if the moaning came from her or the wind outside. She was lost, transported until he lifted and kissed his way up to her lips.

"Better than chocolate," he said and jerked her to

the edge of the dresser where he stood between her thighs.

"I want you," Layala said, gliding her tongue over his chest, tasting the salt of his skin and the sweetness of chocolate.

"Yes, Lady." A slow serpentine smile spread. "Anything you command."

IN BETWEEN TRAINING, they spent the allotted two days in that bedroom, drowning in pleasure, aching for the need to be touched and caressed. It was as if the more they made love, the stronger she felt, invigorating her with an unseen power. Thane even commented on her skin having a golden luster it didn't before. And if it was possible his green eyes were even brighter. She wanted him more and more with every look he gave her, every kiss he stole. Since their violent separation, they hadn't had the time to spend alone like this— to just be.

Light fingers trailed along the curve of Layala's waist and over her hip, waking her from her sleep. Layala rubbed her eyes and combed stray hair off of her face. The window was left open to let in a cool, night breeze that smelled of lilac and lavender. Thane lay next to her; the silky blanket covered him from the waist down, but he was naked underneath. She had the urge to slide her leg over his hips, but he looked troubled as he stared at the wall behind her. She

wasn't sure he even realized he had woken her up. "What's wrong?"

He pulled his gaze to hers. "Huh?"

"You seem... lost."

"Oh." He was quiet and resumed sliding his fingers along her hip. "I had a dream that woke me."

"What about?"

"My father... Again." They both waited in silence for several beats before he went on. "Like before but worse. His corpse tells me I am like him." He swallowed hard. "And sometimes I wonder, what if I am?"

Layala's cheeks warmed at the absolute fury she felt that he could believe he was anything like Tenebris. "You're nothing like him. Not even a little. You do bad things for the good of other people. You are good in here." She pressed her hand over his heart. "And the only good thing Tenebris ever did was bind us together as mates."

The corner of his mouth turned up slightly. "For that I am thankful."

She hated that he harbored any guilt or conflict at all when it came to Tenebris. The wicked king didn't deserve to occupy even a piece of Thane's precious heart. "I want you to know and remember that I love you more than I hate him."

His eyebrows rose. That seemed to surprise him.

"Does only a magic spell make us mates? Or can I call you that without it? Because I feel like we were destined to be together. As if the fates would see to it no matter what happened. Do you feel that way?" She

took a lock of his dark-brown hair between her fingers. Couldn't they be more? Magic may have brought them together, but it didn't make them fall in love.

"Maybe your soul is mated to mine. A soul mate." He inhaled deeply. "I've felt like I've known you for as long as I can remember. And maybe it was because of our mate bond but sometimes I feel—more. I would find you in every life, in every realm. I will be drawn to you for eternity. So yes, call me your mate. I will always call you mine."

PIPER'S BOOTS clacked lightly on the marble floor. Layala watched her fire-haired friend in the mirror's reflection. The other three Ravens waited outside in the hallway while Layala got ready. Thane sat on the bed tossing a small white ball up over and over again, dressed in bronze dragon-scale armor and prepared for the fight that would take place in an hour. Layala held a hairpin between her teeth and fought with the tangles that matted the back overnight. Where was Tifapine when she needed her?

"Let me do it," Piper demanded, snatching the brush right out of Layala's hand. "And we need something to make you look fierce, edgy." She jerked the comb through Layala's hair.

"I don't look fierce?"

"No, you look like a fairy-tale princess."

The brush snagged on a knot, Layala winced, and

Piper mercilessly jerked out pieces of her hair. "I'm wearing armor. And I have a sword that I'm quite skilled at using, I might add. That's fierce."

"It's your face. Stunning—beautiful, but it doesn't incite fear." Piper set the brush on the side table and worked her fingers through.

Layala rolled her eyes. "Oh, but Thane's does?"

"Yeah." She pushed Layala's head to one side and started a braid down above her ear. "He looks like he'll tear your head off and that's when he's not angry. It's his general vibe."

Thane chuckled.

"My general vibe is 'piss off'."

"True," Piper said, with a laugh. "But I have an idea." After she finished braiding, she pulled a small, round, golden case from her pocket. It almost looked like a locket. Piper grabbed Layala's shoulder and spun her around, so they faced one another. "While you two were... living in fantasyland, I found out some things about this match." Piper popped open the case and inside contained ebony and crimson powder. She dipped her fingertip inside the black and then dragged it across Layala's forehead.

"What things? Thane asked.

"Prince Ronan is easily swayed by a couple demure smiles and teasing comments for one." Piper brushed the black power over Layala's eyes and the bridge of her nose. "I think he'd divulge every family secret to me at this point."

"Because he wants to hump you," Thane said and

leaned back on the pillows with his hands behind his head. "He might even want more. That dragon is fascinated with you. Keep stringing him along."

"Tell him to get in line," Layala said and winked at Piper. "You got a host of males after you lately." Although Fennan seemed to have backed off completely. He and Piper hadn't spoken much since they arrived here.

"Don't move. You'll mess this up," Piper said, as a flush flooded her cheeks. "Anyway, I asked for a tour of the area where you'll be fighting. It's a massive arena. It could hold at least ten thousand. There is blood stained in the dirt, and several doors all around the base of the walls to the fighting area. I think, to let things in."

Layala nibbled on her lower lip. "What kind of things?"

"He didn't say, and we didn't go look but I heard— wailing—screeching."

Layala looked over Piper's shoulder at Thane. Her throat suddenly felt dry. "You mean like pale ones?"

"What if they are dragon shifted *and* cursed?" Piper lowered her voice. "Can you imagine?"

Thane jumped out of bed and his footfalls interrupted the silence. "The dragons stay here in the mountains to avoid the curse. They don't want pale ones here, let alone dragon ones. Don't worry about that." He smiled at Layala. "You look phenomenal. Excellent idea, Piper."

Layala twisted to see but Piper grabbed her arm

and forced her back. "I'm not done." She rubbed her thumb in the crimson and then swiped one line from Layala's lower lip, to the bottom of her chin. "Alright, now you can look."

War paint. It's the only thing she could describe it as. The black smeared over her eyes and forehead like a mask and three red runes centered just below her hairline, and the line on her chin made the look all the more fierce. Her light-blue eyes stood out like bright orbs against the ebony paint. "What do those runes mean?"

"It's Old Elvish, not Black Mage's runes, don't worry. And it means 'goddess of war'."

Layala grinned and really looked at herself in the mirror. She did look like a goddess of war. "Piper, you're the greatest. Thank you."

"Whether you are a descendant of them or not, you're worthy of the title."

THE GROUND VIBRATED with the stomping and roaring of thousands of dragon shifters. The sound deadened the rasps of the vultures circling high above. Layala dragged deep breaths in; vultures waited to consume dead flesh, Maker, she hoped it wouldn't be hers. The sand-colored arena stood nearly as high as the walls surrounding the city. Vines snaked up and around the massive three levels of arched doorways large enough to fit a fully-shifted dragon. Overhead they flew in by

the hundreds, shimmering a rainbow of colors. Some swooped low to blast wind, stirring up the dirt into little dust devils. Thane took hold of Layala's hand and gave it a gentle squeeze. That was enough to calm her even if a little.

Prince Ronan kept walking while Layala, Piper and Thane stared up. "Maker bless and watch over them," Piper murmured, then kissed the inside of her fingers and held her hand to the sky.

Ronan turned around and walked backward. "They will need that blessing today." He smiled. "It's not too late to back down."

"You can tell your brother that as well so long as he hands over the scepter." Thane strode forward, tugging Layala with him. They stepped into a tunnel and the chink of their armor bounced off the walls. The dozen guards surrounding them marched in perfect sync.

I am brave. I am strong. I am a goddess of war. Layala's stomach cramped despite her self-talk. Dragon shifters hung over the railings tossing blood-red rose petals; they drifted down around them like snowflakes. Layala's boots stomped over the crimson flowers covering their pathway and all she could think was that it was the color of blood.

"A farewell gift," Ronan said over his shoulder.

They thought this was the end of the elf king and his beloved. Layala tried to ignore it but the thought of them tossing rose petals as a goodbye made her skin crawl.

She looked up to see if they laughed at their attempt, if they mocked, but one face stood out among them.

Holy Maker above—Varlett.

It had been a week since they'd seen her in Newarden. Had she been here this entire time? Why show her face now? She smiled and blew a handful of scarlet rose petals out of her palm.

"Varlett is here," Layala whispered.

Thane looked up nonchalantly. "You're sure?"

"I saw her."

"Varlett and the rest of them can rot in hell. I am the Warrior King, and you are Layala Lightbringer, and this is not where we will meet our end."

She pushed all fear down and locked it away in that deep darkness she used to hide her magic in. Her face became stone. The spirit of the warrior washed over her, swimming through her veins until every muscle tensed ready to strike, until she was detached from the fear of loss, of death, of anything, the same she-elf who came to that castle to assassinate her enemies. She was not prey. She was the predator.

Prince Ronan stopped in the center of a massive archway leading out onto the dirt floor of the arena. Layala looked past him to where Prince Yoren already waited for them in the center. His huge wings protruded from his human form, but his skin shifted into silvery, shiny dragon scales. The hairs on Layala's body prickled. If intimidation had a physical form, it would be him. And it didn't help that the walls had skulls inlaid among

the stone or that the crowd chanted, "Yoren! Yoren! Yoren!" until the sound vibrated through her chest.

Ronan placed one hand on Layala's shoulder and the other on Thane's. "All you have to do is get the scepter. Once you hold it, it's over."

Was Ronan truly on their side? Or did he only like to play games with his brother and cause problems for his family in general? He was difficult to read. But Layala nodded and raised her chin.

Ronan pursed his lips. "Remember what I said about other obstacles. Watch your back. This match is rigged against you." He glanced over his shoulder at his brother, who paced back and forth like a caged wolf. "Get him to shift. It sounds counterintuitive but the scepter will be larger and easier to take. It adjusts with him. He'll avoid shifting if he can. It will make him appear weak if he has to take the form against elves."

"It will be easier to grab but he'll be much harder to take down and kill," Thane said.

"You don't have to kill him. I suggest you don't, or my mother may kill your mate for spite and let you live to suffer." Ronan smirked and winked at Layala. "Remember you're of goddess blood, Layala." He stepped out of the way. "May the Maker and All Mother bless you with victory."

Layala reached back and tugged her sword handle; it scraped on its way free. In her left grip, she held a shield nearly half her size; one she could duck behind

to escape a fire blast. But she rarely used shields in her training and not once in battle; it was heavy and disturbed her balance. Thane equipped himself with two swords, an ax and several daggers. Layala checked her belt one more time; her trusty throwing stars latched all around her hips made of the same metal as her dragon sword.

"Ready?" Thane asked.

She nodded once and side by side they stepped out into the open. The chanting and cheering shifted to "boos" and roaring. Layala's skin itched and crawled with the force of her magic's reaction. It wanted to lash out and fight, strangle and maim. The dragons among the crowd wouldn't be able to come down here and join the fight, would they?

"Remember what we talked about?" Thane asked, chin held high, chest out. One sword swung at his side. The other remained in its scabbard on his back for now.

"Yes." She'd thought about their plan all night and morning.

"Don't let that temper of yours take over. Keep your head clear, look for weakness. If we stick together, we'll survive this."

Layala's breaths came faster the closer they drew. Each footstep felt like it led to her doom—to the loss of him, again. She raised up her shield to neck level and held her sword at chest height. "I don't know if the shield is going to work for me."

"If it hinders you, toss it. You can always pick it back up."

Prince Yoren jumped side to side and rolled his shoulders. He wore only loose-fitting deep-red pants that hung low on his hips; no shoes, no armor, one sword and one ax. Gold bracers with a single rune mark clamped around his wrists and mid-forearms. What did that symbol mean? His silver scales glinted in the sun which seemed to be growing hotter by the moment. Sweat trickled down Layala's back and between her breasts, dampening her under clothes. The tight fitting, thick armor didn't help and neither did the nerves.

A loud female voice boomed, echoing around the circular arena, "Crown Prince Yoren Drakonan, protector and guardian of the god's scepter, welcomes the challengers Layala Lightbringer, elven mage and future Queen of Palenor, and High King Thane Athayel of Palenor, known as the Warrior King." There was a pause for the crowd to boo, hiss, and spit. Red petals showered from everywhere splattering across the arena floor. "May the All Mother condemn the interlopers and bring favor to our most-cherished Prince Yoren Drakonan."

CHAPTER 37

Layala ground her teeth at the condemnation. These people were going to be upset soon. The booing changed to the thousands of dragon shifters shouting, "Yoren! Yoren! Yoren!" rising up like a storm cloud on rushing wind. The wailing and screeching Piper talked about was muffled and its origins indecipherable but nearby. Layala narrowed her eyes against the glaring sun trying to focus on Prince Yoren. The scepter hung just below his throat. Thane lifted his left hand, and the force of his magic coated the air like a bitter tang... yet nothing happened.

Prince Yoren held up his arm showing his right bracer and smiled. "Nice try." They shield against magic then?

A low growl rumbled in Thane's chest. "I guess I won't be searing his brain until he surrenders. I don't know how effective those bracers will be against you, however. Let's find out." Thane stepped to the right,

and Layala moved to the left, circling him, surveying his stance, the way he moved.

Prince Yoren's dark eyes followed Layala. Did that mean he saw her as the bigger threat or wanted to take out the weakest first? She didn't wait to see. The magic burning inside Layala's body rushed out like a wave. Her vines grew twisting around Prince Yoren's legs—and held. Thane struck quick and hard. Prince Yoren twisted and blocked the blow with his ax and a blast of red light shot from the end of it and hit Thane's chest with a pop. Thane flipped end over end until he landed on the ground at least twenty feet away.

Layala swung and connected with his sword. His ax came down a beat later, smashing into her shield. The hit vibrated up her arm and stung all the way to her shoulder and sent her stumbling back. *Shit.* Numbness took over her shield hand. It hit the dirt and she kicked it aside. He was strong, much stronger than she anticipated. No one had ever hit her that hard. It was like the force of a lightning strike.

Vines snapped and broke with a single hack of his ax, and he was free.

Stomping toward her with a sneer of disgust and fury, he said, "You die first, elf witch."

Where did the hate come from? She supposed there was no room for leniency now. Layala lowered her chin and gripped her sword in both hands. "Come and try." Layala inhaled and imagined her vines punching free. The roar of them bursting through the ground rivaled the crowd. One pointed end shot

straight at his chest, hit like a hammer, and slammed him on his back into the dirt. He grunted and cut it off like the head of a snake and rolled onto his feet in one swift move. That hit didn't even hurt him?

Thane sprinted across the arena with a war cry, jumped up with his swords overhead and hacked down at the dragon. He was met with crossed weapons, but Thane's blow sent Prince Yoren staggering. Thane slashed at his opponent with wild fury, the speed of his swords blurred and the clank of metal on metal punched like rapid drumbeats. Prince Yoren hissed in pain as Thane's blade slashed across his chest, leaving a slice in his dragon scales from left shoulder to right peck. The crowd grew louder, more vicious.

Layala raced to get behind him. Thane had Prince Yoren on the defense, ready to fall. Suddenly the ground dropped out beneath her, and she was falling. She clawed, nails scraping the dirt rising around her until she hit the ground—hard, crashing onto her side. The impact made it hard to draw in breath. A screeching wail pierced her ears. Her head snapped up in time to see jagged talons slash across her arm, leaving rakes in the armor and slicing into her skin. Layala hissed, holding in a wail and punched the point of her sword at a small dragon the size of a wolf—no, it was different from a dragon. Its front legs were connected to its wings, a green wyvern. It dodged her blow and hissed sticking out a long snakelike tongue then stood up on scaly hind legs, making it loom ten

feet tall. Another scurried out from the shadows, and then another. Maker above, there were three in this pit. Her boot slammed into its gut, and she swung hard and fast, slicing through its membranous wing, and its paw. It screeched, flailing around, splattering bright-green blood across Layala's chest. It spilled into her wounded left arm and burned like acid. *Shit, that hurts!* She furiously wiped the blood until the other two screamed so high and loud her eardrums throbbed. *Forget this.* She raised a hand and a vine shot out of it. One end wrapped around her wrist and the other hooked onto the opening above and she pulled herself up and out. Three wyverns burst out of the pit after her, soaring into the air, flying around erratically.

But they were just a distraction. A dagger stuck out of Prince Yoren's ribs, and a line of red dripped down his scales. His left wing had a three-inch tear in the membrane, and Thane hardly appeared winded as they circled one another. No one matched the Warrior King in one-on-one combat. Thane would pick him apart... So why hadn't he shifted yet? And why hadn't Thane taken him down?

Two of the wyverns circling above took a sudden downturn and darted toward Thane and Prince Yoren while the third dove at her, wings pinned to his back, wicked jaws snapping. She cringed at the white foam bubbling out of the sides of his mouth and his black wagging tongue. Were these things diseased? Layala waited until the beast was seconds from slamming

into her and then dove. It crashed into the dirt and skidded into a roll. Feet carrying her like the wind, Layala drew up her sword and drove it straight down through the back of the wyvern. It clawed at her blade, hissed, and howled a moment but swiftly went limp.

She whirled around to Thane fighting off the other two at his back, and Prince Yoren, swinging weapons at his front. The wings of one cracked and buckled under the invisible force of Thane's magic. The yowl coming from that thing's mouth chilled her to the core. Prince Yoren's swords still came at him with rapid speed. But Thane bent and weaved like it was a dance he knew well, avoiding every one of their strikes with ease. A quick swing of his sword caught the remaining hovering wyvern in the mouth, slicing off his snout and it crumpled to the ground, dead. For a moment, Layala watched, mouth hanging ajar. It wouldn't matter how many years she trained. She'd never actually best him. Only if he allowed it. His gift was the sword, and he was the harbinger of death.

With a pounding heart, she rushed forward. Thane was trying not to kill Prince Yoren, she realized, or this would be over already. Layala's power whipped out, a vine sprang up from the ground behind Prince Yoren and circled around his neck. He dropped both weapons and clutched at it as he was yanked into a backbend. Thane reached forward; he was inches from grabbing the scepter. Then Prince Yoren exploded; his flesh expanded, filling the space with his dragon form a hundred feet high. That scepter now out of reach,

dangling seventy feet in the air. Smoke roiled out of his nostrils, and he lowered his wide chin. Two eight-foot horns grew out the top of his head and one centered on his nose. His jaws opened wide, and the burst of his roar sent Layala scrambling for her shield.

The crowd absolutely lost it. If she thought they were loud before, they may as well have whispered.

He took a huge intake of air, and a chill ran down Layala's spine. She knew what came next. She slid her hand through the loop and lifted the shield. Thane crashed into her, driving her hard to the right until they hit the ground and rolled over and over. The heat of the fire blast melted the shield where she dropped it several yards away. Thane's weight on top of her made it difficult to breathe.

"I didn't trust that shield," Thane said, shoving up and bringing her up with him. "Thankfully."

The metal shield was nothing but a shiny pile of goo melting into the sand now. Layala gulped. "*Holy Maker.*"

"I'll distract him. You get onto his back and get that scepter," Thane said and sheathed both his swords. He snatched two throwing stars from her belt and took off before she could even muster a response. Maker above, he was infuriating sometimes.

Two wyvern screeches came from the hole again and moments later they burst free. *Maker, more of these things?*

Prince Yoren's massive tail whooshed through the air, careening toward Thane. He dropped onto his

belly and it sailed right over him... but it came for her now skidding across the ground flinging up dirt. *Shit.* Layala pumped her arms and legs, running straight at the arena wall. The dragons above chanted, "Kill her! Kill her! Kill her!" They leaned over the railing, waiting to see if she'd be squashed.

If they survived this, nothing would scare her. Layala clenched her teeth together hard, ran up the wall, pushed back and flipped over the tail. She landed in a squat, one fist on the ground, then Prince Yoren's tail crashed. The impact rumbled the arena and cracked the stone all the way to the railing. The frenzied crowd screeched their obscenities and continued to chant, "Kill her". One dragon shifter fell over the barrier and into the arena. The two green wyverns dropped into dives and descended on the male and started tearing into his flesh before he could shift. He screamed and then they tore out his throat. With their talons lodged into his back they lifted and then dropped him from a hundred feet where he hit with a sickening thud. The crowd loved that.

Layala shook her head and jumped up, letting her vines grow rampant, allowing her magic to assume control. Vines cracked the ground open and appeared mid-air, wrapping around Prince Yoren's wings, cinching them together like a vice. He roared and tossed his head wildly, reared up and clawed at the vines attacking him. Layala jumped onto a growing stalk and rose into the air, hair whipping behind her with the speed of ascent. *Come on, come on. Closer.* Her

magic curved and brought her straight over Prince Yoren's spine. With a deep breath, she dropped onto the back of Prince Yoren's scaly neck and gripped one of his horns. *Hold on!* The dragon prince bucked and jerked around trying to shake her free. The slashes in her arm burned with her effort to stay on and bled even more. He pitched hard right; Layala cursed, and her feet slipped out from under her. She dangled a hundred feet high. Thane looked small from here and oh, Maker, the height made her dizzy. Her vines curled around her waist then hooked around the horn, securing her to Prince Yoren.

A roar of pain ripped from Prince Yoren and his giant paws clawed at his face. Blood oozed out of his eye where one of the throwing stars embedded. Thane screamed, "Now Layala!"

A door in the arena wall opened and three massive gray wolves came out of the shadows, larger than the wyverns and more viscous. Their snapping jaws and snarls strangled her chest as they sprinted at Thane's back. "Behind you!" she shouted.

He turned, drawing out his sword, and Layala moved faster. He couldn't be left to fight them and the dragon at once. With a vine wrapped around her wrist, she jumped over the side and swung down under his neck. The scepter dangled there, ripe, and ready for the taking. She reached out with one hand, and it spun away with his jerky movement. *Shit, shit shit.*

She watched Thane take down one wolf with a sword through its chest and the other crumpled under

with his magic. Prince Yoren still stomped and wailed about in pain, swiping at the throwing star embedded in his eye. His giant tail struck out and smashed Thane and the last wolf, sending them flying. He hit hard against the arena wall with a crack and fell face-first into the dirt. Then Prince Yoren charged for him.

"No!" Layala cried. She had to get the scepter before he could reach Thane. "Get up!" she screamed. The momentum of Prince Yoren's forward motion swung her back toward the scepter again. She reached for it with one arm and held onto her vine with the other. She couldn't miss this time. *So close!* The golden rod spun in a circle until it slammed into her chest, and she grabbed hold. Her vines curled around the chain, and it snapped. *Holy Maker above, I have the scepter!*

Her magic controlled her descent until her feet hit the ground in front of Prince Yoren, blocking his path. She took several steps to the left, drawing Prince Yoren's attention away from Thane. She raised the scepter with both hands over her head. It was as long as her torso and heavy.

Prince Yoren heaved deep breaths. One eye bled over his shining silver scales and dripped onto the dirt ground. Layala turned to make sure Thane was breathing. He slowly pushed up to his hands and knees. Thank the Maker.

The crowd went silent, the breeze and the call of the vultures loud. In this land, that was the sound of triumph for the elves. She grinned and turned in a half

circle showing everyone that she beat the dragon and held the scepter proudly. *Take your red rose petals and shove them up your ass.* The deep rumble of a dragon's throat made Layala whirl around, clutching the scepter to her chest. Prince Yoren's one good eye pinned on Thane. He lowered his head and opened his jaws wide; immense teeth gleamed in the sunlight. He growled and sucked in a massive breath, the kind of inhale that would release armor-melting fire.

She gasped. Ronan said they only had to get the scepter. This should be over. She didn't think. She just ran and stood firm on the path to block Thane.

As if in slow motion, a mass of orange flames burst from the dragon's mouth. She slammed her eyes shut. Thane's beautiful face flashed across her mind, smiling, and laughing. When he was truly happy, he had the best laugh, the kind that drew others in and made them want to laugh too. Could his promise to find her in every life be true? Would he find her again in another time? Looking back, she and Thane locked eyes. He reached toward her from his knees. "No, Layala run!"

NO.

No. She was Layala Lightbringer; the blood of the gods ran through her veins. Lay down and die? Never. She thrust out her free hand and roared with the fury of the dragon's fire that careened toward her. Her body felt ablaze, not with the dragon's breath but with the might of the sun. The squall of blazing orange flames arched around her the same way water spread around

rock. It crackled and sizzled, deafening in its violent assault, but she felt none of the scorch.

Somewhere in the distance, Thane bellowed her name, a heartbreaking cry that said he thought she was gone, but she'd conjured a protective shield of some kind. Her brows furrowed. Somewhere deep down she knew she was capable of this, but how could it be? It wasn't vines and lilies protecting her but an invisible force more powerful than flame and fury. *Touch it*, something seemed to say. Slowly, she reached forward with her fingertips as the assaulting fire hammered. Fingers brushed against the shield. It was no hotter than the air she breathed. Her magic hummed with an uncomfortable intensity. Instinct said to place her palm flat against it. Unafraid, she did. The shield curled forward, and a bright, white light burst into an explosion that rocked the ground. The combined force of her newfound power and the fire, burst and crashed into Prince Yoren. With a keening yelp, his colossal form hurtled backward. He flailed until his head slammed into the arena's stone wall. He didn't get up.

Goddess of war indeed. She grew a slow, almost maniacal smile. Thane was right all along. They *should* fear her. All of them. A swell of pride bubbled in her. She took down a dragon. Where had this power come from?

A wild mane of dark hair and the terrified face of her lover appeared before her. Thane grasped at her shoulders then her face as if he couldn't believe she

stood before him. The sorrow melted into disbelief, and he pulled her into his chest. "I thought you were dead. I thought—how did—what—" he stumbled over his words like a child learning to speak.

She couldn't explain what she did, so she slowly shook her head with her jaw hanging open.

With a sigh of relief, Thane grabbed her face between his dirty, gritty palms and kissed her hard on the mouth. "I love you. I love you." He kept repeating between kisses. "Don't ever scare me like that. Don't you dare leave me." A salty dampness from his face rubbed off onto hers.

"I'm still here." Somehow. She smiled up at Thane and wiped a tear from his cheek with her thumb. It was in that moment, the silence around them invaded. Her gaze swept across the arena where ten thousand dragon shifters watched.

Ronan leapt over the ledge from the canopied area he sat in with his royal parents and Piper and dropped to the ground. He marched toward them with determination. His silvery-blond hair waved behind him as regal as any cloak. Layala tensed, gripping the scepter tighter. It was hers, fair and square. She didn't expect applause when they defeated the dragon prince, but silence was worse than boos and jeers.

Prince Yoren's dragon morphed into his human form, and he groaned, clutching at the back of his head. At least he wasn't dead. Maybe that was what the crowd waited to see. But still only the caw of

crows, squawk of vultures, and Ronan's heavy footfalls broke the quiet.

Ronan stopped before Thane and Layala. He looked back and forth between them and then lowered to one knee. No praise left his lips, but the gesture said more than words.

Layala gripped Thane's hand. She didn't know what she expected but it wasn't that.

Soon, many in the stands sunk to their knees, like a wave they caught on. Thane squeezed her hand back, keeping her steady. His head turned, taking it all in. The red canopy shielding the king and queen from the bright sun, snapped in the wind. The queen smiled and lowered to her knees and the king followed.

"They're—they're," she could hardly believe what played out before her very eyes, "kneeling to us. The entire dragon court."

Thane cleared his throat. "I believe they're kneeling to you."

CHAPTER 38

A group of guards marched out from one of the large arena doors with spears in hand. Their leader was the male with salt-and-pepper hair they'd first encountered outside the castle a few days ago. Layala stiffened, itching to reach for her sword, and tamped down her bubbling magic. She doubted they came looking for a fight after the display of honor she had just witnessed but it was hard to pack down that instinct to always be ready.

The lead guard placed his palm flat over his stomach dipped from the waist then stood erect. "Congratulations on successfully earning the scepter, son and daughter of Runevale. You have proven to us you are descended from the old gods. Please, come with us to a secure area."

LAYALA'S black gown glittered from shoulder to feet, hugging every curve of her body like a glove. The high neck covered her cleavage but the sleeveless nature of it allowed the cool breeze in. The scepter now hung on a chain around her neck, shrunk to about an inch long, even smaller than when Prince Yoren wore it.

The rakes across her forearm from the wyvern attack itched, almost like they scabbed now. She hadn't removed the bandage to see but she had a feeling her body healed more rapidly than it ever had before, like her mate. As if the more she used her magic the stronger she grew and the more the traits of the gods showed in her.

The dewy glass in Layala's hand *tinked* with ice as she brought the lip of the cold white wine to her lips and stared out at the gathering. She didn't want to be here among the richly-dressed onlookers who watched her with a newfound curiosity. The whispers behind hands and lips close to ears said some believed she and Thane were sent from the gods. Others were more skeptical and questioned their place here. They were strangers after all, who came in and defeated their prized prince in front of the entire dragon kingdom. Not everyone believed the legends long foretold. Some, she gathered, didn't believe in other realms at all. They were just fables from an earlier age.

There would only be one way to find out and that was using the scepter and stone in the security of the temple. The temple built to the old gods was close by, or at least that was what the king and queen relayed to

them earlier. Anxiety coursed through her, anticipation for what might happen when they did put the two magical items together and she was stuck tapping her toes at this social gathering, forcing a smile at people she cared nothing for. It was a waste of time. Meanwhile Varlett must be lurking in the shadows somewhere set on ruining their plans. What hand did she have to play? She wouldn't show herself without one. That wicked gleam in her eye before the match reeked of aspirations.

Thane stayed close to her side. His suit sleeve brushed against her skin at all times. He spoke with Leif, Siegfried, and Prince Ronan as if this were any old event back at his own castle. Prince Yoren sat on his throne next to his parents. He smiled at her occasionally, and she was thankful there were no harsh feelings between them.

Talk of the food and wine and important guests arriving carried on. She glanced around wondering where Piper and Fennan were. She hadn't seen them since they stepped away several minutes before. She spotted them in the corner not far away, and the tension on Piper's face was enough for her to tune everyone else out and strain to hear them.

"You're seriously going to be angry with me?" Piper snapped. "For what? You've barely spoken to me since we arrived here."

Fennan's leaned his back against the wall. "I thought you were too preoccupied with Prince Ronan to even notice."

Piper rolled her eyes. "And so what if I am? What if I appreciate that he actually shows me he likes me."

"He only sees you as something to conquer, Piper."

"You don't know that."

Fennan lifted his shoulder. "Fine, don't believe me."

"You're such an ass." Her hands curled into fists at her sides. "You don't want me, but you don't want anyone else to have me either. You say you loved me since you were seventeen, but you slept your way through a quarter of the court. And I get it. You're charming, handsome, and a high-ranking Raven. You can have anyone you want. So I thought I could just wait until you had your fun. I thought I'd wait until you finally noticed me for something other than your sparring partner. But then I realized that if you loved me, you would have shown me. I'm done waiting for you, Fennan."

He stiffened and stood taller. "Piper..." When he didn't go on, she shook her head and started to walk away.

He grabbed hold of her arm, his red-brown eyes pleaded with her to stay. Layala wanted to jump in and side with Piper. Everything she said was spot on. How could he be in love with Piper for so long and yet ignore her for others? But Layala stayed at Thane's side, pretending like she wasn't eaves-dropping.

"I realized I loved you in that cell. I'm sorry I didn't see it before. I said I loved you since I was seventeen

because when I thought back on it, I have. I have loved you that long. I was just too stupid to see it sooner."

She tugged out of his grasp. "The others are watching us. Ronan is watching us."

"I don't care," Fennan said.

"Well, I do."

"You're going to choose him over me? You've known him for a week."

"I don't know what I want so right now, I'm choosing me." Piper stepped away from him and started back toward their group. Layala found staring into her glass prudent and scratched the back of her arm.

Thane leaned down. "Don't say anything."

Layala chuckled. "I won't."

Ronan looked like he was about to make a comment, so Layala blurted out, "Do you know Varlett? The dragon shifter who worked closely with the Black Mage."

Thane's eyes flashed wide, a silent tell that he didn't want her to say more. Prince Ronan ran his fingers through his long silvery hair. "I do. She isn't allowed here. She earned her banishment a few centuries ago. Why do you ask?"

Not allowed? Should she alert him and the guards that Varlett was here then? At that very moment, the golden-haired dragon shifter stepped out from behind a large pillar. She raised the glass of wine in her hand practically begging Layala to start a brawl. Layala was no longer just a young elf mage afraid to use her

magic. She was a descendant of gods and a powerful mage. "Excuse me for a moment," Layala said, and stepped away.

She slipped around groups of chattering people in extravagant gowns and suits. The light string music picked up pace to something easy to dance to. If she wasn't so focused, she'd find herself swaying to the tune, lost in the wistful melody.

"Congratulations," a pair said as she passed by.

A male tipped his glass toward her. "I'm in awe of your power, elf. Truly magnificent. Goddess blood among us once again."

Layala gave a brief smile but kept her gaze pinned on Varlett until she disappeared into the shadows. She wouldn't be stupid and go anywhere alone with her but in the public eye where Varlett was forbidden, was the best place to confront her. Layala set her glass on an empty table and with a dagger in hand and her magic thrumming through her like its own heartbeat, she stood opposite of the bitch who nearly gutted the love of her life.

Varlett's smile made Layala's skin itch. "You think because you won one match against a dragon, you're big and bad now?" Varlett cooed and then sipped her wine.

"What are you doing here?" Layala snapped. Her hand twitched to plunge the blade straight into her chest. She had no dragon scales to protect her at the moment, but rash decisions only brought trouble. Varlett obviously had something.

"Stopping you from making a huge mistake." Her heels tapped as she strode forward. "If you put that scepter and stone together, you won't survive and if you do, you'll be changed, cursed just like Zaurahel."

Layala's stomach dropped, but she played it off. That's what she and Thane discussed at length, whether or not it was worth the risk. "You're just desperate now because I'm close to finding out how to end your pathetic dead lover's curse for good."

Pushing her hair over her shoulder, Varlett cackled. "You are so naive." She curled her black-taloned fingers around her glass, tapping them rhythmically. "That's never going to happen. Not even a line to the gods could give you the power to do that. You're not strong enough and neither is your prince. How's that wound of his anyway? Bet it left a nasty scar. I'm surprised the bastard survived." Her golden eyes looked brighter than usual against her brown skin. Her gaze flicked to where Thane stood, watching them, but he hadn't moved. "I hope he has a limp cock too."

The hairs on the back of Layala's neck raised and an angry heat flooded her body. "I think you're scared." Layala arched an eyebrow. "And you'll say anything to deter us. But your words have no power over me, and you have no authority here." Layala turned and took a few steps away.

"I found your aunt or whatever you call her. I still can't believe your parents chose her, a simple human of all people to raise you."

The music and hundreds of voices muted as if she

stuffed cotton into her ears, and the drum of her heart grew loud. Layala froze.

"That bitch is tough for an old thing. She thought she could squirt slumber berry juice in my eye, and it would work on me."

Layala whirled around, driving the point of the dagger at Varlett's chest. She pressed it against her skin but not enough to do any damage. "Where is she?"

"Come with me and I'll give her back to you. We'll make a bargain. You give me what I want, and I'll give you what you want."

Her chest heaved up and down with heavy breath, but she pulled back. For all Layala knew Varlett was lying, and she wasn't going to play this game. But the slumber berries comment rang true. With a thumping heart, she turned away for the second time and tucked the dagger back into her calf sheath. *Don't turn around no matter what she says.*

"She screamed and cried when I killed that stupid boy. He tried to defend her." She clicked her tongue. "Ren, I think his name was. Such a shame too. He had the most innocent brown eyes."

Layala's legs suddenly went weak, and her steps faltered. The wind wrenched from her lungs like a gut punch. Ren—Ren was dead? How else would she know he had brown eyes unless she saw him? Her chin trembled and hot tears burned. She couldn't turn around, wouldn't allow Varlett to witness the anguish warring inside. If what she said was true... Maker above, not

only had Novak died but Ren too? All because of her. A sob caught in her throat, but she blinked back the tears and drew in a cleansing breath. This wouldn't crumble her. She wasn't that girl they kept starved and weak in the tower anymore. She wouldn't allow words or even lies to tear her apart in the middle of this party where so many watched her. She only slightly turned her head to say, "I'll soon see you on the battlefield." She couldn't risk fighting her here and now or even alerting the guards if she held Aunt Evalyn captive.

Thane met her stare from across the dancing couples in the center and moved toward her. He pushed through them with no care for manners. He meant to charge around her to go after Varlett, still leaning against the wall with an arrogant smirk, but Layala grabbed his arm so hard her hand ached. "We need to use the stone and scepter now."

THE MASSIVE, heavy doors to the temple creaked open. A pair of guards who stood at the top of the light-gray stone steps, nodded as Thane, Layala, the four Ravens, and Prince Ronan stepped inside. To avoid drawing a crowd, they snuck out a side door and along a well-manicured path through lush gardens with gazebos and water fountains. Layala glanced back, paranoid that Varlett followed them. But of course, she would. She didn't want them to find a way to end the Black Mage. But she wouldn't risk attacking, would she?

Three dragon shifters, two demi-gods, and four Ravens vicious and deadly in their own right, would be a lot to handle for anyone no matter if she delved into the dark magics.

The hall they walked into stood at least a hundred feet high. "This is the most warded place in Adalon. We've prepared for this day, in case things should go awry," Ronan said. "So, if another Void is created it will be contained inside these walls. Let's hope that doesn't happen."

Their footsteps echoed in the vast chamber above. Along the wall, twenty-foot statues made of gray marble stood. Five on each wall. All the females were to the left, the males to the right. Each adorned with details that Layala assumed had something to do with their characteristics. One female held an open book in her palms, another with serpents climbing up her arms, their heads blossomed into blooms on her shoulders, and she wore a crown of moon and stars. The center female carried a bow with an arrow knocked back, pointing up toward the sky. Maybe a goddess of battle or hunt? The final two stood back-to-back with a line of flowers between their feet and a sun behind their heads, their faces identical. Birds and other small creatures climbed on the left twin and the right had a tree growing out of her palm. Could Layala be descended from one of them?

"There are more," Prince Ronan said. "These are just the ones our people had contact with or so the

stories say. In Runevale there are many gods and goddesses."

Layala turned her attention to the males, the first with an ax raised, ready for battle. The second held a ball of flame that hovered over his palm, real fire. Was it spelled to burn all the time? The third sat with a harp in his hands and a flute tied around his neck that hung at his chest. She wondered about the stories the dragons must have. The second from the end held a trident in hand and stone waves crested around his legs. And the last carried an hourglass frozen with the sands of time in the top end.

The walls were covered in murals of warriors riding chariots pulled by winged horses, dragons soared among the clouds with riders on their backs. Small windows let in the evening sunlight, staining everything with a golden glow. It was truly beautiful here, divine as it should be.

Ronan stopped at the end of the room and placed his hands behind his back. "And here, before the All Mother and the Maker you shall put the stone and scepter together, and hope you are found worthy." Behind Ronan at the front and center of the temple, a male and a female sat on two massive thrones. They wore crowns. He held a hooked staff, and she, a balancing scale equally weighted.

Layala lightly bit down on her lower lip. What if she and Thane were simply powerful mages and not worthy? Would they die? Would they be burned to ash for their impudence? It was hard to know the truth

from a lie when the elves portrayed Rhegar as the hero who died to save everyone from the Black Mage while the dragons claimed he worked with him.

Thane pulled the stone from within his suit pocket and held it in his open palm. He inspected it for a moment, as if he hadn't memorized every nick and rough edge. Perhaps he was just as nervous as she about the whole thing. But if they ever wanted to rid the world of the Black Mage, this was the only choice.

Taking hold of the golden chain around her neck, Layala slipped the scepter over her head. She plopped it into her hand, and it grew to fit the width of her palm, and about twelve inches in length. Did it suddenly get hotter? Layala fanned her face and smiled nervously at Thane.

He pinned her with a concerned stare. "Are you sure you want to do this?"

"Yes," she answered despite the uncertainty swimming through her. She felt like a fish circling bait that didn't know it was about to get ensnared. She turned to the others who watched them with obvious anxiety. "Maybe you all should wait outside in case—something bad happens."

Piper shook her head. "No. If anything happens, I'm going down with you."

Ronan gave a single nod. "We're not leaving."

Fennan, Leif and Siegfried all agreed. "We're with you," Fennan said.

"No matter what," Leif added.

Well, so be it. Thane raised the stone. Layala

483

tipped the end of the scepter toward him. They locked eyes—what if this was the last moment they had together? What if this was the end? "It's alright," Thane breathed. "I'll always find you." He grasped under her hand. One beat. The stone was inches away. Two, it touched the metal. Three, it settled into place. For half a breath, nothing happened, then a golden light burst from the stone, a beam straight up into the rafters above scattering small birds. The scepter shook, almost as if it fought to break free. She gripped it with her other hand and Thane did the same.

"Keep holding tight," Thane breathed. "Don't let go."

The sensation vibrated up her arms, growing more uncomfortable with each passing moment. Then it just stopped. The golden light showered down shimmering like snowflakes, until a whirl of wind brought the glitter together into the form of a... female. The golden gleam outlined her shape but most of her body was transparent other than her long hair that floated on air like she was suspended in water.

"Who has summoned me?" she asked. Her light voice lilted around the chamber as soft and beautiful as a harp.

Thane and Layala exchanged a glance. If it worked, she expected a voice or something like the portals, but this was a person. If it didn't, she thought she'd be dead. She glanced about the temple to make sure everything was still in place and that all her friends

were alive. They stood mouth open staring with the golden light reflected in their eyes.

"We have," Thane answered.

Her doe eyes lined with long glittering lashes blinked a few times. "And why have you summoned me?"

"We need answers," Layala said. "Are you able to give them?"

"I am the goddess of knowledge. I can give answers as I please as long as it doesn't disrupt the balance in Adalon."

A direct line to the gods... so it was true. It was all real. Layala swallowed hard, nervous to know the answer but there was one thing she must know before anything else. "Where is Evalyn, the woman who raised me?"

"She is being held prisoner by the elf king, Tenebris, near the city of Doonafell."

Shit. Varlett didn't lie. Layala chewed on her lower lip, deciding if she could handle the truth of Ren being dead if she asked.

Thane spoke up, "Why was a Void created the last time this scepter and stone were used and not now?"

The golden female smiled. "Zaurahel Everhath was given what he deserved."

"It is said that Layala can destroy the curse on our land, including the Void and the Black Mage—how?"

She smiled and little golden butterflies fluttered off her hand. "In part that is true. For the curse on your land and your people to be destroyed, you must bring

485

the one you call the Black Mage out of the endless sleep. You must bring him back into reality, and she can do that."

"Bring him back?" Thane balked. "No, that can't be the answer. He can't be allowed back."

Was this a trick? And the endless sleep? Everyone assumed he was dead and gone with something holding him to the land, but he was here and—asleep? Layala's mouth hung slightly ajar. To destroy him, she must bring him back? That made no sense whatsoever. "Why me?" she blurted out before the goddess could answer Thane.

The question she wanted to selfishly know more than anything else.

Her wide doe-like eyes shifted to Layala. "You can bring back the Black Mage because of the blood connection you share." She turned to Thane. "And in order for the curse to be broken, he must live once again. The key is his heart."

So Thane had been right. She was a descendant of the Black Mage, Maker, it made her sick to think she could be related to someone so cruel and hideous. "To kill him, right? In physical form. Stab him in the heart."

The goddess looked away as if wondering what she may or may not say. "That would end him, yes. In his slumber state it's impossible, and in his waking state, for a mortal, that would be *nearly* impossible."

That's all she needed to know. She could pierce his

heart, mortal or not. It was nearly impossible, not impossible.

Thane shifted slightly. "But she and I share the blood of the gods, and are you saying he's not mortal?"

"Neither of you has embraced who you truly are. Much of your power lies dormant. And if he was immortal, a blade to the heart wouldn't kill him, but he's powerful and has grown even more so in his slumber."

Layala hid and fought what she was for years, only using her magic when it was necessary. Hadn't she wished she was someone else? Hadn't she wanted to be rid of her power? And hadn't Thane done the same? His own people didn't even know what he was capable of—he didn't even know.

There was no more hiding. No more running. She was the queen piece on this board, and it was time she put on her crown. "So, how do we wake him?"

CHAPTER 39

Dragon wings lifted and lowered in great whooshes. Wind rushed past, whipping the hairs around Thane's face like reeds in a storm. Throaty calls from dragon to dragon reverberated around them. He, Layala, and Piper rode in the air just above leafy green treetops, while below, five hundred Ravens rode on horseback beating the drums of war. Intel told Thane that his father waited for them with an elven army of three thousand five hundred near the border of the Void. And only the Maker knew how many pale ones lurked beyond the misty shadows inside. The Palenor soldiers knew Thane and the Ravens were coming and they would fight for who they believed was their rightful king.

Thane's charcoal Raven armor hugged his body, trapping the heat from the sun, and his underclothes were damp despite the cool wind at this altitude. He'd imagined this scenario a hundred times in the past few days. The moment his Ravens would clash with their

own. Nightmares still plagued his sleep; his father's rotten corpse seemed to follow him even while awake now. Accusing him of murdering his own people. *You became me. You are me. A bloody king.* His father cackled pointing with a gray, decaying hand.

Hypocrite.

Murderer.

How could they have come to civil war? He swiped a hand over the back of his sweaty neck. And how many Ravens would he sentence to death going against his own father? They were vastly outnumbered even with the help of three dragons. Thane hoped their presence would be enough of a surprise to get his father to surrender before they lost half their fighters. Tenebris may be wicked, evil, but he wasn't a fool, and they didn't have weapons to break through dragon scales—the only problem was Thane didn't want his own people slaughtered.

His eyes felt heavy from lack of sleep, but his body hummed with the adrenaline that rushed through him in anticipation of battle. Shining armor glinted; their numbers stretched in a row as if they stood guard of the Void itself.

"Take me to the ground," Thane said. They were only a quarter of a mile away from meeting the enemy.

Vaper tucked her wings and the sudden drop tickled Thane's stomach. They hit the ground in a spray of grass and dirt. Smoke shot out of Vaper's nostrils like steam from a tea kettle.

"I'll lead them from the ground not from the safety

489

of the sky." He glanced up to find Prince Ronan and Piper soaring by. A great roar echoed across the plain and brought chills to his skin. Prince Ronan and his two personal guards volunteered after the meeting with the Goddess of Wisdom, but that was all House Drakonan would spare. They still feared what the pale one curse might do.

"You're a noble leader, Prince Thane," Vaper's raspy voice rumbled. Her massive head lifted a little higher, glossy bronze scales shimmered in the sunlight. "May the Maker bless your sword and may your arrows fly true."

"Thank you."

A gust of wind from Vaper's wings billowed up dirt and debris and she shot into the sky. The sound of beating wings alone would put fear into his father's soldiers.

Mathekis was nowhere to be seen and he'd yet to spot Varlett in the skies or on the ground, but his father, mother, sister, and Aldrich sat on white horses in the front of the army. Typically, High King Tenebris stayed out of the line of duty, far behind the protection of soldiers, and not once had his mother or sister been on a battlefield, least of all at the front of it. He knew exactly why his father dragged his mother and sister out here. His father's horse shifted slightly, and Thane's heart lurched. Evalyn stood with a rope around her wrists and his father held the other end. Even from here he could see her dress was tattered at the ends and torn in places. Dirt and grime covered

her from boot to head. Frazzled bits of black and silver hair came loose from the tie in the back. Layala might not think clearly here so he must. He didn't care for her the same way Layala did, but she'd still become a soft spot for him, despite her apparent dislike of him.

His stomach knotted but he trudged forward until a great winged shadow cast over him. Layala and Dax hovered above. A vine shot down and with a crash, rooted itself in the ground. Thane smiled. Layala jumped off the dragon's back and swung onto her vine, sliding down the smooth stalk as gracefully as she danced. Her boots hit the ground with a thud, and she stood tall. She tugged her raven-winged helmet down tighter and adjusted the neck of her armor, breath hitching a little. There was just something about seeing her in full battle armor that captivated him. A smile played at the corners of her mouth and those bright blue eyes met his. "You didn't think I'd let you face your family alone, did you?"

She hadn't seen Evalyn yet, he presumed. His jaw clenched.

"What is it?" she asked.

He turned to look at them, still a hundred yards away across grassy fields sprinkled with tiny white and purple wildflowers. A place too beautiful to have blood spilled across it. They weren't close enough to smell the stinking bogs of the Void yet, so the air was fresh and calming. A white flag rose up in Aldrich's hand and the five of them moved ahead.

"You need to allow me to negotiate," Thane said. "Her life depends on it."

Worried eyes scanned the horizon. He saw the moment Layala spotted Evalyn. Her face fell slack, but her fury electrified, and the heavy weight of her magic clouded around them. "I'm taking his head now."

"No," Thane said. "You knew this would happen. You knew they had her. Now is the time to remain calm. They have a white flag—"

"Screw the white flag. He has Evalyn. This only ends one way, Thane," Layala said, lifting her chin slightly. "I'll put a throwing star right through his forehead." The terror on her face was evident despite her demeanor.

"He wouldn't bring her out in the open unless he had something up his sleeve. Do not attack." He ground his teeth. Years of battle with his father told him all he needed to know. Tenebris was cunning and smart. Evalyn was his best tool against them, and he'd use it well. "Or you may very well put her in a grave."

She pulled her hand away from her belt of weapons and swallowed hard but said, "I trust you. Do you have a plan?"

"I expected Evalyn to be held somewhere else. I'm working on one." The glare she shot him turned his stomach. He didn't want to ever see disappointment in her in regard to him. He'd have to come up with something fast. If Layala lost Evalyn, he feared what she might do. They marched side by side. "Do you see Mathekis or Varlett?"

Her bright-blue eyes darted back and forth along the line of soldiers. "No. They must be hidden in the mist. Piper and Ronan will fly to the edge of the Void and burn down the pale ones who dare cross."

That was the plan anyway, but plans could change in battle. Thane looked over his shoulder. His Ravens came to a stop; the horses stamped and tossed their heads eager to push forward. "Unless the pale ones are behind us."

A firm line formed on Layala's lips. She turned, searching the wooded area to the left and the vast rolling green hills to the right side. "There is only that grove of trees. We'd have seen them from above if they hid in there."

"I hope so," Thane replied, though nerves tightened his stomach. Those trees were thick and tall, so to see bodies on the darkened floor would be difficult.

Layala and Thane stopped and waited for his family and Layala's to meet them. Though Evalyn's face was bruised, and her wrists bled from the rope burns, she defiantly held her head high. Talon's horse snorted, and tails swished at flies, but for a moment no one said anything. His sister's chin trembled, on the verge of tears. She wore a pink dress, and her chocolate-brown hair was pulled up with small curls around her face. Thane shook his head. She had no business being here, let alone in a pink dress with lace. She was barely eighteen and looked every bit the child she still was at the moment.

Somehow Orlandia held her tongue, though if glares

could cut, Layala would be sliced to ribbons. Why his mother could be so blind to the truth and place blame on Layala made him boil inside. Layala's lazy stare gave no indication that any of this bothered her, but he knew she was terrified of what could happen to her aunt.

"I hope it was worth it," he said to Aldrich. This was the first time Thane came face to face with Aldrich since he'd injured him back at Kail's place, and the inconvenient pain of seeing him ride beside their father hurt more than he thought it would. The white flag at the end of the pole shifted slightly in the breeze, casting a wavering shadow on Thane's chest. Aldrich didn't meet Thane's gaze. Coward.

Tenebris's horse pawed at the ground, and the reins pinged against the silver armor around the horse's chest and shoulders. He jerked Evalyn's rope, and she winced as it went taut. "We can do this the easy way or the hard way." He looked straight at Layala. "I can be merciful. Your aunt can live."

Thane lifted his chin and took in a deep breath through the nose. "You have two options. You can surrender but the cost is your head, High King. You can save the lives of hundreds, if not thousands, if you give yourself over to be executed for the many crimes you have committed. It will be swift and painless but just. Or you can choose to fight but you will die along with your soldiers, and *my* mercy will not be found."

Tenebris threw his head back in maniacal laughter. The sound grated on Thane's nerves.

"You are in no position to make any demands, Thane. You think your five hundred and a handful of dragons scare me?" He tugged on the rope again to make a point, and Evalyn squeaked, face scrunching in pain.

Layala took a step forward and Tenebris held up a finger. "She's been poisoned and only I know the antidote. Don't come any closer."

Poisoned? Her lips did have a purple tinge and upon further inspection, her bloodshot eyes rang alarm bells. Shit. The only exchange he'd accept would be Layala for Evalyn.

"It's alright, Laya," Evalyn said, tears gleaming. "I've made my peace."

"Shut up," Tenebris snapped and jerked the rope for the third time.

Thane's body tensed, ready to spring into action as blood rushed down Evalyn's arms in streams. He could hardly bear to see any female abused let alone one he cared for.

A glint of metal flashed from Layala's hand and then a quiet gasp. Thane's heart clenched. She'd thrown that star, the one he asked her to stay. He fully expected to see blood streaming down his father's face but... his brows furrowed, had she missed? Suddenly Orlandia screamed with the kind of pain he'd never heard from her before, then her hand clamped over her mouth.

That star found its mark—blood oozed down

Talon's neck. The sharp metal embedded in the hollow of her throat on the left side.

A wave of nauseating heat washed through him. What had Layala done? Thane whirled on her, heart racing and breaking at once. "Laya," his voice came out thick and splintered.

"I put that where it would hurt the most." Layala's voice was cruel, clipped. He hadn't heard her sound so vicious in a long time. She stared down Tenebris with blazing hatred. "She has about a minute before she bleeds out. Give me Evalyn and the antidote or your precious daughter dies."

"You bitch," Tenebris growled.

"Do it!" Orlandia screeched and slid off her horse. Her soft hands pawed at Talon's dress and over her arms. Talon choked and slumped into Orlandia's arms. The wheezing sound of Talon trying to breathe was like searing needles pricking Thane's chest. Suddenly he found it hard to drag in his own breath. This was his little sister; he always promised to protect her and watch over her.

The white flag hit the ground and Aldrich slid in to scoop Talon in his arms. He looked up at Tenebris who had yet to move.

Thane warred with himself; go to Talon and save her or wait out his father... did Tenebris love Talon more than his power? Could he risk waiting? Talon didn't have much time. But if he didn't, they lost the leverage *and* Evalyn.

"My baby!" Orlandia wailed. The hysteria in her

voice cut deep. Her shaking hands swiped over Talon's forehead. "Stay with me, my sweet girl," she crooned. She turned to Thane now with helpless, pleading eyes. "Your baby sister is dying! Are you going to let your senseless feud kill her?!"

Thane couldn't help it. His feet moved almost on their own accord. But a gloved hand grasped around his wrist and jerked him to a halt. "Don't you dare." Layala didn't sound like herself. "You wait," she commanded, even quieter but more vicious. Whether by some unknown power or his own uncertainty, he stilled.

Tenebris let out a roaring scream of anger, dropped the rope and kicked Evalyn in the back, sending her stumbling forward.

Layala rushed with arms outstretched to catch her. "The antidote!"

A small vile flipped end over end; Thane snatched it out of the air and handed it to Layala, then his feet slammed, closing the distance to his family in seconds. He only spared Aldrich a glance then carefully pulled the throwing star loose and tossed the bloody metal piece. Her chest barely moved with breath. Her lips were colorless and that flush she usually had in her cheeks—gone. "Hold on, Talon," he murmured, slicing open his palm. He dipped his finger into the blood and drew the healing rune on her throat and then dug the knife into his flesh, inflicting pain. Her body went into convulsions, Aldrich cradled her tighter, but she never took her sea-green eyes from

Thane. She had all the hope in the world that her big brother would save her.

"Remember that time we ran through the pond throwing mud at the swans?" he said to distract her as much as himself from the pain. "Then I fell flat on my face and came up covered in muck. I don't think you've ever laughed so hard."

Her lips parted like she wanted to speak but couldn't. If this didn't work—Maker, it had to. How could Layala sacrifice his little sister for her aunt... anger flared in him, and he dug the knife deeper, grinding his teeth to keep from groaning. The blood rune grew brighter, sizzling as if it boiled and the wound on her neck began to knit itself shut. Come on! Finally, after what felt like a lifetime, she stopped shaking and moments after that the wound sealed shut.

"I remember," Talon said in a weak voice. "You looked like a swamp beast."

Thane smiled at her and stroked droplets of blood off her cheek. "This is no place for you. Go where it's safe."

"Thane please—just forgive daddy. Let's go home. I want to go home with you, with everyone."

"I can't. One day you will understand." He shoved up and pointed at his mother. "Get her out of here!" Orlandia turned to look at Tenebris for approval. "GO!" Thane shouted. Maker, the hold Tenebris held over his mother was infuriating.

But with a startled jump, she nodded and

mounted her horse. Aldrich lifted Talon behind her, and the horses' hooves pounded as they raced away.

Thane's hand inched for the dagger on his hip. He and Aldrich stood face to face now. But out of respect for the peace of a white flag, he didn't draw his weapon. He didn't allow himself to think of the good times he had with Aldrich, but rather the betrayal. "I'll be seeing you on the battlefield. Brother."

Aldrich's golden hair moved with the breeze. "May the best heir win."

Thane walked backward, keeping his gaze on his father and brother. The pure hatred on Tenebris's expression burned away at Thane's empathy for his father. "You will regret this. I'll crush your Ravens until not one is left to rise against me ever again."

Thane looked over his shoulder at his battalion of waiting Ravens and lifted his fist. The horses knickered and neighed, breath shot from their noses as they danced in anticipation of the charge. The soldiers drew their swords, grinding of metal on metal echoed across the plain.

Thane dropped his fist. "FORWARD!"

CHAPTER 40

The empty glass vial plopped to the ground at Layala's side. She tugged on Aunt Evalyn's arm. Her steps were wobbly, and the antidote would take time to counteract the poison. Layala couldn't risk a healing rune not working for poison. Layala suspected poison would require a different kind of magic to withdraw or counteract and so she'd made a calculated move.

She slung Aunt Evalyn's arm across her shoulder and carried them both into a run. "You have to get off this battlefield."

"That was stupid," Aunt Evalyn croaked. "You risked the princess's life."

"Yeah, well," Layala murmured. "Now we're even. She almost got me killed once. And I did what I had to to save you. I knew Thane could heal her."

"Will Thane see it that way?"

She frowned, knowing her action would hurt him,

but this wasn't the time to worry about it. She could ask for forgiveness, but she couldn't ask for him to bring Aunt Evalyn back from the dead if she hadn't taken action. Aunt Evalyn's toes hit a rock and she stumbled. Layala caught her with her other arm. The pounding of hundreds of horse hooves charging their way kept her from answering aloud.

A lone black horse rode out ahead of the others and turned their way. Layala smiled at the white star on his forehead and the thick black mane—Midnight. And it turned out he wasn't alone. Tif rode in the saddle. She looked horrified to be here, but that little creature was braver than she ever thought. Shooting out heavy breath, Midnight stopped before them, and Tif said. "Thought you could use some help."

"You're the best, Tifapine." Layala pushed Aunt Evalyn up until she swung her leg over the other side of Midnight. "Now go. Get far away from here. Both of you."

Tears welled in Tif's eyes. "Be safe."

"And take off Tenebris's head," Aunt Evalyn said. "Too long has he been afforded breath after what he's done."

"I will," Layala vowed to them both. The thundering of feet drew her gaze. Both sides charged now with only moments before they clashed. Layala gave one last look. "If I don't survive this, know I love you both, and tell Thane I loved him and I will find him in the next life. Take my ashes to Briar Hollow and bury

me next to my parents." Before she could let a tear fall, she turned and ran. Because it wasn't just a battlefield she must survive, it was the Black Mage when she woke him.

Her feet flew over the uneven grass, pushing her legs harder with each breath. Thane was out in front of his soldiers by several yards, alone. Maker, he was a bullheaded fool sometimes. He couldn't even wait for his Ravens to catch up with him? Her heart thudded hard against her ribs.

She searched the enemy's side for Tenebris. She didn't know if she could trust Thane to kill his father when it came down to it, so she'd do it for him. Then they could sneak inside the Void and follow their plan. The line of soldiers rushed forward on foot, deep voices roaring and bellowing the way males did before they clashed in battle. Tenebris's soldiers wore silver armor, easily distinguishable from the Raven coal.

There the tyrant king was, sitting atop his horse in the back with Aldrich beside him. They would have to fight through hundreds of soldiers to get to him. Thane was seconds from colliding with the first soldiers. Legs and arms pumped faster. Her heart lurched; he swung both swords, blocking a blow and shoving the tip of his other blade straight through chest armor as if it wasn't even there.

"Fightbringer!"

Layala looked left, one of the Ravens pointed up.

Dax swooped down. His shiny pearl scales glinted in the light like a sword. He dropped low enough she

threw out her magic to hook it like a lasso on his back horn and up and up they went. "Tenebris!" was all she could manage to say through heavy breathing. She gripped her magical stalk, and in seconds she flew over the heads of the soldiers, ready to spring when she was close to Tenebris. She glanced over to Vaper plowing into a row of the enemy, bowling them over, slashing her massive claws. The screams of terror and pain were horrid.

When she finally killed Tenebris, she hoped the soldiers would surrender and turn to Thane. He was once their king, the rightful heir.

When the Ravens' horses collided with the line of Palenor soldiers, a sick crunch of hooves on armor and screams of agony made her want to gag. They were elves, not cursed, not mindless beasts who wanted them dead, but high elves like her, following orders of their king. If she could end Tenebris quickly, it might save them too.

Arrows soared past her head and bounced off Dax. Tenebris was close now, but a swarm of soldiers moved in to block him. Concentrated arrows came down like rain. One deflected off her shoulder. She'd never make it without more protection and Layala had asked Dax not to burn the soldiers down unless it was necessary. It was too gruesome of a way to die. Now if they were pale ones, she'd say burn them all.

Layala held out her hand, summoning that power she once used against the dragon prince. It was in her somewhere, even if she hadn't mastered it.

A warm pulse left her palm and the arrows stuck into a shimmering wall. It formed around her like a bubble. Tenebris had turned his horse and was making a run toward the Void. Coward. Even if he went inside, it wouldn't stop her. Dax barked out a roaring dragon call and swung her around cutting off, Tenebris's escape. She sprang off her vine, landing gracefully on her feet and jerked out her father's sword. She held it out in front of her and Lightbringer's blade caught the sunlight. Tenebris shielded his eyes from the glare. Good. It was only fitting she ended his life with it.

Tenebris's horse reared up, and the fear leaching out of him gave her a level of satisfaction she thought only killing him could bring. Every footstep she took brought her closer to the one thing she'd wanted almost more than anything.

Dax let out another throaty call, and with great whooshes soared back to the main fight.

"Your father cried, you know," Tenebris said, pulling back on his horse's reins in her advance. Layala's vines wrapped around the horse's legs. He wouldn't be running. "Cried like a little girl before his head fell to the floor. It made the strangest sound, like a watermelon being split in half. I'll never forget it."

The hairs on the back of her neck rose along with the flood of heated anger. "Looks like you don't have Mathekis to save you this time."

Somewhere in the distance she heard Thane calling out to her. He was too far away to stop her, if

that's what he wanted. He wouldn't take this moment.

"Layala!" Thane's voice grew louder, more frantic, closer. Dragons roared and screeched. Elves screamed and weapons collided but none of that mattered right then.

She continued with determination. It was only then that she noticed a dark cloud had amassed at her feet and followed her steps. She paused a moment, but whatever it was, didn't stop her. She stood a few feet from Tenebris and raised her chin. "Get off your horse and fight me."

Body visibly shaking, he took out his sword. She was surprised he even had one. After he slid down, all she could think about was how pathetic he looked standing there with his sword awkward in both hands. It was limp to the left side and his stance was all wrong. His armor didn't have a scratch, too shiny, unused.

One hard swing clacked against his sword, and he sucked in sharply, face scrunching in horror. She nailed him again and sent him stumbling to the ground. "That's it? You're the great King Tenebris, the one I feared for so long?"

He rolled onto his back and reached up with one arm to shield himself. "No, please don't." She strode forward and kicked him hard in the face and heard the sickening crack of metal on bone. His head snapped to the side and his temple split from the impact of her

armor-toed boots. She stomped down on his hand like he once had to her. "Stop," he choked.

"Stop?" Layala shook with built-up rage, pressing her weight harder onto his hand, grinding her toes back and forth. She hoped every single one of the bones snapped.

He whimpered, trying to pull his hand away, and slammed his other fist into her armor-covered calf. She barely even noticed the hit.

"Why would I do that?" She dropped down and her fist collided with his cheek, cracking bone. "You're not so tough now that you don't have others to fight for you. You created an assassin the day you took my parents, and a monster the day you took my mate from me. Oh, you may have put me down for a minute, but it only made me stronger." She hit him again and again, letting the fury flow through her. He curled into himself on his side. She stood over him, shaking her head. Maker, he was pathetic.

Among the shouts and the weapons clashing, and dragons roaring, she heard Thane call to her again. This time she looked for him in the fighting and chaos. What if he needed her? But she found Dax and a sleek black dragon—Varlett clawing and biting at each other in midair. A sharp sting seared Layala's thigh, and she nearly dropped from the shock of it. Only the gold hilt of the dagger showed, and the blade must have struck bone. She gasped at the wave of pain that suddenly washed through her and leaned all her

weight to the left. Tenebris got up and ran toward the Void.

With a roar through her teeth, she jerked the blade free, and a wave of nausea hit. It hurt more to pull it out. "You're not getting away, Tenebris!" She took off after him, pushing through the pain and blood pouring down her knee over her shin. A throwing star to the back of his thigh made him arch and cry out then he dropped to his hands, crawling now. Crawling like the worm he was.

With no care as to how much it would hurt her injury, she caught up to him and kicked him hard in the ribs, dropping him to his side, gasping for air. "Wait, wait don't kill me," he begged. Blood flowed down over his left eye and the swelling had already started from her hits. "We can make a deal. Thane can have the throne. You can be queen. I'll—I'll go away, far away."

Angry tears burned her eyes. She imagined her parents might have asked for him to spare them and their pleas fell on deaf ears. With her sword raised and the point angled at his chest, she said, "This is for my parents, for Reina, for all the people you've hurt and murdered, for Thane, and—for me."

"Layala, look out!" Thane bellowed only yards away now.

Varlett's dragon form careened toward her at the speed of a shooting star. Black talons shone in the sunlight, her mighty roar pierced Layala's ears, so loud

she thought her eardrums would burst and bleed. Instead of plunging that blade through Tenebris, she turned to bring up her magical shield, but the hit was like a mountain falling on top of her, driving her into the grass and dirt, whisking the air from her lungs, then those ebony talons wrapped around her body, and she was in the air, rising faster and faster. Her fuzzy mind whirled. The dragon's grip was so tight around her she couldn't move, could hardly breathe. She gripped her sword's handle, laying on her chest, like it was her last line of survival.

She willed her magic to set her free... where were her vines, her shield... anything? "You forgot I know more about magic than you, Layala. You can't hurt me."

"Why didn't you let me kill him!" Layala screamed and her throat burned. "Why!"

"Oh, did I steal your moment? My apologies," she crooned. "But you have more important things to do." Red slashes covered her chest and neck area, gaping wounds that could only be from Dax's talons. But what happened to him? She peered down and his giant body lay off in the field far away from the ongoing battle. When he slowly rose, she sighed in relief.

"I was going to go to him on my own!" She was wracked with an involuntary shudder giving in to his words from her dreams. *Come to me,* he'd said and now she was.

"So you can kill him? I don't think so."

Layala's tense body went limp—defeated, flying a

hundred feet in the air in the clutches of her enemy. She watched Tenebris grow small, and Thane looked up at her with terror. Why couldn't this one thing work out? Why was that wretched elf always sparred?

The black mist swirled in the wake of Varlett's whooshing wings. The black bogs, the stink, and the waiting groups of pale ones littering the ground made her stomach turn. She was in the Void and there was no turning back now.

It only took moments for the landscape to change. As if a desert oasis grew out of seemingly nowhere, thick trees with wide tropical—*red* fronds, shoots of tall bamboo, kapok trees but with thick maroon leaves and massive branches... so unusual. She could hardly believe it. Was it a magic trick? A full red jungle, not devoid of life like everyone thought. She'd never heard of anything like it. But strangest of all, rising in the center, was a single, white brick tower. Its pointed roof peaked out of the canopy of the jungle. She'd expect it to be dark and menacing if anything, but it was— quaint, almost inviting. It reminded her of the mage's tower in Doonafell.

Varlett's great wings beat rapidly as they lowered to a massive clearing at the base of the tower. She opened her paws several feet from the surface and Layala dropped, freefalling until she smacked into the soft dark-brown earth. Facedown on the ground, she spit dirt and leaves, and swiped the back of her hand across her mouth. The pain in her thigh throbbed but she was thankful the forest floor was covered in thick

foliage and reddish moss or that drop would have been excruciating. She slowly pushed herself up, struggling through the stiffening and tingling in her leg and shoved Lightbringer back in her scabbard. The scent of jasmine wafted on the thick, humid air. Lifting her head, she spotted the small white flowers and their green leaves, growing all around the single door in the tower. And that door was covered in—lavender butterflies.

Sharp talons scraped loudly against Layala's back armor then the dragon gripped her left arm and jerked her up. "Move."

The stab wound radiated pain as she limped forward. A small part of her wanted to rely on Varlett's assistance but she tore her arm away. With a shrug, Varlett strode ahead and took hold of the gold ring on the door, the butterflies scattered taking to the air by the hundreds. Layala watched them circle around her in a whirlwind then disappear into the jungle.

She found it odd there were no birds here singing in the trees. Insects hummed and the wind rustled the tops of the red leaves but no familiar bird calls. With a quick glance around the trunks and foliage, she found gleaming eyes watching from the shadows. A pale one leaned out from behind a tree and stared back at her. She jumped, ready to pull Lightbringer again but the creature didn't move to attack, didn't screech, or holler like they'd always done before. He simply watched.

With a deep breath she searched the skies one last time, with hope that Thane and Vaper might show, or

Piper and Prince Ronan. She found only the sun peeking through the dark misty haze.

Layala touched the dagger on her hip, and Lightbringer on her back, ensuring they were there and stepped through the entrance.

Mathekis waited in the shadows. His black eyes gleamed in the dark until he stepped into the light. He looked her up and down and his black lips twisted down. "I suppose there's no time to make you presentable."

She didn't know what about her appearance he didn't approve of, but she couldn't care less what he thought. The small foyer led directly to a set of stairs, short ivory candles lit in small alcoves in the stone walls, but there were no windows to provide light. A wood handrail lined the left side of the wall; she grabbed hold and started her ascent, skin crawling with Mathekis so close behind. A feeling crept over her that the Black Mage would be at the very top. This would be a painful climb.

The first hundred or so steps were like fire searing her bleeding thigh, but soon numbness took over, diluting the pain to a dull ache. She didn't know if that was a good or bad sign, but she didn't stop. She couldn't hear Varlett. The wench was probably already waiting.

She finally reached the top floor, and the smell of jasmine trickled into her senses, again. She stilled. Why did it remind her of... something? She didn't know what. It was like a known but forgotten name on

the tip of her tongue, and all she needed was a reminder.

Varlett leaned against the wall, inspecting her talons as if the wait vexed her. "About time," she said.

"Well, in case you didn't notice, I've been stabbed." If she thought she could beat her in a fight, they'd have it out right then. But until she found a way to break through Varlett's magical shield, that would have to wait.

"Did *you* stab her?" Mathekis accused.

"I haven't touched her," Varlett growled.

"No, you *just* almost crushed me into the ground."

A single torch burned, giving off a low orange light. Layala snatched it off the wall and angrily strode by. At the end of the empty corridor waited double doors. He was in there, wasn't he? She swallowed hard, moving forward, slower now. This had been the plan since they left House Drakonan, but Thane was supposed to be with her, and being here was much different than imagining it. She almost *felt* him, or a sense of longing, something pulling her that way. *It's your blood connection,* the goddess said. *Ugh,* she wanted to vomit the closer she drew.

"About our deal," Varlett's steps were eerily quiet behind her, like she weighed nothing at all. Her voice was suddenly in Layala's mind, "It's silence—what I'm going to require of you."

Layala looked over her shoulder. "What?" Goosebumps slid across her skin. How had she spoken to her mind like that?

Without moving her mouth, she said, "Soon you will know a detail about Zaurahel and me, something you saw. You must never tell him or anyone. You'll know what I'm talking about."

Mathekis looked back and forth between them, eyes narrowed in suspicion.

"You're making no sense," Layala said.

"You'll understand one day," she whispered in Layala's mind. "If your shiny new magic and that black cloud I witnessed around you earlier is any indication, it will be soon."

"Keeping secrets, Varlett?" Mathekis said, casually, as if he didn't care but it was obvious, he did.

"It's between the elf and me."

Was this a riddle? How could Layala know anything about Varlett and Zaurahel?

With Layala's slow limp, they finally reached the end of the short corridor, and she held the torch closer to the shiny black wood. The carvings, similar to the Black Mage's chair, were of lilies and serpents, intertwined together, weaving like an intricate dance. Something about the contrast between those two things was undeniably beautiful.

Steeling her nerves, Layala inhaled deeply. It was now or never. Her magic soared inside, biting at her flesh, ready to unleash hell. No doubt Varlett would have dosed her with katagas serum if they didn't need her magic. Even if they said the Black Mage was in a deep slumber, she had to be ready for the possibility he waited, perfectly alert to fight on the other side.

But she paused with her hand on the door. "Why did you need Tenebris's and Mathekis's help? Why didn't you just bring me here the day I came to your cabin in the mountains?"

"Zaurahel never told me how to wake him. As I said, we had a falling out."

"But he told Mathekis?" She looked at him.

He nodded. "Though from what Varlett says, you already know what to do. I'm here to ensure what you were told was correct."

"And Tenebris?"

"Made a deal with Zaurahel," Varlett answered. "We all have our own secrets and parts to play."

He made a deal four hundred years ago? She didn't even want to know the details. Shoving her shoulder into the doors, she pushed through. Her gaze fell to the stone table and the body lying on top of it. No windows let in light. It was but a round tomb of ivory brick.

Something itched at the back of her mind; something about her dreams reminded her of this. One foot crossed the threshold, then two. She expected to hear Varlett trailing her, but the dragon shifter stood on the other side. Her scrunched, confused face turned to one of panic. Her hands pressed on the air in the middle of the doorway as if it was solid. "I—can't pass through." She even sounded like she was on the other side of a wall.

Mathekis, however, came inside with ease. "Inter-

esting he would bar you, Varlett. You must have really angered him during that fallout."

She let out a low growl. "Fix it, Mathekis."

"You'll wait and be invited in when he wakes."

Layala full-on grinned at the dragon's plight. Even her smallest inconvenience made Layala's day.

"Layala, you must not kill him. Please. The goddess didn't tell you everything."

"I won't allow her to," Mathekis said and folded his hands behind his back, waiting beside the door like a sentinel. "Relax, Varlett."

Layala ignored the dragon's muffled pleas and Mathekis's promises. They wouldn't stop her. She planned for the possibility of them being here.

Her heart hammered with every footstep, quiet taps that seemed so loud now. It was as if a hush fell over everything. The torch in her hand crackled and sizzled, but that was the only sound. The hairs on the nape of her neck rose. The Black Mage's chest didn't move up and down with breath. He was utterly still. Would he somehow be perfectly preserved for four hundred years without a beating heart? Was he a pale one? Her eyes trailed over his black boots, then up the thick leather, fitted pants. At his waist a silver buckle etched with a rune at its center. A deep red leather, silver-studded vest covered his upper body, and an ebony cloak wrapped around his shoulders draped onto the floor. She was mere feet away now.

She gasped. The rushing of her blood throbbed in

her ears. She gulped and took a step back. His ashy, near black hair brushed against his shoulders, curling slightly. His fair skin looked exactly like someone who hadn't seen the sun in hundreds of years, but he wasn't milky white like a pale one, and he didn't have black lips or the dark circles around his eyes. She blinked several times, scrutinizing every inch of his remarkably beautiful face. Maker above, he looked so much like... Thane.

CHAPTER 41

What did this mean? The likeness was uncanny. *She* was supposed to be his relation... was this a magic trick? It must be an illusion to make her hesitate. Thane could trace his royal lineage back for thousands of years on both sides. There was no way he was related to the mage.

Layala glanced over at Mathekis and slowly slid her dagger from her hip. Turning her back to him and blocking his view of what she was doing, she jabbed the sharp point of her blade at his heart. The tip of her weapon didn't even touch the leather armor he wore. A translucent veil shimmered against her weapon, hard as stone, impenetrable and unyielding. The magic protecting him in this state was indeed there.

"It won't work," Mathekis said smugly. "So don't bother trying to kill him."

But if the veil surrounded him, could she even do the spell to wake him? She slowly reached for his face; her fingertips brushed his skin, and she jerked back at

the icy feel. So she could get through the veil if she didn't intend to harm? Clever. There was no other choice then. She drew the sharp edge of her blade across her palm and took a deep breath as blood welled up.

Mathekis watched her with an unnerving hunger, his face contorted as if he could barely contain himself, but he stood completely still. "That's it," he encouraged.

Hand visibly trembling, she hovered it over his mouth and let her blood drip into his slightly-parted lips. The goddess didn't specify how much but when lines ran down the sides of his chin, she set her hand on his armored chest for balance and leaned forward. Her heart hammered; it was suddenly hard to breathe. She once thought she would take the life of Thane, the elf she *thought* was the worst in the realm of Adalon and now, she was about to give life to true evil.

Her skin crawled as her lips grazed his. She stared at his long dark lashes and whispered the words the goddess told her to recite, "I give you my blood so that your heart may beat and my breath so that your lungs may draw air. I give you life," and then she blew into his mouth. She waited. Her heart thumped hard against her ribs, and then his chest rose beneath her hand as he inhaled. Layala jumped. It worked. His light ashen skin took on a vibrancy as if he radiated from the inside.

Now he was vulnerable. Now he could be killed. She threw out her hand, wrapped her vine around

Mathekis's mouth like a gag. Vines circled his body and pinned him there. He roared but he had to speak words to use his persuasive power. Varlett slammed her fists on the invisible wall and scratched her talons against it, but she was powerless to get through.

Swiftly, Layala took the pommel of her sword in both hands and leveled the tip with his heart. The fact he looked so much like the male she loved made her gut churn, but this was the Black Mage. The elf responsible for the death of so many, the one who brought the curse on this land. She drove down with all her strength. Her blade hit and with a loud snap, it broke in half. *Holy shit. Holy shit. Lightbringer!* Shocked, she stared at the fragmented jagged piece lying on his chest. *The magical shield was supposed to be gone. Why didn't it work?* With her mouth hanging open, she picked up the other half of Lightbringer. No. This had to work.

Mathekis broke free of her magic and said, "Do not strike him again."

She felt the power of his persuasion, but it didn't hit like before. She'd grown resilient to his magic somehow. With no time to lose, she tossed the sword, and it clattered on the floor, loud in the silence of this room. Her dagger was swiftly in her hand.

The Black Mage's eyes flashed open, and he bolted upright. Layala gasped and brought up the dagger to jam it into his neck, but a strong hand snaked around her throat before she could strike and retreat. As if ice slid through her veins, every muscle froze. She fought

to move, to jerk away but she couldn't. She tried to scream, to cry for help though it would have been in vain.

Maroon color eyes that seemed to shift and glitter from deep red to vibrant magenta trailed over Layala, starting from the top of her head to her hips and then his stare met hers. All she could think about at that moment was why he looked so much like Thane even though she should be fighting to break free, calling her magic to destroy this evil bastard. But even if they resembled each other, Thane was beautiful like the sun, warm and bright with the power to burn. The Black Mage was the night, cold, full of shadows and darkness and yet, the only time the stars shined.

"Where are we?" His powerful and seductive voice snaked down her spine.

The hold he had over her vocal cords loosed. "Get your hand off me!" she spat.

He gripped her throat hard enough to cut off her air. "I asked you a question and you will answer. If you make a remark like that again, I'll crush your windpipe."

Her skin prickled and her lungs burned for air. She nodded once, and his digging fingers eased slightly. "The Void." Maker, how was she going to get out of this? Just as every inch of her body was held hostage, so was her magic. Her skin tingled with its power, but nothing happened. It felt like that shimmering veil he once had over him was over her now but to keep her magic trapped inside.

His dark brows pulled down slightly. "The Void?"

"In Adalon. In the Kingdom of Palenor."

Thane, please come. Please. Or Prince Ronan, Piper, Fennan, someone. But they were all locked in their own battles. This was supposed to be easy. Bring him to life then kill him all in a matter of seconds. She reached deep inside herself again, searching for her magic, imagining the black vines shooting around, wrapping around him, crushing the life from him.

Mathekis stepped toward them and said, "My Lord, I am here."

The Black Mage barely spared him a glance as his legs slid off the table, and his boots hit the ground. His intimidating stature loomed over her. He glanced over at Mathekis, scrutinizing him a moment and then he was focused on her again. With whatever magic he wielded, he took control of her legs, pushing her to walk backward until she hit the wall. Her heart slammed against her chest. *Why can't I move? How is he doing this?* She was at the complete mercy of this mad elf. His grip on her throat didn't hurt but was uncomfortable. He blinked a few times and whatever confusion he once had vanished. She saw it lift in his malevolent eyes.

"I knew you'd come to me." He paused. "Valeen."

Layala swallowed hard. "My name is Layala. You're mistaken."

"It's her, Lord," Mathekis said. "I'm certain of it."

"Oh, I *know* it is." He licked Layala's blood from his lower lip and then slowly shook his head. "So, it's

games you want? It's been a long time, but I will never forget you."

He was out of his mind. With all her might, she fought to gain control of her dagger. Her right hand shook a little. "I'm an elven mage and my name is Layala Lightbringer." What if she could convince him she was on his side long enough to get away. "I brought you back—to fight with you, and yet you grab me by the throat."

A cruel smirk lifted the corners of his mouth. "More lies." He licked more blood from the corner of his mouth. "You loathe me. I can feel it radiating off you."

He glanced toward the doorway where Varlett still stood, palm flat against the barrier. She looked—sad. Or at the very least, worried. Her gaze bounced back and forth between them. But it wasn't as if Layala had the upper hand here, so her worry was unwarranted.

"Why is *she* here?" he demanded of Mathekis.

"To make amends, Lord."

He let out a low growl and looked down at Layala once again. "You don't remember anything? I don't look familiar to you?"

He did but not for any reason he was thinking. She shook her head.

"And you don't remember Varlett either, do you? At least from before."

What was there to remember? He was long gone by the time she was born. This must be a case of mistaken identity. Maybe she only looked like the

Valeen they once knew, a doppelgänger. "All I know is that Varlett is your very devoted lover."

He smiled. "You must still be young." His hand felt its way up from her throat to her cheek, sending an involuntary shiver through her. He brushed his thumb over her lips. If he moved it any closer, she'd sink her teeth into him. "Twenty-five?" How could he know that? And what did her age have to do with anything? "Maybe twenty-six. Mathekis knew he had to wait until you were the proper age to wake me." He tilted her face side to side. "But your power is weak. You haven't been using it like you should. No one has trained you."

How could he know all this simply by looking at her? Her chest rushed up and down with panicked breath. All she wanted was to be able to move her body again and fight. Her muscles felt so taut and strained they ached.

"I didn't remember in the beginning either." He tsked. "What are we going to do about that, love?" He took the dagger from her hand and held it up. "You tried to kill me with this? You're either misguided or a fool."

Layala gathered all the saliva in her mouth and spit in his face.

He chucked and wiped his cheek. "Maybe you do remember me."

"I don't know what you're talking about, you smug bastard. Release me!"

"If you'd been using your power like you should,

Val, you could break free of my hold." He smiled, showing off his beautiful teeth and the dimple on his left cheek. He even had that small scar across his chin too as she'd seen in her dream. "You had the power to rival even me."

As if his words gave her strength, she curled her right hand into a fist and punched him straight in the jaw. His head snapped to the side, and he growled, low and menacing. When he looked back, darkness clouded his eyes, and he slowly grew a wicked smile. "Ah there you are." He gripped her throat tighter and that iciness in her blood stilled her completely again. "But that won't happen again." He paused looking her over. "I couldn't have asked for a better welcome back gift than to watch you helpless under my touch. I wonder, would you beg me to let you go?"

Her knees suddenly crumpled, and she dropped to the stone. The pain of the impact flared up her injury and she winced. "Thane!" she shouted but her voice echoed around the room as if a sound barrier kept it inside. Was she trapped in here now? The anxiety of being stuck in that tower at Castle Dredwich coiled its way through her. Her breaths came quicker; her composure began to slip.

He smiled again and tapped his finger on his chin. "Thane?" he purred. "Maybe I'll let you go to him if you say, please, Hel let me go. Please, Hel, most wise, handsome, and all-powerful god, show me mercy."

"Piss off," she snarled. She wouldn't beg.

His smooth-as-honey laugh bounced off the tower

walls. "Oh, what fun we're going to have. And I do so enjoy seeing you on your knees but..." He stood from his crouch and with one simple flick of his finger Layala rose and her feet lifted off the ground until her face was level with his. "It's unbecoming." He shoved his palm against her Raven armored chest and pinned her to the wall. The harsh impact stole the breath from her lungs. "See, a queen should never be on her knees."

Layala's eyes widened, *a queen*?

His gaze drug down her form. "This won't do either." With a snap of his fingers, her armor vanished, and a gown of blood red wrapped around her body. Straps wrapped around her neck and his hand slid up the length of her thigh where a slit in the dress revealed bare skin, all the way to her hip. His gaze fell to the stab wound. "Who hurt you?" He didn't sound concerned but almost as if it delighted him. His eyes were fixed on the blood.

Anger and fury burned hot in her chest, as his fingers danced around the throbbing pain. She wanted to tear his hands off her, but she still couldn't move. "Stop touching me."

He finally tore his gaze up. "I asked you a question, love."

She almost felt compelled to answer, as if she couldn't resist. "The elf I hate most in this world hurt me. King Tenebris. More than once. More than anyone ever has."

He cupped his palm over her injury. Warmth radiated from his touch and to her utter surprise, the

throbbing stopped. "Why does that name sound familiar?" he mused.

"He was the elf prince you made a deal with, Lord," Mathekis offered.

The Black Mage tsked again. "Ah, yes. He should know better than to touch what is mine. He and I had a deal, you know. I'd kill his father so he could be king and if he ensured you were brought to me, he'd become a mage. He couldn't resist but neither could the rest of the elves. Oh, the fun back then."

"You tortured and killed and cursed elves because you thought it was fun?" Her voice overflowed with disdain. "That's why you did this?"

"Why? I did it because I could, love," he said in a tone that sounded flirtatious. He stared at her face as if he couldn't look away. "Gods, you are even more beautiful than I remembered. The envy of all in Runevale."

"I'm not Valeen. I'm a descendant of Runevale but I'm not from there. As you said, I'm twenty-five. I was born here." She hoped he would see reason. See that this was a mistake.

His lips hovered an inch from hers, and his wild magenta eyes filled with mischief and delight. "You may be known as Layala Lightbringer but that's not who you truly are. There is only one person who could bring me back. One single female in all the realms. And her name, *your* true name is Valeen. A goddess reborn." He tugged down the collar of his shirt to reveal a lily mark exactly like hers on the left side of his chest. "And you are *my* wife."

CHAPTER 42

T hane grabbed a fistful of his father's hair and dragged him in a slow steady march. The soldiers around them stopped fighting and parted for him. They watched with what he could only describe as relief, that their fight might be over. In the end, this battle came down to who wore the king's crown.

"Thane," Tenebris hit and clawed at his hand. "Stop this. Stop it! I had no choice. I had to ensure she was brought to him."

He vaguely heard his father's begging, barely registering the excuses. "Tell them," Thane said. "Tell them who the High King is."

"I am High King!" he spat.

His fist cracked Tenebris's already bruised cheek, knocking him to the ground. He wrapped his fingers around his father's throat and jerked him up again. Tenebris wheezed, trying to pry his hand away. Then

Thane placed the sharp edge of his sword on his father's neck. Once Layala was taken, his remorse, his hesitation when it came to Tenebris vanished. This was his fault. This battle, the fact that she wasn't in his arms at this very moment. All of it.

The word began to spread through the field. Swords stopped clashing, arrows didn't cut through the air, and the dragons landed, hanging back in the distance. The smell of burning flesh and charred earth overwhelmed the normally pleasant fresh air. The cries of the dying still lingered, and the vultures hovered above but those remaining stood at attention.

"Tell them Thane Athayel is High King of Palenor. Tell them or I will show them by spilling your blood all over this field."

Tenebris's throat bobbed. The caw of a raven circling overhead interrupted the silence, until he said, "I am stepping down. I relinquish my status." He hesitated. "Thane Athayel is your High King."

Both the Ravens and the Palenor soldiers, side by side, differing only in armor and who'd they'd been loyal to moments before, like a wave crashed to their knees.

Still gripping his father's hair, he forced him to turn. The scrunch of pain on his father's face only made him want to squeeze harder. He was so weak.

"I didn't want to do this. I had no choice," Tenebris started. "I made a deal with the Black Mage hundreds

of years ago. Mathekis made sure I upheld it. I was driven to find her, or I'd turn. You understand, don't you? I had to hold up my end of the bargain. Just like you once did."

There was no sympathy for what his father did. He made a selfish choice. "This was for power, nothing more."

"I was stupid. I wanted to be king. I wanted magic which I would only get when she woke him. And by the time I figured out I made a mistake, it was too late."

"How could he know about Layala that long ago?"

"He said he remembered, and he knew she would come."

"Remembered what?" Thane snarled, pressing the blade harder.

"That he was a god and so was she. I thought he was delusional, but I was only thinking of myself."

Thane stared at his father, at the way his skin creased between his light eyebrows. He remembered they were gods? What did that mean? In another life?

"He said that they were being punished, that they had to repent, and they were sent here to learn their lesson..." he licked his lips in hesitation. "And that she was his wife—his eternally-bound mate. I truly didn't know if your mate bond with her would work but you never finished the spell. You never joined your blood in a wedding ceremony to see."

Thane felt the color drain from his face, and he

released his father, moving back in a faltered step. "No." He wouldn't accept that. She was *his* mate, his wife. He felt it in his soul. They belonged together. But something about that statement stirred at the back of his mind. He could almost hear music, a tune he didn't know he knew. Dancing, gowns—a wedding. His? No —not his.

Tenebris stared down at his hands, opening and closing his fingers. It was an odd movement, like he was testing out if they were stiff. "I'm sorry, my son. I should have never dragged you into this." He held out his palms. "My hands were tied."

He wanted to be remorseful now? To apologize now? Thane watched him closely. The fear that once gripped his face vanished. So, he thought Thane would be lenient.

Thane shoved a finger at Tenebris. "The only reason I'm allowing you breath is so Layala can be the one to end you." He looked to the soldiers to his right. "Bind him. And Aldrich, too. Wherever that snake slinked off to."

He needed to get to Layala. The Void was quiet, too quiet for how close they were. Would they have followed Varlett and Layala? Where was Mathekis? Did they wait for the Black Mage to wake? "Battle formations!" Thane shouted. He wouldn't allow them to be caught unprepared. "Make ready for a pale one attack!"

"Oh, Thane, one more thing before you rush off to

her rescue." Tenebris smiled while the soldiers held his arms behind his back. What did he have up his sleeve? What did he know?

He swept out his leg and dropped the Raven to his left. With confusion, Thane watched the other Raven's skin turn an impossible shade of light blue then... frost covered his hair and even his armor until he was a frozen block of ice.

With a start, realization hit him. The Black Mage was awake, his father's deal was upheld, and Tenebris could now wield magic. With Tenebris's palm facing Thane, fingers splayed wide, a blast of frost hit Thane in the chest with the force of a ten-foot-tall ogre swinging a club. The blow sent him flying back into the group of soldiers, knocking them all down.

His body began to convulse. A cold so deep it felt hot seared his center. He watched in horror as the frost covered the Palenor sigil on his chest, then down his torso, moving like flame over oil. Thane slapped his hand over the cold, and it infected his hand and shot up his arm. The soldiers around him scrambled back. *No no no no*, he was paralyzed as the ice covered everything below his neck. It crept up to his chin—he wanted to scream, called his magic to stop it. It fought to warm him, to break free, then he felt it reach the top of his head.

Everything was dark.

An intense darkness like the stars fell from the heavens and the moon lost its luster.

He heard nothing.

Felt nothing...

... but cold. Bitter cold. Was he dead? Was this hell? An eternal punishment for the lives he'd stolen? It didn't feel like he had a body. He couldn't move... was there anywhere to move to?

He felt something now. Shame. His father bested him, killed him with one singular blow? And oh, Maker above, Layala. She was alone with the Black Mage. He left her alone. No, he couldn't leave her. He made her a promise.

The slightest light flickered. Like a spark in the dead of night. He felt it more than saw it, warming his chest. A *thud, thud, thud,* beat from somewhere. Was that a heartbeat?

It went faster. *Thud, thud, thud, thud.*

Heat blossomed and bloomed, melting the ice in his veins, covering his skin.

A glorious light shined so bright it stung his eyes. He blinked back tears, wiggled his fingers, curled his toes. The grass was soft under him. The scent of something burning invaded his nose. Whispers among soldiers started. But his father had his back to him, unaware. Thane shoved up, jerked free his second sword, and in three strides he drove the blade straight into Tenebris's back.

With a startled, strangled cry, he arched.

"I just remembered," Thane said in his ear. "I promised her that I'd destroy anyone who hurt her.

She didn't need to be the one to do it." Tenebris's legs gave way and Thane wrenched the sword free. Blood pooled out, filling the area around his body swiftly. He thought he would feel something as the light left his father's eyes and he stared up at the blue sky. Thought he'd feel the regret and anguish that had haunted him for months. But there was nothing. He may as well have been back in the darkness—cold.

"Vaper!" Thane's voice carried across the quiet battlefield. The bronze dragon rose into the air, and shot over the soldiers, casting a shadow to cover half of them. She landed with a grunt and smoke puffed out her nostrils.

"Yes, High King?"

"Take me to Layala."

THE THUMPING of Layala's heart and a sudden ringing in her ears made the Black Mage sound far away even though he was so close she could feel his body heat spilling onto her. It couldn't be true. She couldn't be his wife—his mate. He was mad...But she wondered what their connection was, and why the pale ones were drawn to her. Rising nausea made her want to vomit. This couldn't be it. It couldn't be real.

His palm slid across the top of Layala's head. Something heavy and round settled there, a halo. Her stomach dropped. Maker above, not a crown. Not for

him. In her shadow on the stone floor, she saw the outline of stars poised above her head. Holy Maker above, she'd seen the likeness of this headpiece before in the temple on the goddess with the serpents wrapped around her arms and…. Blooms at her shoulders.

A dragon's roar made them both look at the door. *Please be him. Please.* Varlett quickly disappeared, and Mathekis tensed, watching the entry with a narrowed gaze.

"Thane, I presume," the Black Mage said with a smirk. "I cannot wait to meet whoever it is you so desperately want to see. This *Thane* you believe can save you from me."

Layala felt sick. A creeping feeling that somehow the Black Mage would know Thane, overwhelmed her. Just like he knew her. That somehow the three of them were connected. She couldn't fathom how but deep down that knowing enveloped her. The same way she knew she would stop Prince Yoren's dragon's fire from scorching her and Thane. The same way she knew to touch the protective shield and it would not burn.

Dark messy hair and Raven armor covered in dried blood appeared in the entryway. Thane peered inside, and with darkness creeping in and a rumbling like distant thunder, he stepped through the barrier. Piper and Ronan tried to follow him, but the magical force barred them. Piper's fist crashed into the invisible shield.

"Thane!" Layala cried in relief. He would break her free of the Black Mage's hold, surely and together they would take him down.

He raised his sword, the point of it leveled at the Black Mage. "Get your hands off her."

The Black Mage's eyes flashed wide for a moment then his finger slid down the side of her face and down her neck until he cupped her chin. His piercing gaze locked onto Thane. "I should have known it would be you, War. Oh, I should have known. The gods wouldn't have it any other way."

Mathekis withdrew his sword and in his commanding tone said, "Leave us, Prince."

"I am the High King of Palenor. You do not command *me*." His booming authority demanded respect.

The Black Mage's eyes smoldered with delight. "He's much more than that. He's the god of war. Tread carefully, Mathekis."

Mathekis halted, looking at his lord with confusion.

What in the realms is he talking about? Thane, the god of war?

Thane's lips parted and his brows furrowed, but he blinked a few times, and something shifted in his gaze, a spark of recognition.

The Black Mage looked to Thane and said, "You did something, didn't you, War? To block me from her? One of my own spells perhaps? Clever." Layala

blinked... *Holy shit*, she only started hearing his voice *after* the mate bond was broken. "She looks perfect doesn't she, cousin, in her rightful crown? Our goddess. The one we both desired."

Did he just call Thane, cousin? How can that be? Unless they're cousins from... before. Was Tenebris even truly Thane's father? Layala's heart beat even harder. A memory just out of reach itched at the back of her mind. Why did this sound so wrong and yet... so right?

"I said, get your hands off my mate," Thane barked, stepping closer but with trepidation. They met eyes. Thane looked worried the Black Mage would hurt her.

"*Your* mate? Oh, dear me." He smirked. "This might hurt a little." Thane looked as confused and furious as Layala felt. "I'll catch you up. I won her over first and you stole my wife from me. You started a vicious war the realms had never seen before." He paused to lick his bottom lip.

Layala gulped. *The book at the dragon court—the war between the gods and realms Thane spoke of.*

"You may have had her for a time but she's my wife. My mate." He swung her around, and then snaked both his arms around her waist, pulling her back flush against his front. To her disgust, his magic still controlled her completely. "I forgot to introduce myself. How silly of me. I am Hel, god of magic and mischief. The magic I was born with, the mischief was earned. King of Villhara, husband to Valeen, goddess of night. You know her as Layala." His tongue slid

across the edge of her ear. "Don't worry, love, together we will get back home, and all those who sought to punish us will bow and profess, *long live the queen.*"

To be continued in book 3: Fate Calls the Elf Queen.
Coming Spring/Summer 2023

Acknowledgments

Acknowledgments to my beta reader team: Jess Boaden, Rachel Theus Cass, Tiffany Boland, Brittany O'Barr, and Sara Coombes. As per usual you ladies leave the funniest comments and make editing such a fun experience. You all also provided invaluable feedback that I desperately needed. Thank you for your honesty and time and fun! I've loved working with all of you, and thank you and appreciate you all so much.

Charity Chimni aka Hawkeyes, my proofreader who catches everything, thank you! She's my behind the scenes lady who helps make things happen.

My husband Travis encourages me to keep writing and living my dreams. He's amazingly supportive and is a wonderful dad.

David Farland, who sadly passed away in 2022, was a wonderful writing instructor. His tips and advice helped me become a much stronger writer and helped me plan this series.

My dad, who made me a lover of the fantasy genre.

The fans of Bow Before the Elf Queen! You all changed my writing career and my life! I still can't believe it sometimes. The Elf Queen series is a best-selling series because of you! Thank you!

About the Author

J.M. Kearl is a fantasy romance author. She writes feisty heroines to love and hunky heroes to fall in love with. She's also a mother of two and happily married to the love of her life. She lives in Idaho but is usually dreaming of somewhere tropical.

Sign up for J.M. Kearl's Newsletter: http://jmkearl.com/newsletter

ALSO BY J.M. KEARL

For more titles by J.M. Kearl, please visit:

http://jmkearl.com

Made in the USA
Coppell, TX
06 November 2022

14747129R00347